The Demon of Devil's Cavern

A Rory Daggett Story

"*The Demon of Devil's Cavern* is a wild ride along some very dark trails in a weird version of the Old West. Fast-paced and highly entertaining. Brennan LaFaro comes out with both guns blazing!"

- Jonathan Maberry, NY Times bestselling author of *Cave 13* and *The Sleepers War*

"With *The Demon of Devil's Cavern*, LaFaro snaps the reins taut and keeps the gallop strong. The characters and events herein are scrawled in dust and sap, framed in rawhide and wire and hung on your heart. A full-bore fire-fueled adventure. I had a blast!"

- John Boden, feller what wrote *Snarl*

"*The Demon of Devil's Cavern* moves like a runaway stagecoach, careening toward its inevitable end. LaFaro returns with a worthy successor to *Noose*, upping the ante with more bullets, more bodies, and more supernatural strangeness. Buzzard's Edge might not be a place you'd want to live, but it's sure fun to visit."

- Josh Rountree, author of *The Legend of Charlie Fish*

"There's a new sheriff in town—and also plot twists, supernatural evils, and mad scientists galore. In this riveting sequel to *Noose*, LaFaro weaves multiple genres into the standard Western mythos. The result? One hell of a tale."

- Drew Huff, author of *Free Burn*

"LaFaro returns to the world of Buzzard's Edge with both six shooters reloaded and ready to fire. *The Demon of Devil's Cavern* sees LaFaro at his best, combining the western horror adventure of *Noose* with all the heart of his *Slattery Falls* trilogy for his best book yet."

- John Lynch, author of *The Warrior Retreat*

THE DEMON OF DEVIL'S CAVERN

A RORY DAGGETT STORY

BY BRENNAN LAFARO

BRIGIDS GATE™ PRESS

BRIGIDS GATE PRESS
Overland Park, Kansas
www.brigidsgatepress.com
Printed in the United States of America

Books by Brennan LaFaro

Buzzard's Edge

Noose
The Demon of Devil's Cavern
Where the Daybreak Ends

Slattery Falls

Slattery Falls
Decimated Dreams
The World You Loved
I Will Always Find You

Standalone Novels

Last Stay

Short Story Collections

Illusions of Isolation: Thirteen Stories

Content Warnings

Blood
Gore
Gun violence
Child death
Murder
Torture
Mob violence

For Tyler Jones,
Whose unapologetic enthusiasm gave the horse a nudge every time the wagon got
stuck.

CHAPTER 1

WE ALL GOT OUR SECRETS

It started with a knock.

A lot of folk in Buzzard's Edge might think it's the names of people I've put in the ground that keeps a man like me up at night. A man who claimed his revenge, but still sleeps with iron under the mattress. But that ain't it.

It's the people I couldn't save. Right up near the top of that list is Sheriff John Harden. If I hadn't let his brains soak into the sand, maybe this whole mess could've been avoided.

Knock, knock.

Passing the evening in the parlor with a couple of books, Alice and I traded suspicious glances at the sharp sound. For a moment, I saw past her rounded cheeks and found the scared, malnourished kid again. Visitors didn't come tapping at our door all too often. She knew what to do. A short-lived smile spread across my face as she slunk behind the sofa, followed by the soft tear of leather. An almost inaudible *click* told me Alice had the revolver we kept hidden in case of emergencies.

I wiped the grin off my face and walked to the door, wriggling my fingers in case they needed to be quick. In Buzzard's Edge, it's only a fool who opens a door without one hand on their weapon. Henry Taff's six-shooter, the same one that killed "Noose" Holcomb, rested cold against my spine, ready to heat up at a moment's notice.

"Who is it?" I stood slightly to the side of the door frame in case they took a mind to blast through the thin wood.

"Sheriff," returned a curt voice.

I cracked the door, but left my drawing hand comfortably on the grip of the gun.

I half-expected a black hole surrounded by sparkling silver in greeting. Instead, the new sheriff's gun hung by her side. She stood chewing her lip with long, thin arms folded across her breasts. At a glance, she was no more than a handful of years older than me, but her eyes held a daring mischief. I was less than sure I could get off a shot before she got her hand to that holster. Hopefully, I wouldn't need to find out.

"Mary McHugh, I presume." I leaned against the door frame, blocking her view inside. "Your reputation precedes you."

She raised an eyebrow and a bit of a smile with it. "Does it now? I could say the same for you, Rory Daggett. Though, you're a mite younger'n I expected. You hear about a vigilante gunslinger living on the edge of town and you picture a scowling old man with crevices carved in his cheeks."

"You're taller than I would've guessed."

"Lord, Mr. Daggett. That how you learned to greet a lady?" She sighed and let her arms fall by her side. "S'pose I'm just glad you was kind enough to use my Christian name. Be insulting to assume you don't know what else they call me."

I studied her eyes, trying to gauge whether she wanted me to say it or bury it deep down. I opted for the risk. "The Demon. Decidedly not all that Christian."

Mary flinched.

"What brings you around, Ma'am?"

"Oh, you can shove that Ma'am bullshit where the sun don't shine, Mr. Daggett. New sheriff in town needs to get to know the sheep she's s'posed to herd. Good, bad, and… noteworthy."

"Noteworthy." I chuckled. "Would you like to come in?"

She smirked and gave me a quick head-to-toe inspection. "Thought you'd never ask."

I stood aside and let her in. Alice peeped out from the side of the sofa, and I flashed her a look that I hoped said, "stay put."

She vanished like a puff of smoke from the end of a pistol.

Mary grunted as she collapsed into a stiff wooden chair. She let it squeal in its death throes, then continued. "Now, as I was sayin', Mr. Daggett—"

"Rory'll do just fine."

"Hm, Rory then. Some say my predecessor, a Mr. Harden, used to lean on you pretty heavily. Some whispers even want me to believe he let you have the run of the place. Let you get away with murder." A shadow passed over her face and covered the playfulness in those eyes.

I settled onto a chair next to Mary's and brushed a hand across my mouth, wiping away my preferred response in favor of something more friendly. "And you won't allow that under your watch, I guess."

"Way I was raised, rules are rules, and the law is the law, Rory." She injected a little venom into my name. "Like science. Some laws don't bend."

"Thing is, Sheriff…" I let the words simmer in the air, hoping she noticed the ice I added. "You're not the only one that hears whispers. The mayor might've caught your name before I had a chance, but I have little doubt what happened at Devil's Cavern played a role in your hire."

She sat straight up, eyes hard.

"Sure sounds like you walked into a trap," I said. "Upwards of ten men gunning for you. Fire rains from a hole in the earth, bullets tear through rock and spit sand. Screaming, cursing, and blood in equal measure. And you're the only one that comes out alive. Crawls out by all accounts, bullets lodged in various body parts and leaking blood like a rust-eaten bucket."

"Wasn't the only thing living in the end." She shook her head and sneered. "Ain't wrong, but that's hardly the whole story."

"I got time."

Mary's eyes shot toward the sofa, and I fought the urge to follow them. "Well, alright then." She sat forward and braced her hands on her knees, settling in to spin a yarn.

"First thing you got to know about Devil's Cavern is it's right inside this great big bowl, about seven miles east of a town called Windfall. Rocky cliffs on all sides of the cave opening and no way in but to climb up and over. One of the strangest natural fixtures you ever laid eyes on. Just about all open space inside those walls, leading to the cave. The mouth of the cavern was barely wide enough to drive a wagon into. Rust-colored walls reached out to touch hands at their highest point, which wasn't much taller than a man giving a piggyback ride to a mule. Inside, it dipped down into the blackest night God ever allowed. Clear blue sky swirled overhead like it was trying to bring balance to all that darkness." She chuckled. "Bert Weymouth was one of the fellas there that day. He used to say, 'Devil's Cavern? Nah, that there's the Devil's asshole.' Anyways, that lack of light provided plenty of places to hide for the men holed up in there."

I narrowed my eyes. "I thought you were alone."

She fixed me with a cool stare that went a ways toward answering the question. "Wasn't alone when the siege started." A beat passed while she held my gaze. "Heard of the Fieldstone Gang?"

I shook my head.

"Guess they haven't made it this far south yet. People up in Windfall, the town I mentioned? They know that name. Shake in their dang boots when they hear it. Gang wears sky blue bandanas tied around their necks, too calm a color for the likes of such men."

"Violent?"

"Brutal, but that ain't the half of it. You believe the stories, those fellas got some darkness in 'em. I don't mean like cruelty. Might sound strange to a boy like you, but there's some goings on that logic just don't account for. *Unnatural* things I saw that day."

I stifled a grin and resolved to hold my tongue.

"Bert got word the gang was hiding out in that cavern and organized a mission to either take 'em in or take 'em out, and we didn't care which. Gerry McCracken was with us too, only other man who passed for the law in Windfall. He gave the orders. That is until a bullet flew out of the cavern and punched his nose through the back of his head. I can still hear the fleshy thump when he fell into the sand. Almost like a rattlesnake gettin' ready to give a warning. Bert and I didn't bother to check on him. A man don't survive having his face rearranged like that."

Her lip curled into something like a smile. "Bert put a hand over my mouth before Gerry even finished bleeding out. Thought I might let out a dainty scream or some shit like that. 'We need to go, Mary. We're outnumbered, outgunned. Damned fool's errand to think they wouldn't be waiting.'"

"Wouldn't be much of a story if you ran," I said, breaking my vow of silence. "What were you doing there in the first place?"

"Extra body is all. One more gun pointed into that dark pit to convince the enemy to lay down their arms and surrender peaceably. A poorly thought-out plan from the get go. Only I wasn't nervous at the miserable odds. Hell, I was shaking less'n half as much as Ol' Bert, senior deputy of Windfall, I'll have you know. You didn't grow up under my daddy's roof without a depth of knowledge regarding how to care for your iron properly and which way to point the fuckin' thing. And my old man, Mr. Daggett, he'd roll over in his grave if he ever saw his little girl turn tail and run from a fight."

I motioned for her to go on.

"So, they got us dead to rights, yeah? Not much for cover except a solitary anthill-looking structure that we ducked behind. We got the sun beatin' down on us, lighting us up clear as day. They got the night surrounding them. Unfair advantage all around."

She paused, staring over my shoulder as if trying to remember a certain detail. That wasn't it, though. She wanted me to ask.

I took the bait with my best edge-of-your seat voice. "So what'd you do next?"

She grinned and slapped a hand on my thigh. Let it linger a bit longer than necessary and then snatched it back. "Put on a light show, of course.

Don't ask me how they knew we was outnumbered, never mind how badly Those bastards fired shots like their ammo might go bad as meat left in the sun." She raised an eyebrow. "Windfall might be half a day north, but it gets plenty hot. Whatever kind of creature the meat comes off, man or beast, it starts to stink if you leave it out. What was I saying? Shit, they knew we didn't stand a chance, and they wasn't being cute. So Bert and I took advantage. Put his hat on the muzzle of a Sharps Carbine Rifle and handed it over my way. Told me, make it look like we was standing up and draw fire. He'd sight the son of a bitch and make an educated guess 'bout their location. A bullet fired into the dark, sure, but with a better-than-average chance of making a connection with their smilin' fuckin' faces."

"No shit," I said. The longer she talked, the more her language lowered to my admittedly juvenile level. Came to the door with a hard-ass attitude, but I thought maybe this was someone I could get along with.

"Yessir, and I told him to go fuck himself. I hadn't known Bert Weymouth long, but I seen him hem and haw his way through some tense situations. Never once did he lift that rifle. In anger or otherwise. Might've been a perfectly competent marksman, but when a nest of grizzled outlaws done drawn a bead on your whereabouts, well, Lord knows, that's a horseshit time to find out. 'Gimme a pistol', I says. Know what? Fucker doesn't even argue. Just slaps the chrome in my hand and starts waving the hat-wearing rifle around like he's trying to fight off a swarm of bees.

"At first, the entrance to the cavern stays dark as a moonless night, and I wonder if them inside didn't know what to make of it. A couple members of the law hidin' behind a rock, maybe caught their asses on fire and decided a brisk breeze was the best way to put it out. Then the men gather their wits and the first cherry blooms from the depths. Some figures dart through my head." She pursed her lips, studying me for a moment. "Yeah, you look like you know what it's like. You don't think about how far a man's head is away from the wink of his gun, but you kill enough men, and your mind finds a place to store that information whether you like it or not. The bright white fire of the shot fades quickly, but you can still see it. So, you know what I did, Mr. Daggett?" Her hand found my leg again. "Roxy?"

"I can guess."

"Put a fuckin' bullet right between that man's eyes. 'Course I didn't confirm that 'til later, but goddammit, I felt it right then."

"The Demon," I muttered, more awe than insult. Mary sat back in her chair, appeared uncomfortable for an instant, then it passed.

"Bert laughed, so help me God, he laughed. See, he knew I'd sent that rotten bandit to a toasty afterlife soon as the gun cracked. He started waving the hat on the gun around again, this time like the person wearing it was dancin' some kind of jig. Didn't make much of a difference because the rest of the Fieldstone Gang did the worst thing they coulda done." Another pause. Three things this woman had: a knack for storytelling, dramatic timing, and my undivided attention.

"What's that, Mrs. McHugh?"

"Miss. Ain't no Mr. McHugh."

"You don't say. So, what happened next?"

"They all fired. Aimless and scared. Like a bunch of kids alone at night trying to murder the stars. Every shot announced the location of the man behind it and, Mr. Daggett, I pride myself on being a patient woman. I lined up every shot careful as you like and dropped them one by one. Counting one, two, three, all the way up to ten. Funny thing of it all is they was so busy thinking they was rainin' down hell they didn't even notice the others dropping like flies all around them. Not until the last one stopped shooting.

"Bert let out a whoop that could wake a sleeping god and we eased down the incline toward the mouth of the cavern. Tell ya, Mr. Daggett, my nerves was janglin' that day. What if there was one more member of the gang than we suspected? All it'd take is one extra fucker lying in wait, ready to spring up and zing off a couple rounds, to make our great victory for naught."

I cleared my throat. "Why do I get the feeling Bert doesn't get to live happily ever after?"

"Cause that's the way life works, Rory Daggett."

"You missed one after all."

"We missed one after all. Apparently collected the brains of the bunch and when he saw his fellow bandits start to sprout new eyeholes, he must have hit the sand until the shooting stopped. Bert let out a holler that made me jump as we trooped in. Impressed by the shots is all, but it was enough. That shrill sound turned wet and my heart sank. Never heard it with a whistle before, but I regret to say I have heard a man try and talk through a blade in the neck during my time on this earth. It's a sound you don't ever forget."

"Jesus."

"You said it." Mary cleared her throat. "So, this last fella, soon as I see him, I wonder if he even had to duck when the shots came. Barely came up to my shoulders. Just tall enough to pull that knife out of Bert's windpipe with another unforgettable sound. Then he spots me."

"Don't remember hearing about any knife wounds on the Demon."

"Don't remember receiving any. Guess he decided the need for subtlety was over. He drew a little peashooter and started filling the air with whip cracks. First one took me by the shoulder, the second went straight through the opposite wrist." She rolled up the sleeve of her right arm to show off a tangle of scar tissue on the inside of her forearm. "In the interest of politeness, I won't show you the next set, but there's a couple to the gut. Least that's what they pulled out. Another right here." She gently laid a hand dead center on her chest, keeping hold of my eyes.

I let out a low whistle, then cut it short, remembering Bert. "Most people don't survive that."

"Well, most people ain't me. Lucky me, the little fucker didn't expect a woman to be armed. Soon as I collapsed from the chest wound, he leaned over me, smiling and showing off a set of stubby brown teeth. I didn't have to work too hard to make a show of my suffering. 'Bleed out like a bitch' he said, and I still don't know what that meant. Not clever, that's for damn sure, but it gave me a pinch of strength, just enough to draw the iron what fell underneath me. A single bright blast sent those little clods of shit he called teeth spiraling out the back of his head. If the echoing shot wasn't so damn loud, I suspect I mighta heard them skitter across the cave floor 'fore he even hit the ground." Her eyes went distant just then, and she squirmed in her seat. "Funny thing happened next. Maybe real, maybe delirium. But the cave pulsed a dull blue."

I scrunched up my brow. "Thanks for the blood?"

"Something like that, I guess. Just a quick flicker and when it died down, something was watching me. Had the outline of a man, duster draped down to his knees and a wide-brimmed hat."

"Something, not someone."

"Just a feeling, but I trust it. Close enough to me to be free of the shadows, but dark as the night is long and with a set of burning blue eyes." She shook her head. "Like I said, I was practically dying. Could've been my brain trying to check out."

"But you don't think so."

"I don't think so. I could feel it, almost. A demon. Name stuck when I shared it with the doctor, just not the way I intended." She bit her lip and raised her eyebrows. "You don't believe me."

"I've seen a lot of strange things. I wouldn't dare to say any of it's beyond the realm of possibility."

She settled back and nodded like I'd actually answered the question.

"So, there you are, miles from civilization. Almost enough bullets in you to fill a revolver, and you used your last bit of strength to squeeze the trigger. I don't get it. How'd you get back to a doctor?"

She shrugged. "I walked."

I laughed. A whole lot louder than I meant to. "Fine, be that way."

"We all got our secrets, Rory Daggett. Mayhaps someday they'll come to call, but I always found it wisest to keep 'em close 'til you ain't got no more cards to play."

I nodded, but kept quiet.

She smirked and squinted her eyes. "Seems like you got something you want to ask, Daggett."

"Not especially. I just have a hard time trusting a person who takes that many bullets and lives to tell the tale. No wonder they call you the Demon."

"Makes you feel any better, I wouldn't have graced myself with that moniker." She softened slightly. I saw it in her shoulders. "I ain't here to ask you to retire the gun or nothin'. Just want to make sure we understand each other."

"I'm all vengeanced out." I let the words hang, wondering if they were true. "Maybe I left behind a fair body count, but only because I got everybody I was aiming for."

"What about the girl? Them whispers sure seem convinced that you didn't pull all those triggers by yourself."

My turn to keep secrets. "What about her? All we want is to be left alone." I stood and took a step toward the door. "Very pleased to make your acquaintance, Ms. McHugh, but I think it's time you left. Me and Alice ain't a threat to your ability to uphold the law. Promise you that."

She raised her hands in mock surrender as she climbed out of the chair, then made for the door. She grabbed the knob, stopping as if to study the wood grain. From the corner of my eye, I saw Alice poke out from behind the sofa, clearly wondering whether this woman was more likely to plant a kiss on my cheek or shackles on my wrists. If that's the case, our thoughts matched just then.

"I want to trust you, Rory. Really, I do. Thing I've discovered in my time on this earth is that it doesn't matter whether you're eight years old or eighty. Once a killer, always a killer. All the same, I hope to see you around." She flashed a coy grin and opened the door.

A distant pop sounded as she stepped into the night air and Mary toppled back into the parlor, skidding to a stop next to my feet. Blood dribbled out of a hole the size of a wheat penny, opened right between her dull, lifeless eyes.

Chapter 2

The Man with All the Scars

Alice darted out from behind the sofa holding the spare revolver, eyes jackrabbit wide.

"Get down," I yelled.

The first bullet splintered the chair next to me. I hit the floor and scrabbled toward Alice. She raised her eyebrows and slapped her hands over her chest to resemble an X.

I grabbed her wrist and pulled her behind cover. "I was just being friendly. Besides, don't you think we have bigger problems?"

As if I'd personally invited the trouble, a hail of bullets started flying overhead like a pissed-off nest of paper wasps. A select few zipped through the sofa back and came to a clanging halt when they met the sheet of steel we'd installed for just such an occasion. Judging by the popcorn-cooking-on-an-open fire barrage of gunfire, the shooter who dropped Mary was far from alone.

Mary.

I snuck a glance from behind the sofa, nearly catching a needle of wood in the eye for my trouble. Her hand lay on the floor, limestone white and palm up. Not so much as a twitch.

I swallowed and turned back to Alice.

Alice set her gun on the floor, then clapped her fists together and wiggled the fingers on her free hand.

I nodded. "Now you're talking." I pulled my gun from my waistband and gave the cylinder a spin. "On three. One. Two. Three."

Alice took off like a shot as I peered over the edge of the battered sofa and came face to face with a mangy man, looking as though he'd bathed in grease and dirt. It was the Winchester clasped in his hands that really caught my attention, though. As soon as I popped up, he squinted two beady, swine-like eyes at me and got the rifle almost to his shoulder before I blew a hole in his throat. Pig Eye fell backward out the door, leaving only his boots in my parlor, and then the shooting started once more in earnest.

Underneath the dining table, Alice slid a finger along an invisible seam and coaxed it open. Raucous shots buried the small click the compartment usually made, and Alice removed its contents, working with her tongue stuck between her teeth. With the item secured, she flashed a look my way, and I stood to fire again. This time, my bullets vanished into the open mouth of the doorway. Little eyes of gunfire erupted in the night air and I thought of Mary, subconsciously knowing where to place a shot based on the location of each powder blast. I emptied my last five bullets into the darkness. Maybe it was my imagination, but it sure seemed like the amount of return fire dwindled a bit.

Out of ammo, I hit the deck again just in time for Alice to plow into me. I banged around on the floor, searching for the loose board. When I found the one with the most give, I jerked it back and removed a box of bullets, then dropped six of them into the open cylinder of my gun, then Alice's, like a mama bird feeding her chicks. Two guns, twelve rounds. That was the escape plan, or at least the second half of it. I looked at Alice and the strange oblong thing cradled in her arms; an arrow with a fat, round end. It teetered on the ends of her fingers, bringing a line of sweat to my forehead. I took it as gracefully as a communion wafer and she picked up her gun.

"Gonna be loud," I said. "You ready?"

I can't say I loved the smile she responded with, but it sure as hell answered my question. I flashed her back one in kind, anyway. Might as well have double the crazy. We stood in sync and Alice fired into the doorway while I threw the projectile as hard as I could. Then we waited, stock still, to watch the sun reclaim the night sky, if only for a second.

The Ketchum grenade illuminated the silhouettes of nearly a dozen attackers before separating the nearest ones from life and limb. As advertised, the triggered black powder made a sound somewhere between a mountain collapsing and a canyon forming.

I looked to Alice. Her jaw hung open.

"And you didn't want that thing in the house?"

As much as I would've liked to marvel all day at the carnage unleashed by that itty bitty container, Alice tugged at my sleeve, and we dashed for the back bedroom. She snagged a rifle and a bowie knife from under her bed while I peeled back the canvas covering her window.

One sentry assigned to the back of the house, clearly under strict orders not to leave his post. Although the impatient dance routine he was currently engaged in made it clear his instructions hadn't accounted for a burst of flames big enough to lick the sky.

I let the canvas close just long enough to brush my right hand forward from my left index finger. Our silent sign for 'knife'. Just in case Alice handed it over and readied the rifle. Another quick peek and I saw that the man outside was still alone and preoccupied. In a burst of speed, I threw myself out the window, skittered across the sand, and buried a fist in the center of his face before the fucker knew what hit him. His nose broke with a sickening crunch. I lowered him to the ground and held a finger to my lips. The sentry's eyes caught a glint of moonlight off the end of the knife and he nodded quickly while I relieved him of his gun. I turned to find Alice beside me, pointing the rifle toward the front of the house.

"Never did hear you coming," I whispered.

Her mouth remained flat as the Sonoran Desert. Her eyes, though Different story. They flicked toward the man on the ground, then met mine with something like concern in them. She gave the sign for knife with a little more fervor.

I shook my head. "We don't know he would've shot first. Benefit of the doubt, Pip. Give 'em a chance to show who they are before you put 'em down."

Gently removing one hand from the rifle, Alice laid her thumb across the palm holding the barrel and waggled her hand back and forth.

I squinted at her. "Blue?"

Then I realized. Although blood leaked from the man's nose and stained the front of his clothes a dark crimson, there was no mistaking the portions of his bandana that remained untouched.

Sky blue.

"That gang followed her here." My voice sounded distant.

Alice stiffened. Her eyes went wide enough to let a wagon pass through, and her finger tightened against the trigger, but didn't squeeze. A soft crunch dancing underneath the crackling flames told me why.

"Might lower that weapon if I was you, little lady." The high, reedy voice came from an outline against the blaze. Its owner was tall and lean. Even as just a shadow, you could tell he didn't have a single sprout of hair on his dome. Three more figures crept out of the night and joined him. Two short and squat like a pair of skunk pigs and the last, a thin and huddled wraith who seemed like a strong desert breeze might pick him up and carry him back to Devil's Cavern. Steam rose from their bodies and the not-so-subtle scent of cooked flesh wafted our way.

With our attention turned to the new arrivals, the sentry popped up and dashed toward the front of the house, vanishing into the hanging smoke and leaving a trail of blood on the sand. The way he took off, like somebody strapped a steam engine to his shoes, made me doubt he'd return.

Hand brushing my revolver, I stood next to Alice. She kept the sight locked on the tall man in the middle, picking him out as the leader. I guess he felt it, too, because he put his empty hands in the air and stepped closer. I didn't much care for the way his yellow eyes crawled over Alice.

"No guns or nothin', girlie. Just little old me."

The bastard sounded about as trustworthy as a fiddleback spider pouring your drink.

Alice's eyes darted toward me and I froze. There was real fear in them, a plea for help. With my free hand, I clapped my first two fingers against my thumb like a mouth slamming shut.

No.

Not yet, anyway.

"And who is little old you?" I called. "Besides a murderer, that is."

"Murderer?" Christ, that voice was grating. "Such a name to pass between two men who barely know each other."

"Well then, kindly introduce yourself, stranger," I said through gritted teeth.

"My name is Victor." He took another step toward us and as the moonlight poured over him, I squeezed the revolver nearly hard enough to bend metal. Common enough name, except I knew the second part before it could escape his lips.

"Jacobs," I said, with a hint of ice on my breath. The first name only shoveled some coal in the fire; it was his appearance that set the train in motion. I knew the stories. He wore boots and wool pants, but nothing above the waist except for a bandana the color of the afternoon sky. For the blink of an eye, I thought he might be covered in burns, the aftermath of having a grenade chucked at him. But when he stepped closer, tiny knots of scar tissue came into relief, just like in the stories people told. Dozens and dozens lining every inch of his bare chest, racing up and down his arms, and climbing his neck.

"It would appear my reputation precedes me," he said, lilting the words up at the end like a question. Three distinct clicks rang out of the darkness behind him and the odds no longer seemed even.

The rifle shook in Alice's hands.

I whipped my free hand around in a quick forward circle while wiggling my fingers, hoping Alice would pick up on my silent instruction. She didn't blow a hole in Jacobs's head, so I guess it worked alright.

"Is it true every one of those little imperfections is someone you killed?" I asked.

When Jacobs smiled, his teeth shone impossibly white, like staring directly into the sun at noon. "I suspect I've missed some here and there. I may even have to add a few more tonight." He tilted his head, and smoke billowed behind him. "Demon's coming for you, friend. Might I have the pleasure of your name before I carve out your eyes as an offering?"

A knife gleamed into existence in his hand. At the same time, the other three stepped forward. None quite as tall as Jacobs, but a little more broad in the shoulder and wearing a much more appropriate amount of clothing. Each had a piece of iron aimed at either me or Alice, and despite the number of bullets that now decorated our parlor, the bandoleers strapped across their chests promised those cylinders weren't empty.

I lowered my revolver and donned my friendliest grin while I waved my right hand in front of my chest as if shooing a fly. "Well, shit, why didn't you ask earlier?" I caught Alice's eye to make sure she'd seen. No betrayal of emotion on her face, but her lips curled up so slightly a magnifying glass could've missed it. "Name's Rory Daggett, but folks in town call me—"

Alice's free hand shot to her mouth, and she unleashed a piercing whistle.

The four men bracing down on us skidded in the tightly packed sand, looking around like they expected the sky to fall. Then maybe just for a second, they thought that was happening after all, because the earth began to shake. The peccary brothers went back to back while Jacobs stared at his feet with a knowing smile. He wound up and whipped his knife toward Alice at the same moment she squeezed the trigger.

The bullet punched through Jacobs's bicep and he let out a banshee-like scream. The knife went just a bit wide, still catching the side of Alice's face and drawing a gorge along her pale-white cheek. Clutching her face, Alice fell to the dirt.

"You shitstain," I screamed, raising my sidearm. Except before I could squeeze a shot off, a broad gray mare broke through the haze and knocked Victor Jacobs fair on his scarred ass.

"Good girl, Ghost." In the passing seconds, I'd almost forgotten about the whistle.

I blocked Alice from the fray and let a few quick shots fly. The skinny wraith dropped like a pile of laundry and spit out a raspy breath before going still. Two gleams of silver caught the moonlight, though Ghost stamped down and relieved the stocky bandits of their weapons and possibly their lives. A storm of dust rose into the air, swallowing the sound of gunfire. When the dust cleared, three ruined bodies sprawled across our backyard and Victor Jacobs was nowhere to be found.

I stared off toward the horizon, searching for any sign of the varmint, and then a soft mewling sound brought me back to earth.

Alice.

She's just a kid.

No matter how many times I repeated the mantra, it always struck me as surreal. A kid, sure, but a kid who knew her way around weapons like a seasoned hunter. If we lived anywhere besides the ass-end of the world, she could probably keep us eating rich. As it stood, vultures taste like stringy shit and most lizards got no meat on their bones.

Blood poured down her cheek from a gash an inch below her eye. The crimson liquid mixed with her tears and fell to the earth, where the sand drank it up.

"Watch out for stragglers," I said to Ghost, and she whinnied in reply. Never met a horse before that could set a patrol, but I had confidence in the old girl. The surviving members of the Fieldstone Gang seemed to have run off into the night with their scorched tails tucked between their legs and I didn't suspect they'd be back. Not without reserves, anyway.

I scooped up Alice and carried her inside, whispering whatever reassurances sprang to mind. Anything that echoed from childhood that the Taffs, the family who raised me, might've said when I hurt myself.

There seemed something irresponsible about laying a little girl on a couch filled with bullet holes, but that's what I had at my disposal. Alice didn't complain none. The blood still flowed even when her tears dried up.

"Might need stitches," I said. "Or at least a little gunpowder, though I don't care to do that so near the eye."

Alice sat up. Confusion rather than fear or pain set across her brow and she clapped her hands to her chest to form an X again.

"Gonna tease the guy who's gonna set your face on fire to fix you?" I asked, then my grin fell away as I realized what she was getting at.

Brick brown blood spattered the floor where Mary had fallen dead. Her body was gone.

CHAPTER 3

ENJOY THE VIEW

Billy Chambers sat forward in his uncomfortable-looking chair. He studied Alice's face by the light of the single sheriff's office window. "Doesn't look so bad." He cracked a grin and leaned back, kicking his legs up on the desk. "Looks like Red Rory did a passable job of patching you up, kid."

"Good Lord, Billy, you have to stop with the nicknames." Billy was the long-time deputy under Sheriff John Harden. Never the fastest horse in the race, but loyal as all get out. I wondered if Mayor Harvey had considered him for Sheriff after John's death. If Billy even wanted the job.

"Dead-Eye Daggett." He pointed to a series of wanted posters that hung over Mary McHugh's deserted desk. "Look real good up there. Wouldn't you say?"

"She's dead, Billy. Mary is."

Billy's grin fell to the floor so fast it just about made a noise. He shook his head quickly. "Can't be. I just saw her last night." His eyes flicked toward the gash on Alice's face. "What happened?" he whispered.

"Made a trip to the outskirts to introduce herself. When she went to leave, someone put a bullet between her eyes. Fell down dead right in the middle of my parlor."

Billy's eyes went wide as the opening of a pint glass. "You see who did it?"

I shrugged. "More or less. Alice and I. We uh… dealt with 'em. All but maybe one or two." My eyes wandered back to the collection of wanted posters. As soon as I found the one I was looking for, I pointed it out to Billy. A bald man with snake eyes. Even his bone structure made him look more reptile than man.

Alice shuddered and turned her attention away from the poster, suddenly finding something of interest in the single unoccupied cell.

"Victor Jacobs." A third voice floated into the room, followed immediately by an impeccably dressed prick. I hadn't even heard the door open.

"Mr. Locke," I said, trying to veil my displeasure. "Shouldn't you be teaching a class right about now?"

"It's a Sunday, Mr. Daggett." His tone sounded bored. "Contributing members of a society keep track of such things."

"That so?"

Thaddeus Locke was a well-traveled northerner who split his time between teaching the young'uns and detective work. Evidently, he had an open invitation to intrude upon sheriff's business whenever it took his pleasure. He talked like an educated man from New England and looked down his nose at the rest of us like he was ten feet tall and didn't have any other choice. Like I said, a prick.

He turned his attention to Billy. "What's all this about Jacobs? The last time I checked he hadn't been seen in the area for six months or more."

Billy looked uneasy. "If Mr. Daggett can be believed, Jacobs was sure as hell in Buzzard's Edge last night. And... he killed Mary, Thad."

Tink, tink, tink.

Alice tapped at the bars of the cell.

Locke put a hand on his chin and focused on the planks of wood that crisscrossed the ceiling. "Two dead sheriffs in half a year and only one witness to both. Peculiar."

Fire kindled in Alice's eyes. Crossing the room, she put her right hand under her chin and flicked it forward. The open hand became an accusatory pointing gesture directed at Locke's chest.

Billy's brows knit together. "Now what in the devil is that girl doin'?"

"American sign language." Locke's voice held a trace of amusement. "Although what she just suggested I do to myself is not one of the early lessons." He looked to Billy with pride upon his face. "They taught it in Connecticut."

"We got a book we been working out of," I said softly. I shook my head at her before she decided to mime stabbing someone who understood our language.

"My concern stands, Mr. Daggett. I don't suppose you brought Sheriff McHugh's body with you?"

"They took it. Same gang she thought she wiped out single-handedly to get everybody's attention. They came back for her." My voice came out more timid than I meant it to. Something about Locke's way with words brought all the holes in our story to light. Shit, I knew it to be the truth and even I doubted us. Prick he might be, but a half-decent detective. I bet the students fucking hated him.

"And how many did you kill this time?"

I didn't answer. Sounded rhetorical anyway, like he had a response prepared for any number I could've thrown at him.

Locke's eyes narrowed. He leaned against Mary's desk and folded his arms. He had opened his mouth to speak when Billy cut him off.

"Don't, Thad," he said, with steel in his eyes.

Locke closed his mouth with an audible pop and motioned for Billy to have the floor.

"Sounds like a tall tale, I grant you that, but Rory's the guy who brought Noose Holcomb's gang to justice."

"Frontier justice, perhaps," said Locke. He sighed and looked out the window. "Another five deaths with a lone witness."

Alice held up two fingers. Locke ignored her.

Billy's cheeks grew sunburn red. "John Harden trusted Rory Dagget with his life, and I'll be damned if I'm gonna spit on his grave by trying to railroad Rory for some shit he didn't do. Dammit, Thad, you got such a hard-on for this mystery-solving bullshit, tell me why they'd come into town to share this story? Ain't nobody knew where Mary went last night. He wanted to kill her, all he would've had to do was stay put with his thumb up his ass."

I clapped Billy on the shoulder. "Vivid, Billy. Thank you."

"So, what is it you hoped to accomplish by coming here?" asked Locke.

A heat rose in me and I tried not to let it show. "Report a murder, Thad. Just trying to be a contributing member of society, you know?"

He scowled at me.

"Besides," I added. "Might be a wanted killer in town, and I figured that's just up your alley." I leaned toward Locke and lowered my voice "The stories about the scars all over Jacobs's body? One for each victim? That's true. He's covered in 'em like chiggers on a whore's mattress. Pardon my French, sir."

"Such language in front of a child," said Locke.

I cleared my throat and let a little confidence trickle back in. "Thad, my friend, that child has been to hell and back." I looked to Alice. Her face remained impassive. "And she carries herself far better than most grown men." I weighed my next words, clucked my tongue and threw caution to the wind. "Shoots better, too. Never seen the girl miss." I put a hand on his shoulder, gave it a squeeze. "She ever decides she wants to put a bullet in a man's head, that fella better get real used to having three eyes."

Locke peeled my fingers off his shoulder like he was picking up a wagon-squashed rabbit off the road. The heat in his eyes said everything as he considered his next words.

"Billy," I said and waited for him to meet my eyes. "Thank you, my friend. I'm sorry about Ms. McHugh. Truth be told, I kind of liked her."

"Yeah." He lowered his gaze to the uneven floorboards. "Yeah, me too."

Alice stepped toward the door, and I recognized my cue to leave. She pulled it open and let a hot breeze pour in. Locke grabbed my arm. He spoke softly so Billy could only guess at his words from across the room. "Two sheriffs in six months," he repeated. "Even you have to admit it's strange."

"I won't argue it."

He nodded. "All I'm saying is I haven't caught as many criminals as I have by ignoring coincidences." He let go of me and I could still feel his iron-like grip pressing into my bicep. "I'll be watching you, Mr. Daggett."

"Enjoy the view, Daisy." I shut the door in his face.

The entrance to the sheriff's office remained closed as me and Alice walked away. I almost expected Locke to poke his ugly mug out and shoot a glare our way, or offer up one last parting shot, but he evidently kept a cooler head than I did.

Hands in my pockets, I kicked at anything larger than a grain of sand as we strolled down the crowded street toward home. "Bunch of bullshit," I mumbled, flicking a glance toward Alice and anticipating a smart-ass response.

Instead, she bit her lip and tapped the side of her temple with outstretched fingers.

"Yeah, I know you know." I sighed. "We cleaned up an entire gang for this town. A witch, even. Not saying that should hold a day in our honor or nothin' like that, but maybe some fuckin' peace is all I'm asking. At least a little benefit of the doubt when it comes to accusations."

With palms held horizontal, Alice tapped the ends of her fingers together, then switched the top hand and repeated the motion with a shrug. An icy wave rippled through her blue eyes.

I chuckled. "Shit kid. Okay, maybe not entirely for the town. Maybe a little bit for us, but the point stands."

My heart skipped a beat as I looked up. Lynch's Tavern loomed over us on the right, except with Emmett Lynch riding old Charon's ferryboat, the place was under new ownership.

"Saloon at the End of the World," I read under my breath. "Seems a bit dramatic, don't it?"

I tipped my hat at the young man sweeping the front porch, a Mr. Jeffery, if memory served. He squinted at me from behind small round spectacles, let a smile flicker, then disappeared inside.

"Well, now. Attitude seems to be catching."

Alice flicked her hand from under her chin again.

"Fuck it, indeed."

"Rory Daggett!" A boisterous shout caught my breath in my lungs. It took me a moment to realize it beamed down from above like the voice of God.

"Morning, Mayor Harvey." I tipped my hat.

"And how are you this fine morning?" He leaned against the edge of his balcony, straining the wood beneath a set of tree-trunk thick arms. Behind him, a sleepy-looking woman peered down, then lost interest and sauntered away. I'd lived in Buzzard's Edge my whole life and had little for comparison, but I wondered if every town's mayor set up their office over a brothel. His smile, which just a moment before burst with child-like glee, dropped. "You don't look well, my friend."

"Rough night, sir." I kicked at the dirt. "Might want to stop by the sheriff's office and have a talk with Billy when you're good and ready to greet the day."

His gaze flitted between Alice and I, eyes narrowed to pinpricks. She forced a smile and some of the suspicion faded away.

"Yes," he said. "I'll do that. Are you sure there's nothing I can do for you right now?" His eyes darted to the room behind him, and I hoped he wasn't trying to invite me inside for a quickie.

"No, sir. Just need to get on home. Lots to do. Go talk to Billy. If you need me after that, you know where I am." I tried to inject some conviction into my voice, but Locke's accusations had rattled me and there was no sense in pretending otherwise.

He let out a laugh that all but shook the sand under my boots, and his jowls flapped in the morning breeze. "The offer always stands. Be well, Rory." A dainty arm slunk over the mayor's shoulder and pulled him back inside.

We walked in silence for a few minutes, passed McGregor's General Store, Meyer's Cooperage, Barron's Apothecary, and a boarded-up shop with the name Svensson stenciled over the doorway. The buildings thinned, giving way to open desert. I nodded a hello to Mr. Durgin, the barber, and he returned a friendly wave as we exited the town proper.

Nothing but packed sand and a distant view of the Blackjack Mountains between us and home.

"I heard a lot about him. Jacobs," I said, surprising myself.

Alice raised her eyebrows, but kept her pace. She studied each step like the upturned desert sand might contain great secrets.

"When I spent all that time learning about Noose's gang. For a hot minute, I thought Jacobs might be involved. Turned out to be a couple killings linked to Jacobs in the same region where Crane was tossing his murder chemicals into the general public. Not much more than that, though. Plus, he never showed up to try and kill me."

I looked for any kind of reaction. Alice only watched her feet crunch through the sand, watched a spiny lizard zip across her path.

"We were lucky to get out of there in one piece," I murmured. "And no doubt about it, we'll have to watch our backs with twice as much vigilance."

She clapped her fists and when they popped apart, her fingers wriggled like shrapnel.

"Oh, you bet. I'll see if I can get my hands on another grenade." I chuckled, then felt the grin slip off my face. "I'm serious, though. Noose was a bad guy, hurt a lot of people and it didn't seem to bother him much. He was in it for the money, though. Only reason he popped his head up at the end there, isn't it?" I shook my head. "This Jacobs guy, though. I didn't have time to count the scars all along his body last night. If the stories can be believed, I wouldn't have time to count them if he stood butt naked in front of me for an hour. Every one self-inflicted. Every one showing off somebody he killed."

Alice tensed, probably thinking how easily that number could have included us.

I let a beat pass. "I didn't read nothin' about him being part of a gang. Always struck me as death for hire, though I can't argue with that sky blue bandana. Short of it is, Mary got on his list somehow, and you saw how that went. Now, I worry he's not going to let us go at a stern warning and a couple of horse-hoof bruises. I wouldn't be surprised if Victor Jacobs is out there right now, plotting to kill us."

The farmhouse poked its head over the horizon, and Alice came to a stop. She nodded for a second as if confirming a thought, then held her left hand out toward home, sideways like she was about to slice it in half. Her right hand shot up, pointer and middle fingers outstretched like a gun, and stabbed past her open palm. Then, her left hand dropped dead by her side, and she lifted her right, fist closed and thumb pointing straight ahead.

She let it float in the air for a moment, then glanced sideways to see if I took her meaning.

"God damn right." I wrapped an arm around her shoulder, felt some tension unfurl as we picked up our pace.

We kill him first.

Chapter 4

Whistle and Glass

Nine dead. At least that's the closest we could drive a stake to an accurate count. The mess of body parts from the Ketchum Grenade made getting an exact number a little tougher.

The mid-day sun beat down and Ghost nickered the occasional encouragement as we dug behind the stables. Unfortunately, it wasn't like either me or Alice were new to playing hide the body in the backyard. Usually had a few less to contend with, though.

I watched Alice ripping up chunks of the earth to replace with fresh Fieldstone fodder. Her arms had gained a little meat over the last few months. I thought of her stumbling out of the dark in my parent's house when we first met, appearing more corpse-like than some of the fuckers we were now committing to the earth. Her arms looked better fit to poke the fire in a hearth than lift a weapon back then, but I'll be damned because that's exactly what she did.

Many times and again. And still, I had no idea where she'd learned it all. Didn't even know her last name. The sign language went a long way, but maybe there were just some conversations we weren't ready to have yet.

Alice must have caught me staring because she cocked an eyebrow, then dropped her shovel and gave the sign for "help", followed by something less polite.

"Just resting my weary limbs," I said and topped off the freshest grave. Ghost wandered over and promptly christened the churned patch of dirt, drawing a rare belly laugh out of Alice. She didn't let them fly often, and the first time she did, I suspected she might be convulsing, but whenever she allowed something funny to crack that exterior, it did my heart a spot of good.

And that was alright.

"Come on." I grabbed Ghost's bridle and steered her toward the stable. "Let's get you fed. Then we can go wash up. Been a long day."

Alice closed her eyes, and for the second it took to reopen them, she looked just about eight years old again.

We went inside and waited for Mayor Harvey to show up, for Thad Locke.

A couple days passed and, we waited still.

What did I say about knocks before?

Two nights out of four, someone knocks at your door on the edge of town, it's bound to make you a little paranoid. Not to mention, ever since the first guest, you discover there's a killer who knows where you live and keeps a bare patch of skin to carve your memory into, well, it makes a man cross the parlor with a little more care.

Knock, knock.

Quicker than a diving dragonfly, Alice leapt behind the sofa, and I heard the ratchet of a spinning cylinder. Myself, I decided gun out and one finger making acquaintance with the trigger might supply me with a superior advantage.

"Curse the damn fool who didn't think to add a window by the door." I smirked toward Alice, but she was well hid. I lifted the gun and threw the door open. Thaddeus Locke stood on the front porch, painted red by the setting sun, arms crossed behind his back. What he might be hiding there I couldn't guess, though he didn't seem too put out by having a revolver aimed at his chest.

"There's been a development," he said.

That's when I noticed the others. I lowered my revolver and put a hand on Locke's shoulder as I stepped past him onto the porch. A small army of twenty or so surrounded the house. Herschel McGregor wrapped white knuckles around a two-barrelled rifle as he glared up at me. Guess he never forgave me for drawing down on a little old biddy in his store. Can't say I blamed the man. Paul Barron, the town apothecary, clutched a pitchfork and ground his teeth as he squinted, pupils like grains of sand. Christopher Durgin, noted barber, carried no visible weapon. Cloth-wrapped knuckles told me he was prepared to deal damage with his bare hands. Clearly no longer in a waving mood, Durgin danced with a restlessness, and I couldn't decide whether that was down to fear or adrenaline. Other familiar faces flickered in the crowd, none of them friendly.

"They're here for you," Locke said softly. "And the girl."

My cheeks grew hot and I stared from angry face to angry face, as if I could keep them from advancing with a glare. "What the hell are you talking about? Where's Billy? With McHugh gone, that'd leave him in charge. He don't answer to a schoolmarm, Locke."

"Deputy Chambers was assigned to remain at the office."

I clenched my teeth. "Assigned by who? Harvey?"

A new voice called out. "That'd be me, Mr. Daggett." I recognized it immediately, but couldn't bring myself to search out its owner. "Or Rory, if you like."

"Mary," I whispered.

As if summoned, Mary McHugh strode out from the side of the farmhouse, hand hovering slightly north of the iron in her holster. The kindred spark that lived in her eyes the last time I'd seen her was nowhere to be found. Instead, a snarl climbed the side of her face. A slight imperfection dotted the space between her eyebrows, so faint I might have imagined it if I hadn't seen a bullet punch through it and cleaned the mess it left on my floor.

"We thought you were dead. He shot you." I felt my lower jaw dangling. Locke stepped back as if he feared I might drool on his boots. "Jacobs," I finished weakly.

Mary marched up the steps and stopped with her nose less than an inch from mine. Through gritted teeth, she said, "Only person who took a shot at me the other night was that little girl you got hidden away in there. Lucky she can't aim worth a damn." She spat. "I heard you was trouble, Rory Daggett, and I heard some shit about the little Hellspawn, too, but I figured I'd give you the benefit of the doubt. Get to know you."

She turned to face the gathered masses, leaning against the porch railing and raising her voice to preacher-level. "Told him how the law is the law, and we don't tolerate nobody who thinks they's above it. Ain't that right?"

A chorus of affirmations volleyed back, and my heart scaled its way up my throat. This couldn't be the Mary from the other night. Sure, she looked the same, sounded the same, but Mary McHugh's brains leaked all over my damn floor, then she up and vanished.

Riling up the crowd, she said, "So he says, 'here in Buzzard's Edge, don't nobody have the right to tell me what to do. Don't you know who the fuck I am?'"

She let the words hang, a series of gasps biting at their heels. I searched the faces in the crowd, waiting for the first glimmer of recognition that those words sounded nothing like me. It never came. "That's when the little she-devil popped out of the bedroom and took a shot at me, then another. Rage blazing on her face, teeth showing like a wild beast. Then she took another." Mary paused, lowering her voice a little. "Can see the ricochets against the front door, you don't believe me."

"That's horseshit, Mary, and you know it," I said. "What the fuck are you playing at?"

Locke pulled a pistol out from behind his back and smacked me across the jaw with the butt end. An explosion of light danced in front of my eyes and I opted to shut up for the moment.

"What happened next?" shouted a disembodied voice from the crowd. The sun dropped a hitch and the number of people became more difficult to be sure of.

Even as the light faded, a grin lit up Mary's face. That seasoned storyteller look from the cavern story. Was even a single fucking word of that true?

"I'm glad you asked," she said. "I reached for my revolver to return the girl's fire, and that's when the lights went out. An unfathomable pain upside the back of my head, and then darkness all around. Last thing I recall was cruel laughter, surrounding me like water flooding in. Next thing I know, I'm waking up in an alley. Just this morning. Mr. Durgin, himself, found me scorched by the mid-day sun like a common drunk."

Locke nodded along to confirm he'd heard this tale before.

"S'true," called out the wily barber, still mashing his fists together and waiting for someone to give him the go ahead to settle my hash.

"No telling what they might've done to me while I was unconscious. And for so long." She paused and stared down at her feet. "S'pose I oughta be grateful they didn't see fit to kill me. More than Mr. Harden can say."

With pain still radiating through my jaw, I fought the urge to tackle the lying bitch right down the stairs and bash her brains out on the closest rock. Thaddeus Locke likely saw the intent in my eyes because he raised the end of his gun a little. He flicked his eyes toward Mary, looking for any signs she might have more to say.

"Will you come quietly, Daggett?" His voice didn't quite beg, but that wasn't far off.

"Not a damn word she said is true."

"I don't recall asking that question." He leaned in. "Where's the girl?"

I met his eyes, determined not to let mine wander toward the house. He squinted and I don't know whether I gave something away or he just guessed the most logical place.

"In the house," he said. "Careful. According to Mr. Lynch, she's quite the shot."

"Hell she is," Mary grumbled. Locke stared at her a moment, then turned away.

Chris Durgin barreled past Locke and held a hand out toward the door. "Emmett Lynch is dead, sir."

Locke rolled his eyes. "From a very well-placed bullet, is my understanding."

"Oh." Durgin's cheeks reddened, and he pulled the door open. "Little gir—"

Thunder roared and Durgin's hat blew clear off his head, floating to the ground with a smoking hole in the middle. Most of the brave souls who had banded together to haul us outlaws to the gallows dropped to the sand, as well.

"I'm hit!" Durgin cried. "She's killed me."

Locke sighed and stepped toward the oaf. I saw my opportunity.

I drove a boot into the side of Locke's knee. The detective unleashed a feral yell as he toppled into Durgin and knocked him down the stairs. Locke's pistol clattered to the front porch and I kicked it away. Mary stepped toward me, reaching toward her holster. I raised my revolver, but wasn't about to prove this murderous mob justified. I smacked her upside the temple and knocked her back down the stairs where she flipped head over heels into a collected mass of townspeople hiding from an eight-year-old girl.

I glanced into the open parlor and confirmed my suspicions. Alice was gone, maybe out the back, but sure as shit not sticking around to break bread with anyone she'd fired at. I lined up another shot and kicked Locke in the face, then hopped down the stairs, landing next to Durgin, red from screaming, but decidedly unshot.

From the ground, McGregor grabbed my pant leg and snarled something obscene. I took the opportunity to snatch his rifle and rake him over the back with it until I felt his fingers let go.

The others started to climb to their feet. Mary dug through the sand for her iron and the rest advanced with club-like weapons and ill intentions. I stepped back toward the porch, armed with a rifle and a revolver, unwilling to use either for its intended purpose.

What would Noose think? A silly thought, but I couldn't keep it from my mind. I knew. He'd laugh his fucking head off at Rory Daggett wielding two firearms and willing to go to the gallows rather than take a life that didn't deserve taking.

I raised the rifle, watched it tremble in my hands, and found Paul Barron square in my sights. He held the pitchfork a little less tightly, shaking. A flop sweat formed on his forehead and dribbled down his cheeks, caught in his thick mustache. The anger drained from his face, replaced by fear. He thought me a killer, believed every word Mary said.

One shot to prove him right, that's all. The rest of the posse would flee like roaches again after seeing what I did to Paul. The trigger bit into my finger, begged me to pull it. I started to squeeze.

Then a couple things made an attempt to save my immortal soul.

A whistle and glass.

As if ordained by the gods themselves, a vial of darkest black plopped onto the sand between Barron and me. Everybody knew the stories about the mad scientist Simon Crane and his vials of death. What they might not know is that Alice and I had kept a few for a rainy day. All our eyes widened to the size of hot plates and the bodies of men and women scattered away from the wretched glass like it contained the eleventh plague. Shit, for all I knew, it did.

I rolled for cover and a piercing whistle shredded my ears. Suddenly, I knew where the vial came from. I'd have a talk with the lovely little shit later about putting me in a spot where I might end up itching my face off.

The posse grew more puzzled by the minute, and they struggled to their feet once more. A gray beast appeared and knocked them aside like a bad hand of cards. Ghost didn't even slow down as I hopped on behind Alice and we took off west, away from the town.

No one fired a shot that day. No one except Alice, and that was just a warning, but the message was loud and clear. They wanted to rip us limb from limb and hang the leftover parts, and it was all down to something going on in the viper-mad mind of Mary McHugh.

As we raced toward the horizon, a group of dusk-darkened figures surrounded our farmhouse. The closest was Mary, stepping into the last trickles of sunlight to make herself known. She unbuttoned the top of her shirt and I considered turning away, unsure why her last act might be to put on a lewd show. Instead, she untucked a bandana the color of tomorrow morning's sky.

The Demon was coming.

CHAPTER 5

INTO THE BLACKJACKS

"You better wipe that smile off your face," I said to Alice. "I'm still mad at you."

Darkness swallowed the farmhouse, and that was alright, because at least it meant the posse hadn't burned it to the ground. Once in a lifetime was sufficient for watching your home reduce to cinders. A mile or two after the angry shouts died down, Ghost settled into a leisurely trot and eventually to a walk as she took us away from Buzzard's Edge, away from home. Canter long enough, maybe all the way until sunrise and we'd run square into the Blackjack Mountains. Truth be told, that might be the best place to lay low until we figured out how exactly a woman with a bullet in her brain walked out of our parlor and returned a few days later to accuse us of trying to put it there.

Alice kept her smile as I climbed down and walked beside the horse. Her eyes went wide as her mouth formed a mock frown and she waved her arms.

"That supposed to be me? Yeah, fuckin' hilarious. Me trying to get away from a glass vial of death that you threw. I guess you knew it wouldn't break, yeah?"

She waved a hand at me in dismissal, then held out two fists and cocked her thumbs against invisible hammers. After she dropped her imaginary guns, she cupped her hand and pretended to pour something into the breeze.

I looked dumbly at her until my brain caught up. "Wait. Black powder? You threw a vial of black powder. Good Christ, they were right, Pip. You are a monster."

Alice stiffened and turned away. The grin slid off her face.

"Shit," I said. "I'm sorry. I didn't mean it like that."

She held a single claw-like hand up by her shoulder, then let it drop.

"I know you didn't shoot at her. Came from outside and you were right behind me. 'Sides, Ms. McHugh clearly ain't all she pretends to be." I let a beat pass. "You catch that bandana?"

Alice pushed out a single flat hand and wriggled her fingers.

"Blue as a river. Got that right."

The last blink of sun disappeared, and the moon took its shift. No company except the distant howl of a coyote.

"I wonder what it all means."

When I woke up to the sun blazing overhead and the sand scratching at my back, I had two thoughts.

Firstly, thank the gods nothing bit me, stung me, or shot me while I slept. Second was that Alice was still out cold. I could tell by her breathing. With a groan, I climbed to my feet, the morning sun still too bright to let me open my eyes all the way. My mouth tasted like dried shit and I probably looked much the same way. Behind us stretched an endless expanse of desert, inviting in some weird kind of way, but with every moment that passed, the gallows waiting to the east seemed a more likely possibility. A vulture passed overhead, its dark shadow reinforcing that morbid line of thought.

The Blackjack Mountains loomed before us, surprisingly close. We must have covered a fair bit of ground before settling in for the night. A soft stir and Alice was awake and on her feet. She always did sleep lightly and move with a quiet grace.

"Don't suppose you packed some supplies before you jumped out the back window, did you?"

Alice held up her middle finger, sign language old as time itself.

I held up my hands in surrender. "Joke, I swear. Still, I could use some water at the least and Ghost ain't gonna make it much farther, neither."

Alice tilted her head toward the mountains.

"Just what I was thinking. Better chance of water, and it's still early. We go now, might make the trip in a couple hours and outrun the worst of the heat."

The sun had other ideas and beat down relentlessly. Every step brought the mountains closer, in theory, but the spit of land before us never seemed to shrink. Until it did. One moment, the sweat pouring down my forehead dried into rolling grains of salt and the next, luxurious shade bathed our footsteps as the sand darkened, then gave way to a hearty patch of Foothills Palo Verde trees.

The surrounding landscape gradually shifted from dull grays and browns to a vivid stretch of green as we trooped into the Blackjacks. The lush plant life promised salvation in return for just a little more patience. We navigated thinning spaces and moved hopefully forward when suddenly Alice froze.

My gut went cold, and without releasing the reins, I dropped a hand to my holster. Had someone followed us? Were there others in these mountains who might not take kindly to our unexpected arrival?

Slowly, Alice touched her pinky to her thumb, raising the other three fingers in the air, then cupped her ear.

My stomach settled. "I hear it, too."

Ghost bucked forward, nearly pulling my shoulder from the socket. Rather than let her go, I allowed myself to be dragged along. Alice gave chase, stifling laughter as I swatted branches and tried not to lose my damn horse.

Ghost plunged through a clearing and splashed into a thin trickle of running water, then she stuck her muzzle in and tried to suck the mountain dry. Alice and I demonstrated a little more decor, or maybe we were just waiting to see that the horse didn't keel over from tainted river water. Patience waned and we scooped up handfuls of icy goodness that tasted as though the sun had never touched it. The chill ran all the way down my throat and dropped into my stomach like a blessing. Certainly the best moment we'd had in the last few days.

Alice's closed eyes, nodding head, and upturned smile spoke of agreement. Water dribbled down her chin, depositing small drops in the soil, and she eased onto her backside, appearing content. No concerns about dirty pants or wet boots. Happiness beamed off her like sun rays in that moment and even the scar on her cheek seemed on its way to healing.

Then her eyes shot open and my heart missed a beat.

Blue bandanas. Cocked rifles. A snake-like grin hovering over hundreds of puckered scars. The gleam of a knife. I saw it all and I saw none of it in the space of a second, and suddenly Alice's eyes changed from wide and alert to a suspicious squint. She stood and brought all her fingers together into a point, then touched them to her cheek with it, never taking her eyes off the path ahead.

My eyebrows tangled up as I tried to remember that sign, and then I saw what caught her eye.

A cabin in the woods.

We may have neglected food, but we had firepower in spades. The carefree little girl dipping her toes in the creek became a hardened warrior in the space of a single breath as we approached the house, spaced far enough apart that a single shooter could only threaten one of us. From twenty feet behind, Ghost quietly expressed her discontent at being tied to a tree. She kept her voice down, though. A smart horse knows when to not give the game away.

Though the treeline wasn't dense by any stretch of the imagination, it did provide sufficient cover from the cabin's windows. Backs pressed against trunks, we watched for any movement, signs of life. None came. The wood appeared weather-worn yet not all that old, and the longer we stared down the front door, the more prevalent the sense of abandonment became. Someone had lived here, someone had loved this place, but that was another lifetime. Now, this was just wood stacked in a very particular pile.

Alice scraped her middle finger across the back of her left hand.

"Yeah," I whispered. "I think you're right." I took another glance. "Watch my back just in case?" I stepped forward without waiting for her say-so. It was hardly the first time the girl had covered my ass.

The front porch screamed under my weight, a last call for help against the skinny fucker and the little girl intruding on the property. A light breeze whistled through the shack as if to put the final nail in the coffin and declare its solitude. Still, I froze in front of the closed door.

Should I knock? Call out? Barge in?

Sucking in a breath, I pushed the door and held my revolver out in front of me. When the flimsy wooden door rattled against the wall, I nearly jumped out of my skin. Quaint as the cabin looked from the outside, there seemed even less to the inside. A pile of blankets standing in for a bed littered the corner, holes nibbled in the sheets. Some crates lined the walls. Clothing strewn across the top promised nothing fancy. My eyes roamed the room, searching for any sign of inhabitants, and found nothing.

I released that breath.

A hand landed on my shoulder, and I nearly let my newly filled bladder go. I spun and found Alice there, shaking her head. There was something sad about the motion. Then she nodded toward the wall next to the door.

A.M.

W.B.

She ran her middle finger across the back of her left hand again, softer this time.

Empty.

Something bad had happened there. No evidence, just a feeling.

I closed my eyes and listened to the breeze for a second. It contained a hint of danger but compared to the blazing wildfire waiting for us back in Buzzard's Edge, it would do. I caught Alice's eye. She felt it, too. It was written all over her face.

"Guess we got a place to stay."

She moved a closed hand toward her mouth and my stomach answered in kind.

"I'll grab Ghost and let's see what we can do."

The place wasn't sprawling by any means. Room enough for a grown man, a stubborn kid, and a rather large horse. Wasn't my idea. I tried to tie Ghost to the porch, but the way she hits you with those big brown eyes is far more criminal than anything I've ever been accused of.

Some of the clothes packed away looked about my size, a nice boon depending how long we might be stuck there. Stowed away under the shirts and away from the prying sunlight, we found food, preserved and sealed away in jars. Black mold floated inside a few. We set those aside to dispose of later. Opening the rest was as fun as a game of Russian Roulette. I'd never before smelled fruit so fermented I just about got drunk from the fumes. That jar got stowed back under a stack of pants, in case I got desperate. Others stunk to high heaven, threatening to evacuate the already meager contents of my stomach. Those went straight outside where we could move them away later. Maybe bury them or consult a priest.

Not everything was a loss, though. The people who'd lived in this cabin before we stumbled upon it knew what they were doing and clearly had no plans to trek down to Buzzard's Edge any more often than necessary. Judging by the state of things, they'd been gone years, maybe a decade, and yet some of their stores survived. Grateful for that, Alice and I dug in. Ghost, too.

Following the feast, a nap seemed in order. Seemed downright required.

CHAPTER 6

COYOTE AND VULTURE

A.M. and W.B. may not have stocked the kind of mattress the president sleeps on, but it did the trick. Didn't hear Alice complaining about it, neither. She rolled out of bed a few minutes after me and silently studied her surroundings, taking in the faded wood of the walls and the mess we'd made of the previous residents' stores. Judgment usually rested easy on her face, never did feel uncomfortable hanging up its hat there. Not that day, though.

"So, the daring outlaws and their trusty steed escape the wily clutches of the ruthless Sheriff McHugh, back from the dead, against all odds, and set on their capture." I waggled a finger. "No, no. Their execution, at the hands of the very people they swore to defend."

Alice huffed and blew a few strands of crystal blonde hair out from in front of her eyes.

"It is not overdramatic." I let my eyes wander, tracing over the cracks between floorboards. "Seriously, though. Thought a bit of time and travel might help me digest what happened. Doesn't make any more sense now than it did yesterday."

She raised the middle three fingers on her right hand, spread the thumb and pinky out to the side, then brought the whole deal forward and down.

"Just stay here? It's got simplicity going for it. I'll give you that." I tapped my toe against a loose wooden plank and bit my lip. "Okay, say we do. We camp out here for a couple days, weeks. How do we know they won't come looking for us?"

Alice thought for a moment, then unleashed a flurry of waving hands and head nods. A quick swipe across her chin, a single upraised pointer finger swirling at the ceiling, a little two-fingered devil horn, and a pinch like she was trying to snatch something imaginary out of the air in front of her eyes. A few more rapid-fire signs peppered the bunch, though I caught the gist of it, and the kid had a damn good point.

She could've killed us at the farmhouse when she was close enough to flash a bandana. You think the Demon couldn't have made that shot?

"So we stay," I said.

Fingers pointed, pinky and thumb jutting out, forward and down motion.

We stay.

It's a strange thing to brag about, no question, but we made that place shine. Alice brushed years of dust out the front door and into oblivion while I separated the usable goods from the refuse and hauled off the rotten bits.

Even clean, the cabin reminded me of a coffin, due in no small part to its size and the meager amount of natural light peeking through the cracks. Giving over a space the size of a kitchen to a horse hardly helped with the cramped feeling. With the cobwebs banished, the next order of business involved pulling the tarps down from the windows and letting some of that healthy sunshine in. A man who spends his whole life in Buzzard's Edge looks outside and sees a wide spectrum of color, everything from sandy yellow to rocky brown. Adding the lively shades of green those mountains offered… I didn't hate it. Somehow, it made the sun seem less like a villain in its own right; a bringer of life as opposed to a rogue scourge set to suck the liquid and life out of anything that walked.

That unfettered daylight made busywork chores like sorting clothes more manageable, and I took a certain amount of pride in the work. I think we both did. Honoring the memory of those who came before us and left us a roof in our time of need.

Every so often, a series of clumps resonated through the floor. Alice's grab-my-attention signal for when she found items of interest. Some empty jars we could use to store water, a can of jarred pickles that appeared free of disease, a dinky little pistol that seemed like it might not even shoot through an open window. And of course, the serape. Red and gold fabric, faded from use, but sewn with care. I slipped it over my head and Alice silently laughed so hard her shoulders shook and she almost fell over.

"Lots of fellas wear these. Good protection from the sun, you know?"

She refused to embrace my logic.

Except for the serape, most of the items left by good ol' A.M. and W.B. were men's clothes, maybe a little wider around the waist than what I usually wore, but not by much. The deeper we dug into boxes, the more apparent it became that none of the former cabin-dwellers wore the same size as a lean eight-year-old girl. At least the creek would provide a nice place to wash clothes. A few weapons graced the bottom of a long crate, notably a six-inch-long hunting knife. Alice stared, mesmerized by the gleam.

"Might do alright in a fight," I said, "but what you really want that for is skinning an animal, getting the good meat off before you roast it."

Her brows dropped and disappointment bunched them together.

"Now here." I reached into the basket and whistled. "Here's your prize. Seen one of these before?"

Alice lifted the tightly strung bow, sized for a grown man and not far off from the length of her body. Beneath it lay a quiver of arrows.

"Quality stuff, by the looks. Never messed with this type of thing myself, but when it comes to gear for hunting animals or putting down people looking to do you harm, it's all the same, right? Long as it don't rust and dull, it plays."

She ran a cautious finger along the side of one of the arrowheads and cracked a grin.

"Exactly," I said, laying the bow back down with something like reverence.

With all the hustle of the day, it was easy to forget there was a mob who wished for nothing more than to wash their hands in our blood. At least, that was the case until the sun dropped below the trees and every little sound reminded me of a boot step or a rifle hammer clicked into place.

Alice and I sat on either side of an open window, hands holding iron.

The *crack* of a snapped stick.

The *splash* of something landing in the water.

The rustling *crunch* of a heavy limb pressing down on the dirt.

"I'm gonna look," I whispered.

Alice's head shook, so fast it almost didn't happen.

"On three. One. Two—"

I shot up with the revolver outstretched, ready to blast one in the chest and forehead of anybody creeping up on the cabin. Two glowing green eyes stared back from the depths of the woods. Eerie as the sight was, it settled my stomach a bit.

I gave Alice a light tap on the shoulder and she hopped to her feet, still shaking a little.

"Human eyes don't shine like that," I said, and she nodded. "Maybe we should go hunting tomorrow. What do you think?"

Alice didn't answer, just stared out into the night. She watched the creature for another moment until the eyes blinked back into the darkness, though it was hard to shake the notion they were still watching.

"You were scared for me," I said, slipping a little more confidence than I felt into my voice.

Alice got that look that usually meant she was going to hit me, then her eyes softened. She brought her right hand flat from her chest and clapped it against her open left. A second later, she pulled the two hands apart as if taking off a coat. She held that gesture for a moment, then pointed to herself and stooped down to pick up the canvas tarps from the floor.

My throat tightened as I helped her hang them back up and shut out the night.

"Yeah, kid. You're all I have, too."

"Gonna get gored by a wild pig trying to defend myself with this stupid thing." I pulled an arrow back against the tight string and tried to aim at the broad side of a tree. "They got wild pigs up here?"

From the corner of my eye, I watched Alice place a finger in front of her lips. The morning sun glinted off her hair in a way I could claim distracted me if I fucked up. I stowed that away.

Deep breath in and I let go of the arrow and watched it miss the trunk so badly the breeze it created didn't even rustle the leaves.

"Ah, perfect. I was aiming for the grass thirty feet yonder. Fuckin' bullseye." I leaned the bow against a more spindly tree, one I hadn't tried to shoot through the heart, then crossed my arms like a sulking child. "I see something out here with meat on its bones, I'm going to pull my revolver and shoot it. And you can't stop me."

With a quick-draw roll of her eyes, Alice pointed to one ear and then waggled two flat palms as if trying to jump out of the shadows and scare me. Then she grabbed an invisible rope, hauled it up, and let her tongue hang out.

"I don't remember that last one in the book, but I see your point about drawing unwanted attention. Fine, we'll use the bow."

Another few unsuccessful practice rounds and I was ready to send an arrow flying past something more lively. "Follow the creek," Alice had signed. Clearly, she'd been listening to someone smarter than me. Living things needed water and it would lead us back to the cabin when we'd either caught supper or given up. With slow, careful steps, trying not to make any more noise than necessary, we searched the space between the trees for whatever had watched us with those green eyes the night before. The land was less arid at this altitude, but the snakes and other bitey critters would adapt to the color scheme. The stores of A.M. and W.B. failed to compete with the selection of remedies at Barron's Apothecary, even if they did keep a nice wardrobe, some fine hunting tools, and enough jarred food to keep us fed if the hunting trip failed to pan out.

The sun climbed higher in the sky, blazing down through the canopy to roast my exposed patches of skin, and for a while, that seemed the only movement. Then something swished across the stream a ways down. Alice and I froze, watched, not daring to take a breath. My lungs felt about to burst when a coyote popped its head out from the brush. It lapped up some water, taking no note of the strangers watching from an arrow's flight away. Barely moving a single finger, Alice gestured up. I locked the arrow into place, pulled it back, and aimed.

"I don't like it," I whispered.

Alice shot me a look like I'd claimed to be the son of a river toad.

"Henry Taff and me, we got most of our supplies from McGregor's General, but every so often we'd go hunting. 'Course we always used a gun. Point is, he always told me it was bad luck to shoot a coyote."

Alice rested four fingers against her temple and then pulled them into a closed fist away from her head.

I kept the string taut and stared down the coyote, still filling its belly with the cool mountain spring, not a care in the world. "Maybe luck's not the right word. Henry always used to say the coyote had, like, a partner in crime."

My eyes flicked up and found only the sun trickling through the dense canopy. For now. Alice caught the motion and mimicked a bird's beak, opening and closing.

"Yep, not just any bird, though. Vulture. You got two of the most unlovable things the wild ever conjured up, put 'em both in the fucking desert. Figure neither one stands a chance unless they got the other watching their back. So yeah, not luck. Protection. You fuck with one, you get both."

Now we were both checking the skies for stray shadows.

"What do you think?" I grinned at her. "Do we chance it?"

She held up a hand, appearing less sure of herself than a moment before, then dropped it. A muffled smacking noise rang through the clearing. The coyote stiffened and lifted its head from the water. Its big green eyes darted around the woods and stumbled upon us before she dashed into a crowded sprig of trees.

I lowered the bow. "Well, there goes the chow. Fresh chow, anyway."

Alice wasn't listening. Her head was turned toward the sky. A shadow the shape of a dagger crossed over us, then vanished, leaving only the mid-day sun.

"See, now ain't you glad you listened to me? Hungry, sure, but not all scratched up by big, nasty talons. 'Sides, I think I saw something that looked like a pickled rutabaga in one of those jars."

She closed her eyes and shook her head, trying the hide the faintest hint of a grin, as we followed the stream back to the cabin.

Almost a week of unproductive hunting, missed shots, and eating shitty pickled vegetables that floated in jars like pieces of a dismembered creature passed before I got the bright idea to put the bow in Alice's hands. A last ditch effort before I stopped giving a shit about being heard by civilization and started unloading bullets into vermin. She had to rest the bottom of the weapon into a divot on the ground, but still managed to bury an arrow in the target tree on attempt number one.

"Good enough for me," I said, and we set out.

Not twenty feet up the stream sat the fattest cottontail I'd ever laid eyes upon. Like a reward for good behavior sprawled out on a serving dish. The rushing whoosh and twang of the string were the only sounds she made. Not enough to give the rabbit pause from its mouthful of greens before Alice's arrow sliced through its neck.

We'd only just strung the rabbit up by its feet and gone inside to check on Ghost when two sharp knocks came at the cabin door. I'd had about all I could take of these fucking knocks and if it was another posse looking to drag our asses back to town and hang us high, I wouldn't struggle over whether or not to pull the trigger this time.

Alice usually hid at the sound of company. This time, a fed-up look crossed her face, and she picked the rifle up from the dusty floorboards and aimed it squarely at the door. I crept over to the window and tried to peek out without exposing myself. The trees swayed gently. Not a soul in sight.

Another knock. This time a voice followed, shaken a little by panic.

"You in there, Rory? It's Billy."

Billy fucking Chambers.

I opened the door and poked the barrel of my revolver between his startled eyes.

"Come on in, friend. We were just about to start a fire."

41

CHAPTER 7

THE OTHER SIDE OF THE FIRE

Alice relieved Billy of his sidearm and directed him toward the bed where he collapsed in a sweaty heap and eyeballed the cabin's interior as if the shadows might burst to life.

We sat across the room, guns not quite trained on him, but not pointed away either.

"How'd you find us?" I asked.

Billy looked at his boots like somebody might've scribbled the right answer across the toes. When he got tired of looking, he glanced past Alice and met my eyes. "They said you went west. Only thing west for some time is the mountains."

"Been almost a week. Either you scoured the whole range, and you don't look like a man lost in nature, or you knew this place was here." I rested my thumb against the hammer and saw him catch it. "Cut the shit, Billy."

He pursed his lips like he was about to spit, then he did. So to speak. "This was a while back, now. A couple fellas from back east moved out here, built this place. One of 'em came into town every so often. Nice guy. Quiet. Andrew, his name was."

I caught Alice's eye and suspected we both had the same thought.

A.M.

Billy continued. "Andrew smiled when he said his pleases and thank you's, but always had a glint of nervousness in his eyes." Billy chuckled. "Harden used to say he looked like a man who didn't want to be remembered, and I guess he was right on that count."

The grin that accompanied Billy's laughter dropped off his face like he'd forgotten about the guns that hadn't quite grown to trust him. "Say, y'all have me at a disadvantage. And… and you know me." I heard the hurt in his voice. "Don't s'pose you could lower those things a mite? Maybe even move this story outside to cook up that animal you got hung up out there. Long trip, and I could use something to eat."

Alice narrowed her eyes and held up ten fingers. Without lowering her gaze, she mashed them together like clay.

"She's got a real good point, Billy. How do we know there ain't another crowd out there waiting to haul us in?"

Slowly, he took off his hat and lowered his head. When he picked it up, his eyes glistened. "I came 'cause I needed your help. Thought you maybe could use some of mine." Silence filled the cabin. "Way I see it, Doubtin' Daggett, is you can walk me outside with a gun barrel in each ear, pull the triggers if I'm lyin'. 'Sides, if there was a crew out there, how long you think they're gonna wait?"

His eyes met mine when he asked the question. I struggled to argue the point.

"Just hungry is all," he muttered.

"Ah fuck, Billy. Get up. Let's go."

True to his word, Billy led the way outside and not a single shot rang out. Not so much as a pair of coyote eyes watching from the inky darkness. We pushed the night back with a small fire, manageable and shielded from the view of any potential wanderers in the woods.

"Lordy," said Billy. "Never seen a rabbit this size. God as my witness, I thought you too bagged yourself a mongrel pup. What you figure they eat up here?"

Alice sat before the fire, alert but focused on the juices running down her lips. She ate like a middle-of-the-pecking-order predator. Attention on the meal, sure, but not at the expense of losing track of her surroundings.

"Guess they just grow bigger out here. You were saying, about this Andrew fella? Got a last name?"

Billy's eyes went wide and glassy. "Oh yeah. Martin. Won't never forget that. So, Andrew came down about once a month and I guess maybe three or four trips went by before an older gent came looking for him. His father. Not nearly so polite, that fucker. Had a bit of… what you call it? Thinks the world fuckin' owes him something."

"Entitlement," I said, quietly. "Let me guess, you pointed him in the right direction and now guilt bubbles in your gut every time you think about it."

Billy squirmed. Uncomfortable like something had reached through the grass and poked him in the backside. "That's the thing I liked least, actually. He only condescended hisself to Buzzard's Edge to round up some lawmen and a couple guns. He knew exactly where Andrew was." Billy shook his head. "If I'm honest, I think about Andrew at least once or twice a month. His daddy? I can't even remember the guy's name." He spat. "I was tied up with somethin' or other, maybe just left to man the sheriff's office or some such shit, but I heard tell that Andrew's daddy walked from the edge of town to the cabin like he was on a string. Cocked his head every so often to make you think he was hearin' voices. Real unnatural like. When they got up there, they found Andrew livin' in this here cabin with another man. Wes Bradley was his name."

A.M.

W.B.

"Livin'… together?"

Billy gave me a look like I had rocks in my head. On further reflection, it was exactly the type of question a rock-brained individual might ask. "It connected a lot of dots," he said with a shrug. "But they weren't botherin' nobody. Certainly seemed to rub the father the wrong way, though. He started spoutin' preachery bullshit at the both of them." Billy wrapped his arms around his knees, looked down, resembling a scared child all of the sudden.

Alice stopped chewing and raised an eye toward Billy as if she didn't trust what he might do next.

"What happened then?"

He rocked on his behind and bit his lip. We let a moment go by as the breeze fluttered through the trees, stealing some warmth from the fire.

"You won't believe me."

"Not too long ago, I melted a fuckin' witch after she made me imagine I was on a train inside a saloon. Try me."

He nodded as though it all made perfect sense. "Somethin' living in these mountains. Like a man, I guess, but made of light. Right before John Harden's eyes, it ripped that preacher man right in two." Billy glanced over my shoulder. "Probably not ten feet from where we sit. Then the glowing creature took Andrew, vanished under the afternoon sun with him. Didn't leave behind so much as a fingernail."

I raised an eyebrow. "Christ almighty, John told you all this?"

He shook his head. "John made it clear real damn quick he didn't want to talk about it. The story came from Wes Bradley after they hauled him across the desert and slapped him in a cell. Left me all alone with him."

I furrowed my brow as a heat rose in my stomach. "How do you know the kid wasn't lying to save his skin?"

Billy took a minute to answer. "You didn't hear him tell it. The heartbreak in his every word. Didn't make no explanations for the glowing monster, neither. Seems to me, a man who dreamed up that tale would know the whys and wherefores, but this kid didn't pretend to have a clue what life'd thrown at him." Billy took a shaky breath. "So either he was good enough to join a theater troupe, he was out of his mind, or he was telling the truth. I choose to believe the third."

"What happened to him? Wes?"

"We hanged him. We couldn't come to terms with the parts of the world that didn't make no square sense to us, so we hanged him." Billy wiped at his eye and I looked away. "I will cherish the memory of John Harden until the day I die, Rory, but the thing that haunts me most about Wes Bradley is that we chose to put a man to death rather than believe something we couldn't understand."

The world blurred as I shook my head. "I knew John. He wouldn't do that. There's more to the story. Something he didn't tell you."

A joyless smile crept onto Billy's face. "I'm sure there was a thousand things he didn't share with me, and I want you to know, I don't tell you this to hurt you or to sully my friend's name. S'just ain't nobody perfect and makes the best choice every time. Everyone's got ghosts they got to live with and the way they handle those ghosts says a lot about a man." He glanced at Alice, who continued scowling from the other side of the fire. "Or about a woman."

Billy licked his lips. "I'm awfully thirsty. Don't suppose you know where a fella could get a drink around here?"

I pointed at the creek. Billy shook the spirits away and walked toward the sound of the stream.

"Well I'll just about be," he said, letting water dribble down and get stuck in his chin whiskers. "If that ain't the best damned water ever graced my tongue."

"There is something to it, isn't there?" I squatted down by Alice and took my own mouthful. "Like it steered clear of the atmosphere of Buzzard's Edge and is all the more pure for it."

Billy nodded with a thoughtful expression. "Speaking of tainted air, I s'pose you know why I come?"

"Pretty good idea," I said.

Alice held out an index finger and circled her ear, then moved a flat palm from chin to chest.

"Now that ain't nice," I said through a laugh. "Accurate as shit, though."

Billy chuckled. Seemed even he had gleaned a little bit of sign language. Context, maybe.

"Don't understand it entirely, myself," he said. "After you left the sheriff's office that day, Locke spat some accusations, mostly thin nonsense." Billy raised his eyebrows. "He don't seem to like you, none."

"Somebody shit in his hat, but it wasn't me." I gestured for Billy to go on.

"Hm, so he goes on his way. Little over a day later, he's back with Mary hobbling behind him. I just about pissed myself at the sight of her."

Alice pointed at her leg and ran her fist around in a circle.

"Exactly. What do you mean 'hobble'? Nothin' wrong with her legs by the time we ran into her."

"Just what I say. Looked like she got run over by a big ol' beastie. It was her head that bothered me most, though. Had a bandage wrapped around it, little spot of blood poking out right above the eyes."

"Right where they shot her. Huh."

"What I thought. Got her some water and a chair and she spouted a story about how you and the kid ambushed her."

My face went hot. "Bet it was the same particulars as the campfire tale she broke out at the farmhouse, in front of most of the damn town. She say Alice took a shot at her? Missed?"

"She did."

I sucked in a deep breath. "Claimed I knocked her out, and that would account for a seeping head wound, but here's where I start to get troubled, Billy."

Alice held out four fingers on each hand, then let the ones on the right dribble down like blood.

"No bandage around her head when we saw her, and the wound you mentioned?" I shook my head. "Not much more than a beauty mark. Caught my attention, but I guess I didn't have time to dwell on it with an angry mob calling for my head. Not to mention this little brat throwing vials of black powder at me."

Alice flashed a sign so quickly, I doubt Billy even noticed it. Thumb joined to pointer and the other three fingers sticking up like a rooster tail. "Asshole," she said, with a grin on her face.

I clapped my arms to my chest in an X. "You know it. So what the hell does it mean?"

Alice made the 'asshole' sign with both hands and then twirled the top one around.

"Shit," I whispered.

Billy went white. "What'd she say?"

I caught his eye before I spoke. "Ghost."

He started to laugh, but it caught in his throat when neither Alice or me joined him. "Seriously?"

"Maybe not a ghost exactly, but are you telling me this would be the first time in Buzzard's Edge's illustrious history that something more than natural grabbed you by the balls and shook?"

Billy watched the setting sun bounce off the river. He didn't say a word. Didn't have to. I knew what he was thinking. The glowing men in the mountains. Right in this very spot. Not just a story. Something that had done irreversible harm to a human being.

Finally, he spoke. "For the sake of argument, and I ain't sayin' I agree with the two of you, but what if she did have some sort of communion with the dead? Ability to overcome it, if you like. What on God's dusty ass earth would we do about that?"

Alice closed her fist and pointed her thumb at her mouth. My stomach grew heavy and filled with ice. Almost like I'd guzzled a barrel of the creek water in one sip.

I cleared my throat. "I know someone who might be able to point me in the right direction."

Billy nodded. "Where can we find them?"

"Uh-uh. Gotta be just me. Can you stay here with Alice?" I snapped my fingers. "No, shit. What if they miss you at the sheriff's office?"

Billy hushed up and refused to meet my eyes.

"Billy," I whispered. "What took you so long to get here?"

"Her and Locke. They stopped trusting me the moment Mary McHugh's dead ass strolled back into town. Gave me round the clock duty, pointless little jobs, and didn't let me leave. Even brought meals by and had me sleeping in the cell. Said it was just 'til they got the current situation sorted, but it didn't feel right, Rory. You know?"

"What's she doing down there?" I asked the question out loud, but it was as much for me as Billy.

"No idea, and that's the truth. After a few days of that I started imagining what kinds of things they might have planned for me. Decided I had to get away at the first opportunity. Slipped out this morning past some big brute she'd stationed outside the door. Had to knock him upside the head with a chair leg, I'm afraid. Guess I'm just glad they didn't follow me here."

As soon as he dropped the last line, we all got real quiet. The stream burbled a little louder. A lone bird sang in the trees, out past its bedtime.

Bugs chittered, searching for other bugs to fuck. Not a hint of humanity except for our own ragged breathing. Alice remained silent, worry written across her face, either at the prospect of me wandering back into a town that wanted me strung up or who I was sneaking in to see.

"You're welcome to stay here, Billy. I'm heading out tonight, though."

"Won't even tell me the name of the person that's gonna get us out of this mess?" Billy asked.

"An old friend. I just hope he sees it that way."

CHAPTER 8

THE SALOON AT THE END OF THE WORLD

Ghost seemed almost offended when I led her out of the cabin. A quick drink from the creek and the prospect of stretching her legs set her at ease, however. I shook Billy's hand and clapped him on the back, then brought Alice in for a hug and whispered a promise into her ear.

"I'll be back before you know it."

I knew that girl well. If I failed to honor my pledge, she'd chase me into hell and give me a look that spoke a thousand words. With a preview of that glare, she let me go and stepped back toward the cabin.

I nodded toward Billy. "Take good care of him, Pip."

He probably rolled his eyes. I don't know. By then, my back was to the cabin, and I was pointed at Buzzard's Edge like a Colt pistol ready to deal some damage. A slap on Ghost's rump and we were off. She navigated through the trees like she'd grown up in those mountains and knew them inside out. More than once my heart slammed against the wall of my chest thinking the devil mare was about to splatter me upside a tree and hit the desert with nothing but my headless corpse holding the reins.

Through equestrian skill or blind luck, we blew out into the sand, kicking up a dust cloud behind us. I hoped it might make anyone watching from a distance fear what rode in on the wind. I'd be careful. I promised Alice as much, but heaven help the first person who looked at me wrong.

The sun dropped quickly, and the desert cooled. From the burning plains of hell itself to the inside of an icebox in less time than it took to whistle the first movement of *Moonlight Sonata*. The dim glow of the moon made sneaking into Buzzard's Edge simpler, though it would also draw a flock to my destination.

A mile or so outside the town proper, I came across an abandoned farmhouse, burnt to a fucking crisp some time ago by the looks of it. Clearly, the owners had either perished with the fire or abandoned the ashy ruins to start over elsewhere.

Their loss, my gain.

Ghost was a beautiful horse who became downright ornery if she wasn't reminded of that fact regularly, but she stood out in a crowd. A stranger hiding underneath a wide brim is one thing; doesn't attract much attention unless they fire their pistol into the air. A stranger who rides in on the well-known horse of a wanted man. That's a different story entirely.

I held Ghost's muzzle. Otherwise, she wouldn't grace me with her attention. "Be an hour, maybe a bit more, but I'll be back." She knickered softly in a way that said, "I ain't happy about it, but what choice do I have?"

A spigot behind the husk of the farmhouse spat some dust before it turned on the flow. I filled a stray pail and left it by Ghost, who promptly turned her back on me.

I swear that horse descended from royalty somewhere down the line.

The shadows leapt to life as I crept across the open sand. The sounds of civilization made sure I couldn't possibly wander off in the wrong direction.

Was it always this loud?

The exile Mary forced me and Alice into suddenly seemed a whole lot lonelier.

The buildings grew on the horizon. Candles and lantern light rivaled the moon and silhouettes stared out from the packed streets. A cold sweat trickled down the back of my neck. Deserted streets might comfort me, but they sure as hell wouldn't hide me. Taking that first step like I was the fucking mayor himself, I set on down the street. Measured pace. I felt eyes studying me, crawling over the serape and stetson of the two boys who'd kindly lent us the use of their cabin, and I fought the urge to look back. A mite suspicious if a stranger doesn't return your glare, but preferable to getting in a fight with some whiskey-soused asshole who doesn't like the look of you.

I recognized a few faces, casual acquaintances who sold dried meat or boots and tried their damndest not to make eye contact. Since the time I accidentally robbed Herschel McGregor's store, I tried not to wander into town any more than necessary. Other faces reflected the firelight enough to give me a clear look and held no familiarity. In a town this size, those men worried me more.

The crowd grew thicker the closer I got. Elbows poked into my gut and their owners blew acrid belches in my face. Only one place in town that served the type of rotgut that made a man's breath smell like a carcass left rotting under the Arizona sun.

Why the fuck the new guy decided to name it the Saloon at the End of the World when it wasn't even at the end of the country was beyond me. I'd never passed a word with Mr. Jeffery and hadn't been inside his establishment in the couple of months since he took over after Emmett Lynch's timely demise. Jeffery displayed a careful nature combined with the innocent look of a man who had no idea what went on in his back room.

False confidence had gotten me this far, so I called on it once more and gave the door a shove, dodging the swinging batwing and strutting over to the bar. Inside, it smelled like liquor and sweat, with a hint of flatulence. The aroma mixed passably with the brash notes of somebody committing indecent assault on a piano. I paused a couple feet from the bar. I swear I could almost see the previous bartender's brain fleeing out the back of his skull after Alice popped out and let him have it.

From behind the bar, Mr. Jeffery studied me over the top of his rounded glasses. I'd passed no less than thirty sets of prying eyes and managed to keep them clueless. Jeffery wasn't fooled. He knew it was me. I should have turned and run. Instead, I nodded. He tapped another server on the shoulder and whispered something in the man's ear, never taking his eyes off me, then pushed around the side of the bar and gestured toward a table.

"You shouldn't be here," he said as I plopped down across from him.

"I don't intend to disagree. Mr. Jeffery, isn't it?" I kept my hand beneath my serape. Not on my revolver, but not too far away.

"Make it Robert. I'll refrain from saying your name, if you don't mind. One thing I've learned in Buzzard's Edge, especially lately, is that there are unwelcome ears everywhere." His eyes flitted toward the door. "Even when you own the building."

"Robert, then. Let me ask you. Wouldn't be no skin off your back to gather up a small group and haul me in front of the new sheriff. Seems to me, there's people in the room who got an affinity for posse work. So why am I sitting unassaulted instead of being dragged through the streets?"

For a moment, Jeffery teased a smile, then it transformed into something more uneasy. "You've been out of town a week, right?"

"Close enough to it."

He shook his head. "I can't shake the feeling that was the plan. Things don't change in such a short span unless somebody thought real hard about it and set up the pieces on the chessboard."

A ruckus broke out at the bar. Broken glass. The sound of meat thwacking away at meat. The sound of violence and familiarity.

"What changed?"

Robert Jeffery flashed a glance around the room, letting his eyes bounce off every customer and crevice. When he spoke, it was just over a whisper. "Deputies. McHugh said Billy Chambers could no longer be trusted, and she needed a right-hand man. Only problem is she hired something more like fifteen. Outsiders, every one of them."

An image of Mary standing at the edge of my property flickered to mind, sky blue bandana bared for me and Alice to see as we retreated toward the mountains. It wouldn't surprise me to learn those deputies hid their true colors the same way.

He held up a hand. "I'm not a judging man, but none of these fellas seem fit for law enforcement. Vicious men, drunk with power. That and moonshine. Don't suppose you heard about Chris Durgin?"

My stomach dropped, thinking of Alice's warning shot that nearly scared the life out of Durgin. My look must've answered the question, because Jeffery nodded and kept on going.

"First order of business for the new deputies was to blame him for letting you get away. If he hadn't started screaming and distracting everybody, then the townspeople would have dropped you to the ground and hauled you in, but that ain't the way it went. Whole show started with embarrassment, then it got mean. I'll spare you the details, but Christopher Durgin died sobbing in the street, frightened as a little kid before he choked to death on his own blood."

A nasty mix of guilt and rage bubbled in my stomach, threatened to erupt if somebody so much as glanced my way twice. I allowed a few deep breaths before trying to spit out something coherent. When the words finally came, there were only four. "Son of a bitch."

"You're not kidding." Jeffery's eyes settled on the bar and told him he could leave it alone for another minute or two. "They're patrolling the streets night and day looking for you. I don't know what their aim is, but two things are obvious to me."

"Yeah?"

"First, they need you gone to see their plan through. Can't rightly say what it might be or why, but tell me it doesn't feel that way."

"My friend kind of jumped to the same conclusion. Second?"

"You don't want to get caught by these fuckers." He lowered his eyebrows and tilted his head. "Why are you here, anyway? Wasn't me you were looking for."

While the roiling in my stomach kicked up again, a grin fought its way onto my face. "Don't suppose you know what you have in that backroom, do you?"

His eyebrows shot up near the top of his forehead and he returned my smile. "Son, why do you think I decided to call it the Saloon at the End of the World?"

Robert Jeffery closed the door behind me, opting to get back to work rather than join the fun. The moment the door clicked home, the bright storm of lantern light died and the susurrus of drunken bellows and hearty laughter dropped like God himself had called for the music to dim to a new dynamic.

It was cold back there and my fingers trembled as I reached for some matches. As my ears adjusted to the unnatural quiet, the struck match seemed to roar. The flickering light danced along the dull gray walls and found a deserted table and two chairs, even revealed a cracked-open closet. Spiderwebs and a thick layer of dust made me wonder if Jeffery or his employees ever set foot in this room.

Why do you think I decided to call it the Saloon at the End of the World?

"Maybe not," I whispered.

It seemed to echo in the solitude until a brash, tuneless voice called out from the dark and sent a shiver up my spine.

"Shoo fly, don't bother me."

The melody vanished as if it had never existed in the first place. Silence claimed the space. Then the chair closer to me scraped along the floorboards.

"Won't you have a seat, Rory?"

"Mighty kind of you, George." I sat.

From across the table, the other chair scraped back and settled a foot or so away from the wall. I held up the match and wasn't surprised when the light revealed only empty air. Real or illusion, Noose's blood still spattered the top of the table. The heat of the flame crawled toward my fingers. I shook out the match and didn't bother lighting a new one. Perfect darkness settled in front of my eyes.

"Time is very strange when you're dead. S'pose that probably ain't too tough to guess, but feels like it's been a while since you came by."

I shrugged, unsure whether he could see me in the dark. "Four, five months. Can you blame me? Alice's eyes just about popped out of her head when I told her."

"So don't tell her." I heard the smile in his voice.

"That's the difference between you and me, George. I'm not an asshole."

"First visit makes sense, I guess. Closure and curiosity. When you didn't come again, I figured it was a one-off. Disappointed me, really. You'd think being a ghost'd be interesting. Not beholden to all those fuckin' earthbound rules…"

"You dangled from a noose without dying, laughed at everybody while you were doin' it. I watched you get shot in the chest when I was a kid. Earthbound rules didn't exactly limit your bullshit before."

"Fair point," he said. "Mostly, I mean spending eternity in a dusty backroom ain't so glamorous. Especially with people afraid to set foot in here. Shoulda blown my brains out somewhere more interesting." The table rattled as if he'd dropped a fist on it. "Anyways, you got me off track, Shoo Fly. Point is, what brought you back this time?"

I chewed my lip, trying to figure the best way to put my thoughts.

"Ho-ly shit." Noose let out a laugh that seemed to shake the room. I'd almost forgotten the crowd just a wall away. "You need my help," he said. "Well, shit. Let's hear it. Rory Daggett took out a fuckin' platoon of outlaws by his lonesome. Can't fuckin' wait to hear what's got him stumped."

I opened my mouth to speak, and he interrupted.

"It's a woman, ain't it?"

I cleared my throat. "In a manner of speaking."

"Ha! Li'l Rory Daggett looking to get his wick wet, and you come to me for advice. Ain't that something?"

"Jesus Christ, will you shut up for a second? I ain't lookin' for advice on love." I chuckled while I waited for him to butt in. He stayed silent. "Who knows? Maybe you would be the most logical choice. Most fellas talk to their daddies about that shit. You took mine."

"Aww, that stings, Shoo Fly." He passed it off like a joke, but there was a little more seriousness to his tone than I was used to.

"Whole town's looking for me. Think I tried to kill the new sheriff."

"Well, you're in one of my hidey holes. Other's up in the mountains. Served me and the crew you dismantled damn well for years."

I shook my head, then remembered he couldn't see me in the dark. Or maybe he could. "Got that part figured. We found an abandoned cabin up there."

"Shit, luxury. We always just lived out of caves."

I sighed. "Real problem comes in with the sheriff herself."

"A woman. I knew it." He sounded downright gleeful.

"I saw her die. And now she's got it out for me."

The room felt empty all of the sudden, like that declaration had sucked the air from the cramped quarters and Noose's smartass ghost along with it.

"Still there?" I asked.

"You saw her die and now she's after you. I got that right?"

"About the size of it. I figured, who do I know with the ability to court death and walk away?" My cheeks burned and once again, I hoped he couldn't see me. "For a while, anyway."

"Guilty as charged. And you want to know if maybe there's some witchcraft involved?"

I shifted in my seat, clenched my teeth as the chair legs scraped the floor again. "And how to stop it. If it ain't too much trouble."

"Merella's gone," he whispered. "Ain't her doing."

I knew she was, had seen her dissolve to nothing but rags and bones. Still, my stomach dropped to my toes when he said it. "I guess I didn't think it—"

"Some days," he cut in. "I wonder why it is I'm stuck here, and she's not. You know? I mean, answer's gotta be some kind of eternal punishment, right? But then where is she?"

"I—"

"Rhetorical question, you fuckin' idiot. She's crossed over. Wherever that might be. Do me a favor, look behind you."

I spun quickly, half expecting a trick, and found only darkness.

"Nothin' there, right? Yeah, nothing there. Any time somebody comes back here, I expect them to drop whatever's in their hands and stare in awe, but must be only the dead can see it."

"What do you see, George?"

"Ain't much bigger than a knot in the side of a barrel. Little bubble of the bluest light you ever saw in your life. Sometimes it flashes. Pulses. Like it has a heartbeat. Other times I forget it's even there. Tell you, Rory Daggett, sometimes I wonder if she's in there. Watchin' me, maybe."

"Merella," I said.

Noose didn't answer. The darkness seemed to thicken like he didn't want me saying her name.

"You're so bored here, why don't you find out?"

Noose chuckled. "Ain't it obvious?"

I waited for him to say it.

"I'm a fuckin' coward. One of these days, though. You'll come back to hear my sweet singing voice, and I won't answer your calls."

"Know what? I hope you're right."

"Shit," he said. "Got me all turned around, you wily fucker. What was we talking about?"

"Immortality."

"A 'course. Witchcraft is hardly the only path to everlasting life."

His voice slithered, dangling a secret just out of reach.

"You remember Simon Crane?" he asked. "Tall, scrawny motherfucker. Brilliant as the day is long and somehow still scared of his own shadow?"

"Certainly rings a bell. Last I saw him, Meyer was sloughing him off the backside of my horse to fit him for a casket. Hardly the picture of immortality."

"The man, for certain. Not long for this world. You asked me the first one of my crew to get himself killed, and I'd have laid every red cent on Crane. But a man need not live forever for his legacy to go on." He let a pause fill the room and, for the first time, I considered lighting another match. I held back, imagining how Noose might interpret the action, and a little afraid of what he might look like after all this time if he did suddenly show himself.

"Most folks 'round here know his name for his destructive potions. The one that makes people peel their faces off, a classic. A booger green batch makes people try and rip their neighbor to shreds. Another one made anyone around when it went off violently ill 'til they upchucked everything in 'em wasn't nailed down. Ever hear about the stuff that liquified a person from the inside out?"

I shook my head.

"Thought not. Only saw him use it once, myself."

Shit, I guess he could see me.

"Real nasty one, though. On the surface, sounds the same as the vomiting concoction, but no, this one'd make the person on the receiving end get a real funny look in their eyes, like they glimpsed the future. Hell, maybe they did. No telling what some of Crane's shit caused in terms of side effects. Anyway, their legs would swell like two over-soaked sponges and rather than burst, just refuse to hold their body up any longer, so the torso crashed down and this storm of chunky, bloody goo leaked out of every pore. Nothing but stained skin and a putrid fucking smell left behind. Only time we saw it in action, Dorrance threw up on his own boots and told Crane he'd punch his fuckin' head off his body if he ever got it in his mind to use it again."

My stomach swam, and I held up a hand. "I truly hope this ain't the point of the story."

"Nah, I s'pose I digress. Point is, the horrific ones were all people talked about, but it was Crane's work alongside his family that first caught my attention, made me recruit him. Most of the other shit he discovered by accident trying to peek into what else was out there beyond just Buzzard's Edge."

I raised an eyebrow. "Other states? Cities?"

"Christ, kid, that little girl know what a simpleton she got lookin' out for her? Crane had his eye on places you can't take a train to. Places where the demons of the Bible hail from, or maybe not. I never read the fuckin' thing. Used to call it a dark frontier, or some such bullshit."

A moment passed and the din from the next room crept through the walls. Noticeably softer, like the rabble was starting to tuck in for the night.

"When I killed him…" I started. "When he died, he chucked a glass vial at me, but it got him instead. He started batting at the air like he was fighting off invisible monsters, seeing things that weren't there. What do you make of that?"

"I suspect I make of it exactly what you do. Simon Crane tried to transport your mind, if not your body, to some kind of literal hell, and got a whiff of his own medicine. Sure sounds like he didn't like the taste and his body shut down for it."

I leaned forward. "What else was he working on?"

"Way to cheat death, by the sound of it. Talked about it like it was his life's work. Couldn't be contained to a thimble-sized bottle of glass, said if it got to the point we needed to make use of it, there'd be some travel involved."

Icy tendrils snaked their way up my spine. "Travel where?"

"Somewhere north of here. Not all that far, but I never liked to get too far away from Buzzard's Edge if I could help it. Besides, until you murdered my Merella, didn't seem all that pressing. As you well know, I drank that sorrow and chased it with a bullet. Shit, this is the first time I've even thought of his resurrection pit since the skinny fucker dropped dead."

I stood quickly and the scrape of the chair tried to claw at me, but my head was too busy spinning to pay it any mind. Sweat beads formed on my forehead and I swear if they dripped down and touched me, I'd jump out of my skin.

"Family," I said, but my voice sounded far away. "You said he worked with his family."

"A sister. Never met her, but just as smart as him the way he told it." When Noose spoke again, his voice contained a note of concern, wholly unfamiliar coming from the arrogant, carefree outlaw. "Rory, you don't look so good."

"What was her name? You remember?" My voice trembled. I already knew.

"Mary Crane."

I might've tripped over my own feet next, but the door to the back room crashed in and never gave me the chance.

CHAPTER 9

WE GOT AN EXECUTION

The roar of the night crowd vanished as the saloon's lanterns interrupted my makeshift séance. I spun to face the doorway, filled by three figures, two about the size of Dakota grizzly bears swaying behind a familiar lithe female form.

"Mary," I said, allowing a touch of resignation into my voice. I turned back toward the table and sat. If a bullet were coming, the direction I faced wouldn't make much of a difference. Even though Noose's chair remained pulled back, he'd taken off for greener pastures. Maybe even for the light. Either way, the backroom felt deserted.

I placed my palms flat on the table. The weight of the revolver tugged at my side. With the serape in the way, I couldn't hope to get at it before one of them blew me out of my seat.

Footsteps clopped across the wooden boards like horseshoes against packed earth, advanced on me and stopped so close I could feel warm breath on my neck.

"How'd you find me?" I asked.

A moment passed before she spoke. "An effective sheriff has eyes all over. Stranger shows up in town, sneakin' through the streets at night, about the same height and build as a wanted man, them eyes take notice."

Whole truth or not, the notion held a lake's worth of water. I barely had experience chasing outlaws, save for a select few. What the fuck did I know about being one? The moment Robert Jeffery mentioned the slew of deputies, blue bandanas presumably tucked beneath their clothing, hiding in plain sight, I should've run. Hell, maybe he was a fly on the wall for Ms. McHugh.

Not McHugh. Crane.

"There's a pair of pistols pointed at your skull, Mr. Daggett, and plenty more ready to come running if I need 'em."

"So formal. What happened to Rory?"

She ignored me.

"Take that revolver out and put it on the table. Don't move any quicker than a sunset."

I reached beneath the serape and smelled the adrenaline-laced sweat of the behemoths with their guns pointed my way. Two apes searching for any excuse to add to the crimson stain on the table. Henry Taff's revolver clinked as I set it down and it scratched along the table as I slid it away. For a second I had this crazy hope that Noose might pick the thing up and rain hell one last time, slaughter everybody in the room but me. Maybe even grace my palm with the last remaining bullet for old time's sake. His chair remained still and the sense of being watched from his direction never came back.

Then Mary filled the seat. She picked up my revolver from the table, gave it a spin on one finger, and made it disappear.

"Could've shot you back at the farmhouse, you know. You and the girl."

I glanced at the monstrous bodyguards.

She leaned back in Noose's chair. "Don't you mind these two. Quiet as they come and trustworthy to boot."

"I arrived at the same conclusion. About killing us, that is. So why didn't you?"

"Truth is, you're more useful to me as a boogeyman than a corpse. So I gave you the opportunity to skedaddle. Not gonna lie, Rory. Small part of me kind of hoped maybe you saw some sense, took off west and just kept going 'til you hit ocean."

"Seeing sense has never been my strong suit."

"So what brought you here, anyway?" she asked. "Didn't come all the way back for a drink. Nah, too smart for that."

"Came back to talk to a ghost, Miss Mary. Someone told me once that dead men tell no tales, but I know a guy who bit the bullet and just don't shut up." I took a deep breath. "Seemed to know a bit about your family, actually."

"That so?" She studied me with steel-hard eyes as I tried not to let show any cracks in the armor. "Gentlemen, I got this handled. You can step outside for a minute."

The floorboards trembled as the guards made for the door. I waited until I heard it shut. "They don't know who you are."

"Don't need to. Awful hard to build trust in a town your brother helped terrorize. The Fieldstones are a loyal group, but they like their drinks and gossip as much as the next fella."

I nodded. "My friend had some wild ideas about happenings in the northern part of the state. Maybe not too far outside of... Windfall, was it? Got me wondering about that story you told me the night we met."

"You want to know how much is true?"

"If you want to share."

She shook her head. "Ain't about to waste my evening laying all my cards on the table, but I s'pose you worked out some by now."

I tapped my fingers on the table. "If I had to guess, those two gentlemen that just stepped out got blue bandanas somewhere on their person. Doubt you killed a single member of the Fieldstone Gang and at this point, it wouldn't surprise me if you were the one who put bullets in Gerry and Bert. Oh, and the demon you saw? Horseshit to keep people from poking around Devil's Cavern. Guess the only demon is you, after all. Am I close?"

"You ain't far." Mary tilted her head. "Though I don't know that I'd write off *something* living up there." She shifted in her chair. "Whole thing happened to kill two birds with one stone. Get the town of Windfall to lay off the Fieldstone Gang and make a name for myself. Once that story spread, I had, shall we say, employment opportunities, coming in left and right. Just had to wait for the right one."

"Why here?"

She smirked. "You were the one that brought up family, Rory. Think I wouldn't want the chance to get back at the man who killed my brother?"

"And yet you let me run off."

"Killing a man ain't the only way to make him pay."

"Point taken." I shook my head. "He killed himself. Messing with that red liquid."

The smile dropped from her lips. "Bullshit," she whispered.

I shrugged and changed the subject. "What about all the bullet holes? The scars? Had to go that far to sell the story?"

"Exactly that." Her voice remained cool. "Words only go so far. When that new sheriff strolls into town, she better be battle-tested and a little haggard. I was too damn pretty, Rory."

I wanted to disagree, but she wasn't wrong.

"My turn to ask a question." She held my gaze for a minute before speaking again. "You saw me take a bullet to the head and die. You know you did, so why are we dancing around it?" She leaned forward. "What do you know?"

I blew out a breath while I weighed bringing up the resurrection pit Noose had mentioned. "I know you got some dark secrets that might be too big for my limited mind to wrap around. And if I asked about how you've come back to life twice now, you'd probably dodge the question, anyway." She gave her eyebrows a little bounce and I let a flicker of a smile trace the corner of my lips.

"We all got our secrets," she said, climbing to her feet and heading toward the door. A quick knock and the brutes were back. "Grab him."

Two burly arms hauled me to my feet and yanked my hands behind my back. The man's hand was so massive he wrapped his fingers around both my wrists in one go. I suspect I could've broken the hold, except Mary had no reason to keep me alive. Yet here I was. Despite her alternate means to make me suffer, I wondered if she'd hesitate if I forced her to put a bullet in my brain.

I squinted as they marched me out into the saloon. My eyes adjusted and I understood they hadn't emptied the place, just filled it to the brim with fear. Patrons took up every stool. A portly fella sat in front of the piano, his hands too shaky to make the keys sing properly. Ruffians all but melted into the walls, trying to find any place to look that wasn't me. Every soul in the Saloon at the End of the World kept quiet like their life depended on it. Probably it did. Every soul except a single hopelessly stupid one.

"Barely a week and you've got them all too afraid to let out a fart," I said. "I wonder why that is, Miss Crane." The words barely crossed the room before I regretted them. Confusion clouded the face of my escort.

"Crane?" A dozen voices whispered the name in harmony.

Something exploded in Mary's eyes. It blew and for a minute, seemed to raise the temperature in the room. Then the easygoing Sheriff McHugh made an appearance, leading with a mischievous smile.

She held up a hand to stop my forward progress.

"Everybody out." The words came out barely above a whisper, yet no one struggled to hear them. The room cleared faster than a buttered bullet. The guard loosened his grip on me. "Not you," she said. "You can stay. Might need a witness."

With squinted eyes, Mary watched the rabble funnel out the exit. When the last person shoved out the batwing doors, her voice echoed through the breathless saloon. "How about you, Mr. Jeffery?" She let a beat pass. "You think I'm kiddin', Mr. Jeffery, just you go ahead and make me search you out."

She fixed her eyes on mine the whole time. It went on for hours, days, and then the clink of glass rattled from behind the bar. Robert Jeffery stood, trembling hands in the air.

You fuckin' fool.

I considered saying it out loud, but it wouldn't have reached his ears in time.

I never saw Mary pull my gun. It was simply in her hand and outstretched. An explosion loud enough to level a city bounced off the walls. My legs wanted to run, but I made myself watch as the bullet entered the side of Robert Jeffery's mouth and tore through the other cheek, ripping his jawbone free and sending it crashing into a selection of top-shelf liquor. His eyes sprung open like he could handle the pain, but not the surprise. He teetered for a moment with a ragged tongue hanging from his open mouth like a dead snake nailed to a flagpole, then he collapsed bonelessly to the floor, shattering a few more of those toppled whiskey bottles. A series of muffled cries told me he was still alive back there.

Mary narrowed her eyes at the barrel of the weapon as if accusing it of a crime.

"You shot him," Mary said to me. "Man offered you aid and succor, a place to lie low, and you shot him in the mouth. Poor Mr. Jeffery may not survive the night." She shrugged. "Even if he does, he won't have much to say to clear your name."

I shook my head dumbly, and the words refused to reach my tongue.

"First you attack the sheriff," she said. "Hold her hostage, then sneak back into town to murder Mr. Jeffery, a pillar of the community. And when that's not enough, you kill a deputy of the law?"

Before her guard could react, Mary lifted the revolver again and pulled the trigger, decorating the black and white piano keys with the back of the ox's head. A sense of child-like surprise stuck on his face as he toppled to the floor.

"What the—?" My words cut off as she turned the revolver on me.

"I'd say mind what you call me next time, Rory, but you're a pain in the ass. I think we're all out of next times." She leaned in, pressing the gun barrel to my forehead, and grabbed me by the front of the pants, squeezing my crotch. I willed myself not to react. Not overly challenging, given the situation. "Damn shame. We could've had some fun."

Mary let go and took a step back. "Oh, and Mr. Daggett, Rory if you like, I ain't so sure we need you upright and awake to get you to your execution."

She swung the butt of the gun and a sharp pain opened up on the side of my head. The Saloon at the End of the World twisted itself in circles and turned black at the edges while my knees quit trying to keep me upright.

This place is gonna need another new owner, I thought, before the dirty floorboards rose to catch my face and the shadows at the edges of my vision overtook the rest of the world.

It was wet when I came to. Wet, and it smelled like sour food. But I was relatively sure I hadn't been executed.

"As a dog returneth to his vomit, so a fool returneth to his folly."

Fucking Christ. I knew that voice, high and thin, like it was singing from the back legs of a locust, and didn't much take its owner for a man of faith.

Victor Jacobs.

The spinning room looked sort of like the sheriff's office and the bars dancing in front of my eyes just about confirmed it. Daylight cut through the iron cell and recommended I shut my eyes. I weighed a witty retort to Jacobs's scripture, then opted to throw up again instead.

He laughed and tossed his legs up on the desk. "I guess Mary hit you a pinch harder than she meant to," he said, bringing his thumb and pointer together.

A fucking pinch.

"Yeah, I don't know about that. I suspect she hit me exactly as hard as she meant to." I rubbed my splitting head. "How's that bullet in the arm treating you?"

His mouth flattened and his yellow eyes crawled over me. "As well as Alice's scar is treating her, I would imagine. Next time I won't miss."

"Neither will she, shithead. Do us both a favor and leave her out of this. Otherwise, I might have to do something unholy to you when I get out of here."

"How much do you even know about the girl?"

"I'm not going down that road. Not with you." Ice settled in my stomach, and I let the silence hang. "So, you part of the grand plan? Take over the town, take vengeance on me, or whatever it is that Miss Mary has in mind?"

"Part of the plan," he repeated, seeming to taste the words. I imagined those knots of stringy, puckered flesh beneath his shirt, a lost soul screaming inside each one as the bald fuck pondered his existence. "Well now, I guess I never thought about it in that regard. I was simply promised a reprieve from boredom. Of course, such things often arrive with unanticipated… rewards." He lowered his feet to the floor and hoisted himself out of the chair, crossing to the window. "It's almost lovely, wouldn't you say? The changes she's wrought upon this incipient hellhole in a short time. Buzzard's Edge always had kind of an ugly quality to it. Festering might be the better word, but it pulled a shiny mask over the top and hid the rot. Now…"

He looked toward me and suddenly I missed my blurry vision. It would've kept me from seeing the glee in his eyes.

"Streets are empty most of the day. Anyone who steps outside? My god." He sucked a deep breath in through his nose. "You can practically smell the fear. Thing most people don't realize, Mr. Daggett, is how much better their lives would be without that constant need for law and order. Buzzard's Edge got all bent out of shape over a sheriff and look where it got them."

"I'm sorry. Might be the knock on my head setting in, but I didn't understand a fuckin' word you just said."

He flashed a serpentine smile at me, barely contained rage hidden beneath contempt. Without a word, Jacobs reached into his vest pocket and plucked out a vial. Maybe something I wouldn't have put much stock in an hour before, but knowing Mary Crane's familial connections, the whole damn thing screamed that my day was about to get worse. He laid it on the desk with an innocent clink and walked toward my cell.

"You don't know who she is, do you?" he asked.

"Simon Crane's sister, crazed scientist extraordinaire, and member of a gang of bandits who didn't want you in their ranks." I laid my head down on the floor and shut my eyes. "That about right?"

"Not even close, sweetheart." More than his words, his tone sent a shiver up my spine.

"You don't sound surprised, though. Must mean she let you in on the secret."

He chuckled, dark and humorless. "I knew Mary Crane long before she became Mary McHugh." A pause. "Tell me, Mr. Daggett, why do you suppose one joins up with a gang?"

"Shit, that's easy. Every coyote needs a buzzard."

He didn't speak right away, and I fought the urge to open my eyes and see if he appeared as perplexed as the silence suggested. "I don't know what that means," he said, quietly, then cleared his throat.

"No, Mr. Daggett. A man joins a gang for surface-level reasons like money and power, respect, but ultimately what that man craves is leadership. The guidance of someone who can take you to a place that the majority of the population cannot hope to touch. Mary Crane is that person."

I pulled my hat down to keep the light from cutting through my eyelids, leaving the brim just above my mouth so he could see my obnoxious smirk. "If you're looking to set your bullfrog loose in her pond, just say it. We're all friends here."

Jacobs roared and slammed a bare fist against the bars. They unleashed a *clang* I would've earlier guessed you needed metal on metal to produce. Lifting my hat, I squinted out at him.

"Kindly fuck off, Vic. I got a headache and I'd like to sleep it off some more."

His fist still pressed against the bars; he glared at me, angry pink skin pinched around his eyes and teeth clenched so tight a belch couldn't have passed without turning sideways. Heavy breath lifted his arms and shoulders like grass in a stiff breeze, slowly growing a little further apart as he got himself under control.

"You've suffered a head injury, Mr. Daggett." That grimace transformed slyly into a smile. "It would be… unwise to leave you to your own recognizance. Instead, a responsible man would follow the doctor's orders. Don't you agree?"

The splintered wood poking into my backside suddenly felt cold and sharp. The stink of my vomit seemed thicker than before. Noxious. I needed to get out of that cell.

"As I was saying, before I was so rudely interrupted, Mary is the kind of leader who can take us to unexplored and wondrous places."

I did not care for that *us*.

Jacobs continued, turning his back on me and sauntering back toward the desk. "We simply need to trust and allow her to light the way. And to open our eyes, that much is crucial." A light scrape filled the room as he dragged the vial across the desk and picked it up, staring into it the way a mother might fix her eyes on a newborn child. He stepped forward, and I saw this one glowed a dark, unearthly red, the same damn color as the one that had killed Simon Crane.

"Victor. I don't know what she told you to do with that. I don't know what you think it does—"

"She told me to break it, then to get very far away, very quickly." His voice filled with wonder and the crimson liquid inside reflected in his eyes. "What do *you* think it does?"

I grabbed the bars and my knuckles whitened. When I spoke, I tried my damndest to keep my voice level. "I've seen what it does. It drives you mad, then it kills you. Do not break that, Jacobs, I'm warning you."

"Warning me? That's quite rich. I'm envious, though. I wonder what you'll see in your final moments. What might reach out and welcome you in. I'm tempted to join you." He took a step backward. "But I think not today. Don't worry about the girl, Daggett. I'll see that she's taken care of."

Anger clenched my stomach as I grabbed at him through the bars, straining as the metal dug into my skin. My outstretched fingers missed him by feet. "We can work something out, Jacobs. Don't do it!"

A small shake of the head. He appeared almost sad.

Then he tossed the vial toward the bars as he slipped out the door. I'd caught one before, cradled it inside a hat and returned it to sender. I could do it again. I pressed my shoulder as far into the bars as it would go, then a bit farther and watched the vial arc toward my outstretched fingers. As glass brushed my fingertips, I shoved once more and closed my hand around empty air.

Glass tinkled and red smoke began to rise before I even understood I'd missed.

CHAPTER 10

DARK FRONTIER

Red mist fluttered into the air. Each cloudy patch transformed into a mass of writhing bats, blasting out of the mouth of a cave and taking wing to block out the sun as it streamed in through the single jailhouse window. Their shrieks filled my ears, and I stumbled back, catching an ankle against the bars and falling on my ass.

The hard wood that met my backside developed some sudden and surprising give. Grains of what felt like sand shifted aside like they were pouring into the bottom half of an hourglass under my weight. The sensation troubled me, but only until the bars of my cell began to melt, dripping pitch-black globs from the top, like wax down the side of a candle. Crimson bats swooped around the room, looking for all the world like they might try and flit through the spaces between the bars if only their otherworldly bat bodies were a little slimmer. Each drip of iron ate away at the integrity of my prison. It wouldn't be too long before the bats joined me for supper. Every passing critter left a hazy trail in its wake that seemed to eat away at reality, a blood-red campfire smoke that solidified in place of the oak plank walls of Sheriff Harden's office.

I closed my eyes and shook my still-splitting head, then tapped a few fingers against my temple. That wasn't right. John Harden was dead, replaced by the type of demon who might approve of what their office was quickly turning into.

Imagination, that's all.

I snapped my eyes open, hoping to find the world returned to a familiar state.

"Oh, this is much worse," I muttered, and clambered to my feet.

Crimson-black sand speckled with some pearlescent flakes settled around my boots, the worn flooring of the sheriff's office a distant memory. It

71

resembled the Sonoran Desert a little because that's what I knew, but appeared formed from the ashes of a burned building, a few molten embers still in the mix. When I shifted my weight, the pebbles crunched and popped under my feet. A dozen pools of inky blackness gurgled in the sand, liquid remnants of the prison bars. Something about that made my blood run cold. I wasn't an idiot. I remembered the broken vial and Simon Crane's overlarge eyes as he traversed a world like this one. This had to be some sort of waking nightmare, and I could deal with the bars vanishing while my eyes were closed—that was dream logic—but that only works if they're gone, gone. Watching the cursed sand drink their remains made it more real somehow.

A distant bellow caught my attention, and I lifted my eyes from the sand to find the walls of the jail a distant memory. The thing that made that noise, it sounded massive. The bats seemed gone for the moment, but their wispy trails now painted the sky an ugly midnight gray, like the rising air of a house fire. Through cracks in the cloud, crimson red fire blazed. Molten metal waiting at the seams to pour out and smother the landscape. The charred sand stretched for miles in every direction, no hint Buzzard's Edge ever existed. Whatever hellish concoction Simon and Mary Crane had brewed must have stolen the land, the buildings, the people from under my feet 'cause I sure as shit hadn't taken a step.

Crane had his eye on places you can't take a train to. Places where the demons of the Bible hail from, Noose had said.

Dark frontier.

A phantom wind blew across the sunless terrain and cut straight through my clothes. Quickly, and with a mounting sense of panic, I glanced down to be sure I was still wearing some. The serape was gone, but my shirt and pants hadn't deserted me as easily as my surroundings and my good sense. One thing going my way, at least.

I jumped back as something wriggled beneath my boot. I shook my head to try and clear it again. Surprisingly, it made no more difference this time around. From the sooty sand, a curious eyeball stared up at me.

The words "dead body" rang through my head, then the eye blinked.

"Hoo boy, Rory. You gotta get out of here," I said.

Then the bellow again. Low and deep, almost like a grunt slapped out of a hog, if that swine stood ten feet tall with a gut the size of a steam engine. I brushed a hand past my holster and found it empty. Super. Then the smell hit. Or maybe it was always there. Something bestial. I'd watched a coyote from downwind some days ago, a wild creature with a less-than-pleasant musk to it, and that appetizer of stink was nothing compared to the malignant funk riding in on the icy wind.

I squinted against the dim red light occupying the distance. Patches of unfiltered blackness, hidden away from the fiery light, danced in their solitude. The kind of darkness so complete it appears to move whether or not there's something in there. Against my better judgment, I risked a step forward. Maybe a little movement would swing the world back upright.

No such luck. Things remained dismal.

The darkness roiled again, and this time I was pretty positive it wasn't my adventurous mind trying to make things more interesting. A single leg poked out first, silhouetted as it crunched into the oil-black sand. Slow and sure. A second leg dug in next to it, long and thin as a tent pole and stretching up toward a round body about the size of a full-grown bull. Several more spindly legs entered the light and then the fucking thing was off and running, racing across the desert sand like it was slick as glass. The beast unleashed another one of those tired bellows. Sweat began to drip down the back of my neck.

A warning? A battle cry? God help me if that king-size creature was scared of something bigger.

Closer it came, cutting the distance in half, then half again with a couple flicks of those too-many-to-count legs. Its profile scampered into view, revealing hairs and a pair of dripping fangs poking out of a slavering maw. Two eyes I couldn't have hidden under my hat stared me down and I had my answer. I wasn't a pitiful creature to be warned. I was a meal.

A sand spider, I thought. Not quite right, but the closest approximation my mind could pull off.

Whatever it was, it was fast as hell, and all running would do was make me have to guess when it was about to overtake me. With no revolver and no idea if that would even help, timing remained my best weapon. I braced to hit the ground the moment before the spider grabbed me, giving my bad knee a pep talk and begging it not to seize up when I rolled and took off to seek some kind of cover in this barren hellhole.

The enormous beast stampeded closer, and I gritted my teeth.

Then the ground opened up.

Sort of.

Solid ground slurped up the spider like a master trapper had laid a blanket over a freshly dug pit and waited for their quarry to stumble over it. When the last leg kicked into the air and disappeared with a flourish of charred sand, a thin seam of red outlined the shape of the animal's body. A second passed, and the ground rumbled like an upset stomach.

That's when I decided whatever else might be out there, it was better than hanging out by the spider pit.

I eased through the twilit plain with nothing but the remnants of a headache and the dim hope something might materialize on the horizon. Some more bellows honked from far away, but never came closer. Like they heard what happened to their brother and feared the great wandering morsel hobbling through the magic desert.

Small creatures burst out of the shadows from time to time, always in a rush to get somewhere and never very mindful of me. Potato bug-like things the size of stray dogs roamed the desolate wasteland, clicking by without a care in the world and rolling into a ball to squirt away when one of those bellows threatened their peaceful existence. More than a few times, a scythe-like feature sprang up out of the sand and sliced along the horizon before something sucked it down again. It was too dark to be sure, but the scythe sure looked like the tail end of an inhumanely large bark scorpion. The hunched shadow of a vulture prowled in the distance, at least three times bigger than your average buzzard and with flickering flame-filled eyes. It watched me, seeming more interested in waiting for me to collapse than earning its dinner outright.

The liquid fire that blinked in the sky seemed to fade, no longer casting a hellish pall of judgment over me. At first, I thought what passed for the sun was setting, but gradually, a light blue haze began to take over. A calming shade that suddenly made this place feel less like the embodiment of Hades. Trap though it might be, I suspected I was going in the right direction.

Step after pained step until finally, jagged shapes broke through the flat monotony. A shadow soared overhead and made me hit the ground, but my gaze locked on the outcrops dotting the horizon.

Buildings, I thought, but didn't say, lest the buzzard from on high hear, and swoop down to pick me up for a ride. I watched it soar off, wings the width of a Conestoga wagon, until shadows consumed it and the unsettling movement of air gave way to that cold, light breeze once more.

How could a place that looked so much like hell be so fucking cold?

Another pair of eyeballs snapped open in the sand, their gaze following me as I climbed to my feet and brushed cursed dust off my clothes. I treaded carefully, not wanting to step on the disembodied orbs for fear of some breed of bad luck. They squinted, blinked away some grains of sand, then closed and vanished. I watched the space for a moment, convinced they'd open again. Swirled in with the sand were a variety of white flecks. Fingernails and chunks of skin by the look.

"God, I fucking hate this place."

A low hiss disrupted the quiet, and I caught sight of the vulture off to my left again, displeased by my continued existence, but seemingly unwilling to do anything about it.

I stopped. "Or maybe you're going the same way I am."

The guttural caw climbed in pitch, approaching something like a whining screech before fading away to silence. It continued staring and I felt a little less menace pointed in my direction. Not quite enough to go pet the damn thing, but a change in the atmosphere nonetheless. The smoldering ember in its eyes, considerably more stark in the blazing blue light of the town on the horizon, moved toward the odd shapes in the distance.

"I'm going, I'm going." I gave it what I thought was a stern look. "You try and eat me, I swear I'll give you the worst case of indigestion you ever had. Got it, Beaky?"

A vision of Alice popped into my mind, twirling a finger around her ear. *She ain't wrong*, I thought. *You* are *arguing with a mangy bird.*

The shapes grew as I got closer, putting unnatural angles and jagged edges on display. It looked like a graveyard full of broken headstones. At first my heart sank, believing I'd stumbled on nothing but a rock formation. The blue glow convinced me otherwise. It shot out from beneath the structures like a miniature sun and cast its light into the sky. Only then did I realize the crimson overcast wasn't gone. It was overwhelmed.

Soft, sparse crunches told me the vulture was at my back. At the first sign of swift movement, I'd be ready, but it seemed in no hurry. Then it stopped suddenly. So did I. A shadow flitted from one structure to the next, momentarily blocking out the blue light.

"Please don't let it be another spider," I said, reaching toward a nonexistent gun at my hip. It wasn't big enough, though. Another blaze of shadow darted from object to object, disappearing into the side of the structure like it was a front door. The first two set off a reaction and soon enough, humanoid figures popped up all over the field. First five, then upwards of a dozen or more. Most of the fuckers didn't stay still long enough to count. Some moved fast as a windstorm, others peered from their solitary perches, content to simply observe my approach. Then everything stilled.

"You don't belong here," called a disembodied voice. It sounded wet and wavery, like someone had dunked its owner's head in a horse trough.

I let my eyes roam among the shadows, as unmoving as the warped headstones that populated this place. "I don't even know where here is. Don't suppose you could let me in on the secret?"

"What a quandary. Many new arrivals don't make it past the guardians." The voice seemed to come from a different direction this time, maybe multiple directions.

"Not to brag, but I ain't most people."

"Most certainly don't gain the assistance of one of the guardians." A second voice, just as unsteady, but higher. Maybe a woman.

I spun around and caught the vulture resting on its haunches, watching this otherworldly scene play out. It seemed smaller than before, closer to the size of a young kid than a thunderbird.

I turned back. "You still haven't told me where I am."

"The land of the dead, Rory Daggett. The dark frontier." Definitely a woman's voice. I knew it, but from where?

The hair stood up on my arms at the sound of my name. "I'm not dead."

"No? You sound unsure." Flat, emotionless. That's how I was used to hearing it. The watery quality gave it undeserved life. "What's the last thing you remember?"

A series of weights dropped in my stomach, each heavier than the last, and sent a rush of cold wind roaring through my limbs.

"Red mist." The words practically dribbled out of my mouth.

"A mist you know to be deadly. And now your guide tells you you're in the land of the dead. You are not a stupid man, Rory Daggett."

Then it clicked.

"Merella."

"No longer. Not here."

"I spoke to him, you know. George."

A pause. I listened for anything I could pick out of the silence. Fondness, loneliness, even anger. But it was as cold as the rest of this place. I pushed my luck.

"He told me… He wonders if maybe you're checking in on him from time to time. Afraid to take the leap of faith, that one. But, if that *is* you watching him, and you offered up some proof, I believe he'd take your hand and follow you. Wherever it took him."

"No longer," she said. "Not here." Something changed in her voice. The detachment in every deceased speaker in this world of the dead seemed lifted, if only for a moment.

"Rory," said a different voice. No underwater quality. Brimming with desperation. It sounded miles away. Behind me, the vulture continued its vigil.

"They're coming," she said, and the icy formality had returned. "They're coming and they seek to break down the walls. Be warned, it will not go the way they intend. And if you return again, Rory, you will not be allowed to leave. Not for anything. Do you hear me?"

A sharp pain bit into my shoulders. I winced and slapped at whatever was attacking me. Nothing there. Pressure grabbed at my ankles, threatening to pull me off my feet. I collapsed to the ground and felt my lungs freeze up. I tried to answer Merella, but the words were trapped inside. Ignoring the pain, I reached out a hand.

"Do you hear me?" The rolling waves of emotion in her voice frightened me more than the loss of control over my body.

"Do not let them break the walls."

My head throbbed as the wind whipped across my body, biting at any exposed skin. My eyelids pulled down to shut out the light coming from the crooked obelisks trying to escape the ground. I clenched my eyes shut against the burning in my lungs and darkness took over my vision, punctuated at the edges by rays of clean blue light. It fought against the black as my mind struggled to stay conscious.

"Rory!" That voice in the distance again. I swear I knew it.

Then the cold vanished, replaced by a comfortable warmth. Too hot, if anything, but I was in no position to complain. The weight on my head slipped away like rain dripping off the side of a roof.

I braced myself to open my eyes. Fear clenched my bones, assuring me that despite the temperature change, the hellish dark frontier waited on the other side of consciousness. I eased one eyelid open to find two things that brightened my day immensely.

Both the Arizona sun and Alice stared down at me.

CHAPTER 11

NOT A SOUL

"Christ on a crutch, hoss. We thought you was done for."

I don't think I'd ever been so happy to hear Billy's mix of confusion and innocent warmth.

And I thought I was a new resident of the dark frontier, as well. The words formed in my mind and tiptoed toward my tongue. Only they got caught up in a coughing fit along the way. Desert dust trickled down my throat and once the hacking started, I worried it wouldn't stop.

Alice touched her thumb to her pinky, holding the other three fingers up, then shook her head when Billy went cross-eyed. She mimed pouring a glass of water into her open mouth. Billy's eyes went wide with understanding, and he dashed off. The tickle remained in my throat, but the cough settled, and I took in my surroundings.

The run-down exterior of the sheriff's office loomed overhead, promising a bit more malice than it used to. At least the walls had grown back and there was nary a bat in sight. Down the road stood Durgin's Barber Shop and a pang of guilt stabbed at my stomach as I remembered the story of his last moments.

Died sobbing in the street.

A breeze whistled around the buildings and rolled grains of sand aimlessly down the street. It met no resistance.

Where are all the people?

Alice's gaze followed my own. When I met her eyes and asked the unspoken question, she aimed middle fingers down and pointers forward, then spun her hands in a circle while lifting her shoulders.

She'd noticed, too, and hadn't a damn clue.

Scurrying footsteps approached and once more, I reached for an empty holster. Billy rounded the corner, slopping water over the rim of a pint glass. The Saloon at the End of the World stood just around the bend, and as I reached for the water, a second wave of guilt swarmed over me. Another man possibly dead, and the blame rested on my shoulders.

Robert Jeffery, whose blood stained the floor of his saloon. Hell, maybe even stained the glass in my hand. I didn't check. I considered asking for an update on Jeffery's condition, but held my tongue. Mary Crane wasn't the type to rush him to the sawbones.

The tepid drink didn't compare to the fresh stream water by the cabin, but it banished the dust and grit, and allowed me to pass a couple words.

"What happened?"

A sly grin lit up Billy's face, though it didn't chase the worry from his eyes. "You weren't gone more than an hour when this 'un huffed and hopped off the couch. Didn't say a word. Well shit, I guess she wouldn't. Just threw a rifle over her shoulder, picked up a knife and six-shooter, then walked out the door."

True enough, the hunting knife from the cabin hung at Alice's side.

"Shocking," I said, and lowered my eyes so he wouldn't think I was judging his caretaking abilities.

"Flew all the way down the mountain in the goddamn dark," said Billy. "Didn't even flinch at the howls."

"And you came right along for the ride. How noble."

Alice grabbed her shoulders and exaggerated a shudder passing through her body.

"Hey now, it was cold." Billy's eyes darted around. "And dark. Either way, something lit a fire under her ass, like she knew you hit a snag in your plan."

"Well, good intuition and all, but I wasn't in trouble quite that quickly."

"Guess she sees the future, then. Anyways, we walked straight through the night, so forgive me if I am tired and a little grumpy, and then stumbled on a deserted version of Buzzard's Edge. Early, yeah, but not a soul in the streets. You ever seen such a thing?"

"Can't say I have." I drained the rest of the glass and climbed to my feet. "So, I guess you don't have an answer for where everybody got off to, then."

Billy traded a look with Alice. "We just got here."

I shook my head and felt something cold run through my veins, like the wind in that dark frontier. The memory stopped my mind dead to rights. Was that real? Was any of it real?

"How'd you know where to find me?"

The two of them passed another look and a blanket of fear dropped over Alice's face. Her hands remained still by her side, and she nodded at the former sheriff's deputy. A look that said, *you tell him.*

"You was screamin', Rory. Didn't even realize it was you at first. Worked a case one time where somebody was peeling the skin off bodies and leaving them all over Buzzard's Edge. The sound coming from the sheriff's office just now?" He sucked in a breath and closed his eyes. "Same sound I'd expect someone to make if that was happening to them. Losin' their skin, that is."

I must've looked properly horrified because he dropped his gaze and continued. "Didn't know what we'd find in there, but Miss Alice practically knocked the door off its hinges with a bony-ass shoulder. Found you in the cell, twisting and turning on the ground like a bunch of ghosts was tearing you limb from limb. When I saw a hint of red floating about the air, saw the broken glass on the ground, it all came back."

Alice took a few steps away and started fiddling with her revolver, like she didn't want to hear the next part. Billy tilted his head in her direction and lowered his voice. "Dragged her out of there before I thought of grabbing you. Figured that's what you'd want."

My face drained of blood and my head nodded of its own accord. "You did the right thing."

He chewed on his tongue and considered it for a moment. "Half expected her to run back in when she saw you, but I told her to stay put, and she did. On reflection, I didn't give her much choice. Had my shirt pulled over my face and was through the doorway before she could argue. 'Sides, she didn't know where we keep the spare cell key." He chuckled. "Of course, you didn't see her take out the door. I expect she might've bent the bars if it meant getting you out. From there, it was dragging you away from the red shit poisoning the air and slapping at you until you came to."

Billy's words went in my ears and bounced around, but it was Alice who had my attention. He kept his voice down and still she heard every word. I could tell by watching her shoulders, her breathing, the occasional shake.

"Still with us, Rory?"

He'd stopped talking and waited for a reaction. When I didn't snap to attention, he must have assumed there was still something wrong with me.

"Sorry, Billy." I faked a smile.

"Sure you're alright, buddy?"

"I will be."

I clapped him on the shoulder and walked toward Alice, jamming my hands in my pockets. Under the bright sun, the scar running down her cheek almost disappeared for a moment. "Please tell me you don't feel like you let me down."

She shrugged and kept her eyes fixed on some point in the distance.

"'Cause it sure seems like you're the one who got the cavalry down here in time. Another few minutes in that mess, and I… I might not've come back."

She turned toward me, a question knit across her eyebrows. I knew the very one and had no intention of answering it until I understood a little better.

"So, listen—"

My heart quit beating in my chest and my tongue dried up. Alice gave the silence a moment, then stared up at me, eyes glowing with concern. Then she followed my gaze far off to a shadow-riddled alley a few buildings up.

Peering out from the shadows was a man. He wore John Harden's clothes, even donned a shiny little sheriff's badge that flickered out from the darkness. But it couldn't be John. John was dead. A grimy boot stepped into the street and the sun cast its light upon the man's ruined face. Still, the shadows seemed to hold claim over a piece of the man, making him appear not quite solid. Shards of bone dotted pale pink flesh, torn to shreds by the boot of an ox-sized man. Not only did this interloper appear to be dressed like John, he also sported the same injuries that had killed my friend. The kind of injuries that would seriously hinder a man from standing upright.

"Tell me you see that," I whispered.

Shadow John swayed side to side, just enough motion to help me trust my eyes.

The blend of "Oh shit" and "My poor crazy friend" that took over Alice's face answered my question without any hand signals. I could ask Billy, but I suspected I already knew what was what.

Shadow John put a finger to his lips and slid sideways down the alley, like a glug of whiskey dumping over the side of a glass. Even if I ran, I knew I'd find nothing down that alley.

"Never mind, think I'm just, uh, a little overtaxed is all." I shook my head to clear it and Alice relented, though a trace of suspicion remained behind her eyes.

"I'm good. Promise." I kept the words low, no sense in letting Billy know about the dark frontier or giving him a taste of what had followed me home.

"What do you say, Red Rory. Think we dallied long enough? Ready to get to the bottom of the case of the town that didn't have no people?"

"I think if you don't quit with the nicknames, Billy, I'm gonna let Ghost shove a hoof up your ass." As soon as the words left my mouth, my stomach dropped. "Ghost, shit. She's still tied up just outside town."

"Think she's okay?" asked Billy.

"Been less than half a day, I should think, and she had some water handy. She'll be fine, if a little unhappy. Think we should go get her 'fore we do anything else, though."

Alice put her thumb to the side of her temple and flicked her first two fingers into the air.

"That's two votes," I said. "Sorry Bill. Don't need yours."

"Let's just pretend I would've agreed then. Say, Rory, you ain't armed."

For the thousandth time I felt the empty holster hanging at my hip, expecting there to be some weight there.

"Lucky for you," said Billy, pulling my sparkling revolver from behind his back, "it weren't far from the keys."

"Don't s'pose you grabbed my serape from there, did you?"

"That ugly tablecloth you was wearing?"

"Harsh. Well, it was nice while it lasted." I held up Henry Taff's revolver, my revolver. "Ah, Beautiful Billy, you've made my day."

"That mean you need me to come up with a matching nickname."

I flipped out the cylinder. Still loaded.

"Don't you fuckin' dare."

The streets stayed quiet, and the dead kept to the shadows. More than once, I thought I saw a pair of eyes watching me pass, so I kept my focus on the packed dirt before me. Like if I didn't let on that I saw them, they couldn't demand anything of me. Alice noticed; I could tell. Not a minute went by where she wasn't swinging her head around like a weathervane on a windy day.

I traced my way past the saloon, sweat dripping down the back of my neck. If George Holcomb poked his hole-riddled head out the front door, my rational mind might just take a permanent break. Somehow, he was easier to face when I didn't have to look him in the eye. The buildings thinned out then disappeared and before long, we came upon the ashy ruins of that farmhouse. Who'd lived there and did their story contain just as much tragedy as Andrew and Wes? The kind of sorrow that kept the blood flowing through the veins of Buzzard's Edge.

Ghost was hungry as a baby who slept through the night and fit to be tied, to put it kindly. Showing up empty-handed failed to improve her mood, so I made promises of oats or veggies in town, which she turned her nose up at.

"You know," said Billy. "My pa had a horse like this one, bit of a fuckin' attitude. Never lived in the dang house, but a picky eater and you got the sense she'd only carry you if she felt up to the task. Used to make this sound like a squealin' pig when she was pissed off. I won't say I seen the horse smirk at me, certainly had a look, though."

"Smug, I know the one." I yanked on Ghost's bridle and steered her back toward Buzzard's Edge. "How'd your pa break her of the habit?"

"Oh, one well-placed shot and we never heard another complaint."

Ghost trotted toward town with some sass in each step, always keeping to the opposite side of me that Billy walked on. When the bare desert turned into Buzzard's Edge streets, the dirt grew darker, harder packed most likely, though I always imagined it was because it held a little less sunshine.

"Nobody by the sheriff's office. Not so much as a rattlesnake fart on our way out of town. Guess we should try another direction. Stands to reason there's got to be someone left behind," I said. My eyes wandered the desolate terrain, and I hoped I didn't look as nervous as I felt.

"Shh," said Billy, his eyes fixed on Alice. She'd drawn her gun and bent her knees, pulling close to the wall as she crept down a thin side street.

"What's down there?" I whispered through gritted teeth.

Billy stood stock still. His eyebrows lowered into a look of concern and then I heard it, faint but undeniably present. A scream. If the ones that brought Billy and Alice running were screams of mania, of a mind lost to the dark frontier, this one spoke of agony. The kind of feral shout a man might unleash after a jab with a hot poker or the removal of surplus fingers at knifepoint.

"Sweet Jesus," said Billy. He put a hand on Alice's shoulder and stopped her short. "Is that...?"

Alice brought her hands together twice in a muffled clap and looked at me.

"Yeah, Billy, I'd say it's coming from exactly where you're thinking."

He turned toward me, his own gun drawn and dangling listlessly by his side. His eyes reminded me of a beaten dog, wet and frightened. "What business do those devils have in the schoolhouse?"

CHAPTER 12

SCHOOLHOUSE SIEGE

The Josiah Dennis Schoolhouse clashed blood red against the light blue sky, more than a little reminiscent of the fiery haze of the dark frontier. Named after one of the town founders, its church-like steeple pointed toward the heavens from the end of a narrow dirt road. A man with a decent arm could throw a rock and hit the front door from any business on the stretch, yet there was a separation. Dry, empty patches of earth to make sure none of that commerce leached into the school and infected the minds of the town's children.

Worse than the blood-red paint job were the screams still trickling out into the afternoon air. Deep and guttural. Not a sound one might hear from a child, but disturbing, nonetheless. When Billy had mentioned the schoolhouse, I had a moment of doubt, quickly quashed by a few steps in that direction. We tied Ghost in front of Nola's Tailor Shop and set out.

Billy peeked from behind the edge of a dilapidated outhouse and flipped open the cylinder, seeming surprised to find it still loaded. "What's the plan?" His voice shook.

"Plan?" I asked, cracking a grin and leaned against the raggedy wooden wall of the butcher's shop, thankful that even the sunshine beating down on the meat didn't cause quite as bad a stink as the shithouse hiding Billy. "Who needs a plan when you got two men with a bad idea and a little girl who could shoot the toes off a tarantula two roads away?"

Billy grumbled. "I don't think they even got toes."

"Even better."

"You know, I don't think it's exactly a good time for jokes."

"Deal with it. It keeps my head right." I sucked in a deep breath and locked eyes with Alice. She holstered her revolver and drew the rifle from behind her back, then stepped into a shadow and nodded straight ahead.

Billy watched her every movement without emotion. "Those our marching orders?"

"You seen the girl shoot?"

"Heard your stories. Good enough for me, I s'pose."

"On three?"

Billy went to check the cylinder again, then stopped himself. "On three."

"Billy, try not to shout. It'd let those fuckers know we were coming."

A single nod, quick and without blinking.

"One."

"One," he whispered in return.

"Two."

"Two."

Gun raised, I dashed into the street, leaving Billy to finish the count by his lonesome.

Two open windows—one on either side of the main door—peered down like watchful eyes as I landed at the base of the schoolhouse porch. Not a living creature to be found in either one, but the pained screams continued drifting out. The way the shouts intensified, so suddenly I hadn't realized they'd relaxed in the first place, suggested the victim was far from alone.

Billy dropped to the dirt on the other side of the stairs, mumbling something that began with the letter F, but keeping it low enough to avoid drawing attention. Then the first bullet came whizzing past my ear, sounding more like a whistle than a life-threatening projectile. I barely had time to judge the direction before a blast roared from down the street and a skinny weasel-like individual tumbled out the window and cracked his head on the steps. From the corner of my eye, I caught a shadow dart away from the body, disappearing as quickly as it came. I blinked a few times and found only a lifeless husk settled a few feet from me. His mind soup dribbled down the stairs and perversely I thought, "Somebody's going to have to clean this up before the kids come back."

Whether it was Alice's true aim or the fall that killed him was up for debate, but the volley of shots that followed ignited the powder keg. The panels at the base of the steps hid Billy and me from the worst of the shooting. We passed a glance, then alternated popping up like gophers and laying down fire while the other man reloaded. Judging by the variety of passing figures and the other two bodies that took a fatal shot and fell out the fuckin' window, Mary Crane had left a veritable army behind in case I survived. Or maybe she knew Alice would show up and bring hell along for the ride.

The gunfire continued with a diminished density. Simple math, Daggett. Less people equals less guns being fired at the same time.

"We made a dent, sounds like," yelled Billy, clearly arriving at the same conclusion.

"A dent ain't the same as a hole. I'm short of satisfied."

Alice's rifle conducted the choir. Every time it struck a deep percussive note, a voice rang out in ugly harmony. After a particularly melodic scream preceded a body tipping over the railing and crunching into the dirt at my feet, I caught Billy's eye and pointed toward the sky. Without an affirmation he leapt halfway up the stairs and plastered himself flat against the wall between the door and the window. Keeping low, I mirrored his movements and took up position on the other side.

For the moment, the gunfire had stopped, but it'd done so of its own accord. At least one member of the Fieldstone Gang presumably waited inside, saving another bullet or two to make a final stand. I didn't dare speak a word to Billy and the way he pressed his lips together until they turned white as grubs, told me he was of the same mind.

Bracing myself to catch a bullet in the head, I peeked around the corner into the window. A devastating blast erupted, and I hit the deck. Splinters of wood rained down as I rolled to the side. Billy started forward and I waved him off. Warm dribbles of blood leaked down my stupid face. I wiped it out of my eyes and prepared for the trigger-happy bastard to lean out the window and finish me off. The remnants of the shot or the wood or whatever nipped at my raw skin. I stifled a groan.

Then I didn't. An idea took hold, and I let it sing.

A pleasant warmth kindled in my chest as I lay there, revolver held aloft.

"Two left in there, Billy. At least one has a weapon and horseshit aim. Third guy just looks like a pulpy mess. Figure that's our screamer."

Billy stayed still as a statue, staring at me as though the last near miss had knocked something vital loose. I tried to flash him a grin, hoped it cut through the blood streaming down the side of my face.

"Tell you what, Billy," I called, louder than necessary. "You kick that door in, you can probably shoot faster than the yellow coward. Maybe put the first two bullets in his balls. Just for fun." I let a beat pass. Billy remained still, looking petrified. "Wait!" I screamed. "Billy, don't leave me! Come back. No, Billy! Alice! Don't go! Come back!"

A touch overdramatic, but I like to think I was in the sales business just then.

Tentative footsteps creaked inside the wooden schoolhouse. Closer they came, and I forced out a whimper. "Please," I whined. Another step. The click of a hammer being pulled back. With all the gunfire, I didn't much trust my ears, but I thought the shooter must be close enough to the window to reach out and wave.

One last creak, drawn out across an endless expanse of time. I closed my eyes.

Bang.

The sweet sound sailed through the still air and the groaning footsteps gave way to a two-hundred-pound body slapping to the floor like a slab of meat hitting the chopping block. An unwelcome and unexpected noise in the Dennis Schoolhouse that the butcher down the street no doubt knew like sweet music.

Finally, I exhaled and dragged a sleeve across my eyes to get rid of the excess blood. I hopped to my feet and put lead into the knee of the last man standing. I'd climbed through the window and hurdled a few desks, covering half the distance of the one-room schoolhouse before his iron even hit the floor with a hollow *clang*. He followed it to the ground, making no effort to pick it up.

"Hurts like shit, don't it?" I put the burning barrel of the gun to his forehead and let him whimper. Billy plowed through the door with Alice not far behind, guns raised and faces mean. Alice spun slowly, taking in every inch of the large room. Billy's gun dropped to his side, threatening to spill out of his loosened fingers. His eyes weren't on me or the shaking cur clutching his useless leg. They rested on the hitching mass of bruises and blood splayed across the teacher's desk.

In contrast to the blood-soaked mess, Billy went pale as a ghost.

"Mr. Locke," he said. "That you?"

When the reply came, it was little more than a gurgle. Still, it sounded affirmative. I mashed the gun barrel into the cheek of the lone survivor. In his twenties if he was a day, but the snot bubbling out his nose and getting caught above his lip made him look like he belonged in that school building to get an education. I guessed I could give him one.

"Doesn't seem Mr. Locke can answer for himself at the moment. That him?"

The sharp tang of piss filled the room, and the man nodded, quick and sharp.

"Listen carefully, Dribbles. I'm fighting the urge to flip this here gun around and beat you to death with the handle. And I don't even like Locke all that much. Only thing keeping your brains on the inside, for the moment, is that the man who gave me this gun? I don't think he'd approve. But... we're going to talk, and if even one of your answers reeks of a lie, I'm going to forget all about that just long enough to cave your fuckin' skull in."

"I'd do what he says." Billy crossed his arms as Dribbles looked his way for succor.

"Let's start with your name. Otherwise, I'm gonna keep calling you Dribbles or escalate to somethin' more vulgar."

"D-Daniel." The words sputtered out of his mouth like a man blowing bubbles in his beer.

"Dribblin' Daniel," said Billy. "How 'bout that?"

I rolled my eyes. "Got a last name, Daniel?"

"Yes. Yes, sir."

"And would you care to share it?"

"Bartlett. Daniel Bartlett." I eased the revolver away from his cheek and watched the white ring from the barrel regain some color. Alice stared on, dead-eyed, with hands crossed behind her back. A real role model might have known what was about to happen and told her to leave the room. I held my tongue. She'd seen worse.

"That's the formalities out of the way, then. So, next question. Where's the whole town gone and got to?"

Daniel's eyes flicked away. "Don't know."

Billy whistled. "You was doin' so well."

I flipped the revolver and cracked him upside the temple with it, hard enough to thwack but not quite enough to crunch. Too much crunch and the answers wouldn't be worth a tin shit. A thread of blood trailed slowly down the side of his face and joined the pool of bodily fluids collecting above his upper lip.

"If you're gonna lie, Daniel, treat me with a little respect. Make somethin' up, but if you expect me to believe the Lord up and raptured a couple hundred people and your reaction to that miracle was to head to the school and beat up the teacher, well that's just disrespectful."

Bartlett spat red on the floor. "They left."

"Slightly better, even tiptoeing on the edge of truth. Not helpful, though." I cleared my throat. "Okay, that question was a tough one. Let's start with something easier and circle back to the bigger challenges later."

Daniel said nothing, just quivered like a bucket of water in a windstorm.

"Take that as a yes." I looked toward Locke. Red soaked his clothes, though on closer inspection, maybe not as much as I originally thought. The ornery fucker might live after all. His prone form let out a groan and confirmed my disappointment.

"Why'd they leave you and your crew to beat on Mr. Locke here? Jacobs and Crane?"

"Crane? Who the hell is that?" A cloud of confusion edged into his eyes. Apparently, this was a well-guarded secret. I'd have to remember to thank Noose for the privileged information.

"McHugh," I amended.

The cloud floated off, never to burden the dull shine in the young man's eyes again. Something else flickered there, not quite cunning. More like an animalistic survival cue, flickering to tell me from that point on, I'd hear as much truth as Dribbling Daniel had in him.

"Ms. McHugh said she didn't care for the way Locke looked at her, talked to her. A little bit of distrust written across his face went a long way. Said, hole up somewhere and make sure he wouldn't grow to become a thorn in anyone's side. Said, make it slow. Make it hurt."

Billy leaned forward, arms crossed in front of his chest. "And that was a job requiring…" He turned his head from side to side and glanced out the window. "…seven men, all armed to the teeth."

The hint of a smile appeared on Daniel's face, then he smothered it. He looked afraid of what might happen if that flicker caught a spark. "She said we might could expect company. Company that had the penchant for shootin' first and asking questions later. Guess she was dead on."

"I don't recall shooting first," I said.

From behind us, Locke shifted, scraping against the rough grain of the desk and unleashing another dramatic moan.

Alice stepped forward and held up an index finger, waggling it side to side.

Daniel's eyebrows shot toward his forehead. "That little girl scolding me?"

"Shit no. That's just Alice getting impatient." I tilted my head toward her. She lowered her hand to the knife at her side and glared. "That little finger wag means 'where?' Evidently she feels we've rounded back to the most important question. So, spill it, Danny."

He settled back, a misplaced look of arrogance growing on his face. "Know how many people have died in town the last week?"

"Not counting the six around here with the piss poor aim?"

"Twenty-three. You believe that, Daggett? Twenty-three." The waver in his voice had dried up considerably. "A few lost to Ms. McHugh's temper, but the majority punished, or straight up murdered by members of the Fieldstone Gang, or Mr. Victor Jacobs, hisself."

"Get to the point or I'll give you a matching bruise on the other side of your head," I said.

"Alright, alright." He held up his hands in mock surrender. "Thought she was crazy bringing us in to act as deputies, but we found out right quick. People are always looking for a sigil. A blue bandana, they know to turn and run. A shiny, silver star and they don't seem to care what you done and what else you look like. They'll obey those orders like a dumb old mutt lookin' for its next meal. Gettin' to the point, Mr. Daggett, all we had to do was cover up that badge at night, don that light shade of blue and claim allegiance to Rory Daggett and his little girl. Un-fuckin'-believable how fast you can rile up a town when you give them someone to hate."

Sweat trickled down my brow. I traded glances with Billy and Alice. They didn't seem to be faring any better. Locke muttered something that dripped with fury and lacked his usual sense of refinement.

"Turns out Sheriff McHugh stumbled across some information. Rory Daggett and his accomplices been spotted north of Buzzard's Edge, mingling with the Fieldstone Gang and plotting an attack on the town."

"North." My voice sounded far off.

"Little place called Devil's Cavern. Whole town is on their way up there as we speak."

"Women and children, too?"

That smile that had been threatening to make an appearance for the last few minutes finally reared its ugly head.

"All hands on deck."

"Why? What's she got planned?"

Daniel's lips began to part, then his skull burst, flinging shards of bone and scraps of brain in every direction. It seemed to unfold a split second before the ring of a discharged pistol battered my ears, echoing through the classroom.

With a scowl etched on his face, Locke propped himself up on one elbow. A thin line of smoke wafted toward the ceiling, trailing from the gun in his hand.

CHAPTER 13

SCAFFOLDING

My jaw dropped suddenly south, and I fought the urge to beat the ever loving shit out of Thaddeus Locke. I'd've laid down a wager Billy couldn't pull me off before I broke every bone in the son of a bitch's body.

The only thing that kept me from diving at him was a swift patch of shadow rushing by the edge of my vision.

"The fuck you do that for?" Billy's shouts swirled away into nothingness as my head spun to chase the movement.

Daniel Bartlett's body lay prone on the floor, sans most of the head. Wisps of smoke so dark gray they looked to be floating off a wood fire drifted into the air.

"Anybody else seeing this?" My words came out as a whisper and disappeared as Billy grabbed Locke by the shirt collar and shook him like a dirty rug.

The sooty film formed something halfway solid a couple feet off the ground which then sprouted arms, legs, and a head. On that head, smoke boiled and slithered, mimicking the features of the man that lay dead at its feet. As the last bit of dark mist escaped Daniel Bartlett's body, an expression of abject terror appeared on the ethereal figure's face. Its eyes lit on me, and the mouth opened and closed, sending my heart into a wild rhythm. I knew what it looked like when a man flapped his lips because the words wouldn't come. Bartlett's ghost, or soul, or what have you, had the words, and they were flowing freely. Just weren't making any sound

"Daniel," I said. From the corner of my eye, I saw Alice's head whip in my direction. Billy and Locke remained buried in their aggressions.

Suddenly, the shadowy figure jerked backward like he'd tripped. His charcoal gray eyes went impossibly wide, and it happened again. Another step back. Toward the student coat closet and its endless supply of shade peering out from a half-closed door. My legs locked and all I could do was whisper his name once more before two black jets twined with brightest blue struck like rattlesnakes and yanked Daniel Bartlett into darkness unknown. His eyes shone a lighter gray than the rest of him, the last piece visible, begging as something dragged him toward the dark frontier.

The moment his eyes vanished into the coat closet, my legs found their courage and launched me after him. I battered down the door and tumbled into an empty room. No children in the classroom, no coats in the closet. The door cast a small shadow, though nothing moved inside. No longer hungry, the threat had retreated.

The shouts coming from the classroom dropped to nothing. Two grown men ready to tear each other's throats out, now silenced by their companion up and tossing himself into a closet for no apparent reason.

A shadow passed across the doorway and a momentary panic took hold. Then I saw the person who cast it and my heart slowed. I'd killed several men and seen a couple of ghosts in the last twenty minutes, never mind surviving a chemical attack, yet in the moment, Alice told me everything'd be alright. Amazing girl, learning to tell me what's what with a flick of her wrist and an outstretched finger. Sometimes I forgot she could say more with her eyes, then most people could with a thousand words.

She reached a hand out. It said she knew something was wrong, but I was all she had, and we'd conquer the problem together.

I took it.

We stepped out of the coatroom and found Billy and Locke, still wrapped together in violence, posed so still it looked like some great sculptor was chipping away at marble to recreate that moment. The only thing that moved was their eyes.

"What exactly was that all about, Daggett?" Locke's voice was hoarse. No surprise since we'd heard him screaming from halfway across town.

"You just shot a man in the middle of telling us what the sheriff's game was and you got the fuckin' audacity to ask me that? Christ almighty Billy, will you finish choking this blockhead out?"

"My pleasure." He leaned in.

I laughed, and somehow that made Locke's face drop further than my unexplained actions from a moment before. I pulled Billy off of Locke and dusted the front of his shirt for all the good it did. Spots of blood climbed up and down the stiff material. Locke pulled his own shirt closed, but not before I saw what they'd done to him. A rusty red knife on the floor and some sizable chunks of flesh told me everything that first glance had missed.

I closed my eyes for a second to collect my thoughts and wipe the blood off the metaphorical slate. "Thad, I think you're an asshole. I'm not sure what I did to you in a previous life, but it must've been akin to fucking your wife in the town square. Thing is, if we believe Bartlett, and I do, sure as hell sounds like the only four people who know what Mary Crane is up to are in the room. And we're about as outnumbered as a beetle stuck in an anthill."

"Mary *Crane?*" The color drained from his face. Billy's didn't look much more lively.

"Oh, I got some fun stories for the two of you. 'Fore we get to that, let's say we promise not to kill each other and not to make stupid fucking moves without a conversation first. Yeah?"

Billy stared at his boots and nodded.

"I can live with that," mumbled Locke.

"Good. I propose we go up north toward Devil's Cavern before Mary can enact whatever plan she's got in mind."

Billy huffed. "Same plan Thad blew out of Bartlett's head and all over the damn walls."

Alice stifled a laugh and I hate to admit I nearly had the same reaction.

"Billy, kindly shut the fuck up."

"Shuttin' the fuck up, Rory."

"He's got a point, Thad. Don't suppose you were privy to something that makes Bartlett's last piece of information unnecessary?"

With a grunt, Locke lowered his feet to the floor and stood, nearly stumbling over before regaining his balance. He met each of our eyes, Alice's too, then buttoned the front of his waistcoat. I knew a nervous habit when I saw one and didn't expect I'd love the words about to spill out.

"She's going to kill them all," he whispered.

The temptation to hop on Ghost and ride north was so overwhelming it almost made me itch. Except with one of our party in desperate need of patching up, finding a place to regroup before we set out seemed a wise decision. The school resembled a graveyard and offered little in the way of first aid and who knew if the sheriff's office was potentially still lethal? The saloon popped into my mind for a heartbeat, but it currently harbored a ghost who scared me a bit more shitless than it had the day before. With all other options exhausted, we headed for the farmhouse.

"Won't they think to look for us there?" asked Billy, trotting alongside Ghost as she ferried Locke toward my home.

"Who? Seems like everybody that wanted to string me up is miles north by now." As the buildings spread out and gave way to farmhouses, horses nickered and whinnied at my gorgeous gray mare. She kept her eyes trained forward, hearing every bit of attention, yet ignoring it all.

"I suspect that might be a boon in our favor. The horses," Locke called down from on high.

It took a minute for the cogs to click into place. "Good thinkin', Lincoln. No way Buzzard's Edge has more horses than people, right?"

"I've never taken a census, but I sincerely doubt it," said Locke.

"Oh shit," said Billy. "So they must be on foot."

"Exactly," I said. "Determined and pissed off, maybe scared, but completely able to be caught by four expert equestrians such as ourselves."

There's no feeling quite like home, and when the roof you built with your own two hands rises over the horizon, your body develops an odd mixture of rejuvenation and exhaustion. A refreshed mind set at ease by the comfort of home, thankfully un-burnt to the ground, and the urge to crawl into your own bed and just let the town that attacked you be marched to its doom. My stomach dropped at the last thought.

I brushed it aside with a smile sent Alice's way. "Home again, home again, jiggety-jig."

She rolled her eyes, but failed to hide the smile that came with it.

"Locke," I said. "I think maybe you better tell us the finer details of Mary's plan."

He hesitated, and I prayed to any god who'd listen he hadn't lied. "It'll take some time and I'd like to get cleaned up first. Though I daresay the shirt is a loss. One of my favorites. Perhaps the waistcoat can be salvaged." He glanced down and shook his head. "Pardon my rambling. It sounds like, for the moment, time may be on our side. I suggest we take advantage."

Alice wrinkled her nose at me. "Yeah," I said. "Guess I could use a wash myself."

With all the blood washed away, Locke appeared a little further from death, though a variety of bruises decorated his face and he walked with a slight hitch in his step. He planted himself on our bullet-pocked sofa and let out a sigh that had traveled a long way from his pained groans at the schoolhouse.

"Everything put back together?" I asked.

"I've had a fair amount of training in treating wounds, more than a few times on myself."

I forced a smirk his way. "It's delicate. Know what I mean?"

He nodded, but something in his eyes told me he didn't necessarily know where I was going. He'd take the ride, though.

I shifted in the chair, hoping all the gunfire earlier that week hadn't relieved it of its structural integrity. "Half of me wants to throw in right now, grab a few more horses and everything we can get our hands on that goes bang, then ride for the cavern."

"But the other half of you is scared."

Twenty-four hours earlier, that voice would've contained a tone that made me want to knock his teeth down his throat. No judgment in it, now. Amazing what a near-death experience can do for you.

"That's part of it, only part, though." I looked to the doorway for any sign of Billy or Alice. None came. Still washing up or getting dressed, then. "Mary meant to kill me there. That shit she dosed me with, it's deadly. Timing and luck saved my ass." I chuckled. "Timing, luck, and a tenacious little girl."

"You're probably right." Locke's eyes betrayed nothing.

"Still, what if it's some kind of trap? What if me showing up half-cocked is exactly what she wants. I killed her brother. It's obvious she's got some kind of hate boner for me."

Locke sat forward, a spark in his eye. "You called her Mary Crane."

"Exactly the Crane you're thinking of. So, Thad, you ready to spill what tipped her off that you weren't such a loyal dog after all?"

"Scaffolding, Rory." He eased off the sofa and paced the room. Every wince and grimace spoke of lingering pain, but I recognized a man who needed to move his body to move his mind.

"Scaffolding," I repeated. "Have to help me out there."

"One thing builds upon another. Small at first, yes, but as each layer is gradually added, the length, width, even volume increases."

"There's that teacher speak."

He ignored me. "The men she deputized buttoned their shirts to the neck. Filthy, brazen men who couldn't be bothered to tuck in their shirts or go outside to break wind. Yet they wore their collars as though they expected to add a necktie at any moment."

"No shit. Hiding something?"

"Unquestionably."

"A blue bandana, I don't wonder. What else?"

"The wanted posters increased at the sheriff's office. Seven new additions in the course of two days. Excessive, but not entirely suspicious with a change in the law and a brand new most wanted man in Buzzard's Edge. As an assistant to the sheriff's office, I familiarized myself with the new faces and their crimes. With the exception of your face plastered on the board, I recognized not a single man. And the crimes were... piddling. Public intoxication, carrying a firearm within the town limits. Some things that are not even illegal in Buzzard's Edge and others that would fail to draw the eye of even a suspicious lawman."

"What'd you make of that?"

Locke grinned, and it reached up to dot his eyes. Ever the smartest guy in the room. "An excuse to replace the old posters, cover them up and let them be forgotten. Because despite shaved faces and different hairstyles, a trained eye would note similarities between the new arrivals and the old outlaws."

"But you're not a stupid man. You'll have kept all that to yourself. Especially surrounded by unfriendlies. So, the original question. What tipped her off?"

The smile turned into a smirk and something cruel flickered in his eyes. "You. Well, the girl, anyway."

"Alice. Do go on."

"John Harden was a friend, Rory. A dear friend. I moved around a lot before I settled in Buzzard's Edge." A shadow passed over his face and my heart stopped, thinking something dead was about to crop up, but then it vanished like it had never been there. "It is my belief that we all keep parts of ourselves hidden away. I daresay mine may be darker and buried deeper than most."

"I'm here if you care to unburden yourself."

"Not today, I think. Thank you all the same." He cleared his throat. "I never knew if John Harden saw that, but I pride myself on my intuition. I believe he did. And he offered me a home anyway. That trust went both ways. When John told a story, I listened. When he made a claim, I believed."

"Except when it came to me."

He shook his head. "Oh no, especially when it came to you. Because if anyone were ever going to put my livelihood or my new home at risk, it would be you. A man who couldn't help but do the right thing, even if it wasn't the smart thing." Locke stared out the window. I kept my gaze from wandering after his, afraid if I turned my head, I might see another dead man. Maybe even John himself, spoken back to life or something that passed for it.

"He always hated that I gave you a hard time. Told me if I couldn't trust Rory Daggett, then I might just be hopeless."

My throat tightened.

"So even though I tried not to let it show, I always listened when you talked. And when you said that you'd never seen Alice miss a shot, I made a note of that. The last straw, Rory, was when Mary told me that little girl had her dead to rights, murder in her eyes, point blank range, and missed."

"God damn."

"Mary announced the sighting of you and Alice keeping company with the Fieldstone Gang at Devil's Cavern. Rounded up the entire town and ordered them to gather guns, knives, pitchforks, sticks, rocks. Anything they could carry. She commanded them to kill the two of you on sight. An eight-year-old girl about to be murdered by an angry mob. I could not stomach it, and I told her as much. I asked her in front of those loyal brigands and a host of townspeople if she really had no qualms about killing a child."

"And she turned on you faster than a Mojave green with a yanked tail."

"Yes, that's exactly what I was going to say. A single word and she had me dragged away. She assigned a battalion to stay behind, and they worked me over until you showed up. They asked no questions, begged no answers. They simply collected pain like a miser collects gold."

"You said she was going to kill them all."

Locke turned away from me, stared out the window once more. I risked a look and found only the blazing sun beating down on the endless grains of sand spanning from my front door to Devil's Cavern. Not a single specter looming, waiting for me. I'd almost forgotten anything else existed when he spoke again. "Alice was the last straw, but not the last piece of the scaffolding. She told the group to make my death last, make it hurt. Then she turned to leave. Her back was to me, but her words came clear as day. 'He's a tough nut, he'll hold out, but still, I expect he'll be the first sacrifice of many.'"

Locke let the words hang in the air. I searched my mind for anything to add, coming up empty.

"You didn't ask for advice earlier," he said. "Not directly, but the unspoken request was there. You might as well have said, 'I don't know what to do.' The truth is, I don't know what the right thing to do is, either.

The choice that's going to keep us all safe. Perhaps there isn't one. But I know what you will do. You'll ride north because you think there's a chance you can save some of those people. You've seen something, Rory. Something you're not sharing. I can tell just by looking at you. As you said, if you'd ever like to unburden yourself, I'm here, but I suspect you're not quite ready yet."

"On my way."

"And I'm coming with you."

I considered faking surprise, but the son of a bitch was a detective, after all.

"You're hurt," I said.

"I can ride a horse, shoot a gun, and think on my feet."

Billy stepped into the room, Alice close behind him. He looked cleaner, but still tired. "So, we're going." It wasn't a question. "I was up that way with John once. Wasn't much to see, but I reckon I could find it again."

"That's just about perfect, Billy," I said. "How far?"

"Half a day's ride. Give or take."

I chewed my lip and raised an eyebrow at Locke. "You confident about the time they left?

He nodded. "And even more so that they will be on foot."

Alice stood in the doorway, bloodshot eyes fixed on something outside.

"Okay," I said. "Let's take a couple hours. Rest up, eat something, and grab as much firepower as you can."

I leaned back in the chair and pulled my hat over my face to shut out the world. A moment of peace before we jabbed the day with a red-hot poker.

CHAPTER 14

DEVIL POINTS THE WAY

I tried for a nap, but it didn't take. Tried to eat something, but it wouldn't stay down, so in the end, I resorted to becoming a low-life horse thief. Figured my neighbors would forgive my transgressions if I pulled their asses out of the proverbial fire.

A couple hours later, as the sun flirted with the horizon, we ran out of excuses to wait any longer and saddled up.

I helped Locke mount a chestnut brown gelding with the disposition of a wooden rocking horse. The little tics and grimaces Locke let show through were likely outnumbered by the ones he tried to hide. I suspected if his horse were to throw him, he might not get back up. Billy sat astride a midnight black mare, a beauty with a white spot shining like a beacon from the center of its chest. Alice and I both fit on Ghost without giving the old girl too much to bear.

The four of us traded looks. Each one said the same. Whatever waits on the other side, here we go.

The Sonoran Desert opened wide to let us in. For all the isolation and sense of solitude that Buzzard's Edge held, it was easy to forget the country that ran parallel to the Blackjack Mountains contained none of the life-granting greenery, rushing water, or scenic views. The stretching desert had its breathtaking parts, but the further the sun dipped below the horizon, the better they hid.

Billy led the way, keeping an eye on the mountains until darkness wrapped them up, then turning his gaze to the north star. It would point us in the general direction of Devil's Cavern, and we'd figure the rest out as we approached. Billy kept the pace modest with a mind to save the horses and on the off-chance we might overtake the group of travelers. If we caught them before they arrived, it drastically reduced the chances of mass sacrifice, but stumbling on them in the dark increased the risk of pitchforks in the stomach and rocks to the head.

Alice gripped me tight as the stars drew us forward and I kept my eyes low, afraid if I let my guard down, the sky might crack open to reveal the crimson light behind the world. The dark frontier made for a hell of an experience, but not one I had any wish to revisit, especially on a permanent basis, and the very last thing I wanted was to drag my friends and family with me.

Hours passed. Coyotes howled. Lowly creatures skittered through the sand, taking refuge behind rocks, their sounds lost to pounding hoofbeats. Cactuses and hardy trees boasted unusual shapes. Buzzards bedded down for the night, or maybe watched to see what kind of fools pressed on into the night; making a note of the direction we traveled in case we left meaty corpses that might cook in the morning sun and make an easy task of filling their bellies.

Both of Alice's hands clung tightly to my shirt, unable to form words even if a pressing question occurred to her. Our conversation was going to have to be more one-sided than I'd grown used to.

As subtle as possible, I leaned back on the reins to let Billy and Locke gain some ground on us.

"How you holding up?" I shouted, as the ground raced beneath us.

A single squeeze. Old hat. One for yes, two for no. Yes meaning 'I'm alright' in this case.

It was easier to pick out a lie when looking into her eyes, but something still felt off.

"Awfully hard to believe, considering… well, everything."

No squeeze. Maybe as honest as we were going to get.

"Confession time, Pip." I let a beat pass. "I'm scared. The shit you all rescued me from? Same stuff that plucked Simon Crane's mind away from him and flew off with it, killed him a couple minutes later. McHugh's his sister, by the way. Funny fuckin' world, ain't it?"

A squeeze.

"Agree. I'm getting off the beaten track." Up ahead, Billy and Locke took turns swiveling their heads around to check on us. They made no move to slow to our pace.

"I saw where it took him. Place the locals call the dark frontier. Unnatural things aplenty, a sky lit up the color of a burning house, and a city made of broken headstones. People that lived there, I knew some of them, I think. All dead. And that's exactly what the dark frontier is, some kind of land that collects and holds the dead."

Two squeezes.

"Yeah, I get that. Thought about it a lot. Sure as shit sounds crazy. Like I imagined dodging a spider the size of a rockslide and gettin' watched by eyeballs under my feet, all the time I was really thrashing around a jail cell floor waiting for death to take me. But it ain't so farfetched as all that. Don't forget who I went into town to talk to in the first place."

One squeeze.

"Thing is, since you and Billy saved my ass, seeing the dead figures hasn't exactly stopped. Saw one right in the street outside the sheriff's office." I shook my head. "Even Dribbles, the kid Locke shot… Shit, I don't know what I saw. Shadowy ghost left his body after his face blew to kingdom come and something dragged him away into the coatroom. I… I guess I tried to save him. Whole lotta fuckin' good it did."

One squeeze.

"You believe me?"

One squeeze.

"Look, I don't know what we're walking into, but what Noose said about Mary Crane, what Jacobs said about her. Wild-sounding shit. Like she wants to open a path to that dark frontier, let the dead roam free, let those monsters out. Fuck if I know. But she's got an army of pissed off people, connections to some dark shit, and a plan. I don't care for any of that."

Two squeezes.

"So that's how I'm holding up. Tell you something though, kid. Be a lot worse off if you hadn't shown up for me."

One last squeeze.

"Yeah, that's what we do."

Hard to know for sure with the darkness and the speed we traveled at, but I could've sworn a vulture passed overhead just then.

Silence rolled back in, quickly overtaken by the midnight noises of land-of-the-living wildlife and pounding hoofbeats. I gave Ghost the notice to catch up. Billy and Locke never said a word.

A few watering holes and leg-stretching stops later, a glorious swathe of pinks and purples told us the sun would be with us soon.

"We must be close now," said Locke, eyeing Billy.

"Must be. We ain't rode long enough to miss it. Definitely be easier to find by daylight, though. Especially…" Billy snuck a glance at Alice and snorted.

"What? What is it?" I asked.

"Well, the natural formation 'round the cavern is big enough, I s'pose. Doesn't mean you couldn't miss it on your way by. There's a promontory, John called it. A thin, rocky ledge jutting out and up into the sky. Light hits it just right and the red clay comes to life. Can't miss it."

I stifled a laugh. "This *promontory* have a name the locals use?"

Billy lowered his voice. "It does. But maybe I don't want to say it in polite company."

"Alice? She curses more than I do. Eight years old and a woman don't make her polite company."

He dropped his eyes. "Some 'round here call it the Devil's Pecker."

Locke rested a hand on Billy's shoulder and managed to keep a straight face. "Such language in front of a child. You ought to be ashamed, Mr. Chambers."

Alice crossed her arms and shook her head. She squinted over his shoulder and pointed.

I stifled a laugh. "I think what my accomplice means to say is that particular johnson is standing at attention off in the distance there."

Any embarrassment forgotten, Billy's eyes went wide with wonder. A sense of awe overtook his voice. "We're close, then. A couple miles close."

Locke's tone turned deadly serious. "I don't see any people."

"We didn't pass them." I searched the distance for any sign of life. "They're waiting for us."

Guns loaded and drawn, we walked our horses to the closest rock structure that didn't resemble Satan's schlong, tied them up, and crept forward. Four on four hundred might be pitiful odds, but the element of surprise could only help.

Just as Billy said, the Devil's Pecker steered us toward a growing array of rocky outcrops that cut through the flat plains of the Sonoran Desert, home to coyotes, vultures, and outlaws alike.

"Hear that?" asked Billy, his face going white as the underside of a horned lizard.

"Yes," said Locke. "Voices. Lots of them."

"Could be just on the other side," I said. "Mary said the whole thing was like a big bowl. Only way was up and over."

Locke raised an eyebrow. "Do you think we can trust her?"

"My god, no." I nodded toward the rock wall. "Let's climb."

We dug in like bighorn sheep, guns tucked in holsters, grabbing at crumbling handholds as we scaled the rough cliff face. Nowhere near impossible, hell, maybe not even difficult to a man who knew his way around a natural obstacle like this, but I'd lived my whole life in a town as flat as a drunk run over by a hay wagon. I could barely climb a ladder.

Alice scaled the fucking thing like a flea making its way up a horse's leg, and even Locke demonstrated some experience. Not bad for a man on the verge of death half a day ago. Billy and I poured sweat, huffing and puffing like old men. When Alice and Locke reached the top, a full two minutes ahead of me and Billy, they lay flat on their stomachs and peered down the other side. Their feet and faces disappeared out of view and when they returned, fear was etched across their features, Alice's especially, in a way that drove spikes into the pit of my stomach.

"What is it?" I whispered through gnashed teeth.

"Climb faster, Daggett," said Locke. "This is not something I wish to describe."

Ten feet from the top and the roar of the crowd grew louder. It sounded like the type of mob that showed up at a public hanging, thirsty for death and looking to indulge that wanton lust for violence any way they could. Often, you saw men and women wound so tight, they appeared ready to race up those gallows and kick the stool away themselves if the law didn't get to it fast enough.

What's it I always say about Buzzard's Edge vibrating with hate?

I grabbed at the last dusty ledge, instead finding Locke's outstretched hand. He pulled me up from a crouched position and I did the same for Billy. Crawling like bloated gila monsters through the dirt and grit until we reached the other side. Pebbles sprinkled down a rock face as haggard and threatening as the one we'd just surmounted.

That wasn't what caught my attention.

My head swam, and I thanked the invisible stars I was laying down because otherwise I'd have skittered off the edge like a discarded pebble. Suddenly, I was back in the dark frontier. The sky was blue as a Fieldstone bandana and the sun beat down trying to cast some much-needed light on the world, but all those rays succeeded in doing was to reflect off the crimson pools dotting the land. Bodies floated in each one like flies covering a piece of rotten fruit.

CHAPTER 15

SENTRIES

I rolled to the side and viciously heaved my guts. Billy did the same. Thankfully, the clamor of the township covered any raucous noise my body made as it rebelled. When I'd relieved my stomach of its contents, I looked to Locke. Straight-faced and serious, but showing no sign of illness.

How dark that secret must be, I thought.

I braced myself to look again, still able to picture the horrific scene in my mind.

Too late. We've arrived too late. They're dead. They're all dead.

Everything in me wanted to scream the words. I almost did, until Alice grabbed my hand. I stared at her balled-up little fist, whitening around the knuckles. The cut drew down the side of her cheek, still somewhat fresh from Jacobs's knifework, but beginning to scar over.

We looked over the edge together. There never was any shielding that girl from the reality of things.

The bodies strewn about in pools of blood were only the beginning. At the base of the cliff, open desert stretched around the bottom of the bowl like an ancient Roman theater, every inch of crimson sand pointed toward a rock formation on the far side. A man passing along the high-up rim might never notice the craggy mouth, Devil's Cavern, but on that day, you couldn't miss it.

Light like blue fire flowed from its entrance.

People gathered around the entrance, raising weapons in the air and shouting. It was impossible to make out individuals from our distance, but the noise shook the ground itself. The object of their cheers became immediately obvious. A battle taking place before our eyes.

Dozens of blood-soaked Buzzard's Edge residents battered each other with a dizzying array of pointed and cruel implements mere feet from where the dead lay. Every so often a gunshot rang out to interrupt the bloodlust, then its roar died away as men with knives plunged them into men with clubs. The tides turned as men with clubs bashed in the skulls of men with knives. A tall woman whose name was something like Mildred or Marnie, dress torn to shreds, drove a spade into the face of an unfamiliar man with a bushy beard. The sickening squelch as it split his skull resonated to the hilltop. At least I imagined it did. Farm tool still lodged between his eyes, the man fell like a downed tree. A mist of red shot into the air, reminding me of the splintered glass, the contents of the vial that caused madness. No sooner had the man settled into the wet dirt than the woman ripped the spade free, unleashed a scream, and turned her violence toward the next victim. A squirt of inky black blasted into the air from the man's downed corpse and shot toward the mouth of the cavern.

Bushy beard's soul. I fucking knew it.

Elsewhere, children launched rocks at the frenzied town people. Some of them no older than Alice, with hate scrawled across their faces. The projectiles snapped bones and tore at skin, though the combatants showed no sign of slowing their anger. A single well-placed shot shredded the ear of a skinny young man I'd only ever heard called Slim Tim, close enough to the cradle he likely did not need to shave, yet about to meet his fate at the hands of a dozen Davids trying to take out this poor excuse for a Goliath. The skinny teenager held his ear to his head and spun, swinging a cavalry sword to ward away the incoming storm of rocks. They flew into the air, nearly enough to blot out the sun, and a second later, all seemed to find their mark.

Slim Tim collapsed, his face a misshapen collection of bruises and bumps even his mother wouldn't recognize. Still, the rocks rained down, pummeling his lifeless body. I was still waiting for the shadowy exodus to confirm his death when an insignificant chime of glass breaking entered the fray. The children, arms still full of rocks, became lost in a purple mist. Their arms gave out, dropping the rocks to the desert floor, and the kids stared around in confusion, seemingly struggling to come to terms with the carnage that surrounded them.

I reached out and tapped Locke on the shoulder. "You recognize any of 'em?"

"Every one." His voice shook, maybe with anger, maybe fear or just loss. I neglected to ask for clarity.

As clouds of violet poured over the battlefield, the figures at the cavern's mouth set to action. Tens of men, no longer bothering to hide their blue bandanas, streamed into the open expanse and began plucking up the dead. Grabbing men, women, children, and those that the naked eye couldn't identify as any of the three, then dragging them through a mush of blood and dirt toward the cavern's glowing entrance. I kept watch for any sign of Mary or Jacobs, but neither showed themselves. Wave after wave, the Fieldstone Gang dragged the dead away and disappeared down into the earth. Each time one of the rogues emerged, they were alone.

"What the fuck?" Billy voiced the thoughts no doubt echoing through each of our heads.

"What the fuck, indeed," I answered.

The remaining townspeople of Buzzard's Edge swayed slightly, weapons either dropped to the ground or held loosely by their sides. Their shoulders hung in a relaxed fashion. It looked like a sad excuse for dancing, like Brahms entertaining the masses with a violin concerto. The yelling, screaming, and more visceral sounds of wood and metal pounding flesh had ceased, replaced only by the delicate scrape of boots on sand.

The dead no longer burdened the fields.

No, someone's hauled them off to the dark frontier.

Even as the thought formed, I knew it was true.

He'll be the first sacrifice of many, Locke had said.

The Fieldstone Gang returned to the mouth of the cave, taking up their previous positions, pressed against the stone walls. Silence reigned.

"She's inside. Gotta be," I whispered.

"I'm sure you're right," said Locke. "But how on earth do we get to her?"

I made to shake my head and froze with my neck at an uncomfortable angle as one more person exited the mouth of the cavern. From across the way, features meant jack shit. Far too blurry without some kind of looking glass. This person wore no shirt, donned no hat, and the sun shined off their bald pate. With the good graces of a closer inspection, I was sure I'd find their upper body covered in tiny knots of scar tissue and a piece of fabric wrapped around one bicep to staunch a bullet wound.

Victor Jacobs strutted out to the middle of the field, surrounded by the entranced sheep he'd led to this butcher's block. He held his hands in the air, stretching high as you like, trying to Icarus the sun. Rays diving from that selfsame ball of light glinted off the items in his hands. Somehow I doubted these ones contained the same calm, violet mist. With a cheer from the Fieldstoners, he tossed the vials into the crowd and a luminescent green haze erupted.

Booger green. Noose's words. *Makes people try and rip their neighbor to shreds.*

No sooner did the emerald cloud begin to dissipate overhead than the tines of pitchforks, barrels of rifles, and rock-loaded arms lifted into the air and spat on the ceasefire.

With more than a little guilt floating over me like a chemical mist, I rolled away. I'd seen enough the first time. Glancing from Locke to Alice, I'd never seen such bloodless countenances under the Arizona sun, excepting Billy, who was a slightly softer shade of green than the mist. I racked my brain for anything to say to drown out the sounds of death rattles and jagged metal piercing flesh.

"We gotta get our hands on that purple shit."

Alice pointed her index and middle fingers toward each other, then used them to trace her waistline.

"I never noticed if that color was in the belt we took from Crane," I said. "Didn't have much of a mind to touch it, if I'm honest. 'Sides, it's locked up at home."

"Bringing science to fight science would have been a wise move," said Locke.

"We were in a rush!"

He held up his hands in surrender. "So, how do we get from point A to point B without traipsing through the center of the action and springing several new holes?"

It was a damn good question, as evidenced by the collective silence of the crew.

"Okay, table that for a second," I said. "Say we figure that out. What comes next? We don't know how deep in there Mary is, or what she has to fight us with, don't even know what exactly it is that's making the inside of the earth light up like an underwater firecracker." I huffed, chest heaving with anxiety and a hefty dose of panic.

"We didn't think this through," said Billy.

"Understatement of the fucking year." I kicked some sand and watched it flutter into the air and rain down on the death match below.

"Hey!" A voice roared, and I nearly slipped over the edge like the dust in question. "The fuck are y'all doin' up here?"

Always clear the area, Daggett. Might as well be rule number one, but the rules get awful slippery the second you lay eyes on the kind of bloody death going on below us.

The voice's owner stumbled out from behind a rock formation I would've pegged as too small to hide him, swaying back and forth in an unsteady manner. Hate-filled eyes squinted from above a sky-blue bandana. Coal-black stubble lined the parts of the cheeks that poked out from beneath and long, greasy hair drained out the back of his hat, swishing in the wind against his oversized towncoat. The man's gun jumped from target to target, unable to decide which one to blow from the face of the earth.

Locke popped to his feet, hands raised in surrender, and made the decision easier. "Thank goodness you've come." Palms out, he walked toward the enemy. Locke had stowed his iron away and worry creased his face. "These… brigands have taken me captive." He motioned toward the man's bandana. "They've stolen my effects, and had you not come along, they would have thrown me over the edge."

The intruder's gun lowered. Only a little, but I didn't miss it. In the time it took my mind to wonder what Locke's game was, he played his next card.

"Come, relieve them of their weapons and we'll take them to Ms. Crane."

The gun jumped back up and swung toward Locke. "Who the hell is Ms. Crane?"

He huffed out a breath. "Shit." Before Greasy could squeeze the trigger, Locke swatted the gun away with his left hand and mashed a fist upward into the man's sternum. Breath whooshed out of Greasy's lungs and Locke snatched the gun out of the man's flailing hand before he hit the ground, and tossed it to Billy, who nearly juggled it off the side of the cliff. Locke knelt next to Greasy, still gasping for breath. He tore the bandana free, removed the man's hat, and produced a short blade from the end of his sleeve.

"Thad…" I said, waiting for the rest of the words to trickle out. Something akin to 'You don't need to do that' or even just 'Don't' Truth is, I knew what his answer would be—*We're at war*—and I didn't have an argument beyond my loose rule about letting the other guy shoot first. Thaddeus Locke met my eyes as he dragged the razor across the man's throat, then shoved him over the opposite edge, away from the carnage. The corpse disappeared from view before I could glimpse his ash-black soul making for the cave.

As I stared into Locke's eyes, I saw nothing, and it scared the shit out of me. I wasn't quite sure what his secret was, but I could narrow down the list.

He tossed the hat and bandana my way. "Put them on. Patrol the edge of the cliff and go grab a few others." He studied my face. "Kill or incapacitate, your choice, Rory, but if you choose to incapacitate, make sure your decision can't climb back up to bite you."

"Fucking marvelous." Unpleasant moisture seeped into my hair as I put the hat on, and the sour reek of bad breath and moonshine lingered in the bandana. Nonetheless, it transformed me. At least that was the hope. I gave Alice a thumbs up. "Look alright?"

"That's exactly how it looks," said Billy. "Now go clear a path."

The next sentry waited nearly half the length around the bowl. He kept looking up as I approached, then returned his gaze to the mess below. I'd seen enough to last a lifetime, and Locke had just given me an extra peek.

It was then that I wondered if he had orders not to engage with the other lookouts. Unconsciously, I tried to mimic what I could remember of Greasy's gait, walking like I had half a load in my pants and taking my time about it. When I got within shouting distance, the sentry stopped watching the festivities and I tried to read the look in his eyes. I wouldn't put money down on it, but the closest I could guess was relief. Shit, here I was, sweat pouring down my face, thinking he might blow me out of my boots, and this fucker was just bored.

"Hell of a thing, right?" I called.

"Don't think we're supposed to be talkin' to each other." His voice cracked, shot up higher than my heart in my throat and for about the same amount of time. Mary had kids stationed up there.

Kill or incapacitate.

"Nah, they just want you to think that so you won't let your guard down," I said. "Seasoned man knows how to do both. You been here long? I ain't seen you 'round before."

"Couple weeks." No crack this time, but not as deep as it would get someday. If I let it.

I turned my body to face him so I could have been keeping one eye on the gauntlet, if I were so inclined to look. "Where you from?"

"Dusty Streams. Little south of here."

"Yeah? I know it, and what drove you out of there?"

He met my eyes, then quickly dropped his gaze toward the screams below. A flash of green passed over his cheeks. Reflection of the mist, I thought at first, then realized the kid was just sick. Not bored after all.

"Ran away. Got caught out on the trail by a mean-looking bastard. Smelled like a mountain goat, had more hair too." He laughed at his own joke, then let the laughter die. "Gave me a choice. Join up or die."

"Not much of a choice."

His eyes widened. "You don't know the feller I mean, do you? Don't tell him I said that. Jesus, shoulda kept my mouth shut—"

"Relax, kid. Relax." I sucked in a deep breath and prayed I wasn't such a fool as I felt. "I'm gonna offer you a better choice. Give me your bandana and fuck off. Scamper down this here hill and take off back to Dusty Streams. Eight or nine hours if you can find yourself a horse, more if you can't, but it can be done."

"They'll come after me."

"What's your name, kid?"

"Henry."

I grinned, couldn't help it. "Fuckin' hell, that's a good name. Henry, when I'm done here, there won't be enough of these fuckers left to come after you. South you go, and the best of luck to you."

He studied me for a moment, trying to detect a ruse, then untied his bandana and held it out. Not a trace of peach fuzz on him. Probably not a day over fourteen.

"One more thing 'fore you go." I tilted my head behind me. "This shit is probably gonna haunt you for the rest of your life. A ghost always chasing you, makin' you wonder if you could've stopped it." I held the bandana up. "So when that happens, remember that you did everything in your power to make it right. Now get gone."

I watched Henry stumble down the loose rocks, nearly catch himself on a cactus more than once, and eventually find flat ground. He set off into the shade of the Devil's Pecker and, best of all, never turned back once.

"You got one," said Locke. "We needed three."

"Not the way I see it." I glanced toward Alice and tried to ask forgiveness with my eyes. "She stays back. Maybe not all the way, but I'm not putting her in any more danger than I have to and I'm sure as shit not leaving her alone."

A touch of flame burned in her irises, smoldering, but not escalating into a full-grown brushfire. I thought of the vulture in the dark frontier.

"She trusts you, Billy, and so do I. Give her the rifle and the both of you watch our backs. Thad and I are going to scale the outskirts and try not to kill too many people."

"You let the boy go. I could see it from here."

"The boy, exactly. I'm not high on killing everyone we come in contact with, and I'm not willing to take the life of someone who's barely had it more than a decade. Shit, Locke, I'd ask what you would've done, but I don't think I want to know the answer."

"No, you don't."

"Christ, no wonder they booted you out of New England."

Billy watched us argue back and forth, his eyebrows scrunched so hard they formed a canyon in the center.

"It's fine," I said. "We're fine. I trust you. I just… it's been a day."

"For all of us." Locke held out a hand and I shook it.

"Not to kindle the same old fire, but can we at least try it my way?"

He shrugged. "I'm told there's a first time for everything."

I pulled Alice close. "Watch my back. Stay at least a hundred feet away. Drop anyone, and Pip, I mean *anyone* who looks like they're about to put a bullet in me." I made to stand, then paused. "Or a knife."

She nodded and ran through a familiar series of signs.

You're all I have.

"Same, Pip. See you before you know it."

I stood and tied the bandana around my face, then gave Locke a once-over. "Hey Billy, trade jackets with him." I clapped him on the shoulder. "You look too fuckin' fancy. They'll never buy it."

"By the powers, you're right." Locke put on Billy's jacket and resembled a proper scoundrel.

"Wish us luck, beauties." I blew Billy a kiss and set off.

CHAPTER 16

THE GUNSMITH'S FAMILY

With Henry having abandoned his post, the path clearing commenced with minimal incidents. Locke and I established a routine of sorts. Approach slowly and with confidence, gauge resistance, and get the fucker to the ground as quickly as possible. One of us to watch over the violence below and maintain the illusion, the other to tie up the sentry with their own shoelaces and gag him with the bandana. We found a shitty old pistol on each one, but nothing else of note. Evidently the gang leaders didn't trust the peons with the purple peace juice.

At intervals, I couldn't help peeking over my shoulder to check on Billy and Alice. I never once saw them but felt them close. Despite the chaos below, it was comforting to have someone ready to drop any of these blue-sashes that became a problem.

Locke tied up the third sentry and sent him rolling down into a gulley where he could scream into the balled-up bandana to his heart's content. Brushing the dust from his borrowed jacket, Locke shot me a look to say, "My way would be faster."

Sure, hoss, and secure us both a place in whatever passes for hell these days.

With that thought, I surveyed the number of Buzzard's Edge bodies filling up the crimson pools. No way it was less than thirty. A small gathering of shadowy figures flailed their limbs as if fighting the wind. It was no use. The cavern sucked them up like the center of a cyclone. Sooner or later, Victor'd throw the purple shit out again, and that would be our chance.

"We gotta move," I said. "Assuming they follow the same law of routine as last time, we're likely to see everybody calm down real quick so they can drag the bodies away."

"Then what?"

"Then we hope having the high ground is enough."

I held up my revolver and caught the sun with the shiny side, sending a spark back in Alice's direction. What I would've guessed was exactly a hundred feet back, she sprung up from behind a rock, still hidden from any earthbound eyes that wandered toward the heavens.

J, I spelled, swishing an outstretched pinky. A-C-O-B-S. Then I mimicked a gun with my pointer and middle fingers and cocked my thumb. She nodded and set to checking the rounds. Then the familiar ring of broken glass soared up from the base of the valley, followed by violet-tinged smoke.

"Shit, go, go, go," I whispered.

No more sentries in sight, the path along the edge of the bowl took us to the rocky outcrop above the cavern, a formation bursting from the ground as if trying to escape the brutality beneath by fleeing into the sky.

Soot-black remnants of the deceased followed their bodies as the Fieldstone Gang dragged the earthly husks away from center stage and down into the ground. Kind of fucked up how I was almost getting used to seeing those smoky specters. With the killing fields cleared once more, Locke and I peered over the edge, less than twenty feet over the cave mouth.

We waited.

A ways down the trail, so did Alice, Billy at her back and the rifle in her hand.

Jacobs appeared, and the sound vanished from the world. From this distance, the whole thing had the sickly reek of ritual, something this group would keep on doing over and over until every citizen of Buzzard's Edge was shot, stabbed, or bludgeoned and hauled off to some kind of eternal damnation.

Jacobs stopped a few feet from the mouth of the cave. His wiry body appeared coiled, ready to spring. Sweat gleamed on his shirtless, scar-puckered chest as if between appearances, the work below cost him great effort. Only a stone's throw away, it was tempting to pull my revolver and do the deed myself, but Alice could hide faster and draw a little fire while Locke and I ambushed from behind.

Lifting his head as if sniffing the air, Jacobs let a smirk slide across his face and strutted out in the midst of the bloodshed. Alice raised the rifle, the barrel wrapped in a piece of cloth to keep it from catching the sun. Smart girl.

Victor Jacobs's hands plunged into his pockets and came out holding vials of mountain grass green. His reptilian smile seemed to cut his head in half, and I found myself having visions of Alice taking care of that for him.

"Anytime, Pip," I whispered.

The rifle glared down, a little tremble at the end of its barrel.

Sand crunched under Jacobs's slow footsteps. Borrowed time. Then he stopped. He turned his head slowly. It took ages for him to survey all the swaying forms caught in the mindless trap of the purple haze. Without warning, his hands shot into the air, holding the chemical contents aloft. The remaining gang members roared with approval.

Alice stood with the rifle aimed, her pallor white as what I used to think a ghost looked like.

"What's she doing?" asked Locke. He pulled his revolver, didn't draw down on Jacobs, but was ready to do so at a moment's notice.

"Don't," I said. "Wait."

Jacobs's hands jerked back, maybe less than an inch, and Alice's rifle barked. A patch of flesh the size of a fist blasted out the back of Jacobs's shoulder, and he collapsed to the ground, writhing in agony.

"She missed," said Locke.

"She doesn't miss." As much as I believed the sentiment, I couldn't hide the concern in my voice. "Come on, Thaddy. We're up."

Getting down the bowl side of the cliff proved infinitely more fun than getting up in the first place. A quick little rockslide with guns drawn and we were at the bottom. Locke took out the closest Fieldstoner to our landing spot, bursting his head with a single shot. Since the man was midway through pulling his own pistol, and several more were doing the same, I figured later might be a better time for reprimands.

Trusting the other three to cover me, I made straight for Victor to relieve him of those goddamn green vials. Bullets whizzed by my head like diving birds, and I could only hope it was friendly fire designed to take out the fuckers behind me. When I reached Jacobs, he'd rolled away, still clutching his shoulder. The glowing green liquid lay on the sandy desert floor, still contained in its prison. I scooped them up and pocketed them, then cocked the hammer back to finish Alice's work.

That's when a train hit me.

Okay, maybe not really a train, but a man sure as shit the size of a goddamn train. An overpowering musk lit up my nose, one that certainly could've passed for a mountain goat, and as I fought off the ogre's advances, I wondered if I had Henry's abductor at hand. The brute caught me upside the head with a fist the size of a wagon wheel. I rolled with it, which may be the only reason my skull remained intact. The punch glanced off my head and buried itself in the ground like one of those burrowing mice. The dirt didn't quite swallow his fist, but it surprised him enough to allow me to wriggle free and strike out with a whip-sharp crack behind the ear.

Yeah, for all the fucking good it did.

With the bandana lowered around his neck, the big savage bastard smiled, showing all the spots where teeth should be. Enormous, he might be. Pretty quick, too. But a monster that size tends to broadcast every move like they sent you a telegraph scrawled with ill intentions. When he swung, I ducked it and dove for the ground, grabbing at my revolver and trying to remember how many times I'd shot it since the last reload.

Less than four, as it turned out.

He recovered from the missed swing without throwing his back out and lifted his foot to stomp my ever-loving lights out. I dodged the first boot and felt the earth quake beside my head.

And look, I ain't exactly proud of this next part, but staring a boot the size of Texas in the face will make one reevaluate their ethics. So I blasted that devil in his pecker.

The shot thundered and tore through the material, raining down a smattering of blood and meaty bits. The parts left dangling could've been testicles, thigh meat, or innards. I wasn't about to lobby for a closer inspection. Instead, I let gravity take down the big beastie, rolling out of the way even as I regained my footing. Then I let Henry Taff's revolver have one last conversation with the mountain goat's brains.

Another bullet whistled by, dragging me back to the present and the war at hand. Jacobs was nowhere to be seen. By now, Locke had single-handedly dropped a dozen of the bandana'd halfwits guarding the mouth of the cave. Alice and Billy pulled up by my side, covered in dust and letting bullets fly. The swaying townsfolk offset the violence that surrounded them, unintentionally dodging bullets like hail threading a thunderstorm.

Some bodies dropped. Others chose to flee into the safety of the cave, and soon enough, the afternoon air rang with silence. The remnants of the Fieldstone Gang littered the killing fields, heads blown halfway to hell and limbs mangled so fiercely as to cross out any hope of survivors. All the same, Locke walked the perimeter, poking corpses with his boots and leveling his gun at the prospect of movement.

Billy scratched his head with the butt of his revolver. "Shit, I know we still got the big bad science lady to deal with, but don't that seem like it went a little too quickly?"

"Dammit, Billy," I said. "Don't say shit like that." I should've felt nervous, because he was right. Instead, I cracked a smile.

He returned it.

That's when Jacobs burst through a cloud of gun smoke and sand to put a knife to Billy's windpipe. The blade drew a single drop of blood quicker than the smile fell from Billy's face. The smoke cleared to reveal an anthill-shaped outcrop, the perfect hiding spot. Maybe the same damn one from Mary's story.

Alice and I started toward Jacobs, then caught ourselves a few feet in front of him when he waggled the knife and clucked his tongue.

"Kindly drop your weapons unless you'd like to see what the inside of Mr. Chambers's throat looks like," he said.

We passed a glance, then tossed our guns his way. The sand cushioned their fall and muffled any complaints they might make. Even Locke, a few dozen feet away, threw his iron and glared at Jacobs. The chunk missing from Victor's shoulder should have kept him down, but he grimaced and hissed through the pain.

What'd you miss for, Pip?

I looked for the answer to the silent question, but she only had eyes for Jacobs.

"The knife too, girlie."

With a huff, Alice removed the hunting knife from her waist and pitched it away.

"Okay," I said. "You got our attention, but how long you think you can hold a grown man in one arm and keep that knife raised in the other with a bear-bite-sized piece taken out of you?"

"Long enough." He sneered, and his eyes darted from person to person like a trapped animal. He poked the tip of the blade further into Billy's neck and a scarlet drop cascaded down and disappeared behind his shirt collar.

"You're a lucky man, Vic. Alice don't miss all that often."

"From the stories I hear," said Jacobs, "she doesn't miss at all. He smirked at Alice and a low noise crept past her lips. One I'd never heard her make before. Something like a growl. "Must've been something mighty scary to make Alice Svensson miss her mark."

My stomach went so cold it could've turned a puddle to ice. Where had I heard that name before? A distant voice rang in my ears, but it took two tries to catch the words.

"Is that her name, Rory?" It was Locke.

"I don't know." The words fell out of my mouth and the sand ate them up.

"Svensson. You can be sure of that." Jacobs pulled Billy back, just an inch or so, but it sent a message. "You might want to harness your snarling beast, or she's going to get your friend killed."

I put my thumb to my chin and brought my index finger in and out like it was riding the wind from my breath.

Who is this guy?

Without taking her eyes off Jacobs, Alice pressed one palm flat as if against an invisible wall and drove two outstretched fingers on the other hand quickly past it, a stabbing motion.

My head swam with ideas. "Killer, yeah, sure, but—"

"Are you familiar with the name Albert Svensson, Mr. Daggett?"

I'm not sure I could've named my own mother at the moment. Thankfully, Locke saved me.

"The gunsmith? From Buzzard's Edge?" Hands raised, Thad eased toward us, stopping a couple feet from Alice. "People from all over the country sought out his weapons. And then he simply stopped producing them. Disappeared. The market has been poorer for it ever since." Locke's eyes widened. "Is he a relation to the girl?"

"Now you're at the heart of it." Jacobs shuffled a step back. Subtle, but he was retreating toward the cavern's mouth. Toward Mary. "You're not kidding, Mr. Locke. Svensson's work was known and coveted all over. Very prevalent at one time, nearly a decade ago that was, then it began to dry up. Less dead bodies on the receiving end of a Svensson bullet. Whispers circulated, but those in the know? Well, they know."

He glanced toward Alice and his eyes took on a yellow glow. Maybe just jaundice, but it sure looked like concentrated evil.

I put a hand on her shoulder to steady her and she trembled, shaking so hard I worried she might vibrate right into the earth itself.

"It's alright, Pip."

Jacobs jerked the knife and Billy let out a squeal to remind us why we couldn't just rush the bastard.

"The most trustworthy whispers said that Svensson's wife, Anna, gave birth to a little girl. Thing couldn't even cry properly, just let out this soft mewling sound when it was hungry. A strange quirk, to be sure, but the couple took it in stride. Years passed and the child never learned to talk. The pitiful excuses for medical professionals couldn't find a reason, couldn't coax a word from the child. They called her stubborn, said someday she'd grow up and stop being obstinate."

Alice's chest hitched, and a tear fell down the side of her face, curving around the cut on her cheek as if afraid to touch it.

Jacobs continued. "Albert didn't believe them. He put his business on hold and traveled east to find the girl more competent care. When the doctors in Connecticut, Virginia, Massachusetts, and the surrounding states found no cause, the family sailed to Europe." He shook his head. "But you already know how that turned out, don't you?"

Four men and a young woman, and not one of us could plug the silence at that moment.

"Exactly," whispered Jacobs. "The man threw everything he had at travel, doctors, miracle cures, hoaxes. Anything to fix her. The money ran out and the girl, then nearly seven or eight, still hadn't uttered a word. Daddy taught her how to handle a gun, though. That's for damn sure. Thing is, now she had a new baby brother. That one had no trouble crying up a storm." He smirked and my free hand disobediently balled into a fist. Jacobs saw it and took another step back, widening the gap. I traced my eyes along the sand, thinking I still might be able to get at him with a good jump.

"So the Svenssons did what anybody would do. They came home. Daddy figured as long as the sun was hot, people needed to shoot each other. He could start over and make his fortune again."

"Except…"

"Yes, Mr. Daggett. Except. Except their home was gone, storefront boarded up and gone. Taken by the greed of this wretched shithole Albert Svensson was in the process of trying to beg and barter his home back." Jacobs looked around. "A fair bit of the blood this place is drinking belongs to the people that turned him away when he needed them most. So you know where he went?"

"No," I tried to say, but my words were ghosts.

"An abandoned house right up near the center of town. The family that lived there met a… tragic end and the town let it sit and collect cobwebs. Lord only knows how long the Svenssons holed up in there, months it seemed like, while old Albert fought the mayor's office and got exactly nowhere. Living on scraps and huddling together for warmth through the cold nights. Until—"

"Stop." For my sanity, for Alice's. Because I didn't know how long I could keep her from diving for that rifle. "Please, stop."

"Until my pal, Nathan Edwards, asked for a little help. Stake out a house in case some spoiled rich kid returned. Then we gut him. The house was supposed to be empty, and we could live in the lap of luxury until the rich kid showed up. Except it wasn't empty. Second day there, Edwards heard a baby crying on the top floor. Found a whole family stowed away in this little ol' closet. They stank like hell. Daddy tried to fight, but he was barely more than skin and bones. I stuck a bowie knife between his ribs and left him bleeding on the floor while Edwards dragged the others out. Mama had a gun, and that was a little more of a problem because she knew how to use it. Nearly blew a hole through my skull before Edwards wrestled it out of her hands and put a bullet in her guts." He lowered his voice. "Took out the baby she was clutching with that same shot."

Cold sweat lined my brow.

I'm so sorry, Pip.

"Hell of a mess," he continued. "Then this little streak of nothing pops out of a crack in the wall and runs off." He turned toward Alice. "You're looking a little less like a skeleton these days, Alice, but I recognized you right away that first night. How could I not? Paired up with the man who got your family killed."

She looked up at me with those icy blue eyes and my heart just about stopped.

"She was better at hiding in that place than she had any damn right to be. We spent the whole afternoon searching for her and never found a trace. Eventually we figured she must've slipped out a window or the front door and we gave up, set to hiding the bodies in the backyard." He tilted his head toward his shoulder and winced with the pain.

"There's three little knots there. Daddy, Mama, and baby." Jacobs slid his arm from around his captive, keeping the knife against Billy's throat, then slowly lifted his hand and ran a filthy finger over three buds of scarring on his right shoulder, before letting the outstretched digit linger over a small patch of unmarred flesh. "I filched a couple kills that belonged to Nathan, but I doubt he'll say an unkind word about it. Left a little spot for you right next to your family, girlie."

Alice shook with rage. I didn't figure I could keep the pot from boiling over much longer.

"You were out back when I killed him," I said. "Edwards."

The smirk dancing across Jacobs's face dropped.

"Heard the gunshots and everything." I snuck a step forward. "Hell, maybe you even peeked in and saw your friend die. Saw me fucking kill him, and what'd you do? Tossed the shovel and ran for higher ground. You absolute coward. You stand here bragging about killing a couple starving-to-death, down-on-their-luck people and a baby?" I mashed my fist into an open palm and twisted it, and watched Alice's eyes light up. As I pulled my hands apart, I scraped my index fingers against one another, then moved in front of Alice, blocking her from Jacobs's view.

Thankfully, I knew Locke understood our language. I flicked my eyes back to him for the space of a second. All I dared. From behind Alice, he scrunched his eyebrows at me, then gave his arms a quick shake.

Jacobs jabbed the knife deeper into Billy's throat. "Have great care what you say next, Daggett." His yellow eyes locked on mine and filled with alarm. Good.

"I bet you half those scars don't even represent anyone you killed. How about that one?" I jabbed a finger toward his chest. "You swat a fly and give yourself a tally marker?"

"Enough!" shouted Jacobs. He panted, and his eyes darted around the field before settling on the empty patch of sand between me and Locke. "Where'd the girl go?"

"Every coyote needs a buzzard, Vic."

Locke smirked. "Quiet, isn't she?"

I saw Alice coming in the nick of time and lunged for Jacobs's knife, sliding my hand underneath the hilt and throwing it off its axis. Instead of plunging into Billy's neck, it scraped along his cheek, providing a closer shave than he probably would've liked. Maybe it was my heroics that saved him. Maybe it was Alice burying Locke's switchblade into the top of Victor Jacobs's spine.

The serpentine brute dropped to his knees and Alice followed him down, giving the knife a twist as he fell and then yanking it free. His limbs jerked in spasms and the panic in his sickly eyes intensified. Knife in hand, Alice stared down at him. No one spoke a word, with their voice or their hands. Her glare said everything she needed it to.

She knelt beside Jacobs's head and held out her arm. With a few careful strokes, she carved three crisscrossing lines that met at the center into her forearm and held it out toward him.

Three.

One for each person he'd helped to take from her.

"I can't feel my legs," he whispered. "I can't feel anything."

Alice studied the fear in his eyes for a moment, seeming to drink it in. Then she flipped the knife into the air and caught it. In the same movement, she jammed it into Victor Jacobs's ear and the soft gray matter just beyond. The fear faded from his eyes, taking the light with it. A puff of putrid blackness retreated from his desolate carcass and drifted toward the cavern.

Alice collapsed beside him.

CHAPTER 17

ONCE A KILLER

With Jacobs down, Locke sprinted to Billy and checked his wounds while I scooped up Alice and held her close.

"We're okay, Pip. We're gonna be okay." Bullshit, unhelpful words, but really, what do you say to a little girl who just paralyzed and murdered the man who stole her family away from her?

"Nobody said a damn thing to me," I whispered.

She looked up, eyes blue as the Blackjack creek, glistening with fresh tears.

"If there's one person who can understand the fucking twister that's tearing apart your guts right now, it's me. I got you. And you know what? When I let Noose have it, he'd already taken so many people from me one way or another. There was only one person who made me feel like the world wasn't burning down."

Alice laid a hand gently across her chest, all without looking up.

"Damn right, you." I hesitated. "Thing is, I had an advantage you don't. Maybe. Once I put that dog down, I had time to come to terms with the aftermath." I chuckled. "Few months anyway. We got more business to attend to in that cave over there. Least I do, and I don't suspect Locke'd turn his nose up at a fight. Real question is, are you up for it?" I held up a hand. "I wouldn't dare think any less of you if you wanted to stay out here."

Alice put some weight on her legs. Wobbly as they were, they held. Her right hand found her chest once more, then she brought it to her open left and drew them to the side as if spreading her ribs. I knew what came next. I pointed to her.

You're all I have.

"Let's go."

Light poured from the mouth of Devil's Cavern like a sun ray tainted by dirty river water. The bright blue, normally pure and clean, had a soiled quality that made stepping inside the mouth of the cave more than a little frightening. Tendrils of blue light swirled in the darkness, mixing brilliance and murk in an unsettling way.

"I nominate Ragtag Rory to go first, seeing as marching into the gloom was his idea." Billy's voice shook, a trace of the nerves and adrenaline from his brush with death.

"Well now, I'd hate to be thought a coward." I dropped a fresh set of bullets into my revolver and set a foot against the stone below. It had an unnatural smoothness to it. One bad step and I'd slip and slide my way to whatever waited at the bottom. Jagged pillars lined the inside. I imagined Fieldstone members lying in wait, fingers on triggers and shit-eating grins on faces, as Mary and the Windfall lawmen fired into the empty dark.

Each tapping footstep echoed through the cavern and made it sound like ten thousand stragglers were on my tail. Alice tugged at my shirt to let me know I wasn't descending alone. That's when the smell hit. Rot and sulfur, the result of dozens of dead Buzzard's Edge citizens, relieved of their lives under the blazing Arizona sun.

"They dragged them down here," I whispered. It seemed too loud in the rocky underground. "Maybe even upwards of a hundred. So where are the bodies?"

The cavern's silence was the only answer.

Blue haze floated up toward the ceiling like smoke in a burning building and stole any semblance of visibility. I spun to see Billy and Locke holding up the rear, mesmerized by the otherworldly display.

Further and further we walked, and the earth swallowed us up. Not a soul made their presence known, and even the cavern itself seemed to hold its breath. It was hard to tell under the sparse blue light, but the rough walls seemed to slip farther away from our grasp.

"We're approaching something," said Locke. "Can you feel it?"

Hell of it was, I could. The short hairs on the back of my neck stood at attention. Not like a bad batch of goose pimples, more like one of those rare Arizona thunderstorms creeping just over the horizon, and thousands of years of human instinct have conditioned your body to be ready.

I kept on forward, because that was the only way that made sense and the staircase-like tunnel opened to a large room. Blue light slithered down and threaded across the rock walls like exploratory fingers. On the far side of the chamber, a mud-thick pool of liquid roiled. Bright blue, but with cords of black spoiling the waves.

The resurrection pit.

In the center of the chamber, Mary Crane sat on a stone altar, legs crossed, and head bowed as if in some sort of trance. Her body was so still, she could've been dead if it wasn't for the slight rise and fall of her chest, keeping the same rhythm as the pulsing blue light.

The only demon in Devil's Cavern, after all.

I froze and felt a frantic tug at my sleeve, higher up and on the opposite side of Alice. I tried to turn without taking my eyes off Mary, and found Billy, mouth agape and sporting a pallor that did little more than reflect the blue light collected in the cavern.

I kept my voice low. "What is it?"

He extended a trembling finger and let it trail around the room as if drawing an enormous circle.

Bodies lay strewn about the rocky cavern floor. A thick enough layer to resemble carpeting, and make counting a pointless endeavor.

Some I recognized from the town, from the melee. Many of them sported blue bandanas and a bullet hole between the eyes that was eerily similar to the one Mary received the night we met.

"It wasn't enough." Mary's voice echoed around the chamber, riding the acoustics to make it sound like there were several of her. She lifted her head and smiled. "Rory Daggett, you beautiful bastard. Wish I could say I was surprised you made it out of Buzzard's Edge alive."

"What did you do?" I asked.

She lowered her legs over the side of the altar. "I did what any refugee from the dark frontier would do. I tried to free the ones stuck on the other side. It's all I ever wanted to do."

"All Simon wanted to do?" I asked. The temperature in the room seemed to plummet as Mary tilted her head.

"His was a fascination. A need to understand. Then he was taken from me. *You* took him from me." A light chuckle. "Now, I s'pose he understands a bit too well. Know why I came to Buzzard's Edge? Accepted the sheriff's job?"

"We sought you out," said Locke, without much confidence.

"No," I said. "Back at the saloon. You said revenge."

"And that wasn't a lie, but first and foremost to get Simon's body. Mr. Daggett, how many times we run into each other since that first night and you still ain't asked why I'm back up and breathing?"

"Maybe I already know."

"Humor me."

"Okay, how are you still alive? Alice and I saw you take a bullet to the head."

Mary hopped down from the altar and paced the chamber, stepping carefully to avoid the bodies.

"Your eyes didn't deceive you. My crew had orders to blow my brains out and get my body back here posthaste." She held a hand out toward the sour-looking blue waters. "Plop me right in there for a quick soak. Half a minute or so. It don't eliminate every scar, but it gets the blood pumping once more, even if it does warrant a brief trip to the other place."

"Dark frontier," I mumbled.

Mary raised her eyebrows at the words. Hands behind her back, she turned toward the wall. Jets of light crawled along its expanse, and for the first time, I saw the shadows beyond the blue haze. Some human, others far worse. Long, spindly legs and endless, writhing arms belonging to monsters I couldn't imagine, all waiting on the other side of the light. Waiting in the dark frontier.

I fingered my revolver, considered putting another bullet in her head. "You wanted his body to bring him back. Simon."

"That was my noble intention. Shit of it was, nobody knew what happened to his body. No grave marker, no storage. Near as I can tell, this clod here…" She pointed at Billy. "He planted my Simon somewhere in the middle of the desert and forgot about him. So…"

Quicker than she'd shot Robert Jeffery's jawbone off his skull, she raised a pistol and aimed it at Billy. "Do you know how to take down a gate between worlds, Rory?"

Slowly, Billy raised his hands. His face hung like a hound, clearly tired of having weapons pointed at him.

I didn't drop my gun, simply let it dangle off a finger. She hadn't shot Billy yet and a taste of hope lingered in the air. "Can't say I've ever wondered."

The ghost of a smile appeared at the corner of her lips. "Same way you break down any other gate. An army. And if you don't have the manpower to breach the line? Shit, that's simple. You recruit more."

A thundercrack shook the chamber and red mist erupted from Billy's chest. He flopped back and smacked off the cavern floor.

He didn't let out a yell, and maybe that was the worst part.

"Whooooa!" Mary screamed. "Now before y'all get any funny ideas about comeuppance, I'd like you to remember there's a pit what can save lives behind us, and only one person in this room who knows how to use it."

Alice and I rushed to Billy's side. The hitch of his breathing filled the room. He kept silent, but his eyes begged for help.

"Kindly toss your guns down and carry him over to the pool."

Sweat poured down Billy's face as he gasped for breath. He tried to force a smile and gave a little nod as if to say, "It's alright."

Into a clanking metal pile went three revolvers and a rifle. Thad and I carried Billy across the room, dodging corpses while Mary kept her gun trained on us. When we laid him on the stone next to the pool, she shooed us away and straddled his body, leaning down and whispering something into his ear.

"I don't like this," said Thad. His eyes flitted over to our weapons, gauging how fast he could cover the distance and get off a shot. I know because I was doing the same thing.

Mary cradled Billy's head and continued her whispers.

Was it my imagination or was his breathing slowing down? Calming, maybe.

Another moment passed and a few calculations with them They promised the same outcome. With the gun still in her hand, she would put a stop to Billy's shallow breaths and drop at least one of us before I could get my hands on a weapon.

Then she sat up. A thin gray vapor trailed into the air from the hole in Billy's chest. Alice and Locke remained on alert, no trace of shock in their eyes. This was for me alone. Billy's soul floated into the air like a feather on the wind and vanished into the ethereal blue mist that lined the walls. The moment it hit the blue haze, the gate between worlds, a gentle pulse resonated from the place it entered and ran all along the walls. Ghostly hands pressed against the barrier, oblong shapes bulging through like it was made of canvas. It held them back for the time being, but the word *temporary* raced through my mind.

"You killed him. He's gone." My voice was barely more than the wind that carried Billy to the dark frontier.

She brushed cave dust off the front of her shirt as she stood and glazed down at the floor, littered with bodies. She gave Billy's a kick. "It didn't work! God dammit." She surveyed the creatures pushing against the barrier. "It's close, so close. Just one more. I know it." She stared between me, Locke, and Alice, letting her eyes settle greedily on each of us.

"I needed more time, a few more people from above." Her words came fast, and she looked at each member of the Fieldstone Gang lining the floor, neat bullet holes between their eyes and their souls somewhere far away.

"You've been there, Mary. Same as me. You know it's not just Simon coming back through. What about their guardians?" I pointed toward a talon covered in razor-sharp looking barbs. "Is that something you want to deal with on this side?"

Madness swept her face, her hair carrying backward in that chilly, ever-present breeze I remembered from the dark frontier. She didn't answer because she wasn't hearing a word I was saying. Then her gaze landed on Alice and she raised the revolver. I stepped in front of Alice. The gun shook in Mary's hand and tears dripped down her red cheeks.

"This is my last chance, Rory. Don't you dare take it from me!"

"You don't want to do this. It ain't worth it." I risked a step forward.

"The hell it ain't! What if you could have back everyone you lost? You could, Rory. We could. You telling me just sucking it up and sayin' our permanent goodbyes is fair?"

I opened my mouth to speak, but no words came. Harden, Billy, the Taffs, my parents. Alice's family. Even her baby brother. For the space of a moment, all those faces occupied my mind.

"'Cause that's the way life works," I whispered to myself.

"I wasn't thinking clearly before." Mary nodded toward Billy. "Mr. Chambers lived a decent long life. Maybe he even believes he gave it up to save you. Army needs a leader and it ain't gon' be someone satisfied with their ends."

She stepped to the side and tried to find Alice in the gun's sight. "This one's fierce, though. And I seen how she looks at you, Rory. What the girl won't do to get back to her imprinted daddy. Can you imagine it?"

Locke blocked Alice from Mary's new angle. Mary snarled.

"You don't put down that gun, Mary," I said, "I'll tear you into so many fucking pieces, your brother won't be able to find more than a fingernail when he comes through."

"Willing to take that risk." She cocked the hammer. "Shame, Daggett. I never was pretending to be a little sweet on you. We could do this together. Leaders of our very own army of the undead." She stepped forward, keeping the gun level, and whispered in my ear. "Took me less than a week to take over a town and get its residents to walk to their doom. Imagine what we could do by day with a whole 'nother world at our disposal, and mmm, imagine what we could do when the sun goes down."

I sucked in a deep breath and closed my eyes.

"I want to trust you, Mary. Really, I do. Thing is, once a killer, always a killer."

She pulled back and her face fell. The gun, too. Only a hair, but it was enough. I launched myself forward, putting my weight on her wrist. The gun cracked in my ear, but I was already in the air and past caring if it blew a chunk of my arm away. Mary and I hit the ground and rolled. Then I heard the gun clatter away like a stone skipping across a frozen lake. I pulled her to her feet by the shirt collar and met her eyes as I pushed her against the luminescent cavern wall. There should've been fear. Instead, it was more like ecstasy mixed with acceptance. She closed her eyes and nodded.

Before I could decide what to do next, a spiny arm poked through the blue haze and wrapped around her chest, digging its barbed hairs into her skin. That's when the fear entered her eyes.

"No," was all she said before another horrible appendage covered her face and yanked her back, flattening her body against the wall. A few more joined, their bestial smells wafting through the holes in the barrier. They tore at her with the strength of giant monsters and Mary's bones began to crack, reshaping to fit through holes in the veil too small for any human.

I stepped back with my jaw hanging low and my eyes wider than any of the voids claiming Mary Crane.

A rictus of agony overtook her face as her teeth clenched and her eyes threatened to burst. The spiky arms coiled tight like rope and, with a final heave, ripped her remains into the dark frontier, leaving behind nothing but a spray of blood. Miniature red dots filled the air like stars on a cloudless night.

I waited for the beasts to charge through, but for the moment, all was peaceful.

"Rory." Panic filled Locke's voice.

I spun around, but paid no mind to the detective.

Pale as sun-bleached sand, Alice hunched forward, clutching her stomach. Rivulets of red ran out of the bullet wound and through her fingers. Her eyes, squinted to a crack, held mine. She wobbled for a moment, then her legs gave up under her weight and she tumbled to the ground.

CHAPTER 18

The Last Groan

I crossed the chamber in two giant-sized steps and scooped her up. Alice's eyes fluttered for a moment before going still. The rest of her body went as limp as her legs, and then her chest stopped rising and falling.

"No!" A thousand and one words raced through my head, every one tinged red with anger, black with grief. "No" was the only one that escaped as more than an unintelligible scream.

Locke held two fingers to the side of her neck and kept them there for a minute, two. With every passing second, the corners of his mouth drooped further toward the ground. At last, he removed his hand and shook his head, unable to offer comfort. He sat on the cold, hard cavern floor and buried his face in his hands.

From beneath Alice's hands, still clutched to her tiny stomach, a thin gray mist began to climb into the air. With fumbling hands, I tried to catch it and put it back, but no matter how fast you are, no matter how good your reflexes, ain't a man alive who can catch smoke. Eventually, it became hard to see through the wall of tears.

Locke's head shot up. "The pool!"

With the mess of thoughts swirling through my head, I didn't understand at first. Then I did. The blue light lining the walls had dimmed after Mary passed through. Even the resurrection pit, filled to the brim with sky blue muck, lacked the pulse it had when we first entered the room.

But we had to try.

I carried Alice's body, carefully, like it was made of glass, and tried to ignore the cloud of gray leaking out.

Mary said a person could come back. We can call her back.

As we drew closer to the pool, the blue haze sparked to life once more. Shadows writhing along the walls, calling from the dark frontier.

I lowered myself into the pool as it blazed with promise once more, then I laid Alice on her back, allowing her to float across the surface. The liquid was uncomfortably warm, giving the illusion of living skin trailing fingertips across my body.

"Are you sure that's wise?" Locke asked, crouching by the side of the pool. "Going in with her? You don't know how it works."

If you return again, Rory, you will not be allowed to leave.

Fuck it. I'd do it for her.

"Any strange effects the dark frontier is going to have on me, I'd bet they've already begun to show themselves, Thad."

His brows knit in confusion, but he kept any follow-up questions to himself.

Alice floated on the imaginary current as I watched her chest for any sign of returning life.

"Perhaps you need to submerge her," said Locke.

I closed my eyes and begged Alice's forgiveness before sinking her body into the lukewarm sludge. Then I started counting.

One, two, three.

"They're back," Locke whispered. My eyes snapped open, and I spied shadows swaying against the blue light. Hands, claws, and talons pushing out against the thin membrane separating the two worlds.

Six, seven, eight.

A distant rumble shook the walls, and I glanced around the cavern. The dead coming through? The monsters? Silhouettes lined the chamber, watching through the veil. They could have belonged to Mary. They could have belonged to anyone.

Eleven, twelve, thirteen.

"You heard that, too?" Locke studied the ceiling as if expecting rocks to fall.

Another rumble. Less distant.

Sixteen, seventeen, eighteen.

"Pull her up. We have to leave," said Locke.

I shook my head. Something about thirty seconds stuck in my mind. A shard of rock crashed next to the pool, narrowly missing Locke. He skittered away on hands and knees.

Faces pressed against the barrier, stretching it like an undersized shirt and threatening to burst through at any second.

"Now, Rory!"

Twenty-one, twenty-two, twenty-three.

An avalanche of loose stone poured down the cave walls, dropping into the pool. I guided Alice's body away from the debris and continued counting.

Shouts cut through the pounding of rock against the cavern floor. Angry voices, haunting voices. They were almost loose.

"We can't wait any longer, Daggett. We must go. Please, don't make me take the coward's way and leave without you!"

Twenty-seven, twenty-eight, twenty-nine...

"Thirty!" I cried and pulled her up.

Please let that be enough.

"Take her while I get out."

He cradled Alice's body far more gently than bespoke of the murderer I'd seen in action that day. A chunk of boulder collided with his arm. Still, he held her fast. As quickly as my body would allow, I crawled out of the slimy goo and took her back.

All around us, limbs poked through the cerulean mist, little more than shadow remnants. Fingers outstretched and claws grasping, they sought escape. Only tumbling debris kept them at bay.

"Run!"

With one eye forward, and one on the collapsing cavern, I froze at the entrance.

Billy.

Another half minute and maybe I could've saved him too. A stray rock whizzed by my ear like a bullet, declaring that it wasn't meant to be. Maybe Mary was right about that one thing. He'd lived a decent long life.

Locke and I attacked the stone staircase leading out to sunshine and survivors. When the entrance appeared, the cavern's mouth shook like a giant was playing toss with the whole damn mountain. A glance behind us made it clear the cavern was gone, buried along with any further chances at resurrection and, with any luck, an encroaching army of the dead. Alice's cold, damp body in my arms. I'd done all I could. Right?

The ever-expanding rockslide made it look like the mouth was closing. Calling on reserves I didn't realize I had, I made a final push for daylight with Locke by my side. We threw our bodies out onto the sand as Devil's Cavern gave its last groan. Thousands of pounds of rock collapsed inward like a stoved-in skull. Where once stood a prominent crown at the edge of the bowl, now lay a cautious path to freedom.

A glorious sight, but I had no time for it.

I set Alice in the sunlight and searched for any signs of life. Color in the face, a hitch in the chest, movement in the hands. My fingers found the spot on the side of her neck, trying to detect the faintest heartbeat.

"Come on. Come on, come on, come on."

Locke laid a hand on my shoulder with a clear message.

"I'm sorry, friend."

My shoulders fell. Tears gathered at the edge of my vision, but they weren't ready to fall. Even the breath in my lungs wasn't ready to come out yet. I took Alice's hand and squeezed it as I felt the first tear pop free. Her shirt was pulled up just past the belly button. Squinting my eyes, I used my free hand to pull it up a little further. A small imperfection where the bullet had taken her, crisscrossed with white scar tissue, stared back at me.

"Holy shit," I whispered, not quite allowing myself to hope. "Come on, Pip. If anyone can fight their way back…"

Her eyes shot open, and she sucked in a breath. Alice sat up and barely made it to an upright angle before I wrapped her in a crushing hug.

"I thought I lost you, Pip. Christ, I thought I lost you."

As was tradition, she said nothing. Just squeezed back.

CHAPTER 19

A NEW SHERIFF IN TOWN

It was Thaddeus Locke who figured out how to snap all those swaying citizens back to life, get them to walk on their own two feet back to Buzzard's Edge. Said he took the idea from the story of Billy saving my sorry ass at the poison-filled sheriff's office.

A sharp yell and an unexpected smack brought Mayor Harvey back to the present. He shook his gelatinous cheeks, and we stepped back, half worried he might still have some of that violence juice kicking around his system.

Nothing but confusion, and a little hunger as it turned out, though I couldn't help staring at him with new, slightly colder eyes, knowing the role he'd played in Alice's circumstances.

With every person we woke, the job grew a little easier and before we knew it, we had the survivors back in the land of the living and ready to continue their pursuit of the outlaw, Rory Daggett. Thankfully, Locke stood by my side, and we told everybody as much of the story as we could stomach.

"Good God. Billy Chambers," said Mayor Harvey as he removed his hat, placing it over his heart. The vicious sun nipped down and reddened his balding dome. "Man was the law in this town going back sometime. His kind heart will be missed."

"That it will," I said. "Would've made a hell of a sheriff with Mary gone."

"Hmm," said Harvey, and I figured he was thinking I was angling for the job. Let him. I had about as much interest in being sheriff as getting a shave from a scorpion. "Need to put together a committee, I s'pose, in order to make it official. But I do think Mr. Thaddeus Locke'd make a fine sheriff. If he'd be willing to do the job?"

The people of Buzzard's Edge let loose a loud cheer.

A shadow passed over Locke's face, but it was gone, fast as any vulture that might've cast it. My stomach dropped a little before finding its footing. The man had a secret, and it wasn't a pleasant one. We'd come a long way in the last day or so, but if the town was going to give him such a position, I'd need to keep tabs.

Nonetheless, I congratulated my friend.

"If it's all the same," said Locke, with some red in his cheeks, "I'll wait until it's official to make a speech, but if elected, I would be willing to serve."

I thought back to what he'd said, about John Harden seeing through his exterior and being willing to give him the benefit of the doubt. Imperfect, Harden might've been, but I had a damn hard time demonizing the man.

The town let out another hoot at Locke's words.

"Well, hell, that's as settled as can be for the moment." Harvey cleared his throat and looked embarrassed. "How many good folks would you say are buried beneath that load of rock?"

Locke and I traded a look.

"Could be upwards of a hundred," I said. "Both gang members and townspeople."

"My, my. Well, I don't s'pose this is the day for it, with the injured living to care for, but perhaps once we've taken a census, we might gather a crew to retrieve the bodies and give them a proper burial."

My heart sputtered, and it took an awful lot of restraint to keep from screaming. "Mr. Mayor, I appreciate the sentiment, but I wonder if it might be the right move to let the dead rest where they are."

Harvey tilted his head and studied me. I couldn't even meet his eye as visions of undead soldiers and creatures marched through my mind. I hoped to hell that half a mountain was enough to trap them in the dark frontier. It would have to be.

"Thoughts, Mr. Locke?"

Thad nodded. "I think they've earned that rest. After today."

"Hm," said the mayor. "Very well, then. Now, if one of you'd kindly point me toward home, I say we get going."

Outside the bowl, we found a cache of horses belonging to the Fieldstone Gang. Thirty at a count, nowhere near enough for everybody to have a ride, but it was a start. Along the other side, we found the three horses that bore us to Devil's Cavern. Ghost was less than pleased at a day left in the hot sun with no water but couldn't hide her enthusiasm at the sight of me and Alice. I knew her too well. Locke reclaimed his horse and gave Billy's to an injured walker.

It was Mr. Meyer, the town's undertaker and skilled woodworker, who set a course south. A man of many talents, and few words, he brushed the hair out of his eyes and started walking like he was out for an afternoon stroll. Conversation was sparse and included no mention of the violence inflicted upon the others. Not even much talk about those lost to Devil's Cavern. We left out the parts about the dark frontier and giant spiders. The human brain can only stretch so far coming out of a phase of purple-induced euphoria.

The group of several hundred sauntered south at a steady pace, and as the sun began to seek the horizon to our west, Alice and I fell back, away from the crowd.

She rode Ghost and I walked by her side.

"I know you probably don't want to talk much, and I can understand that, but I've been thinking."

Alice tapped her chin with four fingers.

"You sure you want to give me permission to talk? Once I get started, I've been known to have difficulty stopping."

She closed her fist and raised an outstretched pinky to her nose

"Made a mistake, my ass." I laughed. "But I'm glad to see your sense of humor made the trip back with the rest of you."

A smile crossed her face that made the sunset look plain in comparison.

"I've been thinking about your daddy, and I don't wish to speak ill of the dead. Especially since it sounds like he gave his last breath to protect your family. It's just all I can think of is the time, energy, and money he put into trying to fix you, Pip. Guess I can't fault a man who would go to that length for his daughter, but..."

I stared straight ahead, afraid of what her smile might turn into

"From where I'm standing, there ain't nothing to fix." I let the words breathe a minute and looked up. Her smile was smaller, but undeniably present. A single tear dropped down her cheek, climbing up and over the raised scar before it reached her chin.

"Svensson." I said the word slowly, trying it out. "I can get used to that. Strange I never asked you for it, right? I've been thinking about that, too. And I guess I never needed to know. Always thought of you as a Daggett."

Alice closed her fist, letting thumb and pinky stick out, then rocked it back and forth.

I could hardly keep my eyebrows from shooting up to my hairline. "Really? Well, it's just a name, but it's sure as shit yours if you want it."

I turned back toward the south, but from the corner of my eye, caught her flicking fingers and spelling out a series of letters, twelve in all.

Alice Daggett.

We said nothing more for a while. Just let the crunch of the sand, the howl of the coyotes, and the call of the buzzards speak for us. And that was alright.

After a spell, I found the courage to ask the other thing on my mind.

"What'd you see over there? While you were… you know."

A beat went by, then two, while Alice looked away. Maybe trying to find the right words, maybe trying to ignore the question completely. Finally, with the reins still clasped tight, she held her hands up, flat palms facing toward her and moved the right in front of the left.

"Next? I don't understand, what do you mean—"

She did the sign again, a little more aggressively, clapping her hands together as they passed. Then she made a V with her right hand and pointed to her eye.

My guts tied in knots and my feet locked in place as if swallowed by the sand, hand still on the harness. When Ghost ran out of slack, she skidded to a stop, registering her displeasure with a soft knicker.

I shook my head, trying to find any other explanation for Alice's words. Except I knew what that science-y shit could do, what the dark frontier could do. Hadn't I gained the ability to see the dead? What made this so far-fetched?

"Let me get this straight, Pip. You saw what happens next?"

Alice nodded and looked down at Ghost. When she picked her head up, her arms came with it, crossed into an X over her chest with clenched fists. Then her arms dropped, and she opened her fists into outspread palms.

Everything.

My eyes widened and the rest of the town pulled further away. No one noticed us stragglers.

"Tell me what happens next."

LAGNIAPPE

During a staff meeting one gloriously stormy night, the idea of having a "Lagniappe" near the end of some of the works published by Brigids Gate Press was discussed. The staff unanimously voted in favor of the idea.

Lagniappe (pronounced LAN-yap) is an old New Orleans tradition where merchants give a little something extra along with every purchase. It's a way of expressing thanks and appreciation to customers.

The Lagniappe section might contain a short story, a small handful of poems, or a non-fiction piece. In this book, it is an exemption to the anthology's guideline of no fractured fairy tales.

***

For the lagniappe for this book, the author decided to throw in an extra story, *Miles and Miles*, for all of his readers. Hope y'all enjoy it!

142

MILES AND MILES

George Holcomb pulled out his favorite chair. The scrape of the legs against the weathered floorboards was lost to the din from inside the saloon. A great fucking calamity. Clearly, Buzzard's Edge had something to celebrate tonight.

Death relieved a man of his need to breathe, but allowed him to sigh still. There was some kind of irony in that. George let out a frustrated burst of air from his nonexistent lungs and took a seat. Though the room was steeped in pitch black, he could see the tacky blood emblazoned on the table. An everlasting tribute to his unceremonious end. He tapped on the table and sighed again.

Change nothing and nothing changes, he thought.

Across the room, a bullet of blue hung in the air as if by magic, taunting him with its everlasting light. It pulsed once, twice, then expanded, first to the size of a closed fist, then bigger than a horse's head. George squinted. This was new. As it grew, it shone so bright he could hardly bear to look at it. Nor could he look away.

Against the backdrop of sunny afternoon blue, a silhouette eclipsed the light, and a hint of cinnamon filled the air. The figure watched him. George dug his fingers into the table and waited.

"Come and take my hand," said a familiar voice. It wavered and echoed as though it had crossed miles and miles to get to him, but he knew the voice. He would have known it anywhere.

One of these days, though. You'll come back to hear my sweet singing voice, and I won't answer your calls.

For the first time since that bullet had passed through his gray matter, George felt a true smile take up residence on his face.

ACKNOWLEDGEMENTS

I wrote *Noose* in September of 2021 and since then I've returned to that world for multiple short stories and now the novel you hold in your hands. Every time I start a new Buzzard's Edge story, there's a certain fear that I won't be able to find the voice again, capture the same energy as the first book, but a few hundred words in and I'm home. It's damn near impossible for a writer to choose their favorite of their characters, but put a gun to my head, and it's Alice. That's why pulling the curtain back a bit on her life before she met Rory both thrilled and hurt me to write. A lot of readers loved her inclusion in the first book, and it only felt right to give her a little more spotlight this time around. In truth, the book belongs to her, even as she helps Rory turn his attention to parental issues of a different sort.

A quick note, as mentioned the first time around. These stories include magic, ghosts, and immortal-ish beings. By necessity, they're going to take some liberties with history and geography. I've done so again this time around in the interest of story. Specifically, let's talk American Sign Language. While it was employed in New England schools as early as 1814, and feasibly, could've made its way west, most textbooks at the time taught only the hand signals for letters as opposed to full words. Still, the way this language is wrapped into American history fascinated me and opened the door for a new layer of storytelling. Forgive me my exaggerations and fabrications.

A tremendous thank you to Heather and Steve at Brigids Gate Press for breathing new life into these books. Also to Andrew Robert, who gave these books their first home. Thank you to Val Halvorson for the amazing cover, capturing the perfect mix of pulp, horror, and emotion.

A writer's journey can be lonely. Having Tyler Jones fall in love with the first book and consistently remind me it's a story worth telling, told in a manner only I could do, has planted my ass in front of the writing desk on many an occasion. Candace Nola is a light in the darkness that always has a word of encouragement when life makes its best attempts to overwhelm. This book could not have succeeded without her sharp editorial eye. Patrick McDonough has been there since the beginning and continues to heap praise on these books. At times it feels undeserved, but it's always appreciated. Erica Robyn reads every word I commit to the page and does more to build up both me, and horror as a genre, than just about anyone else out there.

Aron, Dallas, and Dustin listen to me prattle endlessly about characters that exist solely in my head and grant me the gift of time to relocate them to paper. Thank you all, and I love you endlessly.

Lastly, thank you to every reader who's taken a chance on a book with my name on the cover. You're the reason we tell stories. Hope you enjoyed the ride and I'll see you where the daybreak ends.

ABOUT THE AUTHOR

Brennan LaFaro is a music teacher by day, horror writer by night, living in southeastern Massachusetts with his wife, two sons, and his hounds. He is the author of the *Slattery Falls* trilogy, the *Buzzard's Edge Saga*, as well as *Illusions of Isolation* and *Last Stay*. You can read his short fiction in various anthologies and find him on Twitter at @brennanlafaro or at www.brennanlafaro.com.

149

More from Brigids Gate Press

MELINDA WEST: MONSTER GUNSLINGER

KC Grifant

KC Grifant comes out guns blazing with *Melinda West: Monster Gunslinger*—a devious action-packed adventure set in a very weird version of the Old West. Fast, furious, and a hell of a lot of fun!"—Jonathan Maberry, *NY Times* bestselling author of *Son of the Poison Rose* and *Relentless*

In an Old West overrun by monsters, a stoic gunslinger must embark on a dangerous quest to save her friends and stop a supernatural war.

Sharpshooter Melinda West, 29, has encountered more than her share of supernatural creatures after a monster infection killed her mother. Now, Melinda and her charismatic partner, Lance, offer their exterminating services to desperate towns, fighting everything from giant flying scorpions to psychic bugs. But when they accidentally release a demon, they must track a dangerous outlaw across treacherous lands and battle a menagerie of creatures—all before an army of soul-devouring monsters descend on Earth.

Supernatural meets *Bonnie and Clyde* in a re-imagined Old West full of diverse characters, desolate landscapes, and fast-paced adventure.

BLOOD ON THE SOIL, TERROR ON THE WIND

Ed. Kenneth W. Cain

Whether in an old weathered mine shaft, somewhere off the beaten path, out in the woods, or right here in the middle of this ghost town, danger awaits. We're going to take you way back, drop you right smack dab in the middle of the Old West at its finest. But we're not just going to give you shootouts and bullet wounds and blood splatter. Yes, those things are prominently featured, but there's so much more to this anthology of western horror.

Maybe it's a well-known creature popping in for a visit, or some new creepy crawly monster sucking out your soul, we're going to turn the Old West inside-out and explore its guts to the fullest. There are new adventures to be had, monsters both familiar and unfamiliar to be thwarted… And we're not always going to be the victors. Life in the Old West is hard, trying at its best, and it can wear you down quick.

So, prepare yourself to be transported back in time. Get yourself up on that rickety stagecoach, draw your guns, and let's get going. There's vast territory to cover here, and your journey begins now.

THE PRISONERS OF STEWARTVILLE

Shannon Felton

Stewartville. A town living in the shadow of the prisons that drive its economy. Haunted by the ghosts of its past. Cursed by the dark secrets hidden beneath. A town so entwined with the prisons waiting outside the city limits that it's impossible to imagine one without the other, or to ever imagine escaping either.

When a teenage boy digs into the history of the town, he discovers a tunnel system beneath Stewartville, passageways filled with dark secrets. Secrets leading not to freedom, but to unrelenting terror.

Stewartville. Where the convicts aren't the only prisoners.

HELL ON HIGH

Michael Clark

Prepare for adventure as Juliana, a nineteen-year-old Brazilian, finds herself forced to run from an occult overlord, leaving her sister in peril. Temporarily safe, Juliana works to save money for Vilma's rescue—and along the way, meets Patrick, a rich-boy mountain climber with friends in high places.

Angus Addison wants to see his corporate flag on the summit of Mount Everest—carried there by the first woman in history—but the Himalayas are no joke. Failure could cost both sisters their lives.

Juliana weighs the risks and rewards—for even if she raises the cash, she still must figure a way to free Vilma from the same man she ran from—a man known to his disciples as *The Farmer*.

Visit our website at: www.brigidsgatepress.com

E-Z DICKENS SUPERHERO 'ΗΡΩΕΣ ΒΙΒΛΊΑ 'ΕΝΑ ΚΑΙ Δ'ΥΟ

ΑΓΓΕΛΟΣ ΤΑΤΤΟΟΥ (TATTOO ANGEL): ΤΑ ΤΡ'ΙΑ (THE THREE)

Cathy McGough

Stratford Living Publishing

Πίνακας περιεχομένων

Αφιέρωση

Για την Dorothy που πίστεψε.

ΒΙΒΛΙΟ ΠΡΩΤΟ:
ΑΓΓΕΛΟΣ ΤΑΤΤΟΟΥ (TATTOO ANGEL)

ΠΡΟΛΟΓΟΣ

Τ Ο ΠΡΏΤΟ ΠΛΆΣΜΑ ΠΈΤΑΞΕ πάνω στο στήθος του Ε-Ζ και προσγειώθηκε, με το πηγούνι μπροστά και τα χέρια στους γοφούς του. Γύρισε μια φορά, δεξιόστροφα. Περιστρέφοντας πιο γρήγορα από το φτερούγισμα των φτερών του αναδύθηκε ένα τραγούδι. Το τραγούδι ήταν ένα χαμηλό βογγητό. Ένα θλιβερό τραγούδι από το παρελθόν, για να γιορτάσει μια ζωή που δεν υπήρχε πια. Το πλάσμα έγειρε προς τα πίσω, το κεφάλι ακουμπούσε στο στήθος του Ε-Ζ. Η περιστροφή σταμάτησε, αλλά το τραγούδι συνέχισε να παίζει.

Το δεύτερο πλάσμα συμμετείχε, κάνοντας το ίδιο τελετουργικό, ενώ περιστρεφόταν αριστερόστροφα. Δημιούργησαν ένα νέο τραγούδι, χωρίς τα μπιπ-μπιπ και τα ζουμ-ζουμ. Γιατί όταν τραγουδούσαν, η ονοματοποιία δεν ήταν απαραίτητη. Ενώ στην καθημερινή συζήτηση με τους ανθρώπους ήταν απαραίτητη. Αυτό το τραγούδι επικάλυψε το άλλο και έγινε μια χαρούμενη, υψίφωνη γιορτή. Μια ωδή για τα πράγματα που έρχονται, για μια ζωή που δεν έχει ακόμη ζήσει. Ένα τραγούδι για το μέλλον.

Ένας ψεκασμός διαμαντόσκονης έσκασε από τις χρυσές κόγχες των ματιών τους καθώς στράφηκαν σε απόλυτο συγχρονισμό. Η διαμαντόσκονη ψεκάστηκε από τα μάτια τους πάνω στο σώμα του Ε-Ζ που κοιμόταν. Η ανταλλαγή συνεχίστηκε, μέχρι που τον κάλυψε με διαμαντόσκονη από την κορυφή ως τα νύχια.

Ο έφηβος συνέχισε να κοιμάται βαθιά. Μέχρι που η διαμαντόσκονη τρύπησε τη σάρκα του - τότε άνοιξε το στόμα του για να ουρλιάξει, αλλά δεν βγήκε κανένας ήχος.

"Ξυπνάει, μπιπ-μπιπ".

"Σηκώστε τον, ζουμ-ζουμ."

Μαζί τον σήκωσαν, καθώς άνοιξε τα μάτια του.

"Κοιμήσου περισσότερο, μπιπ-μπιπ".

"Μην αισθάνεσαι πόνο, ζουμ-ζουμ."

Αγκαλιάζοντας το σώμα του, τα δύο πλάσματα δέχτηκαν τον πόνο του μέσα τους.

"Σήκω πάνω, μπιπ-μπιπ", πρόσταξε.

Και η αναπηρική καρέκλα, σηκώθηκε. Και, τοποθετημένο κάτω από το σώμα του E-Z, περίμενε. Όταν μια σταγόνα αίματος κατέβηκε, η καρέκλα την έπιασε. Την απορρόφησε. Την κατανάλωσε - σαν να ήταν ένα ζωντανό πράγμα.

Καθώς η δύναμη της καρέκλας αυξανόταν, κέρδιζε και αυτή δύναμη. Σύντομα η καρέκλα μπορούσε να κρατήσει τον αφέντη της στον αέρα. Αυτό επέτρεψε στα δύο πλάσματα να ολοκληρώσουν το έργο τους. Το έργο τους να ενώσουν την καρέκλα και τον άνθρωπο. Να τους δέσουν για πάντα με τη δύναμη της διαμαντόσκονης, του αίματος και του πόνου.

Καθώς το σώμα του εφήβου έτρεμε, οι πληγές στο δέρμα του επουλώθηκαν. Η αποστολή ολοκληρώθηκε. Η διαμαντόσκονη ήταν μέρος της ουσίας του. Έτσι, η μουσική σταμάτησε.

"Τελείωσε. Τώρα είναι αλεξίσφαιρος. Και έχει υπερδύναμη, μπιπ-μπιπ."

"Ναι, και είναι καλό, ζουμ-ζουμ."

Η αναπηρική καρέκλα επέστρεψε στο πάτωμα και ο έφηβος στο κρεβάτι του.

"Δεν θα έχει καμία ανάμνηση από αυτό, αλλά τα πραγματικά του φτερά θα αρχίσουν να λειτουργούν πολύ σύντομα μπιπ-μπιπ".

"Τι γίνεται με τις άλλες παρενέργειες; Πότε θα αρχίσουν, και θα ξίναι αισθητές ζουμ-ζουμ;"

"Αυτό δεν το γνωρίζω. Μπορεί να έχει σωματικές αλλαγές... είναι ένα ρίσκο που αξίζει να πάρουμε για να μειώσουμε τον πόνο, μπιπ-μπιπ".

"Σύμφωνοι, ζουμ-ζουμ."

ΑΙΤΙΑ

ΌΛΕΣ ΟΙ ΟΙΚΟΓΕΝΕΙΕΣ ΕΧΟΥΝ διαφωνίες. Κάποιες διαφωνούν για κάθε μικρό πράγμα. Η οικογένεια Ντίκενς συμφωνούσε στα περισσότερα πράγματα. Η μουσική δεν ήταν ένα από αυτά.

"Έλα μπαμπά", είπε ο δωδεκάχρονος E-Z. "Βαριέμαι και αυτή τη στιγμή παίζουν ένα Σαββατοκύριακο με τους Muse στο δορυφόρο".

"Δεν έφερες τα ακουστικά σου;" ρώτησε η μητέρα του Laurel.

"Είναι στο σακίδιό μου στο πορτμπαγκάζ". Εκείνος αναστέναξε.

"Μπορούμε πάντα να σταματήσουμε να τα πάρουμε...".

Ο Μάρτιν, ο πατέρας του αγοριού που οδηγούσε, έλεγξε την ώρα. "Θα ήθελα να φτάσουμε στην καλύβα στα βουνά πριν νυχτώσει. Η Μούσε είναι εντάξει μαζί μου. Εξάλλου, θα είμαστε εκεί σύντομα".

Η Λόρελ γύρισε τον επιλογέα του δορυφορικού συστήματος στο ολοκαίνουργιο κόκκινο κάμπριο αυτοκίνητό τους. Δίστασε για μια στιγμή στο Classic Rock. Ο εκφωνητής είπε: "Ακολουθεί ο ύμνος των Kiss I Wanna Rock N Roll All Night. Μην αγγίξεις τον επιλογέα".

"Περιμένετε, αυτό είναι ένα καλό τραγούδι!" φώναξε το αγόρι.

"Τι, δεν έχει άλλους Muse;" ρώτησε η Λόρελ, κρατώντας το χέρι της στον επιλογέα.

"Μετά τους Kiss, εντάξει;"

"Kiss λοιπόν", είπε ο Μάρτιν, καθώς άνοιγε τους υαλοκαθαριστήρες του παρμπρίζ. Δεν έβρεχε ακόμα, αλλά οι κεραυνοί βροντούσαν. Κλαδιά και άλλα συντρίμμια μπαινόβγαιναν στο όχημά τους καθώς ανέβαιναν το βουνό.

Η Λόρελ φτερνίστηκε και έβαλε έναν σελιδοδείκτη στη σελίδα της. Σταύρωσε τα χέρια της τρέμοντας. "Αυτός ο άνεμος σίγουρα ουρλιάζει. Σε πειράζει να ανοίξουμε την οροφή;"

"Ψηφίζω ναι", είπε ο Ε-Ζ, αφαιρώντας κλαδιά από τα ξανθά μαλλιά του. THWACK.

Δεν υπήρχε χρόνος να ουρλιάξει -όταν η μουσική έσβησε.

Τα αυτιά του αγοριού χτυπούσαν ακόμα από τον ήχο σε συνδυασμό με την έκρηξη των τεσσάρων αερόσακων. Το αίμα έσταζε στο μέτωπό του καθώς άγγιζε αυτό που βρισκόταν στα πόδια του: ένα δέντρο. Το αίμα συγκεντρώθηκε μέσα και γύρω από τον ξύλινο εισβολέα. Έτρεξε το δάχτυλό του κατά μήκος του κορμού του δέντρου. Το ένιωσε σαν δέρμα- ήταν το δέντρο και το δέντρο ήταν αυτός.

"Μαμά; Μπαμπά;" αναφώνησε με το στήθος του να φουσκώνει. "Μαμά; Μπαμπά; Σε παρακαλώ, απάντησε!"

Έπρεπε να καλέσει βοήθεια. Πού ήταν το τηλέφωνό του; Η πρόσκρουση της σύγκρουσης το είχε πετάξει μακριά. Το έβλεπε, αλλά ήταν πολύ μακριά για να το φτάσει. Ή μήπως ήταν; Ήταν catcher, και κάποιοι έλεγαν ότι το χέρι του ήταν σαν λάστιχο. Συγκεντρώθηκε, τεντώθηκε και τεντώθηκε μέχρι να το πιάσει.

Το σήμα ήταν ισχυρό, καθώς τα ματωμένα δάχτυλά του πάτησαν το 9-1-1, και μετά αποσυνδέθηκε. Για να τον βρουν, έπρεπε να χρησιμοποιήσει τη νέα ενισχυμένη υπηρεσία. Πληκτρολόγησε Ε9-1-1. Αυτό έδωσε στις αρχές την άδεια να έχουν πρόσβαση στην τοποθεσία, τον αριθμό τηλεφώνου και τη διεύθυνσή του.

"Υπηρεσίες έκτακτης ανάγκης. Ποιο είναι το επείγον περιστατικό σας;"

"Βοήθεια! Χρειαζόμαστε βοήθεια! Σας παρακαλώ. Οι γονείς μου!"

"Πρώτα πείτε μου, πόσο χρονών είστε; Πώς σε λένε;"

"Είμαι δώδεκα χρονών. Με φωνάζουν Ε-Ζ".

"Παρακαλώ επιβεβαιώστε τη διεύθυνση και τον αριθμό τηλεφώνου σας."

Το έκανε.

"Γεια σου E-Z. Πες μου για τους γονείς σου. Μπορείς να τους δεις; Έχουν τις αισθήσεις τους;"

"Δεν μπορώ να τους δω. Ένα δέντρο έπεσε πάνω στο αυτοκίνητο, πάνω τους και στα πόδια μου. Βοήθεια! Σας παρακαλώ."

"Λαμβάνουμε τη θέση σας τώρα."

Ο E-Z έκλεισε τα μάτια του.

"E-Z;" Πιο δυνατά, "E-Z!"

Το αγόρι συνήλθε. "Εγώ, συγγνώμη, εγώ..."

"Στέλνουμε ένα ελικόπτερο. Προσπάθησε να μείνεις ξύπνιος. Η βοήθεια είναι καθ' οδόν".

"Σας ευχαριστώ", τα μάτια του έπεσαν κλειστά, τα άνοιξε με το ζόρι. "Πρέπει να μείνω ξύπνιος. Είπε να μείνω ξύπνιος". Το μόνο που ήθελε να κάνει ήταν να κοιμηθεί, να κοιμηθεί για να τελειώσει όλος ο πόνος.

Πάνω του, δύο φώτα, ένα πράσινο και ένα κίτρινο, τρεμόπαιξαν μπροστά στα μάτια του. Για ένα δευτερόλεπτο, νόμιζε ότι είδε μικροσκοπικά φτερά να χτυπούν καθώς τα δύο αντικείμενα αιωρούνταν.

"Είναι σε άσχημη κατάσταση", είπε το πράσινο, πλησιάζοντας για να τον δει από κοντά.

"Ας τον βοηθήσουμε", είπε το κίτρινο αιωρούμενο ψηλότερα.

Ο E-Z σήκωσε το χέρι του, για να χτυπήσει τα φώτα που τρεμόπαιζαν. Ένας υψηλός ήχος πόνεσε τα αυτιά του.

"Συμφωνείς να μας βοηθήσεις;" τραγούδησαν τα φώτα.

"Συμφωνώ. Βοηθήστε με".

Τότε όλα μαύρισαν.

ΕΠΙΔΡΑΣΗ

Ο Sam, ο θείος του E-Z ήταν στο νοσοκομείο όταν ξύπνησε. Το αγόρι δεν έκανε την ερώτηση - πού ήταν οι γονείς του - γιατί δεν ήθελε να ακούσει την απάντηση. Αν δεν ήξερε, θα μπορούσε να προσποιηθεί ότι ήταν καλά. Ότι θα έμπαιναν στο δωμάτιό του και θα τον αγκάλιαζαν από λεπτό σε λεπτό. Αλλά στο πίσω μέρος του μυαλού του ήξερε, στην πραγματικότητα πίστευε ότι ήταν νεκροί. Το φαντάζόταν στο μυαλό του, πώς θα έριχνε πίσω τα σκεπάσματα και θα έτρεχε προς το μέρος τους και θα έρχονταν όλοι μαζί σε μια ομαδική αγκαλιά και θα έκλαιγαν για το πόσο τυχεροί ήταν. Αλλά για μισό λεπτό, γιατί δεν μπορούσε να κουνήσει τα δάχτυλα των ποδιών του; Προσπάθησε ξανά, συγκεντρώθηκε πολύ, αλλά δεν συνέβη τίποτα.

Ο Σαμ που παρακολουθούσε είπε: "Δεν υπάρχει απλός τρόπος να σου το πω αυτό", ενώ εκείνος πάλευε να συγκρατήσει έναν λυγμό.

"Τα πόδια μου", είπε ο E-Z, "εγώ, δεν τα νιώθω".

Ο θείος Σαμ έσφιξε το χέρι του ανιψιού του. "Τα πόδια σου..."

"Ωχ, όχι. Μη μου πεις. Απλά μην το πεις".

Ξήλωσε το χέρι του από τον θείο του. Κάλυψε το πρόσωπό του, δημιουργώντας ένα φράγμα ανάμεσα στον εαυτό του και τον κόσμο, καθώς τα δάκρυα κυλούσαν στα μάγουλά του.

Ο θείος Σαμ δίστασε. Ο ανιψιός του ήταν ήδη δακρυσμένος, ήδη πενθούσε κι όμως έπρεπε να του πει για τους γονείς του. Δεν υπήρχε εύκολος τρόπος να το πει, οπότε το ξεστόμισε: "Οι γονείς σου. Ο αδελφός μου και η μαμά σου... δεν τα κατάφεραν".

Το να ξέρει και να ακούει τις λέξεις ήταν δύο διαφορετικά πράγματα. Το ένα το έκανε γεγονός. Ο Ε-Ζ πέταξε το κεφάλι του προς τα πίσω και ούρλιαξε σαν πληγωμένο ζώο, τρέμοντας και θέλοντας να φύγει μακριά, οπουδήποτε. Απλά μακριά.

"Ε-Ζ, είμαι εδώ για σένα".

"Όχι! Δεν είναι αλήθεια. Λες ψέματα. Γιατί μου λες ψέματα;" Τριγύριζε, έσφιγγε τις γροθιές του και τις χτυπούσε στο στρώμα, καθώς μαινόταν και μαινόταν χωρίς να λέει να σταματήσει.

Ο Σαμ πάτησε το κουμπί κοντά στο κρεβάτι. Προσπάθησε να τον ηρεμήσει, αλλά ο Ε-Ζ ήταν εκτός ελέγχου, χτυπιόταν και έβριζε. Δύο νοσοκόμες έφτασαν- η μία έβαλε τη βελόνα, ενώ η άλλη μαζί με τον Σαμ προσπαθούσαν να τον κρατήσουν ακίνητο και του ψιθύριζαν απαλά ότι όλα θα πάνε καλά.

Ο Σαμ κοίταζε, καθώς ο ανιψιός του στη χώρα των ονείρων ή όπου κι αν βρισκόταν τώρα - συγκέντρωσε ένα χαμόγελο. Φύλαγε αυτό το χαμόγελο, σκεπτόμενος ότι θα περνούσε καιρός μέχρι να ξαναδεί ένα τέτοιο χαμόγελο στο πρόσωπο του ανιψιού του. Θα ήταν ένας μακρύς και δύσκολος δρόμος μπροστά του. Ο ανιψιός του θα έπρεπε να αντιμετωπίσει την ημέρα που η ζωή του θα κατέρρεε κατά μέτωπο. Μόλις το έκανε αυτό, θα μπορούσε να παλέψει και μαζί θα μπορούσαν να του χτίσουν μια ολοκαίνουργια ζωή. Νέα - διαφορετική - όχι την ίδια. Τίποτα δεν θα ήταν ποτέ ξανά το ίδιο.

Και όλα αυτά επειδή βρέθηκαν στο λάθος μέρος τη λάθος στιγμή. Θύματα της φύσης: ένα δέντρο. Ένα δέντρο που έγινε το όπλο της φύσης λόγω της ανθρώπινης αμέλειας. Η ξύλινη κατασκευή ήταν νεκρή, με τις ρίζες πάνω από το έδαφος να διεκδικούν την προσοχή τους εδώ και χρόνια. Και όταν του είπαν ότι είχε σημαδευτεί με ένα X για να κοπεί την άνοιξη - ήθελε να ουρλιάξει.

Αντ' αυτού, κάλεσε τον καλύτερο δικηγόρο που γνώριζε. Ήθελε κάποιος να πληρώσει - να πληρώσει το λογαριασμό για δύο ζωές που κόπηκαν πολύ νωρίς και για τα διαλυμένα πόδια και τη ζωή του ανιψιού του.

Αλλά ποιο ήταν το νόημα; Τίποτα δεν μπορούσε να αλλάξει το παρελθόν - αλλά στο μέλλον θα βοηθούσε τον ανιψιό του να βρει το δρόμο του. Εκείνη τη στιγμή ο Σαμ διαμόρφωσε ένα σχέδιο.

Ο Σαμ έμοιαζε με μια ενήλικη εκδοχή του Χάρι Πότερ (χωρίς την ουλή.) Ως ο μοναδικός εν ζωή συγγενής του E-Z, θα αναλάμβανε τη φροντίδα του ανιψιού του. Ένας ρόλος που είχε παραμελήσει στο παρελθόν. Θα προσπαθούσε να μοιάσει στον μεγαλύτερο αδελφό του Μάρτιν - όχι να τον αντικαταστήσει.

Αποτίναξε τις δικαιολογίες, που έβραζαν μέσα του. Προσπαθούσε να τον κάνει να χρησιμοποιήσει τη δουλειά για να τον απαλλάξει από τις ευθύνες. Θα έφευγε με τα πόδια, θα έσβηνε όλες τις υποχρεώσεις. Τότε θα μπορούσε να σταματήσει να κατηγορεί τον εαυτό του. Να μισεί τον εαυτό του για όλο τον χαμένο χρόνο.

Ενώ ο ανιψιός του κοιμόταν, τηλεφώνησε στον διευθύνοντα σύμβουλο της εταιρείας λογισμικού του. Ως ένας καταξιωμένος ανώτερος προγραμματιστής στην κορυφή του τομέα του - ήλπιζε ότι θα έβρισκαν έναν συμβιβασμό. Τους είπε τι ήθελε να κάνει.

"Σίγουρα, Σαμ. Μπορείς να εργαστείς εξ αποστάσεως. Τίποτα δεν θα αλλάξει. Κάνε αυτό που πρέπει να κάνεις. Είμαστε μαζί σου. Πρώτα η οικογένεια - πάντα".

Όταν αποσυνδέθηκε, επέστρεψε στο κρεβάτι του ανιψιού του. Προς το παρόν, θα μετακόμιζε στο σπίτι της οικογένειας, ώστε ο E-Z να παραμείνει κοντά στους φίλους του και στο σχολείο του. Μαζί θα έβαζαν και πάλι τα κομμάτια μαζί και θα έχτιζαν ξανά τη ζωή του. Αυτό θα γινόταν αν δεν φρίκαρε τελείως. Ως εργένης, είχε ελάχιστη έως καθόλου εμπειρία με παιδιά - πόσο μάλλον με εφήβους.

****

ΦΟΎ ΒΓΉΚΑΝ ΑΠΌ ΤΟ *νοσοκομείο - με την επιταγή της μοίρας -*
δεν είχαν άλλη επιλογή από το να δημιουργήσουν έναν δεσμό που
ξεπερνούσε το αίμα.

Ο Ε-Ζ αντιστάθηκε, αρνούμενος ότι μπορούσε να τα κάνει όλα μόνος
του. Στο τέλος δεν είχε άλλη επιλογή από το να δεχτεί την προσφερόμενη
βοήθεια.

Ο Σαμ προχώρησε - ήταν εκεί γι' αυτόν - σαν να ήξερε τι χρειαζόταν ο
ανιψιός του πριν τον ρωτήσει.

Και ήταν εκεί για τον Ε-Ζ τη δεύτερη χειρότερη μέρα της ζωής του - όταν
του είπαν ότι δεν θα περπατούσε ποτέ ξανά.

"Ελάτε μέσα", είπε ο Δρ Χάμερσμιθ, ένας από τους κορυφαίους
χειρουργούς ορθοπεδικούς νευρολόγους.

Στο αναπηρικό του καροτσάκι, ο Ε-Ζ μπήκε μέσα, ακολουθούμενος από
τον Sam.

Ο Χάμερσμιθ φημιζόταν για τη διόρθωση των μη διορθώσιμων και
επρόκειτο να τον διορθώσει. Σε προηγούμενες διαβουλεύσεις είχε υποσχεθεί
στον νεαρό ότι θα έπαιζε ξανά μπέιζμπολ.

"Λυπάμαι", είπε ο Χάμερσμιθ. Μετά από μερικά δευτερόλεπτα άβολης
σιωπής, τη συμπλήρωσε ανακατεύοντας μερικά χαρτιά.

"Για ποιο πράγμα ακριβώς λυπάσαι;" ρώτησε ο Ε-Ζ, σπρώχνοντας με όλη
του τη δύναμη να προχωρήσει μπροστά στη θέση του. Αδυνατώντας να φέρει
εις πέρας το έργο του, παρέμεινε εκεί που βρισκόταν.

"Αυτό που ζήτησε", είπε ο Σαμ, κινούμενος αβίαστα μπροστά στη θέση του.

Ο Χάμερσμιθ καθάρισε το λαιμό του. "Ελπίζαμε ότι, εφόσον όλα λειτουργούσαν κανονικά, η παράλυση θα μπορούσε να είναι προσωρινή Γι' αυτό σας έστειλα για περισσότερες εξετάσεις και σας πρότεινα κάποια φυσικοθεραπεία. Δεν υπάρχει καμία αμφιβολία τώρα, λυπάμαι που στο λέα E-Z, αλλά δεν θα περπατήσεις ποτέ ξανά".

"Πώς μπορείς να του το κάνεις αυτό;" ρώτησε ο Σαμ.

Η οριστικότητα των λόγων του βυθίστηκε στο μυαλό του. "Πάρε με από εδώ, θείε Σαμ!"

"Περιμένετε", είπε ο Χάμερσμιθ, μη μπορώντας να τους κοιτάξε. στα μάτια. "Ζήτησα βοήθεια, από συναδέλφους σε όλο τον κόσμο. Το συμπέρασμά τους ήταν το ίδιο".

"Ευχαριστώ πολύ".

"E-Z, ήρθε η ώρα να προχωρήσεις. Δεν θέλω να σου δώσω άλλες ψεύτικες ελπίδες. "

Ο Σαμ σηκώθηκε, βάζοντας τα χέρια του στις λαβές της αναπηρικής καρέκλας.

"Θα πάρουμε μια δεύτερη γνώμη και μια τρίτη και μια τέταρτη!"

"Μπορείτε να το κάνετε αυτό", είπε ο Χάμερσμιθ, "αλλά το κάναμε ήδη. Αν υπήρχε κάτι καινούργιο, εκεί έξω - κάτι που θα μπορούσαμε να αξιοποιήσουμε - τότε θα το κάναμε. Τα πράγματα μπορεί να αλλάξουν κατά τη διάρκεια της ζωής σας E-Z. Ο τομέας της έρευνας των βλαστοκυττάρων σημειώνει πρόοδο. Στο μεταξύ, δεν θέλω να ζεις τη ζωή σου για τα αν και τα ίσως".

Στη συνέχεια, απευθυνόμενος στον Σαμ,

"Μην αφήσεις τον ανιψιό σου να χαραμίσει τη ζωή του. Βοήθησέ τον να ξαναχτίσει και να επιστρέψει στη γη των ζωντανών. Α, και λυπάμαι που το αναφέρω αυτό, αλλά θα χρειαστούμε σύντομα την αναπηρική καρέκλα πίσω

- φαίνεται ότι έχουμε μια μικρή έλλειψη. Αν δεν σας πειράζει να κάνετε άλλες διευθετήσεις".

"Ωραία", είπε ο Σαμ, καθώς έφυγαν από το γραφείο του Χάμερσμιθ χωρίς να μιλήσουν. Έβαλε την αναπηρική καρέκλα στο πορτμπαγκάζ, έδεσε τις ζώνες ασφαλείας τους και έβαλε μπροστά το αυτοκίνητο.

"Όλα θα πάνε καλά".

Ο E-Z που είχε δάκρυα να κυλούν στα μάγουλά του, τα σκούπισε. "Λυπάμαι".

"Δεν χρειάζεται ποτέ να μου ζητάς συγγνώμη, μικρέ, που δείχνεις τα συναισθήματά σου".

Ο Σαμ χτύπησε τις γροθιές του στο τιμόνι και μετά βγήκε από το σημείο στάθμευσης τρίζοντας τα λάστιχα.

Οδήγησαν χωρίς να μιλήσουν για λίγες στιγμές, μετά έπιασε το χέρι του και άνοιξε το ραδιόφωνο. Χάλασε τη σιωπή ανάμεσα στους δυο τους και έδωσε στον E-Z την ευκαιρία να τα κλάψει χωρίς να νιώσει αυτοσυνειδησία.

Μέχρι να στρίψουν στην είσοδο του σπιτιού τους, ήταν ήρεμοι και πεινασμένοι. Το σχέδιο ήταν να χαζέψουν μερικά προγράμματα και να παραγγείλουν πίτσα.

Λίγες μέρες αργότερα έφτασε ένα ολοκαίνουργιο αναπηρικό καροτσάκι.

Δ ΎΟ ΦΏΤΑ: ΈΝΑ ΚΊΤΡΙΝΟ και ένα πράσινο τρεμόπαιξαν κοντά στο νέο αναπηρικό αμαξίδιο του E-Z.

"Αυτό δεν κάνει, μπιπ-μπιπ".

"Συμφωνώ, δεν κάνει καθόλου. Χρειάζεται κάτι πιο ελαφρύ, πιο δυνατό, πυρίμαχο, αλεξίσφαιρο και απορροφητικό, ζουμ-ζουμ".

"Ξέρεις-ποιος είπε ότι δεν πρέπει να χάνουμε χρόνο - οπότε, ας το κάνουμε, πριν ξυπνήσει ο άνθρωπος, μπιπ-μπιπ."

Τα φώτα χόρεψαν γύρω από την αναπηρική καρέκλα. Το ένα αντικατέστησε το μέταλλο και το άλλο τα λάστιχα. Όταν ολοκλήρωσαν τη διαδικασία, η καρέκλα έμοιαζε ίδια με πριν, αλλά δεν ήταν.

Ο E-Z ψιθύρισε στον ύπνο του.

"Πάμε να φύγουμε από εδώ! Μπιπ μπιπ!"

"Ακριβώς πίσω σου! Ζουμ ζουμ!"

Και έτσι έκαναν, ενώ ο μικρός κοιμόταν.

ΈΝΑΝ ΧΡΟΝΟ ΑΡΓΟΤΕΡΑ, ΚΑΙ ο Ε-Ζ έβλεπε ότι ο θείος Σαμ ήταν πάντα εκεί. Όχι ότι είχε αντικαταστήσει τους γονείς του. Όχι, ποτέ δεν θα μπορούσε να το κάνει αυτό, στην πραγματικότητα δεν θα προσπαθούσε - αλλά τα πήγαιναν καλά. Ήταν φίλοι. Ήταν κάτι περισσότερο από αυτό, ήταν οικογένεια. Η μόνη οικογένεια που είχε απομείνει στον κόσμο για τον δεκατριάχρονο.

"Θέλω να σας ευχαριστήσω", είπε, προσπαθώντας να μην δακρύσει.

"Δεν χρειάζεται να με ευχαριστείς, μικρέ".

"Αλλά το κάνω, θείε Σαμ, χωρίς εσένα θα είχα πετάξει την πετσέτα".

"Είσαι φτιαγμένος από πιο δυνατό υλικό από αυτό".

"Δεν είμαι. Μετά το ατύχημα φοβάμαι, εννοώ πραγματικά φοβάμαι. Βλέπω εφιάλτες".

"Όλοι φοβόμαστε- βοηθάει αν μιλάς γι' αυτό. Εννοώ αν θέλεις να μου μιλήσεις γι' αυτό".

"Συμβαίνει μερικές φορές τη νύχτα - όταν κοιμάσαι. Δεν θέλω να σε ξυπνήσω".

"Είμαι δίπλα και οι τοίχοι δεν είναι τόσο χοντροί. Απλά φώναξέ με και θα είμαι εκεί. Δεν με πειράζει."

"Ευχαριστώ, ελπίζω να μη χρειαστεί, αλλά είναι καλό να το ξέρω".

Επέστρεψαν να δουν τηλεόραση και δεν ξανασυζήτησαν το θέμα.

Μέχρι που ένα βράδυ, όταν ο Ε-Ζ ξύπνησε ουρλιάζοντας και ο Σαμ όπως είχε υποσχεθεί ήταν εκεί.

Άναψε το φως. "Εδώ είμαι. Είσαι καλά;"

Ο E-Z ήταν γαντζωμένος στην άκρη του κρεβατιού, σαν κάποιος που ήταν έτοιμος να πέσει σε γκρεμό. Τον βοήθησε να ξανακαθίσει στο στρώμα.

"Καλύτερα τώρα;"

"Ναι, ευχαριστώ".

"Έχεις όρεξη να μιλήσεις γι' αυτό; Μπορώ να φτιάξω λίγο κακάο".

"Με ζαχαρωτά;"

"Είναι αυτονόητο. Επιστρέφω αμέσως."

"Εντάξει." Ο E-Z έκλεισε τα μάτια του για ένα δευτερόλεπτο, και οι υψηλοί θόρυβοι συνεχίστηκαν. Έκλεισε τα αυτιά του και παρακολούθησε τα κίτρινα και πράσινα φώτα που χόρευαν μπροστά στα μάτια του. Έβγαλε τα χέρια του, ακούγοντας τα γυμνά πόδια του θείου του καθώς χτυπούσαν κατά μήκος του διαδρόμου.

"Ορίστε", είπε ο Σαμ, βάζοντας μια κούπα με ζεστό κακάο στο χέρι του ανιψιού του. Πάρκαρε στην αναπηρική καρέκλα, όπου ήπιε και αναστέναξε.

Με το αριστερό του χέρι, ο E-Z χτύπησε τον αέρα, σχεδόν χύνοντας το ποτό του.

"Τι κάνεις;"

"Δεν το ακούς; Αυτόν τον ήχο που διαπερνάει τα αυτιά;"

Ο Σαμ άκουσε προσεκτικά, τίποτα. Κούνησε το κεφάλι του. "Αν ακούς κάτι παράξενο, γιατί προσπαθείς να το διώξεις;"

Ο E-Z επικεντρώθηκε στο ζεστό του ρόφημα, και μετά κατάπιε ένα μίνι-μαρσμάλοου. "Υποθέτω ότι δεν μπορείς να δεις τα φώτα τότε;"

"Τα φώτα; Τι είδους φώτα;"

"Δύο φώτα: ένα πράσινο και ένα κίτρινο. Περίπου στο μέγεθος της άκρης του δαχτύλου σου. Εδώ πάνω-κάτω - από το ατύχημα και μετά. Τρυπάνε τα αυτιά μου και αναβοσβήνουν μπροστά στα μάτια μου. Με ενοχλούν".

Ο Σαμ πήγε στο κεφαλάρι και κοίταξε από την οπτική γωνία του ανιψιού του. Δεν περίμενε να δει τίποτα - και φυσικά δεν είδε - η προσπάθεια ήταν για καθησυχασμό. "Όχι, αλλά πες μου περισσότερα, για να καταλάβω καλύτερα πώς ξεκίνησε".

"Στο ατύχημα, είδα δύο φώτα, κίτρινα και πράσινα και, μη γελάσεις, αλλά νομίζω ότι μου μίλησαν. Γι' αυτό βλέπω εφιάλτες".

"Τι είδους φώτα; Εννοείς, σαν τα χριστουγεννιάτικα φώτα;"

"Ε, όχι, όχι σαν τα χριστουγεννιάτικα φώτα. Δεν είναι τίποτα. Έχουν φύγει τώρα. Πιθανώς διαταραχή μετατραυματικού στρες, ή αναδρομή στο παρελθόν".

"Το μετατραυματικό στρες ή η αναδρομή σε φλασμπακ είναι δύο εντελώς διαφορετικά πράγματα. Αναρωτιέμαι αν, θα πρέπει να μιλήσεις σε κάποιον. Εννοώ σε κάποιον, εκτός από εμένα."

"Εννοείς τους φίλους μου;"

"Όχι, εννοώ έναν επαγγελματία."

POP.

POP.

Είχαν επιστρέψει και πάλι. Ανοιγόκλειναν μπροστά στη μύτη του και τον έκαναν να αλληθωρίζει. Συγκρατήθηκε. Προσπάθησε να μην τα διώξει. Καθώς ο Σαμ πήρε το φλιτζάνι του με το ένα χέρι και ένιωσε το μέτωπό του με το άλλο, χτύπησε τον αέρα. "Φύγε μακριά μου!"

Ο Σαμ κοίταζε τον ανιψιό του να παγώνει, σαν γλυπτό από πάγο στο Χειμερινό Φεστιβάλ. Ο Σαμ χτύπησε τα δάχτυλά του μπροστά στα μάτια του, αλλά δεν υπήρξε καμία αντίδραση. Ο E-Z αναστέναξε και έγειρε προς τα πίσω, πήρε μια βαθιά ανάσα και μέσα σε δευτερόλεπτα ροχάλιζε σαν στρατιώτης. Ο Σαμ τράβηξε τα σκεπάσματα προς τα πάνω. Φίλησε τον ανιψιό του στο μέτωπο και μετά επέστρεψε στο δωμάτιό του. Τελικά έπεσε για ύπνο.

Την επόμενη μέρα, ο Σαμ πρότεινε στον E-Z να γράψει τα συναισθήματά του, ίσως σε ένα ημερολόγιο. Εν τω μεταξύ, θα ρωτούσε για να κλείσει ένα ραντεβού με έναν επαγγελματία.

"Εννοείς ψυχίατρο;"

"Ή έναν ψυχολόγο. Και στο μεταξύ, να τα γράφει. Όταν τους βλέπεις, πώς μοιάζουν - κατέγραψε τις εμφανίσεις".

"Ένα ημερολόγιο, εννοώ, σε ποιον μοιάζω, στην Όπρα Γουίνφρεϊ;"

"Όχι", είπε ο Σαμ. "Μικρέ, βλέπεις εφιάλτες, ακούς υψηλούς θορύβους και βλέπεις φώτα. Μπορεί να είναι σημάδι, όπως είπες, μετατραυματικού στρες ή κάτι ιατρικό. Πρέπει να το ερευνήσω και να μιλήσω με τον γιατρέ σου, να πάρω τη συμβουλή του. Εν τω μεταξύ, το να γράφετε τις σκέψεις σας, να κρατάτε ημερολόγιο μπορεί να βοηθήσει. Πολλοί άνδρες έχουν γράψει ημερολόγια ή έχουν κρατήσει ημερολόγιο".

"Να μου πεις κάποιον του οποίου το όνομα θα αναγνώριζα;"

"Για να δούμε, ο Λεονάρντο ντα Βίντσι, ο Μάρκο Πόλο, ο Κάρολος Δαρβίνος".

"Εννοώ κάποιον από αυτόν τον αιώνα".

"Έχεις ήδη αναφέρει την Όπρα."

Η ΨΥΧΙΚΉ ΥΓΕΊΑ ΤΟΥ E-Z βελτιώθηκε μετά από μερικές συνεδρίες με έναν θεραπευτή/σύμβουλο. Ήταν καλή και δεν έκρινε τον έφηβο, όπως φοβόταν ότι θα έκανε. Αντίθετα, του προσέφερε προτάσεις και συγκεκριμένες στρατηγικές για να τον ηρεμήσει και να τον βοηθήσει. Εκείνη, όπως και ο θείος του Σαμ, του είχε επίσης προτείνει να τα γράψει όλα - σε ένα ημερολόγιο ή ένα ημερολόγιο.

Αντ' αυτού, συνέγραψε μια μικρή ιστορία για μια σχολική εργασία εμπνευσμένη από το αγαπημένο πουλί της μητέρας του: ένα περιστέρι. Αφού πήρε άριστα στην εργασία του, ο δάσκαλός του έβαλε την ιστορία του σε έναν επαρχιακό διαγωνισμό συγγραφής. Στην αρχή, ήταν αναστατωμένος που συμμετείχε στην ιστορία του χωρίς να τον ρωτήσει. Αλλά όταν κέρδισε, ήταν απίστευτα χαρούμενος. Έκτοτε, η δασκάλα του έβαλε την ιστορία του σε έναν διαγωνισμό σε όλη τη χώρα.

Ενώ ο ανιψιός του εντρυφούσε στην τέχνη της συγγραφής, ο Σαμ ασχολήθηκε με ένα νέο χόμπι: τη γενεαλογία. Ένα βράδυ, όταν έτρωγαν μαζί δείπνο, ξεσπάθωσε:

"Τώρα που έγραψες ένα διήγημα και είχες κάποια επιτυχία, ίσως θα έπρεπε να προσπαθήσεις να γράψεις ένα μυθιστόρημα".

"Εγώ; Μυθιστόρημα; Αποκλείεται".

"Έχεις αίμα συγγραφέα", αποκάλυψε ο θείος Σαμ. "Εντοπίζοντας την ιστορία μας, ανακάλυψα ότι εσύ και εγώ είμαστε συγγενείς με τον μοναδικό Κάρολο Ντίκενς".

"'Ίσως θα έπρεπε να γράψεις ένα μυθιστόρημα, τότε." Γέλασε.

"Δεν είμαι εγώ αυτός με το βραβευμένο διήγημα".

Τα πράσινα και κίτρινα φώτα τρεμόπαιξαν πάνω από το πιάτο του. Τουλάχιστον δεν μπορούσε να ακούσει εκείνο τον ψηλό θόρυβο με τον θείς Σαμ να βροντοφωνάζει.

".... Εξάλλου, εσύ κι εγώ, είμαστε ξαδέλφια διαχρονικά με τον Κάρολς Ντίκενς. Κοίταξε όλα όσα έχεις ξεπεράσει. Είσαι ένα καταπληκτικό παιδί - τι έχεις να χάσεις;"

Το όνομά του είναι Ezekiel Dickens, και αυτή είναι η ιστορία του.

ΚΕΦΑΛΑΙΟ 1

Τ Α ΠΡΩΤΑ ΔΕΚΑΤΡΙΑ ΧΡΟΝΙΑ της ζωής του ήταν γνωστος με διάφορα ονόματα. Ιεζεκιήλ, το όνομα της γέννησής του. E-Z, το παρατσούκλι του. Πιάντης στην ομάδα του μπέιζμπολ. Συγγραφέας διηγημάτων. Γιος των γονιών του. Ανιψιός του θείου του. Καλύτερος φίλος. Τώρα είχαν ένα νέο όνομα γι' αυτόν.

Όχι ότι τον πείραζε η λέξη "γ". Στην πραγματικότητα, κάποιες από τις εναλλακτικές λύσεις τις προτιμούσε λιγότερο. Όπως τα σχόλια που έλεγαν κάποιοι άνθρωποι, επειδή νόμιζαν ότι ήταν πολιτικά ορθά. "Α, να το παιδί που είναι καθηλωμένο σε αναπηρικό καροτσάκι". Το είπαν αυτό ενώ τον έδειχναν - σαν να πίστευαν ότι είχε και αυτός πρόβλημα ακοής. Ή έλεγαν: "Λυπήθηκα που άκουσα ότι είσαι χρήστης αναπηρικού αμαξιδίου, τώρα". Αυτό τον έκανε να ανατριχιάσει. Αλλά αυτό που τον έστειλε στα άκρα, ήταν το "Α, εσύ είσαι το παιδί που χρησιμοποιεί αναπηρικό καροτσάκι τώρα". Βλέποντας κάποιον, ειδικά ένα νεότερο άτομο σε αναπηρικό καροτσάκι, κάποιοι άνθρωποι ένιωθαν άβολα. Αν ένιωθαν έτσι, γιατί έπρεπε να πουν κάτι;

Αυτό ξύπνησε μια ανάμνηση από πολύ παλιά. Μια ανάμνηση των γονιών του, που παρακολουθούσαν την ταινία Bambi στην τηλεόραση ένα βροχερό απόγευμα Σαββάτου. Η μαμά έφτιαχνε τα διάσημα ποπ κορν της. Είχαν σόδα, M&Ms, ζαχαρωτά και τα αγαπημένα Twizzlers του μπαμπά. Ο Θάμπερ, το κουνέλι, είπε: "Αν δεν μπορείς να πεις κάτι καλό, μην πεις καθόλου τίποτα". Όταν πέθανε η μητέρα του Μπάμπι, ήταν η πρώτη φορά που είδε τη μητέρα και τον πατέρα του να κλαίνε για μια ταινία. Επειδή ήταν τόσο σοκαρισμένος από τη συμπεριφορά τους, ο ίδιος δεν έχυσε ούτε ένα δάκρυ.

Κάποιοι από τους βλάχους στο σχολείο, τον αποκαλούσαν "παιδί των δέντρων". Μερικοί ήταν συναθλητές του που κάποτε τον θαύμαζαν όταν ήταν βασιλιάς πίσω από το πιάτο. Σιχαινόταν την αναφορά στο παιδί των δέντρων. Δεν λυπόταν τον εαυτό του (όχι τις περισσότερες φορές) και δεν ήθελε να τον λυπάται κανείς.

Όταν ήρθε η ώρα να επιστρέψει στο σχολείο εκείνη την πρώτη μέρα, το έκανε με τη βοήθεια των φίλων του. Ο PJ (συντομογραφία του Paul Jones) και ο Arden τον στήριξαν και τον πίεσαν, όπως χρειαζόταν. Σύντομα έγιναν γνωστοί ως The Tornado Trio. Κυρίως επειδή όπου πήγαιναν επικρατούσε χάος. Τότε ήταν που ο E-Z έμαθε να περιμένει το απροσδόκητο.

Έτσι, όταν οι φίλοι του πετάχτηκαν ένα πρωί για να τον πάρουν για το σχολείο μερικούς μήνες αργότερα - και μετά είπαν ότι δεν θα πήγαιναν - δεν εξεπλάγη και πολύ. Όταν του είπαν ότι έπρεπε να του δέσουν τα μάτια - αυτό δεν το περίμενε.

Στο πίσω κάθισμα ρώτησε. "Πού πάμε;" Καμία απάντηση. "Θα μου αρέσει;"

"Ναι", είπαν οι φίλοι του.

"Τότε γιατί ο μανδύας και το στιλέτο;"

"Επειδή είναι μια έκπληξη", είπε ο Πι Τζέι.

"Και θα το εκτιμήσεις περισσότερο, μόλις φτάσουμε εκεί".

"Λοιπόν, δεν μπορώ να το σκάσω". Εκείνος χλεύασε.

Η μητέρα του Άρντεν πάρκαρε. "Ευχαριστώ μαμά", είπε.

"Τηλεφώνησέ μου όταν χρειαστεί να σε πάρω", είπε.

Οι δύο φίλοι βοήθησαν τον E-Z να μπει στο αναπηρικό καροτσάκι του και έφυγαν.

"Είναι μόνο ιδέα μου ή αυτή η καρέκλα μοιάζει πιο ελαφριά κάθε φορά που τη βγάζουμε έξω;" ρώτησε ο Άρντεν.

"Εσύ φταις!" Απάντησε ο Πι Τζέι.

Καθώς διέσχιζαν το χνισόπεδο έδαφος, ο E-Z μπορούσε να μυρίσει φρεσκοκομμένο γρασίδι. Όταν οι φίλοι του έβγαλαν το μαντήλι με τα μάτια - βρισκόταν στο γήπεδο του μπέιζμπολ. Δάκρυα έτρεξαν στα μάτια του όταν είδε τους πρώην συμπαίκτες του, την αντίπαλη ομάδα και τον προπονητή Λάντλοου. Φορούσαν πλήρη στολή και ήταν παρατεταγμένοι κατά μήκος της φρεσκοστρωμένης με κιμωλία βασικής γραμμής.

"Καλώς ήρθατε πίσω!" ζητωκραύγασαν.

Ο E-Z έσβησε τα δάκρυα με το μανίκι του καθώς η καρέκλα πλησίαζε στον αγωνιστικό χώρο. Από τότε που το ατύχημα του είχε στερήσει το όνειρο να παίξει επαγγελματικό μπέιζμπολ, απέφευγε το παιχνίδι. Με έναν κόμπο στο λαιμό, ήταν τόσο γεμάτος συγκίνηση που δεν μπορούσε να πάρει ανάσα.

"Έχει χάσει τα λόγια του", είπε ο Πι Τζέι, δίνοντας στον Άρντεν ένα σπρώξιμο με τον αγκώνα του.

"Πρώτη φορά συμβαίνει αυτό".

"Ευχαριστώ, παιδιά. Δεν είχατε άδικο που είπατε ότι ήταν έκπληξη".

"Περιμένετε εδώ", έδωσαν οδηγίες οι φίλοι του.

Ο E-Z έμεινε μόνος του για να απολαύσει τη θέα του διαμαντιού του μπέιζμπολ. Το μέρος που κάποτε ήταν το αγαπημένο του μέρος στη γη. Δάκρυσε ξανά, βλέποντας το πράσινο γρασίδι να λαμπυρίζει στο φως του ήλιου. Τα σκούπισε όταν οι φίλοι του επέστρεψαν κουβαλώντας μια τσάντα με εξοπλισμό.

Ο Άρντεν έσκυψε: "Έκπληξη, φίλε, σήμερα πιάνεις!".

"Τι εννοείς; Δεν μπορώ να παίξω με αυτό!" είπε, χτυπώντας τα χέρια του στα μπράτσα της αναπηρικής καρέκλας.

"Ορίστε, κοίτα αυτό, όσο θα σε εξοπλίζουμε", είπε ο Πι Τζέι, καθώς παρέδωσε το τηλέφωνό του και πάτησε το play.

Ο E-Z παρακολουθούσε έκπληκτος τους παίκτες σαν κι αυτόν, να μπαίνουν στο γήπεδο του μπέιζμπολ. Κοίταξε πιο προσεκτικά τις καρέκλες τους, οι οποίες είχαν τροποποιημένες ρόδες. Ένας παίκτης κύλησε μέχρι το γήπεδο, συνδέθηκε με τη μπάλα και έκανε ζουμ στις βάσεις.

"Ουάου! Αυτό είναι φοβερό!"

"Αν μπορούν να το κάνουν αυτοί, μπορείς κι εσύ!" είπε ο Άρντεν, καθώς έβαζε τα προστατευτικά γονάτων στα πόδια του φίλου του, ενώ ο Πι Τζέι ασφάλιζε το προστατευτικό στήθους. Καθώς έβγαιναν στον αγωνιστικό χώρο, οι φίλοι του του πέταξαν τη μάσκα του catcher και το γάντι του.

"'Ετοιμοι οι μπαλαδόροι!" φώναξε ο προπονητής Λάντλοου.

Ο πίτσερ πέταξε την πρώτη γρήγορη μπαλιά ακριβώς στη ζώνη και την έπιασε.

Η δεύτερη ρίψη ήταν ένα pop up. Ο E-Z πήγε να την πετύχει, κάνοντας ζουμ και σηκώνοντας τον εαυτό του ψηλά. Έφτασε. Ξαφνιάστηκε ακόμα και ο ίδιος όταν την έπιασε. Δεν το είχαν προσέξει, αλλά είχε σηκωθεί. Ο πισινός του είχε φύγει από το κάθισμα της καρέκλας του, και δεν είχε ιδέα πώς το είχε κάνει.

"Ουάου", είπε ο Πι Τζέι, "αυτό ήταν εξαιρετικό πιάσιμο".

"Ναι, πιθανότατα θα το είχες χάσει, αν δεν ήταν η καρέκλα".

Ο E-Z χαμογέλασε και συνέχισε να παίζει. Όταν το παιχνίδι τελείωσε, ένιωσε καλά. Κανονικά. Ευχαρίστησε τα παιδιά που τον επανέφεραν στο ρυθμό των πραγμάτων.

"Την επόμενη φορά, θα χτυπήσεις", είπε ο PJ.

Ο E-Z χλεύασε καθώς η μαμά του Άρντεν τους πήγαινε από το drive through και μετά πίσω στο σχολείο. Αν βιαζόντουσαν, θα προλάβαιναν να φτάσουν εγκαίρως πριν αρχίσει το επόμενο μάθημά τους. Οι μαθητές μποτιλιαρίστηκαν στους διαδρόμους, καθώς εκείνος κυλούσε προς το ντουλάπι του. Οι συμμαθητές του άκουσαν το χαστούκι-χτύπημα των ελαστικών στο λινέλαιο του δαπέδου - και χώρισαν το δρόμο.

Ο Ε-Ζ ήταν το πρώτο παιδί που απαιτούσε πρόσβαση σε αναπηρικό αμαξίδιο στο σχολείο του, αλλά ήταν ήδη ένας θρύλος πριν χάσει τη χρήση των ποδιών του. Χρειάστηκε πολλά για να ζητήσει βοήθεια, αλλά μόλις τα έκανε, την πήρε. Είχε ήδη τον σεβασμό τους ως αθλητής, είχε κερδίσει ένα σωρό τρόπαια ο ίδιος και ως μέλος της ομάδας. Έπρεπε να κερδίσει ξανά τον σεβασμό τους ως ο νέος του εαυτός.

Μετά τον αγώνα επέστρεψαν στο σχολείο και ολοκλήρωσαν τη μέρα τους. Καθώς ήταν μόνο μισή μέρα, ο Ε-Ζ ήταν αρκετά κουρασμένος όταν η μαμά του Άρντεν και οι φίλοι του τον άφησαν μετά το σχολείο.

Αφού τους ευχαρίστησε, μπήκε μέσα.

"Γύρισα σπίτι, θείε Σαμ".

"Το βλέπω αυτό, είχες μια καλή μέρα", είπε ο Σαμ.

"Ναι, ήταν μια καλή μέρα". Τεντώθηκε και χασμουρήθηκε.

"Έλα. Έχω κάτι να σου δείξω. Μια έκπληξη".

"Όχι άλλη μία", είπε ο Ε-Ζ, καθώς ακολουθούσε τον θείο του στο διάδρομο. Πέρασε πρώτα δεξιά, το δωμάτιο των γονιών του - προορισμένο να γίνει μια μέρα ξενώνας. Μέχρι τότε, ήταν ακριβώς όπως το είχαν αφήσει - και έτσι θα παρέμενε μέχρι ο Ε-Ζ να αποφασίσει διαφορετικά.

Κάθε τόσο ο θείος Σαμ προσφερόταν να τον βοηθήσει να ψάξει το δωμάτιο, αλλά ο ανιψιός του έλεγε πάντα το ίδιο πράγμα.

"Θα το κάνω όταν θα είμαι έτοιμος".

Ο Σαμ συμφώνησε απρόθυμα. Ήταν αποφασισμένος να προχωρήσει ο ανιψιός του. Αυτό ήταν το πρώτο βήμα προς αυτή την κατεύθυνση. Από τότε, είχε μιλήσει με τον σύμβουλό του, ο οποίος είπε ότι ο Σαμ θα έπρεπε να ενθαρρύνει τον Ε-Ζ να μιλάει περισσότερο για τους γονείς του. Είπε ότι το να τους κάνει μέρος της καθημερινότητάς του θα τον βοηθούσε να θεραπευτεί πιο γρήγορα. Συνέχισαν κατά μήκος του διαδρόμου, πέρασαν το μπάνιο και σταμάτησαν στο κουτί ή στην αποθήκη.

"Ta-dah!" Είπε ο θείος Σαμ καθώς τον έσπρωχνε μέσα.

Ο E-Z έμεινε άφωνος καθώς αντίκρισε το πρόσφατα μεταμορφωμένο γραφείο. Στο κέντρο, τοποθετημένο μπροστά στο παράθυρο που έβλεπε στον κήπο, υπήρχε ένα γραφείο. Πάνω σε αυτό ήταν στημένο ένα ολοκαίνουργιο PC για παιχνίδια και ένα ηχοσύστημα. Γλίστρησε την καρέκλα του κάτω από το γραφείο - τέλεια εφαρμογή - και έτρεξε τα δάχτυλά του κατά μήκος του πληκτρολογίου. Κοντά του υπήρχε ένας εκτυπωτής, στοιβαγμένος με χαρτί και ένας κάδος απορριμμάτων - όλα σχεδιασμένα σε απόσταση αναπνοής.

Στα αριστερά του υπήρχε μια βιβλιοθήκη. Γύρισε πιο κοντά. Το πρώτο ράφι περιείχε βιβλία για τη συγγραφή και κλασικά βιβλία. Αναγνώρισε αρκετά από τα αγαπημένα βιβλία των γονιών του. Το δεύτερο περιείχε τρόπαια, μεταξύ των οποίων και το βραβείο για τη συγγραφή του. Το τρίτο και το τέταρτο περιείχαν όλα τα αγαπημένα βιβλία της παιδικής του ηλικίας. Τα δύο κατώτερα ράφια ήταν άδεια. Τα μάτια του έτρεξαν κατά μήκος της κορυφής του ράφι, χρειάστηκε να σηκώσει την καρέκλα του προς τα πίσω για να δει τι υπήρχε εκεί πάνω.

Ο Σαμ μπήκε στο δωμάτιο δίπλα του. Έβαλε ένα χέρι στον ώμο του ανιψιού του.

"Εκείνοι, δεν ήμουν σίγουρος αν ήταν πολύ νωρίς. I..."

Το κομμάτι της αντίστασης: μια οικογενειακή φωτογραφία. Ένα δάκρυ κύλησε στο μάγουλό του καθώς θυμήθηκε την ημέρα της φωτογράφισης. Ήταν σε ένα μικρό στούντιο φωτογραφίας στο κέντρο της πόλης. Ήταν όλοι ντυμένοι καλά. Ο μπαμπάς με το μπλε κοστούμι του. Η μαμά με το καινούργιο μπλε φόρεμά της και ένα κόκκινο κασκόλ δεμένο στο λαιμό της. Εκείνος με το γκρι κοστούμι του - το ίδιο που φορούσε και στην κηδεία τους.

Πάλεψε να συγκρατήσει έναν λυγμό, θυμούμενος το σκηνικό στο στούντιο του φωτογράφου. Το στούντιο περιείχε τα πάντα χριστουγεννιάτικα - παρόλο που ήταν μόλις Ιούλιος. Χαμογέλασε, σκεπτόμενος τα φτηνά χριστουγεννιάτικα στολίδια και το ψεύτικο τζάκι.

Εβδομάδες αργότερα, η κάρτα ήρθε με το ταχυδρομείο, αλλά για τους γονείς του εκείνα τα Χριστούγεννα δεν έφτασαν ποτέ. Έστριψε την καρέκλα του προς την έξοδο και κατευθύνθηκε προς τον διάδρομο με τον θείο του να τον ακολουθεί.

"Ξέρω ότι θα πάρει χρόνο. Λυπάμαι αν το παρατράβηξα πολύ νωρίς, αλλά έχει περάσει πάνω από ένας χρόνος και εμείς, εγώ και ο σύμβουλός σου, θεωρήσαμε ότι ήρτε η ώρα".

Ο E-Z συνέχισε να πηγαίνει. Ήθελε να φύγει μακριά. Να αποδράσει στο δωμάτιό του και να αποκλείσει τον κόσμο, τότε κάτι του ήρθε στο μυαλό. Κάτι κρίσιμο. Ο θείος του δεν μπορούσε να γνωρίζει την ιστορία της φωτογραφίας. Αν ήξερε, δεν θα την είχε βάλει εκεί. Μετά απο όλα όσα είχε κάνει γι' αυτόν, του όφειλε μια εξήγηση. Σταμάτησε.

"Δεν τη χρησιμοποιήσαμε ποτέ, προοριζόταν για τη χριστουγεννιάτικη κάρτα μας, αλλά δεν έφτασαν ποτέ μέχρι τα Χριστούγεννα".

"Λυπάμαι πολύ. Δεν το ήξερα".

"Το ξέρω ότι δεν το ήξερες, αλλά αυτό δεν το κάνει να πονάει λιγότερο".

Εξαντλημένος τόσο σωματικά όσο και ψυχικά κινήθηκε πιο κοντα στο δωμάτιό του. Ο εσωτερικός του διάλογος συνεχίστηκε με θετική ενίσχυση. Υπενθυμίζοντάς του ότι όλα θα φαίνονταν καλύτερα το πρωί. Γιατί σχεδόν πάντα έτσι γινόταν.

"Ήταν γραφτό να είναι ένα μέρος για να γράφεις. Να θυμάσαι, είσαι ένας βραβευμένος συγγραφέας τώρα και έχεις συγγραφικό αίμα".

Είχε φτάσει σχεδόν στο δωμάτιό του - γιατί δεν τον είχε αφήσει ο θείος του να φύγει; Η ψυχραιμία του φούντωσε.

"Έγραψα ένα διήγημα, αλλά αυτό δεν σημαίνει ότι μπορώ να γράψω περισσότερα ή ότι θέλω να γράψω. Λέτε ότι στις φλέβες μου κυλάει το αίμα του Τσαρλς Ντίκενς, αλλά αυτό που θέλω είναι να γίνω catcher στους Ντότζερς του Λος Άντζελες. Ακριβώς επειδή με αποκαλούν "αγόρι του δέντρου" - δεν σημαίνει ότι πρέπει να συμβιβαστώ. Γιατί να πρέπει να συμβιβαστώ;"

"Μακάρι να μην τους άφηνες να μπουν στο μυαλό σου".

"Είμαι δεντρόπουλο! Αν δεν ήταν αυτό το γαμημένο δέντρο!" αναφώνησε καθώς έκανε μια απότομη στροφή και χτύπησε τον αγκώνα του στον τοίχο. Το όχι και τόσο αστείο, αστείο κόκαλο του πονούσε σαν τρελό.

"Είσαι καλά;"

Ο E-Z γρύλισε μια απάντηση και συνέχισε προς το δωμάτιό του. Είχε σκοπό να χτυπήσει την πόρτα πίσω του. Αντ' αυτού, σφηνώθηκε μισό μέσα και μισό έξω από την πόρτα. Τότε οι ρόδες της καρέκλας του μπλόκαραν.

"ΓΑΜΟΣ!"

Ο Σαμ απελευθέρωσε την καρέκλα χωρίς να πει λέξη. Έκλεισε την πόρτα βγαίνοντας.

Ο E-Z άρπαξε μερικά άθραυστα αντικείμενα και τα πέταξε στον τοίχο. Για να ηρεμήσει τον εαυτό του, οραματίστηκε τους γονείς του, να του λένε πόσο περήφανοι ήταν γι' αυτόν. Του έλειπε αυτό. Αλλά, αν ο μπαμπάς του ήταν εδώ τώρα, θα τον έβριζε που ήταν τόσο παλιόπαιδο. Και η μητέρα του θα τον έβριζε, αλλά με πιο ευγενικό και ευγενικό τρόπο. Σκούπισε τα δάκρυα. Ένιωσε το τσίμπημα της ντροπής και το σώμα του έπεσε κάτω από την απόλυτη εξάντληση στην αναπηρική του καρέκλα.

Ο θείος Σαμ ρώτησε μέσα από την κλειστή πόρτα: "Είσαι καλά;".

"Αφήστε με ήσυχο!" απάντησε ο E-Z. Παρόλο που χρειαζόταν τη βοήθειά του. Χωρίς αυτόν, δεν μπορούσε να φορέσει τις πιτζάμες του ή να πέσει στο κρεβάτι. Θα έπρεπε να κοιμηθεί στην καρέκλα, με τα ρούχα του. Βαθιά μέσα του ήξερε πάντα την αλήθεια. Αν σταματούσε να νοιάζεται, τότε θα σταματούσαν να νοιάζονται και όλοι οι άλλοι. Τότε θα ήταν πραγματικά μόνος του.

Έφερε την καρέκλα του στο παράθυρο και κοίταξε τον νυχτερινό ουρανό. Μουσική. Ήταν το μόνο πράγμα που τους συνέδεε πραγματικά ως οικογένεια. Βέβαια, είχαν τις διαφορές τους στα μουσικά είδη, αλλά όταν έβγαινε ένα καλό τραγούδι στο ραδιόφωνο, το άφηναν στην άκρη.

Μια ψωριασμένη μαύρη γάτα περπάτησε στο γκαζόν. Η μητέρα του πάντα ήθελε να πάνε στη Νέα Υόρκη και να δουν τις Γάτες στο Μπρόντγουεϊ. Μακάρι να είχαν πάει μαζί. Να δημιουργήσουν μια ανάμνηση. Τώρα δεν θα το έκαναν ποτέ. Αυτό το τραγούδι, κάτι για τις αναμνήσεις τον έκανε να πιάσει το τηλέφωνό του. Επέλεξε έναν σκληρό ροκ ύμνο και ανέβασε την ένταση. Χρησιμοποίησε τις γροθιές του για να χτυπήσει τον ρυθμό στα μπράτσα της καρέκλας του, καθώς παραληρούσε και φώναζε τους στίχους.

Μέχρι που το ροκάνισε τόσο δυνατά που έπεσε από την καρέκλα του και χτύπησε στο πάτωμα. Στην αρχή, βλέποντας το δωμάτιό του από το έδαφος, ήθελε να κλάψει. Αντ' αυτού, άρχισε να γελάει και δεν μπορούσε να σταματήσει.

"Είσαι καλά εκεί μέσα;" ρώτησε ο Σαμ.

"Χμ, θα μπορούσα να χρησιμοποιήσω τη βοήθειά σου". Το στομάχι του πονούσε από τα πολλά γέλια.

Η αρχική αντίδραση του Σαμ ήταν συναγερμός - όταν είδε τον ανιψιό του στο πάτωμα να κρατάει το στομάχι του. Όταν συνειδητοποίησε ότι το κρατούσε από τα γέλια, έπεσε στο πάτωμα δίπλα του.

Αργότερα, όταν ο Σαμ έφευγε, είπε: "Θα γίνεις καλά, μικρέ".

"Θα είμαστε εντάξει."

Τότε ήταν που συμφώνησαν να κάνουν τατουάζ.

ΚΕΦΑΛΑΙΟ 2

"Λ ΥΠΑΜΑΙ, ΔΕΝ ΜΠΟΡΩ ΝΑ παίξω μπέιζμπολ μαζί σας σήμερα".

"Έλα", είπε ο Άρντεν. "Δεν ήσουν τόσο κακός την τελευταία φορά".

"Άντε χάσου", απάντησε ο E-Z. Ανέπτυξε ταχύτητα για να συναντήσει τον θείο του και συγκρούστηκε με τη Μαίρη Γκάρνερ, την επικεφαλής μαζορέτα.

"Ω, συγγνώμη, Μαίρη".

Ήταν η πρώτη φορά που την έβλεπε μετά το ατύχημα. Κοίταξε ψηλά, καθώς τα μαλλιά της έπεσαν σαν κουρτίνα στα μάτια του: μύριζαν κανέλα και μέλι.

"Ηλίθιε", είπε. "Πρόσεχε πού πας".

Έκανε πίσω και απομακρύνθηκε. Η συνοδεία της την ακολούθησε.

Εκείνος χαμογέλασε, έσκυψε το λαιμό του για να την παρακολουθήσει. Οι φίλοι του ήρθαν δίπλα της και έκαναν το ίδιο. Ο Άρντεν σφύριξε.

Έριξε μια ματιά πάνω από τον ώμο της και χτύπησε το πουλί προς την κατεύθυνσή τους.

"Θεέ μου, είναι φανταστική", είπε ο Πι Τζέι.

"Είναι καυτή", είπε ο Άρντεν.

"Πολύ".

Βγαίνοντας πλέον από το σχολείο, ο Πι Τζέι ρώτησε: "Πες μας λοιπόν γιατί δεν θέλεις να παίξεις σήμερα".

"Ναι, βοηθήστε μας, να καταλάβουμε", είπε ο Άρντεν, τραβώντας μια γκριμάτσα και σταυρώνοντας τα μάτια του. "Είμαστε άχρηστοι χωρίς εσένα".

"Κοιτάξτε, ο θείος Σαμ κι εγώ κάναμε μια συμφωνία. Να κάνουμε κάτι μαζί -κάτι σημαντικό- μετά το σχολείο σήμερα".

Οι φίλοι του σταύρωσαν τα χέρια τους εμποδίζοντας την πορεία της καρέκλας του.

"Εξακολουθείς να σκοπεύεις να μας αποκλείσεις - και δεν μας λες καν τς γιατί;" είπε ο κοκκινομάλλης PJ.

"Είσαι τελείως μαλάκας".

"Δεν θα σου κάναμε ποτέ κάτι τέτοιο".

Απομακρύνθηκαν, επιταχύνοντας τον ρυθμό τους.

Ο E-Z επιτάχυνε, αλλά δεν ήταν αρκετό. "Περιμένετε! Θα κάνουμε τατουάζ!"

Οι φίλοι του σταμάτησαν στην πορεία τους.

"Θα κάνω ένα τατουάζ στη μνήμη της μαμάς και του μπαμπά μου - φτερά περιστεριών, ένα σε κάθε ώμο".

"Θα έρθουμε μαζί σας".

"Σκέφτηκα ότι μπορεί να νομίζετε ότι είμαι γλυκανάλατος".

Συνέχισαν να περπατούν χωρίς να μιλούν για λίγο.

"Ο θείος Σαμ θα με συναντήσει στο μαγαζί με τα τατουάζ".

ΚΕΦΑΛΑΙΟ 3

Ό ΤΑΝ Ο ΣΑΜ ΕΙΔΕ τον ανιψιό του με τους φίλους του εξεπλάγη.

"Νόμιζα ότι αυτό το σύμφωνο ήταν μεταξύ μας, δηλαδή μυστικό;"

"Τα παιδιά ήθελαν να με πάνε σε ένα παιχνίδι - έπρεπε να τους το πω".

"Εντάξει, εντάξει. Αλλά δεν συνηθίζω να αντικαθιστώ τους γονείς τους ή να δίνω άδεια εκ μέρους των γονιών τους". Στη συνέχεια, προς τον PJ και τον Άρντεν: "Δεν έχω πρόβλημα που είστε εδώ, αλλά μόνο οι γονείς σας μπορούν να εγκρίνουν τα τατουάζ σας".

"Περιμένετε!" Είπε ο PJ. "Ποτέ δεν σκέφτηκα καν να κάνουμε τατουάζ".

"Οι δικοί μου θα πουν σίγουρα όχι", είπε ο Άρντεν. Οι γονείς του είχαν προβλήματα, τα οποία εκμεταλλεύτηκε πλήρως. Έκανε σαν να μην τον ενοχλούσαν οι συνεχείς καβγάδες τους τις περισσότερες φορές. Κάθε τόσο, όταν δεν άντεχε άλλο, αναζητούσε καταφύγιο στο σπίτι ενός φίλου του.

"Και το δικό μου." Ο Πι Τζέι ήταν ο μεγαλύτερος και είχε δύο αδελφές ηλικίας πέντε και επτά ετών. Οι γονείς του τον ενθάρρυναν να δίνει το καλό παράδειγμα και τις περισσότερες φορές το έκανε. Επικεντρώνοντας την προσοχή του σε ένα μέλλον στον αθλητισμό, κρατούσε τον εαυτό του σε καλό δρόμο.

Μοιραζόμενοι μια φωτεινή στιγμή, οι έφηβοι έδωσαν ο ένας στον άλλον ένα high five.

"Τι;" ρώτησε ο Σαμ.

"Θα τους πούμε γιατί το κάνει ο E-Z και ότι θέλουμε τατουάζ για να τον υποστηρίξουμε", είπε ο PJ.

Ο Άρντεν έγνεψε.

"Περιμένετε ένα λεπτό. Δηλαδή, εσείς οι δύο κρετίνοι θέλετε να χρησιμοποιήσετε το θάνατο των γονιών μου ως δικαιολογία για να κάνετε τατουάζ;"

Ο Σαμ άνοιξε το στόμα του, αλλά του ξέφυγαν τα λόγια.

Ο Πι Τζέι και ο Άρντεν ήταν κατακόκκινοι και κοιτούσαν το πεζοδρόμιο.

Ο E-Z τους άφησε να ξεφύγουν. "Δεν με πειράζει".

Ο Σαμ έκλεισε το στόμα του, καθώς αυτός και τα δύο αγόρια σχημάτισαν έναν ημικύκλιο γύρω από την αναπηρική καρέκλα.

"Υποσχέσου μου όμως ένα πράγμα - δεν επιτρέπονται πεταλούδες".

"'Ει, τι έχετε εσείς με τις πεταλούδες;" ρώτησε ο Σαμ.

ΚΕΦΑΛΑΙΟ 4

ΓΙΑ ΝΑ ΜΗΝ ΤΑ πολυλογώ, ο PJ και ο Arden έπεισαν τους γονείς τους να τους αφήσουν να κάνουν τατουάζ.

"'Έρχομαι σε ένα λεπτό", είπε ο τατουατζής, ρίχνοντας μια ματιά και στους τέσσερις. Απέναντι από τον καθρέφτη, βρισκόταν ένας εύσωμος άνδρας πελάτης που πρόσθετε άλλο ένα τατουάζ στη συλλογή των πολλών του. Αυτό το νέο ήταν ανάμεσα στον αντίχειρα και τον δείκτη του. "Είσαι ο Σαμ;" ρώτησε ο άντρας που έκανε το τατουάζ.

Το στομάχι του Σαμ ένιωσε μια μικρή αναγούλα, καθώς είχε διαβάσει ότι το χέρι ήταν ένα από τα πιο επώδυνα σημεία για να κάνεις τατουάζ. "Ναι, μίλησα μαζί σας στο τηλέφωνο. Αυτός είναι ο ανιψιός μου E-Z και οι φίλοι του, ο PJ και ο Arden".

"Και οι τέσσερις σας θέλετε τατουάζ, σήμερα; Γιατί εγώ περίμενα μόνο δύο από εσάς".

"Λυπάμαι γι' αυτό. Μπορούμε να το αναβάλουμε, αν χρειαστεί, ή μπορώ να κάνω το δικό μου σε άλλη μέρα", είπε ο Σαμ ευχόμενος.

"Για καλή μου τύχη, η κόρη μου θα έρθει σύντομα να με βοηθήσει. Οπότε, καλώς ήρθατε στο Tattoos-R-Us. Μπορείτε να περιμένετε εκεί. Πάρτε ένα ποτήρι νερό. Υπάρχουν επίσης μερικά φυλλάδια που ίσως θέλετε να δείτε. Ίσως σε βοηθήσουν να αποφασίσεις πού θέλεις το τατουάζ σου. Κάθε περιοχή του σώματος έχει ένα κατώφλι πόνου". Ο γεροδεμένος τύπος που έκανε τατουάζ χασκογέλασε.

"Ευχαριστώ", απάντησε η Σαμ καθώς προχωρούσαν προς το χώρο αναμονής. Μόλις κάθισε σε έναν καναπέ, το γόνατό του που χοροπηδούσε προκάλεσε ανατριχίλα στην Πι Τζέι και τον Άρντεν. Διέσχισαν το δωμάτιο και κοίταξαν τον πίνακα ανακοινώσεων. Για να ηρεμήσει τα νεύρα του, ο Σαμ φλυαρούσε. "Τους έψαξα στο διαδίκτυο, λειτουργούν εδώ και είκοσι πέντε χρόνια, και αυτός ο άνθρωπος που μιλήσαμε είναι ο ιδιοκτήτης. Έχουν άριστη θέση στο Better Business Bureau. Επιπλέον, πολλές κριτικές με πέντε αστέρια στην ιστοσελίδα τους".

Όλα τα βλέμματα στράφηκαν καθώς μια εντυπωσιακή γυναίκα ντυμένη με γκόθικ ενδυμασία μπήκε στο χώρο. Ήταν γύρω στα τριάντα και, κρίνοντας από τα χαρακτηριστικά της, η κόρη του ιδιοκτήτη. Είχε τατουάζ σε κάθε κομμάτι της εκτεθειμένης σάρκας και σποραδικά σκουλαρίκια παντού αλλού.

"Συγγνώμη που άργησα", είπε, αγγίζοντας τον πατέρα της στον ώμο. Έριξε μια ματιά στον χώρο αναμονής και του ψιθύρισε κάτι. Χάρισε ένα οδοντωτό χαμόγελο και στράφηκε προς τους πελάτες.

"Γεια σας, είμαι η Τζόσι". Άπλωσε το χέρι της και έσφιξε το χέρι του καθενός από αυτούς. "Αυτός εκεί πέρα είναι ο Ρόκι. Είναι ο ιδιοκτήτης και εγώ είμαι η κόρη του".

"Είμαι ο Σαμ, και αυτός είναι ο ανιψιός μου E-Z και οι δύο φίλοι του, ο Πι Τζέι και ο Άρντεν". Έπεσε αντί να ξανακαθίσει.

Η Τζόσι πήγε να του φέρει ένα ποτήρι νερό.

Ο E-Z σκεφτόταν πόσο θα πρέπει να πονούσε το τρύπημα στη γλώσσα της, και μετά είπε στον θείο του: "Δεν χρειάζεται".

"Με αποκαλείς κότα;" είπε, με όλο του το σώμα να τρέμει, καθώς η Τζόσι του έβαλε το ποτήρι στο χέρι. Καθώς το σήκωσε προς τα χείλη του, έχυσε λίγο νερό.

"Εσείς είστε παρθένοι για τατουάζ, σωστά;" ρώτησε η Τζόσι.

Ο E-Z σκέφτηκε ότι είχε μια γλυκιά φωνή, σαν τη Στίβι Νικς, την αγαπημένη τραγουδίστρια του πατέρα του από τους Fleetwood Mac, που τραγουδούσε για τη Ριάνον, τη μάγισσα.

Δεν χρειάστηκε να απαντήσουν, καθώς η σιωπή τους τα έλεγε όλα.

"Λοιπόν, είστε σε εξαιρετικά χέρια με τον Ρόκι. Είναι ο καλύτερος καλλιτέχνης τατουάζ στην πόλη. Θα πονέσει, παιδιά. Ναι, θα πονέσει. Αλλά είναι σαν αυτό το είδος του πόνου για το οποίο τραγουδάει ο Τζον Κούγκαρ. Ξέρεις, πονάει τόσο καλά".

Ο Σαμ έκανε μια γκριμάτσα. "Πόσο πολύ πονάει στην πραγματικότητα;"

"Εξαρτάται από το κατώφλι σου στον πόνο - και από το πού επιλέγεις να τον πάρεις. Υπάρχει ένα φυλλάδιο εκεί πέρα, το οποίο χαρτογραφεί τις διάφορες περιοχές του σώματος δίνοντας μια βαθμολογία πόνου".

Ο E-Z ένιωσε το πρόσωπό του να ζεσταίνεται, και η επιδερμίδα των φίλων του είχε μια παρόμοια απόχρωση. Έριξε μια ματιά προς την κατεύθυνση του Σαμ, παρατηρώντας την επιδερμίδα του που είχε αλλάξει σε μια πρασινωπή απόχρωση.

Η Τζόσι συνέχισε. "Μετά το πρώτο σου τατουάζ, μπορεί να σου αρέσει και να θέλεις περισσότερα".

Ο Σαμ σηκώθηκε όρθιος, με το σώμα του να τρέμει από φόβο.

"Ίσως χρειάζεται λίγο καθαρό αέρα", είπε ο E-Z, κατευθύνοντας τον θείο του προς την πόρτα.

Μόλις βγήκε έξω, ο Σαμ βημάτιζε πάνω κάτω στο πεζοδρόμιο, με την καρδιά του να χτυπάει σαν να πήγαινε να πεταχτεί έξω από το στήθος του. "Μακάρι να κάπνιζα".

"Το εκτιμώ που ήρθες εδώ μαζί μου, αλήθεια, αλλά ειλικρινά, δεν χρειάζεται να το κάνεις. Ξέρω ότι κάναμε μια συμφωνία, και αυτό είναι κάτι που θέλω να κάνω -στη μνήμη της μαμάς και του μπαμπά μου- αλλά δεν μου χρωστάς τίποτα. Γιατί δεν πάμε μια βόλτα, να πιούμε έναν καφέ και θα σου στελνουμε μήνυμα όταν τελειώσουμε, εντάξει;".

"Είπα ότι θα είμαι εκεί για σένα, πάντα. Είμαι εδώ για σένα τώρα. Μισώ τις βελόνες. Και τα τρυπάνια. Νόμιζα ότι μπορούσα να το κάνω, αλλά τώρα συνειδητοποιώ ότι ο φόβος είναι πιο δυνατός από εμένα. Είμαι τόσο δειλή".

"Πάντα ήσουν εκεί για μένα, θείε Σαμ. Δεν χρειάζεται να το αποδείξεις σε μένα, σε κανέναν, κάνοντας ένα τατουάζ που δεν θέλεις καν. Τώρα, φύγε από εδώ. Θα σου τηλεφωνήσω όταν τελειώσουμε". Ανέβηκε με το τροχό του στη ράμπα, με τους φίλους του να πέφτουν στη σειρά πίσω του. Έριξε μια ματιά πάνω από τον ώμο του στον Σαμ. Ο καημένος ήταν άκαμπτος σαν άγαλμα.

"Θα είμαι εντάξει. Τώρα, απογειώσου".

Ο Σαμ γέλασε. "Αλλά πριν φύγω, καλύτερα να μου δώσεις το γράμμα που έγραψα χθες το βράδυ, για να προσθέσω τα ονόματα του Πι Τζέι και του Άρντεν. Γιατί χωρίς την άδειά μου - κανένας από εσάς δεν πρόκειται να κάνει τατουάζ".

"Καλή σκέψη", είπε ο E-Z καθώς παρέδιδε το σημείωμα στη γραμμή. Τώρα υπογεγραμμένο ήρθε και πάλι πίσω. Το έβαλε στην τσέπη του και μπήκαν μέσα, όπου τους περίμενε η Τζόσι.

"Εντάξει, είσαι ο επόμενος. Αν είναι να κατουρηθείς πάνω σου, θα σου δείξω πού είναι τώρα η τουαλέτα".

"Δάγκωσέ με", είπε ο E-Z καθώς έφερε την καρέκλα του στη θέση της.

ΕΝΏ Ο ROCKY ΤΕΛΕΊΩΝΕ στο ταμείο, η Josie έδωσε στον E-Z ένα βιβλίο με τατουάζ.

"Το ξέρω ήδη χωρίς να κοιτάξω. Θα ήθελα ένα φτερό περιστεριού, σε κάθε ώμο". Εκεί ήταν πάλι, τα πράσινα και κίτρινα φώτα. Ήθελε τόσο πολύ να τα διώξει, αλλά δεν ήθελε να νομίζει και η Τζόσι ότι είναι τρελή.

Η Τζόσι ξεφύλλισε το βιβλίο. "Αυτά είχες στο μυαλό σου;"

Κούνησε το κεφάλι του και μετά την παρακολούθησε στον καθρέφτη καθώς έπλενε τα χέρια της και μετά φόρεσε ένα ζευγάρι μαύρα γάντια. Έβγαλε τα μελανοδοχεία από την αποστειρωμένη συσκευασία και τα έβαλε στο τραπέζι.

"Έχετε κάποιο σημείωμα, από τον γονέα ή τον κηδεμόνα σας; Υποθέτω ότι δεν είσαι δεκαοκτώ ετών;"

Ο E-Z χαμογέλασε και της έδωσε το σημείωμα.

"Όλα φαίνονται μια χαρά. Και τώρα στα πιο σημαντικά θέματα. Έχεις τριχωτή πλάτη;" Εκείνη χαμογέλασε. "Αν έχεις, θα πρέπει πρώτα να την καθαρίσουμε και να την ξυρίσουμε. Εννοώ ολόκληρη την πλάτη σου".

"Σίγουρα όχι".

Ο ήχος των φίλων του που χασκογελούσαν από τον χώρο αναμονής τον έκανε να χαμογελάσει κι εκείνος. Εν τω μεταξύ, η Τζόσι εξαφανίστηκε στο πίσω δωμάτιο και ακούστηκε μουσική. Για ένα δευτερόλεπτο, Another Brick in the Wall, και μετά καμία μουσική.

"Ει, γιατί το έκανες αυτό;" ρώτησε.

"Απεχθάνομαι οτιδήποτε από τους Pink Floyd". Συνέχισε να στήνει τα πράγματα.

"Δεν μπορείς να το λες αυτό, εκτός αν δεν έχεις ακούσει ποτέ το Dark Side of the Moon".

"Το άκουσα, ήταν χάλια", είπε καθώς του τραβούσε το πουκάμισο πάνω από το κεφάλι. 'Ω!"

POP.

POP.

Και τα δύο φώτα εξαφανίστηκαν.

Ο Ρόκι πλησίασε και στάθηκε δίπλα της. "Τι στο καλό;"

"Πράγματι, τι στο καλό", είπε η Τζόσι.

Αυτό έφερε τον Πι Τζέι και τον Άρντεν κοντά της.

"Δεν το καταλαβαίνω, E-Z. Γιατί να πεις ψέματα;"

"Φυσικά, δεν θα έλεγε ψέματα - ο E-Z δεν λέει ποτέ ψέματα", είπε ο Άρντεν.

"ΤΙ!;" ρώτησε ο E-Z, προσπαθώντας να κάνει ελιγμούς στην καρέκλα του ώστε να μπορεί να δει αυτό που έβλεπαν. "Ψέμα; Για ποιο πράγμα; Πες μου, ό,τι κι αν είναι. Μπορώ να το αντέξω".

Η Τζόσι ρώτησε: "Γιατί είπες ψέματα ότι είσαι παρθένος για τατουάζ;".

✸✸✸

"ΔΕΝ ΤΟ ΕΚΑΝΑ!" ΤΡΑΎΛΙΣΕ ο Ε-Ζ, χωρίς να έχει ιδέα τι εννοούσε.

"Περίμενε ένα λεπτό", είπε ο Άρντεν. "'Ελα, φιλαράκο, αν είπες ψέματα, πρέπει να έχεις καλό λόγο".

"Το παιχνίδι τελείωσε!" Είπε ο Πι Τζέι. "Αν και δεν θα μπορούσε να τα πάρει χωρίς την άδεια ενός ενήλικα".

Ο Ρόκι άρπαξε έναν καθρέφτη χειρός και τον τοποθέτησε έτσι ώστε ο Ε-Ζ να μπορεί να δει αυτό που έβλεπαν. Δύο τατουάζ, το ένα στον δεξιό ώμο του και το άλλο στον αριστερό. Τα φτερά.

"Τι στο...;"

"Μου είπε ότι ήθελε φτερά", είπε η Τζόσι. "Νόμιζα ότι ήσουν καλό παιδί".

"Είμαι! Ειλικρινά, δεν έχω ιδέα πώς βρέθηκαν εκεί, και δεν είναι αυτό το είδος φτερών που ήθελα. Ήθελα φτερά περιστεριών. Αυτά μοιάζουν περισσότερο με, φτερά αγγέλου".

"'Ελα, φίλε", είπε ο Ρόκι. "Αυτά έγιναν από επαγγελματία. Πριν από λίγο καιρό. Και είναι αρκετά εξαιρετικά φτερά αγγέλου. Τα συγχαρητήριά μου σε όποιον τα έκανε. Πες τους, αν ψάχνουν ποτέ για δουλειά, να με δουν".

"Ορκίζομαι στην καρδιά μου, δεν έκανα τατουάζ. Είναι η πρώτη φορά που μπαίνω σε μαγαζί με τατουάζ. Ρωτήστε τον θείο μου. Θα με υποστηρίξει. Αυτός ξέρει".

"Τίποτα από όλα αυτά δεν βγάζει νόημα", είπε ο Άρντεν.

Ο Ρόκι κούνησε το κεφάλι του. "Τουλάχιστον παραδέξου το, μικρέ".

"Εσείς οι δύο θέλετε τατουάζ;" Η Τζόσι ρώτησε με τα χέρια στους γορούς της.

"Όχι", απάντησαν.

"Οι άντρες είναι τόσο ψεύτες", είπε η Τζόσι καθώς έκλειναν την πόρτα πίσω τους.

"Δεν πειράζει, αγάπη μου, ούτως ή άλλως ήρθε η ώρα να φάμε", και ιετά έβαλε την πινακίδα ΚΛΕΙΣΤΟ στην πόρτα.

Ο ΣΑΜ ΕΠΕΣΤΡΕΨΕ ΚΑΙ είδε τα τρία αγόρια να περιμένουν έξω από το στούντιο. Η γλώσσα του σώματός τους ήταν παράξενη. Ο κοκκινομάλλης PJ είχε τα χέρια του σταυρωμένα, ενώ ο λαδοκόκκινος Άρντεν τα χέρια του στους γοφούς. Εν τω μεταξύ, ο ανιψιός του ήταν κοντά στα δάκρυα.

"Δόξα τω Θεώ, θείε Σαμ, δόξα τω Θεώ που επέστρεψες".

Έσπευσε να πλησιάσει. "Ωχ όχι, ήταν τρομερά επώδυνο; Θα χαλαρώσει σε λίγες μέρες. Όλα θα πάνε καλά. Τώρα άσε με να ρίξω μια ματιά". Σφύριξε καθώς ο ανιψιός του έσκυψε μπροστά για να μπορέσει να σηκώσει το πουκάμισό του. "Γαμώτο, αυτά πρέπει να πόνεσαν".

"Πιθανότατα", είπε ο Πι Τζέι.

"Όταν τα πήρε για πρώτη φορά."

"Πρώτη φορά; Τι;"

"Τα είχε ήδη όταν εκείνη του έβγαλε το πουκάμισο".

"Αυτό που δεν μπορούμε να καταλάβουμε είναι, πώς;"

"Τι εννοείς; Μπορώ να σας διαβεβαιώσω ότι δεν τα είχε χθες".

"Βλέπετε, σας είπα ότι ο θείος Σαμ θα με υποστήριζε". Αν δεν τον πίστευαν, θα πίστευαν τον θείο του, αλλά γιατί να πιστέψουν ότι θα έλεγε ψέματα γι' αυτό; Ήξεραν ότι δεν ήταν ψεύτης.

"Σύμφωνα με τον Ρόκι, τα έχει αυτά τα πράγματα εδώ και καιρό".

"Βλέπεις πώς έχουν επουλωθεί;" Ο Πι Τζέι είπε. "Ο Ρόκι και η Τζόσι ενοχλήθηκαν, και είχαν κάθε δικαίωμα να ενοχληθούν, αφού ο E-Z φάνηκε εξίσου έκπληκτος με εμάς που τους είδαμε".

"Κι εσείς οι δύο", ρώτησε ο Σαμ, "πώς πήγαν τα τατουάζ σας;"

"Αποφασίσαμε να μην προχωρήσουμε", είπε ο PJ.

"Δεν το νιώθαμε σωστό".

Ο Σαμ είπε: "Πείτε μας τι συνέβη. Εξηγήσου, φίλε, γιατί δεν μπορώ να καταλάβω ούτε το κεφάλι ούτε τις ιστορίες".

"Δεν μπορώ. Θείε Σαμ, ξέρεις ότι δεν ήταν εκεί χθες. Δεν έχω καμία εξήγηση. Το μόνο που θέλω, είναι να πάω σπίτι μου". Άρχισε να κινείται, χτυπώντας τις ρόδες της καρέκλας του, πιο γρήγορα, πιο γρήγορα ακόμα πιο γρήγορα. Ήθελε να φύγει μακριά, οπουδήποτε μακριά. Αν δεν τον πίστευαν, τότε ας πάνε στο διάολο.

Καθώς πλησίαζε στο τέλος του δρόμου, τα φώτα άλλαξαν από πράσινα σε κόκκινα. Ένα κοριτσάκι μόνο του είχε ήδη πάρει φόρα για να περάσει απέναντι. Κατέβηκε από το πεζοδρόμιο, καθώς ένα τροχόσπιτο γύριζε στη γωνία. Η αναπηρική του καρέκλα σηκώθηκε από το έδαφος και εκτοξεύτηκε προς το μέρος της. Άπλωσε το χέρι του και την άρπαξε. Πάνω στην ώρα για να τη σώσει από το να πέσει κάτω από τις ρόδες του οχήματος.

Τώρα εκτός κινδύνου, το αναπηρικό καροτσάκι ακούμπησε ξανά στο έδαφος και την μετέφερε σε ασφαλές μέρος. Μπροστά του στεκόταν ένας μεγαλύτερος από το κανονικό λευκός κύκνος. Του έκανε ένα μπράβο με το φτερό του και μετά πέταξε μακριά.

"Κύκνος", είπε το κοριτσάκι, καθώς κοίταζε γύρω του για τους γονείς της.

Ο E-Z άδραξε την ευκαιρία να αναμειχθεί στο πλήθος και να εξαφανιστεί πίσω από τη γωνία, μετά χτύπησε τις ακτίνες των τροχών του πιο δυνατά από ποτέ και σύντομα βρέθηκε μερικά τετράγωνα μακριά.

"Το είδες αυτό;" αναφώνησε ο Άρντεν, σταματώντας στη γωνία. "Ωχ", είπε καθώς η γυναίκα πίσω του έπεσε πάνω του. "Ωχ" άκουσε πίσω του, άλλοι πεζοί πίσω του συγκρούστηκαν.

Ο Πι Τζέι κράτησε τη θέση του, καθώς ο τύπος πίσω του έπεσε με βαρέλι πάνω του. Στον Άρντεν είπε: "Ναι, το είδα... αλλά δεν είμαι σίγουρος τι είδα. Τα φτερά του τατουάζ ήταν ένα πράγμα, αυτό ήταν... τι; Ένα θαύμα;"

"Ήταν μια οπτική ψευδαίσθηση", είπε ο Σαμ, καθώς το τηλέφωνό του δονήθηκε. Ήταν ένα μήνυμα από τον Ε-Ζ που του ζητούσε να τον βρει το συντομότερο δυνατό κοντά στο πάρκινγκ του καταστήματος σιδηρικών. "Ο Ε-Ζ με χρειάζεται, θα μπορέσετε εσείς οι δύο να επιστρέψετε στο σπίτι σας ξανά;"

"Φυσικά, κανένα πρόβλημα, Σαμ".

"Ελπίζω να είναι καλά".

Ο Σαμ πήρε το δρόμο της επιστροφής προς το αυτοκίνητο, προσπαθώντας να διατηρήσει την ψυχραιμία του καθώς προσπαθούσε να καταλάβει λογικά τι είχε μόλις συμβεί.

Κανένα από τα αγόρια δεν ήθελε να μιλήσει γι' αυτό που είχαν δει - το αναπηρικό καροτσάκι του Ε-Ζ εν πτήσει.

"Το είδατε αυτό;" ψιθύρισαν άλλοι πίσω τους καθώς μαζεύτηκε πλήθος κόσμου.

"Μακάρι να είχα έτοιμο το τηλέφωνό μου", είπε μια γυναίκα.

Μια δεύτερη γυναίκα με μικρόφωνο και κάμερα έσπρωξε προς τα εμπρός. Όταν άλλαξε το φανάρι, διέσχισε το δρόμο, ακολουθούμενη από ένα ζευγάρι, δακρυσμένο - τους γονείς των μικρών κοριτσιών. Πίσω τους βρισκόταν ο οδηγός του τροχόσπιτου.

"Δόξα τω Θεώ, ήσασταν εκεί", φώναξε. "Δεν την είδα. Είσαι ένα ηρωικό παιδί. Σε ευχαριστώ".

"Μαμά!" φώναξε το παιδί, καθώς η μητέρα της την τράβηξε στην αγκαλιά της. Εκείνη και ο σύζυγός της την αγκάλιασαν σφιχτά, καθώς ο δημοσιογράφος πλησίαζε και ο κάμεραμαν κατέγραφε τη στιγμή.

Σε κοντινή απόσταση έκλαιγε με λυγμούς ο άνδρας που παραλίγο να τη χτυπήσει. Ο δημοσιογράφος και ο φωτογράφος μίλησαν μαζί του. "Την έσωσε, και εμένα. Το αγέρι, το αγόρι στο αναπηρικό καροτσάκι".

Προσπάθησαν να τον βρουν, αλλά είχε εξαφανιστεί. Είχε κρυφτεί, σαν εγκληματίας. Περίμενε να έρθει ο θείος Σαμ να τον σώσει. Προσπαθούσε να καταλάβει τι είχε συμβεί. Προσπαθούσε να μην φρικάρει.

Πίσω στον τόπο του εγκλήματος, δύο φώτα, ένα πράσινο και ένα κίτρινο, έσβησαν το μυαλό όλων όσων βρίσκονταν κοντά. Μετά κατέστρεψαν όλα τα καταγεγραμμένα πλάνα.

"Τι κάνουμε εδώ;" ρώτησε ο δημοσιογράφος.

"Δεν έχω ιδέα", απάντησε ο κάμεραμαν.

Στο δρόμο για το σπίτι, ο E-Z ένιωσε κάπως σαν ήρωας. Αλλά ήξερε ότι ο πραγματικός ήρωας ήταν η καρέκλα- η αναπηρική του καρέκλα που είχε πάρει φόρα.

Ο E-Z Dickens ήταν ένας άγγελος τατουάζ.

✳ ✳ ✳

"ΠΈΤΑΞΑ ΤΟΝ ΘΕΙΟ ΣΑΜ. Πραγματικά πέταξα."

Ο Σαμ μπήκε στο δρόμο και πάρκαρε.

"Το είδες, έτσι; Με είδες να σώζω εκείνο το κοριτσάκι. Δεν θα μπορούσα να προλάβω εγκαίρως, και η αναπηρική μου καρέκλα το ήξερε και σηκώθηκε από το έδαφος και επιτάχυνε προς το μέρος της".

"Ναι, το είδα. Ήταν εξαιρετικό. Εννοώ τον τρόπο με τον οποίο έσωσες το κοριτσάκι από το κακό. Αλλά η καρέκλα σου δεν απογειώθηκε. Ήταν η ορμή, που σε έσπρωχνε προς τα εμπρός. Με την έξαρση της αδρεναλίνης και το πόσο γρήγορα έπρεπε να κινηθείς για να φτάσεις εκεί, ένιωσες σαν να πετούσες - αλλά δεν πετούσες".

"Πέταξα. Η καρέκλα έφυγε από το έδαφος".

"E-Z έλα. Ξέρεις και ξέρω ότι δεν πετούσες. Πρέπει να το ξέρεις αυτό. Θέλω να πω, τι νομίζεις ότι είσαι; Ένας γαμημένος άγγελος;"

Ο Σαμ βγήκε από το αυτοκίνητο, έβγαλε το αναπηρικό καροτσάκι από το πορτμπαγκάζ και γύρισε να βοηθήσει τον ανιψιό του να μπει μέσα. Καθώς το έκανε, ο δεξιός ώμος του E-Z γρατζούνισε την άκρη της πόρτας και φώναξε από πόνο.

"Νερό!" ούρλιαξε. "Αισθάνομαι σαν να φλέγομαι".

Ο Σαμ έτρεξε στην κουζίνα και επέστρεψε με ένα μπουκάλι νερό.

Ο E-Z το έριξε στον ώμο του. Ηρέμησε λίγο, μετά ο άλλος του ώμος ένιωσε σαν να είχε πάρει φωτιά. Έριξε το υπόλοιπο μπουκάλι πάνω του. Ο

Σαμ τον έσπρωξε μέσα στο σπίτι, ενώ ο E-Z προσπαθούσε να του σκίσει το πουκάμισο. Ο Σαμ τον βοήθησε να το τραβήξει πάνω από το κεφάλι του.

"Ωχ, όχι!" φώναξε ο Σαμ, καλύπτοντας τη μύτη του. Οι ωμοπλάτες του ανιψιού του έμοιαζαν τώρα και μύριζαν σαν καμένο κρέας μπάρμπεκιου. Έσπευσε στην κουζίνα για περισσότερο νερό.

Στο δρόμο ο E-Z ούρλιαζε και συνέχιζε να ουρλιάζει, μέχρι που έχασε τις αισθήσεις του.

ΚΕΦΑΛΑΙΟ 5

Ἥ ΤΑΝ ΣΚΟΤΆΔΙ ΚΑΙ ΉΤΑΝ ολομόναχος, μόνο η σκιά του φεγγαριού απλωνόταν από πάνω του στον ουρανό.

Τα χέρια του ήταν σταυρωμένα στο στήθος του, όπως είχε δει πτώματα τοποθετημένα σε μια κηδεία με ανοιχτό φέρετρο. Τα κούνησε. Τώρα χαλαρός τα εναπόθεσε στα μπράτσα της αναπηρικής του καρέκλας, μόνο και μόνο για να ανακαλύψει ότι δεν βρισκόταν μέσα σε αυτήν. Φοβούμενος ότι θα έπεφτε, ξανασταύρωσε τα χέρια του πάνω στο στήθος του. Αλλά περίμενε, δεν έπεσε όταν τα ξεσταύρωσε πριν - το έκανε ξανά και παρέμεινε όρθιος.

Ο E-Z κράτησε το ένα χέρι σταθερά στο στήθος του, ενώ το άλλο, το δεξί του, απλώθηκε όσο πιο μακριά μπορούσε. Οι άκρες των δακτύλων του συνδέθηκαν με κάτι δροσερό και μεταλλικό. Με το αριστερό του χέρι έκανε το ίδιο, βρίσκοντας και πάλι μέταλλο. Σκύβοντας μπροστά, ακούμπησε τον τοίχο μπροστά του και έκανε το ίδιο πίσω του. Καθώς μετακινούνταν, το κάθισμα κάτω από αυτόν μετατοπιζόταν, με ένα πάτημα και ένα δώσιμο σαν σύστημα ανάρτησης. Αυτό το σύστημα ήταν που τον κρατούσε όρθιο, ή μήπως ήταν;

PFFT.

Ο ήχος της ομίχλης που αναδύεται στον αέρα. Ζεστή, ενίσχυσε την αίσθηση της όσφρησης, λούζοντάς τον με ένα μπουκέτο λεβάντας και εσπεριδοειδών.

Κατέβηκε σε έναν βαθύ ύπνο, στον οποίο είδε όνειρα που δεν ήταν όνειρα γιατί ήταν αναμνήσεις. Το ατύχημα - συνέβαινε ξανά και ξανά - σε επανάληψη. Έριξε το κεφάλι του προς τα πίσω και ούρλιαξε.

"Μια στιγμή, παρακαλώ", είπε μια γυναικεία φωνή.

Ήταν μια ρομποτική φωνή σαν αυτή που ακούγεται σε μαγνητοφωνημένο δίσκο όταν δεν υπάρχει άνθρωπος.

Πολύ φοβισμένος για να ξανακοιμηθεί, ρώτησε: "Ποιος είναι εκεί; Ποιος είναι εκεί; Πού βρίσκομαι;"

"Είσαι εδώ", είπε η φωνή και στη συνέχεια γέλασε. Το γέλιο αντηχούσε από το δοχείο που έμοιαζε με σιλό, χτυπώντας τα αυτιά του καθώς ερχόταν και έφευγε.

Όταν σταμάτησε, αποφάσισε να ξεσπάσει. Χρησιμοποιώντας κάθε ίχνος δύναμης, άπλωσε τα χέρια του και έσπρωξε. Ένιωθε ωραία. Να κάνει κάτι, οτιδήποτε -στην αρχή- μέχρι που η κλειστοφοβία πήρε το πάνω χέρι.

PFFT.

Το σπρέι, πιο κοντά αυτή τη φορά, πήγε κατευθείαν στα μάτια του. Το κιτρικό οξύ τσίμπησε, και τα δάκρυα βγήκαν σαν να είχε κόψει κρεμμύδι, και σηκώθηκε όρθιος.

Περίμενε ένα λεπτό...

Έπεσε πάλι κάτω. Κούνησε τα δάχτυλα των ποδιών του. Το έκανε πάλι. Τέντωσε το δεξί του πόδι. Μετά το αριστερό του πόδι. Δούλεψαν. Τα πόδια του δούλευαν. Σήκωσε τον εαυτό του...

Μια φωνή, ανδρική αυτή τη φορά, είπε: "Παρακαλώ παραμείνετε καθιστοί."

Τσιμπήθηκε στο δεξί μηρό και μετά στο αριστερό. Ποιος ήξερε ότι ένα ή δύο τσιμπήματα θα μπορούσαν να είναι τόσο ωραία; Κανείς δεν μπορούσε να τον σταματήσει. Όσο μπορούσε να χρησιμοποιήσει τα πόδια του, θα στεκόταν και πάλι όρθιος.

Υπήρχε ένας θόρυβος από πάνω του, σαν ασανσέρ που κινείται. Ο ήχος γινόταν πιο δυνατός. Κοίταξε ψηλά. Η οροφή του σιλό έπεφτε. Γινόταν όλο και μεγαλύτερο. Τελικά, σταμάτησε τελείως.

"Καθίστε", απαίτησε η ανδρική φωνή.

Ο E-Z σηκώθηκε, αλλά το ταβάνι κατέβαινε όλο και πιο κάτω - μέχρι που δεν μπορούσε πια να σταθεί όρθιος. Κάθισε υπομονετικά, περιμένοντας το πράγμα να υποχωρήσει σαν ασανσέρ που ανεβαίνει προς την κορυφή - αλλά δεν κουνιόταν.

PFFT.

"Αφήστε με να βγω!"

"Πρόσθεσε λάβδανο", είπε η φωνή της γυναίκας.

Οι τοίχοι έκαναν παύση και μετά ψέκασαν μια πολύ μεγάλη δόση.

PPPFFFTTT.

Ήταν ο τελευταίος ήχος που άκουσε.

Π ÍΣΩ ΣΤΟ ΚΡΕΒΆΤΙ ΤΟΥ - αναρωτιόταν αν είχε χάσει το μυαλό του και φανταζόταν ότι όλο το περιστατικό με το σιλό ήταν Ε-Ζ. Ένιωθε αληθινό, μύριζε αληθινό. Και οι δύο φωνές - γιατί δεν εμφανίστηκαν; Έξυνε το κεφάλι του, βλέποντας δύο φώτα μπροστά στα μάτια του. Όπως και πριν, το ένα ήταν πράσινο και το άλλο κίτρινο.

"Εμπρός;" ψιθύρισε, καθώς ένα ψηλόφωνο κλαψούρισμα σαν μάστιγα κουνουπιών του επιτέθηκε. Εκτόξευσε το δεξί του χέρι προς τα πίσω, χτυπώντας με ένα ισχυρό χτύπημα. Όμως, πριν συνδεθεί, πάγωσε, με το χέρι στον αέρα. Τα μάτια του γούρλωσαν, σαν υπνωτισμένο κοτόπουλο.

POP.

POP.

Τα φώτα μεταμορφώθηκαν σε δύο πλάσματα. Το καθένα έσπρωξε έναν ώμο, και ο Ε-Ζ έπεσε στο μαξιλάρι, όπου έκλεισε τα μάτια του και κοιμήθηκε.

"Πρέπει να το κάνουμε τώρα, μπιπ-μπιπ", είπε το πρώην κίτρινο φως.

"Ας βεβαιωθούμε ότι κοιμάται, πρώτα, ζουμ-ζουμ", είπε το πρώην πράσινο φως.

"Εντάξει, ας πιάσουμε δουλειά, μπιπ-μπιπ".

"Έχουμε τη συγκατάθεσή του, ζουμ-ζουμ;"

"Είπε ότι θα το κάνει, αλλά δεν θυμάται. Ανησυχώ ότι δεν είναι δεσμευτική η συμφωνία. Μπορεί να είναι μόνο μια μερική, και ξέρεις ποιος μισεί τις μερικές. Για να μην αναφέρω ότι οι ανθρώπινες μερικές θα πιάνονταν ανάμεσα στα μπιπ-μπιπ'.

"Ναι, τον συμπαθώ πάρα πολύ για να τον αφήσω να γίνει ένα betwixt and betweener ζουμ-ζουμ".

"Το να μου αρέσει δεν έχει καμία σχέση με αυτό. Μην ξεχνάς τι συνέβη στον κύκνο. Για να μην αναφέρω - γιατί οι άνθρωποι λένε αυτό που δεν πρέπει να αναφέρουν πριν αναφέρουν αυτό που δεν θέλουν να πουν;" Χωρίς να περιμένει απάντηση. "Θα ήμασταν σε δύσκολη θέση και ο ξέρεις-ποιος θα ήταν πολύ θυμωμένος μπιπ-μπιπ".

"Αλλά ο άνθρωπος έχει ήδη τατουάζ με τα φτερά του. Οι δίκες δεν ξεκινούν, μέχρι να συμφωνήσει το υποκείμενο". Χτύπησε τα δάχτυλά της και ένα βιβλίο εμφανίστηκε. Κούνησε τα φτερά της δημιουργώντας ένα αεράκι που γύριζε τις σελίδες. "Δείτε εδώ, λέει ότι τα φτερά τοποθετούνται μόνο ΜΕΤΑ την έγκριση του υποκειμένου. Οπότε, όταν είπε ναι, αυτό πρέπει να σφράγισε τη συμφωνία ζουμ-ζουμ". Σήκωσε τα χέρια της και το βιβλίο πέταξε προς τα πάνω, σαν να επρόκειτο να χτυπήσει στο ταβάνι, αλλά αντ' αυτού εξαφανίστηκε μέσα από αυτό.

Πέταξαν, ένα προσγειώθηκε στον ώμο του E-Z και ένα στο κεφάλι του.

"Δεν το έκανα εγώ", είπε, χωρίς να ανοίξει τα μάτια του.

"Κοιμήσου κι άλλο, ζουμ-ζουμ", είπε αγγίζοντας τα μάτια του.

"Σσσς, μπιπ-μπιπ".

"Μαμά, γύρνα πίσω. Σε παρακαλώ, γύρνα πίσω!"

"Είναι πολύ ανήσυχος, ζουμ-ζουμ".

"Ονειρεύεται, μπιπ-μπιπ."

Ο E-Z άνοιξε το στόμα του και ροχάλιζε σαν μωρό ελέφαντας. Το αεράκι τους κρατούσε ψηλά - δεν χρειαζόταν να χτυπήσουν τα φτερά τους. Χασκογελούσαν, μέχρι που έκλεισε το στόμα του. Στέλνοντάς τους σε ελεύθερη πτώση. Χτυπώντας μανιωδώς τα φτερά τους, ανέκαμψαν γρήγορα.

"Ωχ όχι, τρίζει τα δόντια του, μπιπ-μπιπ".

"Οι άνθρωποι έχουν παράξενες συνήθειες, ζουμ-ζουμ."

"Αυτό το ανθρώπινο παιδί έχει περάσει αρκετά. Χορηγώντας αυτά τα δικαιώματα, θα νιώσει λιγότερο πόνο, μπιπ-μπιπ."

Το πρώτο πλάσμα πέταξε πάνω στο στήθος του E-Z και προσγειώθηκε, με το πηγούνι του μπροστά και τα χέρια στους γοφούς του. Το πλάσμα γύρισε μια φορά, δεξιόστροφα. Περιστρέφοντας πιο γρήγορα, από το φτερούγισμα των φτερών του αναδύθηκε ένα τραγούδι. Το τραγούδι ήταν ένα χαμηλό βογγητό. Ένα θλιβερό τραγούδι από το παρελθόν, σε γιορτή για μια ζωή που δεν υπήρχε πια. Το πλάσμα έγειρε προς τα πίσω, ακουμπώντας το κεφάλι στο στήθος του E-Z. Η περιστροφή σταμάτησε, αλλά το τραγούδι συνέχισε να παίζει.

Το δεύτερο πλάσμα συμμετείχε, κάνοντας το ίδιο τελετουργικό, ενώ περιστρεφόταν αριστερόστροφα. Δημιούργησαν ένα νέο τραγούδι, χωρίς τα μπιπ-μπιπ και τα ζουμ-ζουμ. Γιατί όταν τραγουδούσαν, η ονοματοποιία δεν ήταν απαραίτητη. Ενώ στην καθημερινή συζήτηση με τους ανθρώπους ήταν απαραίτητη. Αυτό το τραγούδι επικάλυψε το άλλο και έγινε μια χαρούμενη, υψίφωνη γιορτή. Μια ωδή για τα πράγματα που έρχονται, για μια ζωή που δεν έχει ακόμη ζήσει. Ένα τραγούδι για το μέλλον.

Από τις χρυσές κόγχες των ματιών τους έσκασε ένας ψεκασμός διαμαντόσκονης. Γύρισαν σε απόλυτο συγχρονισμό. Η διαμαντόσκονη ψεκάστηκε από τα μάτια τους πάνω στο σώμα του E-Z που κοιμόταν. Η ανταλλαγή συνεχίστηκε, μέχρι που τον κάλυψε με διαμαντόσκονη από την κορυφή ως τα νύχια.

Ο έφηβος συνέχισε να κοιμάται βαθιά. Μέχρι που η διαμαντόσκονη τρύπησε τη σάρκα του - τότε άνοιξε το στόμα του για να ουρλιάξει, αλλά δεν βγήκε κανένας ήχος.

"Ξύπνάει, μπιπ-μπιπ".

"Σηκώστε τον, ζουμ-ζουμ."

Μαζί τον σήκωσαν, καθώς άνοιξε τα μάτια του.

"Κοιμήσου περισσότερο, μπιπ-μπιπ".

"Μην αισθάνεσαι πόνο, ζουμ-ζουμ."

Αγκαλιάζοντας το σώμα του, τα δύο πλάσματα δέχτηκαν τον πόνο του μέσα τους.

"Σήκω πάνω, μπιπ-μπιπ", πρόσταξε.

Και η αναπηρική καρέκλα, σηκώθηκε. Και, τοποθετημένο κάτω από το σώμα του E-Z, περίμενε. Όταν μια σταγόνα αίματος κατέβηκε, η καρέκλα την έπιασε. Την απορρόφησε. Την κατανάλωσε - σαν να ήταν ένα ζωντανό πράγμα.

Καθώς η δύναμη της καρέκλας αυξανόταν, κέρδιζε και αυτή δύναμη. Σύντομα η καρέκλα μπορούσε να κρατήσει τον αφέντη της στον αέρα. Αυτό επέτρεψε στα δύο πλάσματα να ολοκληρώσουν το έργο τους. Το έργο τους να ενώσουν την καρέκλα και τον άνθρωπο. Να τους δέσουν για πάντα με τη δύναμη της διαμαντόσκονης, του αίματος και του πόνου.

Καθώς το σώμα του εφήβου έτρεμε, οι πληγές στο δέρμα του επουλώθηκαν. Η αποστολή ολοκληρώθηκε. Η διαμαντόσκονη ήταν μέρος της ουσίας του. Έτσι, η μουσική σταμάτησε.

"Τελείωσε. Τώρα είναι αλεξίσφαιρος. Και έχει υπερδύναμη, μπιπ-μπιπ."

"Ναι, και είναι καλό, ζουμ-ζουμ."

Η αναπηρική καρέκλα επέστρεψε στο πάτωμα και ο έφηβος στο κρεβάτι του.

"Δεν θα έχει καμία ανάμνηση από αυτό, αλλά τα πραγματικά του φτερά θα αρχίσουν να λειτουργούν πολύ σύντομα μπιπ-μπιπ".

"Τι γίνεται με τις άλλες παρενέργειες; Πότε θα αρχίσουν, και θα είναι αισθητές ζουμ-ζουμ;"

"Αυτό δεν το γνωρίζω. Μπορεί να έχει σωματικές αλλαγές... είναι ένα ρίσκο που αξίζει να πάρουμε για να μειώσουμε τον πόνο, μπιπ-μπιπ".

"Σύμφωνοι, ζουμ-ζουμ."

Εξαντλημένα, τα δύο πλάσματα αγκαλιάστηκαν στο στήθος του Ε-Ζ και αποκοιμήθηκαν. Χωρίς να γνωρίζει ότι ήταν εκεί, όταν τεντώθηκε το πρωί - έπεσαν στο πάτωμα.

"Ουπς, συγγνώμη", είπε στα φτερωτά πλάσματα πριν γυρίσει και ξανακοιμηθεί.

***

"ΕΙΣΑΙ ΞΥΠΝΙΟΣ;" ΡΩΤΗΣΕ Ο Σαμ, πριν ανοίξει λίγο την πόρτα. Ο ανιψιός του ροχάλιζε, αλλά η καρέκλα του δεν ήταν εκεί που την είχε αφήσει όταν τον βοήθησε να πέσει στο κρεβάτι. Ανασήκωσε τους ώμους του και επέστρεψε στο δωμάτιό του, όπου διάβασε μερικά κεφάλαια του Ντέιβιντ Κόπερφιλντ. Ώρες αργότερα επέστρεψε στο δωμάτιο του ανιψιού του.

"Χτύπα, χτύπα".

"Ε, καλημέρα", είπε ο E-Z.

"Μπορώ να περάσω;"

"Βεβαίως."

"Κοιμήθηκες καλά;"

"Έτσι νομίζω." Τεντώθηκε και στη συνέχεια ακούμπησε στο κεφαλάρι.

"Πώς βρέθηκε η καρέκλα σου εδώ; Νόμιζα ότι την είχα παρκάρει στον τοίχο".

Ανασήκωσε τους ώμους.

"Και κοίτα τα μπράτσα - τα έβαψες;"

Έσκυψε, είδε την κόκκινη απόχρωση, και πάλι σήκωσε τους ώμους. "Τι μου συνέβη;"

"Λιποθύμησες. Αυτό που δεν καταλαβαίνω είναι το γιατί. Είπες ότι ένιωθες σαν να είχαν πάρει φωτιά οι ώμοι σου. Έψαξα στο διαδίκτυο χρησιμοποιώντας την περιγραφή σου και εμφανίστηκε ένα ομοιοπαθητικό φάρμακο. Είναι απίστευτο τι μπορείς να βρεις εκεί. Ανακάτεψα λίγο έλαιο λεβάντας με νερό και αλόη σε ένα μπουκάλι ψεκασμού και το έριξα κατευθείαν στο δέρμα σου. Είπαν ότι θα σας δώσει άμεση ανακούφιση. Δεν αστειεύονταν, γιατί χαλάρωσες και σε πήρε ο ύπνος".

"Ευχαριστώ, νιώθω πολύ καλύτερα τώρα". Προσπάθησε να σηκωθεί από το κρεβάτι, αλλά τα zzzzz πετούσαν μέσα στο κεφάλι του σαν να ήταν ο Wile E. Coyote. "Νομίζω ότι θα μείνω στο κρεβάτι για λίγο ακόμα".

"Καλή ιδέα. Να σου φέρω κάτι;"

"Λίγο τοστ; Με μαρμελάδα φράουλα;"

"Βέβαια μικρέ." Έφυγε από το δωμάτιο, λέγοντας ότι θα επιστρέψει σύντομα. Όταν επέστρεψε με το φαγητό σε ένα δίσκο, ο ανιψιός του προσπάθησε να φάει, αλλά δεν μπορούσε να κρατήσει τίποτα.

"Ίσως λίγο νερό".

Ο Σαμ έφερε ένα μπουκάλι, από το οποίο ο E-Z προσπάθησε να πιει, ακόμα και αυτό δεν μπορούσε να το κρατήσει κάτω.

"Νομίζω ότι θα συνεχίσω να ξεκουράζομαι". Τα μάτια του παρέμειναν ανοιχτά, κοιτάζοντας μπροστά του το τίποτα. "Τι ώρα είναι;"

"Είναι πέντε το πρωί και σήμερα είναι Σάββατο. Είσαι εκτός λειτουργίας εδώ και δώδεκα ώρες. Με τρόμαξες".

Η σύνδεση, η λεβάντα και στα δύο μέρη, φάνηκε παράξενη στον E-Z. Είχε βιώσει μια διασταύρωση στην πραγματική ζωή; Ήταν πάρα πολύ μεγάλη σύμπτωση, αυτό αν το σιλό υπήρχε πραγματικά. Ή μήπως ήταν όνειρο; Περισσότερο μοιάζει με εφιάλτη. Αλλά τα πόδια του λειτουργούσαν μέσα σε αυτό το μεταλλικό δοχείο. Θα πήγαινε πίσω στο λεπτό - θα έπαιρνε οποιοδήποτε ρίσκο - για να ξαναχρησιμοποιήσει τα πόδια του.

"E-Z;"

"Ε, τι; Εγώ. Ειλικρινά, νομίζω ότι θα ήθελα να κλείσω τα μάτια μου και να ξεκουραστώ λίγο ακομα".

Ο Σαμ έφυγε από το δωμάτιο, κλείνοντας την πόρτα πίσω του.

Ο E-Z περιφερόταν μέσα και έξω από τις αισθήσεις του, ενώ το ατύχημα έπαιζε σε επανάληψη. Φορώντας λευκά φτερά, η Stevie Nicks παρείχε το συνοδευτικό soundtrack. Ενώ στο βάθος δύο φώτα - ένα πράσινο και ένα κίτρινο - αναπηδούσαν πάνω-κάτω.

ΓΙΑ ΤΙΣ ΕΠΌΜΕΝΕΣ ΗΜΈΡΕΣ, προσπάθησε να ενώσει τα κομμάτια στο μυαλό του κάνοντας έναν κατάλογο με τα κοινά σημεία:

Λευκά φτερά - λευκά φτερά με τατουάζ στους ώμους του. Η Stevie Nicks είχε λευκά φτερά στο όνειρό του.

Λεβάντα - ο θείος Σαμ χρησιμοποιούσε λεβάντα και αλόη για να απαλύνει τα εγκαύματα. Στο σιλό, η λεβάντα ψέκασε τον αέρα για να τον ηρεμήσει.

Κίτρινα και πράσινα φώτα. Τα είδε μετά το ατύχημα και στο δωμάτιό του.

Αναπηρικό καροτσάκι - είχε πετάξει για να μπορέσει να σώσει το κοριτσάκι. Όταν ήταν catcher, ο πισινός του είχε αφήσει την καρέκλα για να μπορέσει να πιάσει την μπάλα.

Τα μπράτσα - ήταν τώρα κόκκινα. Δεν υπάρχουν παρόμοια περιστατικά. Καμία εξήγηση.

Αίσθηση καψίματος στους ώμους/εμφάνιση τατουάζ στους ώμους. Καμία εξήγηση.

Δεν πίστευε πια στο θεό, όχι μετά το ατύχημα. Κανένας θεός δεν θα άφηνε ένα δέντρο να συνθλίψει τους γονείς του. Ήταν καλοί άνθρωποι, δεν έκαναν ποτέ κακό σε κανέναν. Το τι συνέβη στα πόδια του ήταν εκτός θέματος. Οποιοσδήποτε θεός άξιζε κάτι, θα το είχε σταματήσει πριν συμβεί.

Εκτός κι αν υπήρχε θεός, είχε βγει για φαγητό. Ναι, σωστά.

Αλλαγές συνέβαιναν στο σώμα του και ήθελε απαντήσεις. Βαθιά μέσα του ήξερε ότι ο μόνος τρόπος για να τις πάρει ήταν να επιστρέψει στο καταραμένο σιλό - αν υπήρχε.

ΚΕΦΑΛΑΙΟ 6

Τ ο επόμενο πρωί ο E-Z αιωρούνταν στον αέρα πάνω από το κρεβάτι του, αφού τα φτερά του είχαν φυτρώσει. Καθ' οδόν για να δει τα νέα του εξαρτήματα στον καθρέφτη της ντουλάπας, παραλίγο να πέσει στον τοίχο.

"Όλα καλά εκεί μέσα;" φώναξε ο Σαμ από το διπλανό του δωμάτιο.

"Ναι", είπε, πετώντας στο πλάι, καθώς θαύμαζε τη νέα του δύναμη πτήσης. Τα φτερωτά φτερά τον γοήτευαν. Ειδικά ο τρόπος με τον οποίο τον έσπρωχναν προς τα εμπρός, σαν να ήταν ένα με το σώμα του. Νιώθοντας περισσότερο πουλί παρά άγγελος, προσπάθησε να θυμηθεί τι είχε μάθει στο σχολείο για την ορνιθολογία. Ήξερε ότι τα περισσότερα πουλιά είχαν πρωταρχικά φτερά, ενδεχομένως και δέκα. Χωρίς τα πρωτεύοντα φτερά, δεν μπορούσαν να πετάξουν. Εκείνος είχε περισσότερα από δέκα πρωτεύοντα φτερά στα φτερά του, και περισσότερα δευτερεύοντα επίσης. Δοκίμασε να στρίψει αριστερά, μετά δεξιά, αξιολογώντας την ευελιξία του. Νιώθοντας αβαρής, πετούσε γύρω από το δωμάτιό του. Αιωρήθηκε πάνω από την αναπηρική καρέκλα - την οποία δεν χρειαζόταν πλέον. Με αυτά τα φτερά θα μπορούσε να πετάξει σε όλο τον κόσμο. Τοποθετώντας τα χέρια του στους γοφούς του, σαν τον Σούπερμαν, έδειξε προς την κατεύθυνση της πόρτας. Έφτασε εκεί όταν ο Σαμ την άνοιξε.

"Με κατατρόμαξες!" είπε ο Σαμ, σχεδόν πετώντας από το δέρμα του.

Αιφνιδιασμένος, ο έφηβος προσπάθησε να διατηρήσει τον έλεγχο της κατάστασης. Άλλαξε κατεύθυνση, με σκοπό να πάει στο κρεβάτι. Η μετάβαση όμως, δεν ήταν τόσο εύκολη όσο ήλπιζε, και έπεσε σε ελεύθερη πτώση.

Ο Σαμ έτρεξε για το αναπηρικό καροτσάκι, μετακινώντας το μπρος-πίσω για να το κρατήσει κάτω από τον ανιψιό του.

Ο E-Z συνήλθε και ανέβηκε ξανά.

"Έλα εδώ κάτω, τώρα αμέσως!" φώναξε ο Σαμ, σηκώνοντας τις γροθιές του στον αέρα.

Πέταξε προς το κρεβάτι και προσγειώθηκε με ασφάλεια. Τα φτερά του έκλεισαν σαν ακορντεόν χωρίς μουσική. "Είχε πολύ πλάκα. Ανυπομονώ να πετάξω στο σχολείο".

Ο Σαμ έπεσε στην καρέκλα του ανιψιού του. "Τι ήταν όλα αυτά; Και πιστεύεις στ' αλήθεια ότι μπορείς να πετάξεις με αυτά τα πράγματα στο σχολείο; Θα γινόσουν περίγελος".

"Θα το συνήθιζαν και αντί να με φωνάζουν "tree boy" - θα μπορούσαν να με φωνάζουν fly boy. Ναι, μου αρέσει αυτό".

"Απ' ό,τι είδα, ήταν μια αδέξια προσπάθεια. Και το fly boy ακούγεται γελοίο."

"Ήταν η πρώτη μου προσπάθεια. Θα το μάθω."

Ο Σαμ κούνησε το κεφάλι του, καθώς η περιέργεια τον κυρίευσε και ξεπέρασε τα συναισθήματά του για να φύγει.

"Μπορώ να ρίξω μια πιο προσεκτική ματιά; Εννοώ χωρίς να απογειωθείς;" ρώτησε όρθιος καθώς ο E-Z έστρεφε το σώμα του προς το μέρος του. "Έφυγαν. Εντελώς. Εννοώ τα τατουάζ. Έχουν αντικατασταθεί από αληθινά φτερά - και μπορείς να πετάξεις. Ωχ, αγόρι μου!" Κάθισε κάτω πριν πέσει.

"Ξύπνησα, βγήκαν τα φτερά και το επόμενο πράγμα που θυμάμαι είναι ότι πετούσα".

"Είναι μαγεία. Πρέπει να είναι. Ή ίσως ονειρευόμαστε, εσύ είσαι στο όνειρό μου ή εγώ στο δικό σου και σύντομα θα ξυπνήσουμε και...". Ο Σαμ προσπαθούσε να διατηρήσει την ψυχραιμία του για χάρη του ανιψιού του, αλλά μέσα του η καρδιά του χτυπούσε δυνατά.

"Δεν είναι όνειρο".

"Πώς πετάχτηκαν έξω; Έπρεπε να πεις κάτι; Εννοώ, υπάρχουν μαγικές λέξεις που πρέπει να πεις;"

"Δεν θυμάμαι να έχω πει τίποτα. Υποθέτω όμως ότι θα μπορούσα να το δοκιμάσω". Το σκέφτηκε για μερικά δευτερόλεπτα, παίρνοντας μια πόζα σαν τον Στοχαστή του Ροντέν. "Περίμενε ένα λεπτό, άσε με να δοκιμάσω κάτι". Χτύπησε τον αέρα με μια κίνηση χωρίς ραβδί: "Autem!"

"Πότε έμαθες Λατινικά;"

"Υπάρχει μια δωρεάν εφαρμογή στο τηλέφωνό μου".

"Κι εγώ, μαθαίνω γαλλικά. Δοκίμασε το en haut".

"En haut!" Ακόμα τίποτα. "Lift me up! Qui exaltas me!" Ενοχλημένος σταύρωσε τα χέρια του. "Μάλλον είναι καλό που μπήκες μέσα και με είδες να πετάω, αλλιώς δεν θα με πίστευες!" Αναρωτήθηκε τι έκαναν ο Πι Τζέι και ο Άρντεν - είχε μέρες να τους δει. Το επόμενο πράγμα που ήξερε ήταν ότι τα φτερά του άνοιξαν και αιωρούνταν πάνω από το κρεβάτι του.

"Ρο-ρο", είπε ο Σαμ, καθώς τα φτερά του αναδιπλώθηκαν και ο E-Z έπεσε στο πάτωμα.

"Αυτή θα ήταν μια ωραία στιγμή για να αρπάξεις την καρέκλα μου".

Ο Σαμ χαμογέλασε. "Εύκολο να το λες παρά να το κάνεις. Συγγνώμη. Είσαι καλά;"

"Δεν έχω χτυπήσει. Εννοώ σωματικά, αλλά ψυχικά, ποιος ξέρει;" Γέλασε. "Σε πειράζει να με βοηθήσεις να ανέβω στην καρέκλα μου;"

Ο Σαμ τον σήκωσε και τον εναπόθεσε με ασφάλεια στην καρέκλα. Όταν έγειρε προς τα πίσω, τα φτερά αντί να αποσυρθούν εντελώς, ξαναβγήκαν με όλη τους τη δύναμη. Ο E-Z ανέβηκε και πετούσε σαν την Τίνκερμπελ.

"Ώστε έτσι είναι, ε;" είπε ο Σαμ.

"Πρέπει να το συνηθίσω -δεν είμαι σίγουρος γιατί- αλλά...".

"Λοιπόν, όταν είσαι έτοιμος, έλα κάτω και θα πάμε για πρωινό. Θα φέρω το λάπτοπ μου και μπορούμε να κάνουμε κάποια έρευνα".

"Αυτή είναι μια έξυπνη ιδέα. Θα μπορούσαμε να πάμε στο Ann's Cafe. Και εγώ θα ερχόμουν κάτω - αν μπορούσα". Τα φτερά αποσύρθηκαν όταν ο E-Z βρέθηκε ακριβώς πάνω από την αναπηρική του καρέκλα. "Αυτέ είναι που αποκαλώ εξυπηρέτηση", είπε καθώς έπεσε απαλά στην καρέκλα.

Κουβέντιασαν, ενώ εκείνος ντυνόταν. Στη συνέχεια ο E-Z πήγε στο μπάνιο, ενώ ο Σαμ ετοιμαζόταν.

Καθώς έβγαιναν από το σπίτι και κατευθύνονταν προς το καφέ της Άνν, ο E-Z είχε δύο σκέψεις. Πρώτον, ότι του είχε λείψει να πάει εκεί και δεύτερον, "Έχω να πάω εκεί πάρα πολύ καιρό. Από τότε που..."

"Το ξέρω, μικρέ. Είσαι σίγουρος ότι δεν είναι πολύ νωρίς;"

Το πρωινό στο Ann's Café αποτελούσε παράδοση για την οικογένειά του. Εκτός του ότι άνοιγε νωρίς στις 6 το πρωί, ήταν σε κοντινή απόσταση με τα πόδια. Μέσα υπήρχαν ιδιωτικοί θάλαμοι, στολισμένοι με ψεύτικο δέρμα και κόκκινα καρό τραπεζομάντιλα. Ο μπαμπάς του έλεγε πάντα ότι το μέρος είχε ένα "εξωπραγματικό" θέμα. Η μουσική της δεκαετίας του '60 έπαιζε στα τζουκ-μποξ - τα είχαν στήσει, ώστε ο κόσμος να μην χρειάζεται να πληρώσει. Και αφίσες της Μέριλιν Μονρόε, του Τζέιμς Ντιν και του Μάρλον Μπράντο γέμιζαν τους τοίχους. Το μενού ήταν τεράστιο με τα πάντα, από σάντουιτς Club μέχρι Cheeseburgers και Fondues. Αλλά τα προσωπικά του αγαπημένα ήταν τα πολύ παχιά μιλκσέικ και τα Apple Pancakes.

Μόλις τους είδε, η ιδιοκτήτρια Ann ήρθε αμέσως. "Μου έλειψες". Τον αγκάλιασε.

"Αυτός είναι ο θείος μου ο Σαμ, η Άνν". Έδωσαν τα χέρια. "Ευχαριστώ για την κάρτα και τα λουλούδια παρεμπιπτόντως, ήταν πολύ ευγενικό".

Τα μάτια της γέμισαν δάκρυα. "Τώρα, έλα εδώ. Έχω το τέλειο τραπέζι για σένα".

Ήταν σε μια ήσυχη γωνιά, οπότε δεν χρειαζόταν να ανησυχεί μήπως η καρέκλα του ενοχλήσει το προσωπικό της κουζίνας ή τους θαμώνες.

"Θα ετοιμάσω αμέσως το συνηθισμένο σας πιάτο. Ξέρεις τι θα ήθελες, Σαμ, ή να επιστρέψω;"

"Τι θα πάρεις;"

"Τηγανίτες μήλου α λα mode. Είναι οι καλύτερες στον πλανήτη και η Ανν φέρνει πάντα έξτρα σιρόπι και κανέλα".

"Ακούγεται ωραίο, αλλά νομίζω ότι θα προτιμήσω βαρετό μπέικον και αυγά, με μανιτάρια".

"Έγινε", είπε η Ανν. "Και εσύ θα πάρεις ένα παχύρρευστο μιλκσέικ με σοκολάτα;" Εκείνος έγνεψε. "Καφέ για σένα Σαμ; "

"Μαύρο", απάντησε εκείνος. "Και ευχαριστώ που με καλωσόρισες τόσο πολύ".

"Κάθε θείος του E-Z είναι ευπρόσδεκτος εδώ".

Αφού η Ανν πήγε να φέρει τα ποτά, ξεστόμισε: "Θείε Σαμ, νομίζω ότι μεταμορφώνομαι σε άγγελο".

"Θα πρέπει να πεθάνεις πρώτα", είπε, καθώς η Ανν έβαλε τα ποτά στο τραπέζι και επέστρεψε προς την κουζίνα.

"Ίσως να πέθανα, στο αυτοκινητιστικό ατύχημα. Για λίγα λεπτά. Ποιος ξέρει πόσος χρόνος χρειάζεται για να γίνεις άγγελος; Στις ταινίες, αν φτάσεις στις Περλικές Πύλες, ο μεγάλος άνθρωπος μπορεί να γυρίσει τα πράγματα και να σε στείλει πάλι εδώ κάτω. Αυτό αν πιστεύεις σε τέτοια πράγματα -που εγώ δεν πιστεύω".

"Ούτε κι εγώ. Δεν υπάρχουν άγγελοι. Ούτε διάβολοι. Εκτός από το εσωτερικό του καθενός από εμάς. Εννοώ ότι όλοι έχουμε καλό και όλοι έχουμε κακό μέσα μας. Αυτό είναι που μας κάνει ανθρώπους. Όσο για τους ετοιμοθάνατους, θα μου το έλεγαν αν έπρεπε να σε επαναφέρουν. Δεν είπαν τίποτα τέτοιο".

"Τότε, πώς εξηγείται η ξαφνική εμφάνιση των τατουάζ, και τώρα έχουν μετατραπεί σε αληθινά φτερά; Δεν τα είχα χθες. Οπότε, τι συνέβη μεταξύ χθες και σήμερα; Τίποτα που να δικαιολογεί την ανάπτυξη νέων εξαρτημάτων".

"Όχι απ' ό,τι μπορείς να σκεφτείς", είπε ο Σαμ. Γέλασε.

Ο E-Z μαχαίρωσε μια τηγανίτα και την έχωσε στο στόμα του, αφήνοντας το σιρόπι να τρέξει στο πηγούνι του. Η Ανν έκανε τον εαυτό της να εξαφανιστεί.

"Λοιπόν, σίγουρα δεν φαίνεσαι πολύ αγγελικά αυτή τη στιγμή", είπε ο Σαμ, παίρνοντας μια πιρουνιά ομελέτα. "Μμ, αυτά είναι πολύ ωραία". Μετά από μερικές ακόμα μπουκιές, έβαλε το χέρι του στον χαρτοφύλακά του και έβγαλε το λάπτοπ του. Το άνοιξε και πληκτρολόγησε "define angel". Γύρισε την οθόνη ώστε να μπορούν να διαβάσουν τις πληροφορίες ενώ έτρωγαν.

"Ένας αγγελιοφόρος, ειδικά του θεού", διάβασε ο Σαμ, "ένα άτομο που εκτελεί μια αποστολή του θεού ή ενεργεί σαν να έχει σταλεί από τον θεό".

"Ενεργεί σαν να είναι", επανέλαβε ο E-Z, καθώς έβαζε κι άλλες τηγανίτες στο στόμα του.

Ο Σαμ διάβασε: "Άτυπο πρόσωπο, ιδίως γυναίκα, που είναι ευγενικό, αγνό ή όμορφο. Είσαι αρκετά όμορφη, με τα ξανθά σου μαλλιά και τα γαλάζια σου μάτια".

"Σκάσε".

"Μια συμβατική αναπαράσταση", έκανε μια παύση. " οποιουδήποτε από αυτά τα όντα που απεικονίζεται με ανθρώπινη μορφή και φτερά". Ο Σαμ ήπιε άλλη μια γουλιά καφέ, εγκαίρως για να ξαναγεμίσει η Ανν το φλιτζάνι του.

"Θα πάθετε δυσπεψία, αν διαβάζετε και τρώτε ταυτόχρονα".

Ο E-Z γέλασε.

Ο Σαμ είπε: "Όχι, είμαι στην πληροφορική, οπότε είμαι αρκετά καλός στο multitasking".

Η Ανν χασκογέλασε και απομακρύνθηκε.

"Τι εννοούν με το "αυτά τα όντα";" ρώτησε ο E-Z.

"Λέει ότι στη μεσαιωνική αγγελιολογία, οι άγγελοι χωρίζονταν σε τάξεις. Εννέα τάξεις: Σεραφείμ, Χερουβείμ, θρόνοι, κυριαρχίες (γνωστές και ως κυριαρχίες)", έκανε μια παύση, ήπιε μια γουλιά νερό. Έπειτα συνέχισε: "Αρετές, ηγεμονίες (επίσης γνωστές ως πριγκιπάτα), αρχάγγελοι και άγγελοι".

"Ουάου! Προσπαθήστε να τα πείτε αυτά δέκα φορές γρήγορα". Χαμογέλασε. "Δεν είχα ιδέα ότι υπήρχαν τόσα πολλά είδη αγγέλων".

"Ούτε κι εγώ. Αυτό το φαγητό είναι τόσο καλό, που αναρωτιέμαι συνέχεια αν εσύ κι εγώ ονειρευόμαστε".

"Εννοείς ότι εύχεσαι να ονειρευόμασταν - και τα φτερά μου να εξαφανίζονταν;"

"Θα μπορούσαν να φύγουν τόσο γρήγορα όσο ήρθαν." Πλησίασε τον φορητό υπολογιστή και πληκτρολόγησε "Ο άνθρωπος αποκτά φτερά αγγέλου". Ο E-Z χλεύασε, αλλά έσκυψε πιο κοντά για να δει τι εμφανίστηκε. Ο Σαμ έκανε κλικ σε ένα επιστημονικό άρθρο.

"Όπως είπα, δεν υπάρχουν στοιχεία για φτερά αγγέλου στα αρχεία. Εγώ δεν το πίστευα. Νομίζω ότι εκείνο το περιστατικό, ξέρεις, όταν έσωσα το κοριτσάκι - είχε κάποια σχέση με την εμφάνισή τους. Ήταν το έναυσμα, γιατί το κάψιμο άρχισε αμέσως μόλις γύρισα σπίτι και μετά, λοιπόν, τα υπόλοιπα τα ξέρετε".

"Πώς τα πάτε εσείς οι δύο εδώ;" ρώτησε η Ανν.

"Σας παρήγγειλα άλλες δύο τηγανίτες, E-Z, ως συνήθως. Εκτός κι αν μπορείς να φας περισσότερα;"

"Τέλεια."

"Κι εσύ, Σαμ;"

"Απλώς ένα γέμισμα", είπε, προσφέροντας την άδεια κούπα του, την οποία εκείνη πήρε και επέστρεψε με γεμάτη μέχρι το χείλος. Ένα κουδούνι χτύπησε στην κουζίνα και εκείνη πήγε να πάρει τις τηγανίτες.

Ο Ε-Ζ έριξε πάνω τους σιρόπι σφενδάμου, ακολουθούμενο από μια κουταλιά βούτυρο. "Είσαι η καλύτερη", είπε στην Ανν. Εκείνη χαμογέλασε και τους άφησε να τελειώσουν το γεύμα τους.

Ο θείος Σαμ παρακολουθούσε τον ανιψιό του με προσοχή. Μακάρι να είχε παραγγείλει τις τηγανίτες μήλου, αλλά ήταν ήδη χορτάτος.

"Τι;"

"Δεν ξέρω, είναι σαν όταν δοκιμάζεις το φαγητό, το πρόσωπό σου φωτίζεται σαν άγγελος στο χριστουγεννιάτικο δέντρο".

Ο Ε-Ζ άφησε κάτω το πιρούνι του. "Πολύ αστείο. Είσαι κανονικός κωμικός".

Όταν τελείωσαν το φαγητό, ο Σαμ ρώτησε: "Αφού διάβασες για τους αγγέλους, άλλαξες γνώμη; Θέλω να πω, πιστεύεις ακόμα ότι θα μεταμορφωθείς σε έναν. Και αν ναι, τι πρόκειται να κάνεις γι' αυτό;"

"Τι εννοείς θα κάνω; Έχω φτερά, μπορώ κάλλιστα να τα χρησιμοποιήσω".

"Όπως το βλέπω εγώ, αν δεν τα χρησιμοποιήσεις, αν αρνηθείς την ίδια τους την ύπαρξη - τότε θα φύγουν".

Ο Ε-Ζ κούνησε το κεφάλι του. "Δεν είναι επιλογή. Είδες τι συνέβη. Βγήκαν, χωρίς να κάνω τίποτα και σου είπα, όταν ξύπνησα το πρωί πετούσα πάνω από το κρεβάτι μου. Πετούσα, γαμώτο μου".

"Ε-Ζ, σκέφτομαι το μέλλον. Ίσως πρέπει να μιλήσεις σε κάποιον, πρέπει να μιλήσουμε σε κάποιον γι' αυτό".

"Το ατύχημα συνέβη πριν από ένα χρόνο, ο σύμβουλος είπε ότι είμαι καλά. Εξάλλου, όλα αυτά είναι καινούργια".

"Θα μπορούσε να καθυστερήσει. Κάτι μπορεί να το προκάλεσε".

"Ας δούμε τα γεγονότα. Πρώτον, είχα τατουάζ, ενώ δεν έκανα τατουάζ. Νούμερο δύο, η καρέκλα μου ανασηκώθηκε από το έδαφος και έσωσε ένα κοριτσάκι - επιπλέον, ανασηκώθηκα από τη θέση μου για να πιάσω μια μπάλα σε έναν αγώνα. Το αρνιόμουν αυτό μέχρι πρόσφατα... Νούμερο τρία, τα τατουάζ έκαιγαν σαν κόλαση. Νούμερο τέσσερα, εμφανίστηκαν αληθινά φτερά. Νούμερο πέντε, μπορώ να πετάξω. Σου θυμίζει τίποτα από αυτά κάτι; Εννοώ σε άλλες περιπτώσεις".

"Αυτό είναι που δεν καταλαβαίνω. Πώς θα μπορούσε να συμβεί αυτό, αλλά το μυαλό είναι ένας εξαιρετικά ισχυρός υπολογιστής. Είναι αυτό που μας διαχωρίζει από το ζωικό βασίλειο και ο λόγος που ο άνθρωπος επιβίωσε για τόσο πολύ καιρό. Έχω ακούσει ιστορίες, όπου ένα άτομο βρισκόταν σε ακραίο κίνδυνο και έφτασε βοήθεια. Ή, όπου ένα άτομο είχε παγιδευτεί κάτω από ένα όχημα - και ένας περαστικός κατάφερε να σηκώσει το αυτοκίνητο για να του σώσει τη ζωή".

"Έχω διαβάσει γι' αυτό- ονομάζεται υστερική δύναμη - αλλά δεν έχω ακούσει ποτέ για μια περίπτωση όπου τα φτερά μεγάλωσαν".

"Ίσως τα φτερά, εμφανίστηκαν, για να σε σώσουν".

"Από τι; Από τον πολύ ύπνο;" γέλασε. "Θα ήταν ωραία στο ατύχημα. Θα μπορούσα να πετάξω τη μαμά και τον μπαμπά για να φέρουν βοήθεια αντί να περιμένω εκεί με ένα ματωμένο κορμό πάνω μου. Να με κρατάει κάτω. Δεν είναι θαύμα. Εγώ, δεν ξέρω τι είναι θείε Σαμ, το μόνο που ξέρω είναι ότι είναι".

"Κουβεντιάζουμε. Αξιολογούμε. Ανταλλάσσουμε ιδέες. Προσπαθούμε να βρούμε απαντήσεις."

"Θα ήταν ωραίο να έχουμε απαντήσεις, αλλά... ποιος θα ήταν ένας ειδικός που θα μπορούσαμε να ρωτήσουμε σε αυτή την περίπτωση;"

"Τι θα λέγατε για έναν ιερέα ή έναν παπά;"

Ο E-Z κούνησε το κεφάλι του. Είχε να μπει σε εκκλησία από την κηδεία των γονιών του.

"Τι έχουμε να χάσουμε;"

"Υποθέτω ότι αξίζει μια προσπάθεια, αλλά. Ω, ω."

"Τι είναι;"

"Νιώθω να πιέζει τις ωμοπλάτες μου. Πρέπει να φύγω, και δεν ήρθαμε εδώ με το αυτοκίνητο. Συγγνώμη, πρέπει να βιαστώ. Τα λέμε στο σπίτι". Έφυγε γρήγορα από το καφέ και συνέχισε να πηγαίνει, μέχρι που τα φτερά του ξεπρόβαλαν από την κουκούλα του και σηκώθηκε από το έδαφος. Στο σπίτι συνειδητοποίησε ότι δεν είχε κλειδί, αλλά δεν μπορούσε να παραμείνει στη βεράντα - όχι με τα φτερά έξω. Δοκίμασε λατινικά για να τα κάνει να ξαναμπουν μέσα - αλλά τίποτα δεν έπιασε. Έτσι, πέταξε ψηλά και κατάφερε να μπει μέσα από το παράθυρο της κρεβατοκάμαράς του χωρίς να τον δει κανείς.

"E-Z!" φώναξε ο Σαμ όταν έφτασε στο σπίτι. "E-Z!"

"Είμαι εδώ πάνω."

"Είσαι καλά; Ήρθα εδώ όσο πιο γρήγορα μπορούσα".

"'Ελα μέσα, κάθισε. Κανένα σημάδι ότι έχουν αποσυρθεί - ακόμα."

Βλέποντας το ανοιχτό παράθυρο. "Να υποθέσω ότι ήρθατε με αεροπλάνο εδώ;"

"Ναι, ευτυχώς που ξέχασα να κλειδώσω το παράθυρό μου χθες το βράδυ. Μπορούμε κάλλιστα να συνεχίσουμε τη συζήτησή μας, μέχρι να μπορέσω να βγω ξανά έξω".

"Ξέρω έναν ιερέα. Αν κάποιος μπορεί να βοηθήσει, αυτός μπορεί".

Δύο ώρες αργότερα, με μελωδίες να ακούγονται από το ραδιόφωνο, ήταν καθ' οδόν για να δουν τον ιερέα. Το Take Me to Church του Hozier γέμιζε τους αιθέρες. Σύμπτωση; Δεν το σκέφτηκαν και τραγούδησαν μαζί με τους στίχους με όλη τους τη φωνή. Ευτυχώς με τα παράθυρα ανοιχτά κανείς δεν μπορούσε να τους ακούσει.

Σ ΤΗΝ ΕΚΚΛΗΣΊΑ ΔΕΝ ΥΠΉΡΧΕ πρόσβαση για αναπηρικό αμαξίδιο και υπήρχαν πολλές σκάλες που έπρεπε να ανέβουμε.

"Πήγαινε εσύ κάτω από τη σκιά της μεγάλης βελανιδιάς και εγώ θα πάω να βρω τον πατέρα Χόπερ", πρότεινε ο Σαμ.

"Αυτό είναι το πραγματικό του όνομα;" Ο Ε-Ζ γέλασε.

"Απ' όσο ξέρω. Εσύ μείνε εδώ και θα επιστρέψω αμέσως".

"Θα το κάνω."

Ο έφηβος έβγαλε το τηλέφωνό του. Αν και απολάμβανε τη σκιά που του παρείχε το δέντρο - καθιστούσε αδύνατο να δει την οθόνη του. Επανατοποθέτησε την καρέκλα του, παρατηρώντας ένα ασυνήθιστο βουητό στον αέρα. Έναν θόρυβο, ο οποίος φαινόταν να προέρχεται από το ίδιο το δέντρο.

Κοίταξε ψηλά, προσπαθώντας να διακρίνει αν επρόκειτο για πουλί, όταν ο τόνος ανέβηκε και η ένταση αυξήθηκε. Έκανε σίγαση του τηλεφώνου του. Ο ήχος τελείωσε και ένας νέος ήχος άρχισε. Αυτός ήταν μελωδικός-υπνωτιστικός και έπεσε σε μια ονειρική κατάσταση.

Το κεφάλι του γέρνει προς τα εμπρός, μέχρι που ένας νέος ήχος τον ξύπνησε. Ψίθυροι, που προέρχονταν από πάνω από το κεφάλι του. Φωνές που έβγαιναν από το φύλλωμα του δέντρου. Σταύρωσε τα χέρια του, καθώς ένα ρίγος τον διαπέρασε, κάνοντας τα φτερά του να ελευθερωθούν. Πριν το καταλάβει, η καρέκλα του σηκώθηκε από το έδαφος. Έσκυψε τα κλαδιά καθώς ανέβαινε στην καρδιά της τεράστιας βελανιδιάς.

"Αφήστε με κάτω!" διέταξε.

Συνέχισε να σηκώνεται. Καθώς τα άκρα του συνδέονταν με το δέντρο, αίμα έσταζε στους πήχεις και στο κεφάλι του.

"Σταμάτα! Ηλίθιε..."

"Αυτό δεν είναι πολύ ωραίο, μπιπ-μπιπ", είπε μια μικροσκοπική υψηλή φωνή.

"Νόμιζα ότι είπες ότι ήταν υπέροχος όταν ήταν ξύπνιος ζουμ-ζουμ", είπε μια δεύτερη φωνή.

"Ουάου!" είπε ο E-Z, προσπαθώντας να συνέλθει και να αποφύγει να τρελαθεί εντελώς. Πήρε μερικές βαθιές ανάσες. Ηρέμησε. "Ποιες, τ. και πού είσαι;"

"Ποιοι είμαστε πράγματι, μπιπ-μπιπ".

Για άλλη μια φορά, τα ίδια φώτα, ένα πράσινο και ένα κίτρινο χόρεψαν μπροστά στα μάτια του.

Από περιέργεια, είπε: "Γεια".

Το κίτρινο φως εξαφανίστηκε.

Μια κραυγή.

Μετά εξαφανίστηκε το πράσινο.

"Τι στο...; Εσείς οι δύο, ό,τι κι αν είστε, κόψτε το αυτό. Μοι χρωστάτε μια εξήγηση. Ξέρω ότι με παρακολουθούσατε. Βγείτε έξω και αντιμετωπίστε με!"

POP.

Ένα μικροσκοπικό πράσινο πράγμα που έμοιαζε με άγγελ προσγειώθηκε στη μύτη του. Μια παράξενα αντιπαθητική, σχεδόν σαν μπιφτέκι μυρωδιά αναδύθηκε προς το μέρος του. Κάλυψε τη μύτη του.

"Καλημέρα, E-Z, μπιπ-μπιπ", είπε το πράγμα με μια υπόκλιση.

Όταν είπε το όνομά του, έχασε τον έλεγχο των φτερών του. Ταλαιπωρήθηκε και ταλαντεύτηκε στον αέρα σαν πουλί που μαθαίνει να πετάει. Θέλησε τα φτερά του να ξαναβγούν, αλλά εκείνα τον αγνόησαν. Κρατήθηκε από τα μπράτσα της καρέκλας του καθώς έπεφτε.

POP!

Τώρα ήταν δύο. Ο καθένας έπιασε ένα από τα αυτιά του και κατέβασε αυτόν και την καρέκλα του με ασφάλεια στο έδαφος.

"Άουτς", είπε ο E-Z τρίβοντας τα αυτιά του καθώς ο ιερέας και ο θείος του έρχονταν από τη γωνία. "Ε, ευχαριστώ, νομίζω".

POP.

POP.

Τα δύο πλάσματα εξαφανίστηκαν.

"E-Z, αυτός είναι ο πατέρας Μπράντλεϊ Χόπερ και είναι πρόθυμος να βοηθήσει".

Ο Χόπερ άπλωσε το χέρι του, ο E-Z έκανε το ίδιο. Καθώς η σάρκα τους ενώθηκε, ο έφηβος εξαφανίστηκε.

Ο Χόπερ και ο Σαμ παρέμειναν πλάι-πλάι, με τα μάτια τους παγωμένα. Και οι δύο κοιτούσαν το τίποτα σαν δύο κούκλες σε βιτρίνα καταστήματος.

ΚΕΦΑΛΑΙΟ 7

Τ Α ΠΟΔΙΑ ΤΟΥ E-Z ακούμπησαν στο έδαφος και στην αρχή τυφλώθηκε από το λευκό. Έβαλε το ένα πόδι μπροστά από το άλλο, πρώτα περπατώντας, μετά κάνοντας τρέξιμο επί τόπου, και μετά ξεσπώντας σε πλήρες τρέξιμο. Πέταξε τον εαυτό του στον τοίχο, αναπηδώντας, σαν να βρισκόταν σε κάστρο που πηδούσε.

POP

POP

Δεν ήταν πια μόνος του. Μπροστά του υπήρχαν δύο πολυπτέρυγα πράγματα, μέσα σε λουλούδια. Το ένα ήταν πράσινο, το άλλο κίτρινο. Καθώς πλησίαζε, τα φτερά τους, γύριζαν σαν καλειδοσκόπιο γύρω από χρυσά μάτια.

Άγγιξε πρώτα τα πέταλα-φτερά του πράσινου λουλουδιού. Δεν είχε ξαναδεί ποτέ ένα πλήρως πράσινο λουλούδι, πόσο μάλλον ένα με μάτια. Τα μάτια που αναγνώρισε από την προηγούμενη συνάντησή τους. Τα φτερά γαργάλησαν το δάχτυλό του και το πράσινο λουλούδι γέλασε. Απέφυγε να πλησιάσει πολύ κοντά με τη μύτη του, περιμένοντας μια μυρωδιά τυριού να ανεμίζει προς τα εμπρός - αλλά δεν το έκανε.

Το δεύτερο λουλούδι, κίτρινο, είχε περισσότερα πέταλα-φτερά από το άλλο. Τα πέταλα ανταποκρίνονταν στο άγγιγμά του, όπως τα κοράλλια που κινούνται στον ωκεανό. Τα χρυσά μάτια σε αυτό το λουλούδι, είχαν καθορισμένες βλεφαρίδες. Έσκυψε για να το δει από κοντά.

Καθώς συνέχισε να παρατηρεί τα δύο, ένα PFFT γέμισε τον αέρα. Μαζί του βγήκε μια ισχυρή και πιο αρρωστημένα γλυκιά μυρωδιά που τον έκανε να αισθανθεί ναυτία. Οπισθοχώρησε, καλύπτοντας τη μύτη του και σκουπίζοντας το τσούξιμο από τα μάτια του.

Το κίτρινο λουλούδι μίλησε. "Το όνομά μου είναι Ρέικι και σε φέραμε εδώ μπιπ-μπιπ".

"Πού ακριβώς είναι εδώ; Και γιατί δουλεύουν τα πόδια μου;"

"Δεν έχει σημασία πού, E-Z Ντίκενς, ούτε γιατί είσαι όπως είσαι μπιπ-μπιπ".

Διέσχισε το δωμάτιο και σήκωσε το κίτρινο λουλούδι με το δεξί του χέρι και το πράσινο με το αριστερό. ΠΟΥΣΗ! Αυτή τη φορά τον χτύπησε μια πικάντικη ομίχλη και άρχισε να φτερνίζεται και συνέχισε να φτερνίζεται.

"Σας παρακαλώ, αφήστε μας κάτω, πριν μας ρίξετε, μπιπ-μπιπ".

"Υπάρχει ένα κουτί χαρτομάντιλα, εκεί πέρα ζουμ-ζουμ".

"Ω, συγγνώμη." Τα άφησε κάτω, πήρε ένα χαρτομάντιλο - αλλά δεν το χρειαζόταν πια. Κράτησε την απόσταση, ακουμπώντας την πλάτη του σε έναν λευκό τοίχο.

"Σας φέραμε εδώ τώρα, μπιπ-μπιπ".

"Είμαι ο Χαντζ, παρεμπιπτόντως, ζουμ-ζουμ".

"Επειδή έπρεπε να το ξέρεις, μπιπ-μπιπ".

"Ότι δεν πρέπει να μιλήσεις στον ιερέα, για τα φτερά σου ζουμ-ζουμ".

"Στην πραγματικότητα, δεν πρέπει να μιλήσεις σε κανέναν για τίποτα, μπιπ-μπιπ."

Ακουμπώντας το χέρι του στον τοίχο, περπάτησε, σκεπτόμενος καθώς το έκανε. "Πρώτα απ' όλα, γιατί λες μπιπ-μπιπ και ζουμ-ζουμ;"

Η Ρέικι και ο Χαντζ έριξαν τα μάτια τους. "Δεν έχετε ακούσει για την ονοματοποιία;"

"Φυσικά και έχω".

"Τότε θα έπρεπε να ξέρεις, μπιπ-μπιπ".

"Ότι προσθέτει ενθουσιασμό, δράση και ενδιαφέρον, ζουμ-ζουμ".

"Για να διασφαλιστεί ότι ο αναγνώστης ακούει και θυμάται, μπιπ-μπιπ."

"Τι θέλετε να μάθουν, ζουμ-ζουμ."

Γέλασε. "Αυτό ισχύει αν διαβάζεις κάτι, αλλά δεν είναι απαραίτητο σε μια συζήτηση. Θυμάμαι τι λέει ο Ρέικι επειδή το λέει αυτός και θυμάμαι τι λέει η Χαντζ επειδή το λέει εκείνη. Υποθέτω ότι ο ένας από εσάς είναι κορίτσι και ο άλλος αγόρι - είναι σωστό αυτό;"

"Ναι", επιβεβαίωσε η Χαντζ. "Εγώ είμαι κορίτσι. Ουφ, χαίρομαι που δεν χρειάζεται να λέω συνέχεια ζουμ-ζουμ".

"Κι εγώ είμαι αγόρι. Θα μου λείψει να λέω μπιπ-μπιπ".

"Μπορείς να τα λες αν θέλεις, αλλά είναι λίγο ενοχλητικό και κατά τη διάρκεια της συζήτησης η επανάληψη μπορεί να είναι βαρετή".

"Δεν θέλουμε να είμαστε βαρετοί!"

"Αυτό θα αναιρούσε το σκοπό μας, που σας φέραμε εδώ."

"Εντάξει", είπε ο E-Z. "Λοιπόν, τώρα ας επιστρέψουμε σε αυτό που είπες πριν αρχίσουμε να μιλάμε για ένα λογοτεχνικό μέσο". Κούνησαν το κεφάλι τους. "Αν δεν μπορώ να πω σε κανέναν τι μου συμβαίνει, τότε είμαι μόνος μου σε αυτό το πράγμα - ό,τι κι αν είναι. Έσωσα ένα μικρό κορίτσι. Υποθέτω ότι είχε να κάνει κάτι με σένα;"

"Ναι, έχεις δίκιο σε αυτή την υπόθεση μπιπ, ουπς, συγγνώμη".

"Θέλω να μάθω τι είναι αυτό και γιατί μου συμβαίνει;"

"Κλείσε τα μάτια σου", είπε ο Χαντζ.

"Θα το κάνω, αλλά όχι αστεία πράγματα".

Τα λουλούδια χασκογέλασαν.

Τα πόδια του έφυγαν από το έδαφος και προσγειώθηκε σε ένα διαφορετικό δωμάτιο. Σε αυτό το δωμάτιο, όπως και πριν, στην αρχή τυφλώθηκε από το λευκό. Καθώς τα μάτια του εξοικειώθηκαν με το περιβάλλον, πρόσεξε τα βιβλία. Ράφια και ράφια στοιβαγμένα με τόμους ουρανοκατέβατους.

"Μη φοβάσαι", είπε ο Χαντζ.

Δεν φοβήθηκε. Στην πραγματικότητα, ήταν εκστασιασμένος. Γιατί σε αυτό το δωμάτιο, όχι μόνο μπορούσε να χρησιμοποιήσει τα πόδια του, αλλά μπορούσε να νιώσει το αίμα να πάλλεται μέσα τους. Οι αισθήσεις του αυξήθηκαν- η μυρωδιά του παλιού βιβλίου πλανιόταν προς το μέρος του. Μύρισε το γλυκό άρωμα prunus dulcis (γλυκό αμύγδαλο). Σε συνδυασμό με την πλανιφόλια (βανίλια) δημιουργούσε μια τέλεια ανισόρροια. Η καρδιά του χτυπούσε, το αίμα του έτρεχε - ποτέ δεν είχε νιώσει πιο ζωντανός. Ήθελε να μείνει, για πάντα.

Μέσα στα παπούτσια του, η κίνηση κάθε δαχτύλου του τον ευχαριστούσε. Θυμήθηκε ένα παιχνίδι με το οποίο έπαιζε όταν ήταν μικρό παιδί. Έβγαλε τα παπούτσια και τις κάλτσες του και άγγιξε κάθε δάχτυλο του ποδιού λέγοντας το στιχάκι: "Αυτό το γουρουνάκι πήγε στην αγορά".

"'Έχει χάσει το μυαλό του", είπε η Ρέικι, καθώς ο E-Z αναφώνησε: "Γουί!".

"Δώστε του μια στιγμή. Αυτό είναι ένα πολύ καταπληκτικό μέρος".

Ο E-Z φόρεσε πάλι τις κάλτσες του. Γλίστρησε μέσα στο δωμάτιο στα λευκά πατώματα που γυάλιζαν σαν παγωμένο φύλλο. Γέλασε, καθώς εκτοξεύτηκε στον πρώτο και μετά στον δεύτερο τοίχο, αναπήδησε και προσγειώθηκε στο πάτωμα. Δεν μπορούσε να σταματήσει να γελάει, μέχρι που παρατήρησε ότι κάτι περίεργο συνέβαινε με τα βιβλία από πάνω του. Κούνησε το κεφάλι του, όταν ένα πετάχτηκε από το ράφι στο χέρι του. Ήταν ένα βιβλίο του προγόνου του, του Καρόλου Ντίκενς. Το βιβλίο άνοιξε από μόνο του, ξεφύλλισε από την αρχή ως το τέλος, και μετά πέταξε πίσω στο σημείο απ' όπου ήρθε.

"Καλώς ήρθατε στη βιβλιοθήκη των αγγέλων", είπε ο Ρέικι.

"Ουάου! Απλά ουάου! Δηλαδή, εσείς οι δύο είστε άγγελοι;"

"'Έχεις δίκιο", είπε ο Χαντζ. "Και βρίσκεστε εδώ, επειδή έχουμε οριστεί ως μέντορές σας".

"Διορισμένοι; Από ποιον; Τον Θεό;" ειρωνεύτηκε.

Ο Χαντζ και η Ρέικι κοίταξαν ο ένας τον άλλον, κουνώντας τα λουλουδάτα κεφάλια τους.

"Ο σκοπός μας".

"Είναι να σας εξηγήσω την αποστολή σας".

"Επίσης, να σας δείξουμε τον δρόμο. Να σας βοηθήσουμε", είπαν μαζί.

"Αποστολή; Ποια αποστολή;" Το μυαλό του παρασύρθηκε. Στο μυαλό του άκουσε το θέμα από το Mission Impossible. Είδε τον Τομ Κρουζ να πέφτει με καλώδιο σε μια αίθουσα υπολογιστών. "Έι. Περίμενε ένα λεπτό! Εσείς οι δύο ήσασταν στο δωμάτιό μου, έτσι δεν είναι; Και με παρακολουθείτε από το ατύχημα".

"Περιμέναμε την κατάλληλη στιγμή για να συστηθούμε", είπε η Ρέικι. "Ελπίζαμε να το κάνουμε με λιγότερο επίσημο τρόπο, αλλά όταν ήσουν...."

"...πήγαινες να μιλήσεις με τον ιερέα, έπρεπε να πιέσουμε".

"Λοιπόν, σίγουρα πήρατε τον χρόνο σας. Νόμιζα ότι είχα παραισθήσεις", είπε πιο δυνατά απ' ό,τι ήθελε.

POP.

Η Ρέικι εξαφανίστηκε.

"Τώρα κοίτα τι έκανες!" Είπε ο Χαντζ.

POP.

Καθώς είχαν φύγει και δεν είχε ιδέα πού, πότε ή αν θα επέστρεφαν. Παρόλα αυτά, δεν επρόκειτο να χάσει ούτε λεπτό. Έπεσε στο πάτωμα και έκανε είκοσι κάμψεις, ακολουθούμενες από τον ίδιο αριθμό αλμάτων. Τα μάτια του τσούχτηκαν από την έντονη ακτινοβολία και ευχήθηκε να είχε γυαλιά ηλίου.

ΤΙΚ-ΤΑΚ.

Ένα ζευγάρι γυαλιά ηλίου εμφανίστηκε από το πουθενά. Τα φόρεσε, ενώ το στομάχι του γουργούριζε. Έβγαλε μια selfie και μετά έλεγξε την ώρα. Κάτι περίεργο συνέβαινε με το ρολόι. Είχε τρελαθεί. Και οι αριθμοί δεν σταματούσαν να αλλάζουν. Το στομάχι του γρύλισε ξανά.

TICK-TOCK.

Ένα τσίζμπεργκερ και πατάτες τηγανιτές εμφανίστηκαν, τώρα τα χέρια του ήταν γεμάτα. Σκέφτηκε ένα παχύρρευστο μιλκσέικ σοκολάτας με ένα κεράσι μαρασκίνο από πάνω.

TICK-TOCK.

Ένα πολύ μεγάλο μιλκσέικ, με ένα κεράσι στην κορυφή, έφτασε σε ένα λευκό τραπέζι που δεν υπήρχε εκεί πριν. Ή μήπως ήταν; Ίσως δεν το είχε προσέξει, αφού και τα δύο ήταν λευκά.

Πριν αρχίσει να τρώει, απολάμβανε τη μυρωδιά του, και στη συνέχεια, με κάθε μπουκιά, τη γεύση του. Ήταν σαν να μην είχε ξαναφάει ποτέ του τσίζμπεργκερ ή πατάτες τηγανιτές. Και το κεράσι, είχε τόσο γλυκιά γεύση, ακολουθούμενο από τη σοκολατένια σοκολάτα. Καταβρόχθισε το γεύμα του όρθιος. Το φαγητό είχε πάντα καλύτερη γεύση όταν το κατανάλωνε όρθιος. Αυτή η παραγγελία είχε τόσο καλή γεύση που ήταν γελοία.

Όταν τελείωσε, δεν ευχαρίστησε κανέναν για το γεύμα. Στη συνέχεια έστρεψε την προσοχή του στη βιβλιοθήκη και, μια λευκή σκάλα που δεν είχε προσέξει πριν. Και μόνο η σκέψη της ήταν αρκετή για να κάνει τη σκάλα να κινηθεί πιο κοντά του, σαν να ήθελε να του φανεί χρήσιμη. Ανέβηκε πάνω της και αυτή κινήθηκε, σαν δίσκος σε πίνακα Ouija, περνώντας από το ένα ράφι μετά το άλλο με βιβλία. Μετά, σταμάτησε.

Καθώς σκαρφάλωνε, διάβαζε τους τίτλους στις ράχες. Εκείνα ακριβώς μπροστά του ήταν του Καρόλου Ντίκενς, και κάθε τόμος είχε το δικό του ζευγάρι φτερά.

Το ένα πετούσε προς το μέρος του, "Χριστουγεννιάτικη ιστορία". Ξεφύλλισε μερικές σελίδες, για να του δείξει ότι επρόκειτο για Πρώτη Έκδοση, που εκδόθηκε στις 19 Δεκεμβρίου 1843. Καθώς συνέχιζε να κινεί τις σελίδες, θαύμαζε τις εικονογραφήσεις. Πόσο λεπτομερείς ήταν και μάλιστα έγχρωμες. Και στο βάθος, πίσω από τον Τάινι Τιμ και την οικογένειά του σε μια από τις ζωγραφιές, κάτι κουνιόταν. Τα μάτια. Δύο ζευγάρια. Ο Χαντζ και η Ρέικι! Παραλίγο να του πέσει το βιβλίο. Αφού είχε φτερά, επέστρεψε εκεί που έμενε στο ράφι. Εν τω μεταξύ έχασε την ισορροπία του, έπεσε από τη σκάλα και κρατήθηκε για να κρατηθεί. Όταν σταθεροποιήθηκε ξανά, κατέβηκε σταδιακά και πάτησε τα πόδια του γερά στο έδαφος. Αναρωτήθηκε γιατί τα φτερά του δεν είχαν πεταχτεί για να τον βοηθήσουν. Όλα τα άλλα εδώ είχαν φτερά που λειτουργούσαν, μάλιστα οι άγγελοι είχαν πολλά ζευγάρια φτερών. Στον κόσμο εκεί έξω, τα πόδια του δεν λειτουργούσαν, ενώ εκείνος είχε φτερά, τα οποία λειτουργούσαν. Εδώ, όπου κι αν βρισκόταν, τα πόδια του λειτουργούσαν, αλλά τα φτερά του ήταν πλέον ανενεργά.

Έξυνε το κεφάλι του. Μακάρι να ήταν εδώ ο θείος Σαμ. Κι όμως, δεν μπορούσε να του μιλήσει. Ήταν απαγορευμένο. Μα γιατί; Τι θα μπορούσαν να του κάνουν; Οι άγγελοι τον παρακολουθούσαν από το ατύχημα. Υπέθεσε ότι ήταν καλοί άγγελοι, αφού δεν τον είχαν πειράξει - ακόμα. Η νοσταλγία της πατρίδας του όρμησε πάνω του σαν γιγαντιαίο κύμα, απειλώντας να τον παρασύρει.

"Θέλω να πάω σπίτι!" φώναξε, καθώς το τηλέφωνό του δονήθηκε. Πριν προλάβει να το ξεκλειδώσει...

POP.

Η Ρέικι το άρπαξε και το πέταξε...

POP.

Hadz, ο οποίος το πέταξε στον πιο μακρινό λευκό τοίχο. Αναπήδησε, χτύπησε στο πάτωμα και έσπασε σε κομμάτια.

"Μου χρωστάς τετρακόσια δολάρια για ένα καινούργιο τηλέφωνο! Ελπίζω εσείς οι άγγελοι να έχετε μετρητά".

Ο Χατζ έφτασε και χαστούκισε τον E-Z στο πρόσωπο με το φτερό του. Τα φτερά γαργαλίστηκαν, αντί να τον πληγώσουν. "Τώρα εσύ, E-Z Ντίκενς, κάτσε εδώ". Μια λευκή καρέκλα πίεσε την πλάτη των ποδιών του και τον ανάγκασε να καθίσει.

"Και σταμάτα να είσαι μαλάκας", είπε ο Ρέικι.

"Ουάου! Μπορούν οι άγγελοι να το λένε αυτό; Τι είδους άγγελοι είστε τέλος πάντων; Άγγελοι σε εκπαίδευση; Εγώ είμαι ο τύπος που θα σε βοηθήσει να κερδίσεις τα φτερά σου;"

Συνειδητοποίησε ότι είχαν ήδη φτερά. Για την ακρίβεια, αρκετά ζευγάρια από αυτά. Έτσι, το σημείο που προσπαθούσε να πει φάνηκε περιττό καθώς αιωρούνταν από πάνω του.

"Εγώ είμαι ο τύπος που θα σε βοηθήσει ή εσύ πρέπει να με βοηθήσεις; Γιατί αν είσαι εσύ, που είπες ότι είσαι, τότε κάνεις απαίσια δουλειά. Δεν πρόκειται να πω μια καλή κουβέντα για κανέναν από τους δυο σας σύντομα".

"Περιμένουμε μια συγγνώμη".

"Λοιπόν, θα την περιμένετε για πολύ καιρό. Γιατί διψάω".

TICK-TOCK.

Εμφανίστηκε μια κούπα με μπύρα ρίζας σε ένα παγωμένο ποτήρι. Την κατέβασε με μια γουλιά. "Επειδή με έφερες εδώ, χωρίς τη συγκατάθεσή μου. Και..."

"ΣΚΑΣΕ!", είπε μια βροντερή φωνή, καθώς περιφερόταν από έναν από τους λευκούς τοίχους.

Ήταν τόσο ψηλή όσο το ταβάνι. Στην πραγματικότητα, ψηλότερη. Ήταν στραβή, αλλά τεράστια σε μέγεθος και ανάστημα. Τα φτερά της ακουμπούσαν τους τοίχους και το ταβάνι. "ΚΡΑΤΗΣΕ ΤΗ ΓΛΩΣΣΑ ΣΟΥ!", απαίτησε ο υπερμεγέθης άγγελος, τραβώντας τα φτερά της προς τον E-Z με ένα SWOOSH μέχρι που βρέθηκε ακριβώς μπροστά του.

"Ε-Ζ Ντίκενς, σε κάλεσαν εδώ μπροστά μου", είπε ο τεράστιος άγγελος. "Είμαι ο Οφάνιελ, κυβερνήτης του φεγγαριού και των αστεριών. Και αυτοί, είναι οι υφιστάμενοί μου. ΔΕΝ ΠΡΕΠΕΙ να τους φέρεσαι με αυθάδεια. ΠΡΕΠΕΙ να τους φέρεστε με καλοσύνη και σεβασμό, γιατί είναι τα ΜΑΤΙΑ και τα ΑΥΤΙΑ μου για εσάς. Χωρίς αυτούς δεν είστε ΤΙΠΟΤΑ".

Τραύλισε μια ακατανόητη φράση παλεύοντας με την ανάγκη να φύγει.

"ΜΗΝ διακόπτετε μέχρι να τελειώσω την ομιλία μου", διέταξε ο Οφάνιελ.

Εκείνος έγνεψε, με το σώμα του να τρέμει, πολύ φοβισμένος για να πει μια λέξη.

"Ε-Ζ", βροντοφώναξε η φωνή του. "Έχεις σωθεί. Σε σώσαμε, για έναν σκοπό".

Η Ρέικι και ο Χαντζ πετάχτηκαν πιο κοντά και κάθισαν στους ώμους του Οφάνιελ.

"Μείνε ακίνητος", πρόσταξε ο Οφάνιελ.

Δίπλωσαν τις φτερούγες τους, γέρνοντας προς τα μέσα για τα μη χάσουν ούτε μια λέξη.

Ο Ε-Ζ σημείωσε νοερά να τους ρωτήσει πώς να διπλώνει τα φτερά του τόσο αποτελεσματικά όσο εκείνοι τα δικά τους. Αυτό θα γινόταν αν έπαιρνε πίσω τα φτερά του.

Ο Οφάνιελ συνέχισε. "Όταν πέθαναν οι γονείς σου, E-Z Ντίκενς, θα έπρεπε να είχες πεθάνει και εσύ. Ήταν το πεπρωμένο σου. Αυτό που αλλάξαμε για τους δικούς μας σκοπούς. Υποστηρίξαμε με επιτυχία την περίπτωσή σου. Υποσχεθήκαμε ότι θα έκανες αξιοσημείωτα πράγματα. Ότι θα βοηθούσες τους άλλους. Σε σώσαμε και σου χρωστούσαμε ένα χρέος. Ένα χρέος το μεγαλύτερο μέρος του οποίου πλήρωσες πλήρως παραδίδοντας τα πόδια σου".

Παραδόθηκαν; Αυτό ακούστηκε σαν να είχε επιλογή. Ότι είχε πάρει την τελική απόφαση να μην ξαναπερπατήσει ποτέ, πράγμα που ήταν ψέμα. Άνοιξε το στόμα του για να μιλήσει, αλλά η φωνή του Οφάνιελ βροντοφώναξε.

"Υπάρχει ακόμα ένα χρέος, ένα χρέος που μας χρωστάς".

Ο E-Z πήρε μια μεγάλη ρουφηξιά αέρα. Ήθελε να μιλήσει, αλλά δεν μπορούσε. Τα χείλη του κινήθηκαν, αλλά δεν βγήκε κανένας ήχος. Πώς τολμά αυτός, ο άγγελος, να παίρνει αποφάσεις γι' αυτόν και να του λέει ότι του χρωστάς ένα χρέος;

"Σου δώσαμε εργαλεία - μια ισχυρή καρέκλα. Αυτό για να σε βοηθήσει. Για να μπορέσεις μια μέρα να είσαι εδώ με τους γονείς σου και να περπατάς μαζί μας, μαζί τους, στον αιώνα τον άπαντα". Ο Οφάνιελ δίστασε για λίγα δευτερόλεπτα, για να το αφήσει να περάσει στην αντίληψή του. "Μπορείς να μου κάνεις μια ερώτηση σήμερα, αλλά μόνο μία. Να είναι καλή".

Αντί να σκεφτεί την ερώτησή του, ο E-Z ξέσπασε: "Πότε θα μπορέσω να ξαναδώ τους γονείς μου;".

"Όταν θα έχεις εξοφλήσει το χρέος σου στο ακέραιο".

"Μια ακόμη ερώτηση, παρακαλώ."

"Θα υπάρξει χρόνος για ερωτήσεις και θα υπάρξει χρόνος για απαντήσεις. Προς το παρόν, είσαι υπό τη φροντίδα των υφισταμένων μου. Μπορείς να τους κάνεις ερωτήσεις και μπορούν να επιλέξουν να σου απαντήσουν. Ή μπορεί να επιλέξουν να μην απαντήσουν. Θα είναι δική τους επιλογή να απαντήσουν ναι ή όχι. Με τον ίδιο τρόπο θα έχετε την επιλογή αν θα τους απαντήσετε όταν σας κάνουν ερωτήσεις. Να τους φέρεστε όπως θα θέλατε να σας φέρονται και να μην αποκαλύπτετε λεπτομέρειες σχετικά με αυτόν τον τόπο ή τη συνάντησή μας. Μην μιλήσετε γι' αυτό, για τίποτα από αυτά σε κανέναν άνθρωπο. Επαναλαμβάνω, κρατήστε αυτά τα θέματα μόνο για τον εαυτό σας".

Ακόμα δεν μπορούσε να μιλήσει. Χωρίς να το ζητήσει, ο Οφάνιελ προχώρησε στην απάντηση της επόμενης ερώτησής του.

"Αν αθετήσεις αυτή την υπόσχεση, τα φτερά σου θα γίνουν σαν ζυμαρικά -αδύναμα- και δεν θα μπορέσεις ποτέ να ξεπληρώσεις το χρέος σου".

Σκέφτηκε μια άλλη ερώτηση.

"Ναι, όταν έσωσες εκείνο το κοριτσάκι - το κάψιμο - ήταν μέρος της διαδικασίας. Τα φτερά σου πρέπει να καούν, να δυναμώσουν, να δεθούν μαζί σου, έτσι, θα είσαι προετοιμασμένη για την επόμενη πρόκληση".

Σκέφτηκε, κι αν δεν το θέλω.

Ο Οφάνιελ γέλασε και πέταξε στο ψηλότερο σημείο του δωματίου. Στη συνέχεια εξαφανίστηκε μέσα από το ταβάνι.

ΚΕΦΑΛΑΙΟ 8

Τ
Ο ΕΠΌΜΕΝΟ ΠΡΆΓΜΑ ΠΟΥ ήξερε ήταν ότι βρισκόταν πάλι στο αναπηρικό καροτσάκι του και αντιμετώπιζε τον Ιερέα.

"Θείε Σαμ, πρέπει να φύγουμε. ΤΩΡΑ."

"Ω", είπε ο Σαμ, καθώς έβλεπε τον ανιψιό του να απομακρύνεται με το τροχό. "Ζητώ συγγνώμη που σπατάλησα το χρόνο σας, αυτός ε, πρέπει να πάει σπίτι του". Ο Σαμ βιάστηκε να προχωρήσει, ενώ ο Χόπερ τον ακολουθούσε. Πήρε φόρα, πρόλαβε τον ανιψιό του και παίρνοντας τον έλεγχο των χειρολαβών έσπρωξε την αναπηρική καρέκλα. Ο Χόπερ έτρεξε και σύντομα περπατούσε δίπλα τους, αν και λαχανιασμένος.

"Κατάλαβα, τότε πραγματικά δεν έχεις φτερά, Ε-Ζ".

Έριξε μια ματιά πάνω από τον ώμο του, σήκωσε ένα υποτιθέμενο ποτήρι στα χείλη του και μετά γούρλωσε τα μάτια του.

"Δεν έχω πρόβλημα με το ποτό", είπε προκλητικά ο Σαμ.

Και πάλι, ο έφηβος γούρλωσε τα μάτια του, καθώς πλησίαζαν στο πάρκινγκ. Ο ιερέας δεν τους ακολούθησε.

Μόλις έφτασαν στο αυτοκίνητο, ο Σαμ είπε, προσπαθώντας να πάρει ανάσα, "Τι στο διάολο ήταν αυτό;", καθώς άνοιξε την πόρτα και βοήθησε τον ανιψιό του να μπει μέσα.

"Ας φύγουμε πρώτα από εδώ". Καθυστερούσε τον χρόνο του γιατί δεν μπορούσε να του πει τι συνέβη. Έπρεπε να σκεφτεί ένα πειστικό ψέμα - και ποτέ δεν ήταν καλός ψεύτης. Η μητέρα του τον έπιανε πάντα στα πράσα γιατί τα αυτιά του πάντα κοκκίνιζαν όταν έλεγε ψέματα.

"Περιμένω μια εξήγηση", είπε ο Σαμ, σφίγγοντας τη λαβή του στο τιμόνι.

Από τα ηχεία του αυτοκινήτου ακούστηκε το Don't Look Back των Boston.

"Συγγνώμη, έπρεπε να φύγω. Δεν νομίζω ότι ο Χόπερ θα μπορούσε να βοηθήσει και δεν ήθελα να μάθει τίποτα περισσότερο από ό,τι του είχες ήδη πει".

"Ακόμα δεν μου εξήγησες γιατί υπαινίχθηκες ότι είχα πρόβλημα με το ποτό".

"Α, αυτό. Μου ήρθε στο μυαλό και το είπα χωρίς να το σκεφτώ. Λυπάμαι".

"Είμαι περήφανος που δεν συμμετέχω στο αλκοόλ. Σίγουρα, θα πια μια μπύρα πού και πού. Για να είμαι κοινωνικός σε μια εκδήλωση της δουλειάς. Αλλά δεν είμαι σαν τους άλλους μεθύστακες του IT. Και δεν θα γίνω ποτέ".

Ο E-Z δεν σκεφτόταν αυτά που έλεγε ο θείος Σαμ. Αντιθέτως, μελετούσε τις πληροφορίες που του είχε πει ο Οφάνιελ. Χρωστούσε, στους αγγέλους, που τον έσωσαν και είχε ανταλλάξει τα πόδια του για τη ζωή του. Το παζάρι από τους αγγέλους, ήταν για τον δικό τους σκοπό - και τώρα περίμεναν από αυτόν να πληρώσει το χρέος - αλλά πώς;

Το μόνο που ήξερε σίγουρα ήταν ότι έπρεπε να κερδίσει. Όποια καθήκοντα κι αν του έβαζαν στο δρόμο του, έπρεπε να τα ξεπεράσει. Με τη βοήθεια της Ρέικι και του Χαντζ - όσο μικροί κι αν ήταν, θα πλήρωνε αυτό που του χρωστούσαν. Τότε, αν μη τι άλλο, θα έβλεπε ξανά τους γονείς του. Υπέθεσε ότι αυτό σήμαινε ότι θα πέθαινε και θα συναντιόντουσαν στον παράδεισο, αν υπήρχε τέτοιος τόπος. Θα το μάθαινε σύντομα.

ΚΕΦΑΛΑΙΟ 9

Ε ΠΙΣΤΡΕΦΟΝΤΑΣ ΚΑΙ ΠΑΛΙ ΣΤΟ σπίτι, ο έφηβος πήγε κατευθείαν στο δωμάτιό του.

"Αν χρειάζεσαι τη βοήθειά μου", ήταν το μόνο που κατάφερε να πει ο Σαμ πριν ο ανιψιός του χτυπήσει την πόρτα του.

Ο Ε-Ζ κάλυψε το πρόσωπό του με τα χέρια του. Ήταν το κάτι άλλο, το να έχει ξανά τα πόδια του. Χτύπησε τις γροθιές του στα μπράτσα, καθώς τα φτερά του βγήκαν και τον πέταξαν στο κρεβάτι. "Ευχαριστώ", τους είπε, σαν να ήταν ξεχωριστά και όχι μέρος του εαυτού του.

"Πρόσεχε", είπε ο Χαντζ, ο οποίος είχε ξεκουραστεί στο μαξιλάρι του. Ο άγγελος πέταξε μέχρι το φωτιστικό και είπε: "Ξύπνα, γύρισε σπίτι".

Ο Ε-Ζ ήταν τώρα αναπαυτικά ξαπλωμένος στο κρεβάτι του, με κλειστά μάτια, σχεδόν κοιμισμένος.

"Απόψε, θα πετάξεις", τραγούδησαν οι άγγελοι.

"Κοιτάξτε, είχα μια κουραστική μέρα, όπως ξέρετε, και το μόνο που θέλω να κάνω είναι να κοιμηθώ".

"Μπορείς να πάρεις έναν πεντάλεπτο υπνάκο", είπε η Ρέικι.

"Μετά, θα σηκωθείς και θα τους επιτεθείς!"

Είχε σχεδόν αποκοιμηθεί ξανά, όταν εισέβαλε ο Σαμ. "Συγγνώμη για την ενόχληση, αλλά ο Πι Τζέι και ο Άρντεν λένε ότι προσπαθούν να σε βρουν όλη μέρα. Έχει τελειώσει η μπαταρία σου;"

"Ε, όχι, έχασα το τηλέφωνό μου", είπε κοιτάζοντας με κακία τους δύο βοηθούς του.

"Ψεύτη, ψεύτη, καίγεται το παντελόνι σου", τον κατσάδιασαν. Ο Σαμ, δεδομένης της έλλειψης αντίδρασης, δεν άκουσε τις ψηλές φωνές τους. Ο Ε-Ζ τους έδιωξε.

"Γι' αυτό αγοράζω πάντα ασφάλεια με το σχέδιό μου. Μην ανησυχείς, θα σου βρούμε αντικαταστάτη αύριο. Έτσι κι αλλιώς είναι καιρός να αναβαθμίσεις. Μπορείς να κρατήσεις τον ίδιο αριθμό τηλεφώνου. Θα ενημερώσω τα παιδιά ότι θα επικοινωνήσεις μαζί τους τότε".

"Ευχαριστώ, θείε Σαμ. Καληνύχτα".

"Καληνύχτα Ε-Ζ."

ΚΕΦΑΛΑΙΟ 10

Σ ΤΟ ΌΝΕΙΡΌ ΤΟΥ, ΒΡΙΣΚΌΤΑΝ σε ένα ταξίδι για σκι με τους γονείς του. Ήταν στην πραγματικότητα μια ανάμνηση, αλλά την ξαναζούσε ως όνειρο.

Ο E-Z ήταν έξι ετών. Αυτός και η μητέρα του διδάσκονταν όλες τις κινήσεις από έναν δάσκαλο σκι. Εν τω μεταξύ, ο πατέρας του - που δεν ήταν αρχάριος όπως εκείνοι - κατέβαινε τον χιονισμένο λόφο.

Έμαθαν πώς να κάνουν σκι στον λόφο των μωρών - έτσι αναφέρονταν στους δοκιμαστικούς λόφους.

"Είστε έτοιμοι;", είπε ο δάσκαλος, "να χτυπήσετε έναν από τους μεγάλους λόφους;".

Είπαν ότι ήταν έτοιμοι. Νόμιζαν ότι ήταν. Αλλά το να λες και να κάνεις είναι δύο διαφορετικά πράγματα.

Στην πρώτη προσπάθεια, δεν έφτασαν μακριά πριν πέσει ένας από αυτούς. Ήταν η μητέρα του, και όταν έσβησε, κάθισε στο κρύο χιόνι γελώντας. Την βοήθησε να σηκωθεί και ξεκίνησαν πάλι.

Αυτή τη φορά, ο E-Z ήταν αυτός που έπεσε, βυθίζοντας το πρόσωπό του στο κρύο λευκό υλικό. Το τίναξε από πάνω του, τον βοήθησε ο εκπαιδευτής, ενώ η μητέρα του περνούσε ψεκάζοντας χιόνι στο δρόμο της. Εκείνος το εξέλαβε ως πρόκληση και επιτάχυνε, περνώντας την με ένα χαμόγελο.

Το επόμενο πράγμα που ήξερε ήταν ότι εκείνη ερχόταν από πίσω του. Χτύπησε κάποια πακτωμένη πούδρα - και τον άφησε για σκόνη - βρίσκοντας τον βηματισμό της. Παρόλα αυτά, έβαλε τα δυνατά του και την έφτασε.

Κατέβηκαν, πλάι-πλάι, μετά χώρισαν, και μετά πάλι μαζί. Όλο αυτό το διάστημα γελούσαν σαν δύο μικρά παιδιά.

Στο κάτω μέρος του λόφου, ντυμένος από την κορυφή ως τα νύχια στα γαλάζια, ήταν ο πατέρας του. Ξεχώριζε, μια γαλάζια φέτα που περιβαλλόταν από παρθένο χιόνι - με ένα αναπηρικό καροτσάκι στα χέρια του.

"Το χιόνι", είπε ο E-Z, εισπνέοντας άλλο ένα ζαχαρωτό. Είχε ακόμα καλύτερη γεύση λιωμένο. Τότε ένιωσε παγωμένο κρύο και ξύπνησε περικυκλωμένος από πάγο στη μπανιέρα. Ο θείος Σαμ ήταν εκεί, καθισμένος δίπλα του.

"E-Z, πραγματικά με τρόμαξες αυτή τη φορά".

"Τι; Τι συνέβη;

"Άκουσα κάποιους θορύβους και έτσι μπήκα μέσα για να σε ελέγξω. Το παράθυρό σου ήταν ορθάνοιχτο, οι κουρτίνες ανεμίζουν. Έπιασα το μέτωπό σου και έκαιγες. Φοβήθηκα ότι θα πάθαινες κρίση. Ακόμα και τα φτερά σου φαίνονταν μαραμένα.

"Σκέφτηκα να καλέσω το 100, αλλά μετά αποφάσισα να μην το κάνω. Εννοώ, δεν μπορούσα να σε πάω στα επείγοντα, όχι με αυτά τα φτερά. Έπρεπε να σε βάλω στο αναπηρικό σου καροτσάκι και να γεμίσω την μπανιέρα με πάγο και να δω αν θα μπορούσα να ρίξω τη θερμοκρασία σου. Πήγαινα και έφερνα πάγο, ζητώντας δωρεές από φίλους στη γειτονιά. Με βοήθησαν πάρα πολύ".

"Αισθάνομαι καλύτερα τώρα, ευχαριστώ", είπε προσπαθώντας να σηκωθεί. Δεν πρόλαβε να φτάσει μακριά, πριν πέσει ξανά κάτω.

"Πρέπει να μου πεις τι συμβαίνει".

"Δεν μπορώ, θείε Σαμ. Πρέπει να με εμπιστευτείς".

Ο έφηβος προσπάθησε να σηκωθεί ξανά. "Περίμενε εδώ", είπε ο Σαμ, καθώς έβγαινε από το μπάνιο και επέστρεφε με το αναπηρικό καροτσάκι. "Ορίστε", έβαλε το θερμόμετρο στο στόμα του ανιψιού του. "Αν είναι φυσιολογικό, μπορείς να μπεις στην καρέκλα".

Ήταν φυσιολογικό, οπότε με μια ρόμπα τυλιγμένη γύρω του, ο E-Z σηκώθηκε από το μπάνιο και μπήκε στην καρέκλα. Τα φτερά του διαστέλλονταν, μετά χαλάρωσαν στη θέση τους και δεν ένιωθαν πια σαν να είχαν πάρει φωτιά.

Καθώς περνούσε από το σαλόνι, έριξε μια ματιά στις ειδήσεις.

"Χθες το βράδυ, ένα αεροπλάνο που συνετρίβη εκτράπηκε", είπε ο εκπρόσωπος. "Το αποκαλούν θαυματουργή προσγείωση, αλλά εδώ είναι μερικά ακατέργαστα πλάνα, τραβηγμένα από έναν από τους τηλεθεατές μας την ώρα που συνέβη".

Παρακολούθησε το βίντεο, το οποίο έδειχνε την προσγείωση του αεροπλάνου, αλλά δεν υπήρχε τίποτα άλλο - ούτε πλάνο του. Ένιωσε ανακούφιση και επέστρεψε στο δωμάτιό του.

"Επιστρέφω αμέσως για να σε βοηθήσω να ντυθείς".

Ήθελε τόσο πολύ να μπορούσε να πει στο θείο του τα πάντα - αλλά δεν μπορούσε. "Ευχαριστώ", είπε αφού είχε ντυθεί.

"Πάντα σε καλύπτω".

"Κι εγώ", είπε ο έφηβος. "Νομίζω ότι θα πάω στο γραφείο μου να γράψω κάτι".

"Καλή ιδέα, έχω δουλειές στο σπίτι στη λίστα με τις δουλειές που θα ήθελα να τελειώσω σήμερα". Άρχισε να φεύγει και μετά γύρισε πίσω. "Ξέρεις, μικρέ, δεν χρειάζεται να γράψεις αμέσως ένα μυθιστόρημα. Μπορείς να κρατάς ημερολόγιο ή ημερολόγιο. Να γράφεις τα πράγματα που μπορεί μια μέρα να ξεχάσεις. Όπως πολύτιμες αναμνήσεις".

"Σκέφτηκα να γράψω κάτι και να το ονομάσω Τατουάζ Άγγελος".

"Μου αρέσει αυτό."

Μόλις μπήκε στο γραφείο του, κάθισε για μια στιγμή και σκέφτηκε το αεροπλάνο - αναρωτήθηκε πώς μπόρεσε να κάνει αυτό που του ζητήθηκε. Δεν θα μπορούσε να το είχε καταφέρει, χωρίς τη βοήθεια του κύκνου και των φίλων του πουλιών, ή χωρίς τη βοήθεια της καρέκλας του. Ακόμη και εκείνοι οι δύο επίδοξοι άγγελοι είχαν βοηθήσει με τον τρόπο τους, ενθαρρύνοντάς τον στο παρασκήνιο.

Συγκεντρώθηκε στο γράψιμο και πληκτρολόγησε τον τίτλο: Ταϊυάζ Άγγελος.

Τα δάχτυλά του ήθελαν να πληκτρολογήσουν περισσότερο, αλλά το μυαλό του ήθελε να περιπλανηθεί. Έγειρε πίσω στην καρέκλα του και κοίταξε την άδεια οθόνη. Χρειαζόταν μια φανταστική πρώτη πρόταση, όπως είχε γράψει ο πρόγονός του Κάρολος Ντίκενς - "Γεννιέμαι".

Όταν δεν άντεχε άλλο τη θέα της λευκής οθόνης κάποια στιγμή αργότερα, πληκτρολόγησε -

Μακάρι να μην είχα γεννηθεί ποτέ.

Και συνέχισε να πληκτρολογεί.

Δεν μπορώ να περπατήσω πια.

Ποτέ δεν θα παίξω επαγγελματικό μπέιζμπολ ή χόκεϊ ή δεν θα πάρω αθλητική υποτροφία.

Δεν μπορώ να τρέξω.

Δεν μπορώ να πηδήξω.

Υπάρχουν τόσα πολλά πράγματα που δεν μπορώ να κάνω.

Αυτά που δεν θα κάνω ποτέ.

Σταμάτησε να πληκτρολογεί, βλέποντας κάτι στο πάνω δεξί μέρος της οθόνης που κινούνταν προς τα κάτω. Κυλούσε.

Δάκρυα. Μικροσκοπικά δάκρυα.

Ενώνονταν. Γίνονταν όλο και μεγαλύτερα.

Κατεβαίνουν στην οθόνη.

Νόμιζε ότι άκουσε κάτι - ανέβασε την ένταση.

"WAH! WAH! WAH!" τραγούδησε μια ψηλή φωνή.

Μια δεύτερη φωνή συνέχισε.

"WAH-WAH!

WAH-WAH!

WAH-WAH!"

Ο Ε-Ζ έκλεισε τον υπολογιστή.

Ήταν μόνο ένα παραλήρημα και ένιωσε καλύτερα γι' αυτό. Ο καθένας χρειαζόταν ένα πάρτι λύπης πού και πού. Είχε βγει από το σύστημά του.

Ήξερε ένα πράγμα με βεβαιότητα - ως συγγραφέας δεν ήταν ο Κάρολος Ντίκενς.

Ο Κάρολος Ντίκενς όμως δεν μπορούσε να πετάξει.

"ΞΎΠΝΑ, ΕΊΝΑΙ ΏΡΑ ΝΑ φύγουμε!" είπε η Ρέικι, πετώντας προς το παράθυρο.

Ο Χαντζ περίμενε στο ανοιχτό παράθυρο. "Έτοιμος;"

Τον περίμεναν λοιπόν να πηδήξει, από τον τρίτο όροφο του σπιτιού του. "Δεν πρόκειται να πάω εκεί έξω! Κοίτα πόσο ψηλά είμαστε".

"Ξεχνάς ότι έχεις φτερά".

"Και αν πέσεις, θα το καταλάβεις."

Τουλάχιστον φορούσε ακόμα τα ρούχα του, όταν τον έριξαν στο αναπηρικό καροτσάκι του. Ανατρίχιασε, κοιτάζοντας κάτω, αναρωτάμενος πώς τα φτερά του ήταν γραφτό να κρατήσουν τόσο αυτόν όσο κι την καρέκλα του στον αέρα.

"Τι θα γίνει με το αναπηρικό μου καροτσάκι;"

"Θυμάσαι τι είπε ο Οφάνιελ; Τώρα - βγες έξω!"

Μόλις βγήκε έξω, τα φτερά του απλώθηκαν πλήρως. Πάνω από τους ώμους του, μπορούσε να δει τα φτερά σε δράση.

Τα μικρά αλλά δυνατά πλάσματα τον σήκωναν ψηλά, όλο και ψηλότερα, οδηγώντας τον έφηβο στον νυχτερινό ουρανό, ενώ τα φωτεινά αστρικά μάτια τον κοίταζαν από ψηλά. Όταν θεώρησαν ότι ήταν έτοιμος, τον άφησαν να φύγει.

"Μπορώ να πετάξω", είπε. "Μπορώ πραγματικά να πετάξω!"

"Σταμάτα να επιδεικνύεσαι", είπε η Ρέικι, "και μπες στο πρόγραμμα".

"Θα το έκανα, αν ήξερα τι ήταν αυτό", είπε χαχανίζοντας.

Ο Χαντζ πέταξε μπροστά. Ο Ε-Ζ και ο Ρέικι σηκώθηκαν πάνω από το σχολείο, δίπλα στο γήπεδο του μπέιζμπολ. Προς τον πυρήνα της πόλης. Τα φώτα στον διάδρομο προσγείωσης κοντά στο αεροδρόμιο ανταγωνίζονταν άμεσα τα αστέρια από πάνω του.

"Τα πας πολύ καλά", είπε ο Ρέικι.

"Ευχαριστώ".

Ο ήχος μιας μηχανής που έπαθε βλάβη, σε ένα τζετ τζάμπο μπροστά τους, τράβηξε την προσοχή του.

"Κοιτάξτε εκεί, αυτό το αεροπλάνο έχει πρόβλημα. Μακάρι να είχα το τηλέφωνό μου για να καλέσω βοήθεια". Ο κινητήρας σφύριξε και το αεροπλάνο έπεσε λίγο και μετά ισορρόπησε.

"Δεν χρειάζεσαι τηλέφωνο. Καλώς ήρθες στη δεύτερη δοκιμασία σου".

"Περιμένεις να κάνω, τι; Να κουβαλήσω το αεροπλάνο στην πλάτη μου; Δεν μπορώ να σώσω ένα αεροπλάνο- δεν έχω αρκετή δύναμη. Δεν μπορώ να το κάνω".

"Εντάξει τότε", είπε ο Χαντζ που είχαν πλέον προλάβει.

"Ένα πράγμα πρέπει να ξέρεις όμως, αν δεν τους σώσεις - όλοι οι επιβαίνοντες θα χαθούν".

"Και οι 293 επιβάτες. Άνδρες, γυναίκες και παιδιά".

"Συν, δύο σκυλιά και μια γάτα", πρόσθεσε η Ρέικι.

Το κεφάλι του γέμισε με κραυγές, από τους ανθρώπους μέσα στο αεροπλάνο. Πώς τους άκουγε, μέσα από τους χοντρούς μεταλλικούς τοίχους; Τα σκυλιά γαύγιζαν και μια γάτα νιαούριζε. Ένα μωρό έκλαιγε.

"Σταμάτα το, κλείσε το και θα το κάνω εγώ".

"Δεν θα το κλείσουμε".

"Αλλά θα τελειώσει, μόλις αφήσετε το αεροπλάνο με ασφάλεια στο αεροδρόμιο, εκεί πέρα".

"Πιστεύουμε σε σένα", είπε ο Χαντζ.

"Αλλά δεν θα με δουν; Αν με δουν, το παιχνίδι θα τελειώσει, εννοώ με τους όρους του Οφάνιελ - δεν θα μπορέσω ποτέ να δω τους γονείς μου".

"Να σε δουν;"

"Αυτό είναι το μικρότερο από τα προβλήματά σου!"

"Τώρα φύγε", είπε ο Χαντζ. "Α, και ίσως χρειαστείς αυτό".

Τώρα είχε μια ζώνη ασφαλείας, για να τον κρατάει στο αναπηρικό του καροτσάκι, καθώς έτρεχε στον ουρανό προς το αεροπλάνο που έπεφτε.

"Θα παρακολουθούμε", φώναξαν.

"Θα με βοηθήσετε, αν σας χρειαστώ;"

"Αυτές είναι οι δικές σου δοκιμασίες, που αποδίδονται σε σένα και μόνο σε σένα. Είμαστε εδώ για να σε ενθαρρύνουμε. Καλή τύχη".

"Για μισό λεπτό, δεν πρόκειται να μου δώσετε κανένα σωστό μάθημα; Να μου δείξετε τι πρέπει να κάνω;"

POP.

POP.

"Ευχαριστώ για το τίποτα!" φώναξε.

Σ ΤΟ ΑΕΡΟΔΡΟΜΙΟ, ΣΤΟΝ Πύργο Ελέγχου Εναέριας Κυκλοφορίας, ένας ελεγκτής παρατήρησε ότι το αεροπλάνο είχε πρόβλημα. Μη μπορώντας να επικοινωνήσει με τον πιλότο, παρατήρησε ένα άγνωστο ιπτάμενο αντικείμενο στο ραντάρ του.

Χρησιμοποιώντας τον Σούπερμαν και τον Mighty Mouse για έμπνευση, ο E-Z σήκωσε τα χέρια του. Τοποθετήθηκε κάτω από το σώμα του πανίσχυρου μεταλλικού θηρίου και συγκέντρωσε όλη του τη δύναμη.

"Σκέφτηκα ότι θα μπορούσες να χρησιμοποιήσεις λίγη βοήθεια", είπε ένας κύκνος μεγαλύτερος από το κανονικό. Εκείνος έγνεψε και τα πουλιά πέταξαν από πολλές κατευθύνσεις. Καθώς το τζετ-τζάμπο συνδέθηκε μαζί του, τα πραγματικά πουλιά ευθυγραμμίστηκαν. Τον βοήθησαν να κρατήσει το αεροπλάνο σταθερό. Να το σταθεροποιήσουν, ώστε αυτός και η καρέκλα του να μπορέσουν να σηκώσουν όλο το βάρος του.

Στο εσωτερικό του τα πράγματα κυλούσαν σαν μπίλιες. Έπρεπε να βιαστεί, και ευχόταν να είχε ένα άλλο σετ φτερών, ή πιο ισχυρά φτερά. Μακάρι να βρισκόταν στο λευκό δωμάτιο. Συγκεντρώθηκε στο έργο του και προετοιμάστηκε διανοητικά για την κάθοδο. Ρίχνοντας μια ματιά κάτω παρατήρησε ότι και η καρέκλα του είχε φτερά, στα υποπόδια και στις ρόδες. "Σας ευχαριστώ", ψιθύρισε σε κανέναν. Έπειτα στα πουλιά: "Το έχω τώρα, σας ευχαριστώ για τη βοήθειά σας".

Έτοιμος πλέον, κατέβασε το τζάμπο, κρατώντας το σταθερό και επίπεδο. Άγγιξε το μπροστινό μέρος του αεροπλάνου στην άσφαλτο. Στη συνέχεια, καθώς το σύστημα προσγείωσης δεν είχε κατέβει, έπρεπε να φύγει από τη μέση. Τέντωσε το δεξί του χέρι, όσο πιο μακριά μπορούσε να φτάσει, και τοποθέτησε την καρέκλα του μακριά από τη μέση του αεροπλάνου. Κατέβασε το κέντρο του αεροπλάνου και στη συνέχεια την ουρά. Τα κατάφερε! Ναι! Απομακρύνθηκε υπό τους τρομακτικούς ήχους των ουρλιαχτών σειρήνων που πλησίαζαν από όλες τις κατευθύνσεις με τη μορφή πυροσβεστικών οχημάτων, ασθενοφόρων και περιπολικών.

Πριν τον εντοπίσουν, πέταξε μακριά. Οι ευγνώμονες επιβάτες που βρίσκονταν μέσα τον επευφημούσαν, τον φωτογράφιζαν και τον κατέγραφαν στα τηλέφωνά τους. Σύντομα επέστρεψε με τον Hadz και το Reiki.

"Τα πήγες πολύ καλά. Είμαστε περήφανοι για σένα, προστατευόμενε".

Χαμογέλασε, μέχρι που ένιωσε τα φτερά του σαν κάποιος να τους έβαλε φωτιά. Το επόμενο πράγμα που ήξερε ήταν ότι έκαιγε και πονούσε τόσο πολύ, που ήθελε να πεθάνει. Ευχήθηκε να πεθάνει. Τον λαχταρούσε. Τώρα σε ελεύθερη πτώση, με την καρέκλα του στραμμένη προς τα κάτω, είχε τα μάτια του ορθάνοιχτα και περίμενε τα χείλη του να φιλήσουν το έδαφος. Τότε παρασύρθηκε από τους δύο αγγέλους, οι οποίοι τον πήγαν στο σπίτι του και τον έβαλαν για ύπνο.

Ο πόνος δεν μειώθηκε, αλλά ο E-Z ήξερε ότι σήμερα δεν θα πέθαινε. Θα ήταν ασφαλής για άλλη μια μέρα. Μια άλλη δοκιμασία. Το μόνο που έπρεπε να κάνει ήταν να επιβιώσει από αυτή.

$$***$$

"Πότε θα αρχίσει να δουλεύει η διαμαντόσκονη;" ρώτησε ο Hadz. "Πονάει ακόμα πάρα πολύ".

"Ήταν μια νέα θεραπεία, οπότε δεν μπορώ να πω πότε - αλλά θα δράσει - κάποια στιγμή".

"Ελπίζω να αντέξει τόσο πολύ!"

"Με τη βοήθεια του θείου Σαμ, θα τα καταφέρει. Μόλις ξεκινήσει, θα δούμε σημάδια. Κάποιες σωματικές αλλαγές."

Ο E-Z συνέχισε να ροχαλίζει

POP.

POP.

Και για άλλη μια φορά εξαφανίστηκαν.

ΚΕΦΑΛΑΙΟ 11

ΜΙΑ ΜΈΡΑ ΑΡΓΌΤΕΡΑ, ο Ε-Ζ είχε σχεδιάσει τη μέρα του. Πρώτα έπρεπε να ετοιμάσει το σακίδιό του για τη σαββατιάτικη εκδρομή στο πάρκο. Θα έτρωγε πρωινό, θα έγραφε λίγο και μετά θα έφευγε. Ενώ ετοίμαζε το σακίδιό του, άκουσε τις ψηλές φωνές του Χαντζ και της Ρέικι πριν τις δει.

"Σας ακούω", είπε.

POP.

Ο Χαντζ εμφανίστηκε πρώτος.

POP.

Μετά η Ρέικι - και οι δύο με την πλήρως μεταμορφωμένη αγγελική μεγαλοπρέπειά τους.

"Καλημέρα", τραγούδησαν με αρρωστημένα γλυκιά ομοφωνία.

Ο Ε-Ζ έχωσε ένα τετράδιο στο σακίδιό του και μερικά στυλό αγνοώντας τα. Ήλπιζε να βρει κάτι εμπνευσμένο για να γράψει στο πάρκο. Έρτασε κάτω για να κλείσει το θερμουάρ του σακιδίου του, όταν παρατήρησε ότι οι δύο άγγελοι κάθονταν πάνω στο φερμουάρ.

"Ω, συγγνώμη. Παραλίγο να μη σας δω εκεί".

"Ουφ, παραλίγο", είπε η Ρέικι.

Ο Χαντζ έτρεμε πάρα πολύ για να ξεστομίσει έστω και μια λέξη.

Πετάχτηκαν στους ώμους του καθώς έστρεφε την καρέκλα του προς την κλειστή πόρτα.

"Πρέπει να σου μιλήσουμε", είπε ο Χαντζ.

"Είναι... σημαντικό. Κάναμε κάτι..."

"Σε μένα;"

Αιωρήθηκαν μπροστά στα μάτια του.

"Ναι. Ενώ κοιμόσουν πριν από μερικές εβδομάδες".

"Πριν από μερικές εβδομάδες! Εντάξει, ακούω..." Στην πραγματικότητα, προσπαθούσε να μην τα τινάξει όλα στον αέρα. Η σκέψη ότι θα του έκαναν οτιδήποτε. Ενώ κοιμόταν. Χωρίς την άδειά του. Ήταν μια τρομερή παραβίαση της εμπιστοσύνης. Έσφιξε τις γροθιές του. Σιωπή. Σταύρωσε τα χέρια του. Δεν επρόκειτο να τους διευκολύνει.

Ο Σαμ χτύπησε την πόρτα: "Πρωινό E-Z, χρειάζεσαι βοήθεια;".

"Όχι, είμαι εντάξει. Θα είμαι εκεί σε λίγα λεπτά". Σιωπή εκτός από τους ήχους έξω από τη Σαμ που επέστρεφε στην κουζίνα.

"Πρώτα απ' όλα", είπε ο Χαντζ, "κάναμε ό,τι κάναμε μόνο για να σε βοηθήσουμε".

"Με τις δοκιμασίες. Κάναμε κάτι για να σε βοηθήσουμε να πετύχεις τους στόχους σου".

"Εννοείς ότι θα μπορούσατε να με είχατε βοηθήσει, με το αεροπλάνο; Σίγουρα θα μπορούσα να χρησιμοποιήσω τη βοήθειά σας. Ευτυχώς, τα καταφέραμε χάρη στον κύκνο και τα πουλιά".

"Ε, ναι, σχετικά με αυτό, η βοήθεια δεν επιτρέπεται - ούτε από φίλους ούτε από πουλιά. Αναφέραμε το εν λόγω περιστατικό στις αρμόδιες αρχές".

Ο E-Z κούνησε το κεφάλι του, δεν μπορούσε να πιστέψει αυτό που άκουγε. "Μη μου πείτε ότι κάποιος έκανε κακό στον κύκνο ή στα πουλιά; Καλύτερα να μη μου το πεις αυτό... Α, και γιατί ακριβώς μου μίλησε ο κύκνος, στα αγγλικά. Το έκανε ξέρεις."

"Αυτό το θέμα είναι εμπιστευτικό", είπε ο Χαντζ, φτερουγίζοντας κοντά στο πρόσωπό του με τα χέρια στους γοφούς. Η Ρέικι πήρε την ίδια στάση, και τα φτερά τους άγγιξαν τα βλέφαρά του.

"Ε, κόφτε το", είπε, πιο δυνατά απ' ό,τι σκόπευε.

"Όλα καλά εκεί μέσα;" ρώτησε ο Σαμ μέσα από την κλειστή πόρτα

"Είμαι καλά", είπε, κουνώντας το χέρι του μπροστά από το πρόσωπό του εκτοξεύοντας τα πλάσματα σε όλο το δωμάτιο. Ο Ρέικι χτύπησε στον τοίχο και γλίστρησε κάτω. Ο Χαντζ που βρισκόταν ήδη πιο κάτω προσπαθησε να πιάσει τον Ρέικι, αλλά ήταν πολύ αργά. Και οι δύο άγγελοι έπεσαν κατακόρυφα και προσγειώθηκαν στο πάτωμα.

"Συγγνώμη", είπε ο έφηβος. Μετακίνησε την αναπηρική του καρέκλα πιο κοντά τους. Αναρωτήθηκε αν είχαν αστέρια που γυρνούσαν στο κεφάλ τους σαν χαρακτήρες καρτούν της παλιάς εποχής. Παλιά του άρεσε αυτό όταν συνέβαινε στον Γουάιλ Ε. Κογιότ. Τριγύρισαν λίγο, οπότε τους έβαλε στο κρεβάτι. Όταν οι άγγελοι συνήλθαν, είπε: "Συγγνώμη και πάλι. Δεν ηθελα να σας χτυπήσω. Τα φτερά σας με γαργαλούσαν στα μάτια".

"Ναι, το έκανες!" Είπε η Ρέικι.

"Και εμείς, δεν θα το ξεχάσουμε".

Ένιωσε άσχημα. Ήταν τόσο μικρά- δεν είχε συνειδητοποιήσει ότι ένα απλό χτύπημα θα μπορούσε να τα στείλει να πετάξουν έτσι. Ήταν σαν να τα είχε χτυπήσει έξω από το πάρκο και μόλις που τα είχε αγγίξει.

"Σχετικά με αυτό..." είπε ο Ρέικι.

Ο Χαντζ πρόσθεσε: "Όσο κοιμόσουν, σου κάναμε μια τελετουργία'.

Ο E-Z διατήρησε και πάλι την ψυχραιμία του, αλλά μόλις και μετά βίας. "Μια τελετουργία είπατε;" Τον κοίταξαν, ένοχοι σαν την αμαρτία. "Αν ήσασταν άνθρωποι, θα σας έριχναν στο κρατητήριο επειδή μου κάνατε οτιδήποτε χωρίς την άδειά μου. Είναι επίθεση σε βάρος ανηλίκου. Θα ήσουν στη φυλακή..."

Οι άγγελοι έτρεμαν και κρατιόντουσαν ο ένας από τον άλλο.

"Δεν είχαμε άλλη επιλογή".

"Το κάναμε για το καλό σας".

"Το καταλαβαίνω αυτό, αλλά αυτή τη στιγμή η συγγνώμη σας ΔΕΝ γίνεται δεκτή".

"Αρκετά δίκαιο", είπαν οι άγγελοι. "Προς το παρόν." Έψαλαν: "Καλέσαμε δυνάμεις, τις μεγάλες και απατηλές δυνάμεις πάνω και γύρω σας. Τους ζητήσαμε να σας βοηθήσουν αυξάνοντας τη δύναμη, το θάρρος και τη σοφία σας. Με απλά λόγια, πιστεύαμε ότι χρειαζόσουν περισσότερα και έτσι τα προκαλέσαμε για σένα".

"Κατάλαβα. Η συγγνώμη εξακολουθεί να ΜΗΝ γίνεται δεκτή".

"Το κάναμε με τη μικρότερη δυνατή ταλαιπωρία για εσάς", είπε ο Χαντζ.

Ο Ε-Ζ εξέτασε αυτή την τελευταία πληροφορία. Ενώ ταυτόχρονα κοιτούσε την αναπηρική του καρέκλα. Φαινόταν όντως διαφορετικό τώρα, εκτός από την προφανή αλλαγή του χρώματος των μπράτσων.

"Τι συμβαίνει με την καρέκλα μου τελευταία;" ρώτησε. "Είναι σαν να έχει δικό της μυαλό".

Οι άγγελοι έτρεμαν και πάλι.

"Τι κάνατε; Ακριβώς; Γιατί υποψιάζομαι ότι όχι μόνο μου επιτέθηκες, αλλά και στην καρέκλα μου".

Τελικά, οι άγγελοι εξήγησαν τα πάντα σχετικά με τη διαμαντόσκονη και το αίμα. Για τις δυνάμεις που είχαν προικιστεί στον ίδιο και στην καρέκλα. "Καθώς οι δυσκολίες του έργου αυξάνονται, θα πρέπει να ανεβείτε σε υψηλότερα επίπεδα".

"Το ξέρω ήδη, γι' αυτό και τα φτερά μου καίγονται. Αυξάνεται η θερμοκρασία τους μετά από κάθε εργασία. Αλλά λέω συνέχεια στον εαυτό μου ότι όλα θα αξίζουν τον κόπο όταν μπορέσω να ξαναδώ τους γονείς μου".

"Αν ολοκληρώσεις τις δοκιμασίες στο προκαθορισμένο χρονικό διάστημα. Και ακολουθήσεις τις οδηγίες με ακρίβεια", είπε ο Χαντζ.

"Περίμενε ένα λεπτό", είπε ο Ε-Ζ χτυπώντας τα χέρια του στα μπράτσα. "Κανείς δεν είπε ότι υπάρχει προθεσμία. Ούτε στο Λευκό Δωμάτιο. Ούτε σε καμία περίπτωση. Και αν υπάρχει κάποιο βιβλίο με κανόνες, που υποτίθεται ότι πρέπει να ακολουθώ, τότε δώστε το μου, για να το διαβάσω. Επίσης, δεν υπήρξε καμία δέσμευση από καμία πλευρά. Κανείς δεν είπε πόσες ολοκληρωμένες δοκιμές απαιτούνται για να σφραγιστεί η συμφωνία. Πρέπει να τα βάλουμε όλα γραπτώς; Υπάρχει τέτοιο πράγμα όπως δικηγόρος Άγγελος ή ακόμα καλύτερα Νομική Βοήθεια Άγγελος;"

Ο Χαντζ γέλασε. "Φυσικά, έχουμε Δικηγόρους Αγγέλων, αλλά πρέπει να είσαι Άγγελος για να δικαιούσαι να έχεις έναν".

Η Ρέικι είπε: "Ολοκλήρωσες την πρώτη εργασία χωρίς καμία βοήθεια από κανέναν. Έσωσες τη ζωή του μικρού κοριτσιού με την πρωτοβουλία της καρέκλας σου, τη δύναμη της θέλησης και την τύχη. Αυτά τα τρία πράγματα μπορούν να σε οδηγήσουν μόνο μέχρις ενός σημείου, γι' αυτό σου δώσαμε περισσότερη δύναμη πυρός. Το περισσότερο που θα μπορούσαμε να ζητήσουμε".

"Το περισσότερο που θα μπορούσαμε να ρισκάρουμε να σου δώσουμε".

"Ει, τι εννοείς να ρισκάρουμε; Εννοείς ότι αυτή η τελετή μπορεί να με βλάψει;"

"Σου κάναμε μια χάρη. Θέσαμε τους εαυτούς μας σε κίνδυνο για να σε βοηθήσουμε. Αν δεν μπορείς να μας συγχωρέσεις τώρα, τότε θα το κάνεις μια μέρα".

"Μιλάμε για αποφυγή της ερώτησής μου! Σκέφτηκες ποτέ να ασχοληθείς με την πολιτική των Αγγέλων - αν υπάρχει κάτι τέτοιο;"

Είπε ο Χαντζ. "Οι άνθρωποι γύρω σου μπορεί να παρατηρήσουν ορισμένες αλλαγές στη φυσική σου εμφάνιση".

"Ναι, μπορεί", είπε η Ρέικι με ένα χαμόγελο.

"Τι εννοείς σωματικές αλλαγές;" φώναξε.

POP.

POP.

Και εξαφανίστηκαν.

Ο E-Z ήταν πάλι ολομόναχος. Καθώς πήγαινε προς την πόρτα, αναρωτιόταν τι εννοούσαν. Ό,τι κι αν ήταν, θα το μάθαινε σύντομα. Στο μεταξύ, σκέφτηκε ότι η καρέκλα του είχε τώρα το αίμα του. Πώς η καρέκλα ήταν η προέκταση του εαυτού του. Μπήκε στην κουζίνα όπου τον περίμενε ο θείος Σαμ.

"ΛOIΠÓN, AYTÓ ΔEN EΞEΛÍXΘHKE ακριβώς όπως το ε ̇χαμε σχεδιάσει", είπε η Ρέικι. "Ήταν πολύ θυμωμένος μαζί μας. Δεν νομίζω ότι θα μας εμπιστευτεί ποτέ ξανά".

"Μας χρειάζεται περισσότερο απ' ό,τι εμείς αυτόν".

"Θα μπορούσαμε να του σβήσουμε το μυαλό, όπως κάναμε και στους άλλους".

"Αν δεν μας συγχωρήσει, δεν μπορούμε να κάνουμε τίποτα γι' αυτό. Το να σβήσουμε το μυαλό του δεν είναι επιλογή. Χωρίς τη συγκατάθεσή του και αν, όχι όταν το μάθει, θα τον αποξενώσουμε για πάντα. Και ξέρεις σε ποιον δεν θα άρεσε αυτό".

"Έχεις δίκιο όπως πάντα", είπε ο Χαντζ.

"Πιστεύεις ότι κάποιος θα προσέξει τις αλλαγές στην εμφάνισή του σήμερα;"

"Το προσέξαμε, έτσι δεν είναι;"

"Ίσως θα έπρεπε να του το είχαμε πει, τουλάχιστον για τα μαλλιά του. ίσως να τον είχαμε κάνει πιο αγαπητό σε εμάς. Αν του το εξηγούσαμε".

"Νομίζω ότι οι αλλαγές θα ήταν καλύτερες αν προέρχονταν από κάποιον άλλον εκτός από εμάς".

"Οι άνθρωποι είναι πολύ παράξενοι", είπε η Ρέικι.

"Αυτό είναι. Αλλά το να δουλεύουμε μαζί τους είναι ο μόνος τρόπος για να προωθηθούμε ως πραγματικοί άγγελοι".

"Για καλή μας τύχη, είναι πολύ καλός".

ΚΕΦΑΛΑΙΟ 12

Ο Ε-Ζ ΚΑΡΦΩΣΕ ΤΟ πιρούνι του σε ένα πιάτο γεμάτο τηγανίτες. Πεθαίνει της πείνας, σαν να είχε μέρες να φάει. Και διψούσε. Πέταξε το ένα ποτήρι μετά το άλλο με χυμό πορτοκάλι. Ξαναγέμισε το πιάτο του με τηγανίτες, συνέχισε να τρώει μέχρι να τελειώσουν όλες.

Ο Σαμ γέλασε όταν είδε τον ανιψιό του και συνέχισε να βουτάει μια φέτα βουτυρωμένου τοστ στον καφέ του.

"Τι είναι τόσο αστείο;" ρώτησε ο Ε-Ζ.

"Τίποτα, υποθέτω".

Οι μόνοι ήχοι στην κουζίνα ήταν από το γλύψιμο, το κόψιμο και το μάσημα. Εκτός από το ρολόι που χτυπούσε στον τοίχο πίσω τους.

"Τι;" Απαίτησε ο Ε-Ζ, παρατηρώντας ότι ο θείος του χαμογελούσε και το έκρυβε πίσω από το χέρι του.

"Υπάρχει κάτι διαφορετικό στο, λοιπόν, ξέρεις, σημερινό σου πρωινό. Θέλεις να μου πεις κάτι; Όπως το γιατί;"

Τα δύο πλάσματα πετάχτηκαν μέσα και κάθισαν το καθένα σε έναν από τους ώμους του Ε-Ζ. Κρυφάκουγαν και δεν του άρεσε καθόλου η απρόσκλητη εισβολή τους, γι' αυτό και τα έδιωξε.

POP.

POP.

Εξαφανίστηκαν.

"Δεν είμαι σίγουρος τι εννοείς".

Ο Σαμ έχυσε στον εαυτό του άλλο ένα φλιτζάνι καφέ. "Είναι για ένα κορίτσι; Γιατί κάθε κορίτσι, θα έπρεπε να σε αποδέχεται όπως είσαι".

Ο E-Z γέλασε. "Όχι κορίτσι. Είσαι εντελώς εκτός πραγματικότητας".

Και οι δύο έμειναν σιωπηλοί για μερικές ακόμα στιγμές bar το ρολόι χτυπούσε.

"Ετοίμασα μια βαλίτσα και θα πάω στο πάρκο αφού γράψω λίγο σήμερα το πρωί. Θα πάρω ένα σημειωματάριο και μερικά στυλό σε περίπτωση που το πάρκο με εμπνεύσει".

"Ακούγεται καλό σχέδιο, αλλά πρώτα θα με βοηθήσεις να συμμαζέψω", είπε η Σαμ σηκώνοντας το κεφάλι της από το τραπέζι.

Ο έφηβος έσπρωξε την καρέκλα του προς τα πίσω και μαζί καθάρισαν γρήγορα. Ο E-Z πήγε στο γραφείο του και έκλεισε την πόρτα πίσω του, όταν ακούστηκε το κουδούνι της εξώπορτας.

Ο Σαμ άφησε τον Άρντεν και τον Πι Τζέι να περάσουν. "Είναι στο γραφείο του και δουλεύει. Σας περιμένει; Αν ναι, δεν μου είπε τίποτα γι' αυτό".

"Του έστειλα ένα μήνυμα, αλλά δεν απάντησε", είπε ο Πι Τζέι.

"Οπότε, σκεφτήκαμε να πεταχτούμε και να τον βγάλουμε έξω σήμερα. Να σιγουρευτούμε ότι θα διασκεδάσει λίγο. Αυτός ο τύπος δουλεύει πάρα πολύ. Η μαμά είπε ότι θα μας πάει εκεί. Απλά πρέπει να το τσεκάρουμε με την E-Z και μετά να της τηλεφωνήσουμε".

"Ο ανιψιός μου είναι ενθουσιασμένος με αυτό το βιβλίο που γράφει. Μπορεί να έχει αντίρρηση".

"Με τον έναν ή τον άλλο τρόπο θα τον πάρουμε από εδώ σήμερα", είπε ο Πι Τζέι.

"Σχεδίαζε να πάει στο πάρκο, αφού γράψει λίγο. Αλλά πήγαινε κάτω, μπορεί να σε συναντήσει εκεί αργότερα;" Ο Σαμ επέστρεψε στην κουζίνα, βγάζοντας λίγο κιμά από την κατάψυξη. Έλεγξε το ντουλάπι για σάλτσα, μακαρόνια, αυγά, κρεμμύδια, φρυγανιά και σπανάκι. Είχε όλα όσα χρειαζόταν για να φτιάξει αργότερα μακαρόνια και κεφτέδες.

Τα δύο αγόρια κατευθύνθηκαν προς το διάδρομο, αφού κρέμασαν τα παλτά τους.

Ο Σαμ φόρεσε το παλτό του. Είχε αναβάλει το κόψιμο του γκαζόν εδώ και καιρό. Σήμερα ήταν η μέρα που θα το φρόντιζε.

Ο E-Z προσπαθούσε να γράψει, αλλά η δημιουργικότητα δεν έτρεχε. Όταν έφτασαν οι φίλοι του - χάρηκε για τη διακοπή. Άνοιξε το Facebook, προσποιούμενος ότι τσέκαρε τις ενημερώσεις. "Γεια σας παιδιά". Γύρισε την καρέκλα του προς το μέρος τους.

"Πω πω φίλε, τι στο καλό έπαθαν τα μαλλιά σου; Πήγατε στο κομμωτήριο χωρίς εμάς;"

"Μήπως τους έδειξες μια φωτογραφία και ζήτησες να σου κάνουν ένα ανάποδο λουκ του Pepe Le Pew;"

"Και τα φρύδια σου επίσης! Δεν ήξερα καν ότι μπορούν να τα βάψουν αυτά;"

Ο E-Z πέρασε τα δάχτυλά του από τα μαλλιά του, έχοντας μηδενική ιδέα για τι πράγμα μιλούσαν. Για μισό λεπτό - σε αυτό αναφερόταν ο Σαμ;

"Και τα μάτια του, είναι επίσης διαφορετικά".

Ο Άρντεν έσκυψε: "Ναι, έχουν χρυσές κηλίδες μέσα τους. Φοβερό!"

"Φίλε, κάνε πίσω, εντάξει;" είπε ο E-Z. "Εσείς οι δύο με φρικάρετε. Το να εισβάλλετε στο χώρο μου δεν είναι ωραίο".

"Τουλάχιστον δεν μυρίζει σαν τον Πέπε", είπε ο Άρντεν κάνοντας πίσω. Ο PJ τον συνάντησε στην άλλη πλευρά του δωματίου, όπου ψιθύριζαν μεταξύ τους.

"Σε πειράζει να βγάλουμε μια φωτογραφία;"

Ο E-Z χαμογέλασε και είπε: "Μοτσαρέλα".

Ο PJ έδειξε τη φωτογραφία που είχε τραβήξει στον Άρντεν. "Βλέπεις!" είπαν κάνοντας τη μεγάλη αποκάλυψη.

Ο E-Z δεν μπορούσε να πιστέψει αυτό που έβλεπε. Τα ξανθά μαλλιά του είχαν μια μαύρη λωρίδα στη μέση και γκρίζες κηλίδες στους κροτάφους. Γκρι! Ζούμαρε, είχαν δίκιο, τα μάτια του είχαν χρυσές κηλίδες. Το μυαλό του γύρισε πίσω στη διαμαντόσκονη, έτσι έμοιαζε η διαμαντόσκονη; Αυτοί οι δύο ηλίθιοι άγγελοι το έκαναν αυτό! Και το καλό που τους θέλω να ξέρουν πώς να το διορθώσουν! Την επόμενη φορά που θα τους έβλεπε, θα τους έκανε να το πληρώσουν. Στο μεταξύ, προσπάθησε να εκτονώσει την κατάσταση.

"Σιγά το πράγμα. Είχα μια δύσκολη νύχτα".

Ο Άρντεν ρώτησε: "Τι δεν μας λες;".

Ο Πι Τζέι πρόσθεσε: "Τα μαλλιά σου γκριζάρουν και είσαι ακόμα στο λύκειο. Νομίζεις ότι αυτό είναι φυσιολογικό;"

"Νομίζω ότι έχει δίκιο- κάνουμε μεγάλο θέμα για το τίποτα. Τι είπε ο θείος σου γι' αυτό;"

"Δεν το πρόσεξε - ή αν το πρόσεξε, δεν είπε τίποτα".

"Τι; Θέλεις να μου πεις ότι ο Σαμ, δεν το πρόσεξε καν;"

"Ήταν τα μάτια του ανοιχτά;"

Ο E-Z προσπάθησε να θυμηθεί. Πρώτα, ο θείος Σαμ τον είχε ρωτήσει αν είχε κάτι να του πει. Αυτό εννοούσε;

"Μια στιγμή", είπε ο E-Z, καθώς πήγαινε προς το μπάνιο. Χρησιμοποίησε τη δεκαπλάσια μεγέθυνση του καθρέφτη για να ρίξει μια πιο προσεκτική ματιά. Έμεινε άναυδος. Τα αστέρια ή οι κηλίδες στα μάτια του ήταν διαφορετικά. Δεν ήταν επιζήμια, στην πραγματικότητα, τον έκαναν να φαίνεται κουλ. Εξέτασε τις γκρίζες τρίχες κατά μήκος των κροτάφων του.

Και λοιπόν; Είχε περάσει πολλά με τον θάνατο των γονιών του. Συν τις καθημερινές πιέσεις του λυκείου. Και να συνηθίσει το αναπηρικό καροτσάκι. Για να μην αναφέρουμε την αντιμετώπιση των αρχαγγέλων και των δοκιμασιών.

Το ότι τα μαλλιά του γκριζάρισαν πρόωρα δεν ήταν πρόβλημα. Μετακίνησε τον καθρέφτη, περνώντας τα δάχτυλά του από τα μαλλιά του.

Η υφή τους ήταν διαφορετική όταν άγγιζε τη μαύρη λωρίδα. Την ένιωθε χοντροκομμένη, σαν τρίχα. Κανένα πρόβλημα, θα έβαζε λίγο τζελ πάνω τους και...

Έξω η μηχανή του γκαζόν έβαλε μπρος. Ο Σαμ έκανε επιτέλους τη φοβερή δουλειά. Πριν από το ατύχημα, το κούρεμα του γκαζόν ήταν η πιο απεχθής εργασία του Ε-Ζ.

"ΓΙΟΎΧΟΥ!" φώναξε ο Σαμ καθώς η μηχανή του γκαζόν έβηξε και σταμάτησε.

Η καρέκλα του Ε-Ζ παραπάτησε προς την μπροστινή πόρτα, η οποία άνοιξε μόνη της. Απογειώθηκε, έχασε τα σκαλιά και προσγειώθηκε στο γκαζόν πίσω από τον Σαμ.

"Γαμώτο!" αναφώνησε ο Σαμ. Είχε χτυπήσει μια πέτρα με τη χλοοκοπτική μηχανή, η οποία πετάχτηκε και τον χτύπησε κοντά στο μάτι του. Σταγόνες αίματος έσταξαν στο μάγουλό του και συγκεντρώθηκαν στο γρασίδι.

Το αναπηρικό καροτσάκι κινήθηκε προς το σημείο όπου βρισκόταν το αίμα, ρουφώντας το με τις ρόδες.

"Είσαι καλά;"

"Είμαι καλά", είπε ο Σαμ. Έψαξε στην τσέπη του, έβγαλε ένα μαντήλι και το κράτησε στην πληγή του.

Ο Άρντεν και ο Πι Τζέι έφτασαν. "Ακούσαμε την κραυγή".

"Είμαι καλά, αλήθεια", είπε ο Σαμ. "Ένα μικρό ατύχημα. Δεν υπάρχει λόγος ανησυχίας ή προβληματισμού. Ας πάμε πάλι μέσα".

Έπιασε τις λαβές του αναπηρικού αμαξιδίου και έσπρωξε. Ήταν εξαιρετικά δύσκολο να κάνει ελιγμούς στο γρασίδι.

Στο μεταξύ ο Άρντεν έφερε τη μηχανή του γκαζόν και την έκρυψε στο υπόστεγο.

"Έχεις πάρει βάρος;" ρώτησε ο Πι Τζέι παρατηρώντας τη δυσκολία που είχε ο Σαμ.

"Έφαγα περίπου είκοσι τηγανίτες σήμερα το πρωί".

"Μήπως η μαύρη λωρίδα είναι πιο βαριά από τα κανονικά σου μαλλιά;" Είπε ο Άρντεν που τους ξανασυνάντησε με ένα χαμόγελο.

"Ω, το πρόσεξαν", είπε ο Σαμ.

"Ναι, με κοροϊδεύουν γι' αυτό από τότε που ήρθαν. Γιατί δεν είπες τίτοτα;"

Τώρα μέσα, ο E-Z έβγαλε ένα τσιρότο και το έβαλε στην πληγή του θείου του.

"Ήταν μια ανεπαίσθητη αλλαγή", είπε ο Σαμ. "Όχι!" χαμογέλασε. "Α, και έχεις σκεφτεί ποτέ να ασχοληθείς με το επάγγελμα του νοσηλευτή; Έχεις λεπτό άγγιγμα".

Ο Πι Τζέι και ο Άρντεν χλεύασαν.

ΚΕΦΑΛΑΙΟ 13

Ο Ε-Ζ και οι φίλοι του επέστρεψαν στο γραφείο του. Αποφάσισε να μείνει κοντά στο σπίτι σε περίπτωση που τον χρειαζόταν ο Σαμ. Ο Σαμ ήταν πολύ απασχολημένος με το μαγείρεμα του δείπνου για να σκεφτεί τι θα μπορούσε να είχε συμβεί με τη μηχανή του γκαζόν.

"Το δείπνο είναι έτοιμο", τηλεφώνησε λίγες ώρες αργότερα. "Έλα να το πάρεις".

Ο Ε-Ζ έδειξε το δρόμο: "Μυρίζει υπέροχα!"

Κάθισαν και μοίρασαν το φαγητό και τα καρυκεύματα.

"Έχεις ήδη μια ωραία λάμψη εκεί", είπε ο Άρντεν στον Σαμ.

Ο Σαμ που μέχρι τώρα δεν ήξερε ότι είχε μια ορατή πληγή και τώρα τη φορούσε με περηφάνια. Μπήκε σε ένα ακόμα κεφτεδάκι και το έβαλε στο πιάτο του.

"Τι συνέβη εκεί έξω τέλος πάντων", ρώτησε ο Πι Τζέι.

"Ήταν μια πέτρα. Πιάστηκε στο χλοοκοπτικό και με χτύπησε". Συνέχισε να σπρώχνει το φαγητό του στο πιάτο. "Πώς πάει το γράψιμο;" ρώτησε τον ανιψιό του στρέφοντας την προσοχή μακριά από τον εαυτό του.

"Δεν είχα χρόνο να ασχοληθώ με αυτό σήμερα το πρωί".

Ο Σαμ άλλαξε θέμα και ρώτησε αν συνέβαινε κάτι στο σχολείο ή στην ομάδα.

"Έχουμε προπόνηση απόψε", είπε ο Πι Τζέι.

"Και ελπίζουμε ότι ο Ε-Ζ θα πιάσει στο αυριανό παιχνίδι".

Ο Ε-Ζ κούνησε το κεφάλι του, για ένα οριστικό όχι και συνέχισε να τρώει.

"Ένα inning, μόνο ένα και αν δεν θέλεις να συνεχίσεις να παίζεις, δεν μας πειράζει", είπε ο Άρντεν.

"Υπέροχη ιδέα", είπε ο θείος Σαμ. "Βούτηξε το δάχτυλο του ποδιού σου Αν δεν αισθάνεσαι καλά, βγες έξω. Τι έχεις να χάσεις;"

Ο Πι Τζέι άνοιξε το στόμα του για να πει κάτι, αλλά αποφάσισε να μην το κάνει. Έσπρωξε ένα κεφτέ στο στόμα του. Μάσησε, ήπιε ένα ποτό "Όταν είσαι εκεί, E-Z, ανεβάζεις το ηθικό όλων. Τα παιδιά σε εκτιμούν πολύ. Πάντα σε εκτιμούσαν και πάντα θα σε εκτιμούν."

"Εντάξει", είπε ο E-Z. "Θα κάτσω στον πάγκο, αν νομίζεις ότι θα βοηθήσει. Μετά το δείπνο, ας πάμε κάτω στο πάρκο να κάνουμε λίγη προπόνηση. Να δούμε πώς θα πάνε τα πράγματα".

"Εντάξει", είπε ο Πι-Τζέι.

Ευχαρίστησαν τον Σαμ για το καταπληκτικό δείπνο.

"Εσύ μαγείρεψες, οπότε θα καθαρίσουμε εμείς", προσφέρθηκε c Άρντεν.

Ο E-Z και ο Πι-Τζέι αντάλλαξαν ματιές.

Όταν ο Σαμ απομακρύνθηκε, ο Πι-Τζέι είπε: "Είσαι πολύ φιλάρεσκος"

Ο Άρντεν εκτόξευσε λίγο νερό προς την κατεύθυνση του PJ, αλλά c E-Z έπιασε το μεγαλύτερο μέρος του στο πρόσωπο.

Ο PJ ανταπέδωσε μια πιτσιλιά που πιτσίλισε στο πάτωμα της κουζίνας, χτυπώντας τα παπούτσια του Σαμ.

"Η σφουγγαρίστρα και ο κουβάς είναι στη ντουλάπα", είπε, αρπάζοντας το παλτό του βγαίνοντας.

Τελείωσαν το καθάρισμα, μέχρι τότε είχαν στεγνώσει ως επί το πλείστον, εκτός από τον E-Z που άλλαξε το πουκάμισό του. Τελικά, έφτασαν στο γήπεδο του μπέιζμπολ και ήταν ήδη κατειλημμένο.

"Υπέροχα", είπε ο E-Z. "Πάμε".

Στην άκρη του γηπέδου, βρίσκονταν μερικά κορίτσια από την ομάδα μαζορετών της αντίπαλης ομάδας. Η μία, μια κοκκινομάλλα κοπέλα, κοίταξε προς την κατεύθυνση του E-Z. Έκανε μια περιστροφή και προσγειώθηκε με ευκολία.

"Υποθέτω ότι μπορούμε να μείνουμε για λίγο", είπε ο E-Z.

Διέσχισαν το γήπεδο προς τους πάγκους. Έπρεπε τουλάχιστον να πουν ένα γεια, αλλιώς θα έμοιαζαν με μαλάκες.

Η μικρή κοκκινομάλλα κοπέλα ψιθύρισε κάτι στη φίλη της και χαχάνισαν.

Ο E-Z ήταν σίγουρος ότι γελούσαν μαζί του.

"'Έχουμε παρέα", είπε η κοκκινομάλλα κοπέλα.

"Ναι, ένας τύπος σε αναπηρικό καροτσάκι με μαλλιά ζέβρα και δύο σπασίκλες", φώναξε ο τρίτος παίκτης του μπέιζμπολ. Περίμενε ότι όλοι θα γελούσαν με το άθλιο αστείο του, αλλά κανείς δεν το έκανε.

"Μην του δίνεις σημασία", είπε η φίλη της κοκκινομάλλας κοπέλας. "Είναι αξιολύπητος".

"Φύγε", φώναξε ο αριστερός παίκτης του γηπέδου. "Δεν υπάρχει χώρος εδώ για έναν σακάτη".

Ο E-Z αγνόησε όλα τα σχόλια. Η καρέκλα του, όμως, δεν το έκανε. Σπρώχνει, στροφάρει σαν ταύρος που προσπαθεί να ξεφύγει από το μαντρί. "Ουάου!" είπε, καθώς η καρέκλα παραπατούσε, σαν άγριο άλογο.

Ο Άρντεν έπιασε τα χερούλια της καρέκλας, και η καρέκλα επανήλθε στην κανονική της λειτουργία.

Πίσω από το πιάτο, ο catcher πέταξε μια μύγα και χάλασε μια ρίψη. "Βλέπω ότι χρειάζεστε έναν αξιοπρεπή catcher", είπε ο E-Z.

Οι μαζορέτες χασκογέλασαν.

"Δώστε μου πέντε λεπτά πίσω από το πιάτο, μόνο πέντε. Αν καταφέρω να πιάσω κάθε ρίψη που στέλνετε προς το μέρος μου, τότε θα σας κάνουμε τη χάρη να μείνουμε".

"Και αν δεν τα καταφέρεις;" ρώτησε ο πίτσερ.

Ο catcher έβγαλε τη μάσκα του. "Μας κερνάς μπιφτέκια και πατάτες τηγανιτές".

"Και μιλκσέικ", πρόσθεσε ο πρώτος παίκτης του μπέιζμπολ.

"Σύμφωνοι", είπε ο E-Z καθώς η καρέκλα του προωθήθηκε μπροστά.

Κάθισε υπομονετικά, ενώ ο Άρντεν έβαλε τις επιγονατίδες του. Ο Πι-Τζέι τράβηξε το προστατευτικό στήθους στο κεφάλι του και έβαλε τη μάσκα του catcher στο πρόσωπό του. Ο E-Z έσφιξε τη γροθιά του στο γάντι του catcher.

"Σωστά, πέτα μου τη μπάλα", πρόσταξε ο E-Z.

"Ελπίζω να ξέρεις τι κάνεις φίλε", είπαν ο Άρντεν και ο Πι Τζέι.

"Έχε μου εμπιστοσύνη" είπε ο E-Z. Πήρε τη θέση του πίσω από το πιάτο. "Ο παίκτης είναι έτοιμος!"

Ο πίτσερ έκανε νόημα στον Άρντεν να χτυπήσει. Εκείνος διάλεξε ένα ρόπαλο και ανέβηκε στο πιάτο.

Ο E-Z έκανε σήμα στον πίτσερ να ρίξει μια ψηλή γρήγορη μπάλα. Αντ' αυτού, ο πίτσερ έριξε μια καμπύλη μπάλα, η οποία ήταν ακριβώς στη ζώνη. Ο Άρντεν έχασε το χτύπημα, αλλά όχι εντελώς, καθώς συνδέθηκε με τη μπάλα ένα τικ και αυτή έφυγε πίσω. Ο E-Z σηκώθηκε από την καρέκλα του και την άρπαξε.

"Ουάου!" φώναξε ο πίτσερ. "Ωραία διάσωση".

"Τυχερός", είπε ο πρώτος παίκτης βάσης.

Οι μαζορέτες πλησίασαν πιο κοντά.

Δεύτερη ρίψη στον Άρντεν, ο τελευταίος έσκασε στο δεξί γήπεδο.

Ο Πι Τζέι ανέβηκε στο ρόπαλο και έκανε άουτ. Ο E-Z έπιασε εύκολα όλες τις μπάλες, αλλά η τελευταία ρίψη έγινε άγρια και παραλίγο να την χάσει. Ο PJ πήγε προς την πρώτη θέση, αλλά ο E-Z πέταξε την μπάλα κάτω και έμεινε εκτός.

Έπαιξαν μέχρι που σκοτείνιασε πολύ για να δουν πια την μπάλα.

Μετά το παιχνίδι, αποφάσισαν ότι ήταν ισοπαλία. Πήγαν σε ένα κοντινό εστιατόριο και ο καθένας πλήρωσε το φαγητό του.

"Θα σας σκοτώσουμε στο αυριανό παιχνίδι" καυχήθηκε ο Μπραντ Γουίπερ, ο αρχηγός της ομάδας.

"Παίζετε Ε-Ζ;" ρώτησε ο Λάρι Φοξ, ο πρώτος παίκτης του μπέιζμπολ.

"Ω, σίγουρα θα παίξει", είπαν ο Άρντεν και ο Πι Τζέι.

"Σίγουρα".

Η κοκκινομάλλα κοπέλα ήταν η Σάλι Σουόν και ψιθύρισε κάτι στον Άρντεν, ο οποίος κούνησε το κεφάλι του. "Ρώτα τον μόνος σου", είπε.

"Να με ρωτήσεις τι;"

Τα μάγουλά της κοκκίνισαν.

"Θέλεις να μάθεις τι συνέβη, σωστά;"

Εκείνη έγνεψε. "Εσύ ζήτησες από τον κομμωτή σου να το κάνει, ή μήπως αυτοί...".

"Έκαναν κάποιο λάθος;" είπε.

Εκείνη έγνεψε.

"Ξύπνησα σήμερα το πρωί και ήταν κάπως έτσι. Τέλος της ιστορίας".

"Τράβα το άλλο", είπε ένας παίκτης. "Τώρα πες μας γιατί είσαι σε αναπηρικό καροτσάκι".

Ο Ε-Ζ είπε την ιστορία του. Όλοι παρέμειναν ήσυχοι όσο το έκανε. Κανείς δεν έφαγε ή ήπιε. Όταν τελείωσε, ανησύχησε ότι όλοι θα του συμπεριφέρονταν διαφορετικά, αλλά δεν το έκαναν.

Μίλησαν για το επερχόμενο Παγκόσμιο Πρωτάθλημα και άλλες κουβέντες σχετικές με τον αθλητισμό.

Αργότερα, όταν οι φίλοι του τον συνόδευσαν στο σπίτι, ήταν όλοι ήσυχοι. Είπε καληνύχτα στα παιδιά και επέστρεψε στο δωμάτιό του. Προσπάθησε να δει τηλεόραση, να γράψει λίγο, αλλά ό,τι κι αν έκανε, συνέχισε να σκέφτεται όλα όσα έχασε. Έπεσε ξανά στο κρεβάτι και κοίταξε το ταβάνι και τελικά έπεσε για ύπνο.

ΚΕΦΑΛΑΙΟ 14

Ο Ε-Ζ κοιμότ αν, ονειρευόταν.

"Ξύπνα Ε-Ζ! Ξύπνα!" είπε η Ρέικι, πηδώντας πάνω-κάτω στο στήθος του.

"Κόφ' το!" αναφώνησε.

Ο Χαντζ ψέκασε λίγο νερό στο πρόσωπό του.

Εκείνος το τίναξε από πάνω του. "Εσείς οι δύο έχετε να δώσετε κάποιες εξηγήσεις και να διορθώσετε κάποια πράγματα. Βάλτε τα μαλλιά μου πίσω όπως ήταν. Και τα μάτια μου επίσης!"

"Δεν υπάρχει χρόνος!" είπαν, καθώς η καρέκλα του αναποδογύρισε, τον έριξε μέσα και μετά πέταξε έξω από το ήδη ανοιχτό παράθυρο.

"Δεν είμαι καν ντυμένος!" Ο Ε-Ζ αναφώνησε.

Η Ρέικι και ο Χατζ χασκογέλασαν και είπαν στον Ε-Ζ να ευχηθεί αυτό που ήθελε να φορέσει. Όταν κοίταξε ξανά κάτω, φορούσε τζιν, μια ζώνη και ένα μπλουζάκι. Κοίταξε τα πόδια του, όπου τα αθλητικά του παπούτσια έδεναν τα κορδόνια τους. Καθώς πετούσαν στον ουρανό, ο Ε-Ζ τους ευχαρίστησε.

"Λοιπόν, μας συγχωρείτε;" ρώτησε ο Χαντζ.

"Δώστε του χρόνο", είπε ο Ρέικι.

Ο Ε-Ζ έγνεψε, καθώς η καρέκλα του ανέβαινε όλο και πιο ψηλά. Πάνω από ένα αεροπλάνο, περνώντας από το αεροπλάνο. Προφανώς δεν ήταν ο προορισμός τους. Συνέχισαν να πετάνε, μέχρι που η αναπηρική του καρέκλα έμεινε εντελώς ακίνητη, και μετά έστρεψε τον εαυτό της προς τα κάτω

"Εκεί είναι", είπε ο Ρέικι.

Κάτω, μια ομάδα ανθρώπων στεκόταν έξω από ένα ψηλό κτίριο γραφείων σε μια συστάδα.

"Το νιώθεις αυτό;" ρώτησε ο E-Z, παρατηρώντας ότι ο αέρας γύρω από το περιστατικό ήταν διαφορετικός. Δονείτο από ενέργεια.

"Ναι", είπε ο Χαντζ.

"Μπράβο σου που το πρόσεξες αυτή τη φορά", είπε ο Ρέικι.

"Εννοείς ότι υπήρχαν δονήσεις και τις άλλες φορές;"

"Ναι, αλλά καθώς οι δυνάμεις σου μεγαλώνουν, θα μπορείς να μηδενίζεις τις θέσεις".

"Και όχι μόνο εσύ, αλλά και η καρέκλα σου μπορεί να τις αντιληφθεί".

"Εννοείς ότι έχω μια σούπερ-ντούπερ έξυπνη καρέκλα; Ήξερα ότι ήταν τροποποιημένη, αλλά αυτό είναι φοβερό!"

Οι άγγελοι γέλασαν.

Η καρέκλα επιτάχυνε, ενώ από κάτω τους ακούγονταν πυροβολισμοί. Είδαν ανθρώπους να τρέχουν, να ουρλιάζουν, να πέφτουν.

Προς το χάος ο E-Z και η καρέκλα του πέταξαν, μέσα στον επερχόμενο καταιγισμό από σφαίρες. Τριγύρισε, καθώς η αναπηρική καρέκλα τις απέκρουσε. Αναρωτήθηκε τι θα συνέβαινε αν η καρέκλα έχανε μία.

"Είμαστε σίγουροι ότι είσαι αλεξίσφαιρος", είπε η Ρέικι χωρίς να τον ρωτήσει. "Ήταν μέρος του τελετουργικού".

"Και η διαμαντόσκονη θα πρέπει να δουλέψει".

"Αρκετά σίγουροι;" είπε, ελπίζοντας ότι είχαν δίκιο. "Αν δουλέψει, τότε είναι ένα καλό αντάλλαγμα για την κατάσταση των μαλλιών μου!"

Οι επίδοξοι άγγελοι γέλασαν.

ΚΕΦΑΛΑΙΟ 15

Η ΑΝΑΠΗΡΙΚΉ ΤΟΥ ΚΑΡΈΚΛΑ έσπρωξε προς τα κάτω, εντοπίζοντας έναν άνδρα στην οροφή του κτιρίου. Πυροβολούσε στο πλήθος από κάτω, και σε αυτούς καθώς τον πλησίαζαν. Το αναπηρικό καροτσάκι γλίστρησε προς τα εμπρός, ο Ε-Ζ άκουσε έναν παράξενο ήχο, σαν αεροπλάνο που κατεβάζει τον τροχό προσγείωσης. Προερχόταν από την αναπηρική καρέκλα, καθώς μια μεταλλική θήκη έπεφτε προς τα κάτω και προσγειωνόταν πάνω στον τύπο. Το όπλο πετάχτηκε από το χέρι του, σε όλη την οροφή πριν το μαραφέτι πιάσει. Ο άντρας προσπάθησε να πετάξει τον Ε-Ζ και την αναπηρική καρέκλα από την πλάτη του, αλλά τίποτα δεν έπιασε.

Μια σειρήνα ακούστηκε στο βάθος και στη συνέχεια έγινε όλο και πιο δυνατή καθώς έκλεινε το κενό.

"Αν σε αφήσω να ανέβεις", ρώτησε ο Ε-Ζ, "θα είσαι φρόνιμος;".

Παρόλο που ο άνδρας έγνεψε συμφωνώντας, η αναπηρική καρέκλα αρνήθηκε να μετακινηθεί.

Ο Ε-Ζ έπρεπε να απενεργοποιήσει το όπλο και να φύγει από εκεί πριν φτάσει η αστυνομία. Αναρωτήθηκε αν κάποιος από κάτω είχε τραυματιστεί. Περίμενε ότι τα ασθενοφόρα ήταν καθ' οδόν. Ωστόσο, αυτός και η καρέκλα του μπορούσαν να πετάξουν τους σοβαρά τραυματισμένους στο νοσοκομείο πολύ πιο γρήγορα.

Κοίταξε το όπλο στην άλλη πλευρά της οροφής. Συγκεντρώθηκε και μετά άπλωσε το χέρι του. Σαν το χέρι του να ήταν μαγνήτης, το όπλο πέταξε μέσα του και το αχρήστευσε δένοντάς το σε κόμπο. Ο Ε-Ζ έβγαλε τη ζώνη του και τη χρησιμοποίησε για να δέσει τα χέρια του σκοπευτή πίσω από την πλάτη του.

Η καρέκλα απογειώθηκε και πέταξε μακριά σαν πύραυλος, καθώς οι πόρτες στην ταράτσα άνοιξαν. Το τροποποιημένο μαραφέτι σηκώθηκε, αιωρούμενο στον αέρα, ενώ ο E-Z παρακολουθούσε μια ομάδα SWAT να κινείται προς τον δράστη και να τον συλλαμβάνει. Η έκφραση στο πρόσωπο του αστυνομικού που βρήκε το όπλο δεμένο στον κόμπο ήταν ανεκτίμητη.

Για ένα ή δύο δευτερόλεπτα, δίστασε αναλογιζόμενος την εντολή του, αλλά υπήρχαν άνθρωποι τραυματισμένοι από κάτω και μπορούσε να τους βοηθήσει γρηγορότερα από οποιονδήποτε άλλον και αυτό έκανε. Θα ανησυχούσε για τις συνέπειες αργότερα και θα ήλπιζε ότι θα καταλάβαιναν.

Ο E-Z προσγειώθηκε κοντά στο πλήθος. Μάζεψε τους τέσσερις που ήταν οι πιο σοβαρά τραυματισμένοι και καθώς ήταν αναίσθητοι, χρησιμοποίησε μέρος της φτερούγας του για να τους κρατήσει με ασφάλεια στην καρέκλα του καθώς πετούσαν στον ουρανό.

Η καρέκλα απορρόφησε το αίμα των τραυματισμένων επιβατών καθώς έσταζε από τις πληγές τους. Το αίμα τους συνδυάστηκε με το αίμα του E-Z και του Σαμ Ντίκενς. Αυτή η συγχώνευση έσπρωξε τις σφαίρες έξω από τα σώματά τους και οι πληγές τους άρχισαν να επουλώνονται.

Χρειάστηκαν αρκετά λεπτά για να φτάσουν στο νοσοκομείο. Μέχρι να φτάσουν, όλοι οι ασθενείς είχαν θεραπευτεί, σαν να μην είχαν συμβεί ποτέ τα τραύματά τους. Έριξαν τα χέρια τους γύρω από τον E-Z και τον ευχαρίστησαν.

Στο πάρκινγκ του νοσοκομείου ο καθένας τους πήδηξε από το αναπηρικό καροτσάκι.

Στην είσοδο περίμεναν συνοδούς με φορεία έτοιμα.

Ο E-Z έριξε μια ματιά προς το μέρος τους. Χαιρέτησε και μετά πέταξε στον ουρανό. Από κάτω του, εκείνοι που είχε σώσει ανταπέδωσαν το κύμα του. Ήλπιζε ότι οι συνοδοί που περίμεναν θα ήταν πολύ ενοχλημένοι που δεν τους χρειάζονταν τελικά.

"Σας ευχαριστώ", φώναξε ένας νεαρός άνδρας, χαιρετώντας τον.

"Ελπίζω να σας ξαναδώ", αναφώνησε μια μεσήλικη γυναίκα.

"Είστε πραγματικός ήρωας!", είπε ένας άνδρας που του θύμιζε τον θείο Σαμ.

"Μου θυμίζεις τον εγγονό μου - εκτός από την περίεργη γραμμή στα μαλλιά σου!" είπε μια ηλικιωμένη γυναίκα.

Οι συνοδοί πλησίασαν τους τέσσερις ρωτώντας: "Χρειάζεται κανείς βοήθεια;".

Ο νεαρός άνδρας είπε: "Δεν θα το πιστέψετε, αλλά με πυροβόλησαν - δύο φορές πριν από λίγο καιρό. Νομίζω ότι λιποθύμησα. Όταν ξύπνησα", τράβηξε το μπροστινό μέρος του πουκαμίσου του που ήταν γεμάτο αίμα, "οι πληγές είχαν φύγει".

Η ηλικιωμένη γυναίκα, της οποίας το φόρεμα ήταν ματωμένο, εξήγησε πως είχε πυροβοληθεί κοντά στην καρδιά της.

"Θα ήμουν νεκρή, αν εκείνο το παλικάρι στο αναπηρικό καροτσάκι δεν μου είχε σώσει τη ζωή".

Οι άλλοι δύο ασθενείς είχαν ανάλογες ιστορίες να διηγηθούν. Επαίνεσαν τον E-Z και τον ευχαρίστησαν ξανά. Παρόλο που δεν ήταν πια μαζί τους.

"Νομίζω ότι πρέπει να έρθετε όλοι ακόμα στο νοσοκομείο", είπε ο πρώτος φροντιστής.

Ο δεύτερος συνοδός είπε: "Ναι, έχετε περάσει μια τραυματική εμπειρία. Θα πρέπει να δείτε έναν γιατρό και να πάρετε το πράσινο φως".

Και οι τέσσερις πρώην τραυματισμένοι πολίτες επέτρεψαν στους συνοδούς να τους βοηθήσουν να μπουν μέσα. Προσπάθησαν να ανεβάσουν τον μεγαλύτερο από τους τέσσερις στο φορείο.

"Είμαι μια χαρά!" αναφώνησε η ηλικιωμένη γυναίκα.

Την ακολούθησαν μέσα στο νοσοκομείο.

"**Κ**ΑΛΎΤΕΡΑ ΝΑ ΤΟ ΚΆΝΟΥΜΕ τώρα", είπε η Ρέικι.

"Είναι λυπηρό όμως. Έκανε τόσο αξιόλογα πράγματα και τώρα κανείς δεν θα το θυμάται".

Σκούπισαν το μυαλό όλων όσων βρίσκονταν στην περιοχή.

"Πραγματικά έκανε καταπληκτική δουλειά".

"Ναι, ήταν καλά επιλεγμένος", είπε ο Χαντζ.

Ο Ε-Ζ επέστρεψε στο σπίτι του, πετώντας εκεί όσο πιο γρήγορα μπορούσε. Ήξερε ότι ο πόνος θα ερχόταν, αλλά όχι πόσο άσχημος θα ήταν αυτή τη φορά. Με το ζόρι κατάφερε να περάσει από το παράθυρο και να ανέβει στο κρεβάτι πριν οι ώμοι του φλεγούν με αποτέλεσμα να λιποθυμήσει.

Οι άγγελοι επέστρεψαν, ψιθυρίζοντας καταπραϋντικά λόγια όταν φώναζε στον ύπνο του. Όταν ο πόνος γινόταν πολύ μεγάλος, τον ανακούφιζαν παίρνοντάς τον πάνω τους.

"Η τρίτη δοκιμασία ολοκληρώθηκε", είπε η Ρέικι. "Τις περνάει με ευκολία".

"Σωστά, αλλά πρέπει να βεβαιωθούμε ότι δεν αναγνωρίζεται. Μπορεί να φαίνεται, αλλά πρέπει να σβήσουμε τις αναμνήσεις. Ανησυχώ όμως, μήπως μας ξεφύγει κάποιος".

"Αν σβήσουμε τα μυαλά όλων όσων βρίσκονται στην περιοχή, όλα θα πάνε καλά".

ΚΕΦΑΛΑΙΟ 16

Το επόμενο πρωί, ο E-Z έτρωγε δημητριακά όταν ο Σαμ μπήκε στην κουζίνα.

"Ο καφές μυρίζει ωραία", είπε ο Σαμ.

Ο έφηβος έβαλε στο θείο του μια κούπα γεμάτη. "Τι;" ρώτησε εκείνος, με μια αίσθηση déjà vu.

"Τι, τι;" Ο Σαμ ρώτησε καθώς πρόσθεσε λίγη κρέμα γάλακτος στην κούπα.

"Με κοιτάς επίμονα", είπε ο E-Z. Κούνησε το κεφάλι του. Μήπως βρισκόταν στη Μέρα της Μαρμότας; Στην ταινία για μια μέρα που επαναλαμβάνεται ξανά και ξανά, με τον Μπιλ Μάρεϊ;

"Α, αυτό. Υπάρχει κάτι που θα ήθελες να μου πεις;" Έριξε έναν κύβο ζάχαρης στον καφέ του.

Αγνοώντας τον θείο του, έβαλε στο στόμα του κορνφλέικς. "Δεν είμαι σίγουρος τι εννοείς".

Ο Σαμ περίμενε τον ανιψιό του να τελειώσει το πρωινό του. "Σε κοίταξα χθες το βράδυ και το κρεβάτι σου ήταν άδειο και το παράθυρο ανοιχτό. Πώς βγήκες έξω με την καρέκλα σου, δεν ξέρω. Σε κάθε περίπτωση, αν πρόκειται να βγεις έξω, πρέπει να μου το πεις. Είμαι υπεύθυνος για σένα και για το πού βρίσκεσαι. Την επόμενη φορά υποσχέσου μου ότι θα με ενημερώνεις πού πας και πότε θα γυρίσεις. Είναι κοινή ευγένεια".

"Ι..."

POP.

POP.

Εμφανίστηκαν ο Hadz και η Reiki. Η Ρέικι πέταξε προς τον Σαμ, φτερουγίζοντας μπροστά στα μάτια του. Για λίγα δευτερόλεπτα, ο Σαμ φαινόταν ζόμπι. Μετά συνέχισε να πίνει τον καφέ του. Σήκωσε το ποτήρι, ήπιε, το άφησε κάτω. Επανέλαβε.

Ο Ε-Ζ θυμήθηκε ένα παιχνίδι για πουλιά - όπου το πουλί βουτάει το κεφάλι του στο ποτήρι και πίνει. Πώς λεγόταν αυτό το πράγμα;

"Πουλί πουλί", είπε ο Σαμ. Κοίταξε το ρολόι του.

Τι στο καλό; Μπορούσε ο θείος του να διαβάσει το μυαλό του τώρα;

"Ποιος δεν μπορεί να διαβάσει το μυαλό του;" Ο Χαντζ είπε χαμογελώντας.

Ο Σαμ σηκώθηκε και με γλαυκά μάτια και κινήσεις σαν ρομπότ πήγε στον νεροχύτη, ξέπλυνε το φλιτζάνι του και το έβαλε στο πλυντήριο πιάτων. Στη συνέχεια, άρπαξε τα κλειδιά του αυτοκινήτου του και έφυγε χωρίς να πει λέξη.

Το στόμα του Ε-Ζ έμεινε με ανοιχτό το στόμα καθώς επεξεργαζόταν τις πληροφορίες και μετά απαίτησε: "Εντάξει, εσείς οι δύο. Τι κάνατε στον θείο μου τον Σαμ; Δεν είχατε κανένα δικαίωμα να... να... κάνετε ό,τι κάνατε". Ήταν τόσο θυμωμένος που το πρόσωπό του είχε κοκκινίσει και οι γροθιές του ήταν σφιγμένες.

POP.

POP.

Το μισούσε αυτό. Κάθε φορά που έκαναν κάτι κακό, εξαφανίζονταν και έπρεπε να τους ζητάει συγγνώμη για να τους κάνει να επιστρέψουν, ενώ δεν είχε κάνει τίποτα κακό.

"Συγγνώμη", είπε. "Σε παρακαλώ, γύρνα πίσω".

POP

POP.

"Ό,τι έγινε, έγινε", είπε ήρεμα. "Αλήθεια διάβασε το μυαλό μου;"

Η Ρέικι είπε: "Ναι, αλλά ήταν ένα μεμονωμένο περιστατικό".

"Αυτό είναι καλό. Δεν θα μπορούσα ποτέ να ξεφύγω με τίποτα".

"Είμαστε η εφεδρεία σου, κατά τη διάρκεια των δοκιμών. Είναι στα χέρι μας να προστατεύσουμε εσένα και τους φίλους σου, συμπεριλαμβανομένοι του θείου Σαμ".

"Τι του κάνατε;" ρώτησε ξανά, καθώς χτύπησε το κουδούνι της πόρτας. Δεν κουνήθηκε, περίμενε να απαντήσουν στην ερώτησή του. Το κουδούνι χτύπησε ξανά. "Μισό λεπτό", είπε. "Πείτε μου τι του κάνατε. ΤΩΡΑ!"

"Του έσβησα το μυαλό", ψιθύρισε η Ρέικι.

"Τι έκανες!"

"Έπρεπε να το κάνουμε, για να προστατεύσουμε εσένα και την αποστολή σου", πρόσθεσε ο Χαντζ.

Ο Πι Τζέι και ο Άρντεν μπήκαν στην κουζίνα. "Η πόρτα ήταν ξεκλείδωτη", είπε ο Άρντεν.

"Ναι, είπαμε στον Σαμ χθες ότι θα σε παίρναμε σήμερα το πρωί".

"Καλημέρα και σε εσάς". Σπρώχτηκε έξω από το τραπέζι.

"Πρέπει να μιλήσουμε, φίλε. Αλλά βιαζόμαστε".

Πήρε το σακίδιο του και το γεύμα του. Πήγαν προς την μπροστινή πόρτα. Στην κορυφή της σκάλας, η καρέκλα πετάχτηκε μπροστά - σαν να ήθελε να πετάξει κάτω. Ζήτησε από τους φίλους του να τον βοηθήσουν να κατέβει τη ράμπα. Ο Άρντεν και ο Πι Τζέι τον βοήθησαν να μπει στο πίσω κάθισμα του αυτοκινήτου. Ο Άρντεν έβαλε το αναπηρικό καροτσάκι στο πορτμπαγκάζ.

"Γεια σας, κυρία Λέστερ", είπε ο E-Z, καθώς τα τρία αγόρια μπήκαν στο πίσω κάθισμα του αυτοκινήτου.

"Καλημέρα", είπε και μετά άνοιξε το ραδιόφωνο. Ο εκφωνητής μιλούσε για μια νέα συνταγή.

"Μόλις ξεκίνησαν", ψιθύρισε ο Πι-Τζέι, "τι έκανες χθες το βράδυ;".

"Τίποτα ιδιαίτερο. Έφαγα. Κοιμήθηκα. Τα συνηθισμένα".

"Δείξ' του."

Ο Πι Τζέι πέρασε το τηλέφωνό του και πάτησε το play.

Ήταν ένα βίντεο στο YouTube. Με εκείνον, στο αναπηρικό του καροτσάκι να πετάει στον ουρανό, μεταφέροντας τραυματίες. Η καρέκλα του ήταν κατακόκκινη, κινούμενη τόσο γρήγορα, σαν μια θολούρα που καίγεται. Τα λευκά του φτερά ήταν ορατά. Και η αντίθεση αυτής της μαύρης λωρίδας στα ξανθά μαλλιά του τόνιζε την εμφάνισή του.

"Δεν καταλαβαίνω", είπε ο E-Z, ενώ έξυνε το κεφάλι του με μηδενική μοιραστή εξήγηση. Περίμενε να έρθουν οι άγγελοι και να σβήσουν το μυαλό των φίλων του - δεν το έκαναν. Περίμενε να σταματήσει ο κόσμος - δεν το έκανε. Αναρωτήθηκε αν θα έβλεπε ποτέ ξανά τους γονείς του; Ήταν αυτό μια δοκιμασία; Έκλεισε το τηλέφωνο και επέστρεψε το τηλέφωνο.

"Φίλε", είπε ο Άρντεν, καθώς η μητέρα του μπήκε με το όπισθεν σε μια θέση στάθμευσης.

"Βιάσου τώρα, αλλιώς θα αργήσεις", είπε καθώς άνοιγε το πορτμπαγκάζ.

"Τα λέμε αργότερα", είπε ο Άρντεν καθώς η μητέρα του έφυγε.

Οι τρεις φίλοι πήραν το δρόμο για το σχολείο χωρίς να μιλήσουν. Το τελευταίο προειδοποιητικό κουδούνι ήταν έτοιμο να χτυπήσει από λεπτό σε λεπτό.

Ο E-Z τροχοδρόμησε κατά μήκος του διαδρόμου, χαμογελώντας στον εαυτό του, ενώ ταυτόχρονα ανησυχούσε για το ποιος άλλος θα έβλεπε το κλιπ. Αν και ήταν καταπληκτικό να βλέπει τον εαυτό του σε δράση. Σαν ένας πιο άνετος Σούπερμαν. Ένας πραγματικός ήρωας. Είχε σώσει ανθρώπους. Έσωσε ζωές. Αυτός και η αναπηρική του καρέκλα ήταν ανίκητοι. Ήταν ένα δυναμικό δίδυμο. Αναρωτιόταν αν χρειάζονταν καν τη βοήθεια των δύο επίδοξων αγγέλων. Ένιωθε ωραία. Κάθε στιγμή. Η διάσωση. Η σωτηρία. Η επιτυχής ολοκλήρωση μιας ακόμη δοκιμασίας. Φοβερό. Μακάρι να μπορούσε να ενημερώσει τους καλύτερους φίλους του για το μυστικό του.

"E-Z Dickens!" φώναξε η καθηγήτριά του κυρία Κλάους.

"Μάλιστα κυρία", είπε ο Ε-Ζ, γυρίζοντας τη σελίδα για να διαβάσει το μάθημα. Αναρωτήθηκε γιατί έχανε χρόνο στο σχολείο. Δεν τον χρειαζόταν πια.

***

Π ΡΟΣΠΆΘΗΣΕ ΝΑ ΜΗΝ ΚΟΙΜΗΘΕΊ κατά τη διάρκεια του μαθήματος. Η κυρία Κλάους τον παρακολουθούσε, περισσότερο από το συνηθισμένο. Κάθε φορά που αποκοιμιόταν, ύψωνε τη φωνή της σαν να το είχε προσέξει.

Αφού χτύπησε το κουδούνι και το μάθημα τελείωσε, οι μαθητές χώρισαν το δρόμο για να τον αφήσουν να βγει πρώτος από την πόρτα. Έριξε μια ματιά σε μερικούς από τους συμμαθητές του, για να τους ευχαριστήσει. Λίγοι είχαν οπτική επαφή. Οι περισσότεροι κοίταξαν αλλού. Δεν είχαν συνηθίσει τη νέα του ιδιότητα - ακόμα.

Στο διάδρομο περίμενε ένα πλήθος συμμαθητών και θαυμαστών. Τα φλας άναβαν, καθώς οι φωτογραφικές μηχανές και τα κινητά έβγαζαν φωτογραφίες. Ήλπιζε ότι η σχολική εφημερίδα ήταν εκεί. Θα έγραφαν ακόμα και ένα άρθρο γι' αυτόν. Περίμενε ένα λεπτό. Δεν θα έβλεπε ποτέ ξανά τους γονείς του - όχι αν το μάθαιναν όλοι! Πώς συνέβη αυτό; Σπρώχτηκε για να περάσει. Συνέχισαν να χειροκροτούν, με την πάροδο του χρόνου όλο και πιο δυνατά. Μερικοί φώναξαν, "Λόγος!"

Ο Πι Τζέι πλησίασε και ρώτησε: "Έχεις δει το Facebook τελευταία;".

Ο E-Z σήκωσε τους ώμους.

"Ρίξε μια ματιά στα τελευταία", είπε ο PJ, δείχνοντας στον φίλο του τα πρωτοσέλιδα.

"Τοπικός ήρωας σε αναπηρικό καροτσάκι". Σταμάτησε να κινείται και έκανε κλικ στο κλιπ. Έλεγε ότι ο τοπικός ήρωας φοιτούσε στο Λύκειο

Λίνκολν στο Χάρτφορντ του Κονέκτικατ. Ο E-Z κατάλαβε σύντομα ότι οι μαθητές νόμιζαν ότι αυτός ήταν ο ήρωας -ήταν- αλλά δεν μπορούσαν να το ξέρουν αυτό. Δεν ήταν γραφτό να ξέρουν τίποτα από αυτά. Υποτίθεται ότι έπρεπε να έχουν σβήσει το μυαλό τους, όπως έκαναν με τον θείο Σαμ. Αλλά δεν είχε σημασία - δεν ζούσε στο Χάρτφορντ Κονέκτικατ. Έκαναν λάθος. Γιατί τότε οι συμμαθητές του χειροκροτούσαν;

Εκείνος πέρασε, αυτοί έφυγαν από τη μέση. Βγήκε κατευθείαν στη βροχή. Ο E-Z αναρωτήθηκε αν θα μπορούσε να χρησιμοποιήσει τις νεοαποκτηθείσες δυνάμεις της καρέκλας του για προσωπικό του όφελος. Παρόλο που δεν υπήρχε κρίση ή δίκη, θα μπορούσε να μαγέψει ή να κάνει τελετουργικά τον εαυτό του να γυρίσει σπίτι; Το σκεφτόταν αυτό καθώς συνέχιζε να κυλάει κατά μήκος του πεζοδρομίου. Η καρέκλα του τον βοήθησε κάποτε να σώσει ένα μικρό κορίτσι, πριν καν αποκτήσει ε δικές δυνάμεις.

Σκέφτηκε μαγικές λέξεις όπως bibbidi-bobbidi-boo και expelliarmus. Δοκίμασε και τις δύο στην αναπηρική του καρέκλα, αλλά καμία από αυτές δεν έκανε τίποτα. Έριξε μια ματιά πάνω από τον ώμο του ακούγοντας βήματα να πλησιάζουν πίσω του. Περίμενε κάποιον από τους φίλους του - αντ' αυτού, ήταν ένας νεότερος μαθητής, ο οποίος ρώτησε: "Πού είναι τα φτερά σου;".

Ο E-Z γέλασε: "Δεν έχω φτερά". Με το σύνθημα τα φτερά του βγήκαν και τον σήκωσαν στον ουρανό. Στην αρχή, σκέφτηκε ωχ όχι, αλλά αποφάσισε να το δεχτεί και να χαιρετήσει το παιδί, πίσω στο πεζοδρόμιο. Το παιδί ήταν τόσο ενθουσιασμένο που δεν είχε καν σκεφτεί να βγάλει το τηλέφωνό του για να απαθανατίσει τη στιγμή. "Σπίτι!", πρόσταξε. Μια λάμψη κόκκινου φωτός τον παρέσυρε στον ουρανό, ακριβώς δίπλα από το σπίτι του, γιατί η καρέκλα είχε κάπου αλλού να βρεθούν.

Συνέχισαν να πετούν μέχρι που βρέθηκαν ακριβώς πάνω από ένα εμπορικό κέντρο. Ένιωθε τον αέρα να δονείται τώρα, τραβώντας τον πιο κοντά στο σημείο που τον χρειάζονταν. Η καρέκλα έδειξε προς τα κάτω, ρίχνοντάς τον σε μια τράπεζα, και στη συνέχεια σταμάτησε στον αέρα. Οι πελάτες από κάτω συνέχισαν να τριγυρνούν - εκείνος ήταν εκτός του οπτικού τους πεδίου. Ακόμα δεν είχε ιδέα γιατί βρισκόταν εδώ.

Είναι άλλη μια δίκη; αναρωτήθηκε. Περίμενε, αλλά δεν ήρθε καμία απάντηση. Αν αυτή ήταν άλλη μια δίκη, τότε ο χρόνος μεταξύ τους γινόταν όλο και λιγότερος. Πού ήταν αυτοί οι δύο άγγελοι - δεν έπρεπε να τον καλύπτουν; Σκέφτηκε τις άλλες δοκιμασίες. Οι περισσότερες από αυτές συνέβαιναν τη νύχτα. Στο σκοτάδι. Κι αν οι επίδοξοι άγγελοι δεν μπορούσαν να βγουν στο φως, όπως οι βρικόλακες; Γέλασε με αυτή την παράξενη σύνδεση και ήλπιζε ότι ήταν αλήθεια. Κατά κάποιο τρόπο, δεν τον πείραζε που αυτή τη φορά ήταν μόνο αυτός και η καρέκλα του. Ο E-Z επέστρεψε στη στιγμή. Οι πελάτες ούρλιαζαν μέσα στο εμπορικό κέντρο. Πετάχτηκε προς τα εμπρός, έξω από την τράπεζα και μέσα σε ένα κοντινό πολυκατάστημα. Ο χώρος ήταν άδειος.

Ακουμπώντας κάτω, οι ρόδες γύρισαν από μόνες τους οδηγώντας τον. Ο E-Z προσπάθησε να πάρει τον έλεγχο. Αλλά και η αναπηρική του καρέκλα ήθελε τον έλεγχο. Επιτάχυνε, όλο και πιο γρήγορα. Στο τέλος, το άφησε να κυριαρχήσει, φοβούμενος μήπως του καταστρέψουν τα δάχτυλα.

Η καρέκλα σταμάτησε εντελώς, όταν στο έδαφος, περίπου 4 πόδια μπροστά τους, βρίσκονταν πελάτες. Οι περισσότεροι ήταν ξαπλωμένοι και μπρούμυτα στο πάτωμα. Κάποιοι είχαν τα χέρια τους στο πίσω μέρος του κεφαλιού τους, κάποιοι άλλοι είχαν τα χέρια τους πίσω από την πλάτη τους.

Σε διάφορες θέσεις, εντόπισε κάμερες ασφαλείας που έδειχναν μόνο στατική εικόνα. Καθόλου καλό σημάδι.

Το αναπηρικό καροτσάκι τράβηξε ξανά προς τα εμπρός, προς μια νεαρή γυναίκα. Ήταν ντυμένη με στολή παραλλαγής και με ένα καπέλο τραβηγμένο κάτω από τα μάτια της. Είχε ανοιχτόχρωμο παρουσιαστικό, πιθανώς φυσικά ξανθό και γαλανά μάτια, τύπος μοντέλου. Στο ένα χέρι κρατούσε μια καραμπίνα και στο άλλο ένα κυνηγετικό μαχαίρι. Η ακινησία της κρατώντας τα όπλα τον προβλημάτισε. Αυτό και η υπερβολική χρήση του κόκκινου κραγιόν της. Ήταν πασαλειμμένο, μετατρέποντας ένα ανατριχιαστικό χαμόγελο σε μια απειλητική γκριμάτσα.

Ο E-Z εξέτασε όσους κινδύνευαν στο πάτωμα. Πόση ώρα βρίσκονταν εκεί; Τι περίμενε; Είχε ζητήσει χρήματα; Ποιος έξω από το κατάστημα, ήξερε ότι διαδραματιζόταν αυτή η σκηνή ομηρίας, αφού οι κάμερες δεν λειτουργούσαν;

Ένας από τους τύπους στον όροφο τράβηξε την προσοχή του. Ο E-Z έβαλε το δάχτυλό του στα χείλη του. Ο τύπος γύρισε από την άλλη μεριά, τότε ήταν που εντόπισε ένα τηλέφωνο στο πάτωμα με ένα κόκκινο φως να πάλλεται. Κατέγραφε τον ήχο. Ήλπιζε να μην το προσέξει η κοπέλα - έμοιαζε σαν να μπορούσε να τα χάσει ανά πάσα στιγμή.

Η καρέκλα του E-Z απογειώθηκε, σαν έκρηξη από κανόνι, και σύντομα βρέθηκε πάνω στο κορίτσι. Το όπλο της πέταξε προς τη μία κατεύθυνση και το μαχαίρι προς την άλλη. Το μεταλλικό περίβλημα της καρέκλας έπεσε προς τα κάτω.

"Κάλεσε το 100", φώναξε ο E-Z. Και προς τους πελάτες στο πάτωμα: "Φύγετε από εδώ!". Έτρεξαν χωρίς να κοιτάξουν πίσω. Τώρα ήταν ολομόναχος με το τρελό κορίτσι. "Γιατί το έκανες αυτό;" ρώτησε.

Εκείνη ψέλλισε τους στίχους ενός τραγουδιού που είχε ξανακούσει: "Δεν μου αρέσουν οι Δευτέρες", και μετά χαμογέλασε, γούρλωσε τα μάτια της και είπε: "Εξάλλου, είναι μόνο ένα παιχνίδι". Ξαναγύρισε να σιγοτραγουδάει το τραγούδι για μερικά δευτερόλεπτα, με τα μάτια της κλειστά. Μετά τα άνοιξε και με άγρια μάτια και γέλια είπε: "Α, και αν χρειαστείς έναν επαγγελματία να βάψει σωστά τα μαλλιά σου, ξέρω κάποιον".

"Ε, ευχαριστώ", είπε, περνώντας τα δάχτυλά του από τα μαλλιά του.

Θυμήθηκε ένα τραγούδι που τραγουδούσε η μαμά του. Μια αληθινή ιστορία, για έναν πυροβολισμό. Το συγκρότημα είχε πάρει το όνομά του από ποντίκια ή αρουραίους.

Κούνησε το κεφάλι του. Η κοπέλα μπροστά του, έμοιαζε με χαρακτήρα από ένα παιχνίδι που είχε παίξει μερικές φορές. Μέχρι και το πασαλειμμένο κραγιόν. Δεν μπορούσε να θυμηθεί ποιο, αλλά ήταν σίγουρος ότι μιμούνταν έναν παίκτη. "Το να παίζεις ένα παιχνίδι είναι ένα πράγμα - κανείς δεν πληγώνεται. Αυτό είναι η πραγματική ζωή. Αν δεν σου αρέσει κάτι - σταμάτα να το κάνεις! Μην κάνεις κακό στους άλλους".

"Φύγε", απάντησε εκείνη, "λες και είχα κάποια επιλογή στο θέμα".

Η αστυνομία εισέβαλε και έπρεπε να φύγει.

Βρήκαν την κοπέλα ασφαλισμένη με τα όπλα της δεμένα με κόμπους στο διάδρομο ασφαλείας σε μια κονσόλα παιχνιδιών.

Κατευθύνθηκε προς το σπίτι του, περιμένοντας να τον χτυπήσει το φοβερό κάψιμο από τα φτερά του. Έφτασε μέχρι εκεί, μέχρι στιγμής όλα καλά. Αλλά ήταν τόσο πεινασμένος, που ανυπομονούσε να φάει ό,τι έβρισκε στα χέρια του.

Σε ετοιμότητα στο ψυγείο, υπήρχε μισό κοτόπουλο, το οποίο έφαγε ενώ περίμενε να λιώσει το τυρί στο τηγάνι. Κατέβασε το ψητό τυρί. Στη συνέχεια έφτιαξε άλλο ένα, ενώ μασούσε ένα μήλο. Όταν τελείωσε το μήλο, έβαλε κουταλιά παγωτό από το δοχείο. Ο πόνος δεν ήρθε ποτέ, αλλά θα είχε σοβαρό πρόβλημα βάρους αν συνέχιζε να τρώει έτσι.

"Θείε Σαμ;" φώναξε, ελέγχοντας αν βρισκόταν κάπου στο σπίτι - δεν βρισκόταν. Πήγε στο γραφείο του και έκανε μερικές εργασίες, μετά έπαιξε μερικά παιχνίδια. Ακόμα κανένα ίχνος του Σαμ. Ούτε SMS. Ούτε κλήσεις ούτε φωνητικά μηνύματα. Ο Σαμ πάντα τον ενημέρωνε όταν αργούσε να γυρίσει σπίτι. Παράξενο. Πού ήταν;

ΚΕΦΑΛΑΙΟ 17

ΉΤΑΝ ΠΕΡΑΣΜΕΝΑ ΜΕΣΑΝΥΧΤΑ ΚΑΙ δεν υπήρχε ακόμα κανένα ίχνος του θείου Σαμ. Ήταν η πρώτη φορά που παρέλειψε να φτιάξει δείπνο, πόσο μάλλον που δεν είπε στον Ε-Ζ πού βρισκόταν. Ήξερε πόσο ανήσυχος γινόταν ο ανιψιός του όταν τα πράγματα ήταν εκτός του ελέγχου του. Τέτοιες στιγμές, το δέρμα του εφήβου είχε φαγούρα, σαν το αίμα του να έβραζε κάτω από την επιφάνεια.

Καθισμένος στην αναπηρική του καρέκλα, έκανε το αντίστοιχο του βηματισμού. Κυλούσε την καρέκλα του στον διάδρομο και κατέβαινε ξανά. Το δύσκολο κομμάτι ήταν να γυρίσει, κάτι που έκανε στο γραφείο του. Καθώς επέστρεφε προς την κουζίνα, άνοιξε την τηλεόραση για να δημιουργήσει λίγο λευκό θόρυβο. Σταμάτησε να παρακολουθήσει πριν επιστρέψει στο διάδρομο και μια εξωσωματική εμπειρία τον κατέλαβε.

Βρισκόταν στο σαλόνι στο αναπηρικό του καροτσάκι και παρακολουθούσε τον εαυτό του στην τηλεόραση μέσα στο αναπηρικό του καροτσάκι. Ο Ε-Ζ κούνησε το κεφάλι του, προσπαθώντας να βγάλει νόημα. Γιατί ο Χατζ και η Ρέικι δεν είχαν σβήσει τις αναμνήσεις τους; Τότε συνέβη - ο δημοσιογράφος είπε το όνομά του και την πραγματική του διεύθυνση, συμπεριλαμβανομένου του προαστίου. Τα είχε όλα σωστά αυτή τη φορά - και δεν σταμάτησε εκεί.

"Ο δεκατριάχρονος Ε-Ζ Dickens, ήθελε να γίνει επαγγελματίας παίκτης του μπέιζμπολ. Και είχε τις ικανότητες. Τότε ένα ατύχημα, του πήρε τους γονείς του - και τα πόδια του. Το ορφανό - που μετατράπηκε σε υπερήρωα - ζει τώρα με τον μοναδικό του συγγενή, τον Σάμιουελ Ντίκενς".

Ήθελε να κλωτσήσει την οθόνη της τηλεόρασης. Το είπαν, έτσι απλά. Λες και όλοι οι υπερήρωες έπρεπε να είναι ορφανοί. Λες και ήταν απαραίτητη προϋπόθεση. Όταν χτύπησε το τηλέφωνό του, ήλπιζε ότι ήταν ο Σαμ - ήταν ο Άρντεν.

"Το βλέπεις;" ρώτησε. "Είπαν σε ΟΛΟΥΣ πού μένεις!"

"Το ξέρω", είπε ο Ε-Ζ. "Το χειρότερο είναι ότι ο θείος Σαμ είναι άφαντος. Πάντα μου τηλεφωνεί, ό,τι κι αν συμβεί".

Ο Άρντεν μίλησε με τον πατέρα του. "Μείνε εκεί, ο μπαμπάς κι εγώ ερχόμαστε αμέσως. Μπορείς να μείνεις μαζί μας, μέχρι εσύ και ο Σαμ να βρείτε τι θα κάνετε. Αφήστε του ένα σημείωμα".

"Ευχαριστώ, αλλά θα είμαι εντάξει εδώ".

"Ο μπαμπάς λέει, χωρίς αν, και και αλλά. Λέει ότι οι δημοσιογράφοι θα σε κυνηγήσουν σαν το άσπρο στο ρύζι - ό,τι κι αν σημαίνει αυτό".

"Δεν είχα σκεφτεί ότι οι δημοσιογράφοι θα έρθουν εδώ. Εντάξει, θα ετοιμαστώ".

Πήγε στο δωμάτιό του, ετοίμασε μια τσάντα διανυκτέρευσης και μετά στην κουζίνα για να γράψει ένα σημείωμα και να το βάλει στο ψυγείο. Ένα όχημα σταμάτησε ξαφνικά απ' έξω, τρίζοντας τα λάστιχα του. Μια πόρτα χτύπησε, έπειτα ακούστηκαν πυροβολισμοί, καθώς θραύσματα γυαλιού πετάχτηκαν έξω από τα παράθυρα. Η μπροστινή πόρτα έσκασε από τους μεντεσέδες της, καθώς η καρέκλα του απογειώθηκε προς τον δράστη, ο οποίος κρατούσε πυρ όσο πλησίαζε.

"Είναι απλώς ένα παιδί", είπε ο Ε-Ζ, εκμεταλλευόμενος τον δισταγμό του. Άρπαξε το όπλο, το έδεσε κόμπο και το πέταξε στο γκαζόν.

Το αγόρι, που ήταν μικρότερο από τον Ε-Ζ, εκμεταλλεύτηκε τα δευτερόλεπτα που πετούσε το όπλο, για να τον ρίξει στο έδαφος.

"Δεν είναι ωραίο", είπε ο E-Z, καθώς η καρέκλα του τον έσπρωξε και έριξε το μεταλλικό κλουβί πάνω στο παιδί που έκλαιγε με λυγμούς και ζητούσε τη μαμά του. "Κάνε πίσω", είπε ο E-Z στην καρέκλα.

Το παιδί ήταν τυλιγμένο σε θέση εμβρύου, τρέμοντας και κλαίγοντας. Η καρέκλα τράβηξε πίσω το κλουβί: το αγόρι δεν κουνήθηκε.

Ο E-Z, τώρα πια πίσω στην αναπηρική του καρέκλα, ρώτησε: "Ποιος σε έφερε εδώ; Και γιατί όλοι αυτοί οι πυροβολισμοί;"

"Δεν είναι κάτι προσωπικό", εξήγησε το παιδί. "Έπρεπε να το κάνω. Μια φωνή στο κεφάλι μου, μου είπε ότι έπρεπε να το κάνω. Αλλιως θα σκότωναν εμένα και την οικογένειά μου. Γι' αυτό έκλεψα τα κλειδιά του πατέρα μου και έμαθα να οδηγώ - γρήγορα".

"Δεν έχεις οδηγήσει τοτέ πριν;"

"Μόνο σε παιχνίδια".

Πάλι παιχνίδια. "Σε ποιον αναφέρεσαι; Ποια είναι τα ονόματά τους;"

"Δεν ξέρω. Παίζω μερικά παιχνίδια στο διαδίκτυο. Μια γυναίκα έμπαινε στο παιχνίδι και μου έλεγε ότι θα σκοτώσει την αδελφή μου. Θα άλλαζα σε άλλο παιχνίδι- μια άλλη γυναίκα θα έλεγε ότι θα σκοτώσει τους γονείς μου. Στο παιχνίδι που έπαιζα σήμερα μια τρίτη γυναίκα μου είπε ότι αν δεν σκοτώσω ένα παιδί που έμενε σε αυτή τη διεύθυνση, θα υπάρξουν άσχημες συνέπειες". Το παιδί πήρε φόρα από τον E-Z, αλλά δεν πήγε μακριά. Η καρέκλα τον έσπρωξε και χαμήλωσε τον βραχίονα.

"Βγάλε με από εδώ!" απαίτησε το παιδί.

Ο E-Z γέλασε- το παιδί είχε αρχίδια. "Κάτσε κάτω", είπε στην καρέκλα του και βοήθησε το παιδί να σηκωθεί στα πόδια του. Το παιδί τον ευχαρίστησε φτύνοντας τον κατάμουτρα. Έσφιξε τις γροθιές του και σκέφτηκε να ξεριζώσει το γαμημένο κεφάλι του παιδιού, αλλά δεν το έκανε. Αντ' αυτού, τον αγκάλιασε. Το παιδί άρχισε πάλι να κλαίει, τα δάκρυά του έπεφταν στους ώμους και τα φτερά του E-Z.

"Σ' ευχαριστώ, φίλε", είπε το παιδί. Έκανε ένα βήμα πίσω, έβαλε το χέρι του πάνω από την καρδιά του και εξαφανίστηκε.

Όταν τελικά έφτασε η αστυνομία, ο E-Z καθόταν στην καρέκλα του στο πεζοδρόμιο. Μετά δεν ήταν. Βρισκόταν πάλι μέσα στο σιλό και ένιωθε κλειστοφοβία μέσα στο απόλυτο σκοτάδι.

✳ ✳ ✳

ΠΡΟΗΓΟΥΜΈΝΩΣ, ΌΤΑΝ ΒΡΙΣΚΌΤΑΝ ΣΤΟ μεταλλικό δοχείο, μπορούσε να κινείται. Τώρα βρισκόταν στο αναπηρικό του καροτσάκι και μόλις και μετά βίας μπορούσε να κινηθεί. Προσπάθησε να κουνήσει τα δάχτυλα των ποδιών του μέσα στα παπούτσια του - δεν μπορούσε να τα νιώσει. Αν τα πόδια του δεν λειτουργούσαν εδώ, τότε ήταν ευτυχής που βρισκόταν στην αναπηρική του καρέκλα. Ήταν μια ομάδα: όπως ο Μπάτμαν και το Μπάτμομπιλ. Ως απάντηση στις σκέψεις του, το αναπηρικό καροτσάκι κουνήθηκε προς τα εμπρός σαν μαστίγιο με λουρί.

"Βγάλτε μας από εδώ', διέταξε ο E-Z.

Ένιωσε μια αίσθηση κίνησης από πάνω του. Μια μετατόπιση του φωτός σαν σύννεφο που προχωρούσε στον ουρανό. Μακάρι να μπορούσε να πετάξει ψηλά και να ξεφύγει από την οροφή, αλλά τα φτερά του δεν είχαν χώρο να επεκταθούν.

Το δέρμα του άρχισε να φουσκώνει και τον έπιασε φαγούρα. Πού ήταν τώρα εκείνο το καταπραϋντικό σπρέι λεβάντας;

PFFT.

"Ευχαριστώ", είπε. Ακόμα και αυτό το πράγμα μπορούσε να διαβάσει το μυαλό του τώρα.

Οι ώμοι του χαλάρωσαν, καθώς διατύπωσε μια λίστα με αιτήματα:

Νούμερο ένα. Ήθελε να πει στον θείο Σαμ τα πάντα. Και εννοούσε τα πάντα. Τίποτα δεν παρέλειπε.

Νούμερο δύο. Ήθελε να το μάθουν ο Πι Τζέι και ο 'ρντεν. Όχι τα πάντα, όπως θα έκανε ο θείος Σαμ. Αλλά αρκετά ώστε να καταλάβουν την πίεση που δεχόταν. Αρκετά ώστε να μπορούν να τον υποστηρίξουν και να τον ενθαρρύνουν. Μισούσε να τους λέει ψέματα. Ήθελε να ξέρουν για τις δοκιμασίες. Γιατί τις έκανε. Λες και είχε κάποια επιλογή στο θέμα.

Νούμερο τρία. Ήθελε να ζητήσουν την άδειά του, πριν τον απαγάγουν. Έτσι θα ήξερε τι να περιμένει στη συνέχεια. Μισούσε να τον ρίχνουν σε αυτό το πράγμα.

Νούμερο τέσσερα. Ήθελε να ξέρει πού βρισκόταν. Γιατί τον έριχναν πάντα σε αυτό το ίδιο δοχείο. Γιατί μερικές φορές τα πόδια του δούλευαν και μερικές φορές όχι. Γιατί άλλοτε η καρέκλα του ήταν μαζί του και άλλοτε όχι.

"Ο χρόνος αναμονής είναι δώδεκα λεπτά", είπε μια γυναικεία φωνή. "Θα θέλατε ένα ποτό;"

"Νερό", είπε, καθώς το μέταλλο στα δεξιά του έφτυνε ένα ράφι με ένα ποτήρι νερό πάνω του. "Ευχαριστώ". Το πέταξε πίσω. Το ποτήρι γέμισε και πάλι μέχρι πάνω. Το άφησε κάτω για αργότερα.

Πιο χαλαρός τώρα, ένα τραγούδι ήρθε στο μυαλό του. Το λάτρευε ο πατέρας του. Η αναπηρική καρέκλα κουνιόταν μπρος-πίσω, καθώς τραγουδούσε τους στίχους. Η καρέκλα ανέπτυσσε δυναμική - σαν να προσπαθούσε να απελευθερωθεί.

Δευτερόλεπτα αργότερα βρισκόταν πίσω στο σπίτι του, στην κρεβατοκάμαρά του με σπασμένα γυαλιά παντού. Μπλε και κόκκινα φώτα πάλλονταν στους τοίχους. Τώρα στο σπασμένο παράθυρο, κοίταξε έξω.

"Είναι εκεί πάνω!" φώναξε ένας δημοσιογράφος.

'''Ο ΧΙ ΠΑΛΙ!" ΦΩΝΑΞΕ, ΤΩΡΑ πίσω στο μεταλλικό δοχείο. "Βγάλτε με από εδώ!" Κλώτσησε με το πόδι του τον τοίχο του σιλό. "Ωχ!" φώναξε. Μετά χαμογέλασε, χαρούμενος που ένιωθε ξανά τα πόδια του και σηκώθηκε. Σήκωσε τη γροθιά του στον αέρα: "Ποιος νομίζεις ότι είσαι και με φέρνεις εδώ, για κάθε σου καπρίτσιο!"

"Η ώρα αναμονής είναι τώρα έξι λεπτά, παρακαλούμε παραμείνετε καθιστοί".

Ιμάντες βγήκαν από τους τοίχους μπροστά του, πίσω του, σε κάθε πλευρά του. Τον έδεσαν στη θέση του. Πάλεψε να απελευθερωθεί, αλλά οι δερμάτινοι ιμάντες μόνο σφίγγονταν. Σύντομα, το μόνο που μπορούσε να κινήσει ήταν το κεφάλι και ο λαιμός του.

PFFT.

"Αχ, λεβάντα", είπε. Κάτω από αυτόν, η αναπηρική του καρέκλα άρχισε να κουνιέται και να τρέμει. "Όλα θα πάνε καλά." "Φοβάστε τόσο πολύ, δειλοί, ώστε να κατεβείτε εδώ κάτω και να με αντιμετωπίσετε;"

PFFT.

PFFT.

Έχασε τη δόση του.

K οιμήθηκε βαθιά μέχρι που η οροφή του σιλό άνοιξε σαν το Houston Astrodome. Και ένα πράγμα κατάπιε το φως. Το ένιωσε, πριν το δει. Έπαιρνε το φως από τον κόσμο του. Κάτω από αυτόν, η αναπηρική καρέκλα έτρεμε, καθώς το πράγμα από πάνω έπεφτε σε ελεύθερη πτώση.

Σταμάτησε τελείως, σαν αράχνη στο τέλος του σχοινιού της.

Ο Εωσφόρος;

Ο Σατανάς;

Περίμενε, πολύ φοβισμένος για να μιλήσει.

"Γεια σου - ο - ο - ο - ο", βρυχήθηκε το φτερωτό πλάσμα, με τη φωνή του να αναπηδά από τους τοίχους.

Ευχήθηκε τόσο πολύ να μπορούσε να καλύψει τα αυτιά του.

Το πλάσμα χαμογέλασε, αποκαλύπτοντας δόντια σαν ξυράφια, ενώ απέπνεε μια βρωμερή σάπια δυσοσμία.

Πνίγηκε, έβηξε και ευχήθηκε να μπορούσε να καλύψει και τη μύτη του.

Το θηρίο γέλασε με βρυχηθμό, ο οποίος βροντοφώναξε πάνω-κάτω στη μεταλλική φυλακή του, σαν να έβγαζε ποπ κορν. Έσκυψε πιο κοντά στο πρόσωπο του εφήβου και ξεστόμισε: "Δεν μιλάω τη γλώσσα σας, κύριε;".

Ο Ε-Ζ δεν απάντησε. Δεν μπορούσε. Ένιωθε πολύ αντιηρωικός. Το γεγονός ότι η αναπηρική του καρέκλα έτρεμε από κάτω του δεν ενίσχυε την αυτοπεποίθησή του.

"ΔΕΝ ΜΕ ΚΑΤΑΛΑΒΑΙΝΕΙΣ;", φώναξε το πράγμα, ταρακουνώντας τη μεταλλική φυλακή μέχρι τα θεμέλιά της. Το πράγμα πλησίασε ακόμα πιο κοντά, "ΚΑΤΑΛΑΒΕΤΕ. ΕΣΥ. ΔΕΝ. ΑΚΟΥΣΕ. ΜΕ;"

Ήταν σαν ένα ομιλούν σύννεφο με ένα κεφάλι στο κέντρο, που ετοιμαζόταν να πέσει πάνω του με κεραυνούς και αστραπές. Σκάβοντας τα νύχια του στα μπράτσα, βρήκε το κουράγιο να πει: "Ναι". Ξαναέκανε τη λίστα με τα αιτήματά του στο μυαλό του.

Το θηρίο βρυχήθηκε και φωτιά πετάχτηκε από το στόμα του. Ευτυχώς για τον E-Z, η θερμότητα ανεβαίνει. Ξαφνικά αισθάνθηκε πολύ πεινασμένος, για μπέικον.

"Μου αρέσει το μπέικον", εξομολογήθηκε το πλάσμα.

Ο E-Z αναρωτήθηκε αν είχε πει δυνατά αυτό το πράγμα για το μπέικον. Ακόμη και με δεδομένο το επιταχυνόμενο επίπεδο φόβου του, ήξερε ότι δεν το είχε πει. Αυτό σήμαινε ένα πράγμα, όλοι μπορούσαν να διαβάσουν το μυαλό του! Ίσιωσε τον εαυτό του και προσπάθησε να προστατευτεί κλείνοντας το μυαλό του. Οι σκέψεις του έτρεξαν σε φαγητά, τηγανίτες στο καφέ της Ανν, ένα παχύρρευστο σοκολατένιο μιλκσέικ, σιρόπι με βούτυρο. Οτιδήποτε για να κρατήσει τον φόβο μακριά και το άγχος χαμηλά. Αυτό ήταν βασανιστήριο, αυτό το πράγμα μπορούσε να διαβάσει τις σκέψεις του και να τον φυλακίσει για πάντα. Υπήρχε κάποια Ένωση Υπερηρώων στην οποία θα μπορούσε να ενταχθεί;

"Μπα, χα, χα!" βρυχήθηκε το πράγμα από τα γέλια.

Ο E-Z ευχόταν τόσο πολύ να μπορούσε να φτάσει τα αυτιά του, αλλά καθώς δεν μπορούσε, παρηγορήθηκε ότι τουλάχιστον είχε αίσθηση του χιούμορ. "Γιατί βρίσκομαι εδώ;"

Το πράγμα δεν απάντησε αμέσως, οπότε προσπάθησε να το ψυχολογήσει με ένα βλέμμα. Ήταν ιδιαίτερα δύσκολο να κρατήσει το βλεμματικό κλείδωμα, αφού η καρέκλα προσπαθούσε συνεχώς να τον πετάξει έξω από αυτό. Έσφιξε τις γροθιές του, τραβώντας αίμα.

Το πλάσμα κινήθηκε με ευκινησία σαν φίδι, με την αφρώδη γλώσσα του να εκτοξεύεται πέρα δώθε καθώς έγλειφε τις γροθιές του E-Z.

"Ιου!" φώναξε. "Αυτό είναι τόσο αηδιαστικό!"

"Κι άλλο παρακαλώ!" απαίτησε το πλάσμα, καθώς το αίμα στη γλώσσα του έλαμπε σαν σταγόνες βροχής.

Ο E-Z είχε φοβηθεί και πριν, τώρα όμως ήταν πολύ πιο φοβισμένος. Μάλλον είχε πετρώσει - αλλά ήταν υπερήρωας. Έπρεπε να μαζέψει δύναμη από κάπου - ακόμα κι αν η καρέκλα ήταν άχρηστη.

"Μπα, μπα, μπα, μπα, μπα, μπα, μπα", τραγούδησε το πράγμα, καθώς πλησίαζε, έπειτα απομακρύνθηκε, έπειτα πλησίασε ξανά. Αναπηδούσε στους τοίχους.

Μετά από λίγες στιγμές, το πλάσμα εγκαταστάθηκε. Σταύρωσε τα πόδια του στον αέρα. Έπειτα έβαλε το μακρύ οστέινο δάχτυλό του στο μάγουλό του. Φαινόταν σαν να περίμενε να έχει μια φιλική κουβέντα.

"Ο Χαντζ και το Ρέικι έχουν αφαιρεθεί από την υπόθεσή σας", ψιθύρισε το πλάσμα. "Αυτοί οι δύο ήταν ηλίθιοι. Λιγότερο από άχρηστοι. Είμαι ο νέος σου μέντορας".

Το σκοτεινό πλάσμα ξεσταύρωσε τον εαυτό του. Πετάχτηκε από πάνω, έκανε μια μισή υπόκλιση με μια φιγούρα και σηκώθηκε ψηλότερα στο δοχείο.

Ο E-Z σκέφτηκε για μερικά δευτερόλεπτα πριν απαντήσει. Εκείνα τα δύο πλάσματα ήταν πιστά σε αυτόν. Τον είχαν βοηθήσει και τον πρόσεχαν - και το πιο σημαντικό, δεν έπιναν ανθρώπινο αίμα.

"Μπορούμε να το συζητήσουμε αυτό;" ρώτησε ο E-Z. Προσπάθησε να χαμογελάσει. Δεν ήξερε πώς φαινόταν από την άλλη πλευρά.

"ΟΧΙ!" είπε το πράγμα, προωθώντας τον εαυτό του πιο κοντά στην έξοδο.

Ο E-Z παρακολουθούσε καθώς παρασύρθηκε προς τα πάνω. Αβοήθητος. Απελπισμένος.

"Περίμενε!" φώναξε, το πράγμα ήταν μισό μέσα και μισό έξω από το κοντέινερ. "Σε διατάζω να περιμένεις!" είπε ο E-Z, καθώς η οροφή άρχισε να κλείνει, και τότε το πράγμα βρέθηκε στο πρόσωπό του σε μια στιγμή.

"Υ-Ε-Σ;" αναρωτήθηκε.

"Θέλω να μιλήσω με το αφεντικό σου, για να πάρουμε πίσω τη Ρέια και τον Χαντζ. Είναι πιο κατάλληλοι για τις δικές μου, τις δικές μου δοκιμασίες. Για την επιτυχία των δοκιμών."

"Δεν μ' αρέσω;", έσκουξε το πλάσμα με φωνή σαν νύχια σε μαυροπίνακα.

"Σταμάτα! Σε παρακαλώ!"

"Το να φέρεις πίσω αυτούς τους δύο ηλίθιους αποκλείεται", το πλάσμα στριφογύρισε σαν χάμστερ σε τροχό.

"Κόφτε το! Με ζαλίζεις! Πάρε με από εδώ!"

"Εντάξει", είπε, σταυρώνοντας τα χέρια του και ανοιγοκλείνοντας τα μάτια σαν τη γυναίκα στην παλιά τηλεοπτική σειρά "Ονειρεύομαι τη Τζίνι".

Το σιλό εξαφανίστηκε, ενώ ο E-Z και η καρέκλα του έμειναν να πέφτουν στο έδαφος.

"Αααα!" φώναξε.

Μετά η αναπηρική του καρέκλα εξαφανίστηκε.

Και καθώς συνέχισε να πέφτει, κούνησε τις γροθιές του στο πλάσμα από πάνω του. Αντιστάθηκε στην πτώση.

"Παρεμπιπτόντως, το όνομά μου είναι Έριελ".

"Arrggghhhh!" αναφώνησε.

Το ήταν πάλι πίσω στο αναπηρικό του καροτσάκι και κρατιόταν για να κρατηθεί. Ακόμα έπεφταν.

ΚΕΦΑΛΑΙΟ 18

CRASH!

Ακριβώς μέσα από την οροφή του σπιτιού του. Η αναπηρική του καρέκλα έγειρε προς τα εμπρός και τον πέταξε στο κρεβάτι. Στη συνέχεια κύλησε στο πάτωμα. Ήταν και οι δύο καλά. Δεν ήταν χειρότεροι από τη φθορά.

Πάνω του, η τρύπα που είχαν κάνει επιδιορθώθηκε μόνη της.

"Α, εδώ είσαι!" Είπε ο Σαμ. "Καλώς ήρθες σπίτι."

Ο E-Z δεν τον είχε καν προσέξει. Είχε κοιμηθεί βαθιά στην καρέκλα στη γωνία.

Ο Σαμ τεντώθηκε και χασμουρήθηκε. Έπειτα παραπάτησε στο δωμάτιο, όπου περίμενε μια κανάτα με νερό. Κατάπιε ένα ποτήρι και μετά πρόσφερε ένα ποτήρι στον ανιψιό του.

"Τι γίνεται με αυτό το κακό πλάσμα, τον Έριελ!" είπε ο Σαμ.

Ο E-Z παραλίγο να φτύσει το νερό.

"Ποιος; ΤΙ;"

συνέχισε ο Σαμ. "Αυτή η Eriel, είναι το πιο βρώμικο, το πιο αηδιαστικό υπερτροφικό ιπτάμενο πλάσμα που δεν θα ήλπιζα ποτέ να συναντήσω!" Έσφιξε τις γροθιές του. "Ελπίζω να μπορείς να με ακούσεις, όπου κι αν βρίσκεσαι! Δεν σε φοβάμαι!"

Το σαγόνι του E-Z σχεδόν έπεσε στο πάτωμα.

Ο Σαμ συνέχισε. "Αυτό το πράγμα με είχε μέσα σε ένα μεταλλικό δοχείο. Τώρα ξέρω γιατί έβλεπες κακό όνειρο. Ήταν όντως σαν σιλό. Μου είπε ότι έπρεπε να του παραδώσω την κηδεμονία σου, αλλιώς θα σε πυροβολούσαν".

"Α, αυτό", είπε ο E-Z. "Υποθέτω ότι είδες όλα τα σπασμένα γυαλιά. Ήταν ένα παιδί, προσπάθησε να με σκοτώσει".

"Τα ξέρω όλα. Παρακολουθούσα τα πάντα μέσα από το σιλό. Το ήξερες ότι υπήρχε μια τηλεόραση με μεγάλη οθόνη εκεί μέσα; Και ένα καλό ηχοσύστημα επίσης".

"Τι; Μόλις ήμουν εκεί, και ο Έριελ δεν μου είπε τίποτα για σένα ή για την ανάληψη της κηδεμονίας". Διέσχισε το δωμάτιο και κοίταξε το ταβάνι: "Είναι αυτό μια δοκιμή, Έριελ; Αν πω κάτι, θα ανακαλέσεις την προσφορά; Δώσε μου ένα σημάδι".

"Σε ποιον μιλάς; Η Έριελ δεν είναι εδώ. Αν ήταν, θα μπορούσαμε να μυρίσουμε τη δυσωδία του από χιλιόμετρα. Όχι, είμαστε μόνοι μας - παρόλο που του ύψωσα τις γροθιές μου. Δεν περίμενα να με ακούσει".

"Πιθανότατα έχει μάτια και αυτιά παντού".

"Λένε ότι ο θεός έχει μάτια και αυτιά παντού. Αν υπάρχει."

"Τι άλλο σου είπε, για μένα;"

"Μου είπε ότι ήταν γραφτό να πεθάνεις μαζί με τους γονείς σου. Αυτός και οι συνάδελφοί του σε έσωσαν - και τώρα, πρέπει να ολοκληρώσεις μια σειρά από δοκιμασίες".

"Ακριβώς. Ορκίστηκα να τηρήσω το απόρρητο, οπότε αναρωτιέμαι γιατί σου αποκάλυψε αυτές τις πληροφορίες".

"Στην αρχή, προσπάθησε να με τρομοκρατήσει, αλλά βγήκες από τη δύσκολη θέση με το παιδί. Με άφησε εδώ στο σπίτι και δεν μπορούσα να σε βρω πουθενά".

"Ναι, επειδή με είχε στο κοντέινερ".

"Με έβαλε και με έβγαλε μερικές φορές, αλλά αρνήθηκα να παραδώσω την κηδεμονία σου. Μετά τη δεύτερη ή την τρίτη φορά, είπε ότι ζήτησες να μου τα πεις όλα και...".

"Έφτιαξα ένα σχέδιο για να του το ζητήσω αυτό. Δεν του είπα ποιο ήταν - αλλά αυτός, όπως και οι περισσότεροι άλλοι τελευταία, μπορεί να διαβάσει τη σκέψη μου".

"Τι εννοείς, όλοι οι άλλοι;"

"Ε, πριν από τον Έριελ, υπήρχαν δύο επίδοξοι άγγελοι που λέγονταν Χατζ και Ρέικι".

"Ω, όντως ανέφερε δύο ηλίθιους. Είπε ότι υποβιβάστηκαν για να δουλέψουν στα ορυχεία διαμαντιών".

"Ο παράδεισος έχει ορυχεία;"

"Αμφιβάλλω αν αυτό το πράγμα ήταν από τον ουρανό - αν υπάρχει τέτοιο πράγμα".

"Σε πειράζει να πάμε στην κουζίνα για ένα σνακ;" ρώτησε ο E-Z. Προχώρησαν κατά μήκος του διαδρόμου, ο Σαμ έβαλε τη σχάρα και ετοίμασε ψωμί με τυρί και βούτυρο. "Όσο κοιμόσουν, έκανα κάποια έρευνα για την Έριελ. Χρειάστηκε λίγο ψάξιμο για να τον βρω, αλλά μόλις περιόρισα την αναζήτηση, βρήκα χρυσάφι". Αναποδογύρισε τα σάντουιτς σε πιάτα και τα μετέφερε στο τραπέζι.

"Ευχαριστώ, ανυπομονώ να τα ακούσω όλα. Σε πειράζει να μπω κατευθείαν στο θέμα;"

"Όχι, πήγαινε." Ο Σαμ παρακολούθησε τον ανιψιό του να τρώει τέσσερις μπουκιές και μετά το σάντουιτς εξαφανίστηκε. Πέρασε το δικό του, χωρίς να νιώθει πεινασμένος. "Ξεκίνησα την αναζήτηση πληκτρολογώντας Έριελ. Δεν μου ήρθε τίποτα. Έτσι, πληκτρολόγησα Αρχάγγελοι και το όνομα Ουριήλ ήταν ακριβώς στην αρχή της σελίδας".

"Νομίζεις ότι είναι το ίδιο;" Έφαγε άλλη μια μπουκιά.

"Αυτό σκέφτηκα κ. εγώ στην αρχή. Μετά βρήκα μια λίστα με τους Αρχαγγέλους και το όνομα Ραντουριέλ στην εβραϊκή μυθολογία. Όταν έλεγξα την περιγραφή του, λέει ότι μπορούσε να δημιουργήσει κατώτερους αγγέλους με μια απλή εκφορά".

"Εννοείς όπως ο Χαντζ και ο Ρέικι; Μισό λεπτό, αν τους δημιούργησε, μάλλον γι' αυτό μπόρεσε να τους στείλει στα ορυχεία".

"Οι σκέψεις μου ακριβώς. Οπότε, νομίζω ότι με βάση αυτές τις πληροφορίες ξέρουμε τώρα ότι ο Eriel, γνωστός και ως Radueriel, είναι αρχάγγελος".

Ο E-Z έγνεψε.

"Έτσι, συνέχισα να σκάβω και βρήκα αυτό. "Ένας πρίγκιπας που ατενίζει μυστικά μέρη και μυστικά μυστήρια. Επίσης, ένας μεγάλος και άγιος άγγελος του φωτός και της δόξας".

"Ουάου, είναι τελείως κακός!

"Μπορεί επίσης να δημιουργήσει κάτι από το τίποτα, εκδηλώνοντάς το από τον αέρα".

"Οπότε, από αυτό συμπεραίνω ότι μπορεί να αλλάξει τη δική του εμφάνιση, καθώς και τις εμφανίσεις των άλλων."

"Σωστά. Και έγραψα μερικές λέξεις." Έσπρωξε το κομμάτι χαρτί στο άλλο άκρο του τραπεζιού. "Μην τις πεις δυνατά όμως. Αν το κάνεις, θα τον καλέσεις". Οι λέξεις στο χαρτί ήταν οι εξής:

Rosh-Ah-Or.A.Ra-Du,EE,El.

"Απομνημόνευσε τις λέξεις σε αυτό το χαρτί, σε περίπτωση που χρειαστεί ποτέ να τον καλέσεις κοντά σου".

"Πώς ξέρουμε ότι θα πιάσουν;"

"Χρησιμοποιήστε τα μόνο αν είναι απαραίτητο. Δεν αξίζει τον κόπο να τον καλέσετε εδώ - εκτός αν είναι η έσχατη λύση".

"Σύμφωνοι." Καθώς τα επαναλάμβανε ξανά και ξανά στο μυαλό του, ένιωσε παρηγοριά γνωρίζοντας ότι ο αρχάγγελος δεν διάβαζε συνεχώς το μυαλό του.

"Ο Έριελ είπε ότι πρέπει να σε βοηθήσω με τις δοκιμασίες. Υποθέτω ότι το να σώσεις εκείνο το κοριτσάκι, ήταν η πρώτη που έπρεπε να κάνεις;"

"Μέχρι στιγμής, έχω κάνει αρκετές. Την πρώτη, ναι, το κοριτσάκι. Τη δεύτερη, έσωσα ένα αεροπλάνο από τη συντριβή".

"Ουάου! Θα ήθελα πολύ να μάθω περισσότερα για το πώς το έκανες. Εκπλήσσομαι που δεν ήσουν στις ειδήσεις".

"Ήμουν, αλλά δεν μπορούσες να καταλάβεις ότι ήμουν εγώ. Την τρίτη, σταμάτησα έναν δράστη στην ταράτσα ενός κτιρίου στο κέντρο της πόλης. Τέταρτον, ένας άλλος σκοπευτής σε ένα εμπορικό κέντρο με ομήρους και πέμπτον, το παιδί έξω που προσπαθούσε να με σκοτώσει".

Ο Σαμ μάζεψε τα πιάτα και τα πήγε στο πλυντήριο πιάτων. "Δεν μπορώ να σου πω πόσο περήφανος είμαι για σένα. Όλα αυτά συμβαίνουν και εγώ δεν είχα απολύτως καμία ιδέα".

"Είχα ορκιστεί να τηρήσω το απόρρητο. Αν το έλεγα σε κανέναν, θα..."

"Θα φρόντιζαν να μην ξαναδείς ποτέ τους γονείς σου - ναι, μου το είπε. Αυτό μου ακούγεται λίγο ύποπτο. Ο Έριελ δεν είναι συναισθηματικός τύπος- ήταν σαν μια μεγάλη μπάλα θυμού που περίμενε έναν στόχο".

"Τον πλήγωσα, όταν νόμιζε ότι δεν τον συμπαθούσα".

Ο Σαμ χλεύασε. "Φαντάσου αυτό το πράγμα, να έχει συναισθήματα". Σηκώθηκε όρθιος. "Θα ήθελες λίγο καφέ;"

"Θα προτιμούσα κακάο". Χασμουρήθηκε. "Ήταν μια πολύ κουραστική μέρα."

"Μπορούμε να μιλήσουμε περισσότερο γι' αυτό το πρωί, αλλά πώς νιώθεις για την προθεσμία; Έχεις ολοκληρώσει πέντε δοκιμές, σε πόσες μέρες;"

"Ήταν τυχαίες. Δεν ξέρω τίποτα για μια σταθερή προθεσμία".

"Η Έριελ μου είπε ότι πρέπει να ολοκληρώσεις δώδεκα δοκιμές σε τριάντα ημέρες. Αν είσαι ήδη δύο εβδομάδες μέσα, τότε θα πρέπει να το ανεβάσουν - πολύ".

"Πρώτη φορά το ακούω αυτό".

"Είπε ότι αν δεν τις ολοκληρώσεις εγκαίρως - θα πεθάνεις".

"Τι;"

"Επίσης, ότι όλοι όσοι έχεις σώσει θα χαθούν. Ο Σαμ έκανε μια παύση, στη σκέψη ότι θα τον έχανε τώρα που μόλις είχαν ξεκινήσει. Η ζωή του θα ήταν πάλι άδεια, μόνο δουλειά, σπίτι, δουλειά, σπίτι. Ο E-Z τον κοιτούσε επίμονα, περιμένοντας. "Συγγνώμη, απλά σκεφτόμουν πόσα σημαίνεις για μένα μικρέ. Αλλά και κάτι άλλο μου είπε- είπε ότι θα πεθάνεις μαζί με τους γονείς σου. Αυτό θα σήμαινε ότι όλα όσα κάναμε, όλος ο χρόνος που περάσαμε μαζί θα εξαφανιζόταν. Και δεν λέω ότι θα μπορούσα ή θα μπορούσα ποτέ να πάρω τη θέση των γονιών σου, αλλά καταλαβαίνεις τι λέω, σωστά; Σ' αγαπώ μικρή μου!"

"Κι εγώ σ' αγαπώ", είπε ο E-Z. Ήθελε να αγκαλιάσει τον Σαμ και ο Σαμ ήθελε να τον αγκαλιάσει, μπορούσε να το καταλάβει και όμως η κίνησή τους. Πήρε μια βαθιά ανάσα: "Αυτό είναι σκληρό. Ακούγεται περισσότερο σαν τον Έριελ όμως".

"Και κάτι ακόμα, είπε ότι κάθε φορά που ολοκληρώνεις μια δοκιμασία, η ψυχή σου αυξάνεται. Μέχρι να φτάσεις τα δώδεκα, θα έχει φτάσει στη βέλτιστη τιμή. Το νόμισμα της ψυχής που μπορείς να χρησιμοποιήσεις, για να δεις και να μιλήσεις ξανά με τους γονείς σου".

Η καρέκλα του E-Z έκανε όπισθεν από το τραπέζι, καθώς η μπροστινή πόρτα έφυγε από τους μεντεσέδες και εκτοξεύτηκε στον ουρανό.

"Αρργκχχχχχ!" Ο Σαμ ούρλιαξε από πίσω του. Γαντζώθηκε από την καρέκλα και τα φτερά του ανιψιού του σαν ακυβέρνητος χαρταετός.

"Κρατήσου!" Είπε ο E-Z. "Νομίζω ότι η Έριελ μας καλεί".

Και πέταξαν.

ΚΕΦΑΛΑΙΟ 19

"ΚΡΑΤΗΘΕΙΤΕ - ΠΑΜΕ ΓΙΑ *προσγείωση*". Η αναπηρική του καρέκλα κατευθύνθηκε προς τα κάτω.

"Μακάρι να είχα και εγώ ζώνη ασφαλείας!" Αναφώνησε ο Σαμ, τυλίγοντας τα χέρια του γύρω από το λαιμό του ανιψιού του.

"Μην ανησυχείς, θα είναι μια ασφαλής προσγείωση".

"Αν δεν αφεθώ πριν από αυτό! Αρργκχχχχ!"

Καθώς κατέβαιναν, ο E-Z εντόπισε έναν κύκλο από αγάλματα. Μην έχοντας τίποτα άλλο να κάνει, τα μέτρησε - ήταν εκατό με κάτι στη μέση. Περίεργο, είχε πάει στο κέντρο της πόλης πολλές φορές, αλλά δεν θυμόταν αυτή την ομάδα από τσιμεντένια τετράγωνα. Οι ρόδες της καρέκλας ακούμπησαν στο έδαφος, αλλά ο Σαμ κρατιόταν ακόμα για να κρατηθεί.

"Είναι εντάξει τώρα", είπε ο E-Z. "Μπορείς να ανοίξεις τα μάτια σου".

Το έκανε. "Θα σκοτώσω αυτόν τον Έριελ την επόμενη φορά που θα τον δω!"

"Σσσς. Μπορεί να γίνει νωρίτερα απ' ό,τι νομίζεις". Αυτό που είχε εντοπίσει στο κέντρο των αγαλμάτων ήταν ο Eriel σε ανθρώπινη μορφή, στα φυσικά χαρακτηριστικά αλλά όχι στο μέγεθος. Επιπλέον, καθόταν σε μια αναπηρική καρέκλα που αιωρούνταν σαν μαγικός θρόνος.

Τα μαλλιά του ήταν κατάμαυρα και κυλούσαν στους ώμους του και κατέβαιναν μέχρι τη μέση του. Τα μάτια του ήταν σαν κάρβουνο και η επιδερμίδα του σαν αλάβαστρο. Το πηγούνι του ήταν καλυμμένο με γένια, σαν σκιά της ώρας των έξι, παρόλο που ήταν πιο κοντά στο μεσημέρι. Τα χείλη του ήταν πολύ κόκκινα, σαν να είχε βάλει φρέσκο κραγιόν. Ενώ η μύτη του έμοιαζε με εκείνη ενός ποδοσφαιριστή που την είχαν σπάσει περισσότερες από μία φορές. Για ρούχα, φορούσε ένα λευκό μπλουζάκι, μαύρο τζιν και στα πόδια του ένα ζευγάρι σανδάλια Jesus.

Ο E-Z γύρισε σε κύκλο, κοιτάζοντας ξανά τους εκατόν δέκα άνδρες. Ήταν όλοι ντυμένοι με μοντέρνα ρούχα. Οι περισσότεροι φορούσαν γυαλιά και power suits. Τότε κατάλαβε την αλήθεια: ο Έριελ είχε μετατρέψει εκατόν δέκα ζωντανούς, αναπνέοντες άνδρες σε αγάλματα.

Και δεν ήταν μόνο αυτό. Συνειδητοποίησε ότι, παρόλο που βρίσκονταν στην κεντρική επιχειρηματική περιοχή, δεν υπήρχε κανένας από τους συνηθισμένους ήχους. Μια κανονική μέρα, τα αυτοκίνητα που είχαν κολλήσει στην κίνηση θα κορνάριζαν και τα καυσαέρια θα γέμιζαν τον αέρα.

Η σιωπή ήταν ενοχλητική, αλλά ο φρέσκος καθαρός αέρας τον έκανε να αναπνεύσει πιο βαθιά. Τον ηρέμησε. Ήξερε ότι ήταν η ηρεμία πριν από την καταιγίδα.

Κοίταξε ψηλά στον ουρανό. Ένα επιβατικό αεροπλάνο είχε σταματήσει στον αέρα. Δίπλα του υπήρχαν πουλιά που είχαν σταματήσει να πετούν. Για φόντο, σύννεφα. Ακίνητα. Ακίνητα.

Τότε τα πάντα πάνω του άλλαξαν από μπλε σε μαύρο.

Και η κάποτε απόκοσμη σιωπή διαλύθηκε.

Αυτό που την αντικατέστησε, ήταν βογγητά. βογγητά. Καθώς οι ρίζες των δέντρων ξεριζώνονταν από τη γη. Και ο αέρας πύκνωσε και τυλίχτηκε γύρω από τους λαιμούς τους. Κλέβοντας την αναπνοή τους.

Και κάτω από τα πόδια τους, το έδαφος άρχισε να τρέμει. Έστασε διάπλατα. Ένας σεισμός. Σκίζοντας. Σκίσιμο.

Και ο ήλιος, το φεγγάρι και τα αστέρια έλαμψαν όλα μαζί, αλλά μόνο για ένα δευτερόλεπτο. Μετά διαλύθηκαν και έσπασαν σε ένα εκατομμύριο κομμάτια.

"Γιατί μετέτρεψες τους ανθρώπους σε αγάλματα; Και γιατί προσπαθείς να καταστρέψεις τον κόσμο;" ρώτησε ο Ε-Ζ. "Και γιατί αιωρείσαι εκεί πάνω σε αναπηρικό καροτσάκι;"

"Ωχ, όχι", φώναξε ο Σαμ, υψώνοντας τις γροθιές του στον αέρα.

Ο Έριελ γέλασε: "Καιρός ήταν να έρθεις εδώ, προστατευόμενε. Πώς τολμάς να μου μιλάς, να μου κάνεις ερωτήσεις. Είμαι ο μεγάλος και ο ισχυρός, αλλά είμαι αληθινός, όχι ψεύτικος όπως ο μάγος του ΟΖ. Υπάρχεις μόνο επειδή επέλεξα να σε σώσω".

"Όταν μου μίλησε η Οφανιέλ στη βιβλιοθήκη των Αγγέλων, δεν σε ανέφερε καν".

Η Έριελ γέλασε και έδειξε ένα κοκάλινο δάχτυλο που τεντώθηκε προς τα κάτω και άγγιξε τη μύτη του Ε-Ζ. "Η περίπτωσή σου δόθηκε σε μένα, αφού οι δύο ηλίθιοι Χατζ και Ρέικι απέτυχαν στα καθήκοντά τους".

"Μη με αγγίζεις!" Το δάχτυλο αποσύρθηκε. "Σε ξαναρωτώ, τι κάνεις εδώ στα χωράφια μου - και γιατί είσαι σε αναπηρικό καροτσάκι;"

"Όλα θα εξηγηθούν", είπε ο Έριελ. Σήκωσε τα πόδια του ψηλά και τους χαμογέλασε. "Μου αρέσουν αυτά τα παπούτσια- είναι πολύ άνετα".

"Δεν είναι παπούτσια, είναι σανδάλια", είπε ο Σαμ, πλησιάζοντας πιο κοντά στην αιωρούμενη καρέκλα.

"Περίμενε, θείε Σαμ, έλα πίσω μου".

Ο Έριελ έριξε το κεφάλι του προς τα πίσω και γέλασε. "Η αλήθεια είναι ένας σκύλος που πρέπει να κυνηγηθεί" - αυτό είναι ένα απόσπασμα από τον Σαίξπηρ που σημαίνει, ότι ο θείος σου πρέπει να εξημερωθεί".

"Γιατί εσύ!" Ο Σαμ φώναξε, σηκώνοντας τη γροθιά του στον αέρα.

" Είναι δύσκολο να νικήσεις έναν άνθρωπο που δεν τα παρατάει ποτέ' - αυτό είναι μια ρήση από τον Μπέιμπ Ρουθ έναν από τους πιο διάσημους παίκτες του μπέιζμπολ που υπήρξαν ποτέ". Η καρέκλα του Ε-Ζ σηκώθηκε από το έδαφος και πέταξε πιο κοντά στην Έριελ.

"Το μπέιζμπολ είναι ένα παιχνίδι ισορροπίας", είπε ο Έριελ. "Αυτή είναι μια φράση του συγγραφέα Στίβεν Κινγκ". Δίστασε, μετά χαμογέλασε με ένα τόσο μεγάλο χαμόγελο που τα μάγουλά του, θα μπορούσαν να καταρρεύσουν καθώς η καρέκλα του E-Z έπεσε σαν να ήταν φτιαγμένη από μόλυβδο. "Ουπς", είπε ο Έριελ, καθώς βροντοφώναξε από τα γέλια.

Δεν χρειάστηκε πολύς χρόνος για να αποκτήσει ο E-Z τον έλεγχο της καρέκλας του και αυτή ανέβηκε σαν ασανσέρ. Προσπάθησε να πάρει τα φτερά του υπό τον έλεγχό του. Όμως δεν υπήρχε χρόνος, αφού είχε μετατραπεί σε σβούρα και γύριζε γύρω-γύρω.

"Arrgghhhhh!" φώναξε, σκαλίζοντας τα νύχια του στα μπράτσα της καρέκλας. Η περιστροφή σταμάτησε, η καρέκλα έπεσε ξανά σαν μολύβδινο μπαλόνι και μετά σταμάτησε.

Και πάλι, προσπάθησε να κάνει τα φτερά του να δουλέψουν. Δεν συνεργάζονταν και το επόμενο πράγμα που ήξερε ήταν ότι στριφογύριζε ξανά. Αλλά αυτή τη φορά ήταν αριστερόστροφα.

"Hhhhgggggrrraaa!" φώναξε.

Η Έριελ γέλασε τόσο δυνατά που ταρακούνησε τη γη.

Από κάτω, ο Σαμ μάζεψε πέτρες από το πεζοδρόμιο και τις πέταξε στην Eriel, η οποία απέφυγε και έσκυψε τις περισσότερες. Μια μεγάλη πέτρα όμως συνδέθηκε με τη μύτη του πλάσματος. "Διάλεξε κάποιον που είναι πιο κοντά στην ηλικία σου!" φώναξε ο Σαμ.

Καθώς το αίμα έτρεχε στο πρόσωπό του, ο Eriel έβαλε τον θείο του E-Z στη θέση του.

"Όχι!" φώναξε ο E-Z καθώς συνέχιζε να περιστρέφεται. Όταν σταμάτησε τελείως, ανάποδα, αυτό που είδε από κάτω δεν μπορούσε να κάνει λάθος. Ο θείος Σαμ ήταν τώρα ένα από τα αγάλματα σε έναν κύκλο: εκεί στέκονταν εκατόν έντεκα άντρες. Ήταν τόσο ζαλισμένος, παρόλα αυτά του ήρθε μια φράση και καθώς ήταν το μόνο που είχε, την φώναξε όσο πιο δυνατά μπορούσε: "Δεν έχει τελειώσει μέχρι να τελειώσει!".

POP.

POP.

Ο Χαντζ κάθισε στον έναν ώμο του εφήβου, ο Ρέικι στον άλλο.

"Αυτό είναι μια ρήση του Γιόγκι Μπέρα και αυτό, είναι από εμένα και τον θείο Σαμ!"

Στα χέρια του κρατούσε τώρα το μεγαλύτερο ρόπαλο του κόσμου, ένα αντίγραφο του 54 ουάνσερ του Μπέιμπ Ρουθ και έλαμπε από τη σκόνη διαμαντιού. Δεν είχε ιδέα πόσο βαρύ ήταν αυτό, καθώς χτύπησε τον Έριελ στο θρόνο του αναπηρικού αμαξιδίου και τον έστειλε να πετάξει από άκρη σε άκρη. Τραγούδησε: "Πες γεια στον άνθρωπο στο φεγγάρι όταν τον συναντήσεις!".

Στο βάθος η ηχηρή φωνή του Έριελ είπε: "Η δοκιμασία ολοκληρώθηκε!".

Ο Χατζ και η Ρέικι χειροκρότησαν. Όπως και οι εκατόν έντεκα άνθρωποι που είχαν επιστρέψει στην ανθρώπινη μορφή τους, συμπεριλαμβανομένου του θείου Σαμ.

"Φυσικά, ξέρετε ότι θα επιστρέψει", είπε ο Χαντζ. "Και θα είναι πολύ θυμωμένος!"

"Ευχαριστώ για τη βοήθειά σου!" Είπε ο E-Z, καθώς αυτός και ο Σαμ πέταξαν στο σπίτι τους.

Ο Ρέικι και ο Χαντζ έσβησαν τα μυαλά των εκατόν δέκα, μετά συνέχισαν τη δουλειά τους στα ορυχεία και ήλπιζαν ότι κανείς δεν πρόσεξε ότι είχαν βρει τρόπο να δραπετεύσουν.

Ο Έριελ συνέχισε να περιστρέφεται εκτός ελέγχου, ενώ συνέτασσε ένα σχέδιο εκδίκησης.

ΕΠΙΛΟΓΟΣ

Μ ΕΤΑ ΑΠΌ ΜΕΡΙΚΈΣ ΠΟΛΥΆΣΧΟΛΕΣ ημέρες, ο Ε-Ζ κοιμήθηκε επιτέλους καλά. Ονειρευόταν ότι έπαιζε μπέιζμπολ και την επόμενη μέρα ο Άρντεν και ο Πι Τζέι πέρασαν για να τον πάνε σε έναν αγώνα. "Δεν έχω όρεξη να παίξω σήμερα, αλλά θα έρθω μαζί για το ηθικό", είπε.

"Βεβαίως", απάντησαν οι φίλοι του.

Μόλις έβαλαν τον Ε-Ζ στο γήπεδο, επέμεναν να παίξει. Τον χρειάζονταν για να πιάσει, και εκείνος συμφώνησε. Όταν ήρθε η πρώτη του φορά να είναι στο ρόπαλο, ήθελε να χτυπήσει μόνος του. Άρπαξε το αγαπημένο του ρόπαλο και ανέβηκε με ρόδα στο γήπεδο. Η πρώτη μπαλιά ήταν ψηλά και την έχασε. Η ζώνη ρίψης του ήταν πραγματικά συμπυκνωμένη, αφού καθόταν.

"Πρώτο στράικ", φώναξε ο διαιτητής.

Ο Ε-Ζ απομακρύνθηκε από το πιάτο. Έκανε μερικές ακόμη δοκιμαστικές κτυπήματα και μετά επέστρεψε πάλι πίσω. Με την επόμενη ρίψη συνδέθηκε με την μπάλα και αυτή έφυγε έξω.

"Δεύτερο στράικ", φώναξε ο διαιτητής.

"Δεν υπάρχει κτύπημα, δεν υπάρχει κτύπημα", φλυαρούσαν τα παιδιά στον αγωνιστικό χώρο.

Ο πίτσερ πέταξε μια στρεβλή μπάλα και ο Ε-Ζ έσκυψε στην μπάλα και συνδέθηκε. Η μπάλα πέταξε, έξω από το γήπεδο. Πάνω από τον φράχτη. Έξω από το πάρκο.

"Πάρτε τις βάσεις", είπε ο διαιτητής. "Το αξίζεις, μικρέ."

Ο E-Z γύρισε γύρω από τις βάσεις, κρατώντας την καρέκλα του από το να πετάξει. Όταν η καρέκλα του ακούμπησε στο κέντρο, οι συμπαίκτες του συγκεντρώθηκαν γύρω του και τον επευφημούσαν. Το απόλαυσε όσο κράτησε.

Μέχρι που προσγειώθηκε ξανά μέσα στο μεταλλικό δοχείο -μόνο που αυτή τη φορά ήταν τυλιγμένος σε μια μπάλα- και ήταν χωρίς καρέκλα. Σαν νεογέννητο μωρό, ανέπνεε βαθιά, καθώς ήταν το μόνο πράγμα που μπορούσε να κάνει. Περίμενε, τα μωρά μπορούσαν να αναποδογυρίσουν τον εαυτό τους. Το μόνο που έπρεπε να κάνει ήταν να συγκεντρωθεί, να συγκεντρωθεί.

Ναι, τα κατάφερε. Το μόνο πρόβλημα ήταν ότι δεν ήταν καθόλου καλύτερα. Ήταν ακόμα τυλιγμένος, μέσα στο σκοτάδι. Περιορισμένος σε έναν χώρο χωρίς φως ή δυνατότητα να κινηθεί σχεδόν καθόλου. Στην πραγματικότητα, το σχήμα του μεταλλικού δοχείου ήταν διαφορετικό αυτή τη φορά. Ήταν πιο λεπτό στο ένα άκρο, σε σχήμα σφαίρας.

Η γνώση αυτού του γεγονότος δεν βοηθούσε καθώς η κλειστοφοβία και το άγχος του έπαιρναν μεγάλες διαστάσεις. Αναρωτιόταν πόσο καιρό θα μπορούσε να συνεχίσει να αναπνέει σε αυτόν τον περιορισμένο χώρο. Όχι για πολύ. Θα του τελείωνε ο αέρας σε χρόνο μηδέν και θα πέθαινε. Εισέπνευσε βαθιά, προσπαθώντας να κρατήσει το επίπεδο άγχους χαμηλά.

Ένα πράγμα ήταν σίγουρο, δεν υπήρχε περίπτωση να χωρέσει η Έριελ σε αυτό το πράγμα μαζί του. Εκτός κι αν ανατίναζε τους τοίχους διάπλατα - πράγμα που ίσως να μην ήταν και τόσο κακή ιδέα.

Ο E-Z χτύπησε τους τοίχους και το ταβάνι. Φώναξε. Ούρλιαζε. Θυμήθηκε το τηλέφωνό του. Μπορούσε να το φτάσει; Δεν ήταν εκεί. Το είχε βάλει στην αθλητική τσάντα για να ακολουθήσει τον κανόνα που απαγορεύει τα τηλέφωνα στο γήπεδο.

Έξω από το κοντέινερ, ακούγονταν ανησυχητικοί ήχοι. Ξύσιμο. Αρουραίοι; Όχι, όχι αρουραίοι. Μπορούσε να αντιμετωπίσει πολλά πράγματα, αλλά όχι αρουραίους. "Αφήστε με να βγω!" φώναξε.

Μια μηχανή ξεκίνησε. Ένα παλαιότερο όχημα, σαν φορτηγό. Το πάτωμα κάτω από αυτόν άρχισε να τρέμει και να κροταλίζει, καθώς η σφαίρα κυλούσε προς τα εμπρός και αναπηδούσε.

Έξω το κοντέινερ αναπηδούσε στους τοίχους. Μέσα, βρισκόταν σε τόσο περιορισμένο χώρο που δεν υπήρχε μεγάλη κίνηση. Αυτό ήταν ένα πλεονέκτημα του να είσαι παγιδευμένος σε μια σφαίρα.

Το όχημα χτύπησε κάτι και το κεφάλι του E-Z συνδέθηκε με την κορυφή του πράγματος. Φώναξε, αλλά ο ήχος έσβησε. Το μεταλλικό δοχείο μετακινήθηκε ξανά, πλάγια. Χτύπησε κάτι και μετά επέστρεψε στην αρχική του θέση. Ο ώμος του πονούσε από την πρόσκρουση.

Ο E-Z αναρωτήθηκε αν αυτό ήταν έργο του Έριελ, αλλά αποφάσισε ότι δεν μπορούσε να είναι. Άρχισε να συμπεραίνει ότι τον είχαν απαγάγει και τον κρατούσαν αιχμάλωτο. Αλλά γιατί τώρα;

"Έι!" φώναξε καθώς το μεταλλικό αντικείμενο κύλησε και προσγειώθηκε στον επίπεδο πάτο - εκεί που ήταν ο πάτος του. Τώρα το βάρος ήταν πιο ομοιόμορφα κατανεμημένο. Ήταν άνετα. Ή όσο πιο άνετα μπορούσε να είναι υπό αυτές τις συνθήκες. Έτσι, παρέμεινε πολύ ακίνητος μέχρι που το όχημα σταμάτησε τελείως και έπεσε με την άκρη στην άκρη.

Πήρε μια βαθιά ανάσα, ηρέμησε και είπε τις λέξεις δυνατά,

"Roch-Ah-Or, A, Ra-Du, EE, El".

Καθώς περίμενε, ρώτησε: "Πού είσαι, Έριελ;

Roch-Ah-Or, A, Ra-Du, EE, El;"

"Με κάλεσες;" Είπε ο Eriel. Η φωνή του ήταν τραγανή και καθαρή, αλλά δεν ήταν ορατός.

"Ναι, Έριελ, νομίζω ότι με έχουν απαγάγει. Είμαι μέσα σε ένα κοντέινερ. Μπορείς να με βοηθήσεις;"

"Ξέρω πάντα πού βρίσκεσαι", είπε ο Eriel. "Η ερώτηση που θα έπρεπε να κάνεις είναι ΘΑ σε βοηθήσω".

"Δεν ήξερα ότι με παρακολουθούσατε 24 ώρες το 24ωρο!" Αναφώνησε ο Ε-Ζ, γινόταν όλο και πιο θυμωμένος όσο περνούσε η ώρα. Πήρε μερικές βαθιές ανάσες και ηρέμησε. Χρειαζόταν τη βοήθεια του Έριελ και ο αρχάγγελος δεν επρόκειτο να τον διευκολύνει. "Δεν μπορώ να δω τον οδηγό αυτού του πράγματος και δεν μπορώ να ανοίξω τα φτερά μου. Και πού είναι η καρέκλα μου; Μου τελειώνει ο αέρας εδώ μέσα. Αν θέλεις να τελειώσω αυτές τις δοκιμασίες για σένα, τότε καλύτερα να με βγάλεις από εδώ και γρήγορα".

"Πρώτα με προσβάλλεις, αμφισβητώντας αν είμαι άγγελος ή όχι, και μετά με ικετεύεις να σε βοηθήσω. Οι άνθρωποι είναι πράγματι πολύ άστατα πλάσματα".

"Το ξέρω. Λυπάμαι. Σε παρακαλώ, βοήθησέ με".

"Έχεις σκεφτεί", πρότεινε η Έριελ. "Ότι αυτό ΕΙΝΑΙ μια δοκιμασία; Κάτι που πρέπει να ξεπεράσεις εσύ ο ίδιος;"

"Μου λες ότι αυτό είναι σίγουρα μια δοκιμασία;"

"Δεν λέω ότι είναι. Και δεν λέω ότι δεν είναι", είπε η Eriel με ένα χαστούκι.

Η Ε-Ζ ήταν έξαλλη. Του έλειπαν τόσο πολύ ο Χατζ και η Ρέικι.

"Είναι τόσο λυπηρό που σκέφτεσαι ακόμα αυτούς τους δύο ηλίθιους. Τώρα Ε-Ζ, αν ήταν μια δίκη, τότε πώς θα έβγαινες από αυτήν;"

"Πρώτα απ' όλα, με βοήθησαν όταν κόντεψες να σκοτώσεις τη γη. Δεύτερον, δεν μπορεί να είναι δίκη, επειδή δεν υπάρχει κανείς για να βοηθήσω".

Ο Έριελ γέλασε. "Θεωρείς ότι δεν είσαι κανείς;" Η Έριελ έκανε μια παύση. "Σήμερα σώζεις τον εαυτό σου και μόνο τον εαυτό σου. Χρησιμοποίησε τα εργαλεία που έχεις στη διάθεσή σου". Δίστασε και μετά γέλασε ξανά. "Σκέψου έξω από το μεταλλικό δοχείο". Το γέλιο του ήταν τόσο δυνατό μέσα στη μεταλλική σφαίρα που πονούσε τα αυτιά του Ε-Ζ. Τα κάλυψε. Τότε δεν άκουσε πια τον Έριελ.

Ο Ε-Ζ έκλεισε τα μάτια του και συγκεντρώθηκε. Αποφάσισε να μαζέψει τις γροθιές του και να προσπαθήσει να σπρώξει τους τοίχους. Όσο κι αν προσπαθούσε, δεν κουνιόντουσαν. Το σχέδιο Β ήταν να καλέσει την καρέκλα του, όπως και έκανε. Φαντάστηκε ότι δεν ήταν μακριά. Μήπως αιωρούνταν από πάνω, περιμένοντας τον E-Z να την καλέσει; Συγκεντρώθηκε τόσο πολύ στο να καλέσει την καρέκλα του, που δεν κατάλαβε ότι κάποιος περπατούσε έξω. Βήματα στο πεζοδρόμιο. Ένας άντρας, με μπότες που χτυπούσαν. Ο άντρας περνούσε γύρω από το όχημα, προς το πίσω μέρος. Ένα κλειδί μπήκε μέσα. Η πόρτα άνοιξε.

"Κυκλοφορεί εδώ μέσα", είπε ο άντρας.

Ένα γέλιο. Όχι το γέλιο του Έριελ. Το γέλιο ενός άλλου άντρα.

Μετά μια κραυγή.

Μετά κι άλλες κραυγές.

Μετά τρέξιμο. Τρέχοντας μακριά.

Κι άλλες κραυγές.

Μετά κίνηση. Το κοντέινερ κινείται. Να τον σηκώνουν στο αναπηρικό του καροτσάκι.

Μετά ανεβαίνει προς τα πάνω, όλο και ψηλότερα. Μακριά προς την ασφάλεια.

"Ευχαριστώ", είπε ο E-Z στην καρέκλα του. "Τώρα πήγαινέ με στο σπίτι του θείου Σαμ".

Ο E-Z ήξερε ότι ο θείος Σαμ θα μπορούσε να τον βγάλει από το κοντέινερ. Θα χρειαζόταν ένα γιγάντιο ανοιχτήρι κονσέρβας, αλλά αν υπήρχε τέτοιο, ο θείος Σαμ θα το έβρισκε.

Η αναπηρική του καρέκλα όμως έφυγε με ταχύτητα προς την αντίθετη κατεύθυνση.

ΒΙΒΛΙΟ ΔΕΥΤΕΡΟ:
ΤΑ ΤΡΙΑ

ΚΕΦΑΛΑΙΟ 1

Πολύ, πολύ μακριά από εκεί που ζούσε ο E-Z Ντίκενς, ένα μικρό κορίτσι χόρευε. Τα μαθήματα μπαλέτου της γίνονταν σε ένα μικρό στούντιο στην κεντρική επιχειρηματική περιοχή των Κάτω Χωρών.

Ήταν ένα όμορφο παιδί, με χρυσά μαλλιά και μια γραμμή φακίδων που απλωνόταν στη μύτη και τα μάγουλά της. Τα πιο αξιομνημόνευτα χαρακτηριστικά της ήταν τα καστανά πράσινα μάτια της. Το χρώμα τους ήταν ακριβώς το ίδιο με αυτό της γιαγιάς της. Το όνειρό της ήταν να γίνει μια μέρα η πιο διάσημη χορεύτρια μπαλέτου των Κάτω Χωρών.

Η ροζ φούστα της ήταν φτιαγμένη από τούλι. Ήταν ένα διχτυωτό, ελαφρύ ύφασμα που χρησιμοποιούσαν οι σχεδιαστές για τις επαγγελματίες χορεύτριες. Η νταντά της είχε σχεδιάσει και ράψει γι' αυτήν τη φούστα. Το κοστούμι - ένα έργο τέχνης από μόνο του - τόσο πολύ που κάθε παιδί στην τάξη ήθελε ένα.

Η Hannah, η νταντά της Lia δέχτηκε πολλά αιτήματα από άλλους γονείς να φτιάξουν στις κόρες τους την ίδια φούστα. Είπε με αποφασιστικότητα στα παιδιά, στους γονείς τους, στους δασκάλους και σε πολλούς άλλους ότι δεν είχε χρόνο να αναλάβει την επιπλέον δουλειά. Αν και θα μπορούσε να χρησιμοποιήσει τα χρήματα.

Ό,τι έκανε η Χάνα, το έκανε επειδή αγαπούσε την προστατευόμενή της, τη Λία. Τη Λία, την οποία αποκαλούσε kleintje, που μεταφράζεται ως μικρή.

Με τα μπαλέτα (μεταφράζεται: μάθημα μπαλέτου) να έχουν σχεδόν τελειώσει, η Λία μάζεψε τα παπούτσια της. Έτριβε τα πονεμένα πόδια της.

Όλοι οι balletdansers (μεταφράζεται: χορευτές μπαλέτου) - ακόμη και τα επτάχρονα όπως η Lia έπρεπε να προπονούνται τουλάχιστον είκοσι ώρες την εβδομάδα.

Αυτή η πρόσθετη εργασία, πέρα από ένα πλήρες σχολικό πρόγραμμα, απαιτούσε αφοσίωση και δέσμευση. Όποιο παιδί δεν μπορούσε να ακολουθήσει, του έδειχναν αμέσως την πόρτα. Ανεξάρτητα από το πόσα χρήματα προσφέρθηκαν να πληρώσουν οι γονείς τους για να τα κρατήσουν στο πρόγραμμα.

Η Lia ήλπιζε ότι μια μέρα θα συναντούσε το είδωλό της Igone de Jongh, την πιο διάσημη χορεύτρια μπαλέτου της Ολλανδίας όλων των εποχών. Από τότε που το είδωλό της αποσύρθηκε, η Λία παρακολουθούσε τις παραστάσεις της στην τηλεόραση.

Η Χάνα φρόντιζε τη Λία τις καθημερινές. Η μητέρα της Λία, η Σαμάνθα, ταξίδευε για επαγγελματικούς λόγους κατά τη διάρκεια της εβδομάδας.

Έξω από το στούντιο χορού, η Hannah και η Lia μπήκαν στο Volkswagen Golf. Σύντομα θα επέστρεφαν στο σπίτι τους.

"Έχεις καθόλου διάβασμα;" Η Χάνα ρώτησε.

Η Λία ένεψε.

"Goed," μεταφράζεται ως καλή. "Πήγαινε να ξεκινήσεις όταν ετοιμάσω το δείπνο", είπε η Χάνα.

"Oke", που μεταφράζεται ως "εντάξει", απάντησε η Λία.

Η Λία πήγε αμέσως στο δωμάτιό της, όπου κρέμασε τη στολή μπαλέτου της, και στη συνέχεια έπιασε δουλειά στο γραφείο της.

Στο σχολείο μάθαιναν για τον θρύλο του Δέντρου της Μάγισσας. Η εργασία τους ήταν να ζωγραφίσουν το δέντρο και να δημιουργήσουν κάτι μαγικό γι' αυτό. Εκείνη σκόπευε να σχεδιάσει ένα περίγραμμα με κιμωλία.

Στη συνέχεια να χρησιμοποιήσει καθαριστικά πίπας για τις ρίζες και γκλίτερ στα φύλλα για το μαγικό στοιχείο.

Παρόλο που είχε φυσικό ταλέντο στην τέχνη, δεν της άρεσε να τη δημιουργεί. Η προτίμησή της ήταν ο χορός. Δεν παραπονιόταν ούτε απέρριπτε εργασίες που δεν της άρεσαν ιδιαίτερα. Δεν ήταν στη φύση της να είναι ανυπάκουη ή ενοχλητική.

Αν και η Λία ζούσε στο Ζούμπερτ της Ολλανδίας, φοιτούσε σε διεθνές σχολείο. Τα αγγλικά της ήταν εξαιρετικά. Το ίδιο το Ζούμπερτ ήταν παγκοσμίως γνωστό ως η γενέτειρα του Βίνσεντ Βαν Γκογκ. Η Λία γνώριζε τα πάντα για τον Βαν Γκογκ, αφού είχε το ίδιο αίμα στις φλέβες τους.

Αφού ολοκλήρωσε την εργασία της, άνοιξε τον υπολογιστή της. Μπήκε και έπαιξε ένα παιχνίδι. Το να φτάσει στο επόμενο επίπεδο θα έπαιρνε μόνο λίγα λεπτά. Σύντομα η Χάνα θα την καλούσε για avondeten (δείπνο).

Κανείς δεν χρειάζεται να το μάθει ποτέ, έλεγε μια μικρή φωνή στο πίσω μέρος του μυαλού της. Η Λία άκουσε τη φωνή, αλλά για να βεβαιωθεί ότι κανείς δεν το έμαθε, έκλεισε την πόρτα του δωματίου της.

Καθώς τα δάχτυλά της έκαναν κλικ στο πληκτρολόγιο, η λάμπα πάνω από το γραφείο της έσβησε με έναν κρότο. Έκλεισε τον φορητό υπολογιστή και άνοιξε ξανά την πόρτα της. Κοίταξε κάτω στο διάδρομο, όπου βρίσκονταν οι εφεδρικές λάμπες αλογόνου. Η νταντά είχε ένα απόθεμα στο ντουλάπι με τα λευκά είδη στην κορυφή της σκάλας. Το μόνο που χρειαζόταν να κάνει η Λία ήταν να βγει έξω, να φέρει μία, να επιστρέψει και να αλλάξει η ίδια τη λάμπα. Τότε θα είχε περισσότερο χρόνο για να παίξει το παιχνίδι της.

Επιστρέφοντας στο δωμάτιό της, εκτίμησε την κατάσταση. Έπρεπε να σταθεί πάνω στην καρέκλα του γραφείου της - η οποία είχε τροχούς. Θα την έσπρωχνε σταθερά πάνω στο κρεβάτι, για να την ασφαλίσει. Ναι, αυτό θα λειτουργούσε.

Η καρέκλα ασφαλίστηκε κάτω από το φωτιστικό και ανέβηκε πάνω της. Κρατώντας τη νέα λάμπα κάτω από το πηγούνι της ξεβίδωσε την παλιά. Την καμένη λάμπα την πέταξε στο κρεβάτι. Παίρνοντας την άλλη λάμπα κάτω από το πηγούνι της, τη βίδωσε.

ΚΡΑΚ!

Η νέα λάμπα εξερράγη.

Θραύσματα γυαλιού, κυρίως μικροσκοπικού μεγέθους, εκτοξεύτηκαν από μέσα του. Στο πρόσωπο και στα μάτια του μικρού κοριτσιού.

Η Λία δεν φώναξε αμέσως, γιατί ένα μπλε φως γέμισε το δωμάτιο κάνοντας τον χρόνο να σταματήσει. Το φως την περικύκλωσε καθώς ανέβηκε στο ίδιο επίπεδο με το πρόσωπό της.

ΣΤΡΟΦΗ!

Εμφανίστηκε ένα μικροσκοπικό αγγελικό πλάσμα που εξέτασε τα μάτια του μικρού κοριτσιού. Στη συνέχεια, αποφασίζοντας ότι ήταν κατεστραμμένα ανεπανόρθωτα, ψιθύρισε: "Θα είσαι, μία από τις τρεις;"

"Ναι", που μεταφράζεται ως ναι, είπε η Λία. καθώς ο χρόνος σταμάτησε.

Ο άγγελος, το όνομα του οποίου ήταν Haniel, έφτασε. Τραγούδησε ένα καταπραϋντικό νανούρισμα στη Λία, ενώ αφαιρούσε το γυαλί.

Στα αγγλικά, οι στίχοι του τραγουδιού ήταν:

"'Ένα θλιμμένο θλιμμένο κοριτσάκι κάθισε κάτω

στην όχθη του ποταμού.

Το κορίτσι έκλαιγε από θλίψη

γιατί και οι δύο γονείς της είχαν πεθάνει".

Στα ολλανδικά, οι στίχοι του τραγουδιού ήταν:

"Asn d'oever van de snelle vliet

Eeen treurig meisje zat.

Het meisje huilde van verdriet

Omdat zij geen ouders meer had."

Ευτυχώς, η μικρή Λία κοιμόταν και έτσι δεν μπορούσε να τρομάξει από τα λόγια του νανουρίσματος.

Όταν ο Haniel τελείωσε με την αντιμετώπιση του χειρότερου μέρους των πληγών της Lia, έβαλε τα χέρια στους γοφούς της και σταμάτησε να τραγουδάει. Η αποστολή είχε σχεδόν ολοκληρωθεί, το μόνο που είχε να κάνει τώρα ήταν να βάλει τα θεμέλια για τα νέα μάτια του προστατευόμενού της.

Τα δύο χεράκια της Λίας είχαν τυλιχτεί σε μπάλες. Σφιχτές μικρές γροθιές. Η Haniel άφησε τα φτερά της να χαϊδέψουν απαλά τα κλειστά δάχτυλα, παρασύροντάς τα να ανοίξουν.

Όταν οι παλάμες της Λία άνοιξαν, ο άγγελος Haniel, χρησιμοποιώντας τον δείκτη της, περιέγραψε το σχήμα ενός ματιού και στις δύο παλάμες. Στα δάχτυλα, σχεδίασε μία μόνο γραμμή σε καθένα, που οδηγούσε από την παλάμη μέχρι την άκρη του δαχτύλου. Το έργο της ολοκληρώθηκε, ο άγγελος Haniel, φίλησε απαλά τη Lia στο μέτωπο, και στη συνέχεια με ένα

SWISH!

εξαφανίστηκε.

Ο χρόνος ξεκίνησε ξανά και η γενναία μικρή μας Λία εξακολουθούσε να μην ουρλιάζει. Το σοκ το κάνει αυτό στο σώμα σας ως αμυντικός μηχανισμός και σταματώντας τον χρόνο, σταμάτησε και ο πόνος. Όταν η Λία τελικά ούρλιαξε, δεν μπορούσε να σταματήσει. Όχι όταν έφτασε το ασθενοφόρο. Ή όταν τη σήκωσαν πάνω σε ένα φορείο μέσα στο όχημα με τη σειρήνα να συμμετέχει στη χορωδία των κραυγών της. Ή όταν την έσπρωξαν σε ένα φορείο στο νοσοκομείο. Ούτε όταν έριξαν ένα μεγάλο φως στο πρόσωπό της, το οποίο ένιωθε αλλά δεν έβλεπε.

Σταμάτησε να ουρλιάζει όταν την νάρκωσαν. Τότε χρησιμοποίησαν την τελευταία λέξη της τεχνολογίας για να αφαιρέσουν το εναπομείναν γυαλί. Ωστόσο, κάθε κομμάτι γυαλιού είχε ήδη αφαιρεθεί. Οι χειρουργοί προχώρησαν και της έδεσαν τα μάτια και στη συνέχεια την πήγαν στο δωμάτιό της για να αναρρώσει.

Μετά την επέμβαση, έφτασε η μητέρα της Lia, η Samantha. Είχε πάρει την πτήση με το κόκκινο μάτι από το Λονδίνο. Συνάντησε τον χειρουργό ενώ η κόρη της κοιμόταν.

"Λυπάμαι, αλλά δεν θα ξαναδεί ποτέ", είπε.

Η μητέρα της Λία έσπρωξε τη γροθιά της στο στόμα της παλεύοντας να συγκρατήσει την επιθυμία να θρηνήσει.

Ο γιατρός είπε: "Μπορεί να μάθει τη γραφή μπράιγ και να φοιτήσει σε σχολείο για άτομα με προβλήματα όρασης. Είναι σε εξαιρετική ηλικία για μάθηση και θα ρουφήξει τις γνώσεις. Σε λίγο καιρό η νοηματική θα της γίνει δεύτερη φύση".

"Αλλά η κόρη μου θέλει να γίνει χορεύτρια μπαλέτου. Έχετε δει ή ακούσει ποτέ για έναν τυφλό επαγγελματία χορευτή;"

"Η Αλίσια Αλόνσο ήταν μερικώς τυφλή. Δεν το άφησε να την κρατήσει πίσω".

Η μητέρα της Λία χάιδεψε το χέρι της κόρης της που κοιμόταν. "Ευχαριστώ, θα βρω λεπτομέρειες γι' αυτήν στο διαδίκτυο. Τα επτά είναι πολύ μικρά για να αναγκαστείς να εγκαταλείψεις ένα όνειρο".

"Συμφωνώ. Τώρα ξεκουράσου κι εσύ λίγο. Η Λία θα ξυπνήσει σύντομα και θα χρειαστεί να είσαι δυνατή γι' αυτήν. Για όταν της το πεις. Αν θέλεις να είμαι κι εγώ εδώ, πες μου το".

"Σας ευχαριστώ, γιατρέ, θα προσπαθήσω να τα καταφέρω μόνη μου πρώτα".

Καθώς έκλεινε η πόρτα, η μητέρα της Λίας άγγιξε τα σημάδια στο πρόσωπο της κόρης της. Τα αποτυπώματα που άφησε έμοιαζαν με θυμωμένες σταγόνες βροχής. Στη συνέχεια κοίταξε τη νταντά της Λίας που κοιμόταν, τη Χάνα. Καθώς περνούσε από δίπλα της για να πάρει λίγο νερό, κλώτσησε κατά λάθος επίτηδες το αριστερό της παπούτσι για να την ξυπνήσει. "Έξω!" είπε, καθώς η Χάνα χασμουριόταν.

Τώρα στο διάδρομο, η μητέρα της Λία, η Σαμάνθα, άφησε τα συναισθήματά της να ξεσπάσουν χωρίς να συγκρατηθεί. "Πώς μπόρεσες να αφήσεις να συμβεί αυτό στο μωρό μου; Πώς μπόρεσες; Τη μια στιγμή ήμουν σε μια επαγγελματική συνάντηση - την επόμενη έπρεπε να διακόψω το επαγγελματικό μου ταξίδι και να προλάβω την πρώτη πτήση από το Λονδίνο! Τι συνέβη; Πώς συνέβη;"

"Μόλις είχαμε επιστρέψει από το μάθημα μπαλέτου. Εγώ ετοίμαζα το δείπνο και η Λία τελείωνε τις εργασίες της. Η λάμπα πρέπει να κάηκε. Πήρε μια άλλη από την ντουλάπα του διαδρόμου και προσπάθησε να την αντικαταστήσει μόνη της και εξερράγη. Όταν ούρλιαξε, ήμουν εκεί σε δευτερόλεπτα και το ziekenwagen (ασθενοφόρο) έφτασε σε χρόνο μηδέν. Προσευχόμουν τα μάτια της να είναι εντάξει, ότι θα γίνει καλά".

"Προσεύχεσαι στον ύπνο σου λοιπόν, έτσι δεν είναι;" ρώτησε η Σαμάνθα, χωρίς να περιμένει απάντηση. "Οι άρτσεν (γιατροί) λένε ότι δεν θα ξαναδεί ποτέ", είπε η Σαμάνθα με ένα άσχημο δηλητήριο στην εκφορά της.

Ν ΤΩ ΜΕΤΑΞΎ, Η Λία έβλεπε ένα όνειρο και πετούσε με έναν άγγελο. Είχε τα χέρια της γύρω από το λαιμό του, καθώς αγκαλιαζόταν στο στήθος του. Η κίνηση της αναπηρικής καρέκλας στον αέρα την κούναγε και την παρηγορούσε.

Τότε το μυαλό της γύρισε και κοίταζε από ψηλά ένα μεταλλικό δοχείο. Το δοχείο καθόταν στο κάθισμα ενός αναπηρικού αμαξιδίου με φτερά. Το μετέφεραν σε ένα μέρος που δεν γνώριζε.

Σήκωσε το δεξί της χέρι και μετά εδώ το αριστερό, και με αυτά μπορούσε να δει ότι υπήρχε ένας άγγελος/αγόρι παγιδευμένο μέσα σε αυτό. Είχε ένα ευγενικό πρόσωπο, με μάτια πιο γαλανά από τον ουρανό με χρυσές κηλίδες που τα έκαναν να λάμπουν παρόλο που βρισκόταν στο σκοτάδι. Τα μαλλιά του ήταν, ως επί το πλείστον ξανθά, εκτός από μερικά γκρίζα στους κροτάφους. Αλλά το πιο παράξενο ήταν μια μαύρη λωρίδα στη μέση. Έκανε το αγόρι να φαίνεται μεγαλύτερο.

Ο άγγελος/αγόρι στο κοντέινερ που επέβαινε στο κάθισμα του αναπηρικού αμαξιδίου πέταξε πιο κοντά στο κοριτσάκι στο όνειρό της. Άγγιξε το δοχείο, και όταν το έκανε, μπορούσε να νιώσει και να ακούσει τον χτύπο της καρδιάς του αγγέλου/αγόρι μέσα. Και όχι μόνο αυτό, αλλά μπορούσε επίσης να διαβάσει τις σκέψεις και τα συναισθήματά του.

Η Λία ξύπνησε και φώναξε: "Μητέρα! Χάνα! Έλα γρήγορα!"

"Εδώ είμαι, αγάπη μου", είπε η μητέρα της, καθώς επέστρεφε στο κρεβάτι της κόρης της.

Η Χάνα σκούπισε τα μάτια της και ξαναμπήκε στο δωμάτιο.

"Δεν υπάρχει χρόνος για σένα, μητέρα, να ρίξεις το φταίξιμο στη Χάνα. Αυτό ήταν ένα ατύχημα. Εξάλλου, η βοήθειά μας είναι απαραίτητη. Σε παρακαλώ, βρες μου χαρτί και μολύβια - ΤΩΡΑ".

"Παραληρεί!" Αναφώνησε η Σαμάνθα. Έλεγξε το μέτωπο της κόρης της για θερμοκρασία. Φαινόταν μια χαρά.

Η Χάνα ανέσυρε τα ζητούμενα αντικείμενα από την τσάντα της και τα έβαλε στα χέρια της Λία.

Χωρίς δισταγμό, η Λία άρχισε να ζωγραφίζει. Γρατζούνησε το χαρτί, σαν εμπνευσμένη καλλιτέχνιδα. Η Σαμάνθα και η Χάνα παρακολουθούσαν με περιέργεια.

Η πρώτη εικόνα που ζωγράφισε, απεικόνιζε ένα αγόρι μέσα σε ένα μεταλλικό δοχείο σε σχήμα σφαίρας. Το δοχείο ακουμπούσε στο κάθισμα ενός αναπηρικού αμαξιδίου και το αναπηρικό αμαξίδιο είχε φτερά. Φτερά αγγέλου. Η Λία γύρισε τη σελίδα και ζωγράφισε μια δεύτερη εικόνα ενός αγοριού/αγγέλου μέσα από όλες τις γωνίες. Από όλες τις πλευρές. Μετά την πρώτη εικόνα, ζωγράφισε πολλές ακόμα μανιωδώς και μετά τις πέταξε στον αέρα.

Οι εικόνες, σαν να τις είχε πιάσει μια ριπή ανέμου - χόρευαν γύρα από το δωμάτιο, ανεβαίνοντας ψηλά και μετά, κάτω και μετά παντού. Σαν να ήταν κάτω από ένα μαγικό ξόρκι. Μια από τις εικόνες κυνήγησε τη νταντά, οπότε εκείνη έφυγε από το δωμάτιο ουρλιάζοντας.

Η Λία έκλεισε σφιχτά τις γροθιές της και μετά μουρμούρισε κάποιες ακατάληπτες λέξεις.

"Να καλέσω τον γιατρό;" ρώτησε η υστερική μητέρα της. "Το μωρό μου, ωχ όχι, το καημένο το μωρό μου!"

Επέστρεψε η Χάνα, τρέμοντας καθώς έβλεπε ότι η Λία είχε ξαναπέσει για ύπνο.

Οι δύο γυναίκες κάθισαν στο κρεβάτι του παιδιού. Την παρακολουθούσαν να κοιμάται ειρηνικά, μέχρι που τελικά παρασύρθηκαν και οι ίδιες στον ύπνο.

Η Λία δεν μπορούσε να δει με τα καστανά μάτια με τα οποία είχε γεννηθεί. Είχαν αντικατασταθεί από μάτια στις παλάμες των χεριών της.

Τα νέα μάτια που τοποθετήθηκαν στις παλάμες της περιλάμβαναν κάθε φυσιολογικό μέρος ενός ματιού. Όπως η κόρη, η ίριδα, ο σκληρός χιτώνας, ο κερατοειδής και ο δακρυϊκός πόρος. Κάθε μάτι της παλάμης είχε και ένα βλέφαρο. Η κορυφή του άρχιζε εκεί που τελείωναν τα δάχτυλα. Το κάτω μέρος τελείωνε εκεί που άρχιζε ο καρπός.

Όσον αφορά τις βλεφαρίδες, κάθε δάχτυλο είχε ένα τατουάζ πάνω του. Από την κορυφή του βλεφάρου μέχρι εκεί που άρχιζε το νύχι, όπως και ο αντίχειρας.

Κάτι που ήταν καλό, αφού κανένα νεαρό κορίτσι δεν θα ήθελε δάχτυλα με τρίχες να φυτρώνουν πάνω τους.

Ειδικά ένα κοριτσάκι σαν τη Λία που ήλπιζε να γίνει μια μέρα σπουδαία χορεύτρια μπαλέτου.

ΚΕΦΑΛΑΙΟ 2

ΌΤΑΝ ΞΎΠΝΗΣΕ, ΟΙ ΠΑΛΑΜΕΣ των χεριών της είχαν μεγάλη φαγούρα. Για την ακρίβεια, είχαν περισσότερη φαγούρα από ό,τι είχαν ποτέ άλλοτε. Αυτό της θύμισε κάτι που είχε πει κάποτε η γιαγιά της. Η γιαγιά έλεγε ότι όταν το δεξί σου χέρι είχε φαγούρα, σήμαινε ότι θα έπαιρνες χρήματα και μάλιστα πολλά. Αν το αριστερό σου χέρι είχε φαγούρα, σήμαινε ότι θα έχανες χρήματα. Ποτέ δεν είπε τι θα συνέβαινε αν και οι δύο παλάμες φαγούριζαν ταυτόχρονα.

Μια αναλαμπή του αγγέλου/αγόρι που ήταν παγιδευμένο στο δοχείο την επανέφερε στην πραγματικότητα. Άνοιξε τις παλάμες της, προετοιμαζόμενη να ξυνθεί. Αντ' αυτού, σοκαρίστηκε όταν είδε τον εαυτό της να αντανακλάται μέσα τους. Χαμογέλασε, σαν να πόζαρε για μια selfie.

Ακόμα δεν ήταν εκατό τοις εκατό σίγουρη αν ονειρευόταν, έστρεψε και τις δύο παλάμες μακριά της. Η πρόθεσή της ήταν να πάρει μια πανοραμική άποψη του δωματίου.

Ήταν διακοσμημένο σαν να κολυμπούσε μέσα σε ένα ενυδρείο. Ψάρια κλόουν και χρυσόψαρα ήταν απασχολημένα να κυνηγούν το ένα την ουρά του άλλου. Συνέχισε να κινεί τα χέρια της σε όλο το δωμάτιο μέχρι να βρει τη Χάνα. Μετά βρήκε τη μητέρα της. Τσίριξε από ευχαρίστηση.

Η μητέρα της Λία, η Σαμάνθα, πετάχτηκε πάνω, όπως και η Χάνα.

"Τι είναι μωρό μου;"

"Μαμά; Μπορώ να σε δω".

"Φυσικά και μπορείς, αγάπη μου".

"Με πιστεύεις;"

"Ναι, φυσικά και σε πιστεύω. Αλλά πες μου κάτι, πριν, γιατί ζωγράφισες μια αναπηρική καρέκλα με φτερά; Οι αναπηρικές καρέκλες δεν έχουν φτερά".

Δεν βλέπει τα καινούργια μου μάτια, σκέφτηκε η Λία. "Σ' αγαπώ, μαμά, αλλά κάποια αναπηρικά αμαξίδια έχουν φτερά και κάποιοι άγγελοι πετούν σε αναπηρικά αμαξίδια με φτερά".

"Κι εγώ σ' αγαπώ, μωρό μου", απάντησε εκείνη. "Ποιο αγόρι/άγγελος; Είδες όνειρο;"

"Υπάρχει ένα αγόρι-άγγελος", είπε η Λία.

"Ένα αγόρι/άγγελος; Πού μωρό μου;"

Η Λία άνοιξε τις παλάμες των χεριών της και σκέφτηκε το αγόρι/άγγελο. Σκέφτηκε τόσο πολύ, που μπορούσε να τον δει, να τον ακούσει, να νιώσει την παρουσία του στο μυαλό της. "Ο άγγελος/αγόρι έρχεται εδώ για να με δει", είπε.

"Εδώ αγάπη μου;" ρώτησε η μητέρα της, ρίχνοντας μια ματιά προς την κατεύθυνση της νταντάς που σήκωσε τους ώμους της.

"Ναι, το αγγελούδι χρειάζεται τη βοήθειά μου. Έρχεται να με δει από τη Βόρεια Αμερική".

"Όταν ζωγράφιζες τις εικόνες", ρώτησε η Χάνα, "ζωγράφιζες από μια ανάμνηση του αγγέλου/αγοριού;"

"Ή από ένα όνειρο;" ρώτησε η μητέρα της.

"Ξεκίνησε ως όνειρο, αλλά τώρα μπορώ να τον βλέπω και όταν είμαι ξύπνια".

"Αν μπορείς να με δεις μωρό μου, τι φοράω;"

"Μπορώ να σε δω μαμά, όχι με τα παλιά μου μάτια. Αλλά με τα καινούργια μου. Φοράς ένα κόκκινο φόρεμα, με μαργαριτάρια γύρω από το λαιμό σου".

Ένας ηλικιωμένος ασθενής που περνούσε από το δωμάτιό της, σταμάτησε στα πόδια του όταν είδε ένα παιδί, να κρατάει τις παλάμες του ανοιχτές μπροστά του. Είναι αυτή, σκέφτηκε, και για να το επιβεβαιώσει δεν χρειάστηκε να περιμένει πολύ. Γιατί η Λία, αισθανόμενη την παρουσία ενός άλλου ατόμου, έστρεψε την αριστερή της παλάμη προς την κατεύθυνση της πόρτας. Ο ηλικιωμένος είδε την παλάμη της να ανοιγοκλείνει τα μάτια της και μετά βγήκε από το οπτικό της πεδίο.

"Μαντεύει", πρότεινε η Χάνα, στρέφοντας την προσοχή της Λία μακριά από την πόρτα.

Μια νοσοκόμα έφτασε και η Λία, που δεν την είχε ξαναδεί, είπε: 'Γεια σας, νοσοκόμα Βίνκε".

"Έχουμε ξανασυναντηθεί;" ρώτησε η νοσοκόμα Χάιντι Βίνκε.

Η Λία χαχάνισε. "Όχι, αλλά μπορώ να διαβάσω την ετικέτα με τα ονόματά σας".

"Λέει ότι μπορεί να δει, με τα νέα της μάτια", είπε η μητέρα της Λία.

"Έλα, έλα", απάντησε η νοσοκόμα Vinke, φροντίζοντας τη μητέρα αντί για το κοριτσάκι. Το παιδί δεν ενοχλήθηκε όταν η νοσοκόμα Vinke πήρε τη μητέρα της έξω για να της μιλήσει ιδιαιτέρως.

"Είναι φυσιολογικό για την κόρη σας να χρησιμοποιεί τη φαντασία της υπό αυτές τις συνθήκες, έχει χάσει την όρασή της. Είναι ένα χαρούμενο πλασματάκι, παρόλο που της συνέβη κάτι τρομερό".

Η Σαμάνθα έγνεψε και οι δυο τους επέστρεψαν στη Λία.

"Πρέπει να είσαι κουρασμένη παιδί μου", είπε η νοσοκόμα Βίνκε, παίρνοντας τους σφυγμούς του μικρού κοριτσιού.

"Δεν είμαι", είπε η Λία. "Μόλις ξύπνησα και δεν θέλω να ξανακοιμηθώ. Αν κοιμηθώ τώρα, μπορεί να τον χάσω".

"Να χάσω ποιον;" Ρώτησε ο Βίνκε, βάζοντας το κοριτσάκι για ύπνο.

"Μα, το αγόρι/άγγελο", είπε η Λία. "Πλησιάζει όλο και πιο κοντά τώρα. Σχεδόν έφτασε - και χρειάζεται τη βοήθειά μου. Ανυπομονώ να τον συναντήσω. Ταξίδεψε πολύ, πολύ μακριά, μόνο και μόνο για να με δει".

"'Έλα, έλα, παιδί μου", γουργούρισε ο Βίνκε. Πίεσε μια βελόνα γεμάτη με φάρμακο που προκαλεί ύπνο στο χέρι της Λία.

Η Λία διαμαρτυρήθηκε, αλλά αμέσως μετά αποκοιμήθηκε.

"Καληνύχτα, καληνύχτα, μωρό μου", γουργούρισε η μητέρα της.

Ο ΗΛΙΚΙΩΜΈΝΟΣ ΕΠΈΣΤΡΕΨΕ ΣΤΟ δωμάτιό του και σήκωσε το τηλέφωνο. Στη συνέχεια ζήτησε μια εξωτερική γραμμή.

"Είναι εδώ", ψιθύρισε στο τηλέφωνο. "Την είδα με τα μάτια μου - εδώ στο νοσοκομείο, στο τέλος του διαδρόμου από το δωμάτιό μου".

Υπήρξε σιωπή και μετά ένα κλικ στην άλλη άκρη. Ο γέρος μπήκε στο κρεβάτι. Άνοιξε την τηλεόραση με το τηλεχειριστήριο.

Το αγαπημένο του πρόγραμμα: Now or Neverland (γνωστό και ως Fear Factor) είχε μόλις αρχίσει. Ήθελε να δει τι θα έκαναν αυτοί οι τρελοί ανόητοι στο επεισόδιο αυτής της εβδομάδας.

ΚΕΦΑΛΑΙΟ 3

ΚΟΜΑ ΣΤΡΙΜΩΓΜΕΝΟΣ ΜΕΣΑ ΣΤΗΝ ασημένια σφαίρα, ο E-Z δεν ένιωθε πια τόσο μόνος. Γιατί στο μυαλό του, μιλούσε με ένα μικρό κορίτσι.

Είχε έρθει στο μυαλό του συνοδευόμενη από μια λάμψη φωτός και μια κραυγή. Είχε τραυματιστεί. Παρακολουθούσε τον άγγελο Haniel να τη βοηθάει. Άκουσε όταν ο Haniel τραγουδούσε ένα τραγούδι στο κοριτσάκι ενώ εκείνη αφαιρούσε το γυαλί.

Αυτό που ακολούθησε ήταν απροσδόκητο. Ο άγγελος Haniel ζωγράφισε γραμμές στην παλάμη και τα δάχτυλα του μικρού κοριτσιού. Ο Haniel χάρισε στο παιδί ένα νέο είδος όρασης. Και τα μάτια της παλάμης.

Ήξερε αμέσως ότι η μοίρα του μικρού κοριτσιού ήταν συνδεδεμένη με τη δική του.

Στην αρχή, αν και μπορούσε να τη δει στο μυαλό του, δεν ήταν σε θέση να επικοινωνήσει μαζί της. Ήταν σαν να έβλεπε ένα τηλεοπτικό πρόγραμμα στο μυαλό του χωρίς ήχο. Στη συνέχεια, όταν το παιδί ονειρευόταν, ήρθε κοντά του και έβαλε τα χέρια της πάνω στη σφαίρα στην οποία ήταν παγιδευμένος. Τότε εκείνος ήξερε τι ήξερε εκείνη και εκείνη ήξερε τι ήξερε εκείνος και συνδέθηκαν.

Οι πρώτες λέξεις που του είχε πει ήταν: "Δεν μου αρέσει το σκοτάδι".

Ο E-Z είχε απαντήσει: "Μη φοβάσαι. Είμαι εδώ. Το όνομά μου είναι E-Z. Και πώς σε λένε;"

"Με λένε Σεσίλια", απάντησε το παιδί. "Αλλά οι φίλοι μου με φωνάζουν Λία. Μπορείς να με φωνάζεις Λία. Είμαι επτά ετών. Πόσε χρονών είσαι εσύ;"

Ο E-Z είχε πιστέψει ότι το παιδί ήταν μικρότερο. "Είμαι δεκατριών ετών", είπε. "Είμαι από τη Βόρεια Αμερική".

"Εγώ ζω στην Ολλανδία", είπε η Λία.

Και οι δύο σιώπησαν καθώς η Λία χρησιμοποίησε τα μάτια της παλάμης της για να τον κοιτάξει μέσα στην ατσάλινη σφαίρα.

"Τι κάνεις εκεί μέσα;" ρώτησε.

Ο E-Z σκέφτηκε πριν απαντήσει. Δεν ήθελε να τρομάξει το παιδί, με την αληθινή ιστορία στο ότι είχε απαχθεί ως δοκιμασία από έναν αρχάγγελο. Ήθελε να της πει την αλήθεια, αλλά δεν ήταν σίγουρος ότι θα μπορούσε να αντέξει την αλήθεια, αφού ήταν τόσο μικρή.

Είπε: "Δεν είμαι πραγματικά σίγουρος γιατί με έβαλαν εδώ μέσα, αλλά νομίζω ότι ήταν, ότι με έβαλαν εδώ μέσα για να σε γνωρίσω". Δίστασε, έξυσε το κεφάλι του και ρώτησε: "Γνωρίζεις την Έριελ;".

Η Λία κολακεύτηκε, που ήρθε να τη δει, αλλά ανησύχησε ότι μεταφέρθηκε με τέτοιο τρόπο προς όφελός της. "Λυπάμαι πολύ, αν αναγκάζεσαι παρά τη θέλησή σου να ταξιδέψεις από εδώ για να με συναντήσεις. Α, και όχι, αυτό το όνομα δεν μου είναι γνωστό".

Ο E-Z ήταν πολύ περίεργος για τη Λία. Από τη στιγμή που είπε ότι ήταν Ολλανδέζα, είχε εντυπωσιαστεί εξαιρετικά από το πόσο εξαιρετικά ήταν τα αγγλικά της.

"Σε ένιωσα, αλλά δεν μπορούσα να σε δω μέχρι που μεγάλωσαν τα μάτια, τα νέα μου μάτια. Πριν από αυτό, μπορούσα να διαβάσω τις σκέψεις σου. Μπορούσες να διαβάσεις τις δικές μου; Α, και σας ευχαριστώ, για τα αγγλικά μου".

"Είδα τι σου συνέβη, το ατύχημα. Λυπάμαι βαθύτατα που πληγώθηκες. Δεν μπόρεσα να σε βοηθήσω, εξαιτίας αυτού του πράγματος". Χτύπησε τις γροθιές του στους τοίχους. Κάλυψε τα αυτιά του, καθώς ο χτυπητός θόρυβος αντηχούσε. "Όταν ονειρεύτηκες, ήσουν μαζί μου. Μέσα στο κεφάλι μου".

Η Λία έκλεισε τη δεξιά της γροθιά, αφήνοντας την αριστερή ανοιχτή και ακουμπώντας τον εξωτερικό τοίχο. Η παλάμη της ανοιγόκλεινε τα μάτια της και μετά έκλεινε, άνοιγε και μετά έκλεινε. Δεν είπε τίποτα, αλλά κοίταξε μπροστά σαν κάποιος που βρισκόταν σε έκσταση.

Ο E-Z αποφάσισε εκείνη τη στιγμή να της πει την ιστορία του.

"Οι γονείς μου σκοτώθηκαν σε αυτοκινητιστικό δυστύχημα. Και έχασα τη χρήση των ποδιών μου".

Σταμάτησε εκεί. Αναρωτήθηκε πόσα έπρεπε να της πει.

Αυτός ο δισταγμός πήρε την απόφαση γι' αυτόν.

Εκείνη κοιμόταν βαθιά.

ΚΕΦΑΛΑΙΟ 4

Π ίσω στο νοσοκομείο, ένας νέος γιατρός είχε βάρδια. Κοίταξε για λίγο το διάγραμμα της Λίας. Βλέποντας ότι η Σεσίλια κοιμόταν ακόμα, ψιθύρισε στη μητέρα της.

"Πρέπει να κατεβάσουμε την κόρη σας στον δεύτερο όροφο, για άλλη μια εξέταση".

"Είναι επείγον;" ρώτησε η μητέρα της Λία. "Κοιμάται τόσο γαλήνια-θα ήταν κρίμα να την ξυπνήσουμε".

Ο γιατρός, του οποίου το καρτελάκι με τα ονόματα ήταν καλυμμένο από τον γιακά του ιατρικού μπουφάν του, χαμογέλασε. "Δεν χρειάζεται να την ξυπνήσετε. Μπορούμε να τη βάλουμε στο μηχάνημα όσο κοιμάται. Μερικοί ασθενείς, ιδίως οι νεότεροι, το προτιμούν έτσι".

Η Σαμάνθα κοίταξε το ρολόι της. "Βεβαίως, θα κατέβω μαζί της".

"Δεν χρειάζεται", είπε ο γιατρός. "Έχω βοηθούς που έρχονται σε λίγο. Εκμεταλλευτείτε τον χρόνο για να πάρετε ένα σάντουιτς ή ένα φλιτζάνι τσάι χαμομηλιού - η γυναίκα μου ορκίζεται σ' αυτό το πράγμα. Τη βοηθάει να χαλαρώσει και να κοιμηθεί".

"Σας ευχαριστώ", είπε η Σαμάνθα, καθώς έφτασαν δύο βοηθοί. Οι δύο εύσωμοι άντρες ντυμένοι με ρούχα του δρόμου σήκωσαν τη Λία από το κρεβάτι και την τοποθέτησαν πάνω σε ένα φορείο με ρόδες. Ο γιατρός τράβηξε μια κουβέρτα από κάτω από το φορείο και την έβαλε πάνω στη Λία. "Θα την κρατήσουμε ζεστή και θα επιστρέψουμε σε λίγο. Μην ξεχάσετε να εκμεταλλευτείτε αυτό το διάστημα για να κεράσετε τον εαυτό σας ένα τσάι ή έναν καφέ".

Όσο η Χάνα κοιμόταν, η Σαμάνθα παρακολουθούσε τους συνοδούς και τον γιατρό καθώς έσπρωχναν την κόρη της στον διάδρομο. Τώρα, στο ασανσέρ που περίμενε, παρακολουθούσε πιο προσεκτικά. Καθώς έκλεισαν οι πόρτες του ασανσέρ, περιπλανήθηκε στον διάδρομο αγνοώντας ένα συναίσθημα που την ενοχλούσε. Το απομάκρυνε, λέγοντας στον εαυτό της ότι πεινούσε και κατευθύνθηκε προς την καφετέρια. Ήταν πολύ απασχολημένη. Κυρίως με μέλη του προσωπικού που φορούσαν χειρουργικές ποδιές.

Καθώς ετοίμαζε και ρουφούσε το τσάι της, της πέρασε από το μυαλό ότι κανένα μέλος του προσωπικού δεν φορούσε ρούχα του δρόμου.

"Με συγχωρείτε", είπε σε έναν από τους γιατρούς. "Τι υπάρχει στον δεύτερο όροφο; Εκεί γίνονται οι ακτινογραφίες και οι σαρώσεις σώματος;"

Εκείνος κούνησε το κεφάλι του: "Ο δεύτερος όροφος είναι το μαιευτήριο".

Η Σαμάνθα σηκώθηκε από την καρέκλα της, ρίχνοντας το καυτό της τσάι και χύνοντάς το στα γόνατά της καθώς το έκανε. Βοηθοί ήρθαν από όλες τις κατευθύνσεις όταν φώναξε.

"Η κόρη μου!" φώναξε. "Ένας γιατρός με δύο βοηθούς μόλις πήραν την κόρη μου, τη Λία, πάνω σε ένα φορείο. Είπαν ότι την πηγαίνουν στον δεύτερο όροφο για κάποιες εξετάσεις. Αν ο δεύτερος όροφος είναι για το μαιευτήριο, γιατί την πήραν μακριά;

Το ξέσπασμά της τράβηξε πολύ μεγάλη προσοχή. Έτσι, ο γιατρός στον οποίο είχε απευθυνθεί αρχικά την έβγαλε έξω.

Επέστρεψαν στο δωμάτιο της Λίας. Η Σαμάνθα εξήγησε τα πάντα με περισσότερες λεπτομέρειες. Ευτυχώς που είχε κοιτάξει το ρολόι της για να τους πει την ακριβή ώρα που είχαν συμβεί όλα αυτά.

"Πρόκειται για σοβαρό ζήτημα", είπε ο γιατρός Μπράουν. "Αφήστε το σε μένα. Έχουμε κάμερες ασφαλείας σε όλο το νοσοκομείο. Ίσως ακούσατε λάθος για τον δεύτερο όροφο; Ίσως να βρίσκεται στον έβδομο όροφο και να κάνει σπινθηρογράφημα αυτή τη στιγμή που μιλάμε. Αφήστε το σε μένα. Καθίστε εδώ και θα επιστρέψω το συντομότερο δυνατό".

Η Σαμάνθα κάθισε και εξήγησε τα πάντα στη Χάνα. Μοιράστηκαν το σάντουιτς με τόνο και προσπάθησαν σκληρά να μην ανησυχούν.

ΕΝΏ Η ΛΊΑ ΚΟΙΜΌΤΑΝ, ο άνδρας που δεν ήταν πραγματικά γιατρός και οι ειδικευόμενοι που δεν ήταν ειδικευόμενοι έφυγαν από το κτίριο. Πήγαν σε ένα αυτοκίνητο που τους περίμενε. Άφησαν το φορείο στο πάρκινγκ.

Ο Δρ Μπράουν κάλεσε συνάντηση με τον Διοικητή. Χρησιμοποιώντας τη βιντεοεπιτήρηση, έγιναν μάρτυρες της απαγωγής της Λία. Ειδοποίησαν την αστυνομία, δίνοντας περιγραφή του οχήματος. Δυστυχώς, οι κάμερες δεν έλαβαν τα στοιχεία της πινακίδας.

"Ας περιμένουμε λίγο", είπε η Έλεν Μίτσελ, η Διοικήτρια του Νοσοκομείου. Σε λίγες μέρες θα έπαιρνε σύνταξη. "Πριν ενημερώσουμε τη μητέρα του μικρού κοριτσιού. Δεν θέλουμε να την ανησυχήσουμε".

"Δεν μπορώ να το κάνω αυτό", είπε ο γιατρός Μπράουν.

"Η αστυνομία μπορεί να φέρει το παιδί πίσω σε χρόνο μηδέν".

"Ελπίζω να έχετε δίκιο. Παρόλα αυτά, είναι μια ανησυχία. Ας ελπίσουμε ότι δεν θα φτάσουν μακριά".

Το τηλέφωνο χτύπησε, ήταν η αστυνομία. Έβγαλαν ανακοίνωση για το κοριτσάκι. Ζήτησαν μια πρόσφατη φωτογραφία της.

"Θέλουν μια πρόσφατη φωτογραφία", είπε η Helen Mitchell.

"Ο μόνος τρόπος για να πάρουμε μία είναι να ρωτήσουμε τη μητέρα της", είπε ο γιατρός Μπράουν.

Η Έλεν έγνεψε, καθώς ο Μπράουν γύρισε να φύγει.

"Πες τους ότι θα τους τη στείλουμε με φαξ το συντομότερο δυνατό".

"Θα στείλω κάποιον από την ομάδα τραύματος", είπε η Έλεν. Στη συνέχεια προς την αστυνομία στο τηλέφωνο: "Είναι τυφλή και μόλις επτά ετών. Γιατί στην ευχή αυτοί οι τρεις άντρες έκαναν τόσο περίτεχνα πράγματα για να την απομακρύνουν από το νοσοκομείο με αυτόν τον τρόπο;".

"Δεν μπορώ να πω", είπε ο αστυνομικός στην άλλη άκρη του τηλεφώνου

ΚΕΦΑΛΑΙΟ 5

Ο E-Z κατάλαβε αμέσως ότι κάτι δεν πήγαινε καλά με τη νέα του φίλη Lia. Έπρεπε να κοιμάται στο κρεβάτι του νοσοκομείου, αλλά το κρεβάτι της ήταν σε κίνηση. Τι στο...

Σκέφτηκε να την ξυπνήσει, αλλά τι θα μπορούσε να κάνει ακόμα κι αν το έκανε; Όχι, καλύτερα να κοιμόταν - μέχρι να μπορέσει να τη βρει και να τη σώσει. Όπως ήταν, ονειρευόταν τον εαυτό της να χορεύει μπαλέτο. Δεν είχε δώσει ποτέ πριν μεγάλη σημασία στο μπαλέτο, αλλά του φάνηκε ότι αυτό το κοριτσάκι είχε ταλέντο. Και χόρευε χρησιμοποιώντας τα μάτια στα χέρια της καθώς κινούνταν στη σκηνή.

Ο E-Z μετέφερε τον εαυτό του στο μυαλό του στη θέση της χωρίς ιδιαίτερη προσπάθεια. Εκεί βρισκόταν, κοιμισμένη στο πίσω κάθισμα ενός κινούμενου οχήματος. Έδειχνε τόσο γαλήνια, επειδή ήταν μακριά στο μυαλό της και έκανε κάτι που αγαπούσε - χόρευε.

Διεύρυνε το οπτικό του πεδίο και είδε τρία κεφάλια. Το ένα που οδηγούσε ήταν κανονικού μεγέθους και αναστήματος. Ενώ οι άλλοι δύο άνδρες έμοιαζαν με ποδοσφαιριστές.

"Επιτάχυνε!" Ο E-Z πρόσταξε την καρέκλα του, αλλά εκείνη το είχε ήδη κάνει.

Πώς θα τη βοηθούσε, όταν ήταν ακόμα παγιδευμένος μέσα στην ασημένια σφαίρα; Έπρεπε να τη διαλύσει σε κομμάτια - και μάλλον νωρίτερα παρά αργότερα. Μέχρι στιγμής, κάθε προσπάθεια να τη σπάσει δεν είχε αποδώσει.

Αναρωτήθηκε γιατί την είχαν πάρει οι άνδρες. Γνώριζαν για τις δυνάμεις της; Πώς θα μπορούσαν να γνωρίζουν; Τα περισσότερα νοσοκομεία είχαν κλειστό κύκλωμα παρακολούθησης, θα μπορούσαν να την παρακολουθούσαν; Δεν έβγαζε κανένα νόημα όμως. Ήταν ένα επτάχρονο τυφλό κορίτσι. Τι ήθελαν από αυτήν;

Καθώς ο E-Z έτρεχε με ταχύτητα στον ουρανό, δεν μπορούσε παρά να αναρωτηθεί γιατί την είχαν απαγάγει. Μήπως σκόπευαν να ζητήσουν λύτρα;

Εν πάση περιπτώσει, αν αυτό ήταν το ζητούμενο, του φαινόταν πιο λογικό. Καλύτερα από το να ξέρουν ότι την είδαν. Με ειδικές δυνάμεις. Παρόλα αυτά, η πρώτη του προτεραιότητα ήταν να ξεφύγει από τη σφαίρα.

Φώναξε. Όπως είχε κάνει πολλές φορές στο παρελθόν, "ΒΟΗΘΕΙΑ!"

"ΒΟΉΘΕΙΑ!

"Γεια σας", είτε ο Χαντζ, ενώ καθόταν στον ώμο του E-Z. "Τι στο καλό κάνεις εδώ μέσα; Αυτό το μέρος είναι πολύ μικρό για σένα". Η Χαντζ γούρλωσε τα μάτια της.

Η E-Z ήταν κάτι παραπάνω από λίγο ενθουσιασμένη που είδε τη Hadz. Άρπαξε το μικρό πλάσμα και την αγκάλιασε σφιχτά στο στήθος του.

"Ε, πρόσεχε τα φτερά", είπε η Χαντζ.

Ο E-Z άφησε το πλάσμα να φύγει. "Σας ευχαριστώ που ήρθατε και ανταποκριθήκατε στο κάλεσμά μου. Σε χρειάζομαι οπωσδήποτε να με βοηθήσεις να βρω πώς θα βγω από αυτό το πράγμα. Ξέρω ότι έχεις απομακρυνθεί από την υπόθεσή μου, αλλά υπάρχει ένα κοριτσάκι που το λένε Λία και κινδυνεύει και με χρειάζεται. Απλά πρέπει να βοηθήσεις. Είμαι σίγουρος ότι η Έριελ θα καταλάβει".

"Ω, άρα δεν θέλεις να συμμετέχεις σε αυτό το πράγμα τότε;" ρώτησε ο Χαντζ.

"Όχι, δεν θέλω να είμαι εδώ μέσα. Θέλω να βγω, αλλά πώς;"

"Απλώς κάνε το", είπε ο Χαντζ.

"Έχω δοκιμάσει τα πάντα. Οι πλευρές δεν μετακινούνται. Κάλεσα τον Έριελ να με βοηθήσει, αλλά μου είπε ότι είμαι μόνος μου σε αυτό".

"Α, δεν θα του άρεσε αυτό. Υποτίθεται ότι δεν πρέπει να βοηθήσω, αλλά ένα πράγμα που μπορώ να σου πω είναι: σκέψου το περιβάλλον σου".

"Αυτό δεν βοηθάει", είπε ο E-Z, προσπαθώντας να μη χάσει εντελώς την ψυχραιμία του. "Ζήτησα από την καρέκλα να με πάει στον θείο Σαμ. Αυτός θα με έβγαζε σίγουρα από αυτό το πράγμα. Αλλά η καρέκλα αγνόησε την επιθυμία μου. Τώρα, ένα κοριτσάκι έχει πρόβλημα και χρειάζεται τη βοήθειά μου. Αν δεν μπορώ να βγω, τότε δεν μπορώ να βοηθήσω τον εαυτό μου και αν δεν μπορώ να βοηθήσω τον εαυτό μου, τότε δεν μπορώ να βοηθήσω εκείνη. Σε παρακαλώ... Πες μου πώς να βγω από εδώ. Βγάλε με με το ζαπ ή κάτι τέτοιο".

Το πλάσμα κούνησε το κεφάλι της και μετά πέταξε προς την κορυφή της σφαίρας. Άγγιξε την άκρη της. "Σκέψου τη φυσική. Αν είσαι μέσα σε μια σφαίρα, με την οποία μοιάζει αυτό το πράγμα, τότε πρέπει να εκτονωθείς. Να πυροδοτηθείς. Σωστά;"

Ο E-Z εξέτασε τις επιλογές του. Θα μπορούσε να πει στην καρέκλα να τον ρίξει, εκτοξεύοντάς τον προς το έδαφος. Το έδαφος θα σταματούσε την πτώση του. Θα έσπαγε τη σφαίρα; Αποφάσισε ότι άξιζε το ρίσκο. "Εντάξει", είπε ο E-Z, "πρέπει να πω στην καρέκλα να με ρίξει, σωστά;".

Το πλάσμα γέλασε. "Είσαι αστείος, E-Z. Αν έπεφτες από αυτό το ύψος, αυτό το πράγμα θα ήταν ενσωματωμένο στο έδαφος. Αυτό υπό την προϋπόθεση ότι δεν θα εκραγεί κατά την πρόσκρουση. Και με εσένα μέσα σε αυτό". Γέλασε ξανά. "Ή αν δεν πέθαινες στην πτώση. Αν πέθαινες, δεν θα μπορούσες να σώσεις το κοριτσάκι. Ε, για ποιο κοριτσάκι μιλάς τέλος πάντων;"

"Τη λένε Σεσίλια, Λία, και είναι στην Ολλανδία, όχι μακριά από εκεί που είμαστε τώρα".

Ο Χαντζ ένιωσε την άκρη του δοχείου που ο E-Z δεν είχε δει, ούτε μπορούσε να φτάσει. Το πλάσμα το έσπρωξε. Ο κύλινδρος απελευθερώθηκε και άνοιξε σαν τουλίπα. Ο Χαντζ βοήθησε τον E-Z να βγει από τη σφαίρα και σύντομα καθόταν στην καρέκλα του, κρατώντας το πράγμα στα γόνατά του. Τα φτερά του E-Z άνοιξαν. Ένιωθε ωραία να τα τεντώνει.

Ο E-Z απογειώθηκε στον ουρανό, κουβαλώντας τον κύλινδρο, τον οποίο έριξε στη Βόρεια Θάλασσα.

Το τρίο, ο E-Z, η καρέκλα και ο Hadz πέταξαν με μεγάλη ταχύτητα και πέταξαν προς τη Βόρεια Ολλανδία, όπου το αυτοκίνητο έτρεχε με μεγάλη ταχύτητα.

"Ευχαριστώ", είπε ο E-Z.

"Παρακαλώ", απάντησε ο Hadz. "Θα μείνω εδώ σε περίπτωση που με χρειαστείτε".

"Φοβερό!"

ΚΕΦΑΛΑΙΟ 6

Ο Ε-Ζ ΠΛΗΣΙΑΖΕ ΤΟ αυτοκίνητο, το οποίο πλησίαζε στο Zaandam. Έλεγξε και η Λία κοιμόταν ακόμα στο πίσω κάθισμα. Δεν ονειρευόταν πια όμως, οπότε ανησυχούσε μήπως ξυπνήσει σύντομα.

Η αναπηρική του καρέκλα άλλαξε πορεία, επιτάχυνε και μηδένισε το αυτοκίνητο, έπειτα αιωρήθηκε πάνω από αυτό. Ο ψεύτικος γιατρός που οδηγούσε, εντόπισε την αναπηρική καρέκλα πίσω τους στον πλαϊνό καθρέφτη.

"Wat is dat vliegende contraptie?" ρώτησε. (Μετάφραση: "Ο παππούς μου είπε ότι είναι ένα παλιοσίδερο..: Τι είναι αυτό το ιπτάμενο μαραφέτι;"

Οι δύο κακοποιοί γύρισαν τα κεφάλια τους.

Ο ένας είπε: "Ik weet het niet, maar versnel het!" (Μετάφραση: "Δεν το βλέπω, αλλά το βλέπω!"): Δεν ξέρω, αλλά επιταχύνετέ το!"

Ο δεύτερος κακοποιός γέλασε και στη συνέχεια έβγαλε ένα όπλο από το ταμπλό. (Μεταφράζεται: ντουλαπάκι γαντιών.) Έλεγξε για σφαίρες. Το έκλεισε και έκλεισε την ασφάλεια.

Το αναπηρικό καροτσάκι του Ε-Ζ προσγειώθηκε στην οροφή του αυτοκινήτου με ένα κρότο.

Ο οδηγός φρέναρε δυνατά, με αποτέλεσμα η αναπηρική καρέκλα να γλιστρήσει προς τα εμπρός. Γλίστρησε στο παρμπρίζ με κατεύθυνση προς τα εμπρός και μετά στο καπό.

Ο Ε-Ζ σηκώθηκε, αιωρήθηκε και γύρισε προς το μέρος τους.

"Τι στο...;" φώναξε ο οδηγός, καθώς έχασε τον έλεγχο του αυτοκινήτου, με αποτέλεσμα αυτό να γλιστρήσει και να κάνει ζιγκ ζαγκ.

Ο E-Z και η αναπηρική καρέκλα απογειώθηκαν, έκαναν πίσω και πιάστηκαν από τον προφυλακτήρα του αυτοκινήτου, με αποτέλεσμα αυτό να σταματήσει εντελώς.

Αμέσως, ο συνοδηγός άνοιξε και ακούστηκαν πυροβολισμοί.

Στο πίσω κάθισμα η Λία ροχάλιζε.

Ο κακοποιός με το όπλο κύλησε έξω από την πόρτα και στη συνέχεια γονατιστός ετοιμάστηκε να ρίξει μια βολή στον E-Z.

Ο Χαντζ εμφανίστηκε από το πουθενά και έβγαλε το όπλο από τ χέρι του κακοποιού. Στη συνέχεια έδεσε τα χέρια του πίσω από την πλάτη του και τα πόδια του πίσω από την πλάτη του σαν να ήταν μοσχάρι σε ρουτέο.

Ο δεύτερος κακοποιός πήγε κατευθείαν στον E-Z, ο οποίος τον έπιασε με λάσο με τη ζώνη του. Ο κακοποιός έπεσε κάτω, ώστε να μπορέσει εύκολα να τυλίξει τη ζώνη γύρω από τα πόδια του.

Ο τύπος προσπάθησε να πηδήξει μακριά, αλλά δεν πήγε μακριά. Τώρα που τον σταμάτησαν, πήγαν για τον γιατρό χρησιμοποιώντας τον μηχανισμό εγκλωβισμού της καρέκλας. Ο γιατρός πιάστηκε και ακινητοποιήθηκε.

Η Λία κοιμήθηκε κατά τη διάρκεια όλων αυτών, ακόμη και όταν ο Χαντζ την έβγαλε από το όχημα και τη μετέφερε σε ασφαλές μέρος.

Ο E-Z τοποθέτησε τους τρεις άνδρες δίπλα-δίπλα στο πίσω κάθισμα του αυτοκινήτου.

"Για ποιον δουλεύετε;" απαίτησε.

Ο Χαντζ πέταξε πάνω του: "Δεν καταλαβαίνουν αγγλικά". Στους άνδρες μετέφρασε την ερώτηση του E-Z. Αφού απάντησε ο ψεύτικος γιατρός, η Hadz μετέφρασε. "Λέει ότι δεν ξέρουν για ποιον δουλεύουν".

"Αυτό είναι γελοίο. Απήγαγαν ένα παιδί από το νοσοκομείο. Ρώτησέ τους πού την πήγαιναν τότε; Και πώς έμαθαν γι' αυτήν;"

Ο Χαντζ μετέφρασε. Ο ψεύτικος γιατρός απάντησε και πάλι: "Μας είπαν να την πάμε στην αποβάθρα και κάποιος θα την περίμενε εκεί. Αυτό είναι το μόνο που ξέρουμε".

Ο E-Z δεν τους πίστεψε, αλλά ο Hadz επιβεβαίωσε ότι πράγματι έλεγαν την αλήθεια. "Τι θέλετε να τους κάνετε;" ρώτησε.

"Μπορείς να σβήσεις το μυαλό τους; Και τα μυαλά αυτών με τους οποίους συνδέονται, Αυτοί οι τρεις είναι γρανάζια στη μηχανή. Θέλουμε να σβήσουμε το μυαλό του ατόμου στις αποβάθρες. Έτσι, να την ξεχάσουν όλοι - για πάντα".

"Έγινε", είπε.

"Ουάου, είσαι γρήγορος!"

Ο E-Z και ο Χαντζ στην καρέκλα επέστρεψαν στο νοσοκομείο, μόλις η Λία άρχισε να ξυπνάει. Κούνησε το κεφάλι της, ένιωσε τον άνεμο να φυσάει τα μαλλιά της και αγκαλιάστηκε στο στήθος του E-Z. Άνοιξε τη δεξιά της παλάμη και κοίταξε τον φίλο της, το αγόρι/άγγελο. Γέλασε και τον αγκάλιασε σφιχτά. Όταν παρατήρησε το μικρό πλάσμα που έμοιαζε με νεράιδα στον ώμο του E-Z, χρησιμοποίησε τα μάτια της παλάμης της για να την κοιτάξει.

"Είσαι τόσο μικρή και χαριτωμένη", είπε.

"Χαίρομαι που σε γνωρίζω", είπε ο Χαντζ. "Και σ' ευχαριστώ".

Πέταξαν προς το νοσοκομείο.

"Είσαι ασφαλής τώρα", είπε ο E-Z.

"Και δεν είσαι πια μέσα σε αυτό το πράγμα", είπε η Λία.

"Ο Χαντζ με βοήθησε να βγω", είπε ο E-Z χτυπώντας τα φτερά του.

"Πού τα βρήκες αυτά;" Ρώτησε η Λία. "Μπορώ να πάρω μερικά;"

Ο E-Z χαμογέλασε. Δεν ήταν σίγουρος πόσα έπρεπε να της πει. Ανησυχούσε τι θα έλεγε η Έριελ αν αποκάλυπτε πολλά. "Τα πήρα αφού πέθαναν οι γονείς μου".

"Μα γιατί;" ρώτησε η μικρή Λία.

"Άρχισα να σώζω ανθρώπους", είπε ο Ε-Ζ.

"Εννοείς ότι δεν είμαι ο πρώτος άνθρωπος που σώζεις;"

"Όχι, δεν είσαι".

Η Χαντζ καθάρισε το λαιμό της, πράγμα που ήταν ένα σήμα για τον Ε-Ζ να σταματήσει να μιλάει.

Πέταξαν σιωπηλά. Το κοριτσάκι αγκάλιαζε το στήθος του Ε-Ζ. Η αναπηρική καρέκλα ήξερε πού έπρεπε να πάει. Η Hadz ένιωθε ότι την χρειαζόταν για άλλη μια φορά.

Ο Ε-Ζ είχε χαθεί στις σκέψεις του. Αναρωτήθηκε αν η διάσωση της Λία ήταν η κύρια δοκιμασία. Ή αν το να βγει από τη σφαίρα είχε ολοκληρώσει το έργο. Ίσως ήταν δύο για ένα! Πόσοι θα ήταν τότε; Έπρεπε να τις γράψει για να τις παρακολουθεί. Αυτό έκανε στο ημερολόγιό του, αλλά τελευταία δεν είχε πολύ χρόνο για να καταγράφει τα πράγματα.

"Σε ακούω να σκέφτεσαι", είπε η Λία. Είχε και τις δύο παλάμες της ανοιχτές. Παρακολουθούσε τον Ε-Ζ εξωτερικά, ενώ άκουγε τι σκεφτόταν μέσα του. "Θέλω να μάθω περισσότερα για αυτές τις δοκιμές. Και θέλω να μάθω γιατί μπορώ να βλέπω με τα χέρια μου αντί για τα μάτια μου. Πιστεύεις ότι αυτός ο Έριελ θα ξέρει;"

POP

Ο Χαντζ δεν περίμενε την απάντηση.

"Το νοσοκομείο είναι από κάτω", είπε ο Ε-Ζ.

Η καρέκλα κατέβηκε αργά, και μπήκαν μέσα στο νοσοκομείο. Ο Ε-Ζ και τα φτερά της καρέκλας εξαφανίστηκαν. Σπρώχτηκε κατά μήκος του διαδρόμου και βρήκε το δωμάτιο της Λίας. Η μητέρα της περίμενε εκεί.

"Συλλάβετε αυτό το αγόρι", φώναξε η μητέρα της Λίας.

Ο Ε-Ζ έμεινε άναυδος. Γιατί ήθελε να τον συλλάβουν; Μόλις είχε σώσει την κόρη της.

"Μα μαμά", άρχισε η Λία.

Η αστυνομία μπήκε μέσα. Έφτασαν πίσω από τον E-Z και του πέρασαν χειροπέδες στα χέρια.

Πριν τις κλείσουν, η Λία ούρλιαξε. Έπειτα άνοιξε τις παλάμες των χεριών της και τις άπλωσε μπροστά της. Από τα μάτια της παλάμης της βγήκε ένα εκτυφλωτικό λευκό φως κάνοντας όλους στο δωμάτιο εκτός από εκείνη και τον E-Z να σταματήσουν εγκαίρως. Η μικρή Λία σταμάτησε το χρόνο.

"Ωραία! Πώς το έκανες αυτό;" αναφώνησε ο E-Z καθώς οι χειροπέδες έπεσαν στο πάτωμα με ένα κρότο.

"Εγώ, δεν ξέρω. Ήθελα να σε προστατέψω. Να σε σώσω". Σταμάτησε, άκουσε. "Κάποιος έρχεται, πρέπει να φύγεις από εδώ. Αισθάνομαι ότι κάποιος άλλος έρχεται και εσύ πρέπει να φύγεις".

"Κάποιος;" ρώτησε ο E-Z. "Ξέρεις ποιος;"

"Δεν ξέρω. Το μόνο που ξέρω είναι ότι κάποιος άλλος έρχεται και πρέπει να φύγεις - αμέσως".

"Θα είσαι, εντάξει; Θα σου κάνουν κακό;"

"Θα είμαι μια χαρά - έρχονται για σένα - όχι για μένα. Φύγε από εδώ, τώρα".

"Πότε θα σε ξαναδώ;" ρώτησε ο E-Z, καθώς έσπασε το παράθυρο του νοσοκομείου και πέταξε έξω περιμένοντας την απάντησή της.

"Θα με βλέπεις πάντα, E-Z. Είμαστε αλληλένδετοι. Είμαστε φίλοι. Φύγε εσύ από εδώ και θα φροντίσω εγώ για τα υπόλοιπα". Του έστειλε ένα φιλί.

Η Λία μπήκε στο κρεβάτι, τράβηξε τα σκεπάσματα μέχρι το λαιμό της και προσποιήθηκε ότι κοιμόταν βαθιά πριν βάλει τον κόσμο να κινηθεί για άλλη μια φορά.

"Τι συνέβη;" ρώτησε η μητέρα της.

Όλα ήταν και πάλι καλά. Η Λία ήταν στο κρεβάτι της σώα και αβλαβής.

Ο κόσμος συνέχισε να κινείται όπως πριν, ενώ ο E-Z έπαιρνε και πάλι το δρόμο για το σπίτι.

"Ευχαριστώ, Χατζ για τη βοήθεια", είπε ο E-Z παρόλο που είχε φύγει. Κατά κάποιο τρόπο, ήξερε ότι όπου κι αν βρισκόταν, μπορούσε να τον ακούσει.

ΚΕΦΑΛΑΙΟ 7

Κ αθώς ο E-Z πετούσε στον ουρανό, συνειδητοποίησε ότι πεινούσε. Από κάτω του ήταν το Big Ben. Αποφάσισε να προσγειωθεί και να πάρει μερικά αγγλικά ψάρια με πατάτες.

Καθώς η καρέκλα κατέβαινε, παρατήρησε ένα λευκό φορτηγάκι να κινείται γρήγορα στο δρόμο. Ήταν παράλληλα με ένα σχολείο. Είδε γονείς σε οχήματα και πεζούς να περιμένουν να παραλάβουν τα παιδιά τους.

Καθώς το φορτηγάκι έστριβε στη γωνία, ανέπτυξε ταχύτητα.

Η αναπηρική του καρέκλα έπεσε μπροστά, πέφτοντας πίσω από το όχημα. Η οδήγηση γινόταν όλο και πιο απερίσκεπτη, καθώς πλησίαζε στο σχολείο. Τα παιδιά άρχισαν να βγαίνουν έξω.

Ο E-Z άρπαξε το πίσω μέρος του φορτηγού. Χρησιμοποιώντας όλη του τη δύναμη, το τράβηξε μέχρι να σταματήσει με ένα τρίξιμο.

Ο οδηγός πάτησε το γκάζι, προσπαθώντας να απομακρυνθεί. Δεν είχε καμία τύχη. Δεν μπορούσαν να δουν τι ή ποιος τους κρατούσε πίσω.

Ο E-Z έσπασε την κλειδαριά του πορτμπαγκάζ, έφτασε μέσα και έβγαλε τα καλώδια βραχυκύκλωσης. Η καρέκλα γκρεμίστηκε προς τα εμπρός και προσγειώθηκε στην οροφή του οχήματος. Ο E-Z χρησιμοποίησε τα καλώδια για να δέσει τις πόρτες της καμπίνας. Ο οδηγός δεν μπορούσε να βγει.

Οι ήχοι των σειρήνων γέμισαν τον αέρα.

Ο E-Z πήρε φόρα και παρατηρώντας ότι αρκετοί άνθρωποι τον φωτογράφιζαν με τα τηλέφωνά τους πέταξε όλο και πιο ψηλά.

Το στομάχι του γκρίνιαξε και θυμήθηκε τα ψάρια με πατάτες. Επειδή δεν είχε βρετανικό νόμισμα, δεν μπορούσε να τα πληρώσει ούτως ή άλλως, οπότε πήρε το δρόμο για το σπίτι του.

Σκεπτόμενος τον θείο του που αναρωτιόταν πού βρισκόταν, σκέφτηκε να αφήσει ένα μήνυμα και άρχισε να το κάνει: "Είμαι στο δρόμο για το σπίτι".

Κλικ.

"Πού είσαι;" ρώτησε c θείος Σαμ.

Ο E-Z χάρηκε που δεν ήταν μήνυμα!

"Πετάω πάνω από τη Βρετανία. Είναι μια ευχάριστη μέρα για πτήσεις, δεν νομίζεις;"

"Τι; Πώς;"

"Είναι μεγάλη ιστορία, θα σου εξηγήσω όταν επιστρέψω".

"Είσαι σε αεροπλάνο;"

"Όχι, είμαι μόνο εγώ και η καρέκλα μου."

Από κάτω, ο E-Z έβλεπε ανθρώπους να τον φωτογραφίζουν. Όταν είδε ένα 747 του τοπικού αερςμεταφορέα να έρχεται προς το μέρος του, κατάλαβε ότι είχε μπλέξει. Πριν προλάβει να πετάξει ψηλότερα, οι κάμερες έβγαζαν φωτογραφίες και τις ανέβαζαν σε όλα τα μέσα κοινωνικής δικτύωσης.

"Συγγνώμη Eriel", είπε, παίρνοντας τον εαυτό του ψηλότερα. "Ξέρετε το ρητό κάθε δημοσιότητα είναι καλή δημοσιότητα; Λοιπόν..." Ο E-Z γέλασε. Αν ο Eriel μπορούσε να τον βλέπει κάθε μέρα και κάθε ώρα, τότε γιατί έτρεπε να τον καλέσει για βοήθεια; Κάτι δεν κολλούσε καλά. Όχι εγώ οι αρχάγγελοι ήθελαν να ολοκληρώσει τις δοκιμασίες.

Μια ανατριχίλα τον διαπέρασε καθώς ο ουρανός άλλαξε, καθώς μαύρα σύννεφα στροβιλίζονταν και πάλλονταν γύρω του. Πετούσε, προσπαθώντας να επιταχύνει το ρυθμό του, αλλά τότε άρχισαν οι αστραπές και έπρεπε να τις αποφύγει. Τότε θυμήθηκε το αεροπλάνο. Μπορούσε να δει ότι έκανε επιτυχή προσγείωση και ότι οι άνθρωποι ήταν σώοι και αβλαβείς. Συνέχισε προς το σπίτι του.

Μετά την καταιγίδα βγήκαν τα αστέρια. Η καρέκλα του χτυπούσε συνεχώς τα φτερά της, ενώ ο E-Z έπαιρνε έναν υπνάκο.

"E-Z;" είπε η Λία μέσα στο κεφάλι του. "Είσαι εκεί;"

Ξύπνησε απότομα, ξέχασε ότι ήταν στην καρέκλα και έπεσε έξω. Άρχισε να πέφτει, αλλά τα φτερά του κλώτσησαν και σύντομα ξαναβρέθηκε στην καρέκλα.

"Είναι όλα καλά, μικρούλα;" ρώτησε.

"Ναι. Νομίζουν ότι ήταν όλα ένα όνειρο, που σου μίλησα. Ζωγράφιζα εικόνες σου. Η μαμά ξέρει την αλήθεια, αλλά δεν θέλει να την αντιμετωπίσει".

"Ω, αυτό σε ανησυχεί;"

"Όχι. Οι δυνάμεις μου αυξάνονται. Τις αισθάνομαι και ξέρω ότι κάτι έρχεται. Κάτι στο οποίο θα χρειαστείς τη βοήθειά μου. Σύντομα θα πάω στο σπίτι μου. Θα ρωτήσω τη μαμά αν μπορούμε να σε επισκεφτούμε. Σύντομα".

"Τι; Η μαμά σου θα πρέπει να τηλεφωνήσει στον θείο μου τον Σαμ και να κουβεντιάσουν;"

"Ναι, αυτή είναι μια έξυπνη ιδέα. Η μαμά έχει δει τις φωτογραφίες και σε έχει γνωρίσει, αλλά δεν θυμάται. Είναι σαν να έχει καθαρίσει το μυαλό της ή σαν οι αναμνήσεις της για σένα να κοιμούνται".

"Είσαι σίγουρος ότι αυτό είναι το σωστό πράγμα που πρέπει να κάνουμε;"

"Είμαι σίγουρη. Πρέπει να είμαι εκεί που είσαι εσύ. Πρέπει να σε βοηθήσω".

Το μυαλό του E-Z έμεινε κενό. Η Λία είχε φύγει.

Ο έφηβος σκέφτηκε τη Λία να έρχεται στη Βόρεια Αμερική. Ήταν ένα μικρό κορίτσι, που έβλεπε με τα χέρια της, ναι, αλλά πώς θα μπορούσε να τον βοηθήσει; Τον είχε βοηθήσει να δραπετεύσει, αλλά εκείνος είχε μπερδευτεί με την εμπλοκή της. Δεν ήθελε να την θέσει σε κίνδυνο. Φώναξε ξανά την Έριελ. Επικαλέστηκε την ψαλμωδία, αλλά δεν συνέβη τίποτα.

Απολάμβανε το τοπίο, αποσπώντας το μυαλό του από το κοριτσάκι για μια στιγμή. Ήταν σχεδόν στο σπίτι του τώρα. Δόξα τω Θεώ, η καρέκλα του ήταν τροποποιημένη και μπορούσε να ταξιδέψει Φ-Α-Σ-Τ!

ΚΕΦΑΛΑΙΟ 8

Α κριβώς μπροστά, ο E-Z εντόπισε την ακτή. Αναστέναξε με ανακούφιση μέχρι που πρόσεξε ένα μεγάλο πουλί να κατευθύνεται κατευθείαν προς το μέρος του. Καθώς πλησίαζε, συνειδητοποίησε ότι ήταν κύκνος. Αλλά όχι ένας κύκνος κανονικού μεγέθους. Ήταν τεράστιος και το ίδιο και το άνοιγμα των φτερών του, το οποίο υπολόγισε για πάνω από εκατόν πενήντα ίντσες. Ήταν ο ίδιος κύκνος που του είχε μιλήσει πριν. Και όχι μόνο αυτό, αλλά παρατήρησε επίσης ένα έντονο κόκκινο φως να τρεμοπαίζει στον ώμο του πουλιού.

Ο κύκνος έστριψε και στη συνέχεια προσγειώθηκε βαριά στους ώμους του. Είχε κάνει ωτοστόπ.

"Λοιπόν, γεια σου", είπε ο E-Z, ρίχνοντας μια ματιά στο όμορφο πλάσμα καθώς σταθεροποιούνταν.

"Χου-χου", είπε ο κύκνος. Μετά κούνησε το κεφάλι του, άνοιξε το ράμφος του και είπε: "Γεια σου E-Z".

"Νομίζω ότι σου χρωστάω τις ευχαριστίες μου", είπε εκείνος.

"Ω, είσαι πολύ ευπρόσδεκτος. Και ελπίζω να μη σε πειράζει που έκανα οτοστόπ", είπε ο κύκνος, ανασηκώνοντας τα φτερά του.

"Κανένα πρόβλημα", απάντησε ο E-Z.

"Αυτός είναι ο μέντοράς μου ο Άριελ", είπε ο κύκνος.

WHOOPEE

Ένας άγγελος αντικατέστησε το κόκκινο φως.

"Γεια σου", είπε, καθισμένος στο γόνατο του E-Z.

"Χάρηκα για τη γνωριμία", είπε εκείνος.

"Πώς μπορώ να σας εξυπηρετήσω;" ρώτησε.

"Ελπίζω ότι εσύ και ο φίλος μου ο κύκνος από εδώ θα μπορέσετε να σχηματίσετε μια συνεργασία".

"Πώς;" ρώτησε.

"Ο προστατευόμενός μου έχει περάσει πολλά. Μπορεί να σας ενημερώσει για τις λεπτομέρειες όταν νιώσει έτοιμος, αλλά προς το παρόν θέλω να τον βοηθήσετε επιτρέποντάς του να σας βοηθήσει με τις δοκιμασίες. Μπορείς να χρησιμοποιήσεις λίγη βοήθεια, ναι;"

"Απ' ό,τι καταλαβαίνω", είπε απευθυνόμενος στην Άριελ. Στη συνέχεια, προς τον κύκνο, "τίποτα εναντίον σου, φίλε". Τώρα προς την Άριελ, "είναι ότι κανείς δεν μπορεί να με βοηθήσει στις δοκιμασίες μου. Αυτό ήρθε απευθείας από την Έριελ και τον Οφάνιελ".

"Το ξεκαθάρισα μαζί τους. Οπότε, αν αυτή είναι η μόνη σου αντίρρηση", έκανε μια παύση και μετά...

WHOOPEE

και εξαφανίστηκε.

Μετά από αυτό ο E-Z και ο κύκνος συνέχισαν να διασχίζουν τον Ατλαντικό Ωκεανό και να πηγαίνουν στη Βόρεια Αμερική. Καθώς πάντα ήθελε να δει το Γκραντ Κάνυον. Θα έπρεπε να το δει κάποια άλλη στιγμή. Ο κύκνος ροχάλιζε και αγκαλιαζόταν στο λαιμό του E-Z.

Ο E-Z έβαλε το χέρι στην τσέπη του και έβγαλε το τηλέφωνό του. Τράβηξε μια selfie με τον κύκνο. Κράτησε το τηλέφωνό του στο χέρι του, σχεδιάζοντας να καταγράψει τον κύκνο την επόμενη φορά που θα μιλούσε. Χρειαζόταν απόδειξη ότι δεν είχε χάσει το μυαλό του.

Κάποια στιγμή αργότερα, ο E-Z μηδένισε το σπίτι του. Ήταν μέρα σχολείου, αλλά ήταν πολύ κουρασμένος για να πάει. Όταν η καρέκλα άρχισε να κατεβαίνει, ο κύκνος ξύπνησε. "Φτάσαμε;"

"Ναι, είμαστε στο σπίτι μου", είπε ο Ε-Ζ, πατώντας το κουμπί εγγραφής στο τηλέφωνό του. "Θέλεις να σε αφήσω κάπου;"

"Όχι, ευχαριστώ. Θα μείνω μαζί σου", είπε ο κύκνος, καθώς μάκρυνε το λαιμό του για να ρίξει μια ματιά στο σπίτι που θα έμενε. "Εσύ κι εγώ, πρέπει να μιλήσουμε".

Ο Ε-Ζ πάτησε το play, αλλά ήταν νεκρός αέρας. Ο κύκνος δεν μπορούσε να ηχογραφηθεί. Παράξενο.

Προσγειώθηκαν στην μπροστινή πόρτα. Ο Ε-Ζ έβαλε το κλειδί του στην κλειδαριά, αλλά πριν προλάβει να την ανοίξει, ο θείος Σαμ ήταν εκεί. Αγκάλιασε τον ανιψιό του και είπε: "Καλώς ήρθες σπίτι". Έξυνε το πηγούνι του και κοίταξε λίγο ανήσυχος όταν είδε τον σύντροφο του Ε-Ζ, έναν εξαιρετικά μεγάλο κύκνο.

"Χαίρομαι που επέστρεψα", είπε ο Ε-Ζ και μπήκε μέσα.

Ο κύκνος τον ακολούθησε με τα πόδια του με τις γάζες να τον ακολουθούν.

"Και ποιος είναι ο φτερωτός σου φίλος;" ρώτησε ο θείος Σαμ.

Ο Ε-Ζ συνειδητοποίησε ότι δεν ήξερε καν το όνομα του κύκνου.

Ο κύκνος είπε: "Άλφρεντ, το όνομά μου είναι Άλφρεντ".

Ο Ε-Ζ έκανε μια επίσημη εισαγωγή.

Στη συνέχεια ο κύκνος περπάτησε στο διάδρομο, στο δωμάτιο του Ε-Ζ και πέταξε πάνω στο κρεβάτι του για να πάρει έναν καλοπληρωμένο υπνάκο.

Ο Ε-Ζ μπήκε στην κουζίνα με τον θείο Σαμ στις ρόδες του.

"Τι στο καλό κάνει αυτός ο κύκνος εδώ;" Έκανε μια παύση, πήρε λίγο γάλα από το ψυγείο. Έριξε στον ανιψιό του ένα ποτήρι γεμάτο. "Δεν μπορεί να μείνει εδώ. Θα πρέπει να τον βάλουμε στην μπανιέρα. Αυτό αν χωράει. Είναι ο μεγαλύτερος κύκνος που έχω δει ποτέ. Πού το βρήκες και γιατί το έφερες εδώ;"

Ο Ε-Ζ καταβρόχθισε το γάλα του. Σκούπισε το μουστάκι του από το γάλα. "Δεν το βρήκα εγώ, αυτό με βρήκε. Και μπορεί να μιλήσει.

Αυτό, αυτός, ήταν εκεί όταν έσωσα εκείνο το κοριτσάκι και όταν έσωσα το αεροπλάνο. Λέει ότι πρέπει να μιλήσουμε".

Ο θείος Σαμ, χωρίς να απαντήσει, περπάτησε στο διάδρομο. C E-Z ακολούθησε από κοντά χωρίς να μιλήσει.

"Μίλα!" απαίτησε ο θείος Σαμ.

Ο Άλφρεντ ο κύκνος άνοιξε τα μάτια του, χασμουρήθηκε και μετα ξανακοιμήθηκε χωρίς να βγάλει ούτε έναν ήχο.

"Είπα, μίλα", είπε ο θείος Σαμ, προσπαθώντας ξανά.

Ο Άλφρεντ ο κύκνος άνοιξε το ράμφος του και ροχάλισε.

"Δεν πειράζει, Άλφρεντ", είπε ο E-Z. "Είναι ο θείος Σαμ μου".

"Δεν μπορεί να με καταλάβει. Και δεν νομίζω ότι θα μπορέσει ποτέ να με καταλάβει. Είμαι εδώ για σένα και μόνο για σένα", είπε ο Άλφρεντ ο κύκνος. Ροχάλισε, έπειτα χουχούλιασε στο πάπλωμα και αποκοιμήθηκε για άλλη μια φορά.

Ο θείος Σαμ κοιτοίσε, ενώ ο κύκνος είχε ζωηρέψει και κοιτούσε επίμονα τον E-Z.

Αυτός και ο θείος Σαμ έκλεισαν την πόρτα φεύγοντας και γύρισαν στην κουζίνα για να μιλήσουν.

Ο E-Z ήταν τόσο κουρασμένος, που με δυσκολία κρατούσε τα μάτια του ανοιχτά.

"Δεν μπορεί αυτό να περιμένει μέχρι το πρωί;", ρώτησε.

Ο Σαμ κούνησε το κεφάλι του.

"Εντάξει, ξεκινάμε. Πρώτον, χτύπησα μια μπάλα του μπέιζμπολ έξω από το πάρκο. Και μετά έτρεξα ή έκανα τροχήλατο γύρο από τις βάσεις. Έπειτα παγιδεύτηκα μέσα σε ένα δοχείο σε σχήμα σφαίρας χωρίς διέξοδο. Μετά μπόρεσα να μιλήσω με ένα κοριτσάκι στην Ολλανδία. Πήγα εκεί για να τη σώσω. Το όνομά της είναι Λία και η μητέρα της θα σας τηλεφωνήσει. Σταμάτησα ένα όχημα από το να βλάψει παιδιά, στο Λονδίνο της Αγγλίας.

Τότε συνάντησα τον Άλφρεντ, τον κύκνο τρομπετίστα. Και τώρα που είσαι ενημερωμένος - μπορώ να πάω για ύπνο;".

"Τι υποτίθεται ότι πρέπει να πω όταν τηλεφωνήσει;" ρώτησε ο Σαμ. "Δεν τους ξέρουμε καν αυτούς τους ανθρώπους, αλλά υποτίθεται ότι πρέπει να τους αφήσουμε να μείνουν εδώ στο σπίτι μαζί μας. Εμείς και ο Άλφρεντ ο κύκνος;"

"Ναι, σε παρακαλώ να συμφωνήσεις. Υπάρχει ένα σχέδιο σε εξέλιξη εδώ και δεν ξέρω ακόμα όλες τις λεπτομέρειες. Η Λία έχει δυνάμεις, μάτια στις παλάμες των χεριών της και μπορεί να διαβάζει τις σκέψεις μου και να σταματάει τον χρόνο. Ο Άλφρεντ ο κύκνος έχει επίσης δυνάμεις, μπορεί να διαβάσει τη σκέψη μου και μπορεί να μιλήσει. Νομίζω ότι οι τρεις μας συνδεόμαστε με κάποιο τρόπο, ίσως λόγω των δοκιμασιών. Δεν ξέρω. Οτιδήποτε μπορεί να συμβεί με την Eriel να με κατασκοπεύει 24-7", είπε ο E-Z.

Προσερχόμενοι στον διάδρομο, άκουσαν το χτύπημα των ποδιών του κύκνου καθώς περπατούσε. "Πεινάω πολύ για να κοιμηθώ", είπε ο Άλφρεντ ο κύκνος.

"Τι είδους πράγματα τρως;"

"Το καλαμπόκι είναι καλό, ή μπορείτε να με αφήσετε να βγω πίσω και να βρω λίγο χορτάρι".

"Έχουμε καθόλου καλαμπόκι;" ρώτησε ο E-Z.

"Μόνο κατεψυγμένα", είπε ο θείος Σαμ. "Αλλά μπορώ να βάλω τους σπόρους κάτω από ζεστό νερό και θα είναι έτοιμοι στο λεπτό".

"Πες του ευχαριστώ", είπε ο Άλφρεντ ο κύκνος. "Πολύ ευγενικό εκ μέρους του."

Ο θείος Σαμ έβαλε το καλαμπόκι σε ένα πιάτο και ο Άλφρεντ έφαγε ό,τι του προσφέρθηκε. Πεινούσε όμως ακόμα και έπρεπε να πάει να αδειάσει την ουροδόχο κύστη του, γι' αυτό ζήτησε να βγει τελικά έξω. Όσο ήταν έξω, θα έπαιρνε μέρος στο γκαζόν.

Ο E-Z και ο θείος Σαμ παρακολούθησαν τον κύκνο για λίγα δευτερόλεπτα.

"Ελπίζω το τσιουάουα του γείτονα να μην πεταχτεί για επίσκεψη", είπε ο θείος Σαμ. "Αυτός ο κύκνος είναι τόσο μεγάλος που θα τον τρομάξει μέχρι θανάτου".

Ο E-Z γέλασε. "Φαντχστείτε τι θα έκανε, αν ο σκύλος μπορούσε νc τον καταλάβει όπως εγώ;"

Ο Άλφρεντ ο κύκνος βολεύτηκε σαν στο σπίτι του. Ήταν σίγουρος ότι θα ήταν ευτυχισμένος εδώ

ΚΕΦΑΛΑΙΟ 9

Α ΡΓΟΤΕΡΑ, ο Άλφρεντ ο κύκνος ζήτησε να μιλήσει ιδιαιτέρως με τον E-Z.

"Μπορείς να πεις ό,τι θέλεις εδώ", είπε ο E-Z. "Ο θείος Σαμ δεν σε καταλαβαίνει, θυμάσαι;"

"Ναι, το ξέρω. Αλλά είναι θέμα τρόπου συμπεριφοράς. Δεν μιλάει κανείς σε κάποιον όταν είναι παρών κάποιος άλλος, ειδικά όταν είναι φιλοξενούμενος στο σπίτι κάποιου άλλου. Θα ήταν, λοιπόν, μάλλον αγένεια. Στην πραγματικότητα, πολύ αγενές".

Ο E-Z μόλις τώρα συνειδητοποίησε ότι ο Άλφρεντ ο κύκνος μιλούσε με βρετανική προφορά.

"Θα μπορούσα να συγχωρεθώ;" ρώτησε ο E-Z.

Ο θείος Σαμ έγνεψε και ο E-Z πήγε στο δωμάτιό του με τον Άλφρεντ τον κύκνο να τον ακολουθεί.

"Εντάξει", είπε ο E-Z. "Πες μου γιατί σε έστειλε εδώ ο Άριελ και τι ακριβώς σκοπεύεις να κάνεις για να με βοηθήσεις;"

Τώρα που ο E-Z βρισκόταν στο κρεβάτι του, ο κύκνος έκανε κύκνους καθώς ζύμωνε το πάπλωμα, προσπαθώντας να βολευτεί.

"Μπορείς να κοιμηθείς στο κάτω μέρος του κρεβατιού", είπε ο E-Z, πετώντας εκεί ένα μαξιλάρι.

"Ευχαριστώ", είπε ο Άλφρεντ ο κύκνος. Κουτρουβαλήθηκε πάνω στο μαξιλάρι και το χτύπησε με τα δικτυωτά του πόδια μέχρι να βολευτεί. Μετά κάθισε οκλαδόν.

"Τώρα, ας ξεκινήσουμε", είπε ο Άλφρεντ.

Ο E-Z, που φορούσε τώρα τις πιτζάμες του, άκουγε τον Άλφρεντ να λέει την ιστορία του.

"Ήμουν άνθρωπος κάποτε".

Ο E-Z έμεινε άναυδος.

"Καλύτερα να μη διακόπτεις μέχρι να τελειώσω", μάλωσε ο κύκνος. "Διαφορετικά, η ιστορία μου θα συνεχίζεται και κανείς από τους δυο μας δεν θα κοιμηθεί".

"Συγγνώμη", είπε ο E-Z.

Ο κύκνος συνέχισε. "Ζούσα με τη γυναίκα μου και τα δύο παιδιά μου. Ήμασταν απίστευτα ευτυχισμένοι, μέχρι που μια καταιγίδα πέρασε και γκρέμισε το σπίτι μας και τους σκότωσε όλους. Εγώ επέζησα, αλλά χωρίς αυτά δεν ήθελα. Τότε ήρθε ένας άγγελος σε μένα, η Άριελ που γνώρισες, και μου είπε ότι θα μπορούσα να τους ξαναδώ όλους, αν συμφωνούσα να βοηθήσω τους άλλους. Μου αρέσει να βοηθάω τους άλλους και αυτό θα μου έδινε σκοπό. Άλλωστε, δεν είχα άλλες επιλογές και έτσι συμφώνησα".

"Έχεις δοκιμασίες;" ρώτησε ο E-Z. Είχε λανθασμένα υποθέσει ότι η ιστορία του Άλφρεντ είχε ολοκληρωθεί.

"Η ιστορία μου δεν έχει τελειώσει ακόμα", είπε ο Άλφρεντ ο κύκνος, μάλλον με θυμό. Στη συνέχεια συνέχισε. "Αυτή είναι η ουσία της ιστορίας μου. Δεν έχω δοκιμασίες, επειδή δεν είμαι άγγελος σε εκπαίδευση. Τα φτερά μου δεν είναι σαν τα δικά σας φτερά. Είμαι ένας κύκνος, αν και μεγαλύτερος από τον συνηθισμένο κύκνο. Το όνομα της φυλής μου είναι Cygnus Falconeri, που είναι επίσης γνωστό ως γιγάντιος κύκνος. Το είδος μου εξαφανίστηκε πριν από πολύ καιρό. Ο σκοπός μου ήταν απροσδιόριστος. Είχα κολλήσει στο ενδιάμεσο και το ενδιάμεσο, παρασυρόμενος στο χρόνο επειδή έκανα ένα λάθος. Αλλά δεν θέλω να μιλήσω γι' αυτό τώρα. Όταν σε είδα να σώζεις εκείνο το κοριτσάκι, τηλεφώνησα στην Άριελ και ρώτησα αν μπορούσα να σε εξυπηρετήσω. Εκείνη με μάλωσε που δραπέτευσα και με έστειλε πίσω στο ενδιάμεσο. Δραπέτευσα ξανά από εκεί και σε βοήθησα με το αεροπλάνο και η Ariel ζήτησε από τον Ophaniel να μου δώσει άλλη μια ευκαιρία. Τώρα έχω έναν σκοπό - να σε βοηθήσω".

"Και ο Οφάνιελ, συμφώνησε; Αλλά τι γίνεται με την Έριελ;"

"Στην αρχή δεν το έκαναν. Αυτό συνέβη επειδή ο Χαντζ και η Ρέικι με ανέφεραν επειδή σε βοήθησα καλώντας τους φίλους μου τα πουλιά. Όταν έμαθα ότι τους έστειλαν στα ορυχεία και δραπέτευσαν ξανά, η Άριελ πρότεινε την υπόθεσή μου και ο Οφάνιελ συμφώνησε. Δεν ξέρω για την Έριελ. Είναι ο μέντοράς σου;"

"Ναι, ανέλαβε τη θέση του Χαντζ και του Ρέικι. Εκείνοι μπαινόβγαιναν, ενώ εκείνος λέει ότι μπορεί πάντα να βλέπει πού βρίσκομαι και τι κάνω".

"Αυτό ακούγεται υπερβολικό. Παρόλα αυτά, θα ήθελα να τον γνωρίσω μια μέρα. Προς το παρόν, είμαστε μια ομάδα. Μπορώ να σε βοηθήσω, ώστε μια μέρα να είμαι κι εγώ πάλι με την οικογένειά μου. Οπότε, όπου πας εσύ E-Z, πάω κι εγώ".

Ο E-Z ακούμπησε το κεφάλι του στο μαξιλάρι του και έκλεισε τα μάτια του. Ένιωθε ευγνώμων για κάθε βοήθεια. Εξάλλου ο κύκνος τον είχε βοηθήσει στο παρελθόν με το αεροπλάνο.

"Δεν θα μπω στο δρόμο σου", είπε ο Άλφρεντ ο κύκνος. "Ξέρω, σκέφτεσαι ότι είμαστε ένα παράλογο ζευγάρι και όταν φτάσει η Λία, θα είμαστε μια ακόμα πιο παράλογη τριάδα, αλλά...".

"Περίμενε", είπε ο E-Z. "Ξέρεις για τη Λία; Πώς;"

"Ω ναι, ξέρω τα πάντα για σένα και ξέρω τα πάντα γι' αυτήν και ξέρω επίσης περισσότερα. Ότι οι τρεις μας είμαστε συνδεδεμένοι. Προορισμένοι να συνεργαστούμε". Τέντωσε τα σαγόνια του, τα οποία έμοιαζαν σαν να προσπαθούσε να χασμουρηθεί. "Είμαι πολύ κουρασμένος για να μιλήσω άλλο απόψε". Πριν περάσει πολύς καιρός, ο Άλφρεντ, ο κύκνος ροχάλιζε.

Ο E-Z πέρασε από το μυαλό του όλα όσα ήξερε για τους κύκνους. Τα οποία δεν ήταν πολλά. Το πρωί, θα έκανε κάποια έρευνα για το είδος του Άλφρεντ.

Αναρωτήθηκε πώς θα ένιωθαν ο Πι Τζέι και ο Άρντεν για τον Άλφρεντ. Χρειαζόταν να τους συστήσει ή θα μπορούσε ο Άλφρεντ να είναι μυστικό;

Φούσκωσε το μαξιλάρι του με τις γροθιές του και ετοιμάστηκε να κοιμηθεί.

Ξύπνησε τον Άλφρεντ και ήταν δύστροπος γι' αυτό.

"Πρέπει να το κάνεις αυτό;" ρώτησε ο Άλφρεντ.

"Συγγνώμη", είπε ο E-Z.

ΚΕΦΑΛΑΙΟ 10

Το επόμενο πρωί, ο Ε-Ζ ξύπνησε με τον θείο Σαμ να χτυπάει την πόρτα του. "Ξύπνα Ε-Ζ! Ο Πι Τζέι και ο Άρντεν είναι ήδη καθ' οδόν για να σε πάνε στο σχολείο".

Ο Ε-Ζ χασμουρήθηκε και τεντώθηκε. Ντύθηκε και στη συνέχεια κάθισε στην καρέκλα του. Αφού ο Άλφρεντ κοιμόταν ακόμα, θα έβγαινε κρυφά να τον δει μετά το σχολείο.

"Δεν μπορείς να πας πουθενά χωρίς εμένα!" Είπε ο Άλφρεντ. Τίναξε τα φτερά του παντού και μετά πήδηξε στο πάτωμα.

"Δεν μπορείς να έρθεις μαζί μου στο σχολείο. Τα κατοικίδια δεν επιτρέπονται".

"Ε-Ζ, έλα, παλικάρι μου!" φώναξε ο θείος Σαμ από την κουζίνα. "Διαφορετικά, θα χάσεις το πρωινό".

Το στομάχι του Ε-Ζ γουργούρισε καθώς η μυρωδιά του τοστ ανέβηκε προς το μέρος του. "Έρχομαι!"

Χωρίς να έχει χρόνο για αντιρρήσεις, ο Ε-Ζ άνοιξε την πόρτα. Μπήκε στην κουζίνα την ώρα που έφτασαν ο Άρντεν και ο Πι Τζέι. Ένα κορνάρισμα απ' έξω τον ενημέρωσε ότι ήταν εκεί.

"Εντάξει, εντάξει!" φώναξε ο Ε-Ζ καθώς άρπαζε ένα κομμάτι ψωμί του τοστ. Προχώρησε κατά μήκος του διαδρόμου με τον νέο του σύντροφο με τα ιστιοφόρα πόδια να τον ακολουθεί.

Ο PJ βγήκε από το αυτοκίνητο για να βοηθήσει τον E-Z να μπει μέσα και ασφάλισε την αναπηρική του καρέκλα στο πορτμπαγκάζ. Καθώς το έκλεινε, είδε τον Άλφρεντ να προσπαθεί να μπει στο όχημα.

"Ε, αυτό το πράγμα δεν μπορεί να μπει στο αυτοκίνητο", φώναξε ο PJ.

Ο Άρντεν κατέβασε το παράθυρο.

"Τι στο καλό είναι αυτό; Μήπως έχασα ένα σημείωμα που έλεγε ότι σήμερα θα είχαμε Show and Tell;" Χασκογέλασε.

"Κύκνος είναι αυτό;" ρώτησε η μητέρα της κυρίας Χειρολαβής Πι-Τζέι.

"Ή μήπως αυτό το πράγμα είναι ο πρόεδρος της λέσχης θαυμαστών σου;" Ο Πι Τζέι ρώτησε με ένα χαμόγελο.

Μόλις μπήκε μέσα στο αυτοκίνητο, ο E-Z απάντησε. "Είμαστε πολύ μεγάλοι για να δείχνουμε και να λέμε", γέλασε. "Ο κύκνος είναι το πρόγραμμά μου. Ένα πείραμα, όπως ένας σκύλος με μάτια για έναν τυφλό. Είναι ο σύντροφός μου στο αναπηρικό καροτσάκι". Έδεσε τον Άλφρεντ στη ζώνη ασφαλείας.

Ο Πι Τζέι πήγε να καθίσει μπροστά δίπλα στη μητέρα του.

Ο Άλφρεντ, ο κύκνος, είπε: "Δεν θα με συστήσεις;".

Η κυρία Χειρολαβή τράβηξε το αυτοκίνητο και πήραν το δρόμο για το σχολείο.

"Άλφρεντ", ο E-Z έριξε μια ματιά στους φίλους του, "να σου γνωρίσω την κυρία Χειρολαβή. Και οι δύο καλύτεροι φίλοι μου, ο Πι Τζέι και ο Άριτεν. Όλοι σας, αυτός είναι ο Άλφρεντ, ο τρομπετίστας κύκνος". Ο E-Z σταύρωσε τα χέρια του.

Ο Άλφρεντ είπε: "Χου-χου". Στον E-Z είπε: "Χαίρομαι απίστευτα που σας γνωρίζω. Μπορείς να μου μεταφράσεις".

"Πώς ξέρεις το όνομά του;" ρώτησε ο PJ.

"Δεν μεταμορφώνεσαι σε, πώς τον έλεγαν, τον τύπο που μπορούσε να μιλάει στα ζώα τώρα, έτσι δεν είναι E-Z; Σε παρακαλώ πες μου ότι δεν είσαι. Αν και, θα μπορούσε να μετατραπεί σε μια πραγματική αγελάδα μετρητών.

Θα μπορούσαμε να εμπορευτούμε το ταλέντο σου. Να ζητάμε ερωτήσεις και να δημοσιεύουμε τις απαντήσεις στο δικό μας κανάλι στο YouTube. Θα μπορούσαμε να το ονομάσουμε "E-Z Dickens, ο ψιθυριστής των κύκνων".

"Εξαιρετική ιδέα!" είπε ο PJ, καθώς η μητέρα του σταμάτησε σε μια διάβαση πεζών. "Πριν από μερικά χρόνια, πιθανότατα θα είχαμε βγάλει εκατομμύρια στο διαδίκτυο. Στις μέρες μας το να βγάλουμε λεφτά στο διαδίκτυο είναι δύσκολο. Έχουν σφίξει πολύ τα λουριά".

"Μην είσαι αγενής", είπε η κυρία Χειρολαβή, καθώς συνέχιζε την πορεία της.

"Το πρόσωπο στο οποίο αναφέρεται είναι ο Δόκτωρ Ντουλίτλ", πρότεινε ο Άλφρεντ. "Ήταν μια σειρά μυθιστορημάτων δώδεκα βιβλίων που έγραψε ο Χιου Λόφτινγκ. Το πρώτο βιβλίο εκδόθηκε το 1920 και ακολούθησαν τα υπόλοιπα, μέχρι το 1952. Ο Χιου Λόφτινγκ πέθανε το 1947. Ήταν επίσης Βρετανός. Ένας άνθρωπος από το Μπέρκσαϊρ, γεννημένος και μεγαλωμένος".

"Ξέρω ποιον εννοούν", είπε ο E-Z στον Άλφρεντ. "Και όχι, δεν είμαι".

Ο Άρντεν είπε: "Ελπίζω ο κύκνος σύντροφός σου να μην μας κλέψει όλα τα κορίτσια σήμερα. Ξέρεις πόσο αγαπούν τα κορίτσια τα φτερωτά πράγματα".

Η κυρία Χειρολαβή καθάρισε το λαιμό της.

"Ήμουν αρκετά γυναικάς δολοφόνος, στην εποχή μου", είπε ο Άλφρεντ, ακολουθούμενος από άλλο ένα "Χου-χου!", το οποίο έστρεψε προς την Πι-Τζέι και τον Άρντεν.

Η Πι Τζέι είπε: "Ο σύντροφος κύκνος σας με τρελαίνει πραγματικά".

Ο Άρντεν ρώτησε: "Ποια ταινία με πουλιά κέρδισε Όσκαρ;"

Ο PJ απάντησε: "Ο άρχοντας των φτερών".

Ο Άρντεν ρώτησε: "Πού επενδύουν τα πουλιά τα χρήματά τους;"

Ο PJ απάντησε: "Στην αγορά πελαργών!"

"Οι φίλοι σου διασκεδάζουν εύκολα", είπε ο Άλφρεντ. "Είναι δύο βλάκες, κομμένοι από το ίδιο ύφασμα. Καταλαβαίνω γιατί σου αρέσουν. Μου αρέσει η κυρία Handle. Είναι ήσυχη και εξαιρετική οδηγός".

Ο E-Z γέλασε.

"Χαίρομαι που απολαμβάνεις το πρωινό χιούμορ", είπε ο Πι Τζέι.

"Δεν το χαίρομαι πραγματικά", είπε ο Άλφρεντ. "Άλλωστε εσείς οι δύο είστε πραγματικοί βλάκες".

Ο Άρντεν και ο Πι Τζέι έκαναν μια διπλή ματιά.

Ο E-Z έκανε επίσης μια διπλή αναπνοή στις διπλές αναπνοές τους. "Τι;"

"Δεν το ακούσατε αυτό;" είπαν οι δύο μαζί. "Ο κύκνος μπορεί να μιλήσει - και μάλιστα με βρετανική προφορά. Φίλε μου, τα κορίτσια θα τον λατρέψουν πραγματικά".

Η κυρία Handle κούνησε το κεφάλι της. "Μην το παίζετε ανόητοι ζητιάνοι εσείς οι δύο!"

Ο E-Z κοίταξε τον Άλφρεντ τον κύκνο που έδειχνε μπερδεμένος.

Ο Άλφρεντ δοκίμασε ένα δικό του αστείο για να δει αν μπορούσαν πραγματικά να τον καταλάβουν. "Γιατί βουίζουν τα κολιμπρί;" ρώτησε.

Τα τρία αγόρια τον κοίταζαν, ήταν σαφές ότι τόσο ο Άρντεν όσο και ο Πι Τζέι μπορούσαν πλέον να τον καταλάβουν.

Ο Άλφρεντ είπε την ατάκα: "Επειδή δεν ξέρουν τις λέξεις, φυσικά"

Ο Πι Τζέι και ο Άρντεν γέλασαν, κάπως έτσι, αλλά κυρίως είχαν φρικάρει.

"Πώς γίνεται να σε καταλαβαίνουν κι αυτοί τώρα;" ρώτησε ο E-Z. "Στην αρχή δεν μπορούσαν, τώρα μπορούν. Νόμιζα ότι είπες ότι μόνο εγώ το καταλαβαίνω. Και γιατί δεν μπορούσε να σε καταλάβει ο θείος Σαμ;"

Τώρα που μπορούσαν να τον καταλάβουν, ο Άλφρεντ αισθάνθηκε αμήχανα. Ψιθύρισε στον E-Z: "Ειλικρινά δεν ξέρω. Εκτός κι αν αυτό για το οποίο είμαι εδώ έχει να κάνει και με αυτούς".

"Και δεν περιλαμβάνει τον θείο Σαμ; Ή την κυρία Χειρολαβή;"

"'Ίσως όχι", απάντησε ο Άλφρεντ.

"Και πού, βρήκες αυτόν τον κύκνο που μιλάει;" ρώτησε ο Άρντεν.

"Και γιατί τον φέρνεις στο σχολείο;" ρώτησε ο Πι Τζέι.

Η κυρία Χερούλια εκνευρίστηκε. "Φέρεστε όλοι σας πολύ ανόητα. Ο E-Z λέει ότι είναι ένας κύκνος σύντροφος. Δεν μπορεί να μιλήσει".

"Πρώτα απ' όλα, δεν είναι απλώς ένας κύκνος είναι ένας Cygnus Falconeri. Γνωστός και ως γιγάντιος κύκνος και ένα είδος που έχει εξαφανιστεί εδώ και αιώνες".

"Δεν έχω δει πολλούς κύκνους στην πραγματική ζωή", είπε ο Άρντεν. "Αυτοί που έχω δει στο κανάλι της φύσης δεν έμοιαζαν τόσο μεγάλοι όσο αυτός όμως. Τα πόδια του είναι τεράστια! Και τι γίνεται αν πρέπει, ξέρεις, να πάει στην τουαλέτα;"

"Ο μέσος γιγάντιος κύκνος είχε μήκος από το ράμφος μέχρι την ουρά μεταξύ 190-210 εκατοστών", πρότεινε ο Άλφρεντ. "Και αν το κάνω, θα χρησιμοποιήσω το γρασίδι - το γήπεδο των σπορ θα πρέπει να μου δίνει άφθονο χώρο για να ταΐζομαι και να κάνω τη δουλειά μου, αν και όταν χρειαστεί".

"Εννοείς ότι τρως το γρασίδι και μετά πας στο γρασίδι;" είπε ο Πι Τζέι.

"Φτου!" είπε ο Άρντεν.

Ήταν φοβερά κοντά στο σχολείο τώρα, οπότε ο E-Z εξήγησε. "Δεν μπορώ να σου δώσω λεπτομέρειες γιατί δεν τα ξέρω πραγματικά. Το μόνο που ξέρω σίγουρα είναι ότι ο Άλφρεντ είναι εδώ για να με βοηθήσει και θα τον βλέπεις συχνά".

"Δεν νομίζω ότι θα τον αφήσουν να μπει στο σχολείο", είπε ο Άρντεν.

"Δεν θα είναι πρόβλημα, αφού είμαι ο σύντροφός σου", είπε ο Άλφρεντ.

Ο Πι Τζέι, ο Άρντεν και ο Άλφρεντ γέλασαν καθώς το αυτοκίνητο σταμάτησε έξω από το σχολείο.

"Τηλεφώνησέ μου αν θέλεις να σε πάρω μετά το σχολείο", είπε η κυρία Handle.

"Ευχαριστώ", απάντησαν οι.

Αφού η καρέκλα του E-Z βγήκε από το πορτμπαγκάζ, η κυρία Handle απομακρύνθηκε από το πεζοδρόμιο.

Οι φίλοι του τον βοήθησαν να μπει μέσα, ενώ ο Άλφρεντ πέταξε πάνω και κάθισε στον ώμο του. Προχώρησαν προς την είσοδο του σχολείου, όπου ο διευθυντής Πίρσον έβαζε τους μαθητές μέσα.

"Καλημέρα παιδιά", είπε με ένα τεράστιο χαμόγελο στο πρόσωπό του. Μέχρι που πρόσεξε τον Άλφρεντ, τον κύκνο. "Τι είναι αυτό το πράγμα;" ρώτησε.

"Είναι ένας σύντροφος κύκνος", είπε ο E-Z.

"Ένας Cygnus Falconerie, για την ακρίβεια", είπε ο Άρντεν.

"Είναι μαζί μας", είπε ο Πι Τζέι.

Ο διευθυντής Πίρσον σταύρωσε τα χέρια του. "Αυτό το πράγμα, το Cygnus whatchamacallit δεν πρόκειται να μπει εδώ μέσα!"

Ο Άλφρεντ είπε: "Δεν πειράζει, E-Z. Ας μην προκαλέσουμε σκηνή. Θα είμαι εδώ όταν τελειώσουν τα μαθήματά σας. Τα λέμε αργότερα." Ο Άλφρεντ πέταξε ψηλά και προσγειώθηκε στην οροφή του κτιρίου. Απολάμβανε τη θέα πριν πετάξει κάτω στο γήπεδο ποδοσφαίρου. Υπήρχε άφθονο γρασίδι για να μασουλήσει. Όταν θα χόρταινε, θα έβρισκε ένα σκιερό σημείο κάτω από ένα δέντρο και θα έπαιρνε έναν υπνάκο.

Ο διευθυντής Πίρσον κούνησε το κεφάλι του και μετά κράτησε την πόρτα για τον E-Z και τους φίλους του. Μέσα ακούστηκε το προειδοποιητικο κουδούνι των πέντε λεπτών.

Αυτή η σχολική μέρα ήταν αδιάφορη για τον E-Z και τους φίλους του.

Ακόμα δεν υπήρχε κανένα νέο από τον Έριελ για νέες δοκιμές.

ΚΕΦΑΛΑΙΟ 11

Ο Άλφρεντ εγκαταστάθηκε στη νέα του ρουτίνα. Τα παιδιά στο σχολείο τον γνώρισαν - αν και μόνο ο Ε-Ζ και οι φίλοι του ήξεραν ότι μπορούσε να μιλήσει.

Εκείνη τη μέρα, έξω από το σχολείο ο Άλφρεντ περίμενε τον Ε-Ζ και τον ρώτησε: "Μπορούμε να μιλήσουμε;".

Ο Ε-Ζ κοίταξε γύρω του- εξακολουθούσε να μην θέλει οι άλλοι μαθητές να τον ακούσουν να μιλάει σε έναν κύκνο. Ψιθύρισε: "Ε, μπορεί αυτό να περιμένει μέχρι να πάμε σπίτι;".

"Κατάλαβα", είπε ο Άλφρεντ. "Ακόμα νιώθεις αμήχανα όταν κουβεντιάζουμε. Το οποίο είναι κατανοητό, αλλά τα παιδιά με αγαπούν εδώ. Στήνονται στην ουρά για να με χαϊδέψουν, να με ταΐσουν. Εξάλλου, ο θείος Σαμ δεν θα είναι στο σπίτι; Πρέπει να σου μιλήσω ιδιαιτέρως".

"Αφού δεν μπορεί να σε καταλάβει ακόμα, θα μου μιλάς μόνος σου ακόμα και όταν είμαστε στο σπίτι".

"Αλλά αυτό είναι ένα θέμα που μας απασχολεί και είναι μάλλον ευαίσθητο στον χρόνο", είπε ο Άλφρεντ.

Ο Πι Τζέι σταμάτησε στο πεζοδρόμιο δίπλα τους. Ο Άρντεν τους ρώτησε αν ήθελαν να τους πάνε σπίτι τους.

"Ε, παιδιά. Λυπάμαι, αλλά σήμερα θα πάω με τα πόδια στο σπίτι με τον Άλφρεντ. Έχει να μου μεταδώσει κάποιες ζωτικής σημασίας πληροφορίες".

Ο Πι Τζέι και ο Άρντεν κούνησαν τα κεφάλια τους. Ο Άρντεν είπε: "Περιμέναμε να μας πετάξουν μια μέρα για ένα κορίτσι - όχι για ένα πουλί". Χασκογέλασε.

"Και τι θα γίνει με το παιχνίδι;" ρώτησε ο Άρντεν.

"Σήμερα είναι σήμερα και ο αγώνας θα γίνει αύριο. Συγγνώμη, παιδιά". Ο Ε-Ζ ανέβασε το ρυθμό. Το αυτοκίνητο σύρθηκε δίπλα του και μετά απομακρύνθηκε με ένα τρίξιμο των ελαστικών.

"Πλονκερς", είπε ο Άλφρεντ.

"Έχουν καλές προθέσεις. Τώρα τι είναι τόσο σημαντικό;"

"Έχεις ακούσει τίποτα από τη Λία τελευταία; Ανησυχώ γι' αυτήν". Ο Άλφρεντ περπατούσε δίπλα στον Ε-Ζ, τσιμπώντας το κεφάλι μιας πικραλίδας καθώς προχωρούσε.

"Γιατί ανησυχείς; Καμια είδηση δεν είναι καλή είδηση, έτσι δεν είναι;"

"Λοιπόν, στην πραγματικότητα, είχα νέα της και υπήρξε μια, ε, λοιπόν, μια νέα αινιγματική εξέλιξη".

Ο Ε-Ζ σταμάτησε. "Πες μου περισσότερα".

"Συνέχισε να περπατάς", είπε ο Άλφρεντ, τσιμπώντας τώρα το κεφάλι μιας μαργαρίτας. "Η Λία και η μητέρα της είναι ήδη καθ' οδόν προς τα εδώ. Θα πρέπει να φτάσουν κάποια στιγμή αύριο".

"Γιατί τόση βιασύνη; Θέλω να πω, ναι, αυτό είναι μια έκπληξη. Το ξέραμε ότι θα έρθουν σύντομα. Τι το περίεργο έχει αυτό;"

"Δεν είναι αυτό το αποοίας άξιο".

"Σταμάτα να χρονοτριβείς και πες το!"

"Η Λία δεν είναι πλέον επτά ετών - είναι πλέον δέκα ετών".

"Τι; Αυτό είναι αδύνατον."

"Πιστεύεις ότι θα έλεγε ψέματα;"

"Όχι, δεν νομίζω ότι θα έλεγε ψέματα, αλλά - αυτό δεν βγάζει απολύτως κανένα νόημα. Οι άνθρωποι δεν μεγαλώνουν από επτά σε δέκα μέσα σε λίγες εβδομάδες".

"Είπε ότι πήγε για ύπνο. Το επόμενο πρωί, μπήκε στην κουζίνα για πρωινό και η νταντά της άρχισε να ουρλιάζει. Έτσι ανακάλυψε ότι είχε γεράσει τρία χρόνια μέσα σε μια νύχτα".

"Ουάου!" Αναφώνησε ο E-Z.

"Και υπάρχουν κι άλλα".

"Κι άλλα. Δεν μπορώ να φανταστώ τίποτα περισσότερο".

"Κατάφερε να πείσει τη μητέρα της ότι δεν υπήρχε λόγος να παραμείνει εδώ για όλη την επίσκεψη. Είναι μια πολυάσχολη επιχειρηματίας. Χρειάστηκε αρκετή πειθώ. Η Λία είπε ότι θα ήταν καλύτερα, δεδομένης της εμπειρίας της Σαμ μαζί σου και των δοκιμών. Η μητέρα της συμφώνησε, υπό μερικούς όρους".

"Όπως;"

"Ότι της αρέσει ο θείος Σαμ".

"Σε όλους αρέσει ο θείος Σαμ."

"Επίσης, ότι θα της εξηγήσεις πώς η κόρη της μπόρεσε να γεράσει έτσι μέσα σε μια νύχτα".

"Και πώς ακριβώς πρέπει να το κάνω αυτό;"

"Για να είμαι ειλικρινής", είπε ο Alfred, "δεν έχω ιδέα. Γι' αυτό και ήθελα να σου μιλήσω ιδιαιτέρως. Θέλω να πω, ο θείος Σαμ ξέρει ότι η Λία θα έρθει, σωστά;"

Ο E-Z ένεψε: "Υποθέτω πως ναι, αν είναι καθ' οδόν".

"Αλλά περιμένει ένα επτάχρονο κοριτσάκι, όταν ένα δεκάχρονο θα εμφανιστεί στο κατώφλι του".

Ο E-Z σταμάτησε ξανά. Ο θείος Σαμ. Δεν είχε καν σκεφτεί ότι ο θείος Σαμ θα έπρεπε να αντιμετωπίσει ένα δεκάχρονο κορίτσι. "Δεν είμαι σίγουρος ότι του ανέφερα ποτέ την ηλικία της Λία!"

Ο Άλφρεντ συνέχισε. "Έχω ακούσει ότι οι άνθρωποι γερνούν γρήγορα. Υπάρχει μια ασθένεια που λέγεται Progeria. Είναι μια γενετική πάθηση, αρκετά σπάνια και αρκετά θανατηφόρα. Τα περισσότερα παιδιά δεν ζουν πάνω από τα δεκατρία και η Λία είναι ήδη δέκα, οπότε πρέπει να το ανακαλύψουμε".

"Πώς είναι αυτό το πράγμα που είπες".

"Progeria."

"Ναι, Progeria, πώς είναι η σύμβαση;" ρώτησε ο E-Z.

"Απ' ό,τι καταλαβαίνω, συμβαίνει κατά τη διάρκεια των δύο πρώτων ετών. Και τα παιδιά είναι συνήθως παραμορφωμένα".

"Η Λία είναι παραμορφωμένη, εξαιτίας του γυαλιού, όχι εξαιτίας κάποιας ασθένειας. Υπάρχει θεραπεία;"

"Δεν υπάρχει θεραπεία. Αλλά E-Z, υπάρχει κάτι άλλο. Έχει να κάνει με τα μάτια στα χέρια της. Είναι καινούργια και η ασθένεια είναι καινούργια. Πολύ μεγάλη σύμπτωση δεν νομίζεις;"

Ο E-Z το σκέφτηκε αυτό και αποφάσισε ότι ο Άλφρεντ είχε δίκιο. Ήταν πάρα πολύ μεγάλη σύμπτωση. Αλλά τι επρόκειτο να κάνει γι' αυτό; Θα έπρεπε να καλέσει την Έριελ; "Ξέρεις τον Έριελ;"

Ο Άλφρεντ επιβράδυνε τον ρυθμό του και το ίδιο έκανε και ο E-Z. Είχαν σχεδόν φτάσει στο σπίτι τους και έπρεπε να το συζητήσουν πριν συναντηθούν με τον θείο Σαμ. "Ναι, έχω ακούσει γι' αυτόν. Αλλά όπως ξέρεις ο Eriel δεν είναι ο άγγελός μου. Γνώρισες τη μέντορά μου, την Άριελ, και είναι ο άγγελος της φύσης, γι' αυτό και βρίσκομαι στην κατάσταση ενός σπάνιου κύκνου. Μπορεί να είναι σε θέση να βοηθήσει, αλλά θα πρέπει να περιμένουμε την επόμενη εμφάνισή της για να το κάνουμε".

"Εννοείς ότι δεν μπορείς να την καλέσεις;"

Ο Άλφρεντ έγνεψε. "Μπορείς να καλέσεις την Έριελ κατά βούληση;"

Ο E-Z γέλασε. "Όχι ακριβώς κατά βούληση, αλλά είναι προσβάσιμος. Αν και, είναι ένας μπελάς στο ξέρεις τι με αυτό και δεν του αρέσει να τον καλούν ή να τον καλούν". Ο E-Z σκέφτηκε ήσυχα και το ίδιο έκανε και ο Άλφρεντ. Το σπίτι τους βρισκόταν πλέον στον ορίζοντα και ο θείος Σαμ ήταν σπίτι, καθώς το αυτοκίνητό του ήταν παρκαρισμένο στο δρόμο. "Νομίζω ότι πρέπει να περιμένουμε να δούμε τι θα γίνει με τη Λία".

"Σύμφωνοι", είπε ο Άλφρεντ, καθώς βγήκε από το μονοπάτι και τράβηξε λίγο χορτάρι από το έδαφος και το μάσησε. Ο E-Z παρακολουθούσε. "Προτιμώ να μην τρώω πολύ γρασίδι- εννοώ γρασίδι του γκαζόν. Είναι αυτό που τρώω όλη μέρα όταν είσαι στο σχολείο - εκτός από τα λίγα λουλούδια που μπορώ να βρω. Αυτή τη στιγμή, έχω όρεξη να φάω λίγο από το υγρό πράγμα, που μεγαλώνει κάτω από το νερό. Είναι πιο φρέσκο και πιο ζουμερό".

"Το καταλαβαίνω απόλυτα αυτό" είπε ο E-Z. "Μου αρέσει να τρώω σαλάτα όταν είναι φρέσκια και τραγανή. Δεν μου αρέσει τόσο πολύ όταν έρχεται σε σακούλες και ο μόνος τρόπος για να την κατεβάσεις είναι να την βουτήξεις σε σάλτσα σαλάτας".

"Μου λείπει το ανθρώπινο φαγητό".

"Τι σου λείπει περισσότερο;"

"Τα τσίζμπεργκερ και οι πατάτες τηγανιτές, χωρίς αμφιβολία. Α, και η κέτσαπ. Πόσο μου άρεσε αυτή η παχιά, κόκκινη γλοιώδης σάλτσα που πάει πάνω σε όλα".

"Ίσως δεν θα ήταν τόσο κακό, στο γρασίδι;" Ο E-Z γέλασε, αλλά ο Άλφρεντ το σκεφτόταν.

"Θα ήμουν πρόθυμος να το δοκιμάσω".

"Ας το βάλουμε στη λίστα με τα αγαπημένα σου πράγματα", είπε ο E-Z.

"Τι είναι η λίστα με τα κουβαδάκια;" ρώτησε ο Άλφρεντ.

ΚΕΦΑΛΑΙΟ 12

Ο E-Z σκέφτηκε την ερώτηση του Άλφρεντ. Ο Άλφρεντ δεν ήξερε τι είναι η λίστα με τα καλάθια... και η φράση επινοήθηκε το 2007. Στην ομώνυμη ταινία των Νίκολσον/Φρίμαν. Εξήγησε χωρίς να μπει σε πολλές λεπτομέρειες.

"Αυτή είναι μια πολύ ενδιαφέρουσα ιδέα", είπε ο Άλφρεντ, φουσκώνοντας τα φτερά του. "Αλλά πειο είναι το νόημα του να κρατάμε μια λίστα με τα πράγματα που μας απασχολούν; Σίγουρα, θα θυμόσουν οτιδήποτε ήθελες πραγματικά να κάνεις;"

"Ξέρεις, Άλφρεντ, δεν είμαι ακριβώς σίγουρος. Υποθέτω ότι μπορεί να έχει να κάνει με την ηλικία. Μεγαλώνεις και χάνεις τη μνήμη σου".

"Λογικό."

Συνέχισαν το ταξίδι τους και έφτασαν στο σπίτι. Όταν ο E-Z ανέβηκε με ρόδα στη ράμπα, ο Άλφρεντ ανέβηκε πάνω. Ο κύκνος χτύπησε τα φτερά του για να βοηθήσει με την ανοδική ορμή. Στην κορυφή, καθώς ο E-Z άνοιξε την πόρτα, άκουσαν μια άγνωστη φωνή.

"Ωχ όχι, είναι ήδη εδώ!" είπε ο Άλφρεντ.

"Θα μπορούσες να με είχες προειδοποιήσει!" απάντησε ο E-Z, αποθηκεύοντας την τσάντα του σε ένα γάντζο στο δρόμο προς το σαλόνι.

"Προφανώς, θα το είχα κάνει, αν το ήξερα!"

Η Λία σηκώθηκε όρθια.

Για τον E-Z η δεκάχρονη Λία έμοιαζε εντυπωσιακά διαφορετική, μέχρι που σήκωσε τις ανοιχτές παλάμες της.

Η Λία έσκουξε, έτρεξε προς το μέρος του και τον αγκάλιασε. Στη συνέχεια αγκάλιασε τον Άλφρεντ και είπε ότι ήταν απίστευτα χαρούμενη που επιτέλους τον γνώρισε.

Η μαμά της Λία, η Σαμάνθα, στεκόταν επίσης όρθια και παρακολουθούσε την κόρη της να αγκαλιάζει το αγόρι που της είχε σώσει τη ζωή. Ο άγγελος/αγόρι στο αναπηρικό καροτσάκι. Η κόρη της είχε αναφέρει τον Άλφρεντ, αλλά όχι ότι ήταν ένας γιγάντιος κύκνος.

Ο θείος Σαμ στάθηκε όρθιος και είπε: "Ω, E-Z! Δόξα τω Θεώ, γύρισες σπίτι!" Πλησίασε τον ανιψιό του. Στη συνέχεια πρότεινε αμήχανα να πάνε στην κουζίνα για να πάρουν αναψυκτικά.

"Είμαστε μια χαρά", είπε η Σαμάνθα.

Ο Σαμ επέμεινε να πάνε στην κουζίνα ούτως ή άλλως.

"Εεε", τραύλισε ο E-Z. "Θα ήθελα ένα ποτό".

Η Σαμ αναστέναξε.

"Μην μπαίνεις σε κόπο για χάρη μας", είπε η Σαμάνθα.

"Δεν είναι καθόλου κόπος", είπε ο Σαμ, σπρώχνοντας την καρέκλα του E-Z προς την έξοδο του σαλονιού.

"Λία, είσαι πολύ όμορφη", είπε ο Άλφρεντ, σκύβοντας το κεφάλι του για να μπορέσει να τον χαϊδέψει.

"Σ' ευχαριστώ", είπε η Λία κοκκινίζοντας. Έριξε μια ματιά προς την κατεύθυνση του E-Z καθώς έβγαιναν από το δωμάτιο, αλλά εκείνος δεν το πρόσεξε, καθώς τα μάτια του ήταν στραμμένα στο θείο του.

Μόλις βρέθηκαν στην κουζίνα, ο Σαμ πάρκαρε τον ανιψιό του. Άνοιξε το ψυγείο και το έκλεισε ξανά. Πήγε στο ντουλάπι, άνοιξε την πόρτα και την έκλεισε ξανά.

"Τι συμβαίνει;" ρώτησε ο E-Z.

"Εγώ, δεν τα περίμενα τόσο σύντομα και τι τρώνε και τι πίνουν τέλος πάντων οι άνθρωποι από την Ολλανδία; Δεν νομίζω ότι έχω κάτι κατάλληλο στο σπίτι. Μήπως να βγω έξω και να πάρω κάτι ιδιαίτερο;"

"Είναι άνθρωποι σαν κι εμάς, είμαι σίγουρος ότι θα δοκιμάσουν ό,τι κι αν έχεις. Μην το σκέφτεσαι πολύ".

"Βοήθησέ με, μικρέ. Τι είδους πράγματα πρέπει να σερβίρουμε; Τυρί και κράκερς; Κάτι ζεστό, σάντουιτς με ψητό τυρί; Έχουμε νερό, χυμούς και αναψυκτικά".

"Εντάξει, ας κάνουμε το τυρί και τα κράκερς για την ώρα. Να δούμε πώς θα πάμε με αυτό. Και έναν δίσκο με διάφορα ποτά".

Ο Σαμ αναστέναξε και τα έβαλε όλα μαζί σε έναν δίσκο. "Ω, χαρτοπετσέτες!" είπε, βγάζοντας μια στοίβα από αυτές από το συρτάρι.

"Όλα έτοιμα;" ρώτησε ο E-Z.

"Ευχαριστώ, μικρέ", είπε ο Σαμ, καθώς σήκωνε τον δίσκο με τα φαγητά και τα ποτά. Πήρε το δρόμο για το σαλόνι με τον ανιψιό του να τον ακολουθεί από πίσω. Ο Σαμ έβαλε τα πάντα στο τραπέζι και μετά πετάχτηκε πάνω λέγοντας: "Πιάτα για τα πλάγια!" και έφυγε από το δωμάτιο, επιστρέφοντας λίγο αργότερα με τα εν λόγω αντικείμενα.

Ο E-Z έριξε μια ματιά προς την κατεύθυνση της Λίας όταν ήπιε το ποτό του. Την έβλεπε ακόμα σαν μικρό κορίτσι, παρόλο που δεν ήταν πια. Τα μαλλιά της ήταν μακρύτερα.

Η μαμά της Λία φαινόταν ακόμα πιο αμήχανη από ό,τι ο θείος Σαμ. Έπαιζε με ένα κράκερ, αλλά δεν το δάγκωσε. Μετακίνησε το ποτήρι με το ποτό μπρος-πίσω αλλά δεν ήπιε από αυτό. Κοιτούσε προς την κατεύθυνση του θείου Σαμ κάθε τόσο, αλλά όχι για πολύ. Στη συνέχεια αναστέναξε πολύ δυνατά και ξαναγύρισε να παίζει με το φαγητό της.

"Πώς ήταν η πτήση σας;" ρώτησε ο E-Z.

"Ήταν εύκολη-εύκολη σε σύγκριση με την πτήση μαζί σου", είπε η Λία. Γέλασε και το αναψυκτικό παραλίγο να βγει από τη μύτη της. Σύντομα γελούσαν όλοι και ένιωθαν πιο άνετα.

Ο Άλφρεντ κουβέντιαζε ελεύθερα, γνωρίζοντας ότι μόνο η Λία και ο Ε-Ζ μπορούσαν να τον καταλάβουν. "Τώρα είμαστε μαζί, οι Τρεις. Όπως ήταν γραφτό να γίνει".

Η Λία και ο Ε-Ζ αντάλλαξαν ματιές.

Ο Άλφρεντ συνέχισε. "Αναρωτιέμαι συνέχεια γιατί μας έφεραν μαζί. Ε-Ζ μπορείς να σώζεις ανθρώπους και είσαι σούπερ-ντούπερ δυνατή, συν το ότι μπορείς να πετάξεις και το ίδιο και η καρέκλα σου. Λία, οι δυνάμεις σου βρίσκονται στην όρασή σου. Μπορείς να διαβάζεις σκέψεις. Από όσα μου είπε ο Ε-Ζ έχεις τις δυνάμεις του φωτός και μπορείς να σταματήσεις τον χρόνο.

"Εγώ, μπορώ να ταξιδεύω, να πετάω στον ουρανό και μερικές φορές μπορώ να καταλάβω πότε θα συμβούν πράγματα πριν συμβούν. Μπορώ επίσης να διαβάζω σκέψεις, όχι πάντα. Επίσης, οι περισσότεροι άνθρωποι αγαπούν τους κύκνους. Κάποιοι λένε ότι είμαστε αγγελικοί. Υπάρχουν ακόμη και εκείνοι που πιστεύουν ότι οι κύκνοι έχουν τη δύναμη να μεταμορφώνουν τους ανθρώπους σε αγγέλους. Δεν ξέρω αν αυτό είναι αλήθεια. Εγώ, ο ίδιος, μπορώ να βοηθήσω όλα τα ζωντανά, αναπνέοντα πράγματα να θεραπευτούν".

Το τελευταίο μέρος ήταν καινούργιο για τον Ε-Ζ. Ήθελε να μάθει περισσότερα.

Ο Άλφρεντ προθυμοποιήθηκε: "Η παράδοση είναι το πρώτο βήμα".

Ο Ε-Ζ και η Lia χάθηκαν σε σκέψεις σχετικά με την εξομολόγηση του Alfred.

"Τι κάνουμε τώρα;" ρώτησε η Λία.

"Κάθε ομάδα χρειάζεται έναν ηγέτη, έναν αρχηγό. Εγώ προτείνω τον Ε-Ζ", είπε ο Άλφρεντ.

"Υποστηρίζω την υποψηφιότητα", είπε η Λία.

Η Λία και ο Άλφρεντ σήκωσαν τα ποτήρια τους στην υγεία του E-Z. Ο θείος Σαμ και η μαμά της Λίας, η Σαμάνθα, συμμετείχαν στην πρόποση. Αν και δεν είχαν ιδέα γιατί όλοι μαζί έκαναν πρόποση.

Ο E-Z τους ευχαρίστησε όλους. Αλλά μέσα του αναρωτιόταν πώς θα λειτουργούσαν όλα αυτά. Πώς, επρόκειτο να οδηγήσει ένα μικρό κορίτσι και έναν σαλπιγκτή κύκνο; Πώς θα τους κρατούσε ασφαλείς και μακριά από κινδύνους;

Ο θείος Σαμ και η Σαμάνθα προσφέρθηκαν να καθαρίσουν, ενώ το τρίο επέστρεψε στο σαλόνι.

"Θα είναι μια καλή ευκαιρία για να γνωριστούν λίγο καλύτερα", είπε ο Άλφρεντ.

"Ναι, η μητέρα δεν έχει ξαναγίνει τόσο νευρική. Με τη δουλειά της, συναντάει πολύ κόσμο και τους μιλάει, ακόμα και σε τελείως ξένους, σαν να τους ήξερε πάντα. Είναι ένα από τα μυστικά της επιτυχίας της, νομίζω. Με τον Σαμ όμως, είναι ήσυχη σαν ποντίκι και νευρική".

"Ίσως φταίει το τζετ λαγκ", πρότεινε ο E-Z.

Ο Άλφρεντ γέλασε. "Όχι, έλκονται ο ένας από τον άλλον. Είστε και οι δύο πολύ νέοι για να το καταλάβετε, αλλά υπήρχε μια αύρα στον αέρα".

"Αλήθεια, η μαμά μου είναι ερωτευμένη με τον Σαμ;"

"Και ο θείος Σαμ ήταν αμήχανος - αλλά δεν συναντάει πολλά κορίτσια αυτές τις μέρες, αφού δουλεύει από το σπίτι και περνάει τον περισσότερο χρόνο του βοηθώντας με. Ψηφίζω, αλλάζουμε θέμα".

"Κι εγώ", είπε η Λία.

"Εσείς οι δύο δεν έχετε καθόλου πλάκα".

"Νομίζω ότι ίσως ήρθε η ώρα να καλέσουμε την Έριελ", είπε ο E-Z. "Πρέπει να είναι αυτός που μας έφερε όλους μαζί. Πρέπει να μας ενημερώσει για το σχέδιο. Να ξέρουμε τι πρόκειται να περιμένει από εμάς και πότε".

"Ποιος είναι ο Έριελ;" ρώτησε η Λία. "Θυμάμαι ότι με ρώτησες πριν αν τον ξέρω".

"Είναι ένας Αρχάγγελος και είναι ο μέντορας των δοκιμασιών μου. Λοιπόν, τις τελευταίες τουλάχιστον".

"Ο άγγελός μου, αυτός που μου έδωσε το χάρισμα της όρασης με το χέρι, ονομάζεται Haniel. Είναι κι αυτή αρχάγγελος. Είναι ο φροντιστής της γης".

Αυτό εξέπληξε τον E-Z. Αν όλοι εργάζονταν για τους δικούς τους αγγέλους, τότε γιατί τους έφεραν μαζί; Ήταν ο ένας άγγελος πιο ισχυρός από τον άλλο; Ποιος ήταν το αφεντικό άγγελος; Ποιος απαντούσε σε ποιον;

"Σίγουρα θα ήθελα να μάθω τι συμβαίνει", είπε ο Άλφρεντ.

"Το μόνο που ξέρω", είπε η Λία, "είναι ότι μετά το ατύχημα με ρώτησαν αν θα ήμουν ένας από τους τρεις. Και τώρα, ορίστε, εδώ είμαστε".

Ο θείος Σαμ και η Σαμάνθα μπήκαν στο δωμάτιο. Κουβέντιασαν για λίγο ακόμα μαζί, μέχρι που η Σαμάνθα που ήταν κουρασμένη από την πτήση πήγε στο δωμάτιό της. Ο θείος Σαμ πήγε επίσης στο δωμάτιό του.

"Ας πάμε στο δωμάτιό μου να μιλήσουμε", είπε ο E-Z.

Η Λία και ο Άλφρεντ ακολούθησαν. Μετά από μερικές ώρες συζήτησης, το τρίο συνειδητοποίησε ότι είχε πολλές ερωτήσεις αλλά λίγες απαντήσεις. Η Λία πήγε στο δωμάτιό της, το οποίο μοιραζόταν με τη μητέρα της. Ο Άλφρεντ κοιμήθηκε στην άκρη του κρεβατιού του E-Z. Ο E-Z ροχάλιζε. Αύριο ήταν μια άλλη μέρα - τότε θα τα έβρισκαν όλα.

ΚΕΦΑΛΑΙΟ 13

Τ Ο ΕΠΟΜΕΝΟ ΠΡΩΙ Η Λία μετέφερε μπολ με δημητριακά στον πίσω κήπο. Ο ήλιος ανέβαινε στον ουρανό, ήταν μια μέρα χωρίς σύννεφα και πλησίαζε στις 10 π.μ. Ο Άλφρεντ μασούλησε στο γρασίδι κοντά στο μονοπάτι.

Η Λία έδωσε στον E-Z το μπολ του, στη συνέχεια κάθισε κάτω από την ομπρέλα στην αυλή και πήρε μια κουταλιά Cornflakes.

"Τα κορνφλέικς της Βόρειας Αμερικής έχουν διαφορετική γεύση από αυτά που έχουμε στην Ολλανδία".

"Ποια είναι η διαφορά;" ρώτησε ο E-Z.

"Όλα εδώ έχουν πιο γλυκιά γεύση".

"Έχω ακούσει ότι χρησιμοποιούν διαφορετικές συνταγές σε διαφορετικές χώρες. Θέλεις κάτι άλλς;" Εκείνη αρνήθηκε με ένα κούνημα του κεφαλιού. "Δεν μπορούσα να κοιμηθώ χθες το βράδυ", είπε ο E-Z, παίρνοντας άλλη μια κουταλιά Captain Crunch.

"Συγγνώμη, ροχάλιζα πολύ;" ρώτησε ο Άλφρεντ καθώς έσπρωχνε το πρόσωπό του στο δροσερό γρασίδι.

"Όχι, ήσουν μια χαρά. Είχα πολλά στο μυαλό μου. Θέλω να πω, είμαστε όλοι εδώ. Οι τρεις - κι εγώ έχω καιρό να κάνω δίκη... Από τότε που υποβιβάστηκαν ο Χατζ και η Ρέικι, δεν ξέρω τι συμβαίνει. Μετα την τελευταία μάχη με την Eriel - την οποία κέρδισα παρεμπιπτόντως - δεν έχω ακούσει τίποτα από την Eriel. Αυτό με αγχώνει. Αναρωτιέμαι τι ονειρεύεται για να κάνει τη ζωή μου δυστυχισμένη".

Ο Άλφρεντ κουνήθηκε πιο μακριά στον κήπο, καθώς ένας μονόκερος προσγειώθηκε στο γρασίδι.

"Στις υπηρεσίες σας", είπε η Μικρή Ντόριτ.

Ο μονόκερος χούφτωσε τη Λία, ενώ εκείνη στάθηκε και τον φίλησε στο μέτωπο.

Από πάνω τους άρχισε μια μπλε γραμμή ουρανογραφίας. Έγραφε τις λέξεις:

ΑΚΟΛΟΥΘΗΣΤΕ ΜΕ.

Η καρέκλα του E-Z σηκώθηκε, "'Ελα!" φώναξε.

Η Μικρή Ντόριτ έσκυψε, επιτρέποντας στη Λία να την καβαλήσει.

Ο Άλφρεντ χτύπησε τα φτερά του και ενώθηκε με τους άλλους.

"Καμιά ιδέα για το πού πάμε;" ρώτησε ο Άλφρεντ.

"Το μόνο που ξέρω είναι ότι πρέπει να βιαστούμε! Οι δονήσεις αυξάνονται, άρα πρέπει να είμαστε κοντά".

"Κοιτάξτε μπροστά", φώναξε η Λία. "Νομίζω ότι μας χρειάζονται στο λούνα παρκ".

Αμέσως, έγινε φανερό στον E-Z πώς τους χρειάζονταν. Το τρενάκι του λούνα παρκ είχε εκτροχιαστεί. Τα βαγόνια κρέμονταν μισά πάνω και μισά έξω από τις ράγες. Και οι επιβάτες όλων των ηλικιών ούρλιαζαν. Ένα παιδί κρεμόταν τόσο επισφαλώς με τα πόδια του πάνω από το πλάι του αμαξιδίου που ήταν σαφές ότι θα έπεφτε πρώτο.

"Θα αρπάξουμε το παιδί", είπε η Λία, παίρνοντας φόρα. Αυτή και η Μικρή Ντόριτ πήγαν κατευθείαν προς το αγόρι. Εκείνος το άφησε, έπεσε και προσγειώθηκε με ασφάλεια μπροστά από τη Λία πάνω στον μονόκερο.

"Σ' ευχαριστώ", είπε το αγόρι. "Είναι όντως μονόκερος ή ονειρεύομαι;"

"Πραγματικά είναι", είπε η Λία. "Το όνομά της είναι Μικρή Ντόριτ".

"Η μαμά μου έχει ένα βιβλίο με αυτό το όνομα. Νομίζω ότι είναι του Καρόλου Ντίκενς".

"Σωστά", είπε η Λία.

"Υπάρχουν μονόκεροι στη Μικρή Ντόριτ; Αν ναι, θα πρέπει να το διαβάσω!"

"Δεν μπορώ να πω με σιγουριά", είπε η Λία. "Αλλά αν το ανακαλύψεις, ενημέρωσέ με".

Ο E-Z άρπαξε ένα-ένα τα αυτοκίνητα που κρέμονταν από πάνω του. Χρειάστηκε λίγη προσπάθεια για να ισορροπήσει, έμοιαζε λίγο με σλίνκι που γέρνει όλο προς μια κατεύθυνση στην αρχή. Αλλά η εμπειρία του με το αεροπλάνο τον βοήθησε και τον ενέπνευσε καθώς σήκωνε τα αυτοκίνητα πίσω στις ράγες. Τα κράτησε σταθερά μέχρι να μπουν όλοι οι επιβάτες με ασφάλεια μέσα.

Χάρη στη βοήθεια του Άλφρεντ, η διαδικασία αυτή ήταν ομαλή. Ο Άλφρεντ, χρησιμοποιώντας τα φτερά του, το ράμφος του και το απόλυτο μέγεθός του, κατάφερε να τους μοχλεύσει προς την ασφάλεια.

"Είναι όλοι καλά;" φώναξε ο E-Z για να τον χειροκροτήσουν όλοι οι επιβάτες.

Η εργασία ολοκληρώθηκε με επιτυχία και ο Άλφρεντ πέταξε μέχρι το σημείο όπου βρίσκονταν η Λία και οι υπόλοιποι. Ήταν μια εξαιρετική τοποθεσία για παρατήρηση.

"Μπορούμε να κατεβάσουμε το αγόρι τώρα;" ρώτησε η Λία.

Ο E-Z της σήκωσε τον αντίχειρα ψηλά.

Από κάτω, ένας γερανός μεταφέρθηκε με σκοπό να σηκωθεί για τη διάσωση. Δεν ήταν ακόμα ούτε κατά διάνοια έτοιμος. Παρακολουθούσε τους εργάτες που στριφογύριζαν με τα κίτρινα προστατευτικά καπέλα τους.

Ο E-Z σφύριξε στον τύπο που χειριζόταν το τρενάκι του τρόμου για να το ξεκινήσει.

Ο χειριστής του τρενάκι ξεκίνησε ξανά τη μηχανή. Στην αρχή τα βαγόνια πήγαιναν λίγο μπροστά και μετά σταμάτησαν. Οι επιβάτες ούρλιαζαν-φοβούμενοι ότι θα εκτροχιαζόταν ξανά. Κάποιοι κρατούσαν το λαιμό τους, ο οποίος είχε τραυματιστεί στο αρχικό συμβάν.

Ο E-Z τοποθέτησε την αναπηρική του καρέκλα στο μπροστινό μέρος των βαγονιών για να παρατηρήσει ότι η θέση τους δεν άλλαξε. Παρατήρησε ότι ο άνεμος είχε δυναμώσει, καθώς τα μαλλιά των επιβατών παρασύρονταν μέσα στα βαγόνια. Ένας ηλικιωμένος έχασε το καπέλο του μπέιζμπολ των LA Dodgers. Όλοι παρακολουθούσαν καθώς έπεφτε στο έδαφος.

"Δοκίμασε ξανά", φώναξε ο E-Z, ελπίζοντας για το καλύτερο, αλλά σκεπτόμενος ένα Σχέδιο Β για κάθε ενδεχόμενο.

Ο χειριστής ανέβασε τον κινητήρα. Για άλλη μια φορά, το τρενάκι κινήθηκε προς τα εμπρός. Αυτή τη φορά λίγο πιο πέρα, αλλά και πάλι κύλησε μέχρι την πλήρη στάση.

Ο E-Z φώναξε εντολές στη Μικρή Ντόριτ: "Σε παρακαλώ, βάλε τη Λία στο έδαφος. Στη συνέχεια, πιάσε μερικές αλυσίδες με γάντζους και στις δύο άκρες και φέρε τες σε μένα".

Ο μονόκερος έγνεψε, κατεβαίνοντας υπό τα "ωχ" και "αχ" του πλήθους που είχε συγκεντρωθεί από κάτω. Ένας τύπος προσπάθησε να την αρπάξει και να πιάσει μια βόλτα, εκείνη τον έσπρωξε μακριά με τη μύτη της και η αστυνομία κινήθηκε για να αποκλείσει την περιοχή.

"Εδώ!" είπε ένας εργάτης οικοδομών. Είχε ακούσει τι ζητούσε η E-Z. Τοποθέτησε ένα μέρος της αλυσίδας στο στόμα της Little Dorrit και έβαλε την υπόλοιπη γύρω από το λαιμό της.

"Δεν είναι πολύ βαριά;" ρώτησε, καθώς η Μικρή Ντόριτ απογειώθηκε χωρίς κανένα πρόβλημα και έφτασε με φτερά μέχρι το σημείο όπου ο Άλφρεντ περίμενε τώρα στο πλευρό του E-Z.

Ο Άλφρεντ χρησιμοποιώντας το ράμφος του, έβαλε τον γάντζο στο μπροστινό μέρος του βαγονιού του τρενάκι του λούνα παρκ. Το ασφάλισε στη θέση του και το προσάρμοσε στην αναπηρική καρέκλα του E-Z.

"Παρακαλούμε παραμείνετε καθιστοί", φώναξε ο E-Z. "Θα σε κατεβάσω, αργά αλλά σταθερά. Προσπαθήστε να μη μετακινείστε πολύ, θα ήθελα το βάρος να είναι σταθερά τοποθετημένο. Με το τρία, πάμε να κυλήσουμε", είπε. "Ένα, δύο, τρία." Τράβηξε, δίνοντας ό,τι είχε και δεν είχε, και το αυτοκίνητο κύλησε μαζί του. Το κατέβασμα ήταν εύκολο, το ανέβασμα, έπρεπε να διασφαλίσει ότι το καρότσι δεν θα έπαιρνε μεγάλη ταχύτητα και δεν θα ξεκολλούσε ξανά. Η Μικρή Ντόριτ και ο Άλφρεντ πετούσαν δίπλα στο αυτοκίνητο, έτοιμοι να δράσουν αν κάτι πήγαινε στραβά.

Η Λία ήταν τόσο φοβισμένη, νευρική και ενθουσιασμένη.

"Μπορείς να τα καταφέρεις, E-Z!" φώναξε, ξεχνώντας ότι μπορούσε να πει τις λέξεις στο μυαλό της και εκείνος θα τις άκουγε.

"Ευχαριστώ", είπε, διατηρώντας τον ρυθμό αργό και σταθερό. Παρόλο που ο E-Z ήταν κουρασμένος, έπρεπε να ολοκληρώσει το έργο που είχε αναλάβει. Καθώς το αυτοκίνητο έστριψε στη γωνία και σταμάτησε εντελώς, μπήκε ξανά μέσα στο τούνελ. Πίσω εκεί όπου είχε ξεκινήσει το ταξίδι του.

"Σας ευχαριστώ!" φώναξε ο χειριστής.

Πυροσβέστες, παραϊατρικοί και νοσηλευτές ετοιμάστηκαν για την επέλαση των επιβατών. Αποβιβάζονταν ταυτόχρονα.

"E-Z! E-Z! E-Z!", φώναζε το πλήθος, με τα τηλέφωνα σηκωμένα να βιντεοσκοπούν το όλο περιστατικό.

"Λέτε να έχουμε χρόνο να πάρουμε λίγο μαλλί της γριάς;" ρώτησε η Λία.

"Και καραμελωμένο καλαμπόκι;" Είπε ο Άλφρεντ. "Δεν είμαι σίγουρη αν θα μου αρέσει, αλλά είμαι πρόθυμη να το δοκιμάσω!"

"Βέβαια", είπε ο E-Z, "θα σου φέρω και τα δύο, μην ανησυχείς! Μπορεί να πάρω και ένα Candy Apple".

Καθώς πήγε να κάνει τις αγορές, παρατήρησε ότι είχαν φτάσει οι δημοσιογράφοι. Είχαν συγκεντρωθεί γύρω από κάποιον που ήταν πολύ ψηλός με κατάμαυρα μαλλιά. Ο άνδρας κρατούσε μπροστά του ένα καπέλο και έμοιαζε με τον Αβραάμ Λίνκολν. Με μια πιο προσεκτική ματιά συνειδητοποίησε ότι ήταν ο Eriel μεταμφιεσμένος. Πλησίασε για να ακούσει.

"Ναι, εγώ είμαι αυτός που έφερε κοντά αυτή τη δυναμική τριάδα. Ο αρχηγός είναι ο Ε-Ζ Ντίκενς και είναι δεκατριών ετών και σούπερ σταρ. Εκτός του ότι είναι το πιο έμπειρο μέλος των Τριών, είναι και ο αρχηγός. Όπως πρέπει να έχετε παρατηρήσει, μπορεί να διαχειριστεί σχεδόν τα πάντα. Είναι ένα σπουδαίο παιδί!"

Ο Ε-Ζ ένιωθε τα μάγουλά του να ζεσταίνονται.

"Τι γίνεται με το κορίτσι και τον μονόκερο;" φώναξε ένας δημοσιογράφος.

"Το όνομά της είναι Λία, και αυτό ήταν το πρώτο της εγχείρημα στον κόσμο των υπερηρώων. Ο μονόκερός της είναι η Μικρή Ντόριτ, και οι δυο τους είναι μια καταπληκτική ομάδα. Έσωσε εκείνο το παλικάρι", έπιασε το αγόρι. Τον έβαλε μπροστά και στο κέντρο για τις κάμερες.

Όταν όλα τα μάτια ήταν στραμμένα πάνω του, ολοκλήρωσε τη φράση του. "Με ευκολία. Η Λία και η Μικρή Ντόριτ είναι υπέροχες προσθήκες στην ομάδα και θα είναι τεράστια βοήθεια για τον Ε-Ζ σε όλες τις μελλοντικές του προσπάθειες".

"Πώς ήταν;" ρώτησε ένας δημοσιογράφος το αγόρι.

"Η Λία ήταν πολύ καλή", είπε το νεαρό αγόρι.

Η σκοτεινή φιγούρα έσπρωξε το αγόρι μακριά. Ξεσκονίστηκε.

"Ο κύκνος τρομπετίστας ονομάζεται Άλφρεντ. Αυτή ήταν η πρώτη του ευκαιρία να βοηθήσει τον Ε-Ζ. Με γενναιότητα, έθεσε τον εαυτό του σε κίνδυνο. Ο Άλφρεντ είναι άλλο ένα εξαιρετικό μέλος αυτής της ομάδας υπερηρώων των Τριών. Θα τους βλέπετε συχνά στο μέλλον". Δίστασε: "Α, και το όνομά μου είναι Έριελ, σε περίπτωση που θέλετε να με αναφέρετε στο άρθρο σας".

Τώρα ο Ε-Ζ ευχόταν να μην είχε συμφωνήσει να μαζεύει καρναβαλικά κεράσματα. Κούρνιασε, στο πλάι, ελπίζοντας να μην τον προσέξουν.

"Νάτος!" φώναξε κάποιος.

Άλλοι που ήταν στην ουρά πίσω του, τον έσπρωξαν προς το μπροστινό μέρος της ουράς.

"Κερνάει το μαγαζί", είπε ο πωλητής, δίνοντάς του ένα από τα πάντα.

"Σας ευχαριστώ", είπε εκείνος, καθώς σηκωνόταν.

"Αυτός είναι! Το αγόρι με το αναπηρικό καροτσάκι! Ο ήρωάς μας!" φώναξε κάποιος από κάτω του.

"Να 'τος, βγάλτε του μια φωτογραφία".

"Ελάτε πίσω για μια selfie, παρακαλώ!"

Ο E-Z έριξε μια ματιά προς το μέρος όπου βρισκόταν ο Έριελ, αλλά τώρα που τον εντόπισαν, κανείς δεν ενδιαφερόταν γι' αυτόν. Το επόμενο πράγμα που κατάλαβε ήταν ότι ο Eriel είχε εξαφανιστεί.

"Πάμε να φύγουμε από εδώ!" αναφώνησε ο E-Z, αναρωτώμενος πού ακριβώς θα έπρεπε να πάνε. Αν πήγαιναν στο σπίτι του, οι δημοσιογράφοι και οι θαυμαστές θα ακολουθούσαν πιθανότατα. Κατά κάποιον τρόπο, του έλειπαν οι μέρες που ο Χατζ και η Ρέικι σκούπιζαν τα μυαλά όλων των εμπλεκομένων - αυτό σίγουρα αποσυμπίεζε τα πράγματα.

Στο δρόμο της επιστροφής, ο E-Z δεν μπορούσε να μην αναρωτηθεί τι σκάρωνε ο Έριελ. Άλλωστε κανείς δεν έπρεπε να γνωρίζει για τις δοκιμασίες του. Ήταν πολύ παράξενο - αλλά ήταν πολύ εξαντλημένος για να μιλήσει γι' αυτό με τους φίλους του. Αντ' αυτού, αναρωτήθηκε γιατί δεν ήταν πλέον σημαντικό να κρατάει κρυφές τις δοκιμασίες του - και πώς θα άλλαζε τα πράγματα. Ήταν καλό που τα φτερά του δεν έκαιγαν πια, και η καρέκλα του δεν φαινόταν να ενδιαφέρεται να πιει αίμα.

"Λοιπόν, αυτό ήταν αρκετά εύκολο", είπε ο Άλφρεντ.

Η Λία γέλασε: "Και ήταν κάπως διασκεδαστικό να σε βλέπω σε δράση E-Z".

"'Ει, κι εγώ τι θα γίνει, βοήθησα κι εγώ!"

"Σίγουρα βοήθησες", είπε ο E-Z. "Και η Μικρή Ντόριτ, σε ευχαριστώ! Δεν θα μπορούσα να τα καταφέρω χωρίς εσένα!"

Η Μικρή Ντόριτ γέλασε. "Χαίρομαι που βοήθησα".

"'Ήσουν καταπληκτική!" Είπε η Λία, χαϊδεύοντας τον λαιμό της.

Κάτι όμως τους απασχολούσε. Ήταν προφανές, ότι ο E-Z θα μπορούσε να τα είχε κάνει όλα μόνος του. Δεν χρειαζόταν βοήθεια.

Ο Άλφρεντ ειδικά ένιωθε ότι, ως τρομπετοελίτης κύκνος, έκανε ό,τι μπορούσε. Αλλά δεν ήταν μεγάλη βοήθεια σε αυτού του είδους τη διάσωση. Όχι ότι κάποιος που είχε χέρια θα μπορούσε να βοηθήσει. Είχε καταβάλει την καλύτερη δυνατή προσπάθεια, αλλά ήταν αρκετή; Ήταν η καλύτερη επιλογή για να γίνει μέλος των Τριών;

Η Λία σκεφτόταν ότι η Μικρή Ντόριτ θα μπορούσε να προσγειωθεί κάτω από το αγόρι και να το σώσει χωρίς να είναι εκείνη στην πλάτη του. Ο μονόκερος ήταν έξυπνος και θα μπορούσε να είχε ακολουθήσει το παράδειγμα και τις οδηγίες του E-Z. Ένιωθε ότι είχε κάνει τόσο δρόμο και για ποιο λόγο; Δεν είχε κανένα νόημα.

Επέστρεψαν και πάλι στο σπίτι τους. Παρόλο που είχαν καταφέρει κάτι υπέροχο μαζί, η διάθεσή τους ήταν πεσμένη.

Η Μικρή Ντόριτ έφυγε και πήγε εκεί όπου ζούσε όταν δεν την χρειάζονταν.

Ο E-Z πήγε αμέσως στο γραφείο του όπου έκανε λίγη δουλειά στο βιβλίο του. Ήθελε να επικαιροποιήσει τη λίστα των δοκιμασιών για να δει πού βρισκόταν. Αποφάσισε να τις πληκτρολογήσει όλες ξανά από την αρχή:

1/ έσωσε το κοριτσάκι

2/ έσωσε το αεροπλάνο από τη συντριβή

3/ σταμάτησε τον σκοπευτή στην ταράτσα

4/ σταμάτησε το κορίτσι στο μαγαζί

5/ σταμάτησε τον δράστη έξω από το σπίτι του

6/ μονομάχησε με τον Eriel

7. βγήκε από τη σφαίρα

8/ έσωσε τη Lia

9/ επανέφερε ένα τρενάκι του λούνα παρκ στις ράγες.

Δεν ήταν σίγουρος αν η σωτηρία του θείου Σαμ ήταν δοκιμασία ή ότι. Ο Χατζ και η Ρέικι είχαν σκουπίσει το μυαλό του. Το ένστικτο του E-Z έλεγε ότι η διάσωση του θείου Σαμ δεν ήταν δοκιμασία.

Ξανακάθισε στην καρέκλα του. Σκεφτόταν την επικείμενη προθεσμία του. Έπρεπε να ολοκληρώσει άλλες τρεις δοκιμασίες σε περιορισμένο χρονικό διάστημα. Κατά κάποιο τρόπο, ήθελε να τις τελειώσει, να τελειώσει με αυτές. Από την άλλη, το να τελειώσει με τη δέσμευσή του τον τρόμαζε.

Εν τω μεταξύ, ο Άλφρεντ αποφάσισε να πάει για κολύμπι στη λίμνη.

Ενώ η Λία και η μητέρα της πήγαν μια βόλτα.

✳✳✳

"ΛOIΠÓN, ΠΩΣ ΉΤΑΝ;" ΡΩΤΗΣΕ η Σαμάνθα.

"Ήταν εξαιρετικά συναρπαστικό και τρομακτικό ταυτόχρονα. Ο Ε-Ζ είναι αξιοσημείωτος. Ατρόμητος", εξήγησε η Λία.

"Και ποια ήταν η δική σου συμβολή;"

Γύρισαν στη γωνία και κάθισαν μαζί σε ένα παγκάκι του πάρκου. Παιδιά έπαιζαν, έτρεχαν πάνω κάτω και φώναζαν. Τόσο η μητέρα όσο και η κόρη θυμήθηκαν πώς η Λία συνήθιζε να παίζει έτσι, ανέμελα, όταν ήταν επτά ετών. Τώρα που ήταν δέκα ετών, το ενδιαφέρον της για το παιχνίδι είχε μειωθεί πολύ.

"Σου, σου λείπει;" ρώτησε η Σαμάνθα.

Η Λία χαμογέλασε. "Πάντα ξέρεις τι σκέφτομαι. Δεν ξέρω πραγματικά, αλλά κάποια μέρα σύντομα, θα ήθελα να δοκιμάσω ξανά να χορέψω. Για να δω πώς και αν θα μπορούσα να προσαρμοστώ".

Κάθισαν μαζί και παρακολουθούσαν, χωρίς να πουν τίποτα.

"Όσον αφορά τη συμβολή μου, ένα μικρό αγόρι κρεμόταν από το αυτοκίνητο και χωρίς τη βοήθεια της Μικρής Ντόριτ, ίσως να είχε πέσει".

"Θα μπορούσε;"

"Ναι, νομίζω ότι ο Ε-Ζ θα τον είχε σώσει και μετά θα είχε καταφέρει τα υπόλοιπα, αν δεν ήμασταν εκεί. Έχει συνηθίσει να κάνει τις δοκιμασίες μόνος του".

"Δεν πιστεύεις ότι εσύ ή ο Άλφρεντ ήσασταν απαραίτητοι;"

"Το ότι ήμασταν εκεί για ηθική υποστήριξη ήταν χρήσιμο, δεν ξέρω. Οι αρχάγγελοι μπήκαν σε μεγάλο κόπο για να μας συγκεντρώσουν. Για να μας πετάξουν μέχρι εδώ από την Ολλανδία, το σπίτι μας. Όταν, με βάση αυτή τη δίκη, δεν νομίζω ότι είμαστε απαραίτητοι".

Η Σαμάνθα πήρε το χέρι της κόρης της στο δικό της και σηκώθηκαν από το παγκάκι και γύρισαν προς το σπίτι.

"Νομίζω ότι το να έχεις μια ομάδα, εφεδρική, είναι καλό πράγμα και είμαι σίγουρη ότι ο E-Z το ξέρει και το εκτιμά. Δεν μοιάζει με παιδί που θα μπορούσε να είναι μοναχικός. Έπαιζε μπέιζμπολ, εξακολουθεί να παίζει απ' ό,τι μου λέει ο Σαμ. Ξέρει ότι οι ομάδες λειτουργούν καλά μαζί, αξιοποιώντας τα δυνατά σημεία του κάθε παίκτη. Όσο για σένα, δεν θα ανησυχούσα ότι δεν ήσουν ο πιο κρίσιμος παράγοντας σε αυτή τη δίκη. Και μην υποτιμάς ποτέ την αξία σου".

"Ευχαριστώ, μαμά", είπε η Λία, καθώς έστριψαν στη γωνία για τον δρόμο τους. "Τώρα, ας μιλήσουμε για τον Σαμ. Σου αρέσει πολύ, έτσι δεν είναι;"

Η Σαμάνθα χαμογέλασε αλλά δεν απάντησε.

$$* * *$$

ΤΑΥΤΌΧΡΟΝΑ, Ο ΣΑΜ ΈΛΕΓΧΕ τον Ε-Ζ. "Είναι όλα εντάξει;" ρώτησε, σπρώχνοντας το κεφάλι του στο γραφείο του ανιψιού του.

"Δεν είμαι σίγουρος. Μπορούμε να μιλήσουμε;"

"Φυσικά, μικρέ".

"Κλείσε την πόρτα, σε παρακαλώ".

"Τι συμβαίνει; Δεν πήγε καλά η δοκιμή της πρώτης ομάδας;"

"Πρώτα, θέλω να σε ρωτήσω, τι συμβαίνει με σένα και τη μαμά της Λίας;"

Ο Σαμ ανακάτεψε τα πόδια του και καθάρισε τα γυαλιά του. "Ας μην το κάνουμε αυτό για μένα και τη Σαμάνθα. Αυτό είναι μεταξύ μας".

"Ω, άρα, υπάρχει μια ΗΠΑ, τότε;" χαμογέλασε.

"Άλλαξε θέμα", είπε ο Σαμ.

"Εντάξει τότε, ό,τι πεις εσύ. Όσον αφορά τη δίκη, πήγε καλά, και μη με σκέφτεσαι άσχημα. Δεν το λέω αυτό επειδή είμαι ξεροκέφαλος, αλλά θα μπορούσα να την είχα ολοκληρώσει και χωρίς τους άλλους".

"Πες μου ακριβώς τι συνέβη. Ποια ήταν η αποστολή σου; Και πρέπει να πω ότι αυτό με εκπλήσσει, αφού πάντα ήσουν ομαδικός παίκτης".

"Το ξέρω. Αυτό είναι που με ενοχλεί κι εμένα. Ήταν στο λούνα παρκ. Ένα τρενάκι του λούνα παρκ βγήκε από την πίστα. Το μπροστινό μέρος του κρεμόταν από την άκρη και οι επιβάτες ξεχύνονταν. Μόνο ένας κινδύνευσε πραγματικά - ένα παιδί που το έπιασε η Λία με τη βοήθεια της Μικρής Ντόριτ, του μονόκερου".

"Φαίνεται ότι η διάσωση αυτή ήταν χρήσιμη".

"Ήταν, γιατί το παιδί ήταν εκπρόθεσμο, αλλά ήμουν εκεί και θα μπορούσα να το είχα σώσει. Στη συνέχεια, έβαλα το καρότσι πίσω στη γραμμή και βοήθησα τους άλλους να μπουν μέσα. Ήταν σαν να σταμάτησε ο χρόνος για μένα - οπότε, θα μπορούσα εύκολα να είχα λύσει αυτή την κατάσταση χωρίς τη βοήθεια κανενός".

"Φαίνεται ότι ο Άλφρεντ, δεν σου ήταν πολύ χρήσιμος. Συμπεραίνεις ότι θα μπορούσες να τα καταφέρεις και χωρίς αυτόν;"

Ο E-Z πέρασε τα δάχτυλά του μέσα από τη σκούρα μέση των μαλλιών του. Η αγκαθωτή αίσθηση τον έκανε κατά κάποιο τρόπο να αποφορτιστεί.

"Ο Άλφρεντ βοήθησε. Αλλά εγώ έψαχνα τρόπους για να τον βοηθήσω. Προσπαθεί τόσο σκληρά. Θέλουμε τόσο πολύ να βοηθήσουμε, αλλά ειλικρινά, είναι αρκετά έξυπνος για να ξέρει ότι του έκανα δουλειά. Οπότε, θα μπορούσε να βοηθήσει και δεν αισθάνομαι καλά γι' αυτό".

"Αυτό κάνουν οι ομαδικοί παίκτες. Προσέχουν ο ένας τον άλλον. Βοηθάει ο ένας τον άλλον".

"Το ξέρω, αλλά όταν διακυβεύονται ζωές, είναι στο χέρι μου να σιγουρευτώ ότι κανείς δεν θα πεθάνει. Αν βρίσκω καθήκοντα για τους άλλους για να τους κάνω να νιώθουν ότι τους χρειάζονται είναι μειονέκτημα και όχι βοήθεια". Αναστέναξε βαθιά, κάνοντας κλικ με τα δάχτυλά του στο πληκτρολόγιο του. Ντροπιασμένος, απέφυγε την οπτική επαφή με τον θείο του.

Μετά από μερικά λεπτά σιωπής, ο E-Z επέστρεψε να δουλέψει το βιβλίο του για να αφήσει τον θείο του να σκεφτεί τα πράγματα. Πέρασε από τις λεπτομέρειες των γεγονότων της ημέρας.

Καθώς ενημέρωνε. Αναλύοντας τα πράγματα. Διαλύοντας τη δίκη και συναρμολογώντας την ξανά, είχε μια αποκάλυψη. Αυτό ήταν κάτι που δεν είχε κάνει ποτέ πριν. Θα μπορούσε να συζητήσει το θέμα με την ομάδα του. Θα μπορούσαν να του πουν πώς τα πήγε, να του κάνουν προτάσεις ώστε να βελτιωθεί. Ναι, υπήρχαν πολλά πλεονεκτήματα στο να είσαι ένας από τους τρεις. Ένιωθε χαλαρός και πιο ευτυχισμένος με αυτή τη γνώση.

"Νομίζω ότι πρέπει να δώσεις περισσότερο χρόνο σε αυτή την κατάσταση της ομάδας πριν αποφασίσεις οτιδήποτε. Πρέπει να είναι ωφέλιμο για σένα να ξέρεις ότι ο καθένας έχει τις δικές του ειδικές δυνάμεις, για να σε βοηθήσει. Σε αυτή την κατάσταση, οι ικανότητές σας ήταν στην πρώτη γραμμή. Αυτό δεν σημαίνει ότι θα είναι πάντα έτσι. Τα πράγματα μπορεί να αλλάξουν για την επόμενη εργασία. Όλα συμβαίνουν για κάποιο λόγο".

"Σκέφτεσαι με τον ίδιο τρόπο που σκέφτομαι κι εγώ τώρα. Όλα είναι πάντα καλύτερα αν δεν χρειάζεται να τα αντιμετωπίσεις μόνος σου. Εσύ μου το έμαθες αυτό".

"Πεινάει κανείς άλλος σε αυτό το σπίτι;" φώναξε ο Άλφρεντ καθώς περπατούσε κατά μήκος του διαδρόμου.

Ο Ε-Ζ έσπρωξε την καρέκλα του προς τα πίσω και απάντησε: "Εγώ!"

Ο Σαμ είπε: "Εσύ τι;"

"Α, ο Άλφρεντ ρώτησε αν πεινάει κανείς".

"Κι εγώ!" Ο Σαμ φώναξε.

"Εγώ πεινάω", είπε η Λία. "Τι έχει για δείπνο;"

Η Σαμάνθα πρότεινε να παραγγείλουν πίτσα. Όλοι ζητωκραύγασαν, εκτός από τον Άλφρεντ. Δεν ήταν οπαδός του τυριού με τις χορδές.

Πέρασαν το βράδυ μαζί, γεμίζοντας τα πρόσωπά τους και παρακολουθώντας μια σειρά για ζόμπι.

"Δεν είναι πολύ τρομακτικό για σένα, έτσι δεν είναι Λία;" ρώτησε ο Ε-Ζ,

"Είναι πολύ τρομακτικό για μένα!" απάντησε η Σαμάνθα. Ο Σαμ έβαλε το χέρι του γύρω της, ενώ η Λία γελούσε και κρατούσε το χέρι της μητέρας της.

ΚΕΦΑΛΑΙΟ 14

Νωρίς το επόμενο πρωί ο Άλφρεντ ξύπνησε με μια κραυγή. Αν δεν έχετε ακούσει ποτέ κύκνο να ουρλιάζει, τότε είστε τυχεροί. Ήταν τόσο δυνατή που ξύπνησε τους πάντες.

Ο E-Z προσπάθησε να ηρεμήσει τον Alfred. Ο κύκνος το μόνο που έκανε ήταν να χτυπάει περισσότερο τα φτερά του και να κάνει έναν τρομερό ήχο. Ήταν σαν να τον βασάνιζαν. Είτε αυτό είτε το τέλος του κόσμου!

Ο θείος Σαμ έφτασε για να ελέγξει τι συνέβαινε.

"Είναι ο Άλφρεντ, αλλά μην ανησυχείς. Το αναλαμβάνω εγώ", είπε ο E-Z.

Σύντομα η Λία και η Σαμάνθα ήρθαν να ερευνήσουν. Η Λία έπεισε τη Σαμάνθα να ξανακοιμηθεί.

Η Λία παρέμεινε, για να βοηθήσει τον E-Z να παρηγορήσει τον Άλφρεντ. Ο οποίος πήγε αμέσως στο παράθυρο, το άνοιξε με το ράμφος του και πέταξε έξω στη νύχτα.

Από πάνω τους, ο E-Z και η Lia άκουγαν τα πλεγμένα πόδια του Άλφρεντ να χτυπάνε στην οροφή.

"Τι περιμένετε εσείς οι δύο!" φώναξε. "Πρέπει να φύγουμε - ΤΩΡΑ!"

Η Λία σκαρφάλωσε έξω από το παράθυρο και στάθηκε τρέμοντας στο περβάζι. Περίμενε μέχρι ο E-Z να μπορέσει να μπει στο αναπηρικό καροτσάκι του και να το ελιχθεί σε θέση αιώρησης.

"Περιμένετε, νομίζω ότι ο μονόκερος είναι επιτέλους καθ' οδόν", είπε ο Άλφρεντ. "Γι' αυτό είμαι εδώ πάνω. Για να δω αν θα ερχόταν".

Η Μικρή Ντόριτ προσγειώθηκε, έβαλε τη μύτη της κάτω από τη Λία και την πέταξε στην πλάτη της.

Πέταξαν με τον Άλφρεντ να τους οδηγεί.

"Πιο σιγά!" φώναξε ο E-Z. Ο Άλφρεντ τον αγνόησε. Συνέχισε, παίρνοντας ύψος και ταχύτητα. Τα φτερά της καρέκλας του E-Z άρχισαν να χτυπάνε όπως και τα φτερά του αγγέλου του. Έπρεπε να δουλέψει γρήγορα για να κρατήσει τον Άλφρεντ στο οπτικό του πεδίο.

Η Λία ανατρίχιασε. "Μακάρι να είχα ένα πουλόβερ μαζί μου".

"Αγκαλιάσου στο λαιμό μου", είπε η Μικρή Ντόριτ. "Θα σε κρατήσω ζεστή".

Ο E-Z ανέβασε το ρυθμό, πλησιάζοντας, και μετά συνειδητοποίησε ότι ο Άλφρεντ έκοβε ταχύτητα. Ή τουλάχιστον έτσι νόμιζε. Αντ' αυτού, είδε ένα θέαμα που δεν θα έσβηνε ποτέ από το μυαλό του. Ο Άλφρεντ είχε παγώσει στον αέρα, με τα φτερά και τα πόδια του τεντωμένα. Σαν να μοντελοποιούνταν σαν X.

Στη συνέχεια, ολόκληρο το σώμα του άρχισε να τρέμει, το οποίο εξελίχθηκε σε τρέμουλο. Φαινόταν σαν να τον έπιανε ηλεκτροπληξία. Και το πρόσωπό του, η έκφραση αφόρητου πόνου πάνω του, έφερε δάκρυα στα μάτια των φίλων του.

"Τι του συμβαίνει;" ρώτησε η Λία. "Δεν μπορώ να το βλέπω πια. Απλά δεν μπορώ", έκλαιγε με λυγμούς.

"Είναι σαν να τον σοκάρουν. Ποιος θα έκανε κάτι τέτοιο;" Καθώς το έλεγε, το ήξερε. Μόνο η Έριελ θα μπορούσε να είναι τόσο σκληρή. Η Έριελ τους καλούσε. Χρησιμοποιώντας αυτή την τεχνική ηλεκτροπληξίας για να τους κάνει να ακολουθήσουν τον φίλο τους τον Άλφρεντ. Μόνο, τι θα γινόταν αν δεν επιβίωνε από τα ηλεκτροσόκ; Καθώς το έλεγε αυτό, μια χούφτα φτερά του Άλφρεντ αποσυνδέθηκαν από το σώμα του και αιωρήθηκαν στον αέρα. Σταμάτησε να τρέμει και άρχισε να πετάει. Πάνω από τον ώμο του είπε: "'Ελα, προχώρα πριν με χτυπήσει ξανά".

"Είσαι καλά;" ρώτησε η Λία.

"Αυτό ήταν το τρίτο, και κάθε φορά γίνεται χειρότερο. Πρέπει να πάμε εκεί που μας θέλουν και γρήγορα. Δεν ξέρω αν μπορώ να ζήσω άλλο ένα - όχι χειρότερο από το προηγούμενο. Ήταν πολύ άσχημο".

Συνέχισαν την πτήση τους, κουβεντιάζοντας καθώς προχωρούσαν.

"Συγγνώμη που τοις ξύπνησα όλους", είπε ο Άλφρεντ τώρα που οι κραδασμοί είχαν σταματήσει.

"Δεν έφταιγες εσύ." Είπε ο E-Z. "Είμαι σίγουρος ότι ξέρω ποιος έφταιγε - και όταν τον δούμε, θα του δώσω να καταλάβει γιατί".

"Τι εννοείς;" ρώτησε η Λία, αγκαλιάζοντας τον λαιμό της Μικρής Ντόριτ. Ήταν τόσο σκοτεινά και κρύα- δεν μπορούσε να σταματήσει να τρέμει.

Ο Άλφρεντ είπε: "Μας κάλεσαν στέλνοντας ηλεκτρικά σοκ σε όλο μου το σώμα. Ήταν σαν τα φτερά μου να είχαν πάρει φωτιά από μέσα προς τα έξω. Τόσο αγενές. Τόσο πολύ αγενές και για ένα λεπτό, νόμιζα ότι βρισκόμουν πάλι στο μεταξύ και στο μεταξύ".

Ολόκληρο το σώμα του κύκνου του έτρεμε στη σκέψη. "Θα δώσω σε όποιον το έκανε αυτό αυτό που του αξίζει όταν τον δω κιόλας!"

Ο Άλφρεντ συνέχισε να πετάει μπροστά από τους άλλους. "Προηγουμένως η Άριελ ψιθύρισε στο αυτί μου για να με ξυπνήσει. Μετά συζητούσαμε μαζί ένα σχέδιο. Το έκανε αυτό ακόμα και όταν ήμουν στο μεταξύ και στο μεταξύ. Ήταν πάντα ευγενική και ευγενική μαζί μου. Αυτή η κλήση ήταν διαφορετική".

"Ακούγεται σαν να το έκανε η Έριελ", παραδέχτηκε ο E-Z. "Δεν είναι πολύ διακριτικός και μπορεί να γίνει λίγο μελοδραματικός και αρκετά αναίσθητος. Για να μην αναφέρω ότι έχει μια αρρωστημένη αίσθηση του χιούμορ".

"Λίγο μελοδραματικός, δεν ξύνει καν την επιφάνεια", είπε ο Άλφρεντ.

"Θα πρέπει να μας πεις περισσότερα γι' αυτό το ενδιάμεσο κάποια στιγμή. Το όνομα ακούγεται χαριτωμένο, αλλά έχω την αίσθηση ότι είναι οξύμωρο", είπε ο E-Z.

"Δεν μου αρέσει να μιλάω γι' αυτό", απάντησε ο Άλφρεντ.

"Ανυπομονώ πραγματικά να γνωρίσω αυτό το πρόσωπο, την Έριελ. ΟΧΙ". Η Λία εξομολογήθηκε. "Είναι σαν να ανυπομονώ να συναντήσω τον Βόλντεμορτ. Η φήμη του προηγείται".

"Α, είσαι φαν του Χάρι Πότερ, λοιπόν;" Είπε ο Άλφρεντ.

"Σίγουρα", παραδέχτηκε η Λία.

Τα αστέρια στον ουρανό από πάνω έστειλαν φανταστική ζέστη. Παρόλα αυτά, έτρεμαν απροετοίμαστοι στον νυχτερινό αέρα.

"Κοντεύουμε να φτάσουμε;" ρώτησε ο Ε-Ζ.

"Δεν ξέρω σίγουρα", είπε ο Άλφρεντ. "Το σοκ δεν έλεγε πού μας κάλεσαν, και δεν μπορώ να πιάσω καμία δόνηση στον αέρα. Το μόνο πράγμα που θα υποδείξει ότι δεν κάνουμε αυτό που αναμένεται από εμάς, είναι ένα άλλο σοκ. Δυστυχώς".

"Δεν θέλουμε να συμβεί κάτι τέτοιο. Ας επιταχύνουμε το ρυθμό".

"Φαίνεται όμως ότι πλησιάζουμε." Ο Άλφρεντ σταμάτησε στον αέρα- τα φτερά του ήταν πλήρως εκτεταμένα. "Ωχ, όχι!" ψιθύρισε, περιμένοντας το νέο σοκ να χτυπήσει. Περίμενε και περίμενε, αλλά τίποτα δεν συνέβη. "Υποθέτω ότι είμαστε σχεδόν..."

Το σώμα του κύκνου δεν έτρεμε και δεν κουνιόταν μόνο αυτή τη φορά. Το σώμα του Άλφρεντ κύλησε ξανά και ξανά. Σαν να έκανε τούμπες στον ουρανό.

Χαλαρά φτερά πετούσαν γύρω του, χορεύοντας στον άνεμο, καθώς ο κύκνος έπεφτε σε ελεύθερη πτώση.

Ο Ε-Ζ πέταξε κάτω από τον τρομπέτα κύκνο και τον έπιασε. "Άλφρεντ; Άλφρεντ;" Ο φτωχός κύκνος είχε λιποθυμήσει. "Έριελ! Εσύ! Μεγάλε τριχωτέ γύπα!" φώναξε ο Ε-Ζ, σηκώνοντας τη γροθιά του προς τον ουρανό. "Δεν χρειάζεται να σκοτώσεις τον Άλφρεντ. Πες μας πού βρίσκεσαι και θα έρθουμε εκεί, αλλά μόνο αν συμφωνήσεις να το κόψεις με τα ηλεκτρικά φορτία. Είναι βάρβαρο. Είναι ένας κύκνος για όνομα του Θεού. Δώστε του μια ευκαιρία".

"Αυτό που είπε", απάντησε η Λία, με τις ανοιχτές παλάμες της στραμμένες προς τον ουρανό.

Για ένα δευτερόλεπτο, αιωρήθηκαν, ακόμα στη θέση τους.

Τότε ένα σοκ χτύπησε την αναπηρική καρέκλα. Μετά χτύπησε τον Ντόριτ, τον μονόκερο. Και όλοι έπεσαν σε ελεύθερη πτώση.

Το γέλιο της Έριελ γέμισε τον αέρα γύρω τους. Ο κόσμος ήταν το Sensurround του και κορόιδευε τους Τρεις όπως κανείς άλλος δεν μπορούσε. Ή θα το έκανε.

ΚΕΦΑΛΑΙΟ 15

ΣΥΝΕΧΙΣΑΝ ΝΑ ΠΕΦΤΟΥΝ ΓΙΑ αρκετό καιρό. Κανένας από αυτούς δεν είχε έλεγχο των ειδικών δυνάμεων ή ιδιοτήτων του.

Περίμεναν σχεδόν ότι τα σώματά τους θα διασκορπίζονταν στο πεζοδρόμιο από κάτω. Το πεζοδρόμιο σηκωνόταν για να τους υποδεχτεί.

Ξαφνικά, η κάθοδος τελείωσε. Ήταν σαν να ήταν όλοι τους προσκολλημένοι σε κάποιον αόρατο μαριονετοπαίχτη.

Μετά από λίγα δευτερόλεπτα, η κίνηση ξεκίνησε ξανά Αλλά αυτή τη φορά ήταν ήπια.

Τους καθοδηγούσε, μέχρι να μπορέσουν να πέσουν με ασφάλεια στα πόδια των αρχαγγέλων Έριελ, Άριελ και Χάνιελ.

"Είχατε καλό ταξίδι;" ρώτησε η Έριελ. Εκείνος βροντοφώναξε από τα γέλια. Οι σύντροφοί του κοιτούσαν χωρίς να γελούν ή να μιλούν.

Ο Άλφρεντ, ξύπνιος πια, πέταξε και προσγειώθηκε, ακολουθούμενος από τον Μικρό Ντόριτ τον Μονόκερο που κουβαλούσε τη Λία.

Ο μονόκερος υποκλίθηκε στους υπόλοιπους καλεσμένους και στη συνέχεια αποσύρθηκε στην άλλη άκρη της αίθουσας.

Ο Έριελ ήταν ο ψηλότερος από τους άλλους τρεις και στεκόταν με τα χέρια στους γοφούς του, φροντίζοντας να μην υπάρχει καμία αμφιβολία για το ποιος ήταν υπεύθυνος.

Ο Άριελ αντίθετα ήταν σαν νεράιδα.

Ο Haniel ήταν αγαλματένιος, εκπέμποντας ομορφιά.

Ο Έριελ βγήκε μπροστά, ανασηκώθηκε από το έδαφος, ώστε να βρίσκεται από πάνω τους. Φώναξε: 'Σας πήρε αρκετό καιρό να έρθετε εδώ! Στο μέλλον, όταν διατάξω την παρουσία σας, θα είστε εδώ αμέσως!"

Ο Haniel πέταξε πιο κοντά στον Alfred. Τον άγγιξε στο μέτωπο. Στη συνέχεια στράφηκε προς τον E-Z και έκανε το ίδιο. Χαμογέλασε. "Χαίρομαι που σας γνωρίζω και τους δύο." Γύρισε προς τη Λία. Η Λία άνοιξε την παλάμη της και οι δυς τους αντάλλαξαν άγγιγμα με τα δάχτυλα της ανοιχτής παλάμης. Η Λία ρίχτηκε στην αγκαλιά του Haniel. Η Haniel τύλιξε τα φτερά της γύρω της, απολαμβάνοντας την εμφάνιση του νέου δεκάχρονοι κοριτσιού.

Η Άριελ φτερούγισε κοντά στην E-Z. Του έκλεισε το μάτι και χαμογέλασε στη Λία. Πέταξε προς τον Άλφρεντ και τον απάλλαξε από τον πόνο του.

"Αρκετά με τη φασαρία!" Ο Έριελ διέταξε με τη φωνή του να βροντοφωνάζει τόσο δυνατά που ο E-Z φοβήθηκε ότι θα ανέβαζε την οροφή.

"Περίμενε ένα λεπτό', είπε ο Άλφρεντ, περπατώντας με τον ήχο των δικτυωτών ποδιών του που χτυπούσαν στο τσιμεντένιο πάτωμα. "Παραλίγο να πάθω ηλεκτροπληξία και θα ήθελα μια συγγνώμη".

Ο Έριελ άνοιξε τα φτερά του διάπλατα, πιο πλατιά, όσο πιο πλατιά μπορούσαν να φτάσουν. Αιωρήθηκε πάνω από τον Άλφρεντ, ο οποίος έτρεμε αλλά κρατούσε τη θέση του. Τα μάτια τους κλειδώθηκαν.

Ο Έριελ ένιωσε ότι ο Άλφρεντ, ο κύκνος τρομπετίστας, ήταν είτε πολύ γενναίος είτε πολύ ανόητος. Όπως και να 'χει, χρειαζόταν βοήθεια.

Ο E-Z κύλησε μπροστά, τοποθέτησε την καρέκλα του ανάμεσά τους. "Ό,τι έγινε, έγινε". Απευθυνόμενος στον Άλφρεντ, "Σταθείτε κάτω". Ο Άλφρεντ το έκανε. Στη συνέχεια, απευθυνόμενος στον Έριελ, "Ξέρω ότι είσαι νταής και ότι αυτό που έκανες στον φίλο μας ήταν ασυγχώρητο και σκληρό. Είναι μεσάνυχτα, οπότε μπείτε στο θέμα - πείτε μας γιατί είμαστε εδώ; Ποια είναι η έκτακτη ανάγκη;"

Ο Έριελ προσγειώθηκε και τα φτερά του δίπλωσαν πίσω από το σώμα του. Φώναξε: "Οι προσπάθειές μου να επικοινωνήσω μαζί σας προσωπικά με τον προστατευόμενό μου έμειναν αναπάντητες. Ό,τι κι αν έκανα, το ροχαλητό σου δεν σε άφηνε να ξυπνήσεις. Έστειλα τον Haniel για τη Lia, αλλά δεν μπόρεσε να την ξυπνήσει χωρίς να ενοχλήσει τη μητέρα της που κοιμόταν δίπλα της. Ως εκ τούτου, καλέσαμε τον Άλφρεντ, ο οποίος επίσης δεν ανταποκρίθηκε για αρκετή ώρα. Η μέντοράς του προσπάθησε να τον πλησιάσει, με τον συνήθη τρόπο της - αλλά οι ψίθυροι της δεν ήταν αρκετά ισχυροί για να τον ξυπνήσουν".

"Ανησύχησα για σένα", είπε η Άριελ.

"Λυπάμαι", είπε ο Άλφρεντ. "Το κρεβάτι του E-Z είναι θαυμάσια άνετο, και ροχαλίζει όντως αρκετά δυνατά. Είχε περάσει πολύς καιρός από τότε που κοιμήθηκα ξανά σε πραγματικό κρεβάτι".

"ΣΙΩΠΉ!" Ο Έριελ ούρλιαξε.

Ο Άλφρεντ έκανε ένα βήμα πίσω, ενώ ο E-Z μετακίνησε την καρέκλα του πολύ πιο κοντά στο πλάσμα.

Ο Έριελ χαμήλωσε τη φωνή του. "Ο Χάνιελ νόμιζε ότι ήσουν νεκρός, κύκνε. Και ως εκ τούτου εγώ, χρησιμοποίησα αυτή την ευκαιρία για να αξιολογήσω τη νεότερη τεχνολογία μας".

"Δεν είχε ξαναγίνει σε ανθρώπους", παραδέχτηκε ο Haniel.

"Σκεφτήκαμε ότι θα ήταν καλύτερο να το δοκιμάσουμε σε κάποιον που δεν ήταν άνθρωπος - ο Άλφρεντ σου ταιριάζει και λειτούργησε άψογα. Είναι αλήθεια ότι όλοι σας αργήσατε να φτάσετε, αλλά φτάσατε εδώ. Όπως λένε, καλύτερα αργά παρά ποτέ".

"Με χρησιμοποίησες ως πειραματόζωο;" Είπε ο Άλφρεντ, κουνώντας το λαιμό του μπρος-πίσω με το ράμφος του ορθάνοιχτο και προχωρώντας στο πάτωμα.

Ο E-Z τοποθέτησε για άλλη μια φορά την αναπηρική του καρέκλα ανάμεσά τους. "Κάτσε κάτω", είπε στον Άλφρεντ.

Ο Έριελ, ο Χάνιελ και ο Άριελ σχημάτισαν ένα ημικύκλιο γύρω από το τρίο.

"Έχεις δίκιο E-Z. Ό,τι έγινε, έγινε. Καλύτερα να το δοκιμάσουν σε μένα, παρά σε εσάς τους δύο. Τώρα τελειώνετε", απαίτησε ο Άλφρεντ.

"Ναι, Έριελ", είπε ο E-Z, "και πάλι ρωτάω, γιατί είμαστε εδώ;"

"Πρώτα απ' όλα", βροντοφώναξε ο αρχάγγελος, "το σχέδιο ήταν οι τρεις σας να σχηματίσετε ένα είδος τρίο".

"Αυτό το έχουμε ήδη καταλάβει μόνοι μας", είπε η Λία. Κρατούσε τις παλάμες της ανοιχτές, ώστε να μπορεί να αντικρίζει ταυτόχρονα όλη τη θέα των τριών αρχαγγέλων. Κοίταζε επίσης γύρω από το δωμάτιο κατά διαστήματα για να αντιληφθεί το περιβάλλον τους. Φαινόταν γνώριμς, με μεταλλικούς τοίχους σαν αυτόν στον οποίο είχε συναντήσει για πρώτη φορά τον E-Z. Μόνο που ήταν πολύ πιο ευρύχωρο.

Ο E-Z κοίταξε γύρω του και κοίταξε τη Lia. Σκεφτόταν το ίδιο πράγμα. Όσο περισσότερο κοιτούσε τους τοίχους, τόσο περισσοτερο έμοιαζαν να τον κλείνουν. Ένιωθε κρύο και κλειστοφοβία, παρόλο που ο χώρος ήταν τεράστιος. Εύχεται το αναπηρικό του αμαξίδιο να είχε ένα κουμπί όπως σε κάποια αυτοκίνητα όπου το κάθισμα θα μπορούσε να θερμανθεί.

"Ησυχία!" φώναξε ο Έριελ. Δεδομένου ότι όλοι ήταν σιωπηλοί, του φάνηκε παράταιρο. Φυσικά, δεν είχαν λάβει υπόψη τους ότι μπορούσε επίσης να διαβάσει τις σκέψεις τους.

Ο Άλφρεντ γέλασε.

Η Έριελ έκλεισε το κενό ανάμεσά τους και ο Άλφρεντ έκανε πίσω. Ο Έριελ έκλεισε ξανά το κενό. Και ούτω καθεξής, μέχρι που ο Άλφρεντ βρέθηκε με την πλάτη στον τοίχο. Ο Άλφρεντ τράπηκε σε φυγή. Ο Έριελ τον σήκωσε με τα πόδια του που έμοιαζαν με νύχια. Τον κράτησε πάνω από τους άλλους.

"Έριελ, σε παρακαλώ", είπε ο Άριελ. "Ο Άλφρεντ είναι καλή ψυχή".

Ο Έριελ τον άφησε κάτω και μετά σήκωσε τις γροθιές του. Κεραυνοί πετάχτηκαν από αυτές και εξοστρακίστηκαν στο μεταλλικό ταβάνι του κοντέινερ. Όλοι εκτός από τον Έριελ έπαιζαν ντότζεμ με τα ιπτάμενα ηλεκτρικά φορτία. Ο Έριελ παρακολουθούσε. Γέλασε. Μέχρι που κουράστηκε από τη διασκέδαση.

Η αυτοπεποίθηση των Τριών είχε δοκιμαστεί.

Ο Έριελ έπιασε τους εναπομείναντες κεραυνούς. Έκανε μεγάλη επίδειξη, καθώς τις έβαζε στις τσέπες του.

"Τώρα λοιπόν", είπε με ένα πονηρό χαμόγελο. "Μια νέα δοκιμασία έρχεται προς το μέρος σας. Σήμερα. Ένας από εσάς θα πεθάνει".

Ο Ε-Ζ σηκώθηκε από την καρέκλα του. Ο Άλφρεντ ούρλιαξε ένα ακούσιο "Χου-χου!" και η Λία ούρλιαξε σαν κοριτσάκι.

Ο Έριελ συνέχισε, αγνοώντας τις αντιδράσεις τους. "Είστε εδώ για να διαλέξετε. Ποιος από εσάς θα πεθάνει σήμερα; Αφού επιλέξετε, θα σας εξηγήσω τις συνέπειες που θα αντιμετωπίσετε λόγω του εν λόγω θανάτου". Ο Eriel πέταξε λίγα μέτρα μακριά και οι άλλοι δύο άγγελοι βρέθηκαν δίπλα του, ένας σε κάθε πλευρά.

Αρχικά, ο Άριελ περιέγραψε τον θάνατο του Άλφρεντ:

"Δεν μπορώ να σας πω λεπτομέρειες για αυτή τη δίκη. Το μόνο που μπορώ να σας πω, είναι ότι Alfred, αν πεθάνεις σήμερα, δεν θα εκπληρώσεις τη συμβατική σου συμφωνία. Ως εκ τούτου, δεν θα ξαναδείς την οικογένειά σου, ούτε τώρα ούτε ποτέ. Ο θάνατός σου, ωστόσο, θα είναι όμορφος. Γιατί όπως και στη ζωή, ο θάνατος ενός κύκνου είναι πάντα όμορφος. Μεγαλειώδης. Γιατί όταν ένας κύκνος πεθαίνει, γίνεται άγγελος. Η μεταμόρφωσή σου θα ήταν μια νέα αρχή για σένα. Ο σκοπός σου θα είναι για τη βελτίωση των ανθρώπων και των ζώων. Θα σας δοθεί ένα νέο όνομα και ένας νέος σκοπός. Θα εκτιμηθείς πραγματικά με κάθε τρόπο. Και η ψυχή σου θα επέστρεφε στο αιώνιο σημείο ανάπαυσής της".

Δάκρυα έτρεξαν στα μάγουλα του Άλφρεντ. Η Άριελ τον παρηγόρησε τυλίγοντας τα φτερά της γύρω από τα φτερά του.

Δεύτερον, ο Haniel είπε για το θάνατο της Lia:

"Παιδί μου, που σύντομα θα γίνεις γυναίκα, όπως η Ariel, δεν μπορώ να σου πω καμία πληροφορία για το έργο που έχεις αναλάβει. Το μόνο που μπορώ να σου πω αγαπητή Σεσίλια, γνωστή και ως Λία, είναι ότι αν πέθαινες σήμερα, τότε δεν θα είσαι πια. Σε καμία μορφή. Ο θάνατός σου θα είναι ακριβώς αυτό, ένας θάνατος. Τελικός. Θα είναι όπως θα ήταν όταν έσκασε η λάμπα, θα είχες πεθάνει. Η φτωχή σας ζωή θα είχε τελειώσει τότε. Και όμως είστε εδώ τώρα, και έχετε πολλά να προσφέρετε στον κόσμο. Δεν έχετε καν ξύσει την επιφάνεια των δυνάμεων που έχετε στη διάθεσή σας. Ωστόσο, αν πεθάνετε σήμερα, αυτές οι δυνάμεις θα παραμείνουν αναξιοποίητες. Θα πέφτατε στο χώμα, από χώμα σε χώμα. Μια απλή ανάμνηση για όσους σε γνώρισαν και σε αγάπησαν. Αλλά και η ψυχή σου, επίσης, θα επέστρεφε στην αιώνια ανάπαυσή της".

Η Λία έκλεισε τα χέρια της για να συγκρατήσει τα δάκρυα που έπεφταν από αυτά. Έπεφταν και από τα μάτια της. Τα παλιά της μάτια. Το σώμα της έτρεμε όταν έκλαιγε με λυγμούς. Ήταν πολύ καταβεβλημένη από τη συγκίνηση για να μιλήσει.

Η μικρή Ντόριτ πλησίασε και σκούντησε το κοριτσάκι στον ώμο. Ο Haniel προσπάθησε επίσης να την παρηγορήσει φιλώντας την στο μέτωπο.

Και τότε η Έριελ άρχισε να διηγείται την ιστορία της E-Z:

"E-Z, έχεις καταφέρει πολλά πράγματα από τότε που πέθαναν οι γονείς σου. Σου έχουν δοθεί δοκιμασίες. Μερικές φορές, συχνά ανυπέρβλητα καθήκοντα για έναν άνθρωπο. Ωστόσο, έχεις καταφέρει να τις ξεπεράσεις με επιτυχία. Έχεις σώσει ζωές. Δεν με απογοήτευσες. Ωστόσο, αισθάνομαστε". Δίστασε ρίχνοντας μια ματιά από άκρη σε άκρη. "Αισθάνομαι ιδιαίτερα ότι έχετε ματαιώσει τις δυνάμεις σας. Μερικές φορές μάλιστα τις αρνήθηκες.

Πήρατε τον χρόνο που σας δώσαμε για να κάνετε τον κόσμο καλύτερο και τον σπαταλήσατε".

Ο E-Z άνοιξε το στόμα του για να μιλήσει.

"Σιωπή!" Ούρλιαξε ο Έριελ. "Μην προσπαθείς να δικαιολογήσεις τον εαυτό σου. Σε βλέπαμε να παίζεις μπέιζμπολ και να σπαταλάς το χρόνο σου με τους φίλους σου, σαν να είχες όλο το χρόνο του κόσμου για να ολοκληρώσεις τα καθήκοντά σου. Λοιπόν, ο χρόνος τελείωσε. Αν πεθάνεις σήμερα, οι δοκιμασίες σου θα είναι ατελείς".

Ο E-Z είχε μια καλή ιδέα για το τι θα ακολουθούσε, αλλά έπρεπε να περιμένει να το πει η Έριελ. Να πει τα λόγια για να γίνει πραγματικότητα.

Όπως υπέθεσε, η Eriel δεν είχε τελειώσει ακόμα. "Μας αφήνεις με ατελείς δοκιμασίες για τις οποίες σώθηκε η ζωή σου. Αυτό θα ήταν ασυγχώρητο. Αν πέθαινες σήμερα, θα έχανες τα φτερά σου. Αυτό είναι για αρχή. Αυτές οι δοκιμασίες που δεν σου είχαν δοθεί ακόμα - δεν θα γίνονταν ποτέ. Διότι ήσουν ο μόνος που μπορούσε να ολοκληρώσει τα καθήκοντα. Η μόνη μας ελπίδα.

"Επομένως, αυτοί που θα έσωζες δεν θα μπορούσαν να σωθούν από κανέναν, σε καμία περίπτωση. Θα πεθάνουν εξαιτίας σου. Όλοι όσοι έσωσες ποτέ κατά τη διάρκεια των δοκιμασιών σου θα πέθαιναν.

"Θα ήταν σαν να μην υπήρχες ποτέ. Ο θάνατός τους θα ήταν οριστικός. Ολοκληρωμένοι. Μηδενική ευκαιρία για μεταθανάτια ζωή για κανέναν τους. Ακόμα και το να τους στείλετε στο ενδιάμεσο δεν θα ήταν επιλογή. Ο θάνατός σας τότε E-Z θα προκαλούσε χάος και θα έφερνε χάος στον κόσμο. Όπως τη μέρα που μονομαχήσαμε. Θυμάσαι πώς ήταν ο κόσμος εκείνη την ημέρα; Έτσι θα ήταν η γη - κάθε μέρα". Ο Έριελ γύρισε την πλάτη του. Τον είδαν να ανοίγει τα φτερά του, σαν να ετοιμαζόταν να φύγει.

Όλοι ήταν σιωπηλοί. Σκεπτόμενοι τη μοίρα τους.

Μετά από λίγο καιρό, ο Έριελ έσπασε τη σιωπή. "Ο Άριελ, ο Χάνιελ και εγώ θα σας αφήσουμε για την ώρα. Μπορείτε να μιλήσετε μεταξύ σας και να αποφασίσετε. Αλλά να είστε γρήγοροι σε αυτό. Δεν έχουμε όλη τη μέρα στη διάθεσή μας".

Το τρίο των αρχαγγέλων εξαφανίστηκε μέσα από το ταβάνι.

ΚΕΦΑΛΑΙΟ 16

ΑΦΟΎ ΈΦΥΓΑΝ ΟΙ ΑΡΧΆΓΓΕΛΟΙ, οι Τρεις ήταν πολύ έκπληκτοι για να πουν οτιδήποτε. Μέχρι που ο E-Z έσπασε τη σιωπή.

"Δεν μου φαίνεται λογικό να μας φέρνουν όλους εδώ μαζί. Να βασανίζουν τον Άλφρεντ. Να μας φέρουν εδώ. Και μετά να μας πουν ότι ένας από εμάς πρέπει να πεθάνει. Και εμείς πρέπει να διαλέξουμε ποιος. Είναι βάρβαρο - ακόμα και για την Έριελ".

Η Λία περπατούσε με σφιγμένες τις γροθιές της. Ήταν πολύ θυμωμένη για να μιλήσει, και δεν την ένοιαζε αν θα χτυπούσε σε οτιδήποτε. Στην πραγματικότητα, όταν το έκανε, το κλωτσούσε.

Ο Άλφρεντ συνέχισε. "Νομίζω ότι αν κάποιος πρέπει να πεθάνει, αυτός πρέπει να είμαι εγώ. Οι δυνάμεις μου είναι εξαιρετικά περιορισμένες. Το πιο πιθανό είναι να μετατραπώ σε σούπα κύκνου, δεδομένης της πολυπλοκότητας των δοκιμασιών. Όπως και στην τελευταία δοκιμασία. Ξέρω ότι με βοηθούσες E-Z. Ήταν ευγενικό εκ μέρους σου, αλλά ήξερα ότι ήμουν βάρος".

Ο E-Z προσπάθησε να διακόψει, αλλά ο Άλφρεντ απλά συνέχισε. "Για να μην αναφέρω ότι μπορεί να γινόμουν εμπόδιο. Να βάλω κάποιον από εσάς σε κίνδυνο. Έχω ζήσει μια θλιβερή και μοναχική ζωή από τότε που μου πήραν την οικογένειά μου. Κάποια μέρα η μοναξιά είναι συντριπτική. Το να είμαι μέλος των Τριών έχει βοηθήσει, αλλά...

"Ακόμα και ως κύκνος, μπορούσα να τους σκέφτομαι. Να τους θυμάμαι, να τους αγαπώ. Και μόνο που ξέρω ότι πέθαναν μαζί και είναι κάπου μαζί μου δίνει γαλήνη. Ακόμα κι αν δεν είμαι μαζί τους, αλλά θα είμαι σήμερα, αν είμαι αυτός που θα πεθάνει. Είμαι πρόθυμος να πάρω αυτό το ρίσκο. Άλλωστε, όταν φύγω, δεν θα λείψω σε κανέναν στη γη".

"Θα μας λείψεις!" Είπε η Λία.

"Φυσικά και θα μας λείψεις!" Ο E-Z συμφώνησε, καθώς διέσχιζε το πάτωμα, παρατηρώντας ένα τραπέζι που πριν είχε ενσωματωθεί στον τοίχο. Πλησίασε πιο κοντά του, πάνω στο οποίο ανακάλυψε μια στοίβα χαρτιά, τα οποία ξεφύλλισε.

"Εκτιμώ το συναίσθημα", είπε ο Άλφρεντ. "Ει, τι κάνεις, E-Z; Από πού ήρθε αυτό το τραπέζι;"

Η Λία άπλωσε και τα δύο χέρια μπροστά της, ώστε να μπορεί να βλέπει ταυτόχρονα τόσο τον E-Z όσο και τον Άλφρεντ.

Ο E-Z συνέχισε να ξεφυλλίζει σελίδες. Σύντομα πετούσαν σε όλο το δωμάτιο. Περιστρέφονταν στον αέρα σαν να είχαν πέσει στο μάτι ενός ανεμοστρόβιλου.

Οι Τρεις μαζεύτηκαν μαζί και παρακολουθούσαν τον καταιγισμό των χαρτιών. Τότε με τη μια έπεσαν στο πεζοδρόμιο.

Η Λία άρπαξε ένα από αυτά και το διάβασε, ενώ ο E-Z και ο Άλφρεντ κοιτούσαν.

"Τι είναι αυτό;" αναφώνησε. "Λέει τα ονόματά μας. Λέει τις ιστορίες μας. Τις δικές μας ιστορίες. Των θανάτων μας".

"Λέει ότι είμαστε ήδη νεκροί!" είπε ο E-Z διαβάζοντας ένα από τα χαρτιά που είχε χάσει.

"Ω", είπε η Λία, με ένα δάκρυ να τρέχει στο μάγουλό της. "Λέει επίσης ότι η μητέρα μου είναι νεκρή, όπως και ο θείος σας ο Σαμ".

Ο E-Z κούνησε το κεφάλι του. "Δεν μπορεί να είναι αλήθεια Δεν είναι αλήθεια. Μας δουλεύουν". Κοίταξε γύρω του. Κάτι στο δωμάτιο είχε αλλάξει. Οι τοίχοι. Ήταν τώρα κόκκινοι. "Μήπως πήγαμε σε άλλη διάσταση ή κάτι τέτοιο; Κοιτάξτε τους τοίχους. Είμαστε κάπου αλλού, όπου το μέλλον είναι ήδη παρελθόν;"

Ο Άλφρεντ σήκωσε άλλη μια από τις πεσμένες σελίδες. Έλεγε για τον θάνατο της γυναίκας του, των παιδιών του και για τον δικό του θάνατο. Κι όμως, όταν κοίταξε τον εαυτό του, ένιωσε τον εαυτό του, ήταν ζωντανός, με φτερά: ένας σαλπιγκτής κύκνος. "Θέλω να φύγω", είπε.

Η Λία χαμογέλασε. "Εννοείς, έξω από αυτό το δωμάτιο ή έξω από αυτή τη ζωή; Κι εγώ θέλω να βγω, εννοώ από αυτό το ανατριχιαστικό μεταλλικό δοχείο, αλλά δεν θέλω να πεθάνω. Το να βλέπω τον κόσμο μέσα από τις παλάμες των χεριών μου είναι παράξενο και δροσερό ταυτόχρονα. Το να μπορώ να διαβάζω σκέψεις, είναι επίσης ωραίο. Όταν σταμάτησα το χρόνο όμως, αυτό ήταν φοβερό. Φανταστείτε να μπορείτε να καλέσετε αυτή τη δύναμη, όπως αν κάποιος κινδύνευε ή αν υπήρχε μια καταστροφή. Φανταστείτε πόσες ζωές θα μπορούσαν να σωθούν; Και τώρα είμαι δέκα χρονών και ποιος ξέρει τι άλλες δυνάμεις μου επιφυλάσσει το μέλλον".

"Θεϊκό", είπε ο E-Z. "Ξέρω πώς ένιωσες, Λία. Έτσι ένιωσα κι εγώ, όταν έσωσα εκείνο το πρώτο κοριτσάκι, όταν έσωσα τα άλλα και όταν έσωσα εσένα".

Οι τρεις τους σχημάτισαν έναν κύκλο και ενώθηκαν με τα χέρια καθώς απήγγειλαν τις λέξεις: "Έχουμε τη δύναμη. Κανείς δεν πεθαίνει σήμερα. Δεν έχει σημασία τι λένε". Γύριζαν γύρω-γύρω, ψέλνοντας το νέο τους μάντρα. Μέχρι που ήταν έτοιμοι να καλέσουν ξανά τους αρχαγγέλους.

ΚΕΦΑΛΑΙΟ 17

Ο Έριελ έφτασε πρώτος, με τα φρύδια του σηκωμένα και τα χείλη του στρεβλωμένα σε περιφρόνηση. Στη συνέχεια έφτασαν η Άριελ και ο Χάνιελ. Οι δύο παρέμειναν πίσω του στη σκιά των τεράστιων φτερών του. Ο Έριελ σταύρωσε τα χέρια του, ενώ οι άλλοι δύο αρχάγγελο. προχώρησαν προς τα πάνω. Αιωρήθηκαν στις αντίθετες πλευρές των ωμων του.

"Αποφασίσαμε", είπε ο Ε-Ζ. "Κανείς δεν θα πεθάνει σήμερα".

Το γέλιο του Έριελ βροντοφώναξε γύρω από το μεταλλικό περίβλημα. Ανέβηκε στον αέρα και μετά σταύρωσε τα χέρια του πάνω στο στήθος του. Η Άριελ και ο Χάνιελ παρέμειναν σιωπηλοί, ενώ το γέλιο του Έριελ δυνάμωσε σε τόνο, αρκετά ψηλά ώστε να πληγώνει τα αυτιά του Άλφρεντ.

Ο Άλφρεντ λιποθύμησε αλλά συνήλθε γρήγορα. Η Λία και ο Ε-Ζ τον βοήθησαν να σηκωθεί. Τον κράτησαν μέχρι να πετάξει η Μικρή Ντόριτ. Λίγες στιγμές αργότερα ο Άλφρεντ καθόταν ψηλά από πάνω τους πάνω στον μονόκερο. Βρισκόταν πρόσωπο με πρόσωπο με την Έριελ.

"Ευχαριστώ, φίλε", είπε ο Άλφρεντ.

"Χαίρομαι που βοήθησα", είπε η Μικρή Ντόριτ.

"Αρκετά!" φώναξε ο Eriel, κινούμενος ψηλότερα από πάνω τους. Τους εκφόβιζε με το μέγεθός του, τη νοσηρότητά του, τη βροντερή φωνή του. "Νομίζετε ότι μπορείτε να αλλάξετε αυτό που θα γίνει; Σας είπα τι πρέπει να συμβεί και δεν έχετε άλλη επιλογή από το να με υπακούσετε. Δεν ήταν έρευνα. Ούτε δημοκρατία. Ήταν μια βεβαιότητα. Γιατί είναι γραμμένο..."

Τότε παρατήρησε ότι το πάτωμα ήταν καλυμμένο με χαρτιά. Πετάχτηκε κάτω και πήρε ένα από αυτά. Μετά σηκώθηκε, ώστε να βρεθεί πρόσωπο με πρόσωπο με τον Άλφρεντ. Στο χέρι του κρατούσε την ιστορία του Άλφρεντ.

"Βλέπω ότι έχεις διαβάσει το μέλλον. Τώρα γνωρίζεις την αλήθεια, ότι ζεις σε ένα παράλληλο σύμπαν. Ό,τι συμβαίνει εδώ, διαχέεται σε όλα τα άλλα σύμπαντα. Σε μέρη όπου υπάρχει τόσο το μέλλον όσο και το παρελθόν".

Η Λία άφησε το δεξί της χέρι και σήκωσε το αριστερό. Τα χέρια της δεν ήταν δυνατά, γιατί ακόμα συνήθιζαν να πρέπει να τα κρατάει ψηλά.

Ο Έριελ πέταξε σε όλο το δωμάτιο προς έναν κόκκινο καναπέ στον οποίο κάθισε. Οι άλλοι άγγελοι τον συνόδευσαν, ένας σε κάθε μπράτσο. Ο Έριελ καθόταν αναπαυτικά με τα φτερά του ούτε εντελώς μέσα ούτε έξω.

Αφού βολεύτηκε, συνέχισε. "Σε έναν από τους κόσμους, και οι τρεις σας είστε ήδη νεκροί. Διαβάσατε την αλήθεια. Σε αυτόν τον κόσμο, υπάρχει ακόμα ελπίδα. Η ελπίδα υπάρχει, εξαιτίας μας, δηλαδή εξαιτίας εμού, του Άριελ, του Χάνιελ και του Οφάνιελ. Επιλέξαμε εσάς τους τρεις ανθρώπους, για να συνεργαστείτε μαζί μας. Σας δώσαμε στόχους και σας βοηθήσαμε όπου και όταν μπορούσαμε. Όσο είμαστε μαζί σας, μόνο εμείς επιτρέπουμε τη συνέχιση της ύπαρξής σας. Μόνο εμείς δίνουμε σκοπό στη ζωή σας. Αν αρνηθείτε να ακολουθήσετε το μονοπάτι που επιλέξαμε για εσάς, τότε ούτε εσείς θα υπάρχετε πλέον εδώ σε αυτόν τον κόσμο. Θα διαγραφείτε, όπως δεν υπήρξατε ποτέ και δεν θα γίνετε ποτέ".

Ο E-Z έσφιξε τις γροθιές του και η καρέκλα του κουνήθηκε προς τα εμπρός. "Στο έγγραφο, το έγγραφο για την άλλη μου ζωή, αναφερόταν ότι και ο θείος Σαμ ήταν νεκρός. Δεν ήταν στο ατύχημα με τους γονείς μου. Δεν αποτελεί μέρος αυτής της συμφωνίας. Τον σκότωσες Έριελ, για να με κρατήσεις εδώ;"

Χωρίς να περιμένει απάντηση, η Λία παρενέβη. "Στο έγγραφό μου λέει ότι η μητέρα μου είναι νεκρή. Πώς μπορεί να είναι αλήθεια αυτό; Σε παρακαλώ, πες μου ότι δεν είναι αλήθεια!"

Ο Άλφρεντ που αισθανόταν τώρα καλύτερα, πήδηξε από την πλάτη της Μικρής Ντόριτ. Πλησίασε πιο κοντά στον καναπέ και ήρθε ξανά πρόσωπο με πρόσωπο με την Έριελ.

Ο E-Z κοίταζε με περηφάνια τον φίλο του Άλφρεντ, τον ατρόμητο τρομπέτα κύκνο.

"Και στα έγγραφα, οι προσευχές μου εισακούστηκαν. Είμαι ήδη νεκρός. Πέθανε μαζί με την οικογένειά μου, όπως έπρεπε να γίνει Θα προτιμούσα να είχα μείνει νεκρός. Να είχα πεθάνει μαζί τους, αντί να μετενσαρκωθώ ως τρομπετοελίπτης κύκνος. Κι αυτό αφού ο Haniel με έσωσε από το μεταξύ και το μεταξύ".

Ο Έριελ έδιωξε τον Άλφρεντ. "Α, ναι, το ενδιάμεσο και το ενδιάμεσο. Είχα ξεχάσει ότι σε είχαν στείλει εκεί. Δεν σου άρεσε και πολύ, έτσι δεν είναι;"

Ο Άλφρεντ κούνησε τον λαιμό του και έκανε μια γκριμάτσα με το ράμφος του. Έδειξε τα μικρά, οδοντωτά δόντια του σαν να ήθελε να δαγκώσει την Έριελ.

"Κάτσε κάτω", είπε ο E-Z καθώς κύλησε προς τον καναπέ.

Ο Άλφρεντ έκλεισε το ράμφος του. Η Λία πλησίασε πιο κοντά. Τώρα οι Τρεις στέκονταν μαζί μπροστά στην Έριελ. Περίμεναν τον αρχάγγελο να πει κάτι, οτιδήποτε. Για πρώτη φορά έμειναν άφωνοι.

Ο E-Z άδραξε την ευκαιρία για να πάρει την κατάσταση στα χέρια του.

"Στις εφημερίδες αναφερόταν ότι ο θείος Σαμ είχε πεθάνει στο ατύχημα με τη μητέρα μου, τον πατέρα μου και εμένα. Δεν ήταν στο αυτοκίνητο μαζί μας, για να συμβεί αυτό, θα έπρεπε να είχε φυτευτεί στο όχημα μαζί μας. Για ποιο λόγο; Εξηγήστε μας εσείς οι λεγόμενοι αρχάγγελοι. Γιατί αλλάζετε την ιστορία για να εξυπηρετήσετε τους σκοπούς σας; Παρεμπιπτόντως, πού είναι ο Θεός σε όλα αυτά; Θέλω να του μιλήσω".

"Κι εγώ το ίδιο!" Η Λία αναφώνησε.

"Κι εγώ το ίδιο!" Ο Άλφρεντ συνέχισε.

Ο Έριελ σταύρωσε τα πόδια του και άνοιξε τα φτερά του. Έβαλε το χέρι του στο πηγούνι του και απάντησε: "Ο Θεός δεν έχει καμία σχέση με εμάς ή εσένα - όχι πια". Χασμουρήθηκε, σαν να τον κούραζε αυτή η εργασία.

"Κι αν σου έλεγα ότι το σπίτι σου καίγεται αυτή τη στιγμή που μιλάμε; Κι αν σου έλεγα ότι ούτε ο θείος Σαμ, ούτε η μητέρα σου Σαμάνθα, η Λία θα ζούσαν για να δουν άλλη μια μέρα;"

"Μπάσταρδε!" αναφώνησε ο Ε-Ζ.

"Ditto!" Είπε η Λία.

"Έλα τώρα", είπε ο Έριελ. "Είμαστε όλοι φίλοι εδώ. Φίλοι, έτσι δεν είναι; Το σπίτι σου μπορεί να πάρει φωτιά, οτιδήποτε μπορεί να συμβεί όσο είμαστε εδώ σε αυτό το μέρος, ανασταλμένοι στο χρόνο. Όσο περισσότερο καθυστερείς να επιλέξεις, τόσο περισσότερο χάος δημιουργείς στον κόσμο". Σηκώθηκε και τα φτερά του άνοιξαν, κάνοντας το τρίο να κάνει μερικά βήματα πίσω.

Συνέχισε: "Ε-Ζ θα διακινδύνευες τη ζωή σου για τον θείο Σαμ, σωστά;". Εκείνος έγνεψε. "Φυσικά και θα το έκανες. Και η Λία, θα διακινδύνευες τη ζωή σου για να σώσεις τη ζωή της μητέρας σου, ναι;" Η Λία έγνεψε.

"Και ο Άλφρεντ, ο αγαπημένος μου μικρός κύκνος τρομπετίστας. Ο φτερωτός μου φτερωτός φίλος. Ποιον από τους δύο θα έσωζες. Αν μπορούσες να σώσεις μόνο έναν από αυτούς;" Ο Έριελ χαμογέλασε, περήφανος για τα στιχάκια που είχε φτιάξει.

"Θα τους έσωζα και τους δύο", είπε ο Άλφρεντ. "Θα διακινδύνευα τη ζωή μου ή θα πέθαινα προσπαθώντας".

"Έχεις μια παράξενη επιθυμία θανάτου, φτερωτέ φίλε μου".

Ο Άλφρεντ όρμησε προς τον Έριελ.

"Y-o-u a-r-e n-o-t m-y f-r-i-e-n-d! Σταμάτα να παίζεις παιχνίδια μαζί μας. Εσύ μας έφερες κοντά. Εσύ μας έφερες μαζί. Γιατί; Για να μας κοροϊδέψεις. Για να κάνεις ένα μικρό κορίτσι να κλάψει. Δεν είσαι παρά ένας, αλλά ένας μεγάλος νταής".

"Ναι", είπε η Λία. "Σταμάτα να μας εκφοβίζεις".

"Αυτό που είπαν", πρόσθεσε ο E-Z.

Η Έριελ τώρα έξαλλη, έγινε από μαύρη σε κόκκινη, από μαύρη σε κόκκινη. Πετάχτηκε σε όλο το δωμάτιο και χτύπησε τις γροθιές του στο τραπέζι.

"Θέλετε την αλήθεια; Δεν μπορείς να χειριστείς την αλήθεια!" Χαμογέλασε. "Μια μικρή παρένθεση, λατρεύω την ερμηνεία του Τζακ Νίκολσον στην ταινία "Λίγοι καλοί άνδρες"".

Ήταν ένα πράγμα στο οποίο συμφωνούσαν τόσο ο Έριελ όσο και ο E-Z. Η ερμηνεία του Νίκολσον σε εκείνη την ταινία ήταν άψογη.

"Σταματήστε τους μελοδραματισμούς και πείτε μας τι θέλετε από εμάς".

"Το κάναμε ήδη", είπε ο Έριελ. "Σας είπα ότι ένας από εσάς πρέπει να πεθάνει σήμερα. Σας είπα να διαλέξετε ποιος. Είναι γραμμένο, ένας από εσάς πρέπει να πεθάνει. Πρέπει να διαλέξετε. Τώρα."

Ο Άλφρεντ βγήκε μπροστά, με τον λαιμό του κύκνου του τεντωμένο. "Τότε θα είμαι εγώ."

Ο Άλφρεντ γονάτισε, με το σώμα του να τρέμει. Χαμήλωσε το κεφάλι του, σαν να περίμενε ότι ο αρχάγγελος θα το έκοβε.

Αντ' αυτού, και οι τρεις αρχάγγελοι χειροκρότησαν. Έκαναν βόλτες στο δωμάτιο. Τραγουδούσαν σαν να ήταν μισθωμένοι κλόουν που έπαιζαν σε παιδικό πάρτι γενεθλίων.

Μετά από μερικά λεπτά απόλυτης τρέλας, οι αρχάγγελοι σταμάτησαν.

"Τελείωσε", είπε ο Έριελ.

Και μετά εξαφανίστηκαν.

ΚΕΦΑΛΑΙΟ 18

Με τον Ε-Ζ στο αναπηρικό καροτσάκι του, τη Lia στη Little Dorrit και τον Alfred τον κύκνο, οι Τρεις πετούσαν στον ουρανό. Συνέχισαν να προχωρούν για μερικά χιλιόμετρα, μέχρι που κάτω από αυτούς παρατήρησαν μια τεράστια μεταλλική γέφυρα.

Ένας νεαρός άνδρας ακροβατούσε στο περβάζι δίνοντας κάθε ένδειξη ότι επρόκειτο να πηδήξει.

Ο Ε-Ζ έβγαλε το τηλέφωνό του και ήταν έτοιμος να καλέσει το 100, ενώ ο Άλφρεντ, χωρίς δισταγμό, πέταξε προς τον άνδρα. Έβαλε το τηλέφωνό του στην άκρη και ακολούθησε μαζί με τη Λία.

Ο Άλφρεντ αιωρήθηκε κοντά στον άνδρα, χωρίς να μπορεί να μιλήσει και να γίνει κατανοητός από αυτόν το μόνο που μπορούσε να πει ήταν: "Χου-χου!".

"Φύγε μακριά μου!" φώναξε ο άντρας, κουνώντας τον καημένο τον Άλφρεντ που το μόνο που προσπαθούσε ήταν να βοηθήσει.

Ο άντρας πλησίασε πιο κοντά στην άκρη, κλώτσησε τα παπούτσια του και τα έβλεπε να πέφτουν στο ποτάμι από κάτω του. Παρακολουθούσε, καθώς το νερό τους προσπερνούσε, τραβώντας τα παπούτσια κάτω από το πεινασμένο στόμα του. Θέλοντας να δει περισσότερα, έβγαλε το μπλουζάκι του - το οποίο ειρωνικά έγραφε, "Το τέλος", στο μπροστινό μέρος του.

Ο νεαρός άνδρας κοίταζε καθώς το αγαπημένο του μπλουζάκι λικνιζόταν και χόρευε στην πορεία του προς τα κάτω. Καθώς το νερό το κατάπινε, ο άντρας άρχισε να τραγουδάει:

"Πάω γύρω από το θάμνο της μουριάς.

Ο θάμνος της μουριάς, ο θάμνος της μουριάς.

Εδώ πάω γύρω από τον θάμνο μουριάς,

Όλα αυτά ένα, ένα ηλιόλουστο πρωινό."

Ο Άλφρεντ τον άκουσε να τραγουδάει. Ήταν εξοικειωμένος με το στιχάκι. Περίμενε να τραγουδήσει κι άλλο στίχο. Στην πραγματικότητα, ήθελε να τραγουδήσει κι άλλο. Αλλά φοβόταν να τον ενοχλήσει. Ο άντρας δεν θα καταλάβαινε, ακόμα κι αν προσπαθούσε να του μιλήσει.

Μέχρι εκείνη τη στιγμή, ο E-Z περίμενε ένα σημάδι από τον Άλφρεντ. Τελικά, πήρε ένα - ο Άλφρεντ είπε σε αυτόν και τη Λία να μην πλησιάσουν περισσότερο.

Ο Άλφρεντ ευχήθηκε ο νεαρός να τον καταλάβαινε. Αν πλησίαζε, θα μπορούσε να τον πιάσει; Πλησίασε, ανοίγοντας τα φτερά του στο έπακρο.

Ο νεαρός τον είδε. "Κύκνος", είπε. Μετά πήδηξε.

Ο σάλπιγγας ήταν μεγαλύτερος από τον μέσο κύκνο. Αλλά όχι αρκετά μεγάλος για να πιάσει έναν ενήλικα άντρα. Προσπάθησε όμως να ανακόψει την πτώση του. Έθεσε τη ζωή του σε κίνδυνο για να τον σώσει. Αλλά ό,τι κι αν έκανε, ο άντρας εξακολουθούσε να πέφτει σαν μολυβένιο μπαλόνι. Στο πεινασμένο στόμιο του ποταμού.

Ο Άλφρεντ, χωρίς να σκεφτεί τον εαυτό του, βούτηξε πίσω του. Κανείς δεν ήξερε πώς σκόπευε να τον βγάλει έξω. Κάποιοι λένε ότι η σκέψη είναι αυτή που μετράει. Σε αυτή την περίπτωση, ο Άλφρεντ τραβήχτηκε κάτω από το βάρος του ανθρώπου.

Μέχρι εκείνη τη στιγμή, ο E-Z αιωρούνταν πάνω από το νερό, ψάχνοντας είτε τον άνδρα είτε τον Άλφρεντ να αναδυθούν ώστε να μπορέσει να τους βοηθήσει. Ούτε η Λία, ούτε η Μικρή Ντόριτ ήξεραν κολύμπι. Και ο E-Z δεν μπορούσε να μπει μέσα για να τους βρει με ή χωρίς την καρέκλα του.

Απογοητευμένος πέταξε προς την ακτή, ψάχνοντας για οποιοδήποτε σημάδι ζωής. Επιτέλους, το είδε, κάτι που κουνιόταν στην άλλη πλευρά.

Έτρεξε προς τα εκεί, μετέφερε τον άντρα εκεί που τον περίμενε η Λία, και μόλις έβηχε, πήγε να ψάξει για κάποιο σημάδι του Άλφρεντ, του κύκνου.

Τότε τον είδε. Μισό μέσα και μισό έξω από το νερό. Να βαδίζει με την παλίρροια.

"Άλφρεντ!" φώναξε, καθώς σήκωσε το κεφάλι του κύκνου, παρατηρώντας αμέσως ότι ο λαιμός του ήταν σπασμένος. Ο Άλφρεντ, ο κύκνος τρομπετίστας, ο φίλος του δεν υπήρχε πια. Η πράξη του Έριελ είχε γίνει.

Η Λία, που παρακολουθούσε κάθε κίνηση του Ε-Ζ, είδε το λαιμό του Άλφρεντ και φώναξε "Όχι!".

Ο Ε-Ζ σήκωσε το άψυχο σώμα του κύκνου πάνω στην αναπηρική του καρέκλα και το κράτησε. Άρχισε κι αυτός να κλαίει.

Πίσω τους, ο άνθρωπος που έσωσε ο Άλφρεντ φώναξε,

"Δεν είμαι νεκρός! Εγώ είμαι, ο Άλφρεντ".

ΚΕΦΑΛΑΙΟ 19

E ARTH PAUSE.

Τα πουλιά σταμάτησαν στη μέση της πτήσης. Όπως και τα αεροπλάνα. Και άλλα ιπτάμενα αντικείμενα, όπως τα μπαλόνια και τα μη επανδρωμένα αεροσκάφη. Οι σφαίρες σταματούσαν να πυροβολούν αφού είχαν βγει από τη θαλάμη. Το νερό σταμάτησε να ρέει στους καταρράκτες του Νιαγάρα. Τα έντομα δεν βουίζουν πια. Ο αέρας έμεινε ακίνητος.

Εμφανίστηκε ο Ophaniel, μαζί με τον Eriel, τον Ariel και τον Haniel. Με τα χέρια στους γοφούς της και το πηγούνι της μπροστά, ήταν κάτι παραπάνω από φανερό ότι ήταν ενοχλημένη.

Αντί να μιλήσει, στράφηκε προς την κατεύθυνση του E-Z.

Εκείνος ήταν παγωμένος, με το στόμα του ορθάνοιχτο. Η τελευταία του λέξη που είχε πει ήταν: "ΟΧΙ ΟΧΙ ΟΧΙ ΟΧΙ ΟΧΙ ΟΧΙ ΟΧΙ ΟΧΙ!"

Τώρα παρατηρούσε τη Λία. Η κοπέλα είχε ένα δάκρυ παγωμένο στο μάγουλό της. Είχε τρέξει από το παλιό της μάτι.

Και τώρα πίσω στην E-Z. Κουβαλούσε ένα πτώμα. Το σώμα ενός νεκρού κύκνου.

Τώρα, στον Άλφρεντ, ο οποίος δεν ήταν πλέον κύκνος. Είχε πάρει τη μορφή ανθρώπου. Ενός πνιγμένου ανθρώπου.

Του ίδιου ανθρώπου που θα τον αντικαθιστούσε στους Τρεις.

"Τώρα, τι δεν πάει καλά με αυτή την εικόνα;" ρώτησε ο Οφάνιελ, ο κυβερνήτης του φεγγαριού των αστεριών.

Κανείς δεν τόλμησε να μιλήσει.

"Έριελ, εσύ είσαι υπεύθυνος εδώ. Πρώτον, χαλάς τη δοκιμασία δεσμού με τον E-Z και τον Σαμ με το να σε βγάζουν -συγχωρέστε με για την έκφραση- από το πάρκο.

"Τώρα, εξαιτίας της βλακείας σου, ο Άλφρεντ ο κύκνος κατέλαβε ένα ανθρώπινο σώμα. Το σώμα του ατόμου που σου είπα ότι θα έπρεπε να είναι μέλος των Τριών.

"Ξέρεις τι έχουμε να αντιμετωπίσουμε. Καταλαβαίνεις τι επιφυλάσσει το μέλλον αν δεν βάλουμε τα πράγματα σε τάξη. Ξέρεις!"

Ο Έριελ υποκλίθηκε στα πόδια του Οφάνιελ, μετά σηκώθηκε από το έδαφος πριν μιλήσει. "Είπα τα λόγια, έγινε".

"Ναι, μίλησες τα λόγια και στη συνέχεια απέτυχες να διασφαλίσεις ότι το έργο θα ολοκληρωθεί, ανόητε!"

Αιωρήθηκε κοντά στον νέο Άλφρεντ. "Λυπάμαι, αλλά αυτό περιπλέκει τα πράγματα, ακόμη και για εμάς. Ακόμα και με τις δυνάμεις μας, το να τον βγάλουμε από αυτό το ανθρώπινο σώμα και να τον ξαναβάλουμε στη μορφή του κύκνου δεν θα είναι τόσο εύκολο. Ίσως χρειαστεί να τον στείλουμε πίσω στο ενδιάμεσο και το ενδιάμεσο! Και δεν του αξίζει αυτό. Στην πραγματικότητα".

Η Άριελ πέταξε στο πλευρό του Οφάνιελ και ρώτησε: "Μπορώ να μιλήσω;"

"Μπορείς, αν έχεις κάποια εικόνα για τον Άλφρεντ που μπορεί να μας βοηθήσει να βγούμε από αυτό το χάος".

"Γνωρίζω τον Άλφρεντ, καλύτερα από οποιονδήποτε άλλον εδώ. Συμφώνησε να είναι αυτός που θα θυσιάσει τον εαυτό του. Θα το ξαναέκανε χωρίς δισταγμό - ακόμα κι αν δεν υπήρχε κάτι γι' αυτόν. Αυτή είναι μια τεράστια θυσία για κάθε ζωντανό πλάσμα, να δώσει τη ζωή του για να σώσει ένα άλλο. Επίσης, θα πρέπει να αναλογιστεί κανείς πόσο πολύ έχει υποφέρει ο Άλφρεντ, τόσο στην ανθρώπινη ύπαρξή του όσο και ως κύκνος. Είναι μια εξαιρετική ψυχή και θα πρέπει να του δοθεί μια δεύτερη ευκαιρία, και μια τρίτη, και περισσότερες!".

Η Έριελ χλεύασε: "Θα έπρεπε να έχει φύγει, πίσω στο μεταξύ και στο μεταξύ για όλη την αιωνιότητα. Δεν είναι άξιος..."

"Δεν σου έδωσα την άδεια να διακόψεις!" Ο Οφάνιελ ούρλιαξε. Για να τον εμποδίσει να διακόψει στο μέλλον, του έκλεισε τα χείλη.

"Είναι αλήθεια αυτό που λες, Άριελ", είπε ο Οφάνιελ. "Ο Άλορεντ συνεργάζεται καλά τόσο με τη Λία όσο και με τον E-Z. Οφείλουμε να του δώσουμε μια δεύτερη ευκαιρία σε αυτό το νέο σώμα. Δεν ήταν γραφτό να βρίσκεται στο ενδιάμεσο και το ενδιάμεσο. Ήταν στο χέρι του Hadz και του Reiki. Θα τους είχαμε εξορίσει στα ορυχεία αμέσως μετά από αυτό. Αντ᾽ αυτού, τους δώσαμε άλλη μια ευκαιρία με τον E-Z.

"Παρόλα αυτά, η Eriel τους έστειλε στα ορυχεία. Οπότε, τέλος καλο, όλα καλά. Ίσως, ο Alfred αξίζει άλλη μια ευκαιρία. Ας δούμε τι θα συμβεί, όπως λένε οι άνθρωποι, ας το παίξουμε με το αυτί. Αν όλα πάνε καλά. Αν όχι, αυτό το σώμα μπορεί να ανακυκλωθεί, αφού το πνεύμα έχει ήδη εγκαταλείψει το κτίριο".

"Ευχαριστώ", είπε η Άριελ, υποκλινόμενη χαμηλά στον Οφάνιελ. "Σας ευχαριστώ πάρα πολύ. Θα παρακολουθώ την κατάσταση. Δεν θα αφήσω τον Άλφρεντ να σε απογοητεύσει".

Η Οφάνιελ ένγεψε, σηκώθηκε και είπε τα λόγια:

ΕΠΑΝΑΛΗΨΗ ΤΗΣ ΓΗΣ.

Ο χρόνος άρχισε να κυλάει και ο κόσμος επέστρεψε όπως ήταν πριν.

Ο Οφάνιελ εξαφανίστηκε πρώτος, οι άλλοι τρεις περίμεναν μερικά δευτερόλεπτα πριν ακολουθήσουν.

ΚΕΦΑΛΑΙΟ 20

"ΑΠΟΚΛΕΙΕΤΑΙ!" ΑΝΑΦΩΝΗΣΕ Ο Ε-Ζ, πλησιάζοντας τον νέο Άλφρεντ. "Άλφρεντ, εσύ είσαι; Μπορείς, αλήθεια, να είσαι εσύ;"

Η Λία δεν χρειαζόταν να ρωτήσει, γιατί ήξερε ήδη. Έτρεξε προς τον Άλφρεντ και τον αγκάλιασε.

Ο Άλφρεντ είπε, με την αγγλική του προφορά, "Ο Έριελ πρέπει να έκανε μια αλλαγή-α-ρόο".

Ο Άλφρεντ, ο οποίος φορούσε μόνο ένα τζιν, ανατρίχιασε. "Παρόλο που κρυώνω, είναι σίγουρα ωραία αίσθηση να βρίσκομαι ξανά σε ένα σώμα". Λύγισε τους μύες του και έτρεξε επί τόπου για να ζεσταθεί. Στη συνέχεια έκανε μερικούς τροχούς πάνω στο γκαζόν, ενώ ο Ε-Ζ και η Λία στέκονταν και παρακολουθούσαν με το στόμα ανοιχτό.

"Τι επιδειξίας!" είπε η μικρή Ντόριτ.

Ο Άλφρεντ που μόλις την είχε προσέξει, πήγε κοντά της και πέρασε το χέρι του κατά μήκος της γούνας της. Την ένιωθε τόσο απαλή και ζεστή, που την αγκάλιασε.

"Αυτή είναι μια μάλλον περίεργη τροπή των γεγονότων", είπε ο Ε-Ζ, πλησιάζοντας πιο κοντά. "Δεν ξέρω τι να το κάνω".

"Ούτε εγώ ξέρω", είπε ο Άλφρεντ, "αλλά μπορούμε να το συζητήσουμε όσο τρώμε; Πεθαίνω της πείνας και ένα τσίζμπεργκερ φορτωμένο με κέτσαπ και κρεμμύδια με μια τεράστια πλευρά πατάτες τηγανιτές θα ήταν σίγουρα ό,τι πρέπει".

"Περιμένετε ένα λεπτό", είπε ο E-Z. "Αν είσαι αυτός ο τύπος, αυτός ο τύπος που δεν ξέρουμε καν το όνομά του - τότε τι θα γίνει αν κάποιος σε αναγνωρίσει;"

Ο Άλφρεντ έσκυψε και άγγιξε τα δάχτυλα των ποδιών του. Ένιωσε το δέρμα στο πρόσωπό του. Τα μαλλιά του. "Θα περάσουμε αυτή τη γέφυρα όταν φτάσουμε εκεί". Χαμογέλασε, σήκωσε το κεφάλι του προς την κατεύθυνση του ουρανού και είπε: "Σ' ευχαριστώ Έριελ, όπου κι αν βρίσκεσαι".

Ένα αεροπλάνο πάνω από τα κεφάλια τους έγραψε στον ουρανό τις λέξεις:

Για άλλη μια φορά στο ρήγμα, αγαπητοί φίλοι.

"Αυτή είναι μια μάλλον παράξενη φράση για ουρανογραφία", παρατήρησε η Λία. "Ξέρει κανείς σας τι σημαίνει;"

Ο E-Z κούνησε το κεφάλι του: "Μπορώ να το γκουγκλάρω". Έβγαλε το τηλέφωνό του.

"Δεν χρειάζεται", είπε ο Άλφρεντ. "Είναι από τον Σαίξπηρ, αποδίδεται στον βασιλιά Ερρίκο. Κυριολεκτικά σημαίνει, 'Ας προσπαθήσουμε άλλη μια φορά'. Πιστεύω ότι ειπώθηκε κατά τη διάρκεια της μάχης. Οπότε, υποθέτω ότι αυτό είναι ένα μήνυμα από την Άριελ μου, που με ενημερώνει ότι μου δόθηκε άλλη μια ευκαιρία". Τα δάκρυα ανέβηκαν στα μάτια του.

Ο E-Z ήταν καχύποπτος για αυτή την αλλαγή των γεγονότων. Ήταν χαρούμενος που ο Άλφρεντ ήταν ακόμα μαζί τους, αλλά αναρωτιόταν με ποιο τίμημα. "Ανησυχώ", παραδέχτηκε ο E-Z.

Η Λία είπε ότι κι εκείνη ανησυχούσε.

"Αχ, μην ανησυχείς. Αν η Άριελ μου έστειλε αυτό το μήνυμα, τότε είναι με το μέρος μας. Εξάλλου, ο άνθρωπος του οποίου το σώμα είμαι μέσα - δεν το ήθελε πια. Προσπάθησα να τον σώσω, αλλά πήδηξε έτσι κι αλλιώς. Ίσως είναι η μοίρα μου να σε βοηθήσω με τις δοκιμασίες σου, E-Z. Ό,τι κι αν είναι, θα το δεχτώ. Θα τα δώσω όλα. Αυτό αφού φορέσω ένα πουκάμισο και μερικά παπούτσια".

"Αναρωτιέμαι ποιες είναι οι δυνάμεις σου τώρα, Άλφρεντ. Εννοώ, αν τις έχεις ακόμα ή αν έχεις άλλες δυνάμεις. Ή καμία. Αφού είσαι πάλι άνθρωπος", ρώτησε η Λία.

Ο Άλφρεντ έξυσε το ξανθό του κεφάλι. "Ε, δεν ξέρω. Το μόνο πράγμα που χρειάζεται θεραπεία εδώ γύρω είναι το πρώην σώμα μου σαν κύκνος. Δεν θέλω να διακινδυνεύσω, αν το θεραπεύσω, να καταλήξω πάλι σε αυτό".

"Αρκετά δίκαιο", είπε η Λία. "Αλλά δεν μπορούμε να αφήσουμε το παλιό σου σώμα κύκνου εκεί, έτσι δεν είναι; Πρέπει να το θάψουμε".

Καθώς κοίταζαν το άψυχο σώμα, αυτό εξαφανίστηκε στον αέρα.

"Λοιπόν, αυτό λύνει το πρόβλημα", είπε ο E-Z.

"Αισθάνομαι ότι πρέπει να πω μερικά λόγια, για το πέρασμα του παλιού μου σώματος. Πειράζει κανέναν;"

Τόσο ο E-Z όσο και η Lia έσκυψαν τα κεφάλια τους.

Ο Άλφρεντ απήγγειλε ένα απόσπασμα από το ποίημα του λόρδου Άλφρεντ Τένυσον με τίτλο:

Ο κύκνος που πεθαίνει:

Η πεδιάδα ήταν χορταριασμένη, άγρια και γυμνή,

Ευρεία, άγρια και ανοιχτή στον αέρα,

που είχε χτιστεί παντού

μια στέγη από θλιβερό γκρίζο.

Με μια εσωτερική φωνή το ποτάμι έτρεχε,

Κάτω του επέπλεε ένας κύκνος που πέθαινε,

και θρήνησε δυνατά.

Εδώ ο Άλφρεντ Χου-Χου και Χου-Χου, μέχρι που τα δάκρυα γέμισαν τα μάτια όλων τους καθώς το ποίημα συνεχιζόταν:

Ήταν μεσημέρι.

Ο κουρασμένος άνεμος συνέχιζε να φυσάει,

Και έπαιρνε τις κορυφές των καλαμιών καθώς πήγαινε.

Στάθηκαν μαζί σε μια στιγμή σιωπής.

Τότε η Λία είπε: "Τώρα πάμε να σου βάλουμε φρέσκα και στεγνά ρούχα και μετά θα πάμε όλοι μαζί σε ένα μπέργκερ. Πεινάω και διψάω κι εγώ".

Ο E-Z κούνησε το κεφάλι του. "Κάποιο φαγητό θα ήταν καλό, αλλά εξακολουθώ να είμαι καχύποπτος με την Έριελ. Κάτι εδώ δεν κολλάει"

"Θα το καταλάβουμε - μόλις φάμε! Οδήγησέ με στον παράδεισο των τσίζμπεργκερ".

Άρχισαν να κινούνται κατά μήκος του περιπάτου της προκυμαίας. Συνέχισαν να περπατούν για αρκετή ώρα. Πριν συνειδητοποιήσουν ότι είχαν χαθεί.

"Είμαι εξαιρετική πλοηγός", είπε η Μικρή Ντόριτ, ο μονόκερος, καθώς πέταξε κάτω για να τους χαιρετήσει. "Ανεβείτε στον Άλφρεντ και τη Λία. E-Z μπορείτε να με ακολουθήσετε".

Ο Άλφρεντ έβαλε το χέρι του στην τσέπη του τζιν του και έβγαλε ένα πορτοφόλι. Μέσα βρήκε μερικά χαρτονομίσματα και την ταυτότητα του σώματος στο οποίο διέμενε τώρα. Το όνομα του νεαρού άνδρα ήταν Ντέιβιντ, Τζέιμς Πάρκερ, ηλικίας είκοσι τεσσάρων ετών. Κρατούσε ψηλά ένα δίπλωμα οδήγησης.

"Ωραία φωτογραφία', είπε η Λία.

"Ναι, είμαι μάλλον όμορφος".

"Ω, αδερφέ", είπε ο E-Z, σπρώχνοντας προς τα εμπρός.

Ψηλά, ψηλά στον αέρα πέταξαν οι επιβάτες της Μικρής Ντόριτ. Ο E-Z ακολούθησε μέχρι να καταλάβει πού βρισκόταν. Αποφάσισε να ζητήσει να προστεθεί ένα GPS στην αναπηρική του καρέκλα. Κρίμα που δεν το είχαν σκεφτεί όταν το είχαν τροποποιήσει.

Την κάθοδο ακολούθησε μια γρήγορη βόλτα σε ένα κατάστημα μεταχειρισμένων ειδών. Ο Άλφρεντ φορούσε τώρα ένα καινούργιο μπλουζάκι, τζιν παντελόνι, αθλητικά παπούτσια και κάλτσες. Ακολούθησε μια σύντομη ουρά πριν αρχίσει η παραγγελία του φαγητού.

Η Μικρή Ντόριτ έκανε τον εαυτό της λιγοστό, ενώ η τριάδα έτρωγε το φαγητό της. Ήταν όλοι πολύ πεινασμένοι.

Ο Άλφρεντ έκανε γουργουρητούς ήχους, πάρα πολλούς για να τους περιγράψει κανείς με λεπτομέρειες. Όταν τελείωσαν το φαγητό, εναπόθεσαν τα σκουπίδια στους αντίστοιχους κάδους. Και πήραν το δρόμο για το σπίτι τους.

Όταν έφτασαν σχεδόν εκεί, ο Άλφρεντ φώναξε στον E-Z: "Πρέπει να μιλήσουμε!"

"Δεν μπορεί να περιμένει μέχρι να προσγειωθείτε;" ρώτησε η Μικρή Ντόριτ. "Αφού τελειώσω εδώ, έχω μέρη, να πάω, ανθρώπους να δω".

"Τι αγένεια", είπε ο E-Z. "Προχώρα, Άλφρεντ ή Ντέιβιντ ή όπως αλλιώς σε λένε τώρα".

"Γι' αυτό ήθελα να σου μιλήσω", είπε ο Άλφρεντ. "Πώς θα εξηγήσεις τη μεταμόρφωσή μου στον θείο Σαμ και τη Σαμάνθα; Ε, θείε Σαμ και Σαμάνθα, θα ήθελα να σας γνωρίσω τον Άλφρεντ, τον τρομπετό κύκνο. Το όνομά του είναι τώρα Ντέιβιντ Τζέιμς Πάρκερ. Χάρη στο σώμα στο οποίο μπήκε και στο οποίο κατοικεί σήμερα. Από τότε που ο νεαρός που ήταν ο προηγούμενος ιδιοκτήτης του σώματος αυτοκτόνησε. Στη γέφυρα της οδού Τζόουνς".

"Θεέ μου", είπε ο E-Z. "Είναι εκατό τοις εκατό η αλήθεια όπως την ξέρουμε, αλλά δεν μπορούμε να τους πούμε την αλήθεια".

"Η μητέρα μου θα λιποθυμούσε αν το λέγαμε αυτό. Γιατί δεν τους λέμε ότι ο Άλφρεντ ο κύκνος πέταξε νότια; Για πιο ηλιόλουστο καιρό. Ή ότι βρήκε ένα ταίρι; Τότε μπορούμε να παρουσιάσουμε τον Άλφρεντ ως D.J., που ακούγεται πολύ πιο φιλικό από τον Ντέιβιντ Τζέιμς".

"Είσαι ιδιοφυΐα", είπε ο E-Z. "Αν και, αφού ο φίλος μου λέγεται PJ, τα πράγματα θα μπορούσαν να γίνουν λίγο μπερδεμένα με έναν DJ και έναν PJ. Εσύ τι λες, Άλφρεντ; Έχεις κάποια προτίμηση;"

"Δεν μου αρέσει ο DJ. Ακούγεται πάρα πολύ κοινότυπο. Θα προτιμούσα να με φωνάζουν Πάρκερ. Ο Πάρκερ ο μπάτλερ ήταν ένας από τους αγαπημένους μου χαρακτήρες στο Thunderbirds".

"Πάρκερ λοιπόν", τελείωσε να λέει ο E-Z, καθώς η Λία έβγαλε μια κραυγή και ο Άλφρεντ λιποθύμησε - το σπίτι τους είχε χαθεί. Κάηκε ολοσχερώς.

ΚΕΦΑΛΑΙΟ 21

"Ωχ, όχι!" ΦΩΝΑΞΕ Ο Ε-Ζ καθώς έτρεχε προς τα φλεγόμενα απομεινάρια. "Πρέπει να βρω τον θείο Σαμ και τη Σαμάνθα. Απλά πρέπει να το κάνω".

Η καρέκλα του αιωρήθηκε πάνω από τα ερείπια- ήταν όλα απανθρακωμένα μαύρα. Ένα δυσδιάκριτο χάος καταστροφής χωρίς ίχνος ανθρώπινης ζωής. Σποραδικά αντικείμενα ήταν ποτισμένα με νερό. Διακοπτόμενα σήματα καπνού υψώνονταν εδώ κι εκεί ανάμεσα στα σβησμένα κάρβουνα.

Ο Ε-Ζ σήκωσε τις γροθιές του στον αέρα. "Έλα εδώ Έριελ, εσύ γιγάντιε..."

"Ιπτάμενε βλάκα!" Ο Πάρκερ ολοκλήρωσε την προσβολή.

Η Λία προσπάθησε να τους ηρεμήσει όλους.

"Γιατί έπρεπε να το κάνεις αυτό; Γιατί; Γιατί;" φώναξε ο Ε-Ζ.

Η Λία έπεσε στο έδαφος. Ακούμπησε το κεφάλι της στο γόνατο του Ε-Ζ και ο Πάρκερ την αγκάλιασε ακριβώς τη στιγμή που ένα αυτοκίνητο σταμάτησε πίσω τους.

Δύο πόρτες άνοιξαν: Ο Σαμ και η Σαμάνθα.

Έτρεξαν και αγκαλιάστηκαν μεταξύ τους- σαν να μην περίμεναν ποτέ να ξαναδούν ο ένας τον άλλον. Όλοι έχυσαν ένα ή δύο δάκρυα, πριν χωρίσουν. Όταν συνειδητοποίησαν ότι η ομαδική αγκαλιά περιλάμβανε έναν άντρα που δεν γνώριζαν.

Ο *άγνωστος ήταν ένας ψηλός άντρας*, ο οποίος δεν θα είχε πρόβλημα να πάρει μια θέση στους Ράπτορς. Ήταν ντυμένος από την κορυφή ως τα νύχια με ένα σκούρο μαύρο ριγέ κοστούμι με ασορτί παπούτσια.

Τα κουμπιά του σακακιού του ξεκούμπωτα αποκάλυπταν ένα μαύρο κοστούμι με γυαλιστερό ύφασμα, πιθανώς μεταξωτό. Τα κατάμαυρα μάτια του και οι ανεμοδαρμένες μπούκλες του έκαναν αντίθεση με την κισσόχρωμη επιδερμίδα του. Έμοιαζε με διασταύρωση νεκροθάφτη και μάγου.

Άπλωσε το χέρι του: "Γεια σας, είμαι ο ασφαλιστής του Σαμ".

Ο θείος Σαμ εξήγησε ότι αυτός και η Σαμάνθα είχαν βγει έξω για να πάρουν κάτι να φάνε. Βλέποντας την έκφραση του E-Z, το δικαιολόγησε: "Δεν είχε μπορέσει να κοιμηθεί λόγω του τζετ λαγκ". Η Σαμάνθα και ο Σαμ αντάλλαξαν ματιές και έγνεψαν. "Η Σαμάνθα κι εγώ..."

"Ω, μαμά!"

Ο E-Z είπε: "Η Σαμάνθα και ο θείος Σαμ κάθονται σε ένα δένδρο - κ-ι-σ-ι-σ-ι-ν-γ".

"Σταμάτα", είπε η Πάρκερ. "Τους φέρνεις σε δύσκολη θέση".

Όλα τα βλέμματα ήταν στραμμένα στον ασφαλιστή. Το όνομά του ήταν Reginald Oxworthy. Μιλούσε στο τηλέφωνο. Φώναζε. "Τι εννοείτε ότι δεν πληροί τις προϋποθέσεις;"

"Ωχ, όχι!" Είπε ο Σαμ

"Είναι πελάτης μας εδώ και χρόνια, πρώτα όταν ζούσε σε άλλη πολιτεία και από τότε που μετακόμισε εδώ. Καλύπτεται, είμαι σίγουρος γι' αυτό". Υπήρξε μια παύση. "Λοιπόν, Κοιτάξτε ξανά!" Έκλεισε το τηλέφωνό του. "Λυπάμαι για όλα αυτά".

Ο Σαμ πλησίασε πιο κοντά και όλοι οι άλλοι τον ακολούθησαν. "Ποιο ακριβώς είναι το πρόβλημα;"

"Ω, κανένα πρόβλημα, για να το πω έτσι".

"Εμένα σίγουρα μου φάνηκε σαν πρόβλημα", είπε η Σαμάνθα. Οι υπόλοιποι έγνεψαν.

Ο Όξγουορθι καθάρισε το λαιμό του. "Τους είπα να ελέγξουν ξανά την πολιτική σας. Δώσε μου ένα", χτύπησε το τηλέφωνό του. "Ένα λεπτό", είπε και απομακρύνθηκε από κοντά τους. Τον ακολούθησαν σαν μια ομάδα ποδοσφαιριστών που είχαν μαζευτεί, ακούγοντας κάθε λέξη που έλεγε. "Ε, ναι. Εντάξει. Το επιβεβαίωσαν λοιπόν. Κανένα πρόβλημα, συμβαίνουν αυτά".

Χάρισε ένα χαμόγελο προς τη μεριά του Σαμ και μετά του σήκωσε τους αντίχειρες. Απομακρύνθηκε από τη συνοδεία και συνέχισε τη συζήτησή του.

Στέκονταν σε μια συστάδα, κοιτάζοντας ό,τι είχε απομείνει από το σπίτι τους. Ένα σπίτι στο οποίο ο Ε-Ζ είχε ζήσει όλη του τη ζωή. Τι θα συνέβαινε τώρα; Θα έπρεπε να ξαναχτίσουν σε αυτή την τοποθεσία; Ένα νέο σπίτι, χωρίς ιστορία ή νόημα. Ένα νέο σπίτι που δεν θα γινόταν ποτέ σπίτι γι' αυτόν. Ποτέ δεν θα ήταν ένα μέρος όπου τα φαντάσματα των γονιών του, αν υπήρχαν φαντάσματα, θα μπορούσαν να τα επισκεφθούν.

Ο Όξγουορθι κατευθύνθηκε προς το μέρος τους. "Λοιπόν, τώρα. Ζητώ συγγνώμη για την καθυστέρηση. Αλλά οι κρατήσεις σας στο ξενοδοχείο έχουν επιβεβαιωθεί. Μπορούμε να ξεκινήσουμε. Να σας τακτοποιήσουμε, όποτε είστε έτοιμοι".

"Σας ευχαριστώ", είπε ο Σαμ. "Καμιά ιδέα ακόμα, ποια ήταν η αιτία της πυρκαγιάς;"

"Μετά από προκαταρκτική έρευνα είναι ενενήντα τοις εκατό σίγουροι ότι η έκρηξη προκλήθηκε από διαρροή αερίου. Αλλά μην ανησυχείς γι' αυτό τώρα. Το συμβόλαιό σας καλύπτει όλα τα έξοδα για τη διαμονή στο ξενοδοχείο. Σας έχω κλείσει τρία δωμάτια. Αυτό θα πρέπει να είναι αρκετό, έτσι δεν είναι;"

"Αυτό θα είναι μια χαρά", είπε ο Σαμ. "Σ' ευχαριστώ, Ρετζ".

"Το συμβόλαιό σας καλύπτει επίσης τα έξοδα, για αντικείμενα αντικατάστασης, είδη πρώτης ανάγκης, φαγητό. Δεν θα χρειαστεί να πληρώσετε ούτε σεντς στο ξενοδοχείο. Οτιδήποτε αγοράσεις, στείλε μου τις αποδείξεις. Κάνε αντίγραφα, τα πρωτότυπα τα κρατάς εσύ. Θα φροντίσω να σου επιστραφούν τα χρήματα".

Ο Σαμ και ο Όξγουορθι έδωσαν τα χέρια.

"Χρειάζεται κανείς να σας μεταφέρει στο ξενοδοχείο;" ρώτησε ο Oxworthy, και η Lia και η Samantha ανέβηκαν στο πίσω κάθισμα της μαύρης Mercedes του.

Ο E-Z και ο Πάρκερ μπήκαν στο αυτοκίνητο του θείου Σαμ.

"Δεν νομίζω ότι έχουμε συστηθεί", είπε ο θείος Σαμ, απλώνοντας τε χέρι του στον Πάρκερ που καθόταν στο πίσω κάθισμα.

"Χαίρομαι που σε γνωρίζω", είπε ο Πάρκερ.

"Α, είσαι κι εσύ Βρετανός", είπε ο θείος Σαμ. "Μιας και το έφερε η κουβέντα, πού είναι ο Άλφρεντ;"

Ο E-Z κούνησε το κεφάλι του. "Θα σου εξηγήσω το πρωί. Κι εσύ μπορείς να συνεχίσεις αυτό που επρόκειτο να μας πεις, για σένα και τη Σαμάνθα".

"Δίκαιο", είπε ο Σαμ, κοιτάζοντας στον καθρέφτη του για να δει ότι ο Πάρκερ κοιμόταν βαθιά. Άναψε το αυτοκίνητο και έφυγε με ταχύτητα.

"Είχαμε όλοι μια αρκετά περιπετειώδη μέρα", είπε ο E-Z.

"Εμένα μου λες".

Συγγνώμη Έριελ, που σου ρίχνω το φταίξιμο, σκέφτηκε ο E-Z. Αν και μια υποψία στο πίσω μέρος του μυαλού του έδειχνε ότι οι ένορκοι δεν είχαν ακόμη αποφασίσει για το θέμα.

ΚΕΦΑΛΑΙΟ 22

ΌΛΙΣ ΌΛΟΙ ΈΦΤΑΣΑΝ ΣΤΟ ξενοδοχείο, τακτοποιήθηκαν στα δωμάτιά τους, με σχέδιο να συναντηθούν αργότερα για δείπνο στις 6 μ.μ.

Ο θείος Σαμ είχε ένα δωμάτιο για τον εαυτό του, αλλά μεταξύ του δωματίου του και του δωματίου του ανιψιού του είχαν μια διπλανή πόρτα. Ο Πάρκερ κοιμόταν επίσης στο δωμάτιο του E-Z, ενώ η Λία και η μητέρα της μοιράζονταν ένα δωμάτιο λίγες πόρτες πιο κάτω.

Αφού εγκαταστάθηκαν, η Λία και η Σαμάνθα αποφάσισαν να ψωνίσουν τα απαραίτητα. Πρώτη προτεραιότητα ήταν τα καινούργια ρούχα, καθώς ό,τι είχαν φέρει μαζί τους είχε χαθεί στη φωτιά.

"Και τα διαβατήριά μας;" ρώτησε η Λία.

"Ευτυχώς που τα έχω πάντα μαζί μου στην τσάντα μου".

"Ουφ!" Οι δυο τους μπήκαν σε ένα κατάστημα με επώνυμα ρούχα και άρχισαν αμέσως να δοκιμάζουν τις τελευταίες βορειοαμερικανικές μόδες.

"Αυτό θα είναι ιδιαίτερα διασκεδαστικό, αφού η ασφαλιστική εταιρεία πληρώνει τα πάντα!" αναφώνησε η Σαμάνθα μέσα από τον τοίχο στην κόρη της που βρισκόταν στο διπλανό δωμάτιο αλλαξιέρας.

"Τίποτα δεν αγαπάμε περισσότερο από μια βόλτα για ψώνια!" είπε η Λία. "Σίγουρα θα πάρω αυτό, και αυτό και αυτό".

Πίσω στο ΞΕΝΟΔΟΧΕΊΟ, ο Parker ροχάλιζε στο κρεβάτι. Ο Ε-Ζ στριφογύριζε στο δωμάτιο και σκεφτόταν τον χαμένο υπολογιστή του. Ευτυχώς που δεν είχε προχωρήσει πολύ στο μυθιστόρημά του "Τατουάζ Άγγελος", αλλά αυτό που τον απασχολούσε περισσότερο, ήταν τα πράγματα των γονιών του. Δεν μπορούσε να πιστέψει ότι είχαν όλα - ΕΛΛΕΙΨΕΙ. Δεν βοηθούσε το γεγονός ότι είχε να τα κοιτάξει πάρα πολύ καιρό. Αλλά γιατί κατηγορούσε τον εαυτό του; Οι ασφαλιστές είπαν ότι η αιτία ήταν η διαρροή αερίου. Είπαν ότι ήταν ενενήντα τοις εκατό σίγουροι. Γιατί συνέχιζε να αισθάνεται ότι έφταιγε για όλα αυτός, επειδή θα μπορούσε να το είχε σταματήσει, να είχε σταματήσει την Έριελ όταν είχε την ευκαιρία.

Ο Σαμ έβαλε το κεφάλι του στο δωμάτιο. "Είστε καλά οι δυο σας;"

Ο Πάρκερ τεντώθηκε.

"Ναι, είμαστε αξιοπρεπείς. Ελάτε μέσα".

"Πάω στα μαγαζιά να πάρω μερικά είδη πρώτης ανάγκης. Εσείς οι δύο θέλετε να μου δώσετε μια λίστα με αυτά που χρειάζεστε ή θέλετε να έρθετε μαζί μου;"

"Αν αυτό περιλαμβάνει φαγητό, είμαι κι εγώ μέσα!" είπε ο Άλφρεντ.

"Πάντα πεινάς!"

"Τι να πω, εδώ και αρκετό καιρό τρώω μόνο χόρτο".

Ο Ε-Ζ έπιασε το βλέμμα του Σαμ και προσποιήθηκε ότι καπνίζει ένα φανταστικό τσιγάρο.

Ο θείος Σαμ χλεύασε, αναρωτώμενος πώς ο δεκατριάχρονος ανιψιός του γνώριζε τέτοια πράγματα. Για να αλλάξουν το θέμα, κλείδωσαν τα δωμάτιά τους και κατευθύνθηκαν προς τον διάδρομο.

"Πού πάμε ακριβώς;" ρώτησε ο E-Z.

"Σωστά, δεν πηγαίνουμε συχνά για ψώνια στην πόλη. Υπάρχει ένα φανταστικό εμπορικό κέντρο, στο οποίο ήθελα να πάω από τότε που μετακόμισα εδώ. Δεν είναι μακριά, οπότε σκέφτηκα να κουβεντιάσουμε στο δρόμο".

"Μπορείς να μας πεις τι συνέβη;" ρώτησε ο Πάρκερ.

"Ναι, πώς εσύ και η Σαμάνθα τα φτιάξατε τόσο γρήγορα". ρώτησε ο E-Z.

"Χμμμ", είπε ο Σαμ.

"Εννοούσα τη φωτιά", είπε ο Πάρκερ, ρίχνοντας στον E-Z μια σταυρωτή ματιά πάνω από τον ώμο του.

Έφτασαν στο κατάστημα. Ο Πάρκερ και ο Σαμ μπήκαν μέσα από τις περιστρεφόμενες πόρτες, ενώ ο E-Z χρησιμοποίησε το κουμπί ανοίγματος της πόρτας για να μπει.

Μόλις μπήκαν μέσα, ο Πάρκερ έσκυψε να ξαναβάλει τα παπούτσια του. Ο E-Z έβγαλε ένα κομψό τζιν σακάκι από την κρεμάστρα και το δοκίμασε. Στριφογύρισε μπροστά από έναν καθρέφτη για να ελέγξει την εφαρμογή του. "Φαίνεται αρκετά καλό".

Ο Σαμ ήρθε να αξιολογήσει την κατάσταση: "Συμφωνώ, είναι ακριβή εφαρμογή. Φαίνεται σαν να φτιάχτηκε για σένα".

"Εσύ τι λες, Άλφρεντ;"

Ο Σαμ έκανε μια διπλή ματιά. Ο Πάρκερ είπε: "Θα σταματήσεις να με αποκαλείς Άλφρεντ; Ποιος ήταν αυτός ο Άλφρεντ τέλος πάντων;"

"Ε, συγγνώμη, φταίει η βρετανική προφορά. Είχε κι αυτός μία. Ο Άλφρεντ ήταν, λοιπόν, ένας φίλος μας".

Ο Σαμ επέστρεψε στο να κοιτάζει ρούχα. Γέμιζε ένα καλάθι με εσώρουχα και είδη υγιεινής.

"Τι λες, Πάρκερ;"

Διέσχισε το πάτωμα για να ρίξει μια πιο προσεκτική ματιά. "Μου ταιριάζει πολύ. Νομίζω ότι πρέπει να το πάρεις. Αλλά θα είναι κρίμα όταν τα φτερά σου σπάσουν και καταστραφεί".

Ο Σαμ πέρασε και ο E-Z πέταξε το σακάκι στο καλάθι του. "Νομίζω ότι πρέπει να πάρετε και μερικά απαραίτητα, όπως εσώρουχα. Εκτός κι αν σκοπεύετε να πάτε κομάντο".

"Ιού!" αναφώνησε ο E-Z.

"Ω, μου είναι γνωστή αυτή η φράση. Η προέλευσή της, είμαι αρκετά σίγουρος ότι είναι στο Ηνωμένο Βασίλειο".

"Καταλαβαίνω γιατί ο ανιψιός μου σε αποκαλεί συνέχεια Άλφρεντ. Κάτι τέτοιο θα έλεγε κι εκείνος".

Ο E-Z κοίταξε τον Πάρκερ για ένα δευτερόλεπτο. Έπειτα ακολούθησε τον θείο του στο δρόμο προς το ταμείο, όπου σταμάτησε, δοκίμασε ένα καπέλο και το πέταξε στο καλάθι.

"Τώρα, πού πήγε ο Πάρκερ;" ρώτησε. Ο Σαμ συνέχισε να κοιτάζει τις καρφίτσες για γραβάτες, ενώ ο E-Z έψαχνε το μαγαζί για τον αγνοούμενο φίλο του.

Ο Πάρκερ στεκόταν ακίνητος στη μέση του διαδρόμου τέσσερα με το δεξί του χέρι ψηλά και το αριστερό κάτω. Η έκφραση στο πρόσωπέ του ήταν αδιαμφισβήτητα σαν ζόμπι.

"Ωχ, όχι!" Είπε ο E-Z καθώς γύριζε προς τα εκεί. "Ε, Πάρκερ", ψιθύρισε. "Τι συμβαίνει; Καλύτερα να προσέχεις, αλλιώς κάποιος θα σε μπερδέψει με μια κούκλα".

Ο Πάρκερ παρέμεινε ακίνητος.

"Σύνελθε", είπε ο E-Z, χτυπώντας τον Πάρκερ με την καρέκλα του. Το σώμα του Πάρκερ έγειρε και μετά αναποδογύρισε. Ο E-Z τον άρπαξε εγκαίρως, κρατώντας τον από το πίσω μέρος του πουκαμίσου του.

Προσπάθησε να ισιώσει τον φίλο του, ώστε να μη μοιάζει τόσο άκαμπτος και σαν κούκλα, αλλά δεν ήταν εύκολη υπόθεση.

Ο θείος Σαμ έσπευσε να βοηθήσει. "Τι συμβαίνει με τον Πάρκερ;"

"Δεν ξέρω. Πρέπει να τον πάρουμε από εδώ".

"Παίρνει ναρκωτικά; Έχει μια περίεργη έκφραση στο πρόσωπό του, σαν να έχει δει ένα φάντασμα ή κάτι τέτοιο".

"Όχι, δεν παίρνει ναρκωτικά, εκτός από λίγο χόρτο που και που. Και δεν υπάρχουν φαντάσματα - για να μην αναφέρω ότι είναι μέρα. Μήπως μπορώ να τον μεταφέρω στην καρέκλα μου; Πρέπει να τον βγάλουμε από εδώ, πριν τον προσέξει κάποιος και καλέσει την αστυνομία.

"Σύμφωνοι. Δεν ξέρω τι λόγο θα έδιναν στην αστυνομία αν την καλούσαν. Υπάρχει ένας τύπος στο κατάστημά μας που μιμείται μια κούκλα! Ελάτε γρήγορα".

"Αστείο", είπε ο E-Z. "Πήγαινε εσύ να κάνεις τσεκ άουτ και εγώ θα μείνω εδώ. Ας σκεφτούμε πώς μπορούμε να τον βγάλουμε από εδώ χωρίς να τραβήξουμε την προσοχή".

Ο θείος Σαμ πήγε να πληρώσει, ενώ ο E-Z παρέμεινε με τον Πάρκερ. Οι πελάτες που ανέβαιναν στο διάδρομο, είχαν πρόβλημα να μπουν μέσα και να τους παρακάμψουν. Ο E-Z έστριβε την καρέκλα του αριστερά, μετά δεξιά, για να εξυπηρετήσει τους αγοραστές.

Στο τέλος, όταν υπήρχαν πολλοί πελάτες ταυτόχρονα, έσπρωξε τον Πάρκερ σε έναν τοίχο. Τουλάχιστον αυτός ήταν μακριά από τη μέση. Στη συνέχεια κάθισε περιμένοντας τον Σαμ.

"Εδώ είμαστε!" φώναξε ο E-Z όταν τον εντόπισε.

"Γιατί κοιτάει προς τον τοίχο; Και τι κάνεις εδώ πέρα;"

"Υπήρχαν πολλοί πελάτες και ήμασταν στη μέση. Σκέφτηκες πώς μπορούμε να τον βγάλουμε από εδώ;"

"Ναι, θα φέρω ένα από αυτά τα φορτηγά", είπε ο Σαμ.

"Γιατί δεν παίρνεις ένα καρότσι;" ρώτησε ο E-Z. "Λιγότερο εμφανές".

"Δεν θα μπορέσουμε ποτέ να τον βάλουμε σε ένα καρότσι. Όχι, εκτός αν θέλεις να βγάλεις τα φτερά σου, να τον σηκώσεις και να τον ρίξεις μέσα".

"Πρέπει να σκεφτώ." Μετά από λίγα λεπτά, συνειδητοποίησε ότι το να πάρει ένα φορτηγό ήταν η καλύτερη ιδέα. "Ναι, πάρε ένα καρότσι και μπορώ να σε βοηθήσω να τον βάλεις μέσα. Μόλις βγούμε από το μαγαζί, μπορώ να τον πετάξω πίσω στο ξενοδοχείο. Το μόνο πρόβλημα θα είναι, όταν φτάσω εκεί, τι θα τον κάνω τότε'.

"Αυτό θα το σκεφτούμε μόλις βγούμε από το μαγαζί". Ο Σαμ πήγε να πάρει ένα καρότσι. Αντ' αυτού, επέστρεψε με ένα καρότσι. Αποδείχτηκε ότι ήταν μια καλύτερη επιλογή. Ανέβασαν εύκολα τον Πάρκερ πάνω του και κατευθύνθηκαν πίσω στο ξενοδοχείο.

"Ας γυρίσουμε πίσω με τα πόδια, αργά και σταθερά", είπε ο E-Z. "Δεν χρειάζεται να πετάξω τελικά. Θα το πάμε όμορφα και ήρεμα, θα πάμε στο δωμάτιό μας και θα τον βάλουμε στο κρεβάτι του".

"Μετά θα επιστρέψω το φορτηγό, έπρεπε να υποσχεθώ ότι θα το επέστρεφα προσωπικά".

"Ακούγεται σαν σχέδιο. Ουπς."

Μια ομάδα αγοραστών καταλάμβανε το μεγαλύτερο μέρος του πεζοδρομίου. Σταμάτησαν, για να τους αφήσουν να περάσουν, και μετά συνέχισαν ξανά τον δρόμο τους και σύντομα επέστρεψαν στο ξενοδοχείο.

Μόλις μπήκαν μέσα, το φορτηγό δεν χωρούσε στο κανονικό ασανσέρ, οπότε έπρεπε να χρησιμοποιήσουν το ασανσέρ υπηρεσίας. Χρειάστηκε να πείσουν, δηλαδή να δωροδοκήσουν τον θυρωρό. Μόλις τα χρήματα άλλαξαν χέρια, τους βοήθησε ακόμη και να βγάλουν το φορτηγό από το ασανσέρ. Προσφέρθηκε επίσης να το επιστρέψει στο κατάστημα όταν τελείωναν. Μια προσφορά την οποία ο Σαμ αρνήθηκε ευγενικά.

Τώρα, έξω από το δωμάτιο του E-Z και του Πάρκερ, το ασανσέρ άνοιξε και βγήκαν η Λία και η μητέρα της. Ο καθένας τους κουβαλούσε πολυάριθμες τσάντες όταν παρατήρησαν τους τύπους και το φορτηγό.

"Ωχ, όχι! Τι συνέβη; ρώτησε η Λία.

"Δεν ξέρω", είπε ο E-Z. "Πήρε μια περίεργη στροφή".

"Ας τον πάμε μέσα", είπε ο Σαμ.

Αφού κατέβασαν τις τσάντες τους, τα κορίτσια βοήθησαν τον E-Z και τον Σαμ να βάλουν τον Πάρκερ στο κρεβάτι.

"'Ίσως έχει κάνει κάποιο ξόρκι;" πρότεινε η Λία.

"Αυτό είναι ένα μάλλον περίεργο άλμα για σένα", είπε η Σαμάνθα. "'Εχεις δει πάρα πολλές επαναλήψεις της σειράς Charmed".

Η Λία γέλασε. "Ναι, ήταν ένα από τα αγαπημένα μου. Εννοώ την προηγούμενη εκδοχή, αυτή με το κορίτσι από το Ποιος είναι το αφεντικό".

"Χαίρομαι που ξέρω ότι βλέπεις και στην Ολλανδία το κανάλι με τα παλιά τραγούδια", είπε ο E-Z. Στη συνέχεια πλησίασε πιο κοντά στην Πάρκερ. "Περίμενε ένα λεπτό. Αναπνέει ακόμα;"

Παρακολούθησαν το ανέβασμα και το κατέβασμα του στήθους του Πάρκερ. Αυτό δεν συνέβη.

"Ελέγξτε για καρδιακό παλμό - ή για σφυγμό", πρότεινε η Σαμάνθα.

"Υπάρχει καρδιακός παλμός", είπε η Σαμ. "Και αναπνέει, αλλά σποραδικά".

Η Σαμάνθα έσκυψε και έπιασε το μέτωπο του Πάρκερ. "Ω, Θεέ μου, έχει πυρετό!"

"Φέρτε λίγο πάγο!" φώναξε ο Σαμ, και στη συνέχεια, ακολουθώντας τη δική του εντολή, έτρεξε έξω στο διάδρομο με τον κουβά με τον πάγο στη ρυμούλκηση.

"Δεν θα έπρεπε να καλέσουμε έναν γιατρό;" ρώτησε η Σαμάνθα.

ΚΕΦΑΛΑΙΟ 23

"ΣΥΜΦΩΝΩ ΜΕ ΤΗ ΜΑΜΑ. Πρέπει να καλέσουμε ένα ασθενοφόρο, ή ίσως το ξενοδοχείο έχει κάποιον γιατρό που μένει εδώ", είπε η Λία.

Ο Ε-Ζ έκανε μια γκριμάτσα, στέλνοντας στη Λία το μήνυμα - πρέπει να ξεφορτωθούμε τον θείο Σαμ και τη μαμά σου.

Ο Σαμ επέστρεψε, με έναν κουβά γεμάτο πάγο. "Πρέπει να τον βάλουμε στην μπανιέρα". Αυτός και η Σαμάνθα άρχισαν να σηκώνουν τον Πάρκερ.

"Περιμένετε!" Είπε η Λία. "Ε, Σαμ και μαμά, γιατί δεν πάτε οι δυο σας να φέρετε πολύ, πολύ πάγς; Θέλω να πω, πρέπει να γεμίσουμε την μπανιέρα πριν τον βάλουμε μέσα, σωστά;"

"Ε, νομίζω ότι προσπαθούν να μας ξεφορτωθούν", είπε ο Σαμ.

"Λυπάμαι", είπε ο Ε-Ζ. "Μπορείς να μας δώσεις λίγα λεπτά για να προσπαθήσουμε να καταλάβουμε την κατάσταση με τον Πάρκερ;"

Η Σαμάνθα και ο Σαμ έγνεψαν και έπειτα έφυγαν από το δωμάτιο.

Ο Ε-Ζ απήγγειλε τις μαγικές λέξεις που κάλεσαν την Eriel:

Roch-Ah-Or, A, Ra-Du, EE, El.

Παρόλα αυτά ο αρχάγγελος δεν εμφανίστηκε. Το γεγονός ότι τον αγνοούσαν ενοχλούσε αφάνταστα τον Ε-Ζ, τώρα που ήξερε ότι τον παρακολουθούσε διαρκάς ο Έριελ.

Η Λία προσπάθησε να επικοινωνήσει με τον Χανιέλ, αλλά δεν έλαβε καμία απάντηση.

Ο Ε-Ζ και η Λία δεν ήξεραν τι να κάνουν όταν η καρδιά του Πάρκερ επιβράδυνε τους χτύπους της και σχεδόν σταμάτησε τελείως.

Χωρίς να τον καλέσουν ή με φανφάρες, η Άριελ έφτασε. Πέταξε κατευθείαν προς τον Πάρκερ. Τοποθέτησε τα χέρια της στο μέτωπό του. Παρακολουθούσαν τις σταγόνες των δακρύων να πέφτουν από τα μάτια της και να προσγειώνονται στα μάγουλά του. Τραγούδησε, τραγουδώντας ένα απαλό τραγούδι, και περίμενε. Όταν εκείνος δεν κουνήθηκε ούτε ανέκτησε τις αισθήσεις του, γύρισε να αναχωρήσει. Αλλά πριν φύγει, θρήνησε: "Έφυγε". Και δευτερόλεπτα αργότερα το ίδιο συνέβη και με εκείνη.

Παρόλο που βρίσκονταν στον 45ο όροφο και παρόλο που ο Άλφρεντ/Πάρκερ ήταν νεκρός. Και πάλι. Ο E-Z τον σήκωσε από το κρεβάτι και τον μετέφερε στο παράθυρο. Έριξε μια ματιά πίσω στη Λία πάνω από τον ώμο του.

Έκλαιγε καθώς αυτός και ο Πάρκερ έπεφταν κάτω.

Πέφτοντας, πέφτοντας. Μέχρι που βγήκαν τα φτερά του E-Z από το αναπηρικό αμαξίδιο. Πέταξαν, αυτός και ο Άλφρεντ, αυτός και η Πάρκερ. Ήταν και οι δύο ίδιοι. Δύο στην τιμή του ενός.

Είχε αρχίσει να παραληρεί, καθώς ανέβαινε όλο και πιο ψηλά. Τα μεταλλικά μέρη της καρέκλας του γίνονταν όλο και πιο ζεστά.

Φοβόταν ότι θα αυτοαναφλεγούν.

Έπρεπε να το διορθώσει αυτό. Απλά έπρεπε να το κάνει. Έπρεπε να βρει την Έριελ.

Η αναπηρική καρέκλα άρχισε να συσπάται, με αποτέλεσμα ο E-Z και ο Άλφρεντ/Πάρκερ να πέσουν.

Προσγειώθηκαν χωρίς καρέκλα στο σιλό, όπου ο E-Z γαντζώθηκε στο άψυχο σώμα του φίλου του.

Δεν άργησε να φτάσει ο Eriel και αιωρούμενος στον αέρα μπροστά τους φώναξε: "Σας το είπα ότι θα συμβεί. Σας το είπα και εκείνος συμφώνησε. Η συμφωνία έγινε".

Ο Ε-Ζ ήξερε ότι αυτό ήταν αλήθεια, κι όμως. "Γιατί του έδωσες τότε ελπίδα και γιατί το απόσπασμα του Σαίξπηρ για το ότι του έδωσες μια δεύτερη ευκαιρία;"

Ο Έριελ κοίταξε το κουτσό σώμα που κρατούσε ο Ε-Ζ. "Αυτό δεν ήταν δικό μου έργο".

"Τότε με ποιον πρέπει να μιλήσω;" ρώτησε ο Ε-Ζ. "Φέρτε τον σε μένα. Ο Θεός ή όποιος είναι υπεύθυνος. Απαιτώ να τον δω!"

ΚΕΦΑΛΑΙΟ 24

Η ERIEL ΞΕΦΟΎΣΚΩΣΕ ΚΑΙ μετά εξαφανίστηκε.

Ο E-Z και ο Alfred/Parker παρέμειναν. Το όνομα Πάρκερ δεν ήταν τίποτα και κανένας γι' αυτόν. Ο Άλφρεντ ήταν φίλος του και τώρα που έφυγε, θα τον θυμόταν ως Άλφρεντ και μόνο ως Άλφρεντ.

Περίμενε κάτι και τίποτα ταυτόχρονα. Ο E-Z αγκάλιασε τη μορφή του νεκρού φίλου του, ευχόμενος να ξαναζωντανέψει.

"Θα θέλατε ένα ποτό;" ρώτησε η φωνή στον τοίχο.

"Θα ήθελα ο φίλος μου να είναι και πάλι ζωντανός. Μπορείς να τον επαναφέρεις και πάλι στη ζωή; Μπορείς σε παρακαλώ να με βοηθήσεις να τον σώσω;"

"Παρακαλώ, μείνετε καθισμένοι".

PFFT.

Η καταπραϋντική μυρωδιά της λεβάντας γέμισε τον αέρα. Αποκοιμήθηκε, σε μια ονειρική κατάσταση όπου ξαναζούσε μια ανάμνηση, μια ανάμνηση που είχε μετατοπιστεί και αλλάξει για να ταιριάζει στην τρέχουσα κατάστασή του.

Εκεί ήταν η μητέρα και ο πατέρας του E-Z ζωντανοί και υγιείς, αλλά νεότεροι. Επέστρεφαν από το νοσοκομείο με ένα αυτοκίνητο που δεν είχε ξαναδεί. Ο πατέρας του, ο Μάρτιν, βγήκε βιαστικά από τη θέση του οδηγού, για να βοηθήσει τη μητέρα του, τη Λόρελ, να βγει από το αυτοκίνητο.

Και μαζί, έφτασαν στο πίσω κάθισμα και σήκωσαν έξω ένα βρεφικό κάθισμα. Κοίταξαν με αγάπη το μωρό μέσα σε αυτό, το οποίο κοιμόταν βαθιά.

"Είναι σαν τον μεγάλο του αδελφό", είπε ο Μάρτιν.

"Ναι, ο E-Z πάντα κοιμόταν στο αυτοκίνητο", είπε η Laurel.

"Έλα μέσα", γουργούρισε ο Μάρτιν.

"Και να γνωρίσεις τον μεγάλο σου αδελφό", είπε η Λόρελ, καθώς το βρέφος άνοιξε για λίγο τα μάτια του και μετά ξανακοιμήθηκε.

Ο E-Z που είχε κοιτάξει έξω από το παράθυρο, με τον θείο του Σαμ δίπλα του. Θέλοντας να βγει έξω και να χαιρετήσει το νέο του αδελφάκι.

"Περίμενε να μπουν μέσα", είπε ο θείος Σαμ.

"Εντάξει", είπε ο επτάχρονος E-Z, με το πρόσωπό του κολλημένο στο παράθυρο, αγκαλιασμένο στα δύο του χέρια.

Η μπροστινή πόρτα άνοιξε: "Γυρίσαμε σπίτι!" φώναξε η μητέρα του Laurel.

Ο E-Z έτρεξε στην εξώπορτα, όπου η μητέρα του και ο πατέρας του τον αγκάλιασαν. Σκύβοντας, παρουσίασαν το νεότερο μέλος της οικογένειας Ντίκενς.

"Είναι τόσο μικρό", είπε ο E-Z.

"Είναι ένας αυτός", είπε ο πατέρας του.

"Ω."

"Θα ήθελες να τον κρατήσεις;" ρώτησε η μητέρα του.

"Εντάξει", είπε ο E-Z, κρατώντας τα χέρια του για να μπορέσει η μητέρα του να βάλει τον μικρό του αδελφό μέσα σε αυτά. "Δεν θέλω όμως να τον ξυπνήσω. Θα τον πειράζε;"

"Όχι, δεν θα ξυπνήσει", είπε η Λόρελ.

"Αν ξυπνήσει, είναι επειδή θέλει να γνωρίσει τον μεγάλο του αδελφέ".

"Έχει όνομα;" ρώτησε ο E-Z, παίρνοντας το νεογέννητο στην αγκαλιά του και αγκαλιάζοντας το κεφάλι του.

"'Όχι ακόμα, θα ήθελες να του δώσεις όνομα;" ρώτησε η μητέρα του. "Ωραία, κράτα το λαιμό του, ακριβώς έτσι... πολύ ωραία. Πώς ήξερες να το κάνεις αυτό; Είσαι τόσο καλός μεγάλος αδελφός".

"Πολύ καλή δουλειά, φιλαράκο", είπε ο μπαμπάς του.

Ο E-Z κοίταξε κάτω στο πρόσωπο του κυνηγιού και είπε: "Μου μοιάζει με τον Άλφρεντ".

Τα δάκρυα κύλησαν στα μάγουλα του E-Z καθώς οι δύο κόσμοι συγκρούστηκαν. Στον ένα κρατούσε το αδελφάκι του που ονομαζόταν Άλφρεντ. Στον άλλο κρατούσε το νεκρό σώμα του Άλφρεντ στο σιλό.

"Ο χρόνος αναμονής είναι τώρα επτά λεπτά", είπε η φωνή στον τοίχο.

"Επτά λεπτά", επανέλαβε ο E-Z.

Σκέφτηκε τον Άλφρεντ, τις δυνάμεις του. Για το πώς μπορούσε να θεραπεύσει άλλες μορφές ζωής, συμπεριλαμβανομένων των ανθρώπων. Αναρωτιόταν αν ο Άλφρεντ, είχε θεραπεύσει τον νεαρό άνδρα. Είχε κάνει ο ίδιος την αλλαγή; Θα ήταν αυτό δυνατό;

"Άλφρεντ", είπε ο E-Z. "'λφρεντ, με ακούς;" Κούνησε το σώμα του φίλου του. "Άλφρεντ!" είπε, ξανά και ξανά, ελπίζοντας ότι ο φίλος του θα μπορούσε να τον ακούσει με κάποιο τρόπο.

Καθώς το ρολόι του τοίχου μετρούσε αντίστροφα, εμφανίστηκε η Άριελ. "Δεν μπορείς να μεταχειρίζεσαι το σώμα, με τέτοιο τρόπο. Είναι ντροπή". Άνοιξε τα φτερά της και πήγε να σηκώσει το κουτσό σώμα του Άλφρεντ από την αγκαλιά του E-Z με σκοπό να το πάρει μακριά.

"'Όχι!" είπε ο E-Z. "Δεν θα τον πάρεις".

Η Άριελ κούνησε τα φτερά της και στη συνέχεια τον δείκτη της προς τον E-Z.

"Ο Άλφρεντ έχει φύγει από το κτίριο, εσύ κρατάς το δέρμα, τη στολή που τον κρατούσε. Ο Άλφρεντ είναι εκεί που έπρεπε να είναι τώρα. Άφησε το σώμα του να φύγει".

Ο E-Z σηκώθηκε όρθιος. Αν ο Άλφρεντ ήταν κάπου με την οικογένειά του, αν αυτό ήταν αλήθεια, τότε ναι, μπορούσε να τον αφήσει να φύγει. Μέχρι τότε κρατιόταν.

"Πού ακριβώς βρίσκεται; Είναι με την οικογένειά του;"

Η Άριελ πετάχτηκε κοντά, εντυπωσιακά κοντά, σχεδόν καθισμένη στη μύτη του E-Z. 'Αυτό δεν μπορώ να το πω."

"Τότε δεν τον αφήνω να φύγει".

"Ωραία", είπε η Άριελ. Ξεφούσκωσε και εξαφανίστηκε.

Πάνω του, στο σιλό εμφανίστηκαν δύο φιγούρες ένας άντρας και μια γυναίκα. Κινήθηκαν προς το μέρος του και αιωρήθηκαν προς τα κάτω. Όλο και πιο κοντά.

Έτριψε τα μάτια του. Ονειρευόταν πάλι; Ήταν η μητέρα του και ο πατέρας του. Ο Μάρτιν και η Λόρελ. Άγγελοι, που ερχόντουσαν να τον υποδεχτούν. Κούνησε το κεφάλι του. Δεν θα μπορούσαν να είναι αυτοί. Δεν μπορούσαν να είναι. Τους ονειρευόταν - να φέρνουν στο σπίτι ένα αδερφάκι. Τώρα ήταν εδώ, μαζί του στο σιλό. Ξεκάθαρα σαν την ημέρα - αλλά κοιμόταν ακόμα; Ονειρευόταν;

"E-Z", είπε η μητέρα του. "Αυτό το άτομο, ο φίλος σου ο Άλφρεντ, είναι νεκρός. Πρέπει να τον αφήσεις να φύγει και να συνεχίσεις τη δουλειά σου. Πρέπει να ολοκληρώσεις τις δοκιμασίες και ο χρόνος τρέχει. Ο χρόνος σου τελειώνει".

Ο πατέρας του E-Z, ο Μάρτιν, είπε: "Είναι ο μόνος τρόπος για να είμαστε όλοι μαζί ξανά".

"Μα του είπαν ψέματα", είπε ο E-Z. "Του είπαν ότι θα είναι με την οικογένειά του. Δεν μπορεί να είναι με την οικογένειά του τώρα, όχι έτσι. Πώς ξέρω ότι δεν μου λένε ψέματα, ότι θα είναι μαζί σου; Πώς ξέρω ότι εσύ δεν είσαι μια χειραγώγηση από τον Έριελ για να με κάνει να εκτελώ τις εντολές του;"

"Ποιος είναι ο Έριελ;' ρώτησε η μητέρα του.

"Δεν ξέρουμε τον Έριελ", είπε ο πατέρας του.

Αυτό δεν έβγαζε κανένα νόημα. Αυτό ήταν το μέρος του Eriel. Είτε τον γνώριζαν είτε όχι δεν είχε σημασία, αυτός ήταν υπεύθυνος για την παρουσία τους εκεί. Ήξερε πώς να τραβάει τις χορδές της καρδιάς του E-Z. Ήξερε πώς να τον κάνει να κάνει αυτό που ήθελε να κάνει.

Τι ακριβώς ήθελε; Και γιατί χρησιμοποιούσε τους γονείς του για να το πετύχει; Ήταν ξεδιάντροπο. Στον αέρα από πάνω του, οι γονείς του αιωρούνταν, ενεργοποιώντας και απενεργοποιώντας το χαμόγελό τους σαν να ήταν μαριονέτες. Τότε ήταν που κατάλαβε με βεβαιότητα ότι τα δύο φαντάσματα, ή ό,τι άλλο ήταν, δεν ήταν τελικά οι γονείς του. Ήταν αποκυήματα της φαντασίας του, ή ενδεχομένως της Έριελ. Αυτό που δεν μπορούσε να καταλάβει ήταν το γιατί. Γιατί τον χειραγωγούσαν τόσο σκληρά και ξεδιάντροπα;

"Ξύπνα E-Z!"

Ήταν πάλι στο κρεβάτι του. Στο σπίτι του.

Αναποδογύρισε και ξανακοιμήθηκε... και προσγειώθηκε ξανά στο σιλό - και πάλι.

ΚΕΦΑΛΑΙΟ 25

Τ ΡΊΑ ΠΡΆΓΜΑΤΑ ΠΟΥ ΈΜΟΙΑΖΑΝ με σιλό αιωρούνταν γύρω από τc δωμάτιο σαν να έπαιζαν το παιχνίδι Follow the Leader.

Δεν ήταν σιλό. Ήταν αυθεντικοί αιώνιοι χώροι ανάπαυσης που ονομάζονται Ψυχοπαγίδες.

Κάθε φορά που ένα ζωντανό πλάσμα χανόταν, υπό την προϋπόθεση ότι το σώμα στο οποίο ζούσε είχε γεννηθεί με ψυχή, θα ζούσε μια μέρα. Οι Ψυχοπαγίδες ήταν πολλές, πάρα πολλές για να τις μετρήσει κανείς. Ο αριθμός τους ήταν πολύ μεγαλύτερος απ' ό,τι μπορούμε να κατανοήσουμε εμείς οι άνθρωποι. Περισσότεροι από ένα googolplex, που είναι ο μεγαλύτερος γνωστός αριθμός.

Όταν έφτασε ο E-Z, όπως και πριν, τοποθετήθηκε στον αναμενόμενο κυνηγό ψυχών.

Ο Άλφρεντ έφτασε μετά, το σώμα του ήταν ακόμα νεκρό και τοποθετήθηκε στην ψυχοπαγίδα του.

Η Λία έφτασε τελευταία, ακόμα κοιμισμένη μέσα στην ψυχοπαγίδα της.

Ο E-Z δεν άργησε να νιώσει κλειστοφοβία.

"Θα θέλατε ένα ποτό;" ρώτησε η φωνή στον τοίχο.

"Όχι, ευχαριστώ", είπε, χτυπώντας τα δάχτυλά του στο μπράτσο της αναπηρικής του καρέκλας, όταν εμφανίστηκε ένας άγγελος. Ένας νέος άγγελος, που δεν είχε ξαναδεί.

Αυτός ο άγγελος ήταν γυναίκα. Ήταν ντυμένη με ένα ρέον μαύρο φόρεμα και καπέλο - σαν να συμμετείχε σε τελετή αποφοίτησης. Στο αυστηρό πρόσωπό της είχε ένα ζευγάρι γυαλιά. Παρόμοια με αυτά που φορούσε η Μέριλιν Μονρόε στην αφίσα στο καφέ. Η διαφορά ήταν ότι σε αυτούς τους σκελετούς έτρεχε κόκκινο υγρό που έμοιαζε με αίμα.

"E-Z", είπε, με μια τρεμάμενη δυνατή φωνή. Η φωνή της αντηχούσε. "Καλώς ήρθατε πίσω στον Ψυχοπαγιδευτή σας".

"Soul Catcher;" είπε. "Έτσι λέγεται αυτό το πράγμα; Σε μένα μοιάζει περισσότερο με σιλό. Λοιπόν, τι είναι η Ψυχοπαγίδα Ψυχής τέλος πάντων;"

"Είναι ένας αιώνιος τόπος ανάπαυσης για τις ψυχές", είπε, σαν να είχε απαντήσει στην ίδια ερώτηση ένα εκατομμύριο φορές στο παρελθόν.

"Αλλά αυτό δεν είναι για όταν οι άνθρωποι είναι νεκροί; Εγώ δεν είμαι νεκρός". Σίγουρα ήλπιζε να μην ήταν νεκρός!

"Περίμενε!" φώναξε.

Και πάλι, έτρεμε τους τοίχους όταν μιλούσε. Και τα δόντια του δονούνταν επίσης. Τόσο πολύ που η προτίμησή του θα ήταν να είναι έξω στο χιόνι, μετά να πρέπει να την ακούσει να ξεστομίζει άλλη μια λέξη.

"Δεν σου είπα ότι είναι ώρα για ερωτήσεις και απαντήσεις. Όπως το βλέπω, έχετε ολοκληρώσει τις περισσότερες από τις δοκιμασίες σας με επιτυχία. Αν και ο Άλφρεντ βοήθησε στη δοκιμή νούμερο δύο. Όπως γνωρίζετε, η μη εγκεκριμένη βοήθεια δεν επιτρέπεται".

Ο E-Z άνοιξε το στόμα του για να υπερασπιστεί τον Άλφρεντ, αλλά το έκλεισε ξανά. Δεν ήθελε να διακινδυνεύσει να υψώσει ξανά τη φωνή της. Σίγουρα ευχόταν να ανέβαζαν τη θερμοκρασία εκεί μέσα. Από την άλλη, ήταν ένας χώρος για ψυχές. Ίσως οι ψυχές να προτιμούσαν την ψυχρή αποθήκευση.

ΤΙΚ-ΤΑΚ.

Μια κουβέρτα ήταν τώρα τυλιγμένη γύρω από τους ώμους του.

"Ευχαριστώ."

"Έχεις δίκιο, όταν πεθάνεις η ψυχή σου θα αναπαυθεί εδώ. Ή θα αναπαυόταν εδώ, αν σε αφήναμε να πεθάνεις. Αλλά σε κρατήσαμε ζωντανό.

Είχαμε καλό λογο να το κάνουμε. Τα πράγματα έχουν αλλάξει όμως Δεν έχει λειτουργήσει. Ως εκ τούτου, θα θέλαμε να ακυρώσουμε την αρχική μας συμφωνία".

"Τι εννοείτε να την ανακαλέσετε; Έχεις πολύ θράσος! Προσπαθείτε να ακυρώσετε μια συμφωνία, τι είναι αυτό μόνο και μόνο επειδή είμαι παιδί; Υπάρχουν νόμοι κατά της παιδικής εργασίας. Εξάλλου, έχω κάνει ό,τι μου ζητήθηκε. Σίγουρα, έπρεπε να τα μάθω όλα στο πόδι. Αλλά μέσα απο τα πυκνά και τα δύσκολα τα κατάφερα. Κράτησα το δικό μου μέρος της συμφωνίας, και εσύ πρέπει να κρατήσεις το δικό σου!".

"Ω ναι, έκανες ό,τι σου ζητήθηκε. Αυτό είναι το πρόβλημα - σου λείπει η πρωτοβουλία".

"Μου λείπει η πρωτοβουλία!" αναφώνησε ο E-Z καθώς έσπαγε τις γροθιές του στα μπράτσα της αναπηρικής του καρέκλας. "Η συμφωνία ήταν να μου στέλνεις δοκιμασίες και εγώ να βρω τον τρόπο να τις κατακτήσω. Έχω σώσει ζωές. Δεν μπορείς να αλλάξεις τους κανόνες στα μισά του παιχνιδιού".

"Σωστά, αυτή ήταν η αρχική συμφωνία. Μετά τα πράγματα πήγαν στραβά με τον Χαντζ και τον Ρέικι - ξέχασαν να σβήσουν τα μυαλά - για ένα πράγμα και έπρεπε να εμπλακεί ο Έριελ".

"Μου έστειλε δοκιμασίες, τις ολοκλήρωσα. Τον κέρδισα ακόμη και σε μια μονομαχία".

"Ναι, το έκανες. Του είχα ζητήσει να αξιολογήσει τους δεσμούς ανάμεσα σε σένα και τον θείο Σαμ".

"Να μας αξιολογήσει;"

"Ναι. Ένας αρχάγγελος δεν προορίζεται να ΔΗΜΙΟΥΡΓΕΙ δοκιμασίες για έναν άγγελο που εκπαιδεύεται. Λόγω της δικής σου, λοιπόν, έλλειψης πρωτοβουλίας, ο Έριελ έπρεπε να εμπλακεί περισσότερο απ' ό,τι θα έπρεπε".

"Περιμένετε ένα λεπτό! Δηλαδή, μου λες ότι έπρεπε να βγω έξω και να βρω τις δικές μου δοκιμασίες; Γιατί δεν με ενημέρωσε κανείς για αυτές τις απαιτήσεις;"

"Ελπίζαμε ότι θα το καταλάβαινες μόνος σου. Υπήρχαν ενδείξεις. Ενδείξεις για τη μεγάλη εικόνα. Κοινά στοιχεία. Ελπίζαμε ότι αν είχες και άλλους να συζητάς τις δοκιμές... Τις δοκιμασίες που έχετε ήδη ολοκληρώσει. Ότι θα εντοπίζατε το πρόβλημα. Να καταλήξετε στο ίδιο συμπέρασμα.

Να μας βοηθήσετε. Ίσως ακόμη και να το κατακτήσετε - χωρίς να χρειαστεί να σας το δώσουμε με το κουτάλι. Σου δώσαμε κάθε ευκαιρία, αλλά δεν το έκανες. Γι' αυτό, θα ακολουθήσουμε άλλο δρόμο".

"Κοινά σημεία; Μπορεί να ξέρω τι εννοείς".

"Αν το καταλάβεις και πάρεις την επιλογή του Υπερήρωα... Αυτό θα μπορούσε να λειτουργήσει. Αρκεί να ήταν όλα πεντακάθαρα. Είχες την πλήρη εικόνα. Ήξερες τους κινδύνους."

"Δηλαδή, θα είμαστε ακόμα ομάδα; Γιατί δεν το διευκρινίζεις; Να το κάνεις εύκολο για μένα;"

"Στο παρελθόν, παρόλο που οι σύντροφοί σου είχαν λάβει δυνάμεις, τις οποίες εσύ δεν κατείχες - δεν τις χρησιμοποιούσες. Αντ' αυτού, οι τρεις σας καθόσασταν - σπαταλώντας χρόνο - περιμένοντας να συμβούν όλα.

Δεν σας φάνηκε περίεργο όταν η Έριελ εμφανίστηκε στο λούνα παρκ; Ανέβαζε το προφίλ των Τριών. Αυτό δεν είναι δουλειά ενός αρχάγγελου. Είναι δική σου δουλειά".

Κούνησε το κεφάλι του. "Δεν ήμουν εκατό τοις εκατό σίγουρος ότι ήταν ο Έριελ, μέχρι που αναγνωρίστηκε στο τέλος. Πριν από αυτό είχα τις υποψίες μου. Ποιος άλλος θα ντυνόταν σαν τον Αβραάμ Λίνκολν;

"Εξάλλου, νόμιζα ότι κανείς δεν έπρεπε να το μάθει. Μέχρι εκείνο το σημείο, νόμιζα ότι οι δίκες ήταν μυστικές. Φοβόμουν μήπως παραβιάσω τη συμφωνία μου μαζί σου. Ο Οφάνιελ είπε ότι αν το έλεγα σε κανέναν, θα έχανα την ευκαιρία να ξαναδώ τους γονείς μου. Ακολούθησα τους κανόνες που μου τέθηκαν. Δεν νομίζω ότι καταλαβαίνεις την έννοια του ευ αγωνίζεσθαι".

"Αυτό δεν είναι παιχνίδι. Οι Αρχάγγελοι μπορούμε να κάνουμε ό,τι θέλουμε!" αναφώνησε, πλησιάζοντας πιο κοντά στο σημείο όπου καθόταν ο E-Z. Έσπρωξε το πηγούνι της προς τα εμπρός. "Αποφασίσαμε ότι σου ταιριάζει περισσότερο το παιχνίδι των Υπερηρώων παρά το παιχνίδι των Αγγέλων. Ήταν τότε, που σας βοηθήσαμε στο τμήμα δημοσίων σχέσεων. Για να σε ενθαρρύνουμε να βρεις τους δικούς σου ανθρώπους να σε βοηθήσουν. Ένας Θεός ξέρει ότι η γη είναι γεμάτη από αυτούς. Πώς τους έλεγε ο Σαίξπηρ, αυτούς που κλαψουρίζουν και ξερνάνε στην αγκαλιά της νοσοκόμας τους".

"Δεν έχω διαβάσει Σαίξπηρ, αλλά είμαι συγγενής με τον Κάρολο Ντίκενς. Όχι ότι αυτό έχει σχέση. Αλλά, εντάξει, λοιπόν, θέλεις να συνεχίσω, ως Υπερήρωας με τον Άλφρεντ, αν ζει και με τη Λία στο πλευρό μου. Μπορούμε εύκολα να έχουμε μεγάλη υποστήριξη και δημοσιότητα από τα ΜΜΕ.

"Είμαι ακόμα αφοσιωμένος σε σένα. Αν μας αφήσεις ελεύθερους, γιατί, ο ουρανός θα είναι το όριο. Γνωρίζουμε πολλά παιδιά στο σχολείο και στον αθλητικό κλάδο. Μπορούμε να δημιουργήσουμε μια τηλεφωνική γραμμή για υπερήρωες και μια ιστοσελίδα. Μπορούμε να χρησιμοποιήσουμε τα μέσα κοινωνικής δικτύωσης για να συνδεθούμε με ανθρώπους από όλο τον κόσμο. Οι άνθρωποι θα κάνουν ουρά για να τους βοηθήσουμε. Θα είναι ένα εντελώς νέο παιχνίδι".

"Α, επιτέλους μιλάει για πρωτοβουλία... αλλά αγαπητό μου αγόρι είναι πολύ λίγο αργά. Όπως είπα και πριν, θέλουμε να απαλλαγούμε από την υποχρέωση απέναντί σας. Δεν είσαι πλέον δεσμευμένος μαζί μας. Δεν έχεις πλέον χρέος να πληρώσεις".

"Μα..."

"Και οι τρεις σας έχετε αποδείξει ότι το κάνετε αυτό μόνο για τον εαυτό σας. Όταν οι άγγελοι πρότειναν για πρώτη φορά ότι θα μπορούσατε να μας βοηθήσετε, να μας εκπροσωπήσετε εδώ στη γη - είχαμε ένα σχέδιο Με τον Άλφρεντ, ήταν το ίδιο. Μετά, ήρθε η Λία. Από τότε, είχαμε κάποια επιτυχία με εσάς τους δύο. Τη συμπεριλάβαμε στην τριάδα... αλλά τώρα έχετε καταστεί άχρηστοι".

"Σώζουμε ανθρώπους, βοηθάμε ανθρώπους".

"Μη μου λες τέτοια. Αν σου έδινα την ευκαιρία να είσαι με τους γονείς σου σήμερα, εδώ και τώρα. Θα πετούσες την πετσέτα. Θα έφευγες χωρίς να νοιαστείς ή να σκεφτείς για εκείνες τις ζωές που θα μπορούσες να είχες σώσει αν οι δοκιμές είχαν συνεχιστεί.

"Το ίδιο και με τον Άλφρεντ, περιμένω - αν επιβιώσει. Θα πήγαινε σε ένα χωράφι με μαργαρίτες με την οικογένειά του χωρίς να ανοιγοκλείσει το μάτι. Και μιλώντας για μάτια, αν η Λία είχε την όρασή της πίσω - θα έφευγε κι αυτή.

"Μετά από προσεκτική σκέψη συνειδητοποιήσαμε ότι κανένας από εσάς δεν είναι αφοσιωμένος σε κάτι άλλο εκτός από τον εαυτό του, ως εκ τούτου, προχωρήσαμε στο σχέδιο Β".

"Περιμένετε ένα λεπτό. Ας ορίσουμε τη δουλειά". Την έψαξε στο Google και με ικανοποίηση διαπίστωσε ότι είχε τέσσερις μπάρες. "Σύμφωνα με ένα διαδικτυακό λεξικό: να εκτελείς εργασία ή να εκπληρώνεις καθήκοντα τακτικά έναντι μισθού ή ημερομισθίου. Δούλεψα για σένα, χωρίς αμοιβή. Εκτός από την υπόσχεση για αποζημίωση. Είχαμε μια προφορική συμφωνία.

"Δεν είμαι σίγουρος για τις λεπτομέρειες της συμφωνίας που είχε κάνει ο Άλφρεντ ή η Λία, αλλά στοιχηματίζω ότι οι άγγελοί τους τούς πρόσφεραν παρόμοια κίνητρα. Εγώ κράτησα το δικό μου μέρος της συμφωνίας και εσύ πρέπει να τηρήσεις το δικό σου. Είμαι δεκατριών ετών και", το έψαξε στο google. "Ναι, όπως σκέφτηκα, σύμφωνα με το Υπουργείο Εργασίας των ΗΠΑ, τα δεκατέσσερα είναι η ελάχιστη ηλικία εργασίας".

Γέλασε και ξαναρύθμισε τα γυαλιά της. Παρατήρησε ότι είχε αίμα στα χέρια της. Τα σκούπισε στο μαύρο της ρούχο. "Οι πρώιμοι νόμοι δεν ισχύουν για τους αγγέλους ή τους αρχαγγέλους. Είναι αφελές εκ μέρους σου να νομίζεις ότι θα ήταν έτσι όμως". Έκανε μια παύση. "Είμαστε διατεθειμένοι να σας προσφέρουμε δύο επιλογές. Την πρώτη επιλογή: Θα παραμείνεις εδώ στην Ψυχοπαγίδα σου για το υπόλοιπο της ζωής σου".

"Τι;"

Τα ίδια τα θεμέλια της Ψυχοπαγίδας του έτρεμαν. Η ιδέα να θαφτεί ζωντανός μέσα σε αυτό το μεταλλικό δοχείο τον αρρώστησε.

"Η ζωή που θα ζήσεις, για τις ζωντανές σου αναπνευστικές μέρες θα περάσει όπως σου υποσχέθηκαν εκείνοι οι ανόητοι αρχάγγελοι. Με τους γονείς σου. Δηλαδή, θα ξαναζήσεις τη ζωή σου με τους γονείς σου από την ημέρα που γεννήθηκες μέχρι την ακριβή στιγμή που έληξε η ζωή τους. Εσύ δεν θα βρεθείς ποτέ σε αναπηρικό καροτσάκι και εκείνο δεν θα πεθάνουν ποτέ". Έκανε μια παύση. "Τώρα, μπορείτε να μιλήσετε".

"Εννοείτε ότι θα ξαναζήσω τη ζωή μου με τους γονείς μου, κάθε μέρα που περάσαμε μαζί, για όλη την αιωνιότητα, ξανά και ξανά;"

"Ναι."

"Ποια είναι η επιλογή νούμερο δύο;"

"Δεν μπορείς να μαντέψεις;" ρώτησε με ένα οδοντωτό χαμόγελο.

Το χαμόγελό της ήταν τόσο ανειλικρινές που αναγκάστηκε να κοιτάξει αλλού.

Εκείνος περίμενε.

"Η επιλογή δύο θα σήμαινε ότι θα επέστρεφες να ζήσεις τη ζωή σου με τον θείο Σαμ". Δίστασε, πλησιάζοντας πιο κοντά, ώστε ο Ξ-Ζ. Κρυωνόταν ήδη, και τώρα τον έκανε ακόμα πιο κρύο με κάθε χτύπημα των φτερών της. Σκεπάστηκε με την κουβέρτα. Εκείνη συνέχισε. "Όπως ίσως έχεις ήδη μαντέψει, δεν θα ξανασμίξεις ούτε θα ξανασμίξεις ποτέ με τους γονείς σου ούτε με τη μία ούτε με την άλλη επιλογή. Θα αναδημιουργούσαμε το παρελθόν. Θα ήταν σαν να ζούσες σε ένα θεατρικό έργο ή σε μια τηλεοπτική εκπομπή".

"Τι! Δεν είναι αυτό που συμφώνησα!" Ο E-Z αναφώνησε. "Θέλεις να πεις Χατζ. Ρέικι, ο Έριελ και ο Οφάνιελ μου είπαν ψέματα;"

"Το ψέμα είναι ισχυρή λέξη, αλλά ναι. Κοιτάξτε το περιβάλλον σας. Οι ψυχές κατατίθενται σε μεμονωμένα διαμερίσματα. Ένα διαμέρισμα προετοιμάζεται εκ των προτέρων για κάθε ψυχή".

"Δηλαδή, λες ότι οι γονείς μου βρίσκονται ο καθένας σε ένα από αυτά τα διαμερίσματα;"

"Ναι, οι ψυχές τους είναι."

"Και μετά τι τους συμβαίνει;"

"Γιατί, αιωρούνται στους ουρανούς."

"Αυτό είναι λυπηρό. Πάντα πίστευα ότι οι γονείς μου θα ήταν μαζί, κάπου. Ξέρω ότι αυτό ήταν το μόνο πράγμα που έδινε στον Άλφρεντ κάποια παρηγοριά. Ότι η γυναίκα του και τα παιδιά του ήταν κάπου μαζί. Σε κανέναν δεν αρέσει να σκέφτεται ότι το αγαπημένο του πρόσωπο πεθαίνει μόνο του. Πόσο μάλλον να περάσει την αιωνιότητα μέσα σε ένα μεταλλικό δοχείο που παρασύρεται από τόπο σε τόπο".

"Ανθρώπινος συναισθηματισμός. Οι ψυχές απλώς υπάρχουν. Δεν ζουν και δεν αναπνέουν, ούτε τρώνε, ούτε νιώθουν πολύ ζέστη ή πολύ κρύο. Οι άνθρωποι δεν καταλαβαίνουν την έννοια".

Εκείνος χλεύασε.

"Δεν θέλω να προσβάλω το είδος σας. Αλλά όταν ένα σώμα πεθαίνει, αυτό που μένει, η ψυχή, είναι μια έννοια που δύσκολα μπορείς να κατανοήσεις. Οι ανθρώπινοι εγκέφαλοι είναι απλά πολύ μικροί για να κατανοήσουν την πολυπλοκότητα του σύμπαντος. Εξ ου και η δημιουργία θρησκευτικών δογμάτων. Γράφεται με όρους του λαϊκού ανθρώπου. Εύκολα διδάσκονται και ακολουθούνται χωρίς καμία απόδειξη".

"Αφού οι ψυχές έχουν μεγαλύτερη αξία από τους ανθρώπους σαν εμένα, πώς θα μπορούσα να ζήσω το υπόλοιπο της ζωής μου σε ένα από αυτά τα δοχεία;"

"Έχουμε κάνει προσαρμογές, όπως τώρα και πριν. Δεν είχες κανένα πρόβλημα να υπάρχεις εδώ μέσα όταν σε φέραμε, έτσι δεν είναι τώρα;"

"Εκτός από την κλειστοφοβία", είπε. "Και τις φορές που χρειάστηκε να με ηρεμήσουν με εκείνο το σπρέι λεβάντας".

"Α, ναι. Η επανεμφάνιση της κλειστοφοβίας θα εξαρτηθεί φυσικά από την επιλογή που θα επιλέξετε. Αν επιλέξετε την επιλογή νούμερο ένα, το περιβάλλον θα σας στηρίξει με κάθε τρόπο μέχρι να είναι έτοιμη η ψυχή σας. Τότε η γήινη μορφή σας μπορεί να απορριφθεί. Οι άνθρωποι προσαρμόζονται και θα το συνηθίσετε. Επιπλέον, θα είσαι με τους γονείς σου, αναβιώνοντας αναμνήσεις. Έτσι θα περάσει η ώρα. Τώρα, πες το όνομα της επιλογής σου!"

"Περίμενε, τι θα γίνει με τα φτερά μου και τα φτερά της καρέκλας μου; Τι θα τους συμβεί;" Δίστασε: "Τι θα γίνει με τις δυνάμεις του Άλφρεντ και της Λία; Αν επιλέξουμε την επιλογή νούμερο ένα, θα επιστρέψουμε στην κατάσταση που θα ήμασταν; Εννοώ προτού εσύ και οι άλλοι αρχάγγελοι εμπλακείτε στις ζωές μας;"

"Φυσικά, δεν πρόκειται να σας βγάλουμε τα φτερά, αγαπητό μου αγόρι, ούτε να αφαιρέσουμε τις δυνάμεις που έχουν ήδη δοθεί σε κάποιον από εσάς. Είμαστε αρχάγγελοι, όχι σαδιστές".

"Χαίρομαι που το γνωρίζω, οπότε, μπορούμε να συνεχίσουμε να είμαστε Υπερήρωες".

"Μπορείτε, αλλά θα πρέπει να δημιουργήσετε τη δική σας δημοσιότητα - γιατί όταν εμείς βγούμε - βγαίνουμε για πάντα".

"Παρακαλώ παραμείνετε καθιστοί", είπε η φωνή στον τοίχο, αν και ο E-Z δεν είχε και πολλές επιλογές.

Ο αρχάγγελος δεν είπε τίποτα. Αντ' αυτού, απέσπασε την προσοχή της καθαρίζοντας τα γυαλιά της και στη συνέχεια βάζοντάς τα ξανά στη θέση τους.

"Κάτι ακόμα", ρώτησε η E-Z, "σχετικά με τον Άλφρεντ".

"Συνέχισε, αλλά κάνε γρήγορα. Μια άλλη έννοια που δεν καταλαβαίνουν οι άνθρωποι, είναι ότι ο χρόνος υπάρχει σε όλο το σύμπαν. Έχω κι άλλα μέρη να βρεθώ και άλλους αρχαγγέλους να δω".

"Εντάξει, θα το κάνω. Ο Άλφρεντ βρίσκεται τώρα σε ένα άλλο ανθρώπινο σώμα. Αν η ψυχή παραμένει μαζί με το σώμα, τότε, υπάρχουν δύο ψυχές εκεί μέσα; Περιμένει ο ψυχοπαγιδευτής δύο ψυχές;"

Ο άγγελος του γύρισε την πλάτη. Καθάρισε τον λαιμό της προτού μιλήσει: "Εγώ, εμείς, ελπίζαμε ότι δεν θα κάνατε αυτή την ερώτηση. Είσαι πιο έξυπνος απ' ό,τι περιμέναμε". Εκείνη έκλεισε τα μάτια της και έγνεψε: "Μμμμ". Τα μάτια της παρέμειναν κλειστά. Ο E-Z κοίταξε να δει αν φορούσε ωτοασπίδες, καθώς φαινόταν να ακούει κάποιον. Ή ίσως το φανταζόταν. Εκείνη έγνεψε. "Σύμφωνοι", είπε.

"Είναι κάποιος άλλος εδώ μέσα μαζί μας;" ρώτησε.

Μια νέα φωνή ακούστηκε από παντού γύρω του. Γιατί όλοι οι αρχάγγελοι είχαν τόσο δυνατές φωνές;

"Είμαι ο Ραζέλ ο Φύλακας των Μυστικών. E-Z Ντίκενς, πρέπει να ακούσεις τα λόγια μου. Γιατί μόλις ειπωθούν, δεν θα τις θυμάσαι. Ούτε ότι ήμουν εδώ. Οι Ψυχοποιοί και οι σκοποί τους δεν σε αφορούν. Ξεπέρασες τα όριά σου και δεν θα το ανεχτούμε! Σας δώσαμε γενναιόδωρα δύο επιλογές. Αποφασίστε ΤΩΡΑ, αλλιώς ο μορφωμένος φίλος μου θα πάρει την απόφαση για εσάς".

Ο E-Z άρχισε να μιλάει, αλλά μετά το μυαλό του έμεινε κενό. Για τι πράγμα μιλούσαν;

Ο αρχάγγελος έκλεισε ξανά τα μάτια, ξεστόμισε τις λέξεις "Ευχαριστώ", και η φωνή του Ραζέλ δεν μίλησε άλλο.

ΉΤΑΝ ΣΑΝ Ο ΧΡΟΝΟΣ να είχε γυρίσει πίσω. "Περιμένεις να αποφασίσω επί τόπου, χωρίς να μου δώσεις χρόνο να το σκεφτώ; Χωρίς να μιλήσω με τον θείο Σαμ ή με τους φίλους μου; Μιλώντας γι' αυτό, τι γίνεται με τον Άλφρεντ, του είπαν ότι θα επανενωθεί με την οικογένειά του; Και η Λία, της είπαν ότι θα ξαναβρεί την όρασή της".

"Εφόσον ο Άλφρεντ έχει φύγει, η απόφασή σου -αν θα επιβιώσει στη γη ή όχι- θα είναι δική του απόφαση. Η νούμερο ένα επιλογή του θα είναι η ίδια με τη δική σου. Θα ήθελε να ξαναζήσει τη ζωή του με την οικογένειά του επανειλημμένα; Καθώς έχει φύγει, μπορεί ήδη να βλέπει ευχάριστα όνειρα γι' αυτούς. Από την άλλη, ποτέ δεν ξέρει κανείς τι κόλπα μπορεί να κάνει το μυαλό. Μπορεί να βρίσκεται σε έναν βρόγχο από εφιάλτες και μόνο εσείς μπορείτε να σώσετε αυτόν και την οικογένειά του κάνοντας τη σωστή επιλογή γι' αυτόν".

"Λέτε ότι δεν θα βγει ποτέ από αυτό; Οριστικά;"

"Αυτό δεν μπορώ να το πω. Το μόνο που ξέρω είναι ότι ο ψυχοπαγιδευτής δεν είναι έτοιμος να συλλέξει την ψυχή του... ακόμα".

"Και η Λία;"

"Τα ανθρώπινα μάτια της έχουν χαθεί σε αυτή τη ζωή, όπως και τα πόδια σου. Μπορεί να ξαναζήσει τις μέρες της όρασης, αλλά μπορεί να προτιμάει να επιλέξεις κι εσύ γι' αυτήν. Εξάλλου, δεν είχε χρόνο να μεγαλώσει και να ωριμάσει όπως ένα κανονικό παιδί. Έχει ήδη χάσει τρία χρόνια από τη ζωή της και αυτό το επεισόδιο της γήρανσης, δεν είμαστε σίγουροι αν είναι ένα μεμονωμένο περιστατικό ή, αν θα ξανασυμβεί".

"Εννοείτε ότι ούτε εσείς ξέρετε τι πρόκειται να της συμβεί;"

"Όχι, δεν ξέρουμε. Εξάλλου, κοιμάται ακόμα".

"Δεν μπορώ να το αποφασίσω αυτό, και για τους τρεις μας, σε μια προθεσμία. Είναι μια μεγάλη απόφαση και χρειάζομαι χρόνο".

"Τότε θα τον έχεις." Εμφανίστηκε ένα ρολόι που μετρούσε αντίστροφα από τα εξήντα λεπτά. "Ο χρόνος σου αρχίζει τώρα. Δώστε μου την απάντησή σας πριν χτυπήσει το μηδέν. Διαφορετικά, όλα όσα έχουμε συζητήσει θα είναι άκυρα. Και θα βρεθείτε πίσω στο ξενοδοχείο με το πτώμα του φίλου σας". Τα φτερά της χτύπησαν και σηκώθηκε όλο και ψηλότερα.

"Περίμενε, πριν φύγεις", φώναξε.

"Τι είναι τώρα;"

"Υπάρχουν κι άλλοι, εννοώ άλλα παιδιά σαν κι εμάς;"

"Χάρηκα που σε γνώρισα", είπε εκείνη.

"Το συναίσθημα σίγουρα δεν είναι αμοιβαίο", απάντησε εκείνος.

ΚΕΦΑΛΑΙΟ 26

ΚΑΘΩΣ ΤΑ ΛΕΠΤΑ ΠΕΡΝΟΥΣΑΝ, ο Ε-Ζ ανέλυσε όλα όσα του είχαν μόλις πει. Εύχεται το σιλό να ήταν αρκετά ευρύ ώστε να μπορεί να κινείται περισσότερο. Τουλάχιστον καθόταν αναπαυτικά στο αναπηρικό καροτσάκι του. Μαζί ήταν σαν το δυναμικό δίδυμο.

"Θα θέλατε να φάτε κάτι;" ρώτησε η φωνή από τον τοίχο.

"Φυσικά και θα ήθελα", είπε. "Ένα μήλο, λίγο ποπ κορν - με γεύση τυρί θα ήταν καλό και ένα μπουκάλι νερό".

"Έρχεται αμέσως", είπε η φωνή, καθώς ένα μεταλλικό τραπέζι έσπρωχνε μέσα από μια σχισμή στον τοίχο που δεν είχε προσέξει πριν. Ήρθε να σταματήσει μπροστά του. Από τη σχισμή βγήκε ένας γάντζος, μεταφέροντας πρώτα το μπουκάλι με το νερό. Στη συνέχεια, ένας δεύτερος γάντζος μετέφερε ένα ποτήρι. Ακολούθησε ένας τρίτος γάντζος με ένα μήλο. Πριν το αφήσει κάτω, ο γάντζος το γυάλισε με μια πετσέτα. Στη συνέχεια, ένας τέταρτος γάντζος πετάχτηκε έξω, μεταφέροντας ένα μπολ με ποπ κορν.

"Σας ευχαριστώ", είπε καθώς τα τέσσερα αγκίστρια που έπιαναν τα χέρια του χαιρέτησαν και εξαφανίστηκαν πίσω στον τοίχο.

"Παρακαλώ."

"Υπάρχει περίπτωση να μου φέρετε τον υπολογιστή μου; Καταστράφηκε στη φωτιά. Σίγουρα θα ήθελα να μπορέσω να κάνω μια λίστα με τα πράγματα για να πάρω αυτή την απόφαση".

"Βεβαίως. Δώστε μου ένα ή δύο λεπτά".

Καθώς τελείωνε το μήλο και σκεφτόταν το ποπ κορν, από μια άλλη σχισμή στον απέναντι τοίχο εμφανίστηκε ο φορητός υπολογιστής του. Ο γάντζος το κρατούσε ψηλά, περιμένοντας τον E-Z να μετακινήσει τα άλλα αντικείμενα για να το φιλοξενήσει. Όταν δεν το έκανε, εμφανίστηκαν γάντζοι από την άλλη πλευρά. Ένας σήκωσε τον πυρήνα του μήλου και εξαφανίστηκε πίσω στον τοίχο. Ένας άλλος έριξε το υπόλοιπο νερό στο ποτήρι. Στη συνέχεια πήρε το άδειο μπουκάλι πίσω από τη σχισμή του τοίχου. Καθώς ήθελε να κρατήσει το ποπ κορν και το ποτήρι με το νερό, τα αφαίρεσε από το τραπέζι. Ο γάντζος άφησε κάτω το φορητό του υπολογιστή, και στη συνέχεια επέστρεψε μέσω της σχισμής του στον τοίχο.

Ο E-Z πίστευε ότι οι γάντζοι ήταν ωραία αξεσουάρ. Θα μπορούσε εύκολα να τα προωθήσει σε μια μεγάλη σουηδική αλυσίδα.

Τώρα που τα άγκιστρα είχαν φύγει όλα, σήκωσε το καπάκι του φορητού υπολογιστή του και το άνοιξε. Πρώτα, έλεγξε το αρχείο του Tattoo Angel, όλα ήταν ακόμα εκεί! Ήταν τόσο χαρούμενος- θα έκλαιγε αν το ρολόι δεν χτυπούσε την ώρα.

"Σας ευχαριστώ πολύ", είπε, χώνοντας μια χούφτα τυρένιο ποπ κορν στο στόμα του. Και μετά άρχισε να πληκτρολογεί. Αποφάσισε να σκεφτεί τον εαυτό του τρίτος. Πρώτον, να γράψει τα υπέρ και τα κατά σχετικά με τον Άλφρεντ. Κατευθείαν ήξερε ότι ο Άλφρεντ δεν θα τον πείραζε να ξαναζήσει το παρελθόν του με την οικογένειά του επανειλημμένα. Θα επέλεγε αμέσως αυτή την επιλογή.

"Παρόλα αυτά, φάνηκε στον E-Z ότι δεν ήταν μια επιλογή που η οικογένειά του θα ήθελε να πάρει. Αφού θα ξαναζούσε αυτό που ήδη υπήρχε και δεν θα προχωρούσε μπροστά. Στη ζωή, πρέπει να προχωράς μπροστά. Να συνεχίσεις να μαθαίνεις και να μεγαλώνεις.

Όσο περισσότερο το σκεφτόταν, τόσο περισσότερο συνειδητοποιούσε ότι θα ήταν σαν να βλέπεις την ιστορία της ζωής σου σε επανάληψη. Φανταστείτε τη ζωή σας είκοσι τέσσερις φορές το εικοσιτετράωρο σε μόνιμη επανάληψη. Χωρίς να ξέρεις ποτέ πότε θα τελειώσει. Ή αν θα τελείωνε ποτέ. Αυτό θα μπορούσε να μετατραπεί σε ένα διαφορετικό είδος κόλασης. Μια που δεν άντεχε να σκέφτεται.

Εκτός αν ήξερε σίγουρα ότι ο Άλφρεντ θα ήταν πάντα σε κώμα. Κάτι στο οποίο είχε υπαινιχθεί ο αρχάγγελος. Τότε γι' αυτόν, η επιλογή του θα απέτρεπε κάθε κακό όνειρο ή εφιάλτη. Ο Άλφρεντ θα ήταν με την οικογένειά του, για πάντα. Ακόμα κι αν δεν ήταν το αληθινό πράγμα... μπορεί να ήταν αρκετό. Θα το επέλεγε;

Έριξε μια ματιά στην ώρα, απέμεναν πενήντα λεπτά. Άρχισε να σκέφτεται την υπόθεση της Λία. Το όνειρό της να γίνει διάσημη μπαλαρίνα είχε διακοπεί. Θα ήθελε να ξαναζήσει την παιδική της ηλικία, γνωρίζοντας ότι αυτό το όνειρο δεν θα εκπληρωθεί ποτέ; Για εκείνη, θα άξιζε να ρισκάρει το μέλλον. Τα μάτια στις παλάμες της την έκαναν ξεχωριστή, μοναδική.. και ήταν συμπαθής. Θα μπορούσε ακόμη και να είναι η πιο πρόσφατη εκδοχή μιας γυναίκας θαύματος, αν ήταν σε θέση να αξιοποιήσει όλες τις δυνάμεις.

"E-Z;" είπε η Λία. "Σε ακούω να σκέφτεσαι, αλλά πού είσαι;"

Ωχ όχι! Τώρα που ήταν ξύπνια θα έπρεπε να της εξηγήσει τα πάντα και θα χρειαζόταν χρόνος και ο χρόνος τελείωνε. Θα έπρεπε να το κάνει, γρήγορα. "Άκου Λία", άρχισε, "έχω μια μεγάλη ιστορία να σου πω, σε παρακαλώ μη με σταματήσεις μέχρι να ολοκληρωθεί η ιστορία. Μας τελειώνει ο χρόνος". Τα εξήγησε όλα, του πήρε δέκα λεπτά. Άλλα δέκα λεπτά πέρασαν. Απομένουν σαράντα λεπτά.

"Εντάξει, E-Z, εσύ σκέψου εσένα και εγώ θα σκεφτώ τον εαυτό μου Ας κάνουμε πέντε λεπτά και μετά θα ξαναμιλήσουμε. Ο χρόνος αρχίζει τώρα".

"Καλό σχέδιο."

Πέντε λεπτά αργότερα και το ρολόι έδειχνε τριάντα πέντε λεπτά που απέμεναν. Ο E-Z ρώτησε τη Λία αν είχε αποφασίσει.

"Έχω αποφασίσει", είπε εκείνη. "Κι εσύ;"

"Κι εγώ", είπε. "Εσύ πρώτος, σε πέντε λεπτά ή λιγότερο αν μπορείς".

"Για μένα η απόφαση είναι πολύ εύκολη, E-Z. Δεν θέλω να μείνω σε αυτό το πράγμα και να ζήσω τη ζωή μου εδώ. Όταν ο Ψυχοπαγιδευτής με φέρει εδώ, όταν θα είμαι νεκρός. Δεν πειράζει. Αλλά δεν θέλω να περιοριστώ με τη βία σε αυτόν τον χώρο. Όχι όταν θα μπορούσα να είμαι εκεί έξω και να νιώθω τη ζεστασιά του ήλιου, να ακούω τα πουλιά, με τον άνεμο στα μαλλιά μου. Για να μην αναφέρω ότι θα περνάω χρόνο με τη μαμά μου, με τον θείο Σαμ και ελπίζω και με σένα. Η ζωή είναι πολύ μικρή για να τη σπαταλάμε και μου αρέσουν τα νέα μου μάτια τις περισσότερες φορές". Γέλασε.

"Συμφωνώ και αν ήμουν στη θέση σου, θα έκανα το ίδιο".

"Ευχαριστώ, E-Z. Τι ώρα μένει τώρα;"

"Είκοσι πέντε λεπτά ακόμα", επιβεβαίωσε. "Να τώρα η σκέψη μου σε ελπίζω λιγότερο από πέντε λεπτά. Δεν με πειράζει που είμαι εδώ μέσα, δεν διαφέρει πολύ από το να είμαι εκεί έξω. Έχω μάθει ότι το να βρίσκομαι σε αναπηρικό καροτσάκι δεν είναι το τέλος του κόσμου. Στην πραγματικότητα, το έχω συνηθίσει αρκετά. Μπορώ να κάνω πράγματα που έκανα πριν, όπως να παίζω μπέιζμπολ, και δεν είμαι εντελώς χάλια σε αυτό. Γαμώτο, θα το παίξουν ακόμα και στους Παραολυμπιακούς Αγώνες.

"Οι γονείς μου δεν θα ήθελαν να σπαταλήσω τη ζωή μου ζώντας στο παρελθόν. Ούτε και ο θείος Σαμ. Δεν είμαι διατεθειμένος να εγκαταλείψω τα πάντα, μόνο και μόνο επειδή εκείνοι οι ηλίθιοι αρχάγγελοι έδωσαν μερικές απρεπείς υποσχέσεις. Οπότε, συμφωνώ μαζί σου. Θα φύγουμε από αυτά τα πράγματα του Ψυχοπαγιδευτή. Θα ζήσουμε τις ζωές μας μέχρι να τελειώσουμε να ζούμε. Και τότε μπορεί να έρθει να μας πιάσει. Χρόνια αργότερα, αφού ελπίζουμε ότι θα έχουμε συνεισφέρει στην ανθρωπότητα και θα έχουμε ζήσει μια καλή ζωή. Θα μπορούσαμε να βρούμε άλλους σαν εμάς. Θα μπορούσαμε να δημιουργήσουμε μια τηλεφωνική γραμμή υπερηρώων και να συνεργαστούμε σε όλο τον κόσμο. Θα μπορούσαμε να χρησιμοποιήσουμε τις δυνάμεις μας για να κάνουμε τον κόσμο καλύτερο. Θα μπορούσαμε να ζήσουμε τη ζωή μας στο έπακρο, να δημιουργήσουμε εμπνευσμένες ζωές για τις οποίες θα ήμασταν περήφανοι και οι οικογένειές μας επίσης".

"Μπράβο!" αναφώνησε η Λία. "Αλλά υπάρχουν κι άλλοι, σαν εμάς;"

"Ρώτησα τον άγγελο που μου τα εξήγησε όλα, αλλά δεν απάντησε. Αυτό με κάνει να πιστεύω ότι υπάρχουν". Έριξε μια ματιά στο ρολόι. "Έμειναν μόνο είκοσι ένα λεπτά".

"Και ο Άλφρεντ; Θα ξυπνήσει ποτέ;"

"Ο άγγελος είπε ότι δεν ξέρει, μόνο ο ψυχοπαγιδευτής ξέρει... αλλά είπε ότι μπορεί να βλέπει εφιάλτες. Αν υπάρχει πιθανότητα, να βρίσκεται σε μια ζωντανή κόλαση, τότε καλύτερα να τον αφήσουμε να φύγει. Η επιλογή νούμερο ένα, το να ξαναζήσει τη ζωή του με την οικογένειά του σε επανάληψη είναι αυτή που του ταιριάζει;"

"Διαφωνώ. Κανείς από εμάς δεν ξέρει με βεβαιότητα, πότε θα έρθει ο ψυχοπαγιδευτής για εμάς. Ο Άλφρεντ δεν θα ήθελε να σπαταληθε εδώ μέσα, επειδή μπορεί να τον βρουν κακά όνειρα. Όχι εκεί που υπάρχει η πιθανότητα, να βοηθήσει κάποιον ή να εμπνεύσει κάποιον. Ήρθαμε εδώ μαζί και πρέπε να φύγουμε μαζί. Κατά τη γνώμη μου, αυτό είναι όλο".

Δεκατέσσερα λεπτά και ο χρόνος περνάει.

Είχε προσεγγίσει το θέμα του Άλφρεντ με έναν μοναδικό τρόπο Είχε δίκιο; Θα επιθυμούσε πράγματι ο Άλφρεντ να εγκαταλείψει την οικογένειά του σε αυτό το σενάριο για ένα αχαρτογράφητο μέλλον; Δεν υπάρχουμε όλοι σε έναν αχαρτογράφητο κόσμο; Αλλάζουμε πορεία, σκύβουμε και βουτάμε. Ανοίγουμε παράθυρα, κλείνουμε πόρτες. Αφήνουμε τα συναισθήματά μας να μας παρασύρουν και μετά να επιστρέφουμε. Όλα έχουν να κάνουν με τη ζωή. Ναι, η Λία είχε δίκιο. Ήταν μια τελειωμένη συμφωνία.

Οκτώ λεπτά έμεναν στο ρολόι.

"Νομίζω ότι έχεις δίκιο, Λία. Είναι όλοι για έναν και ένας για όλους", είπε ο E-Z. "Ο αρχάγγελος μου είπε ότι έπρεπε να πω τα λόγια πριν τελειώσει το ρολόι. Τότε θα βρισκόμασταν όλοι πίσω στο ξενοδοχείο... σαν να μην είχε συμβεί ποτέ αυτό το ιντερλούδιο με τον Ψυχοπαγιδευτή".

"Πιστεύεις όμως ότι θα θυμόμαστε ακόμα για τους ψυχοπαγιδευτές; Είναι σημαντικό για εμάς να μάθουμε από αυτή την εμπειρία. Ακόμα κι αν δεν την μοιραστήκαμε. Έχε στο μυαλό σου ότι καταρρίπτει όλα όσα ξέρουμε για τον παράδεισο και τη μετά θάνατον ζωή".

Πέντε λεπτά έμειναν.

"Πράγματι, αλλά ας το συζητήσουμε αυτό στην άλλη πλευρά". Έσφιξε τις γροθιές του καθώς το ρολόι έδειχνε τέσσερα λεπτά. "Αποφασίσαμε!" φώναξε. "Βγάλτε τους τρεις μας από αυτά, από αυτές τις ψυχοπαγίδες - ΤΩΡΑ!"

Οι τοίχοι του σιλό του E-Z άρχισαν να τρέμουν. "Είσαι καλά, Λία;" φώναξε. Εκείνη δεν απάντησε. Το έδαφος κάτω από τα πόδια του έμοιαζε να κροταλίζει και να βροντάει. Στη συνέχεια άρχισε να γυρίζει, πρώτα δεξιόστροφα, μετά αριστερόστροφα, μετά δεξιόστροφα.

Μέσα του το στομάχι του στριφογύριζε. Ξερνούσε τυρώδες ποπ κορν και μασούσε παντού κομμάτια κόκκινου μήλου.

Ήταν τα μόνα ενθύμια που θα είχε ο Ψυχοπαγιδευτής από αυτόν. Ελπίζω για πάρα πολύ καιρό.

Ευχαριστίες

Αγαπητοί αναγνώστες,

Σας ευχαριστούμε που διαβάσατε το πρώτο και το δεύτερο βιβλίς της σειράς E-Z Dickens. Ελπίζω να σας αρέσει η προσθήκη αυτών των νέων χαρακτήρων και να είστε πρόθυμοι να μάθετε τι θα συμβεί στη συνέχεια.

Θα μπορείτε να διαβάσετε το υπόλοιπο της σειράς πολύ σύντομα!

Ευχαριστώ για άλλη μια φορά τους βήτα αναγνώστες, τους διορθωτές και τους συντάκτες μου. Οι συμβουλές και η ενθάρρυνσή σας με κράτησαν σε καλό δρόμο με αυτό το έργο και η συμβολή σας ήταν/είναι πάντα ευπρόσδεκτη.

Ευχαριστώ επίσης την οικογένεια και τους φίλους μου που είναι πάντα εκεί για μένα.

Και όπως πάντα, καλή ανάγνωση!

Cathy

Σχετικά με τον συγγραφέα

Η Cathy McGough ζει και γράφει στο Οντάριο του Καναδά. με τον σύζυγό της, τον γιο της, τις δύο γάτες τους και έναν σκύλο.

Επίσης από:

ΥΑ

E-Z Dickens Superhero Βιβλίο τρία: Κόκκινο δωμάτιο

E-Z Dickens Superhero Βιβλίο Τέταρτο: Επί Πάγος

103 ΙΔΈΕΣ ΣΥΛΛΟΓΉΣ ΧΡΗΜΆΤΩΝ ΓΙΑ ΕΘΕΛΟΝΤΈΣ

ΓΟΝΕΊΣ ΜΕ ΣΧΟΛΕΊΑ ΚΑΙ ΟΜΆΔΕΣ

+ Παιδικά βιβλία